PERFECT TEMPTATIONS

Seduce Me at Sunrise

AND

Tempt Me at Twilight

PERFECT
TEMPTATIONS

Two Novels in One

Seduce Me at Sunrise

AND

Tempt Me at Twilight

LISA KLEYPAS

St. Martin's Paperbacks

This is a work of fiction. All of the characters, organizations, and events portrayed in these novels are either products of the author's imagination or are used fictitiously.

Published in the United States by St. Martin's Paperbacks, an imprint of St. Martin's Publishing Group

PERFECT TEMPTATIONS: SEDUCE ME AT SUNRISE copyright © 2008 by Lisa Kleypas and TEMPT ME AT TWILIGHT copyright © 2009 by Lisa Kleypas.

For information, address St. Martin's Publishing Group, 120 Broadway, New York, NY 10271.

www.stmartins.com

ISBN: 978-1-250-83282-5

Our books may be purchased in bulk for promotional, educational, or business use. Please contact your local bookseller or the Macmillan Corporate and Premium Sales Department at 1-800-221-7945, ext. 5442, or by email at MacmillanSpecialMarkets@macmillan.com.

Printed in the United States of America

St. Martin's Paperbacks edition / February 2022

10 9 8 7 6 5 4 3 2 1

Seduce Me at Sunrise

Chapter One

Win had always thought Kev Merripen was beautiful, in the way an austere landscape or a wintry day could be beautiful. He was a large, striking man, uncompromising in every angle. His hair was as black as a raven's wing, his brows strong and straight. The irises of his eyes were so dark they were barely distinguishable from the pupil, and his mouth was set with a perpetually brooding curve Win found irresistible.

Kev. Her love, but never her lover. They had known each other since childhood, when he'd been taken in by her family.

He came to Win's bedroom and stood at the threshold to watch as she packed a valise with personal articles from the top of her dresser. A hairbrush, a rack of pins, a handful of handkerchiefs her sister Poppy had embroidered for her. As Win tucked the objects into the leather bag, she was intensely aware of Kev's motionless form. She knew what lurked beneath his stillness, because she felt the same undertow of yearning.

The thought of leaving him was breaking her heart. And yet there was no choice. She had been an invalid ever since she'd had scarlet fever two years earlier. She was thin and frail and given to fainting spells and fatigue. Weak lungs, all the doctors had said. Nothing to do but succumb. A lifetime of bed rest followed by early death.

Win wouldn't accept such a fate.

She longed to get well, to enjoy the things most people took for granted. To dance, laugh, walk through the countryside. She wanted the freedom to love . . . to marry . . . and to have her own family someday.

With her health in such a poor state, there was no possibility of doing any of those things. But that was about to change. She was departing this day for a French clinic, where a dynamic young doctor, Julian Harrow, had achieved remarkable results for patients just like herself. His treatments were unorthodox, controversial, but Win didn't care. She would have done anything to be cured. Because until that day came, she could never have Kev.

"Don't go," he said, so softly she almost didn't hear him.

Win struggled to remain outwardly calm, even as a hot-and-cold chill went down her spine.

"Close the door," she managed to say. They needed privacy for the conversation they were about to have.

Kev didn't move. Color had risen in his tanned face, and his black eyes glittered with emotion he would never allow himself to express.

She went to close the door herself, while he moved away as if any contact between them would prove fatal.

"Why don't you want me to go, Kev?" she asked gently.

"You won't be safe there."

"I'll be perfectly safe," she said. "I have faith in Dr. Harrow. His treatments sound sensible to me, and he's had a high success rate—"

"He's had as many failures as successes. There are better doctors here in London. You should try them first."

"I think my best chances lie with Dr. Harrow." Win smiled

into Kev's hard black eyes, understanding the things he couldn't say. "I'll come back to you. I promise."

He ignored that. Any attempt she made to bring their feelings to light was always met with rock-hard resistance. He would never admit he cared for her, or treat her as anything other than a fragile invalid who needed his protection. A butterfly under glass.

While he went on with his private pursuits.

Despite Kev's discretion in personal matters, Win had no illusions that he'd been celibate. Something bleak and angry rose from the depths of her soul at the thought of Kev sleeping with someone else. It would shock everyone who knew her, had they understood the power of her desire for him. It would probably shock Kev most of all.

Seeing his expressionless face, Win thought, *Very well, Kev. If this is what you want, I'll be stoic. We'll have a pleasant, bloodless good-bye.*

Later she would suffer in private, knowing it would be an eternity until she saw him again. But that was better than living like this, forever together and yet apart, her illness always between them.

"Well," she said briskly, "I'll be off soon. And there's no need to worry, Kev. Leo will take care of me during the trip to France, and—"

"Your brother can't even take care of himself," Kev said. "You're not going. You'll stay here, where I can—"

He bit off the words.

But Win had heard a note of something like fury, or anguish, buried in his deep voice.

This was getting interesting.

Her heart began to thump. "There . . ." She had to pause to catch her breath. "There's only one thing that could stop me from leaving."

He shot her an alert glance. "What is it?"

It took her a long moment to summon the courage to speak. "Tell me you love me. Tell me, and I'll stay."

The black eyes widened. The sound of his indrawn breath cut through the air like the downward arc of an ax stroke. He was silent, frozen.

A curious mixture of amusement and despair surged through Win as she waited for his reply.

"I . . . care for everyone in your family . . ."

"No. You know that's not what I'm asking for." Win moved toward him and lifted her pale hands to his chest, resting her palms on a surface of tough, unyielding muscle. She felt the response that jolted through him. "Please," she said, hating the desperate edge in her own voice, "I wouldn't care if I died tomorrow, if I could just hear it once—"

"*Don't,*" he muttered, backing away.

Casting aside all caution, Win followed. She reached out to grasp the loose folds of his shirt. "Tell me. Let's finally bring the truth out into the open—"

"Hush; you'll make yourself ill."

It infuriated Win that he was right. She could feel the familiar weakness, the dizziness that came along with her pounding heart and laboring lungs. She cursed her failing body. "I love you," she said wretchedly. "And if I were well, no power on earth could keep me away from you. I'd take you into my bed, and show you as much passion as any woman could—"

"No." His hand lifted to her mouth as if to muffle her, then snatched back as he felt the warmth of her lips.

"If I'm not afraid to admit it, why should you be?" Her pleasure at being near him, touching him, was a kind of madness. Recklessly she molded herself against him. He tried to push her away without hurting her, but she clung with all her remaining strength. "What if this were the last moment you ever had with me? Wouldn't you have been sorry not to tell me how you felt? Wouldn't you—"

Kev covered her mouth with his, desperate for a way to make her quiet. They both gasped and went still, absorbing the feel of it. Each strike of his breath on her cheek was a shock of heat. His arms went around her, wrapping her in his vast strength, holding her against the hardness of his body. And then everything ignited, and they were both lost in a furor of need.

She could taste the sweetness of apples on his breath, the bitter hint of coffee, but most of all the rich essence of him. Wanting more, craving him, she pressed upward. He took the innocent offering with a low, savage sound.

She felt the touch of his tongue. Opening to him, she drew him deeper, hesitantly using her own tongue in a slide of silk on silk, and he shivered and gasped and held her more tightly. A new weakness flooded her, her senses starving for his hands and mouth and body . . . his powerful weight over and between and inside her . . . oh, she wanted him, wanted . . .

Kev kissed her hungrily, his mouth moving over hers with rough, luscious strokes. Her nerves blazed with pleasure, and she squirmed and clutched at him, wanting him closer.

Even through the layers of her skirts, she felt the way he urged his hips against hers, the tight, subtle rhythm. Instinctively she reached down to feel him, to soothe him, and her trembling fingers encountered the hard shape of his arousal.

He buried an agonized groan in her mouth. For one scalding moment he reached down and gripped her hand tightly over himself. Her eyes flew open as she felt the pulsing heat and tension that seemed ready to explode. "Kev . . . the bed . . ." she whispered, going crimson from head to toe. She had wanted him so desperately, for so long, and now it was finally going to happen. "Take me—"

Gasping uncontrollably, Kev cursed and pushed her away. Win moved toward him. "Kev—"

"*Stay back,*" he said with such force that she jumped in fright.

For at least a minute, there was no sound or movement save the angry friction of their breaths.

Kev was the first to speak. His voice was weighted with rage and disgust, though whether it was directed against her or himself was impossible to fathom. "That will never happen again."

"Because you're afraid you might hurt me?"

"Because I don't want you that way."

She stiffened with indignation and gave a disbelieving laugh. "You responded to me just now. I felt it."

His color deepened. "That would have happened with any woman."

"You . . . you're trying to make me believe you have no particular feeling for me?"

"Nothing other than a desire to protect one of your family."

She knew it was a lie; she *knew* it. But his callous rejection made leaving a bit easier. "I . . ." It was difficult to speak. "How noble of you." Her attempt at an ironic tone was ruined by her breathlessness. Stupid weak lungs.

"You're overwrought," Kev said, moving toward her. "You need to rest—"

"I'm *fine,*" Win said fiercely, going to the washstand, gripping it to steady herself. When her balance was secured, she poured a splash of water onto a linen cloth and applied it to her flushed cheeks. Glancing into the looking glass, she made her face into its usual serene mask. Somehow she made her voice calm. "I'll have all of you or nothing. You know what words will make me stay. If you won't say them, then leave."

The air in the room was heavy with emotion. Win's nerves screamed in protest as the silence drew out. She stared into the looking glass, able to see only the broad shape of his shoulder and arm. And then he moved, and the door opened and closed.

Win continued to dab at her face with the cool cloth, using it to blot stray teardrops. Setting the cloth aside, she noticed that her palm, the one she had used to grip the intimate shape of him, still retained the memory of his flesh. And her lips still tingled from the sweet, hard kisses, and her chest was filled with the ache of desperate love.

"Well," she said to her flushed reflection, "now you're motivated." And she laughed shakily until she had to wipe away more tears.

As Cam Rohan supervised the loading of the carriage that would soon depart for the London docks, he couldn't help wondering if he was making a mistake. He'd promised Amelia he'd take care of her family. But less than two months after they'd married, he was sending one of her sisters to France.

"We can wait," he had told Amelia only last night, holding her against his shoulder, stroking her rich brown hair as it lay in a river over his chest. "If you wish to keep Win with you a little longer, we'll send her to the clinic in the spring."

"No, she must go as soon as possible. Too much time has already been wasted. Win's best chance of improvement is to start the course of treatment at once."

Cam had smiled at Amelia's pragmatic tone. His wife excelled at hiding her emotions, maintaining such a sturdy facade that few people perceived how vulnerable she was underneath. He was the only one with whom she would let down her guard.

"We must be sensible," Amelia had added.

Cam had rolled her to her back and stared down at her small, lovely face in the lamplight. Such round blue eyes, dark as the heart of midnight. "It's not always easy to be sensible, is it?"

She shook her head, her eyes turning liquid.

He stroked her cheek with his fingertips. "Poor hummingbird," he whispered. "You've gone through so many changes in the past months—not the least of which was marrying me. And now we're sending your sister away."

"To a clinic, to make her well," Amelia had said. "I know it's best for her. It's only that . . . I'll miss her. Win is the dearest, gentlest one in the family. The peacemaker. We'll all probably murder each other in her absence." She gave him a little scowl. "Don't tell anyone I was crying, or I shall be *very* cross with you."

"No, *monisha*," he had soothed, cuddling her closer as she sniffled. "Your secrets are safe with me. You know that."

And he had kissed away her tears, and removed her nightgown, and made love to her slowly. "Little love," he had whispered as she trembled beneath him. "Let me make you feel better . . ." And as he took careful possession of her body, he murmured that she pleased him in all ways, he loved to be inside her, he would never leave her. Amelia's hands had worked on his back like cat paws, her hips pressing upward into his weight. He'd pleasured her with all his love and skill and taken his own pleasure until she'd fallen into a sated sleep.

For a long while afterward Cam had held her nestled against him, the trusting weight of her head on his shoulder. He was responsible for Amelia and her entire family now.

The Hathaways were a group of misfits that included four sisters, a brother, and Merripen, who was a Rom like Cam. No one seemed to know much about Merripen, aside from the fact that he'd been taken in by the Hathaway family as a boy after having being wounded and left for dead by a lawless group of local landowners bent on destroying temporary Romany encampments.

There was no predicting how Merripen would fare in Win's absence, but Cam had a feeling it wasn't going to be pleasant. They couldn't have been more opposite: one so refined and otherworldly; the other hardy, physical, and down to earth. But their connection was like the path of a hawk that always returned to the same forest, following the invisible map etched in its very nature.

When the carriage was properly loaded and the luggage had been secured with leather straps, Cam went into the family's hotel suite. They'd gathered in the receiving room to say their good-byes.

Merripen was conspicuously absent.

They crowded the small room, the sisters and their brother, Leo, who was going to France as Win's companion and escort.

"There, now," Leo said gruffly, patting the back of the youngest, Beatrix, who had just turned sixteen. "No need to make a scene."

She hugged him tightly. "You'll be lonely, so far from home. Won't you take one of my pets to keep you company?"

"No, darling. I'll have to content myself with the human companionship I can find on board." He turned to Poppy, a ruddy-haired beauty of eighteen. "Good-bye, sis. Enjoy your first season in London. Don't accept the first fellow who proposes."

Poppy moved forward to embrace him. "Dear Leo," she said, her voice muffled against his shoulder, "do try to behave while you're in France."

"No one behaves in France," Leo told her. "That's why everyone likes it so much." He turned to Amelia. It was only then that his self-assured facade began to disintegrate. He drew an unsteady breath. Of all the Hathaway siblings, Leo and Amelia had argued the most frequently and the most bitterly. And yet she was undoubtedly his favorite. They had been through a great deal together, taking care of the younger siblings after their parents had died. Amelia had watched Leo turn from a promising young architect into a wreck of a man. Inheriting a viscountcy hadn't helped one bit. In fact, the newly acquired title and status had only hastened Leo's dissolution. That hadn't stopped Amelia from fighting for him, trying to save him, every step of the way. Which had annoyed him considerably.

Amelia went to him and laid her head against his chest. "Leo," she said with a sniffle. "If you let anything happen to Win, I'll kill you."

He stroked her hair gently. "You've threatened to kill me for years, and nothing ever comes of it."

"I've been w-waiting for the right occasion."

Smiling, Leo pried her head from his chest and kissed her forehead. "I'll bring her back safe and well."

"And yourself?" she asked.

"And myself."

Amelia smoothed his coat, her lip trembling. "Then you'd better stop living like a drunken wastrel," she said.

Leo grinned. "But I've always believed in cultivating one's natural talents to the fullest." He lowered his head so she could kiss his cheek. "You're a fine one to talk about how to conduct oneself," he said. "You, who just married a man you barely know."

"It was the best thing I ever did," Amelia said.

"Since he's paying for my trip to France, I suppose I can't disagree." Leo reached out to shake Cam's hand. After a rocky beginning, the two men had come to like each other in a short time. "Good-bye, *phral*," Leo said, using the Romany word Cam had taught him for "brother." "I have no doubt you'll do an excellent job taking care of the family.

You've already gotten rid of me, which is a promising beginning."

"You'll return to a rebuilt home and a thriving estate, my lord."

Leo gave a low laugh. "I can't wait to see what you'll accomplish. You know, not just any peer would entrust all his affairs to a pair of Roma."

"I would say with certainty," Cam replied, "you're the only one."

AFTER WIN HAD BID FAREWELL TO HER SISTERS, LEO SETTLED her into the carriage and sat beside her. There was a soft lurch as the team pulled forward, and they headed to the London docks.

Leo studied Win's profile. As usual, she showed little emotion, her fine-boned face serene and composed. But he saw the flags of color burning on the pale crests of her cheeks, and the way her fingers clenched and tugged at the embroidered handkerchief in her lap. It had not escaped him that Merripen hadn't been there to say good-bye. Leo wondered if he and Win had exchanged harsh words.

Sighing, Leo reached out and put his arm around his sister's thin, breakable frame. She stiffened but did not pull away. After a moment, the handkerchief came up, and he saw that she was blotting her eyes. She was afraid, and ill, and miserable.

And he was all she had.

God help her.

He made an attempt at humor. "You didn't let Beatrix give you one of her pets, did you? I'm warning you, if you're carrying a hedgehog or a rat, it goes overboard as soon as we're on the ship."

Win shook her head and blew her nose.

"You know," Leo said conversationally, still holding her,

"you're the least amusing of all the sisters. I can't think how I ended up going to France with you."

"Believe me," came her watery reply, "I wouldn't be this boring if I had any say in the matter. When I get well I intend to behave very badly indeed."

"Well, that's something to look forward to." He rested his cheek on her soft blond hair.

"Leo," she asked after a moment, "why did you volunteer to go to the clinic with me? Is it because you want to get well, too?"

Leo was both touched and annoyed by the innocent question. Win, like everyone else in the family, thought his excessive drinking was an illness that would be cured by a period of abstinence and healthful surroundings. But his drinking was merely a symptom of the real illness—a grief so persistent that at times it threatened to stop his heart from beating.

There was no cure for losing Laura.

"No," he said to Win. "I have no expectation of getting well. I merely want to carry on with my debauchery in new scenery." He was rewarded by a small chuckle. "Win . . . did you and Merripen quarrel? Is that why he wasn't there to see you off?" At her prolonged silence, Leo rolled his eyes. "If you insist on being closemouthed, sis, it's going to be a long journey indeed."

"Yes, we quarreled."

"About what? Harrow's clinic?"

"Not really. That was part of it, but . . ." Win shrugged uncomfortably. "It's too complicated. It would take forever to explain."

"We're about to cross an ocean, and then half of France. Believe me, we have time."

AFTER THE CARRIAGE HAD LEFT, CAM WENT TO THE MEWS behind the hotel, a tidy building with horse stalls and a

carriage house on the ground floor, and servants' accommo-
dations above. As he had expected, Merripen was grooming
the horses. The hotel mews were run on a part-livery system,
which meant some of the stabling chores had to be assumed
by the horse owners. At the moment Merripen was taking
care of Cam's black gelding. His movements were light,
quick, and methodical as he ran a brush over the horse's shining flanks.

Cam watched for a moment, appreciating his skill.

"What do you want?" Merripen asked without looking at
him.

Cam approached the open stall, smiling as the horse lowered his head and nudged his chest. "No, boy . . . no sugar
lumps." He patted the muscular neck. His shirtsleeves were
rolled up to his elbows, exposing the tattoo of a black flying
horse on his forearm. Cam had no memory of when he'd gotten the tattoo . . . it had been there forever, for reasons his
grandmother would never explain.

The symbol was an Irish nightmare steed called a *pooka*,
an alternately malevolent and benevolent horse who spoke in
a human voice and flew at night on widespread wings. According to legend, the *pooka* would come to an unsuspecting
human's door at midnight and take him on a ride that would
leave him forever changed.

Cam had never seen a similar mark on anyone else. Until
Merripen.

Through a quirk of fate, Merripen had recently been injured in a house fire. As his wound was treated, the Hathaways had discovered the tattoo on his shoulder.

That had raised more than a few questions in Cam's mind.

He saw Merripen glance at the tattoo on his arm. "What
do you make of a Rom wearing an Irish design?" Cam asked.

"There are Roma in Ireland. Nothing unusual."

"There's something unusual about this tattoo," Cam said

evenly. "I've never seen another like it, until you. And since it came as a surprise to the Hathaways, you've evidently taken great care to keep it hidden. Why is that, *phral*?"

"Don't call me that."

"You've been part of the Hathaway family since childhood," Cam said. "And I've married into it. That makes us brothers, doesn't it?"

A disdainful glance was his only reply.

Cam found perverse amusement in being friendly to a Rom who so clearly despised him. He understood exactly what had engendered Merripen's hostility. For a stranger to come in and act as the head of the family was nearly unendurable.

"Why have you always kept it hidden?" Cam persisted.

Merripen paused in his brushing and gave him a cold, dark glance. "I was told it was the mark of a curse."

Cam showed no outward reaction, but he felt a few prickles of unease at the back of his neck.

"Who are you, Merripen?" he asked softly.

The big Rom went back to work. "No one."

"You were part of a tribe once. You must have had family."

"I don't remember any father. My mother died when I was born."

"So did mine. I was raised by my grandmother."

The brush halted midstroke. Neither of them moved. The stable became deadly quiet, except for the snuffling and shifting of horses. "I was raised by my uncle. To be one of the *asharibe*."

"Ah." Cam kept any hint of pity from his expression.

No wonder Merripen fought so well. *Asharibe* were hardened fighters down to the bootstraps, designated as warriors of the tribe.

"Well, that explains your sweet temperament," Cam said. "Was that why you chose to stay with the Hathaways after they took you in? Because you no longer wanted to live that way?"

"Yes."

"You're lying, *phral*," Cam said, watching him closely. "You stayed for another reason." And Cam knew from the Rom's visible flush that he'd hit upon the truth.

Quietly, Cam added, "You stayed for her."

Chapter Two

There was no softness in him. He'd been raised by his uncle to fight on command. There was no mother to plead for him, no father to intervene in his uncle's harsh punishments.

Eventually *gadje* had decided to attack their encampment. There had been gunshots, clubbings, sleeping Roma attacked in their beds, women and children screaming and crying. The camp had been scattered and everyone had been driven off, the wagons set on fire, many of the horses stolen.

Kev had done his best to defend the tribe until he'd been struck on the head with the butt of a gun. Someone else had stabbed him in the back with a bayonet, and then he'd been left for dead. Alone in the night, he had lain half-conscious by the river, listening to the rush of dark water, feeling the chill of hard, wet earth beneath him. With no reason or desire to live, he'd waited without fear for the great wheel to roll into darkness.

But as morning had approached, Kev had found himself gathered up and carried away in a small rustic cart. A *gadjo* had found him and bid a local boy to help carry the dying Romany boy into his house.

It was the first time Kev had ever been beneath the ceiling

of anything other than a *vardo*. He'd been too weak to lift a finger in his own defense.

The room he occupied was not much bigger than a horse stall, holding only a bed and a chair. There were cushions, pillows, framed needlework on the walls, a lamp with beaded fringe. Had he not been so ill, he would have gone mad in the overstuffed little room.

The *gadjo* who had brought him there . . . Hathaway . . . was a tall, slender man with pale hair. His diffident manner made Kev hostile. Why had Hathaway saved him? What could he want from a Romany boy? Kev refused to talk to the *gadjo* and wouldn't take medicine. He rejected any overture of kindness. He owed this man nothing. He hadn't asked to be saved. So he lay there, flinching and silent, whenever the man changed the bandage on his back.

Kev spoke only once, and that was when Hathaway had asked about the tattoo.

"What's this mark for?"

"It's a curse," Kev said through gritted teeth. "Don't mention it to anyone, or the curse will fall on you, too."

"I see." The man's voice was kind. "I'll keep your secret. But as a rationalist, I don't believe in superstitions. A curse has only as much power as one gives it."

Stupid *gadjo,* Kev thought. Everyone knew denying a curse was *very* bad luck.

It was a noisy household full of children. Kev could hear them beyond the closed door of the room he had been put in. But there was something else . . . a faint, sweet presence nearby. He felt it hovering outside the room, just out of reach.

Amid the clamor of children bickering, laughing, singing, he heard a murmur that raised every hair on his body. A girl's voice. Lovely, soothing. He wanted her to come to him. He willed it as he lay there, his wounds mending slowly. *Come to me . . .*

But she never appeared. The only ones who entered the room were Hathaway and his wife, a pleasant but wary woman who regarded Kev as if he were dangerous.

On one or two occasions the children came to look at him, peeking around the edge of the partially open door. There were two little girls named Poppy and Beatrix, who giggled and squealed with happy fright when he scowled at them. There was another, older daughter, Amelia, who glanced at him with the same skeptical assessment her mother had. And there was a tall blue-eyed boy, Leo, who looked not much older than Kev himself.

"I want to make it clear," the boy had said from the doorway, his voice quiet, "that no one intends to do you any harm. As soon as you're able to leave, you'll be free to do so." He'd stared at Kev's sullen, feverish face for a moment before adding, "My father is a kind man, but I'm not. So don't even think of hurting or insulting any of my sisters, or you'll answer to me."

Kev respected that enough to give Leo a slight nod. He'd begun to accept that this odd little family really didn't mean him harm. Nor did they seem to want anything from him.

After a week, Kev's fever had eased and his wound had healed enough for him to move. He woke up early one morning and dressed in the clothes they'd given him.

It hurt to move, but Kev ignored the fierce pounding in his head and the jabbing fire in his back. He filled his coat pockets with a candle stub and a sliver of soap. The first light of dawn shone through the little window above the bed. The family would be awake soon. He started for the door, felt dizzy, and half collapsed onto the mattress. Gasping, he tried to collect his strength.

There was a tap at the door just before it opened.

"May I come in?" he heard a girl ask softly.

Kev's senses were overwhelmed. He closed his eyes, breathing, waiting.

It's you. You're here.

"You've been alone for so long," she said as she approached, "I thought you might want some company. I'm Win."

Kev drew in the scent and sound of her, his heart pounding. Carefully he eased to his back, ignoring the pain that shot through him. He opened his eyes.

He'd never thought any *gadji* could compare to Romany girls. But this one was remarkable, an otherworldly creature, her hair moonlight-blond, her features delicate. She gazed at him with tender gravity, and his entire being responded so acutely that he reached out and seized her.

She gasped but held still. Kev knew it wasn't right to touch her. He didn't know how to be gentle. But she relaxed in his hold, staring at him with those pure blue eyes.

Why wasn't she afraid of him?

"Let go," she told him gently.

He didn't want to. Ever. He wanted to keep her against him, and pull her braided hair down, and comb his fingers through the pale silk. He wanted to carry her off to the ends of the earth.

"If I do," he said gruffly, "will you stay?"

Her lips curved in a sweet, delicious smile. "Silly boy. Of course I'll stay. I've come to visit you."

Slowly his fingers loosened.

"Lie back," she said. "Why are you dressed already?" Her eyes widened. "Oh. You mustn't leave. Not until you're well."

She needn't have worried. Any notion of escaping had disappeared the second he'd seen her. Kev eased back against the pillows, watching intently as she sat on the chair. She was wearing a pink dress. The edges of it, at the neck and wrists, were trimmed with little ruffles.

"What's your name?" she asked.

Kev hated talking. *Hated* making conversation. But he was willing to do anything to keep her with him. "Merripen."

"Is that your first name?"

"No."

Win tilted her head to the side. "Won't you tell it to me?"

He shook his head. He could only share his true name with another Rom.

"At least tell me the first letter," she coaxed. At his silence, she ventured, "I don't know many Romany names. Is it Luca? Marko? Stefan?"

He realized she was teasing him. He didn't know how to respond. Usually if someone tried to tease him, he responded by sinking his fist into the offender's face.

"Someday you'll tell me," she said with a little grin. She made a move as if to rise from the chair, and Kev's hand shot out to take her arm. Surprise flickered across her face.

"You said you'd stay," he said gruffly.

Her free hand came to the one clamped around her wrist. "I will. Be at ease, Merripen. I'm only going to fetch some bread and tea for us. Let go, and I'll come right back." Her palm was light and warm as it rubbed over his hand. "I'll stay all day, if you wish."

"They won't let you."

"Oh yes, they will." She coaxed his hand to loosen, gently prying at his fingers. "Don't be so anxious. My goodness. I thought Roma were supposed to be merry."

She almost made him smile.

"I've had a bad week," he told her gravely.

"Yes, I can see that. How did you come to be hurt?"

"*Gadje* attacked my tribe. They may come for me here." He released her carefully. "I'm not safe. I should go."

"No one would dare take you away from us. My father is a respected man in the village. A scholar." Seeing Merripen's doubtful expression, she added, "The pen is mightier than the sword, you know."

That was something only *gadje* would say. It made no sense at all. "The men who attacked me last week weren't armed with pens."

"Poor boy," she said compassionately. "I'm sorry. Your wounds must hurt after all this moving about. I'll fetch some tonic."

Kev had never been the object of sympathy before. His pride bristled as he watched her go to the door. He was certain she wouldn't come back. And he wanted her near him so badly.

So he fixed her with a sullen stare and muttered, "Go, then. Devil take you."

Win paused at the doorway and glanced over her shoulder with a quizzical grin. "Don't be cross. I'll come back with bread and tea and a book, and I'll stay as long as it takes to have a smile from you."

"I never smile," he told her.

Much to his surprise, Win did return. She spent the better part of a day reading to him, some dull and wordy story that made him drowsy with contentment. No music, no rustling of trees in the forest, no birdsong had ever pleased him as much as her voice. Occasionally another family member came to the doorway, but Kev couldn't bring himself to snap at any of them. He couldn't seem to hate anyone when he was so close to happiness.

The next day the Hathaways brought him to the main room in the cottage, a parlor filled with worn furniture. Every available surface was covered with sketches, needlework, and piles of books. While Kev half reclined on the sofa, the smaller girls played on the carpet nearby, trying to teach tricks to Beatrix's pet squirrel. Leo and his father played chess in the corner. Amelia and her mother cooked in the kitchen.

Win sat close to Kev and combed the tangles from his hair with great care. "Hold still. I'm trying to be—oh, do stop flinching! Your head can't possibly be that sensitive."

Kev wasn't flinching because of the tangles or the comb. It was because he'd never been touched for so long by anyone in his life. But as he glanced around the room, it seemed no one minded or cared about what Win was doing. He settled back with slitted eyes. The comb tugged a little too hard, and Win murmured an apology and rubbed the smarting spot with her fingertips. So gently. It made his throat tight and his eyes sting. He held still, hardly able to breathe for the pleasure she gave him.

Next came a cloth draped around his neck and the scissors.

"I'm very good at this," Win said, pushing his head forward and combing the locks at the back of his neck. "And your hair badly needs cutting. There's enough wool on your head to stuff a mattress."

"Beware, lad," Mr. Hathaway said cheerfully. "Recollect what happened to Samson."

Kev's head lifted. "What?"

Win pushed it back down. "Samson's hair was his source of strength," she said. "After Delilah cut it, he turned weak and was captured by the Philistines."

"Haven't you read the Bible?" Poppy asked.

"No," Kev said. He held still as the scissors bit carefully through the thick waves at his nape.

"Oooooh, how pretty!" the little girl, Beatrix, exclaimed. "May I have it, Win?"

"No," Kev said gruffly, his head still bent.

"Why not?" Beatrix asked.

"Someone could use it to make a bad luck charm. Or a love spell."

"Oh, I wouldn't do that," Beatrix said earnestly. "I just want to line a nest with it."

"Never mind, darling," Win said serenely. "If it makes our friend uncomfortable, your pets will have to make do with some other nesting material." The scissors snipped through another heavy black swath.

Kev was quiet, listening to the family talk while Win cut his hair. It was the oddest conversation he'd ever heard. They moved from one subject to another, debating ideas that didn't apply to them, situations that didn't affect them. There was no point to any of it, but they seemed to enjoy themselves tremendously.

He had never known people like this existed. He had no idea how they'd survived this long.

THE HATHAWAYS WERE AN UNWORLDLY LOT, ECCENTRIC AND cheerful and preoccupied with books and art and music. They lived in a ramshackle cottage, but instead of repairing door frames or holes in the ceiling, they pruned roses and wrote poetry. If a chair leg broke off, they merely wedged a stack of books beneath it. Their priorities bewildered him. He was further mystified when, after his wounds had healed sufficiently, they invited him to make a room for himself in the stable loft.

Kev began to take care of the things the Hathaways paid no attention to, such as repairing the holes in the ceiling and the decaying joints beneath the chimney stack. Despite his terror of heights, he did new coat work on the thatched roof. He took care of the horse and the cow, and tended the kitchen garden, and even mended the family's shoes. Soon Mrs. Hathaway trusted him to take money to the village to buy food and other necessities.

There was only one time his presence at the Hathaway

cottage had seemed in jeopardy, the time he'd been caught fighting some village toughs.

Mrs. Hathaway had been alarmed by the sight of him, battered and bloody-nosed, and demanded to know how it had happened. "I sent you to fetch a round from the cheesemaker, and you come home empty-handed and in such a condition," she'd cried. "Whom were you fighting, and why?"

Kev hadn't explained, only stood grim-faced at the door as she berated him.

"I won't tolerate brutality in this household," Mrs. Hathaway had continued. "Perhaps you should collect your things and leave."

But before Kev had been able to obey, Win had entered the house. "No, Mother," she'd said calmly. "I know what happened—my friend Laura just told me. Her brother was there. Merripen was defending our family. Two other boys were shouting insults about the Hathaways, and he thrashed them for it."

"What insults?" Mrs. Hathaway had asked, bewildered.

Kev had stared hard at the floor with his fists clenched.

Win hadn't flinched from the truth. "They're criticizing our family," she'd said, "because we're harboring a Rom. Some of the villagers don't like it. They're afraid Merripen might steal from them, or put curses on people, or other such nonsense. They blame us for taking him in."

In the silence that followed, Kev trembled with anger and a sense of defeat. He was a liability to the family. He would never be able to live among *gadje* without conflict.

"I'll go," he said. It was the best thing he could do for them.

"You most certainly will not," Mrs. Hathaway had astonished him by saying. "What would it teach my children to let such ignorance and despicable prejudice prevail? No, you'll stay. But you mustn't fight, Merripen. Ignore them, and they'll eventually lose interest in taunting us."

A new voice had entered the conversation. "If he stays," Leo had remarked, coming into the kitchen, "he'll most certainly have to fight, Mother."

Like Kev, Leo had looked much the worse for wear, with a blackened eye and a split lip. He gave a crooked grin at his mother's and sister's exclamations. Still smiling, he glanced at Kev. "I thrashed one or two of the fellows you overlooked," he said.

"Oh dear," Mrs. Hathaway had said sorrowfully, taking her son's hand, which had been bruised and bleeding from a gash where he must have caught someone's tooth with a knuckle. "These are hands meant for holding books. Not fighting."

"I like to think I can manage both," Leo had said dryly. His expression turned serious as he gazed at Kev. "I'll be damned if anyone will tell me who may live in my home. As long as you wish to stay, Merripen, I'll defend you as a brother."

"I don't want to make trouble for you," Kev had muttered.

"No trouble," Leo had replied, gingerly flexing his hand. "Some principles are worth standing up for."

Chapter Three

Constant exposure to the Hathaways had changed Kev. He'd spent years listening to their animated discussions about Shakespeare, Galileo, Flemish art versus Venetian, democracy and monarchy and theocracy, and every other imaginable subject. He'd learned to read, and had even acquired some Latin. He had changed into someone his former tribe would never have recognized.

Kev had never come to think of Mr. and Mrs. Hathaway as parents, although he would have done anything for them. He had no desire to form attachments to people. That would have required more trust and intimacy than he could summon. But he did care for all the Hathaway brood, even Leo. And then there was Win, for whom he would have died a thousand times over.

He would never dare assume a place in her life other than as a protector. She was too fine, too rare. As she grew into womanhood, every man in the county was enthralled by her beauty.

Outsiders tended to view Win as an ice maiden, but they knew nothing of the sly wit and warmth that lurked beneath her perfect surface. Outsiders hadn't seen Win teaching

Poppy the steps to a quadrille until they'd both collapsed to the floor in giggles. Or the occasions she'd gone frog-hunting with Beatrix. Or the droll way she read a Dickens novel with an array of voices and sounds that made the entire family howl at her cleverness.

Kev loved her. Not in the way that novelists and poets described. Nothing so tame. He loved her beyond earth, heaven, or hell. Every moment out of her company was agony; every moment with her was the only peace he had ever known. Every touch of her hands was a sensation that ate down to his soul. He would have died before admitting it to anyone. The truth was buried deep in his heart.

"There," Win said one day after they had rambled through dry meadows and settled to rest in their favorite place. "You're almost doing it."

"Almost doing what?" Kev asked lazily. They reclined by a clump of trees bordering a winterbourne, a stream that ran dry in the summer months. The grass was littered with purple rampion and white meadowsweet, the latter spreading an almondlike fragrance through the air.

"Smiling." She lifted on her elbows beside him and touched his lips with her fingers. Kev stopped breathing.

A pipit rose from a nearby tree on taut wings, drawing out a long note as he descended.

Intent on her task, Win shaped the corners of Kev's mouth upward and tried to hold them there.

Aroused and amused, Kev let out a smothered laugh and brushed her hand away.

"You should smile more often," Win said, still staring down at him. "You're very handsome when you do."

She was more dazzling than the sun, her hair like cream silk, her lips a tender shade of pink. At first her gaze seemed like nothing more than friendly inquiry, but as it held on his, he realized she was trying to read his secrets.

He wanted to pull her down with him and cover her body with his. It had been four years since he had come to live with the Hathaways. Now he was finding it more and more difficult to control his feelings for Win.

"What are you thinking when you look at me like that?" she asked softly.

"I can't say."

"Why not?"

Kev felt the smile hovering on his lips again, this time edged with wryness. "It would frighten you."

"Merripen," she said decisively, "nothing you could ever do or say would frighten me." She frowned. "Are you *ever* going to tell me your first name?"

"No."

"You will. I'll make you." She pretended to beat against his chest with her fists.

Kev caught her slim wrists in his hands, restraining her easily. His body followed the motion, rolling to trap her beneath him. It was wrong, but he couldn't stop himself. And as he pinned her with his weight, felt her wriggle instinctively to accommodate him, he was almost paralyzed by the primal pleasure of it. He expected her to struggle, to fight him, but instead she went passive in his hold, smiling up at him.

Dimly Kev remembered one of the mythology stories the Hathaways were so fond of . . . the Greek one about Hades, the god of the underworld, kidnapping the maiden Persephone in a flowery field and dragging her down through an opening in the earth. Down to his dark, private world where he could possess her. Although the Hathaway daughters had all been indignant about Persephone's fate, Kev's sympathies had privately been on Hades's side.

"I don't see why eating a mere half dozen pomegranate seeds should have condemned Persephone to stay with Hades part of every year," Poppy had said in outrage. "No one told her the rules. It wasn't fair. I'm certain she would never have touched a thing had she known what would happen."

"And it wasn't a very filling snack," Beatrix had added, perturbed. "If I'd been there, I would have asked for a pudding or a jam pasty, at least."

"Perhaps she wasn't altogether unhappy, having to stay," Win had suggested, her eyes twinkling. "After all, Hades did make her his queen. And the story says he possessed the riches of the earth."

"A rich husband," Amelia had said, "doesn't change the fact that Persephone's main residence is in an undesirable location with no view whatsoever. Just think of the difficulties in leasing it out during the off-months."

They had all agreed that Hades was a complete villain.

But Kev had understood exactly why the underworld god had stolen Persephone for his bride. He had wanted a little bit of sunshine, of warmth, for himself, down in the cheerless gloom of his dark palace.

"So the tribe members who left you for dead," Win said, bringing Kev's thoughts back to the present, "they're allowed to know your name, but I'm not?"

"That's right." Kev watched the brindling of sun and leaf shadows on her face. He wondered how it would feel to press his lips to that soft skin.

A delectable notch appeared between Win's tawny brows. "Why? Why can't I know?"

"Because you're a *gadji*." His tone was more tender than he had meant it to be.

"Your *gadji*."

At this foray into dangerous territory, Kev felt his heart contract painfully. She wasn't his, nor could she ever be. Except in his heart.

He rolled off her, rising to his feet. "It's time to go back," he said curtly. He reached down for her, gripped her small, extended hand, and hauled her upward. She didn't check the momentum but instead let herself fall naturally against him. Her skirts fluttered around his legs, and the slim feminine shape of her body pressed all along his front. Desperately he searched for the strength, the will, to push her away.

"Will you ever try to find them, Merripen?" she asked. "Will you ever go away from me?"

Never, he thought in a flash of ardent need. But instead, he said, "I don't know."

"If you did, I would follow you. And I would bring you back home."

"I doubt the man you marry would allow that."

Win smiled as if the statement were ridiculous. She eased herself away and let go of his hand. They began the walk back to Hampshire House in silence. "Tobar?" she suggested after a moment. "Garridan? Palo?"

"No."

"Rye?"

"No."

"Cooper? . . . Stanley? . . ."

"No."

To the pride of the entire Hathaway family, Leo was accepted at the Académie des Beaux-Arts in Paris, where he studied art and architecture for two years. So promising was Leo's talent that part of his tuition was assumed by the renowned London architect Rowland Temple, who said that Leo could repay him by working as his draughtsman upon returning.

Leo had matured into a steady and good-natured young man, with a keen wit and a ready laugh. And in light of his talent and ambition, there was the promise of even more

attainment. Upon his return to England, Leo took up residence in London to fulfill his obligation to Temple, but he also
came frequently to visit his family at Primrose Place. And to
court a pretty, dark-haired village girl named Laura Dillard.

During Leo's absence, Kev had done his best to take care
of the Hathaways. And Mr. Hathaway had tried on more than
one occasion to help Kev plan a future for himself. Such
conversations turned out to be an exercise in frustration for
them both.

"You are being wasted," Mr. Hathaway had told Kev, looking mildly troubled.

Kev had snorted at that, but Mr. Hathaway had persisted.

"We must consider your future. And before you say a word,
let me state that I am aware of the Rom's preference to live
in the present. But you have changed, Merripen. You have advanced too far to neglect what has taken root in you."

"Do you want me to leave?" Kev asked quietly.

"Heavens, no. Not at all. As I have told you before, you
may stay with us as long as you wish. But I feel it my duty
to make you aware that in staying here, you are sacrificing
many opportunities for self-improvement. You should go out
into the world, as Leo has. Take an apprenticeship, learn a
trade, perhaps enlist in the military—"

"What would I get from that?" Kev had asked.

"To start with, the ability to earn more than the pittance
I'm able to give you."

"I don't need money."

"But as things stand, you haven't the means to marry, to
buy your own plot of land, to—"

"I don't want to marry. And I can't own land. No one can."

"In the eyes of the British government, Merripen, a man
most certainly can own land, and a house upon it."

"The tent shall stand when the palace shall fall," Kev had
replied prosaically.

Mr. Hathaway had let out an exasperated chuckle. "I would rather argue with a hundred scholars," he had told Kev, "than with one Rom. Very well, we will let the matter rest for now. But bear in mind . . . life is more than following the impulses of primitive feeling. A man must make his mark on the world."

"Why?" Kev asked in genuine bewilderment, but Mr. Hathaway had already gone to join his wife in the rose garden.

APPROXIMATELY A YEAR AFTER LEO HAD RETURNED FROM Paris, tragedy struck the Hathaway family. Until then none of them had ever known true sorrow, fear, or grief. They had lived in what had seemed to be a magically protected family circle. But Mr. Hathaway complained of odd, sharp pains in his chest one evening, leading his wife to conclude that he was suffering dyspepsia after a particularly rich supper. He went to bed early, quiet and gray-faced. No more was heard from their room until daybreak, when Mrs. Hathaway came out weeping and told the stunned family their father was dead.

And that was only the beginning of the Hathaways' misfortune. It seemed the family had fallen under a curse, in which the full measure of their former happiness had been converted to sorrow. "Trouble comes in threes" was one of the sayings Kev remembered from his childhood, and to his bitter regret, it proved to be true.

Mrs. Hathaway was so overcome by grief that she took to her bed after her husband's funeral, and suffered such melancholy that she could scarcely be persuaded to eat or drink. None of her children's attempts to bring her back to her usual self were effective. In a startlingly short time, she had wasted away to almost nothing.

"Is it possible to die of a broken heart?" Leo asked somberly one evening, after the doctor had left with the pronouncement that he could discern no physical cause of their mother's decline.

"She should want to live for Poppy and Beatrix, at least," Amelia said, keeping her voice low. At that moment, Poppy was putting Beatrix to bed in another room. "They're still too young to be without a mother. No matter how long I had to live with a broken heart, I would force myself to do it, if only to take care of them."

"But you have a core of steel," Win said, patting her older sister's back. "You are your own source of strength. I'm afraid Mother has always drawn hers from Father." She glanced at Kev with despairing blue eyes. "Merripen, what would Roma prescribe for melancholy? How would your culture view this?"

Kev shook his head, switching his gaze to the hearth. "They would leave her alone. Too much grief tempts the dead to come back and haunt the living."

All four were silent then, listening to the hiss and snap of the small fire.

"She wants to be with Father, wherever he's gone," Win said eventually. "Her heart is broken. I wish it weren't. I'd exchange my life, my heart, for hers, if such a trade were possible. I wish—" She broke off with a quick breath as Kev's hand closed over her arm.

He hadn't been aware of reaching out for her, but her words had provoked him irrationally. She was tempting Fate. "Don't say that," he muttered.

"Why not?" she whispered.

Because it wasn't hers to give.

Your heart is mine, he thought. *It belongs to me.*

And though he hadn't said the words aloud, it seemed somehow that Win had heard them. Her eyes widened, darkened, and a flush born of strong emotion rose in her face. And right there, in the presence of her brother and sister, she lowered her head and pressed her cheek to the back of Kev's hand.

Kev longed to comfort her, envelop her with kisses, surround her with his strength. Instead he released her arm carefully and risked a wary glance at Amelia and Leo. The former had picked up a few pieces of kindling from the hearthside basket and was occupying herself by feeding them to the fire. The latter was watching Win intently.

LESS THAN SIX MONTHS AFTER HER HUSBAND'S DEATH, Mrs. Hathaway was laid to rest beside him. And before the siblings could begin to accept that they had been orphaned with such cruel swiftness, the third tragedy occurred.

"MERRIPEN." WIN STOOD AT THE FRONT THRESHOLD OF THE cottage. There was such an odd look on her face that Kev rose to his feet at once.

He was bone-weary and dirty, having just come in from working all day at a neighbor's house, building a gate and fence around their yard. To set the fence posts, Kev had dug holes in ground already permeated with the frost of approaching winter. He had just sat down at the table with Amelia, who was attempting to clean spots from one of Poppy's dresses with a quill dipped in spirit of turpentine. The scent of the chemical burned in Kev's nostrils as he drew in a quick breath. He knew from Win's expression that something was very wrong.

"I've been with Laura and Leo today," Win said. "Laura took ill earlier . . . she said her throat hurt, and her head, and so we took her home at once and her family sent for the doctor. He said it was scarlet fever."

"Oh God," Amelia breathed, the color draining from her face. The three of them were silent with shared horror.

There was no other fever that burned so violently or spread so quickly. It provoked a brilliant red rash from the skin, imparting a fine, gritty texture like the glass paper used to smooth pieces of wood. And it burned and ravaged its way through the body until the organs failed. The disease lingered in the expired air, in locks of hair, on the skin itself. The only way to protect others was to isolate the patient.

"Was he certain?" Kev asked in a controlled voice.

"Yes, he said the signs are unmistakable. And he said—"

Win broke off as Kev strode toward her. "No, Merripen!" And she held up a slim white hand with such desperate authority that it stopped him in his tracks. "No one must come near me. Leo is at Laura's house. He won't leave her. They said it was all right for him to stay, and . . . you must gather up Poppy and Beatrix, and Amelia, too, and take them to our cousins in Hedgerley. They won't like it, but they'll take them in and—"

"I'm not going anywhere," Amelia said, her manner calm even though she was trembling slightly. "If you have the fever, you'll need me to take care of you."

"But if you should catch it—"

"I had a very mild bout of it when I was a young child. That means I'm probably safe from it now."

"What about Leo?"

"I'm afraid he didn't have it. Which may put him in danger." Amelia glanced at Kev. "Merripen, did you ever—"

"I don't know."

"Then you should stay away with the children until this is over. Will go you collect them? They went out to play at the winterbourne. I'll pack their things."

Kev found it nearly impossible to leave Win when she might be ill. But there was no choice. Someone had to take her sisters to a safe place.

Before an hour had passed, Kev had found Beatrix and Poppy, loaded the bewildered girls into the family carriage, and taken them on the half-day journey to Hedgerley. By the time he had settled them with their cousins and returned to the cottage, it was well past midnight.

Amelia was in the parlor, wearing her nightclothes and dressing robe, her hair trailing down her back in a long braid. She sat before the fire, her shoulders hunched inward.

She looked up with surprise as Kev entered the house. "You shouldn't be here. The danger—"

"How is she?" Kev interrupted. "Any sign of fever yet?"

"Chills. Pains. No rise in temperature, as far as I can tell. Perhaps that's a good sign. Perhaps that means she'll only have it lightly."

"Any word from the Dillards? Or from Leo?"

Amelia shook her head. "Win said he meant to sleep in the parlor and go to her whenever they would allow it. It isn't at all proper, but if Laura . . . well, if she doesn't live through this . . ." Amelia's voice thickened, and she paused to swallow back tears. "I suppose if it comes to that, they wouldn't want to deprive Laura of her last moments with the man she loves."

Kev sat nearby and silently sorted through platitudes he'd heard *gadje* say. Things about endurance, and accepting the Almighty's will, and about worlds far better than this one. He couldn't bring himself to repeat any of it to Amelia. Her grief was too honest, her love for her family too real.

"It's too much," he heard Amelia whisper after a while. "I can't bear losing anyone else. I'm so afraid for Win. I'm afraid for Leo." She rubbed her forehead. "I sound like the rankest coward, don't I?"

Kev shook his head. "You would be a fool not to be afraid."

That elicited a small, dry chuckle. "I am definitely not a fool, then."

By morning Win was flushed and feverish, her legs moving restlessly beneath the covers. Kev went to a window and drew open the curtain, admitting the weak light of dawn.

She awakened as he approached the bed, her blue eyes

wide in her red-burnished face. "No," she croaked, trying to shrink away from him. "You're not supposed to be here. Don't come near me; you'll catch it—"

"Quiet," Kev said, sitting on the edge of the mattress. He caught Win as she tried to roll away and settled his hand on her forehead. He felt the burning pulse beneath her fragile skin, the veins lit with raging fever.

As Win struggled to push him away, Kev was alarmed by how feeble she had grown. Already.

"Don't," she sobbed, writhing. Weak tears slid from her eyes. "Please don't touch me. I don't want you here. I don't want you to get sick. Oh, *please* go . . ."

Kev pulled her up against him, her body living flame beneath the thin layer of her nightgown, the pale silk of her hair streaming over both of them. And he cradled her head in one of his hands, the powerful battered hand of a bare-knuckle fighter. "You're mad," he said in a low voice, "if you think I would leave you now. I'll see you safe and well, no matter what it takes."

"I won't live through this," she whispered.

Kev was shocked by the words, and even more by his own reaction to them.

"I'm going to die," she said, "and I won't take you with me."

Kev gripped her more closely, letting her fitful breaths blow against his face. No matter how she writhed, he wouldn't let go. He breathed the air from her, taking it deep into his own lungs.

"*Stop,*" she cried, trying desperately to twist away from him. The exertion caused her flush to darken. "This is madness . . . oh, you stubborn ass, let me go!"

"Never." Kev smoothed her wild, fine hair, the strands darkening where her tears had tracked. "Easy," he murmured. "Don't exhaust yourself. Rest."

Win's struggles slowed as she recognized the futility of

resisting him. "You're so strong," she said faintly, the words born not of praise, but damnation. "You're so strong . . ."

"Yes," Kev said, gently using a corner of the bed linens to dry her face. "I'm a brute, and you've always known it, haven't you?"

"Yes," she whispered.

"And you're going to do as I say." He cradled her against his chest and gave her some water.

She took a few painful sips. "Can't," she managed, turning her face away.

"More," he insisted, bringing the cup back to her lips.

"Let me sleep, please—"

"After you drink more."

Kev wouldn't relent until she obeyed with a moan. Settling her back into the pillows, he let her drowse for a few minutes, then returned with some toast softened in broth. He bullied her into taking a few spoonfuls.

By that time Amelia had awakened, and she came into Win's room. A quick double blink was Amelia's only reaction to the sight of Win leaning back against Kev's arm while he fed her.

"Get rid of him," Win told her sister hoarsely, her head resting on Kev's shoulder. "He's torturing me."

"Well, we've always known he was a fiend," Amelia said in a reasonable tone, coming to stand at the bedside. "How dare you, Merripen? . . . Coming into an unsuspecting girl's room and feeding her toast."

"The rash has started," Kev said, noting the roughness that was rising up Win's throat and cheeks. Her silken skin had turned sandy and red. He felt Amelia's hand touch his back, clenching in a loose fold of his shirt as if she needed to hold on to him for balance.

But Amelia's voice was light and steady. "I'll mix a solution of soda water. That should soothe the rawness, dear."

Kev felt a surge of admiration for Amelia. No matter what disasters came her way, she was willing to meet all challenges. Of all the Hathaways, she had shown the toughest mettle so far. And yet Win would have to be stronger and even more obstinate if she was to survive the days to come.

"While you bathe her," he told Amelia, "I'll fetch the doctor."

Not that he had any faith in a *gadjo* doctor, but it might give the sisters peace of mind. Kev also wanted to see how Leo and Laura were faring.

After relinquishing Win to Amelia's care, Kev went to the Dillards' home. But the maid who answered the door told him that Leo wasn't available.

"He's in there with Miss Laura," the maid said brokenly, blotting her face with a rag. "She knows no one; she is near insensible. She is failing fast, sir."

Kev felt the traction of his short, pared nails against the tough skin of his palms. Win was less robust than Laura Dillard, less sturdy in form and constitution. If Laura was sinking so fast, it hardly seemed possible that Win would be able to withstand the same fever.

His next thoughts were of Leo, who was not a brother by blood but certainly a tribesman. Leo loved Laura Dillard with an intensity that wouldn't allow him to accept her death rationally, if at all. Kev was more than a little concerned for him. "What is Mr. Hathaway's condition?" Kev asked. "Does he show any sign of illness?"

"No, sir. I don't think so. I don't know."

But from the way her watery gaze slid away from his, Kev understood that Leo was not well. He wanted to take Leo away from the death watch, *now*, and put him to bed to preserve his strength for the days to come. But it would be cruel to deny Leo the last hours with the woman he loved.

"When she passes," Kev said bluntly, "send him home. But

don't let him go alone. Have someone accompany him all the way to the doorstep of the Hathaway cottage. Do you understand?"

"Yes, sir."

Two days later, Leo came home. "Laura's dead," he said, and collapsed in a delirium of fever and grief.

Chapter Four

The scarlet fever that had swept the village was a particularly virulent strain, the worst effects falling on the very young and the old. There were not enough doctors to tend the ailing, and no one outside Primrose Place dared to come. After visiting the cottage to examine the two patients, the exhausted doctor had prescribed hot vinegar poultices for the throat. He had also left a tonic containing tincture of aconite. It seemed to have no effect on either Win or Leo.

"We're not doing enough," Amelia said on the fourth day. Neither she nor Kev had had sufficient sleep, both of them taking turns caring for the ailing brother and sister. Amelia came into the kitchen, where Kev was boiling water for tea. "The only thing we've accomplished so far is to make their decline more comfortable. There must be something that can stop the fever. I won't let this happen." She stood rigid and trembling, stacking word upon word as if trying to shore up her defenses.

She looked so vulnerable that Kev was moved to compassion. He was not comfortable with touching other people or being touched, but a brotherly feeling caused him to step toward her.

"No," Amelia said quickly, as she realized he had been about to reach out to her. Taking a step back, she gave a strong shake of her head. "I . . . I'm not the kind of woman who can lean on anyone. I would fall to pieces."

Kev understood. For people like her, and himself, closeness meant too much.

"What is to be done?" Amelia whispered, wrapping her arms around herself.

Kev rubbed his weary eyes. "Have you heard of a plant called deadly nightshade?"

"No." Amelia was only familiar with herbs used for cooking.

"It only blooms at night. When the sun comes up, the flowers die. There was a *drabengro,* a medicine expert in my tribe. Sometimes he sent me to fetch plants for him. He told me deadly nightshade was the most powerful herb he knew of. It could kill a man, but it could also bring someone back from the brink of death."

"Did you ever see it work?"

Kev nodded, giving her a sidelong glance as he rubbed the taut muscles at the back of his neck. "I saw it cure fever," he muttered. And he waited.

"Get some," Amelia finally said, her voice unsteady. "It may prove to be fatal. But they're both sure to die without it."

KEV BOILED THE PLANTS, WHICH HE HAD FOUND IN THE COR-ner of the village graveyard, down to thin black syrup. Amelia stood beside him as he strained the deadly broth and poured it into a small eggcup.

"Leo first," Amelia said resolutely, though her expression was doubt-ridden. "He's worse off than Win."

They went to Leo's bedside. It was astonishing how quickly a man could deteriorate from scarlet fever, how emaciated their strapping brother had become. Leo's formerly handsome face was unrecognizable, turgid and swollen and discolored. His last coherent words had been the day before, when he had begged Kev to let him die. His wish would soon be granted. From all appearances a coma was only hours, if not minutes, away.

Amelia went directly to a window and opened it, letting the cold air sweep away.

Leo moaned and stirred feebly, unable to resist as Kev forced his mouth open, lifted a spoon, and poured four or five drops of the tincture onto his dry, fissured tongue.

Amelia went to sit beside her brother, smoothing his dull hair, kissing his brow.

"If it were going to . . . to have an adverse effect," she said, when Kev knew she meant *if it were going to kill him*, "how long would it take?"

"Five minutes to an hour." Kev saw the way Amelia's hand shook as she continued to smooth Leo's hair.

It seemed the longest hour of Kev's life as they sat and watched Leo, who moved and muttered as if he was in the middle of a nightmare.

"Poor boy," Amelia murmured, running a cool rag over his face.

When they were certain that no convulsions were forthcoming, Kev retrieved the eggcup and stood.

"You're going to give it to Win now?" Amelia asked, still looking down at her brother.

"Yes."

"Do you need help?"

Kev shook his head. "Stay with Leo."

Kev went to Win's room. She was still and quiet on the bed. She no longer recognized him, her mind and body consumed in the red heat of fever. As he lifted her and let her head fall back on his arm, she writhed in protest.

"Win," he said softly. "Love, be still." Her eyes slitted

open at the sound of his voice. "I'm here," he whispered. He picked up a spoon and dipped it into the cup. "Open your mouth, little *gadji*. Do it for me." But she refused. She turned her face, and her lips moved in a soundless whisper.

"What is it?" he murmured, easing her head back. "Win. You must take this medicine."

She whispered again.

Comprehending the scratchy words, Kev stared at her in disbelief. "You'll take it if I tell you my name?"

She struggled to produce enough saliva to speak. "Yes."

His throat tightened, and the corners of his eyes burned. "It's Kev," he managed to say. "My name is Kev."

She let him put the spoon between her lips then, and the inky poison trickled down her throat.

Her body relaxed against him. As he continued to hold her, the fragile body felt as light and hot as flame in his arms.

I will follow you, he thought, *whatever your fate is.*

Win was the only thing on earth he had ever wanted. She would not leave without him.

Kev bent over her, and touched the dry, hot lips with his own.

A kiss she could not feel and would never remember.

He tasted the poison as he let his mouth linger on hers. Lifting his head, he glanced at the bedside table where he had set the remainder of the deadly nightshade. There was more than enough left to kill a healthy man.

It seemed as if the only thing that kept Win's spirit from leaving her body was the confinement of Kev's arms. So he held her and rocked her. He thought briefly of praying. But he wouldn't acknowledge any being, supernatural or mortal, who threatened to take her from him.

The world had become this quiet, shadowed room, the slender body in his arms, the breath that filtered softly in and out of her lungs. He followed that rhythm with his own breath, his own heartbeat. Leaning back against the bed, he fell into a dark trance as he waited for their shared fate.

Unaware of how much time passed, he rested with her until a movement in the doorway and a glow of light awakened him.

"Merripen." Amelia's husky voice. She held a candle at the threshold.

Kev felt blindly for Win's cheek, laid his hand along the side of her face, and felt a thrill of panic as his fingers met cool skin. He felt for the pulse in her throat.

"Leo's fever has broken," Amelia said. Kev could barely hear her over the blood rush in his ears. "He's going to be well."

A weak but steady throb lay beneath Kev's searching fingertips. Win's heartbeat . . . the pulse that sustained his universe.

Chapter Five

The addition of Cam Rohan to the Hathaway family had set the table for new company. It was puzzling how one person could change everything. Not to mention infuriating.

But then, everything was infuriating to Kev now. Win had gone to France, and there was no reason for him to be pleasant or even civil. He was always aware of his need for her, and the unendurable knowledge that she was somewhere far away and he couldn't reach her.

Kev had forgotten how this felt, this black hatred of the world and all its occupants. It was an unwelcome reminder of his boyhood, when he'd known nothing but violence and misery. And yet the Hathaways all seemed to expect him to behave as usual, to take part in the family routine, to pretend the Earth had gone on spinning.

The only thing that kept him sane was the knowledge of what *she* would want him to do. She would want him to take care of her sisters. And refrain from killing her new brother-in-law.

Kev could hardly stand the bastard.

The rest of them adored him. Cam had come and swept Amelia, a determined spinster, completely off her feet.

Seduced her, as a matter of fact, which Kev still hadn't forgiven him for. But Amelia was entirely happy with her husband, even though he was half-Rom.

None of them had ever met anyone quite like Cam, whose origins were as mysterious as Kev's own. For most of his life, he'd worked at a gentlemen's gaming club, Jenner's, eventually becoming a factotum and then owning a small interest in the highly lucrative business. Burdened with a growing fortune, he had invested it as badly as possible to spare himself the supreme embarrassment of being a Rom with far too much money. It hadn't worked. The money kept coming, every foolish investment returning miraculous dividends. Cam sheepishly called it his good luck curse.

But as it turned out, the curse was useful, since taking care of the Hathaways was an expensive proposition. Their family estate in Hampshire, which Leo had inherited last year along with his title, had burned down recently and was being rebuilt. And Poppy needed clothes for her London season, and Beatrix wanted to go to finishing school. On top of that, there were Win's clinic bills. As Cam had pointed out to Kev, he was in a position to do a great deal for the Hathaways and that should be reason enough for Kev to tolerate him.

Therefore, Kev tolerated him.

Barely.

"Good morning," Cam said cheerfully, coming into the dining area of the family's suite at the Rutledge Hotel. They were already halfway through breakfast. Unlike the rest of them, he wasn't an early riser, having spent most of his life in a gambling club where there was activity at all hours of the night.

He was lean and supple with an easy way of moving. Before taking the chair next to Amelia, he leaned down to kiss her head. The locks of his black hair, worn a shade too long, slid apart to reveal a diamond stud glittering in one ear. There had been a time in the not-too-distant past when Amelia would have disapproved of such demonstrations. Now she merely blushed and looked bemused.

Kev scowled down at his half-finished plate.

"Are you still sleepy?" he heard Amelia ask.

"At this rate, I won't be fully awake until noon."

"You should try some coffee."

"No, thank you. I can't abide the stuff."

Beatrix spoke then. "Merripen drinks lots of coffee. He *loves* it."

"Of course he does," Cam said. "It's dark and bitter." He grinned as Kev gave him a warning glance. "How are you faring this morning, *phral*?"

"Don't call me that." Although Kev didn't raise his voice, there was a savage note in it that gave everyone pause.

After a moment, Amelia spoke to Cam in a deliberately light tone. "We're going to the dressmaker's today, Poppy and Beatrix and I. We'll probably be gone till supper." While Amelia went on to describe the gowns and hats and fripperies they would need, Kev felt Beatrix's small hand creep over his.

"It's all right," Beatrix whispered. "I miss them too."

At sixteen, the youngest Hathaway sibling was at that vulnerable age between childhood and adulthood. A sweet-natured little scamp, she was as inquisitive as one of the many pets she had accumulated. Since Amelia's marriage to Cam, Beatrix had been begging to go to finishing school. Kev suspected she had read one too many novels featuring heroines who acquired airs and graces at academies for young ladies. He was doubtful that finishing school would turn out well for the free-spirited Beatrix.

Letting go of his hand, Beatrix turned her attention back

to the conversation, which had progressed to the subject of Cam's latest investment.

It had become something of a game for him to find an investment opportunity that wouldn't succeed. The last time he'd tried it, he'd bought a London rubber manufactory that was failing badly. As soon as Cam had purchased it, however, the company had acquired patent rights for vulcanization and had invented something called the rubber band. And now people were buying millions of the things.

". . . this one is sure to be a disaster," Cam was saying. "There is a pair of brothers, both of them blacksmiths, who have come up with a design for a man-powered vehicle. They call it a volocycle. Two wheels set on a frame, with a little pad to sit on, propelled by pedals you push with your feet."

"Only two wheels?" Poppy asked, perplexed. "How could one ride it without falling over?"

"The driver would have to balance his center of mass over the wheels."

"How would one turn the vehicle?"

"More importantly," Amelia said in a dry tone, "how would one *stop* it?"

"By the application of one's body to the ground?" Poppy suggested.

Cam laughed. "Probably. We'll put it into production, of course. Westcliff says he's never seen a more disastrous investment. The volocycle looks uncomfortable as the devil and requires balance far beyond the abilities of the average man. It won't be affordable or practical. After all, no sane man would choose to pedal along the street on a two-wheeled contraption in lieu of riding a horse."

"It sounds quite fun, though," Beatrix said wistfully.

"It's not an invention a girl could try," Poppy pointed out.

"Why not?"

"Our skirts would make it impossible."

"Why must we wear skirts?" Beatrix asked. "I think trousers would be ever so much more comfortable."

Amelia looked appalled and amused. "These are observations best kept in the family, dear." Picking up a glass of water, she raised it in Cam's direction. "Well, then. Here's to your first failure." She raised an eyebrow. "I hope you're not risking the entire family fortune before we reach the dressmaker's?"

He grinned at her. "Not the entire fortune. Shop with confidence, *monisha*."

When breakfast was concluded, the women left the dining table, while Cam and Kev stood politely.

Lowering himself back into the chair, Cam watched as Kev began to leave. "Where are you going?" he asked lazily. "Meeting with your tailor? Going to discuss the latest political events at the local coffeehouse?"

"If your goal is to annoy me," Kev informed him, "there's no need to make an effort. You annoy me just by breathing."

"Yes, I know." Cam gestured to a chair. "Join me, Merripen. We need to discuss a few things."

Kev complied with a glower.

"You're a man of few words, aren't you?" Cam observed.

"Better than to fill the air with empty chatter."

"I'll go straight to the point, then. While Leo . . . Lord Ramsay . . . is in Europe, his entire estate, his financial affairs, and three of his sisters have been placed in the care of a pair of Roma. It's not what I'd call an ideal situation. If Leo were in any condition to stay, I would have kept him here and sent Poppy to France with Win."

But Leo was not in good condition, as they both knew. He had been a broken man, a wastrel, ever since the death of Laura Dillard. And although he was finally coming to terms with his grief, his path to healing in both body and spirit would not be short.

"Do you actually believe," Kev asked, his voice riddled with contempt, "that Leo will check himself in as a patient at a health clinic?"

"No. But he'll stay close by to keep an eye on Win. And it's a remote setting where opportunities for trouble are limited. He did well in France before when he was studying architecture. Perhaps living there again will help to recall himself."

"Or," Kev said darkly, "he'll disappear to Paris and drown himself in drink and prostitutes."

Cam shrugged. "Leo's future is in his own hands. I'm more concerned about what we're facing here. Amelia is determined that Poppy should have a season in London and Beatrix should go to finishing school. At the same time, the rebuilding of the manor in Hampshire has to continue. The ruins need to be cleared and the grounds—"

"I know what has to be done."

"Then you'll manage the project? You'll work with the architect, the builders, the masons and carpenters, and so forth?"

Kev glared at him with rank antagonism. "You won't be rid of me that easily. And I'll be damned if I work for you, or answer to you—"

"Wait." Cam's hands lifted in a staying gesture, a scattering of gold rings gleaming richly on his dark fingers. "Wait. For God's sake, I'm not trying to get rid of you. I'm proposing a partnership. Frankly, I'm no more thrilled by the prospect than you are. But there's much to be accomplished. And we have more to gain by working together than being at cross-purposes."

Idly picking up a table knife, Kev ran his fingers along the blunt edge and the intricate gilded handle. "You want me to go to Hampshire and oversee the work crews while you stay in London with the women?"

"Come and go as you please. I'll be traveling back and forth to Hampshire every now and again to look over things." Cam gave him an astute glance. "You have nothing keeping you in London, do you?"

Kev shook his head.

"Then it's settled?" Cam pressed.

Although Kev hated to admit it, the plan was not without appeal. He hated London, the grime and clamor and crowded buildings, the smog and noise. He longed to return to the country. And the thought of rebuilding the manor, exhausting himself with hard work . . . it would do him some good. Besides, he knew what the Ramsay estate needed better than anyone. Cam might know every street, square, and rookery in London, but he wasn't at all familiar with country life. It only made sense for Kev to take charge of the estate.

"I'll want to make improvements to the land as well," Kev said, setting down the knife. "There are field gates and fences that need repair. Ditches and drainage channels to be dug. And the tenant farmers are still using flails and reaphooks because there is no threshing machine. The estate should have its own bakehouse to save the tenants from having to go to the village for their bread. Also—"

"Whatever you decide," Cam said hastily, having the typical Londoner's complete lack of interest in farming. "Attracting more tenants will benefit the estate, of course."

"I know you've already commissioned an architect and builder. But from now on, I'll be the one they come to with questions. I'll need access to the Ramsay accounts. And I'm going to pick the land crews and manage them without interference."

Cam's brows lifted at Kev's authoritative manner. "Well. This is a side of you I haven't seen before."

"Do you agree to my terms?"

"Yes." Cam extended his hand. "Shall we shake on it?"

Kev stood, ignoring the overture. "Not necessary."

Cam's white teeth flashed in a grin. "Merripen, would it be so terrible to attempt a friendship with me?"

"We'll never be friends. At best, we're enemies with a common purpose."

Cam continued to smile. "I suppose the end result is the same." He waited until Kev had reached the door before saying casually, "By the way, I'm going to pursue the matter of the tattoos. If there is a connection between the two of us, I want to find out what it is."

"You'll do it without me," Kev said stonily.

"Why not? Aren't you curious?"

"Not in the least."

Cam's hazel eyes were filled with speculation. "You have no ties to the past and no knowledge of why a unique design was inked into your arm in early childhood. What are you afraid of finding out?"

"You've had the same tattoo for just as long," Kev shot back. "You have no more idea about what it's for than I do. Why take such an interest in it now?"

"I . . ." Absently Cam rubbed his arm over his shirtsleeve, where the tattoo was located. "I always assumed it was done at some whim of my grandmother's. She would never explain why I had the mark, or what it meant."

"Did she know?"

"I believe so. She seemed to know everything. When I was about ten years old, she sent me away from the tribe. She said I was in danger. My cousin Noah brought me to London and helped me to find work at the gaming club as a list-maker's runner. I've never seen any of my tribe since then." Cam paused, his face becoming shadowed. "I had to leave my tribe without ever knowing why. And I had no reason to assume the tattoo had anything to do with it. Until I met you. We have two things in common, *phral*: we're outcasts, and we share an identical tattoo. And I think that finding out where it came from may help us both."

In the following months Kev prepared the Ramsay estate for reconstruction. A mild and half-hearted winter had fallen over the village of Stony Cross and its environs, where the Ramsay estate was located. Beige grasses were crisped with frost, and dogwoods had sent up red winter stems to splinter the pale gray landscape.

The crews employed by John Dashiell, the contractor in charge of rebuilding Ramsay House, were hardworking and efficient. The first two months were spent clearing the remains of the house, carting off charred wood and broken rock and rubble. A small gatehouse on the approach road was repaired for the Hathaways' convenience.

Once the ground began to soften in March, the rebuilding of the manor would start in earnest. Kev was certain the crews had been warned in advance that the project was being supervised by a Rom, for they offered no objection to his presence or his authority. Dashiell, being a self-made and pragmatic man, didn't seem to care as long as his payment schedule was met.

Near the end of February, Kev made the twelve-hour journey from Stony Cross to London. He had received word from Amelia that Beatrix had quit finishing school. Even though Amelia had added that all was well, Kev wanted to make certain for himself. The two months' separation was the longest he had ever spent away from the Hathaway sisters, and he was surprised by how intensely he had missed them.

It seemed the feeling was mutual. As soon as Kev arrived at their suite at the Rutledge Hotel, Amelia, Poppy, and Beatrix all pounced on him with unseemly enthusiasm. He tolerated their shrieks and kisses with gruff indulgence, secretly pleased by the warmth of their welcome.

Following them into the family parlor, Kev sat with Amelia on an overstuffed settee, while Cam and Poppy occupied nearby chairs. Beatrix perched on a footstool at Kev's feet. The women looked well, Kev thought . . . all three stylishly dressed and groomed, their dark hair arranged in pinned-up curls except for Beatrix, who had plaits.

Amelia in particular seemed happy, laughing easily, radiating a contentment that could only come from a good marriage. Poppy was emerging as a beauty, with her fine features and her rich auburn-toned hair . . . a warmer, more approachable version of Win's delicate blond perfection. Beatrix, however, was subdued and thin. To anyone who didn't know her, Beatrix would appear to be a normal, cheerful girl. But Kev saw the subtle signs of tension and strain on her face.

"What happened at school?" Kev asked with his customary bluntness.

Beatrix unburdened herself eagerly. "Oh. Merripen, it was all my fault. School is horrid. I *abhor* it. I did make a friend or two, and I was sorry to leave them. But I didn't get on with my teachers. I was always saying the wrong thing in class, asking the wrong questions—"

"It appeared," Amelia said wryly, "that the Hathaway method of learning and debating wasn't welcome in school."

"And I got into some rows," Beatrix continued, "because some of the girls said their parents told them not to associate with me because we have 'Gypsies' in the family, and for all they knew I might be part 'Gypsy,' too. And I said I wasn't, but even if I were, it would be no cause for shame, and I called them snobs, and then there was a lot of scratching and hair-pulling."

Kev swore under his breath. He exchanged glances with Cam, who looked grim. Their presence in the family was a liability to the Hathaway sisters . . . and yet there was no remedy for that.

"And then," Beatrix said, "my problem came back."

Everyone was silent. Kev reached out and settled his hand on her head, his fingers curving over the shape of her skull. "*Chavi*," he murmured, a Romany endearment for a young girl. Since he rarely used the old language, Beatrix gave him a round-eyed look of surprise.

Beatrix's problem had first appeared after Mr. Hathaway's death. It recurred every now and then in times of anxiety or distress. She had a compulsion to steal things, usually small things like pencil stubs or bookmarks, or the odd piece of flatware. Sometimes she didn't even remember taking an object. Later she would suffer intense remorse and go to extraordinary lengths to return the things she had filched.

Kev removed his hand from her head and looked down at her. "What did you take, little ferret?" he asked gently.

She looked chagrined. "Hair ribbons, combs, books . . . small things. And then I tried to put everything back, but I couldn't remember where it all went. So there was a great rumpus, and I came forward to confess, and I was asked to leave the school. And now I'll never be a lady."

"Yes, you will," Amelia said at once. "We're going to hire a governess, which is what we should have done in the beginning."

Beatrix regarded her doubtfully. "I don't think I would want any governess who would work for our family."

"Oh, we're not as bad as all that—" Amelia began.

"Yes, we are," Poppy informed her. "We're odd, Amelia. I've always told you that. We were odd even before you brought Cam into the family." Casting a quick glance at Cam, she said, "No offense meant."

His eyes glinted with amusement. "None taken."

Poppy turned to Kev. "No matter how difficult it is to find

a proper governess, we *must* have one. I need help. My season has been nothing short of disaster."

"It's only been two months," Kev said. "How can it be a disaster?"

"I'm a wallflower."

"You can't be."

"I'm *lower* than a wallflower," she told him. "No man wants anything to do with me."

Kev looked at Cam and Amelia incredulously. A beautiful, intelligent girl like Poppy should have been overrun with suitors. "What is the matter with these *gadjos*?" Kev asked in amazement.

"They're all idiots," Cam said. "They never waste an opportunity to prove it."

Glancing back at Poppy, Kev cut to the chase. "Is it because there are Roma in the family? Is that why you're not sought after?"

"Well, it doesn't exactly help," Poppy admitted. "But the greater problem is that I have no social graces. I'm constantly making faux pas. And I'm dreadful at small talk. You're supposed to go lightly from topic to topic like a butterfly. It's not easy to do, and there's no point to it. And the young men who do bring themselves to approach me find an excuse to flee after five minutes. Because they flirt and say the silliest things, and I have no idea how to respond."

"I wouldn't want any of them for her, anyway," Amelia said crisply. "You should see them, Merripen. A more useless flock of preening peacocks could not be found."

"I believe it would be called a muster of peacocks," Poppy said. "Not a flock."

"Call them a knot of toads instead," Beatrix said.

"A colony of penguins," Amelia joined in.

"A rumpus of baboons," Poppy said, laughing.

Kev smiled slightly, but he was still preoccupied. Poppy

had always dreamed of a London season. For it to turn out this way must be a crushing disappointment. "Have you been invited to the right events?" he asked. "The dances . . . the dinner things . . ."

"Balls and soirees," Poppy supplied. "Yes, thanks to the patronage of Lord Westcliff and Lord St. Vincent, we've received invitations. But merely getting past the door doesn't make one desirable. It only affords one the opportunity to prop up the wall while everyone else dances."

Kev frowned at Amelia and Cam. "What are you going to do about this?"

"We're going to withdraw Poppy from the season," Amelia said, "and tell everyone that on second thought, she's still too young to be out in society."

"No one will believe that," Beatrix said. "After all, Poppy's almost *nineteen*."

"There's no need to make me sound like a warty old crone, Bea," Poppy said indignantly.

"—and in the meantime," Amelia continued with great patience, "we'll find a governess who will teach both Poppy and Beatrix how to behave."

"She'd better be good," Beatrix said, pulling a grunting black-and-white guinea pig from her pocket and snuggling it under her chin. "We have a lot to overcome. Don't we, Mr. Nibbles?"

LATER, AMELIA TOOK KEV ASIDE. SHE REACHED INTO THE pocket of her gown and extracted a small, white square. She gave it to him, her gaze searching his face. "Win wrote other letters to the family, and of course you shall read those as well. But this was addressed solely to you."

Unable to speak, Kev closed his fingers around the bit of parchment sealed with wax.

He went to his hotel room, which was separate from the

rest of the family's at his request. Sitting at a small table, he broke the seal with scrupulous care.

There was Win's familiar writing, the pen strokes small and precise.

> *Dear Kev,*
>
> *I hope this letter finds you in full health and vigor. I cannot imagine you in any other state, actually. Every morning I awaken in this place, which seems another world entirely, and I am surprised anew to find myself so far away from my family. And from you.*
>
> *The journey across the channel was trying, the land route to the clinic even more so. As you know, I am not a good traveler, but Leo saw me safely here. He is now residing a short distance away as a paying guest at a small château, and so far he has come to visit every other day . . .*

Win's letter went on to describe the clinic, which was quiet and austere. The patients suffered from a variety of ailments, but most especially those of the lung and pulmonary system.

Instead of dosing them with narcotic drugs and keeping them inside as most doctors prescribed, Dr. Harrow put them all on a program of exercise, cold baths, health tonics, and a simple abstemious diet. Compelling the patients to exercise was a controversial treatment, but according to Dr. Harrow, motion was the prevailing instinct of all animal life.

The patients started every day with a morning walk outside, rain or shine, followed by an hour in the gymnasium for activities such as ladder-climbing or lifting dumbbells. So far Win could hardly manage any exercises without becoming severely out of breath, but she thought she could detect a small improvement in her abilities. Everyone at the clinic was required to practice breathing on a new device called a spirometer, an apparatus for measuring the volume of air inspired and expired by the lungs.

There was more about the clinic and the patients, which Kev skimmed over quickly. And then he reached the last paragraphs.

Since my illness I have had the strength to do very little except to love, but that I have done, and I still do, in full measure. I am sorry for the way I shocked you the morning I left, but I do not regret the sentiments I expressed.

I am running after you, and life, in desperate pursuit. My dream is that someday you will both turn and let me catch you. That dream carries me through every night. I long to tell you so many things, but I am not free yet.

I hope to be well enough someday to shock you again with far more pleasing results.

I have enclosed a hundred kisses in this letter. You must count them out carefully and not lose any.

Yours, Win

Flattening the slip of paper on the table, Kev smoothed it and ran his fingertips along the delicate lines of script. He read it twice more.

He let his hand close over the parchment, crushing it tightly, and then he hurled it into the hearth, where a small fire was burning.

And he watched the parchment light and smolder, until the whiteness had darkened into ash and every last word from Win had disappeared.

Chapter Six

A t long last, Win had come home.

The clipper from Calais was docked, the hold packed with luxury goods and bags of letters and parcels to be delivered by the Royal Mail. It was a medium-sized ship with seven spacious staterooms for the passengers, each lined with Gothic arched panels and painted a glossy shade of Florence white.

Win stood on the deck and watched the crew employing the ground tackle to moor the ship. Only then would the passengers be allowed to disembark.

Once, the excitement that gripped her would have made it impossible to breathe. But Win was returning to London a different woman. She wondered how her family would react to the changes in her. Of course, they had all changed as well: Amelia and Cam had been married for two years now, and Poppy and Beatrix were now out in society.

And Kev . . . but Win's mind shied from thoughts of him, which were too stirring to dwell on when she was in public.

She gazed at the forest of ship masts, the endless acres of quay and jetty, the immense warehouses for tobacco, wool, and wine. There was movement everywhere, sailors, passengers, provision agents, laborers, vehicles, and live-stock. A profusion of odors thickened the air: goats and horses, spices, ocean salt, tar, dry rot. And above all hung the stench of chimney smoke and coal vapor, darkening as the night pressed close over the city.

Win longed to be in Hampshire, where the spring mead-ows would be green and thick with wildflowers and the hedgerows were in bloom. According to Amelia, the resto-ration of the Ramsay estate was not yet complete, but the manor was habitable now. It seemed the work had gone with extraordinary speed under Kev's direction.

The gangplank was lowered from the vessel and secured. As Win watched the first few passengers descend to the dock, she saw her brother's tall, almost lanky form leading the way.

France had been good for both of them. Whereas Win had gained some much-needed weight, Leo had lost his dis-sipated bloat. He had spent so much time out-of-doors, walking, painting, swimming, that his dark brown hair had lightened a few shades and his skin had soaked up sun. His eyes, a striking pale shade of blue, were startling in his tanned face.

Win knew that her brother would never again be the gal-lant, unguarded boy he had been before Laura Dillard's death. But he was no longer a suicidal wreck, which would no doubt be a great relief to the rest of the family.

In a relatively short time, Leo bounded back up the gang-plank. He came to Win with a wry grin, clamping his top hat more firmly on his head.

"Is anyone waiting for us?" Win asked eagerly.

"No."

Worry creased her forehead. "They must not have received my letter." She and Leo had sent word that they would be ar-riving a few days earlier than expected, owing to a change in the clipper line's schedule.

"Your letter is probably stuck at the bottom of a Royal Mail satchel somewhere," Leo said. "Don't worry, Win. We'll go to the Rutledge by hackney. It isn't far."

"But it will be a shock to the family for us to arrive before we're expected."

"Our family likes to be shocked," he said. "Or at least, they're accustomed to it."

"They'll be surprised that Dr. Harrow has come back with us."

"I'm sure they won't mind his presence at all," Leo replied. One corner of his mouth twitched in private amusement. "Well . . . most of them won't."

EVENING HAD FALLEN BY THE TIME THEY REACHED THE RUT-ledge Hotel. Leo arranged for rooms and managed the luggage, while Win and Dr. Harrow waited in a corner of the spacious lobby.

"I'll allow you to reunite with your family in private," Dr. Harrow said. "My manservant and I will go to our rooms and unpack."

"You are welcome to come with us," Win said, but she was secretly relieved when he shook his head.

"I won't intrude. Your reunion should be private."

"But we will see you in the morning?" Win asked.

Yes." He stood looking down at her, a slight smile on his lips.

Dr. Julian Harrow was an elegant man, supremely composed, effortlessly charming. He was dark-haired, and gray-eyed, and possessed a square-jawed attractiveness that had caused nearly all of his female patients to fall a little bit in love with him. One of the women at the clinic had remarked dryly that Dr. Harrow's personal magnetism not only affected men, women, and children but also extended to potted plants, and the nearby goldfish in a bowl.

As Leo had put it: "Harrow doesn't look at all like a doctor. He looks like a woman's fantasy of a doctor. I suspect half his practice consists of lovestruck females who prolong their illness merely to continue being treated by him."

"I assure you," Win had said, laughing, "I am neither lovestruck, nor am I the least bit inclined to prolong my illness."

But she had to admit, it was difficult not to feel *something* for a man who was attractive, attentive, and had also cured her of a debilitating condition. And Win thought Julian might possibly have feelings for her in return. During the past year especially, when Win's health had rebounded into full vitality, Julian had begun to treat her as something more than a mere patient. They had gone on long walks through the impossibly romantic scenery of Provence, and he had flirted with her, and had made her laugh. His attentions had soothed her wounded spirit after Kev had so callously ignored her.

Eventually Win had accepted that the feelings she had for Kev were not reciprocated. She had even cried on Leo's shoulder. Her brother had pointed out that she had seen very little of the world and knew next to nothing about men.

"Don't you think it's possible your attachment to him was a result of proximity as much as anything else?" Leo had asked gently. "Let's look at the situation honestly, Win. You have nothing in common with him. You're a lovely, sensitive, literate woman, and he's . . . Merripen. He likes to chop wood for entertainment. And apparently it falls to me to point out the indelicate truth that some couples are well-suited in the bedroom but not anywhere else."

Win had been shocked out of her tears by his bluntness. "Leo Hathaway, are you suggesting—"

"Lord Ramsay now, thank you," he had teased.

"*Lord Ramsay*, are you suggesting that my feelings for Merripen are carnal in nature?"

"They're certainly not intellectual," Leo had said, and grinned as she punched him in the shoulder.

After much reflection, however, Win had had to admit that Leo had a point. Of course, Kev was far more intelligent and educated than her brother gave him credit for. As far as she remembered, Kev had challenged Leo in many a philosophical discussion and had memorized more Greek and Latin than anyone else in the family except her father. But he'd only learned those things to fit in with the Hathaways, not because he had any real interest in obtaining an education.

Kev was a man of nature; he craved the feel of earth and sky. And he and Win were as different as fish from fowl.

Julian took her hand in his long, elegant one. His fingers were smooth and well-tended, tapered at the tips. "Winnifred," he said gently, "now that we're away from the clinic, life won't be quite so well-regulated. You must safeguard your health. Make certain you rest tonight, no matter how tempting it is to stay up all hours."

"Yes, Doctor," Win said, smiling up at him. She felt a surge of affection for him, remembering the first time she had managed to climb the exercise ladder in the clinic. Julian had been behind her every step, his encouragements soft in her ear, his chest firm against her back. *A little higher, Winnifred. I won't let you fall.* He hadn't done any of the work for her. Only kept her safe as she climbed.

"I'M A BIT NERVOUS," WIN ADMITTED AS LEO ESCORTED HER to the Hathaways' suite on the hotel's second floor.

"Why?"

"I'm not sure. Perhaps because we've all changed."

"The essential things haven't changed." Leo gripped her elbow firmly. "You're still the delightful girl you were. And I'm still a scoundrel with a taste for spirits and light-skirts."

"Leo," she said, darting a quick frown at him. "You're not planning to go back to your old ways, are you?"

"I will avoid temptation," he replied, "unless it happens to fall directly in my path." He stopped her at the middle landing. "Do you want to pause for a moment?"

"Not at all." Win continued enthusiastically upward. "I love stair climbing. I love doing anything I couldn't do before. And from now on I'm going to live by the motto 'Life is to be lived to the fullest.'"

Leo grinned. "You should know that I've said that on many occasions in the past, and it always landed me in trouble."

Win glanced at her surroundings with pleasure. After living in the austere surroundings of Harrow's clinic for so long, she would enjoy a taste of luxury.

Elegant, modern, and supremely comfortable, the Rutledge was owned by the mysterious Harry Rutledge, about whom there were so many rumors that no one could even say definitively whether he was British or American. All that was known for certain was that he had lived for a time in America and had come to England to create a hotel that combined the opulence of Europe with the best of American innovations.

The Rutledge was the first hotel to design every single bedroom en suite with its own private bathroom. And there were delights such as food service lifts, built-in cupboards in the bedrooms, private meeting rooms with atrium glass ceilings, and gardens designed as outdoor rooms. The hotel also featured a dining room that was said to be the most beautiful in England, with so many chandeliers that the ceiling had required extra reinforcements during construction.

They reached the door of the Hathaways' suite, and Leo knocked gently.

There were a few movements within. The door opened to

reveal a young fair-haired maid. The maid's gaze swept over the both of them. "May I help you, sir?" she asked Leo.

"We've come to see Mr. and Mrs. Rohan."

"Beg pardon, sir, but they have just retired for the evening."

The hour was quite late, Win thought, deflated. "We should go to our rooms and let them rest," she told Leo. "We'll come back in the morning."

Leo stared at the housemaid with a slight smile, and asked in a soft, low voice, "What is your name?"

Her brown eyes widened, and a blush crept up her cheeks. "Abigail, sir."

"Abigail," he repeated. "Tell Mrs. Rohan that her sister is here and wishes to see her."

"Yes, sir." The maid giggled and left them at the door.

Win gave her brother a wry glance as he helped to remove her cloak. "Your way with women never fails to astonish me."

"Most women have a tragic attraction to rakes," he said regretfully.

Someone came into the receiving room. She saw Amelia's familiar form clad in a blue dressing robe, accompanied by Cam Rohan, who was handsomely disheveled in an open-necked shirt and trousers.

Her blue eyes as round as saucers, Amelia stopped at the sight of her brother and sister. A white hand fluttered to Amelia's throat. "Is it really you?" she asked unsteadily.

Win tried to smile, but it was impossible when her lips were trembling with emotion. She tried to imagine how she must appear to Amelia, who had seen her last as a frail invalid. "I'm home," she said, a slight break in her voice.

"Oh, Win! I dreamed—I so hoped—" Amelia stopped and rushed forward, and their arms went around each other, fast and tight.

Win closed her eyes and sighed basking in the soft comfort of her sister's arms.

"You're so beautiful," Amelia said, drawing back to cup Win's wet cheeks with her hands. "So healthy and strong. Oh, look at this goddess. Cam, just look at her!"

"You look well," Cam told Win, his eyes glowing. "Better than I've ever seen you, little sister." Carefully he embraced her and kissed her forehead. "Welcome back."

"Where are Poppy and Beatrix?" Win asked, clinging to Amelia's hand.

"They're abed, but I'll go wake them."

"No, let them sleep," Win said quickly. "We shan't stay for long—we're both exhausted—but I had to see you before retiring for the night."

Amelia's gaze went to Leo, who had hung back near the door. Win heard the quiet intake of her sister's breath as she saw the changes in him.

"There's my old Leo," Amelia said softly.

Win was surprised to see a flicker of something in Leo's sardonic expression—a sort of boyish vulnerability, as if he was embarrassed by his own pleasure in the reunion. "Now you'll weep for a different cause," he told Amelia. "Because as you see, I've come back as well."

She flew to him, and was swallowed in a strong embrace. "The French wouldn't have you?" she asked, her voice muffled against his chest.

"On the contrary, they adored me. But there's no entertainment in staying where one is wanted."

"That's too bad," Amelia said, standing on her toes to kiss his cheek. "Because you're *very* much wanted here."

Smiling, Leo reached out to shake Cam's hand. "I look forward to seeing the improvements you wrote about. It seems the estate is thriving."

"You can ask Merripen on the morrow," Cam replied

easily. "He knows every inch of the place, and the name of every servant and tenant. And he has much to say on the subject, so be forewarned that any conversation about the estate will be a lengthy one."

"On the morrow," Leo repeated, giving Win a quick glance. "He's in London then?"

"Here at the Rutledge. He's in town to visit a placement agency to hire more servants."

"I have much to thank Merripen for," Leo said with uncharacteristic sincerity, "and you as well, Rohan. The devil knows why you've undertaken so much for my sake."

"It was for the family's sake, as well."

As the two men talked, Amelia drew Win to a settee near the hearth. "Your face is fuller," Amelia said, openly cataloging the changes in her sister. "Your eyes are brighter, and your figure is altogether splendid."

"No more tight-lacing," Win said with a grin. "Dr. Harrow says tight corsets compress the lungs, force the spine and head into an unnatural attitude, and weaken the back muscles."

"What else does Dr. Harrow say?" Amelia was clearly entertained. "Any opinions on stockings and garters?"

"You may hear it from the source himself," Win said. "Leo and I have brought Dr. Harrow back with us."

"Lovely. Does he have business here?"

"Not that I know of."

"I suppose since he's from London, he has relations and friends to meet?"

"Yes, that's part of it, but . . ." Win felt herself flush a little. "Julian has expressed a personal interest in spending time with me away from the setting of the clinic."

Amelia's lips parted in surprise. "Julian," she repeated. "Does he mean to *court* you, Win?"

"I'm not sure. I'm not at all experienced in these matters. But I think so."

"Do you like him?"

Win nodded without hesitation.

"Then I'm certain to like him as well. And I will be glad of the chance to thank him personally for what he has done."

They grinned at each other, basking in the delight of being reunited. But after a moment Win thought of Kev, and her pulse began to throb with uncomfortable force, and nerves jumped everywhere in her body.

"How is he, Amelia?" she finally brought herself to whisper.

There was no need for Amelia to ask who "he" was. "Merripen has changed," she said cautiously, "nearly as much as you and Leo. Cam says what he's accomplished with the estate is no less than astounding. It requires a broad array of skills to direct builders, craftsmen, and groundsmen, and also to repair the tenant farms. And Merripen's done it all. When necessary, he'll strip off his coat and lend his own back to a task. He's earned the respect of the workers—they never dare to question his authority."

"I'm not surprised, of course," Win said, while a bittersweet feeling came over her. "He has always been a very capable man. But when you say he has changed, what do you mean?"

"He has become rather . . . hard."

"Hard-hearted?"

"Yes, and remote. He seems to take no satisfaction in his success, nor does he exhibit any real pleasure in life. I think . . ." An uncomfortable pause. "Perhaps it will help him to see you again. You were always a good influence."

Win eased her hands away and glowered down at her own lap. "I doubt that. I doubt I have any influence on Merripen whatsoever. He's made his lack of interest very clear."

"Lack of interest?" Amelia repeated, and gave a strange little laugh. "No, Win, I wouldn't say that at all. Any mention of you earns his closest attention."

"One may judge a man's feelings by his actions." Win

sighed and rubbed her weary eyes. "At first I was hurt by the way he ignored my letters. Then I was angry. Now I merely feel foolish."

"Why, dear?" Amelia asked, her blue eyes filled with concern.

For loving, and having that love tossed back in her face. For wasting an ocean's worth of tears on a big, hard-hearted brute.

And for still wanting to see him despite all that.

Win shook her head. The talk of Kev had made her agitated and melancholy. "I'm weary after the long journey, Amelia. Would you mind if I—"

"No, no, go at once," her sister said, drawing her up from the settee and putting a protective arm around her. "Leo, do take Win to her room. You're both exhausted. We'll have time for talking tomorrow."

"Ah, that lovely tone of command," Leo reminisced. "I'd hoped that by now you would have rid her of the habit of barking out orders like a drill sergeant, Rohan."

"I enjoy all her habits," Cam replied, smiling at his wife.

"What room is Merripen in?" Win whispered to Amelia.

"Third floor, number twenty-one," Amelia whispered back. "But you mustn't go tonight, dear."

"Of course." Win smiled at her. "The only thing I intend to do tonight is go to bed without delay."

Chapter Seven

Third floor, number twenty-one. Win pulled the hood of her cloak farther over her head, concealing her face as she walked along the quiet hallway.

She had to find Kev, of course. She had come too far. She had crossed miles of earth and an ocean, and come to think of it, she had climbed the equivalent of a thousand ladders in the clinic gymnasium, all to reach him. Now that they were in the same *building*, she was hardly going to end her journey prematurely.

The hotel hallways were bracketed at each end with colonnaded light wells to admit the sun in the daytime hours. Win could hear strains of music from deep within the hotel. There must be a private party in the ballroom, or an event in the famous dining room. Harry Rutledge was called the hotelier to royalty, welcoming the famous, the powerful, and the fashionable to his establishment.

Glancing at the gilded numbers on each door, Win finally found twenty-one. Her stomach plunged, and every muscle clenched with anxiety. She felt a light sweat break out on her forehead. Fumbling a little with her gloves, she managed to pull them off and tuck them into the pockets of her cloak.

A tremulous knock at the door with her knuckles. And she waited in frozen stillness, head downbent, hardly able to breathe for nerves. She gripped her arms around herself beneath the concealing cloak.

She was not certain how much time passed, only that it seemed an eternity before the door was unlocked and opened.

Before she could bring herself to look up, she heard Kev's voice. She had forgotten how deep and dark it was, how it seemed to reach down to the center of her.

"I didn't send for a woman tonight."

That last word forestalled Win's reply.

"Tonight" implied that there had been other nights when he had indeed sent for a woman. And although Win was unworldly, she certainly understood what happened when a woman was sent for and received by a man at a hotel.

Her brain swarmed with thoughts. She had no right to object if Kev wanted a woman to service him. She didn't own him. They had made no promises or agreements. He didn't owe her fidelity.

But she couldn't help wondering . . . how many women? How many nights?

"No matter," he said brusquely. "I can use you. Come in." A large hand reached out and gripped Win's shoulder, hauling her past the threshold without giving her the opportunity to object.

I can use you?

Anger and consternation tumbled through her. She had no idea what to do or say. Somehow it didn't seem appropriate simply to throw back her hood and cry, *Surprise!*

Kev had mistaken her for a prostitute, and now the reunion she'd dreamed of for so long was turning into a farce.

"I assume you were told that I'm a Rom," he said.

Her face still concealed by the hood, Win nodded.

"And that doesn't matter to you?"

Win managed a single shake of her head.

He left her momentarily, striding to the window to close the heavy velvet curtains against the smoke-hazed lights of London. A single lamp strained to illuminate the dimness of the room.

Win glanced at him quickly. It was Kev . . . but as Amelia had said, he was altered. He had lost weight, perhaps a stone. He was huge, lean, almost rawboned. The neck of his shirt hung open, revealing the brown, hairless chest, the gleaming curve of powerful muscle. She thought at first it was a trick of the light, the immense bulwark of his shoulders and upper arms. Good Lord, how strong he'd become.

But none of that intrigued or startled her as much as his face. He was still as handsome as the devil, with those black eyes and that wicked mouth, the austere angles of nose and jaw, the high planes of his cheekbones. There were new lines, however, deep, bitter grooves that ran from nose to mouth, and the trace of a permanent frown between his thick brows. And most disturbing of all, a hint of cruelty in his expression. He looked capable of things that *her* Kev never could have done.

Kev, she thought in despair and wonder, *what's happened to you?*

He came to her. Win had forgotten the fluid way he moved, the breathtaking vitality that seemed to charge the air. Hastily she lowered her head.

Kev reached out for her and felt her flinch. He must have also detected the tremors that ran through her frame, for he said in a pitiless tone, "You're new at this."

She managed a hoarse whisper: "Yes."

"I won't hurt you." Kev guided her to a nearby table. As she stood facing away from him, he reached around to the fastenings of her cloak. The heavy garment fell away, revealing her straight blond hair, which was falling from its combs. She heard his breath catch. A moment of stillness. Win closed her eyes as Kev's hands skimmed her sides. Her body was fuller, more curved, strong in the places where she had once been frail. She wore no corset, in spite of the fact that a decent woman always wore a corset. There was only one conclusion a man could have drawn from that.

As he leaned over to lay her cloak at the side of the table, Win felt the unyielding surface of his body brush against hers. The scent of him, clean and rich and male, unlocked a flood of memories. He smelled like the outdoors, like dry leaves and clean, rain-soaked earth. He smelled like Kev.

She didn't want to be so undone by him. And yet it shouldn't have been a surprise. Something about him had always reached through her composure, down to the vein of purest feeling. This raw exhilaration was terrible and sweet, and no man had ever done this to her except him.

"Don't you want to see my face?" she asked huskily.

A cold, level reply. "It's of no concern to me if you're plain or fair." But his breath hastened as his hands settled on her, one sliding up her spine, urging her to bend forward. And his next words fell on her ears like black velvet.

"Put your hands on the table."

Win obeyed blindly, trying to understand herself, the sudden sting of tears, the excitement that throbbed all through her. He stood behind her. His hand continued to move over her back in slow, soothing paths, awakening sensations that had lain dormant for so long. These hands had soothed and cared for her all during her illness; they had pulled her from the very brink of death.

And yet he was not touching her with love, but with impersonal skill. She comprehended that he fully intended to take her, use her, as he had put it. And after an intimate act with a complete stranger, he planned to send her away a stranger still. It was beneath him, the coward. Would he never allow himself to be involved with anyone?

He had closed one hand in her skirts now, easing them upward. Win felt the touch of a cold draft on her ankle, and she couldn't help but imagine what it would be like if she let him go on.

Aroused and panicking, she stared down at her fists and choked out, "Is this how you treat women now, Kev?"

Everything stopped. The world halted on its axis.

Her skirt hem dropped, and she was seized in a fierce, hurtful grip and spun around. Caught helplessly, she looked up into his dark face.

Kev was expressionless, save for the widening of his eyes. As he stared at her, a flush burned across his cheeks and the bridge of his nose.

"*Win.*" Her name was carried on a shaken breath.

She tried to smile at him, to say something, but her mouth was trembling, and she was blinded by pleasure tears. To be with him again . . . it overwhelmed her in every way.

One of his hands came upward. The calloused tip of his thumb smoothed over the gloss of dampness beneath her eye. His hand cradled the side of her face so gently that her lashes fluttered down, and she didn't resist as she felt him bring her closer. His parted lips touched the salty wake of the tear and followed it along her cheek. And then the gentleness evaporated. With a swift, greedy move, he reached for her back, her hips, clutching her hard against him.

His mouth found hers with hot, urgent pressure. She reached up to his cheeks and shaped her fingers over the scrape of bristle. A sound came from low in his throat, a masculine growl of pleasure and need. His arms clasped around her in an unbreakable hold, for which she was grateful. Her knees threatened to give way entirely.

Lifting his head, Kev looked down at her with dazed dark eyes. "How can you be here?"

"I came back early." A shiver went through her as his hot breath fanned against her lips. "I wanted to see you. Wanted you—"

He took her mouth again, no longer gentle. He sank his tongue into her, aggressively searching. Both his hands came up to her head, angling it to make her mouth fully accessible. She reached around him, gripping the powerful stretch of his back, the hard muscles that went on and on.

Kev groaned as he felt her hands on him. He groped at the combs in her hair, tugged them out, and tangled his fingers in the long silken locks. Pulling her head back, he sought the fragile skin of her throat and dragged his mouth along it as if he wanted to consume her. His hunger escalated and drove his breath faster and his pulse harder, until Win realized he was close to losing all control.

He scooped her up with shocking ease. He carried her to the bed and lowered her swiftly to the mattress. His lips found hers, ravaging deep and sweet, draining her with hot, seeking kisses.

He lowered over her, his solid weight pinning her in place. Win felt him grip the front of her traveling gown, pulling so hard she thought the fabric might tear. The thick cloth resisted his efforts, although a few of the buttons at the back of her gown strained and popped. "Wait . . . wait . . ." she whispered, afraid he would rip her gown to shreds. He was too caught up in his savage desire to hear anything.

As Kev cupped the soft shape of her breast over the gown, the tip ached and hardened. His head bent. To Win's astonishment, she felt him biting against the cloth until her nipple was caught in the light clamp of his teeth. A whimper escaped her, and her hips jerked upward reflexively.

Kev crawled over her. His face was misted with sweat, his nostrils flared from the force of his breathing. The front of her skirts had ridden up between them. He tugged them higher and impelled himself between her thighs until she felt the thick ridge of him between the layers of her drawers and his trousers. Her eyes flew open. She stared up into the black fire of his gaze. He moved against her, letting her feel every inch of what he wanted to put inside her, and she moaned and opened to him.

He made a low sound as he rubbed over her again, caressing her with unspeakable intimacy. She wanted him to stop, and at the same time she wanted him never to stop. "Kev." Her voice was shaking. "Kev—"

But his mouth covered hers, his tongue sinking deep, while his hips moved in slow strokes. Shaken and impassioned, she lifted against that demanding hardness. Each wicked thrust caused sensations to spread, heat unfolding.

Win writhed helplessly, unable to speak with his mouth possessing hers. More heat, more delicious friction. Something was happening, her muscles tightening, her senses opening in readiness for . . . for what? She was going to faint if he didn't stop. Her hands groped at his shoulders, pushing at him, but he ignored the feeble shove. Reaching beneath her, he cupped her squirming bottom and pulled her higher, right against the pumping, sliding pressure. A suspended moment of exquisite tension, so sharp that she gave an uneasy whimper.

Suddenly he flung himself away from her, going to the opposite side of the room. Bracing his hands against the wall, he hung his head, and panted, and shivered like a wet dog.

Dazed and trembling, Win moved slowly to restore her clothing. She felt desperate and painfully empty, needing something she had no name for. When she was covered again, she left the bed on unsteady legs.

She approached Kev cautiously. It was obvious he was aroused. Painfully so. She wanted to touch him again. Most of all she wanted him to put his arms around her and tell her how overjoyed he was to have her back.

But he spoke before she reached him. His tone was not encouraging. "If you touch me, I won't be responsible for what happens next."

Win stopped, plaiting her fingers.

Eventually Kev recovered his breath. And he gave her a glance that should have immolated her on the spot.

"Next time," he said flatly, "some advance warning of your arrival might be a good idea."

"I did send advance notice." Win was amazed that she could even speak. "It must have been lost." She paused. "That was a f-far warmer welcome than I expected, considering the way you've ignored me for the past two years."

"I haven't ignored you."

Win took quick refuge in sarcasm. "You wrote to me once in two years."

Kev turned and rested his back against the wall. "You didn't need letters from me."

"I needed any sign of affection! And you gave me none." She stared at him incredulously as he remained silent. "For heaven's sake, Kev, aren't you even going to say you're glad I'm well again?"

"I'm glad you're well again."

"Then why are you behaving this way?"

"Because nothing else has changed."

"*You've* changed," she shot back. "I don't know you anymore."

"That's as it should be."

"Kev," she said in bewilderment, "why are you behaving this way? I went away to get well. *Surely* you can't blame me for that."

"I blame you for nothing. But the devil knows what you could want from me now."

I want you to love me, she wanted to cry out. She had traveled so far, and yet there was more distance between them than ever. "I can tell you what I *don't* want, Kev, and that's to be estranged from you."

Kev's expression was stony and unfeeling. "We're not estranged." He picked up her cloak and handed it to her. "Put this on. I'll take you to your room."

Win pulled the garment around herself, stealing discreet glances at Kev, who was all brooding energy and suppressed power as he tucked his shirt into his trousers. The X of the braces over his back highlighted his magnificent build.

"You needn't walk with me," she said in a subdued voice. "I can find my way back without—"

"You're to go nowhere in this hotel alone. It's not safe."

"You're right," she said sullenly. "I'd hate to be accosted by someone."

The shot hit its mark. Kev's mouth hardened and he gave her a dangerous glance as he shrugged into his coat.

How much he reminded her just now of the rough, wrathful boy he had been when he had first come to the Hathaways.

"Kev," she said softly, "can't we resume our friendship?"

"I'm still your friend."

"But nothing more?"

"No."

Win couldn't help glancing at the bed, at the rumpled counterpane that covered it, and a new surge of heat went through her.

Merripen went still as he followed the direction of her gaze. "That shouldn't have happened," he said roughly. "I shouldn't have—" He stopped and swallowed audibly. "I haven't been with a woman in a while. You were in the wrong place at the wrong time."

Win had never been so mortified. "You're saying you would have reacted that way with any woman?"

"Yes."

"I don't believe you!"

"Believe what you like." Kev went to the door and opened it to glance in both directions along the hallway. "Come here."

"I want to stay. I need to talk with you."

"Not alone. Not at this hour." He paused. "I said come here."

This last was said with a quiet authority that made her bristle. But she complied.

As Win reached him, Kev pulled the hood of her cloak up to conceal her face. Ascertaining that the hallway was still clear, he guided her outside the room and closed the door.

They were silent as they went to the staircase at the end of the hallway. Win was acutely conscious of his hand resting lightly on her back. Reaching the top step, she was surprised when he stopped her.

"Take my arm."

She realized he intended to help her down the stairs, as he'd always done when she was ill. Stairs had been a particular trial for her. The entire family had been terrified she would faint while going up or down the steps, and perhaps break her neck. Merripen had often carried her rather than let her take the risk.

"No, thank you," she said. "I'm able to do it on my own now."

"Take it," he repeated, reaching for her hand.

Win snatched it back, while her chest tightened with annoyance. "Stop ordering me about. I don't want your help. I'm no longer an invalid. Though it seems you preferred me that way."

Although she couldn't see his face, she heard his sharply indrawn breath. She felt ashamed at the petty accusation.

Kev didn't reply, however. If she'd hurt him, he bore it stoically. They descended the stairs separately, in silence.

Win was utterly confused. She had pictured this night a hundred different ways. Every possible way but this. She led the way to her door and reached in her pocket for the key.

Kev took the key from her and opened the door. "Go and light the lamp."

Conscious of his large, dark form waiting at the threshold, Win went to the bedside table. Carefully she lifted the glass globe of the lamp, lit the wick, and replaced the glass.

After inserting the key into the other side of the door, Kev said, "Lock it behind me."

Turning to look at him, Win felt a miserable laugh knotting in her throat. "This is where we left off, isn't it? Me, throwing myself at you. You, turning me away. I thought I understood before. I wasn't well enough for the kind of relationship I wanted with you. But now I don't understand. Because there's nothing to stop us from finding out if . . . if . . ." Distressed and mortified, she couldn't find words for what she wanted. "Unless I was mistaken in how you once felt for me? Did you ever desire me, Kev?"

His voice was barely audible. "It was only friendship. And pity."

Win felt her face go very white. Her eyes and nose prickled. A hot tear leaked down her cheek. "Liar," she said, and turned away.

The door closed gently.

KEV NEVER REMEMBERED WALKING BACK TO HIS ROOM, ONLY that he eventually found himself standing beside his bed. Groaning a curse, he sank to his knees and gripped huge handfuls of the counterpane and buried his face in it. He was in hell.

Holy Christ, how Win devastated him. He had starved for

her for so long, dreamed of her so many nights, and woken to so many bitter mornings without her that at first he hadn't believed she was real.

He thought of Win's lovely face, and the softness of her mouth against his, and the way she'd felt, her body supple and strong. But her spirit was the same, radiant with the endearing sweetness and honest his strength not to go to his knees before her.

She'd asked for friendship. Impossible. How could he separate any part of the unwieldy tangle of his feelings and hand over such a small piece? And she knew better than to ask. Even in the Hathaways' eccentric world, some things were forbidden.

Kev had nothing to offer Win. Even Cam Rohan had been able to provide Amelia with his considerable wealth. But Kev had no worldly possessions, no grace of character, no education, no advantageous connections, nothing *gadje* valued. He had been isolated and maltreated as a boy for reasons he had never understood. But on some elemental level, he felt he must have deserved it.

If Win was well enough to marry someday, it should be to a gentleman.

To a gentle man.

Chapter Eight

In the morning, Leo met the governess.

Poppy and Beatrix had both written to him about having acquired a governess a year earlier. Her name was Miss Marks, and they both liked her, although their descriptions didn't exactly convey *why* they should like such a creature. Apparently she was slight and quiet and stern. She was helping not only the sisters but the entire family learn to acquit itself in society.

Leo thought this social instruction was probably a good thing. For everyone else. Not him.

When it came to polite behavior, society was far more demanding of women than men. If a man had a title and held his liquor reasonably well, he could do or say nearly anything he liked and still be invited everywhere.

Through a quirk of fate Leo had inherited a viscountcy, which had taken care of the first part of the equation. And now after the long stay in France, he had limited his drinking to a glass of wine or two at supper. Which meant he was relatively certain of being received at any dull and respectable event in London that he had no desire to attend.

He only hoped that the formidable Miss Marks would try

to correct him. It might be amusing to set her back on her heels.

Leo knew next to nothing about governesses save for the drab creatures in novels, who tended to fall in love with the lord of the manor, always with bad results. However, Miss Marks was entirely safe from him. For a change, he had no interest in seducing anyone. His former dissipated pursuits had lost their power to enthrall him.

On one of Leo's ambles around Provence to visit some Gallo-Roman architectural remains, he had encountered one of his old professors from the Académie des Beaux-Arts. The chance meeting had resulted in a renewed acquaintanceship. In the months to come, Leo had spent many an afternoon sketching, reading, and studying in the professor's atelier, or workshop. Leo had arrived at some conclusions that he intended to put to the test now that he was back in England.

As he strolled nonchalantly along the long hallway that led to the Hathaway suite, he heard rapid footsteps. Someone was running toward him from the other direction. Moving to the side, Leo waited with his hands tucked in his trouser pockets.

"Come here, you little fiend!" he heard a woman snarl. "You oversized rat! When I get my hands on you, I'll rip out your innards!"

The bloodthirsty tone was unladylike. Appalling. Leo was vastly entertained. The footsteps drew closer . . . but there was only one set of them. Who on earth could she be chasing?

It quickly became clear that she was not pursuing a "who" but a "what." The furry, slithery body of a ferret came loping along the hallway with a frilly object clamped in his mouth. Most hotel guests would no doubt be disconcerted by the sight of a small carnivorous mammal streaking toward them. However, Leo had lived for years with Beatrix's creatures:

mice appearing in his pockets, baby rabbits in his shoes, hedgehogs wandering casually past the dining table. Smiling, he watched the ferret hurry past him.

The woman came soon after, a mass of rustling gray skirts as she ran full bore after the creature. But if there was one thing ladies' clothing was not designed to do, it was facilitating ease of movement. Weighted by layers and layers of fabric, she stumbled and fell a few yards away from Leo. A pair of spectacles went flying to the side.

Leo was at her side in an instant, crouching on the floor as he sorted through the hissing tangle of limbs and skirts. "Are you hurt? I feel certain there's a woman in here somewhere . . . ah, there you are. Easy, now. Let me—"

"*Don't touch me,*" she snapped, batting at him with her fists.

"I'm not touching you. That is, I'm only touching you with the—*ow*, damn it—with the intention of helping." Her hat, a little scrap of wool felt with cheap corded trim, had fallen over her face. Leo managed to push it back to the top of her head, narrowly missing a sharp blow to his jaw. "*Christ.* Would you stop flailing for a moment?"

Straggling to a sitting position, she glared at him.

Leo crawled to retrieve the spectacles and returned them to her. She snatched them from him without a word of thanks.

She was a lean, anxious-looking woman. A young woman with narrowed eyes, from which bad temper flashed out. Her light brown hair was pulled back with a gallows-rope tightness that made Leo wince just to see it. One would have hoped for some compensating feature—a soft pair of lips, perhaps, or a pretty bosom. But no, there was only a stern mouth, a flat chest, and gaunt cheeks. If Leo were compelled to spend any time with her—which, thankfully, he wasn't— he would have insisted on feeding her.

"If you want to help," she said coldly, hooking the spectacles around her ears, "retrieve that blasted ferret for me. Perhaps I've tired him enough that you may be able to run him to ground."

Still crouching on the floor, Leo glanced at the ferret, which had paused ten yards away and was watching them both with bright, beady eyes. "What's his name?"

"Dodger."

Leo gave a low whistle and a few clicks of his tongue. "Come here, Dodger. You've caused enough trouble for the morning. Though I can't fault your taste in . . . ladies' garters? Is that what you're holding?"

The woman watched, stupefied, as the ferret's long, slender body wriggled toward Leo. Chattering busily, Dodger crawled onto Leo's thigh. "Good fellow," Leo said, stroking the sleek fur.

"How did you do that?" the woman asked in annoyance.

"I have a way with animals. They tend to acknowledge me as one of their own." Leo gently pried a frilly bit of lace and ribbon from the long front teeth. It was definitely a garter, deliciously feminine and impractical. He gave the woman a mocking smile as he handed it to her. "No doubt this is yours."

He hadn't really thought that, of course. He had assumed the garter belonged to someone else. It was impossible to fathom this stern female wearing something so frivolous. But as he saw a blush spreading across the young woman's cheeks, he realized it actually *was* hers. Intriguing.

He gestured with the ferret hanging relaxed in his hand and said, "I take it this animal doesn't belong to you?"

"No, to one of my charges."

"Are you by chance a governess?"

"That's no concern of yours."

"Because if you are, then one of your charges is most definitely Miss Beatrix Hathaway."

She scowled. "How do you know that?"

"My sister is the only person I know who would bring a garter-stealing ferret to the Rutledge Hotel."

"Your *sister*?"

He smiled into her astonished face. "Lord Ramsay, at your service. And you are Miss Marks, the governess?"

"Yes," she muttered, ignoring the hand he reached down for her. She rose to her feet unassisted.

Leo felt an irresistible urge to provoke her. "How gratifying. I've always wanted a family governess to annoy."

The comment seemed to incense her beyond all expectation. "I'm aware of your reputation, my lord. I find no cause for humor in it."

Leo didn't think she found cause for humor in much of anything. "My reputation has lasted in spite of a two-year absence?" he asked, affecting a tone of pleased surprise.

"You're *proud* of it?"

"Well, of course. It's easy to have a good reputation—you merely have to do nothing. But earning a bad reputation . . . well, that takes some effort."

A contemptuous stare burned through the spectacle lenses. "I despise you," she announced. Turning on her heel, she walked away from him.

Leo followed, carrying the ferret. "We've only just met. You can't despise me until you really get to know me."

She ignored him as he followed her to the Hathaway suite. She ignored him as he knocked at the door, and she ignored him as they were welcomed inside by the maid.

There was some kind of commotion going on in the suite, which shouldn't have been a surprise considering it was his family's suite. The air was filled with cursing, exclamations, and grunts of physical combat.

"Leo?" Beatrix appeared from the main receiving room and hurried over to them.

"Beatrix, darling!" Leo was amazed by the difference the past two and a half years had made in his youngest sister. "How you've grown—"

"Yes, never mind that," she said impatiently, snatching the ferret from him. "Go in there and help Cam!"

"Help him with what?"

"He's trying to stop Merripen from killing Dr. Harrow."

"Already?" Leo asked blankly, and rushed into the receiving room.

Chapter Nine

After attempting to sleep on a bed that had turned into a torture rack, Kev had awoken with a heavy heart. And other, more urgent discomforts.

He'd been plagued with stimulating dreams in which Win's naked body had been writhing against him, beneath him. All the desires he kept at bay in the daylight hours had expressed themselves in those dreams . . . he had been holding Win, thrusting inside her, and taking her cries into his mouth . . . kissing her from head to toe and back again. And in those same dreams she had behaved in a most un-Win-like manner, delicately feasting on him with a wanton mouth, exploring him with inquisitive hands.

Washing in frigid water had helped his condition marginally, but Kev was still aware of the heat burning far too close to the surface.

He was going to have to face Win today and converse with her in front of everyone, as if everything were ordinary. He was going to have to look at her and not think about the softness between her thighs, and how she had cradled him as he had thrust against her, and how he had felt her warmth even through the layers of their clothes. And how he had lied to her and made her cry.

Feeling wretched and explosive, Kev dressed in the town clothes that the family insisted he wear when in London. "You know how much value *gadje* place on appearance," Cam had told him, dragging him to Savile Row. "You have to look respectable, or it will reflect badly on your sisters to be seen with you."

Cam's former employer, Lord St. Vincent, had recommended a shop that specialized in bespoke tailoring. *You won't find anything that's acceptable in made-to-measure,* St. Vincent had said, flicking an assessing glance over Kev. *No pattern would fit him.*

Kev had submitted to the indignity of having measurements taken, being draped with countless fabrics, and going for endless fittings. Cam and the Hathaway sisters had all seemed pleased with the results, but Kev couldn't see any difference between his new attire and the old. Clothes were clothes, something that covered the body to protect it from the elements.

Scowling, Kev donned a white pleated shirt and black cravat, a vest with a notched collar, and narrow-legged trousers. He pulled on a wool town coat with front flap pockets and a split at the back. (Despite his disdain for *gadje* clothing, he had to admit it was a fine, comfortable coat.)

As was his habit, Kev went to the Hathaway suite for breakfast. He kept his face expressionless, even though his gut was twisting and his pulse was rampaging. All at the thought of seeing Win. But he would manage the situation adeptly. He would be calm and quiet, and Win would be her usual composed self, and they would get past this first unholy awkward meeting.

All his intentions, however, vanished as he entered the

suite, went to the receiving room, and saw Win on the floor. In her underclothes.

She was lying prostrate on her stomach, trying to push upward, while a man leaned over her. Touching her.

The sight exploded inside Kev.

With a bloodthirsty roar, he reached Win in a flash, snatching her up in possessive arms.

"Wait," she gasped. "What are you—oh, *don't*! Let me expl—no!"

He deposited her unceremoniously on a sofa behind him and turned to face the other man. The only thought in Kev's mind was swift and effective dismemberment, starting by ripping the bastard's head off.

Prudently the man had rushed behind a heavy chair, placing it between them. "You must be Merripen," he said. "And I'm—"

"A dead man," Kev growled, starting for him.

"He's my doctor!" Win cried. "He's Dr. Harrow, and—Merripen, don't you dare hurt him!"

Ignoring her, Kev went forward about two strides before he felt a leg hook around his, sending him hurtling to the floor. It was Cam, who pounced on him, knelt on his arms, and gripped the back of his neck.

"Merripen, you *idiot*," he said, struggling to keep him down, "he's the damn doctor. What do you think you're doing?"

"Killing . . . him," Kev grunted, lurching upward despite Cam's restraining weight.

"Bloody hell!" Cam exclaimed. "Leo, help me hold him! *Now*."

Leo rushed over to help. It took both of them to keep Kev down.

"I love our family gatherings," he heard Leo say. "Merripen, what the devil is your problem?"

"Win is in her underclothes, and that man—"

"These are not my underclothes," came Win's exasperated voice. "This is an exercise costume!"

Kev twisted to look in her direction. Since Cam and Leo were still pinning him down, he couldn't look all the way up. But he saw that Win was clad in loose-fitting drawers and a bodice with bare arms. "I know underclothes when I see them," he snapped.

"These are Turkish trousers and a perfectly respectable bodice. Every woman at the clinic wears this same costume. Exercising is necessary for my health, and I'm certainly not going to do it in a gown and cors—"

"He was touching you!" Kev interrupted harshly.

"He was making certain I had the correct form."

The doctor approached with caution. There was a flicker of humor in his alert gray eyes. "It's part of a strength-training system I've developed. All my patients have incorporated it into their daily schedules. Please believe my attentions to Miss Hathaway were entirely respectful." He paused and asked wryly, "Am I safe now?"

Leo and Cam, still struggling with Kev, both answered simultaneously, "*No.*"

By this time, Poppy, Beatrix, and Miss Marks had hurried into the room.

"Merripen," Poppy said, "Dr. Harrow wasn't hurting Win a bit, and—"

"He's really very nice, Merripen," Beatrix chimed in. "Even my animals like him."

"Easy," Cam said quietly to Kev, speaking in Romany so no one else could understand. "This is no good for anyone."

Kev went still. "He was touching her," he replied in the old language, even though he hated using it.

"She's not yours, *phral*," Cam continued in Romany, not without sympathy.

Slowly Kev forced himself to relax.

"May I get off him now?" Leo asked. "There's only one kind of exertion I enjoy before breakfast. And this is not it."

Cam allowed Kev to stand but kept one arm twisted behind his back.

Win went to stand beside Harrow. The sight of her wearing so little, being so near another man, caused muscles to twitch all over Kev's body. He could see the shape of her hips and legs. The entire family had gone insane, letting her dress that way in front of an outsider and acting as though it were appropriate. *Turkish trousers* . . . as if giving them such a name made them anything but underdrawers.

"I insist that you apologize," Win said. "You've been very rude to my guest, Merripen."

Her guest? Kev stared at her in outrage.

"No need," Harrow said hastily. "I know how it must have appeared."

Win glared at Kev. "He has made me well again, and *this* is the way you repay him?" she demanded.

"You made yourself well," Harrow said. "It was a result of your own efforts, Miss Hathaway."

Win's expression softened as she glanced at the doctor. "Thank you." But when she looked back at Kev, the frown returned. "Are you going to apologize, Merripen?"

Cam twisted his arm a bit more tightly. "Do it, damn you," he muttered. "For the sake of the family."

Glaring at the doctor, Kev spoke in Romany. "*Ka xlia ma pe tute.*" (I'm going to shit on you.)

"Which means," Cam said hastily, "'Please forgive the misunderstanding; let's part as friends.'"

"*Te malavel les i menkiva,*" Kev added for good measure. (May you die of a malignant wasting disease.)

"Roughly translated," Cam said, "that means, 'May your

garden be filled with fine, fat hedgehogs.' Which, I may add, is considered quite a blessing among Roma."

Harrow looked skeptical. But he murmured, "I accept your apology. No harm done."

"Excuse us," Cam said pleasantly, still twisting Kev's arm. "Go on with breakfast, please . . . we have some errands to accomplish. Please tell Amelia when she rises that I'll return at approximately midday." And he steered Kev from the room, with Leo at their heels.

As soon as they were out of the suite and in the hallway, Cam released Kev's arm and turned to face him. Raking his hand through his hair, he asked with mild exasperation, "What did you hope to get out of killing Win's doctor?"

"Enjoyment."

"No doubt you would have. Win didn't seem to be enjoying it, however."

"Why is Harrow here?" Kev asked fiercely.

"I can answer that one," Leo said, leaning a shoulder against the wall with casual ease. "Harrow wants to become better acquainted with the Hathaways. Because he and my sister are . . . close."

Kev's stomach suddenly felt as if he'd swallowed a handful of river stones. "What do you mean?" he asked, even though he knew. No man could be exposed to Win and not fall in love with her.

"Harrow is a widower," Leo said. "A decent enough fellow. More attached to his clinic and patients than anything else. But he's a sophisticated man, widely traveled, and wealthy as the devil. And he's a collector of beautiful objects. A connoisseur of fine things."

Neither of the other men missed the implication.

It was difficult to ask the next question, but Kev forced himself to. "Does Win care for him?"

"I don't believe Win knows how much of what she feels for him is gratitude, and how much is true affection." Leo gave Kev a pointed glance. "And there are still a few unresolved questions she has to answer for herself."

"I'll talk to her."

"I wouldn't, if I were you. Not until she cools a bit. She's rather incensed with you."

"Why?" Kev asked, wondering if she had confided to her brother about the events of the previous night.

"*Why?*" Leo's mouth twisted. "There's such a dazzling array of choices, I find myself in a quandary about which one to start with. Putting your behavior of this morning aside, what about the fact that you never wrote to her?"

"I did," Kev said indignantly.

"One letter," Leo allowed. "The farm report. She showed it to me, actually. How could one forget the soaring prose you wrote about fertilizing the field near the east gate? I'll tell you, the part about sheep dung nearly brought a tear to my eye, it was so sentimental and—"

"What did she expect me to write about?" Kev demanded.

"Don't bother to explain, my lord," Cam interceded as Leo opened his mouth. "It's not the way of Roma to put our private thoughts on paper."

"It's not the way of Roma to run an estate and manage crews of workmen and tenant farmers, either," Leo replied. "But he's done that, hasn't he?" Leo smiled sardonically at Kev's sullen expression. "In all likelihood, Merripen, you'd make a far better lord of the manor than I will. Look at you. Are you dressed like a Rom? Do you spend your days lounging by the campfire, or are you poring over estate account books? Do you sleep outside on the hard ground, or inside on a nice feather bed? Do you even speak like a Rom anymore? No, you've lost your accent. You sound like—"

"What's your point?" Kev interrupted curtly.

"Only that you've made compromises right and left since you joined this family. You've done whatever you had to, to be close to Win. So don't be a bloody hypocrite and turn all Romany now that you finally have a chance to—" Leo stopped and lifted his eyes heavenward. "Good Lord. This is too much even for me. And I thought I was inured to drama." He gave Cam a sour look. "You talk to him. I'm going to have my tea."

He went back into the suite, leaving them in the hallway.

"I didn't write about sheep dung," Kev muttered. "It was another kind of fertilizer."

Cam tried unsuccessfully to smother a grin. "Be that as it may, *phral*, the word should probably be left out of a letter to a lady."

"Don't call me that."

Cam started down the hallway. "Come with me. There actually is an errand I want you for."

"Not interested."

"It's dangerous," Cam coaxed. "You might have a chance to hit someone. Maybe even start a brawl. Ah . . . I knew that would convince you."

One of the qualities Kev found most annoying about Cam Rohan was his persistence in trying to find out about the tattoos. He'd pursued the mystery for two years.

Despite a multitude of responsibilities, Cam never missed an opportunity to delve further into the matter. He had searched diligently for his own tribe, asking for information from every passing *vardo* and going to every Romany camp. But it seemed as if Cam's tribe had disappeared from the face of the earth, or at least had gone to the other side of it. He would probably never find them—there was no limit to how far a tribe might travel, and no guarantee they would ever return to England.

Cam had searched marriage, birth, and death records to find any mention of himself or his mother, Sonya. Nothing so far. He had also consulted heraldic experts and Irish historians to find out the possible significance of the *pooka* symbol. All they had been able to do was dredge up the familiar legends of the nightmare horse: that he spoke in a human voice, that he appeared at midnight and called for you to come with him, and you could never refuse. And when you went with him, if you survived the ride, you were changed forever when you returned.

Cam had also not been able to find a meaningful connection between the Rohan and Merripen names, which were common among Roma. Therefore, Cam's latest approach was to search for Kev's tribe, or anyone who knew about it.

Kev was understandably hostile about this plan, which Cam revealed to him as they walked to the hotel mews.

"They left me for dead," Kev said. "And you want me to help you find them? If I see any of them, especially the *rom baro,* I'll kill him with my bare hands."

"Fine," Cam returned equably. "*After* they tell us about the tattoo."

"All they'll say is what I've already told you—it's the mark of a curse. And if you ever find out what it means—"

"Yes, yes, I know. We're doomed. But if I'm wearing a curse on my arm, Merripen, I want to know about it."

Kev gave him a glance that should have felled him on the spot. He stopped at a corner of the stables, where hoof picks, clippers, and files were neatly organized on shelves. "I'm not going. You'll have to look for my tribe without me."

"I need you," Cam countered. "For one thing, the place we're headed to is *kekkeno mushespuv.*"

Kev stared at him in disbelief. The phrase, which translated to "no-man's-land," referred to a squalid plain located on the Surrey side of the Thames. The open muddy ground was crowded with ragged tents, a few dilapidated *vardos,* and a non-Romany group called the Chorodies. They were descendants of rogues and outcasts, mainly Saxon in origin, without customs or manners. Going anywhere near them was virtually asking to be attacked or robbed. It was hard to imagine a more dangerous place in London except for a few Eastside rookeries.

"Why do you think anyone from my tribe could be in such a place?" Kev asked, more than a little shocked by the idea. Surely, even under the *rom baro*'s leadership, they wouldn't have sunk so low.

"Not long ago I met a *chal* from the Bosvil tribe. He said his youngest sister, Shuri, was married long ago to your *rom baro*." Cam stared at him intently. "It seems the story of what happened to you has been told all through Romanija."

"I don't see why," Kev muttered, feeling suffocated. "It's not important."

Cam shrugged casually, his gaze trained on Kev's face. "Roma take care of their own. No tribe would ever leave an injured or dying boy behind, no matter what the circumstances. And apparently it brought a curse on the *rom baro*'s tribe. Their luck turned very bad, and most of them came to ruin. There's justice for you."

"I never cared about justice." Kev was vaguely surprised by the rustiness of his own voice.

Cam spoke with quiet understanding. "It's a strange life, isn't it? A Rom with no tribe. No matter how hard you look, you can never find a home. Because to us, home is not a building or a tent or *vardo* . . . home is a family."

Kev had a difficult time meeting his gaze. The words cut too close to his heart. In all the time they'd known each other, Kev had never felt a kinship with him until now. But

Kev could no longer ignore the fact that they had too damn much in common. They were two outsiders with pasts full of unanswered questions. And each of them had been drawn to the Hathaways and had found a home with them.

"I'll go with you, damn it," Kev said gruffly. "But only because I know what Amelia would do to me if I let something happen to you."

Chapter Ten

Somewhere in England spring had covered the ground with green velvet and coaxed flowers from the hedgerows. Somewhere the sky was blue and the air was sweet. But not in no-man's-land, where smoke from millions of chimney pipes had soured the complexion of the city with a yellow fog that daylight could barely penetrate. There was little but mud and misery in this barren place. It was located approximately a quarter mile from the river and bordered by a hill and a railway.

Kev was grim and silent as he and Cam led their horses through the Romany camp. Tents were loosely scattered, with men sitting at the entrances and whittling pegs or making baskets. Kev heard a few boys shouting at one another. As he rounded a tent, he saw a small group gathered around a fight. Men angrily shouted instructions and threats to the boys as if they were animals in a pit.

Stopping at the sight, Kev stared at the boys while images from his own childhood flashed through his mind. Pain, violence, fear . . . the wrath of the *rom baro,* who would beat Kev further if he lost. And if he won, sending another boy bloodied and broken to the ground, there would be no reward. Only the crushing guilt of harming someone who had done no wrong to him.

What is this? the *rom baro* had roared, discovering Kev huddled in a corner, crying after he had beaten a boy who had begged him to stop. *You pathetic, sniveling dog. I'll give you one of these*—his booted foot had landed in Kev's side, bruising a rib—*for every tear you shed. What kind of idiot would cry for winning?* He hadn't stopped kicking Kev until he was unconscious.

The next time Kev had beaten someone, he'd felt no guilt. He'd felt nothing.

Kev wasn't aware that he'd frozen in his tracks, or that he was breathing heavily, until Cam spoke to him softly.

"Come, *phral.*"

Tearing his gaze away from the boys, Kev saw the compassion and sanity in the other man's eyes. The dark memories receded, and he followed.

Cam stopped at two or three tents, asking the whereabouts of a woman named Shuri. The responses were grudging. As expected, strangers were regarded with suspicion and curiosity.

Kev and Cam were directed to one of the smaller tents, where an older boy sat by the entrance on an overturned pail. He carved buttons with a small knife.

"We're looking for Shuri," Kev said in the old language.

The boy glanced over his shoulder into the tent and called, "There are two men to see you. Roma dressed like *gadje.*"

A singular-looking woman came to the entrance. She was not quite five feet tall, but her torso and head were broad, her complexion dark and wrinkled, her eyes lustrous and black. Kev recognized her immediately. It was indeed Shuri, who had only been about sixteen when she had married the *rom baro*. Kev had left the tribe not long after that.

The years had not been kind to her. Shuri had once been a striking beauty, but a life of hardship had aged her prematurely. Although she and Kev were nearly the same age, the difference between them could have been twenty years instead of two.

She stared at Kev without much interest. Then her eyes widened, and her gnarled hands moved in a gesture commonly used to protect oneself against evil spirits.

"Kev," she breathed.

"Hello, Shuri," he said with difficulty, and followed it with a greeting he hadn't said since childhood. "*Droboy tume Romale.*"

Cam looked at him alertly. "Kev?" he repeated. "Is that your tribal name?"

Kev ignored him.

Shuri stared at him suspiciously. "If it's really you, show me the mark."

"May I do it inside?"

After a long hesitation, she nodded reluctantly, waving both Kev and Cam into the tent.

Cam paused at the entrance and spoke to the boy. "Make certain the horses aren't stolen," he said, "and I'll give you a half crown."

"Yes, *kako*," the boy said, using a respectful form of address for a much older male.

Smiling ruefully, Cam followed Kev into the tent.

The structure was made of rods stuck into the ground and bent at the top, with other supporting rods fastened to it with string. The whole of it was covered with coarse brown cloth that had been pinned together over the ribs of the structure. There were no chairs or tables. The interior of the tent was heated by a small coke fire glowing in a three-legged pan.

At Shuri's direction, Cam sat cross-legged by the fire pan and stifled a grin as Shuri insisted on seeing Merripen's tattoo. Being a modest and private man, Kev cringed inside at having to undress in front of them. But he set his jaw, tugged off his coat, and unbuttoned his vest. Rather than remove the shirt entirely, he unfastened it and let it fall to reveal his upper back and shoulders.

Shuri moved behind Kev to look at the tattoo. Kev's head lowered, and he breathed quietly, his face detached save for a slight frown.

After glancing at the mark of the nightmare horse, Shuri moved away from Kev and motioned for him to dress himself. "Who is this man?" she asked, nodding in Cam's direction.

"One of my *kumpania*," Kev muttered. The word was used to describe a clan, a group united though not necessarily by family ties. Pulling his clothes back on, he asked brusquely, "What happened to the tribe? Where's the *rom baro*?"

"In the ground," the woman said, with a pointed lack of respect for her husband. "And the tribe is scattered. After they saw what he did to you, Kev . . . making us leave you for dead . . . it all went bad after that. No one wanted to follow him. The *gadje* finally hanged him when he was caught making counterfeit money. Before that," Shuri continued, "the *rom baro* had tried to make some of the young boys into *asharibe* to earn coins at fairs and in the London streets. But none of them could fight like you, and their parents would only let the *rom baro* go so far with them." Her shrewd dark eyes turned in Cam's direction.

"My husband was cruel to Kev," she continued. "He put

him in too many fights, and gave him no bandages or salve for his wounds. We tried to help him when we could."

Cam's face was grim. "Why did your husband treat Merripen that way?" he asked quietly.

"The *rom baro* hated all things *gadje*."

Kev looked at her sharply. "But I'm a Rom."

"You're half-*gadjo*," Shuri told him, and smiled at his astonishment. "You never suspected?"

Kev shook his head, speechless at the revelation.

"Holy hell," Cam whispered.

"Your mother married a *gadjo*," Shuri continued. "You wear the mark of his family. But your father left her. And after we thought you died, the *rom baro* said, 'Now there's only one.'"

"Only one what?" Cam managed to ask.

"Brother." Shuri moved to stir the contents of the fire pan, sending a brighter glow through the tent. "Kev had a younger brother."

Emotion flooded Kev, but he fought to conceal it. After he'd spent all his life believing himself to be alone, here was someone who shared his blood. A true brother.

"The grandmother took care of both boys for a while," Shuri continued. "But then the grandmother had cause to think *gadje* might come and take them. So she kept one boy, while Kev was sent to our tribe. I'm sure the grandmother didn't suspect how the *rom baro* would abuse him, or she never would have done it."

Shuri glanced at Kev. "She probably thought that since Pov was a strong man, he would do a good job of protecting you. But he thought of you as an abomination, being half—" She stopped with a gasp as Cam shoved up his coat and shirtsleeve, and showed his forearm to her. The *pooka* tattoo stood out in dark, inky relief against his skin.

"I'm his brother," Cam said, his voice slightly hoarse.

Shuri's gaze moved from one man's face to the other. "Yes, I see," she eventually murmured. "Not a close likeness, but it is there." A curious smile touched her lips. "It is God who brought you together."

"Do you know our father's name?" Kev asked tersely.

Shuri looked regretful. "Pov never mentioned it. I'm sorry."

"No, you've helped quite a lot," Cam said. "Do you know anything about why *gadjos* might have wanted to—"

"*Mami,*" came the boy's voice from outside. "Chorodies are coming."

"They want the horses," Kev said, rising swiftly to his feet. He pressed a few coins into Shuri's hand. "Luck and good health," he said.

Cam and Kev hurried outside the tent. Three Chorodies were approaching. With their matted hair, filthy complexions, rotted mouths, and a stench that preceded them well before their arrival, they seemed more like animals than men. A few curious Roma watched from a safe distance. It was clear there would be no help from that quarter.

"Well," Cam said beneath his breath, "this should be entertaining."

"Chorodies like knives," Kev said. "But they don't know how to use them. Leave this to me."

"Go right ahead," Cam said agreeably.

One of the Chorodies spoke in a dialect unfamiliar to Cam. But as he gestured to Pooka, who eyed them nervously and shuffled his feet, Cam had no difficulty understanding what he wanted.

"Like hell," Cam said, glaring at him.

The Chorodie reached behind his back, produced a jagged knife, and lunged forward with a harsh cry. Kev turned in a nimble sidestep, grabbed the attacking arm and jerked the man off-balance, using his own momentum against him. Before another heartbeat had passed, Kev had flipped him to the ground, twisting the bastard's arm in the process. An audible fracture rent the air, and the Chorodie howled in agony. After prying the knife from the man's limp hand, Kev tossed it to Cam, who caught it reflexively.

Kev glanced at the remaining two Chorodies. "Who's next?" he asked coldly.

They fled without a backward glance, leaving their injured companion to drag himself away with loud groans.

"Well done, *phral*," Cam said in admiration.

"We're leaving," Kev informed him curtly. "Before more of them come."

"Let's go to a tavern," Cam said. "I need a drink."

Kev mounted his bay without a word. For once, they were in agreement.

TAVERNS WERE OFTEN DESCRIBED AS THE BUSY MAN'S RECREATION, the idle man's business, and the melancholy man's sanctuary. The Hell and Bucket, located in the more disreputable environs of London, could also have been called the criminal's covert and the drunkard's haven. It suited Cam and Kev's purposes quite well, being a place that would serve two Roma without blinking an eye. The ale was good quality, twelve-bushel strength, and although the barmaids were surly, they did an adequate job of keeping the tankard full and the floor swept.

Cam and Kev sat at a small table, lit by a turnip that had been carved into a candleholder, with tallow runneling over its purple-tinged sides. Kev drank half a tankard without stopping and set the vessel down. He rarely drank anything except wine, and that in moderation. He didn't like the loss of control that came with drinking.

Cam, however, drained his own tankard. He leaned back

in his chair and surveyed Kev with a slight smile. "I've always been amused by your inability to hold your liquor," he remarked. "A Rom your size should be able to drink a quarter barrel to the pitching. But now to discover that you're half-Irish as well . . . it's inexcusable, *phral*. We'll have to work on your drinking skills."

"We're not going to tell this to anyone," Kev told him grimly.

"About the fact that we're brothers?" Cam seemed to enjoy Kev's visible wince. "It's not so bad, being half-*gadjo*," he told Kev kindly, and snickered at his expression. "It certainly explains why both of us have found a stopping place, while most Roma choose to wander forever. It's the Irish in us that—"

"*Not . . . one . . . word,*" Kev said. "Not even to the family."

Cam sobered a little. "I don't keep secrets from my wife."

"Not even for her safety?"

Cam appeared to think that over, gazing through one of the narrow windows of the tavern. The streets thronged with costermongers, the wheels of their barrows rattling over the cobblestones. Their cries rose thick in the air as they tried to interest customers in bonnet boxes, toys, lucifer matches, umbrellas, and brooms. On the opposite side of the street, a butcher shop window gleamed crimson and white with freshly cut meat.

"You think our father's family might still want to kill us?" Cam asked.

"It's possible."

Absently Cam rubbed over his own sleeve, over the place where the *pooka* mark was located. "You realize that none of this—the tattoos, the secrets, splitting us apart, giving us different names—would have happened unless our father was a man of some worth? Because otherwise, *gadje* wouldn't give a damn about a pair of half-breed children. I wonder why he left our mother? I wonder—"

"I don't give a damn."

"I'm going to do a new search of parish birth records. Perhaps our father—"

"Don't. Let it lie."

"*Let it lie?*" Cam gave him an incredulous glance. "You actually want to ignore what we found out today? Ignore the kinship between us?"

"Yes."

Shaking his head slowly, Cam turned one of the gold rings on his fingers. "After today, brother, I understand much more about you. The way you—"

"Don't call me that."

"I imagine the way you were raised doesn't inspire fond feelings for the human race. I'm sorry you were the unlucky one, being sent to our uncle. But you can't let that stop you from finding out who you are."

"Finding out who I am won't get me what I want. Nothing will. So there's no point in it."

"What is it you want?" Cam asked softly.

Clamping his mouth shut, Kev glared at him.

"You can't bring yourself to say it?" Cam prodded. When Kev remained obstinately silent, Cam reached over for his tankard. "Are you going to finish this?"

"No."

Cam drank the ale in a few expedient gulps. "You know," he remarked wryly, "it was a lot easier managing a club full of drunkards, gamblers, and assorted criminals than it is to deal with you and the Hathaways." He set the tankard down and waited a moment before asking quietly, "Did you suspect anything? Did you think the tie between us might be this close?"

"No."

"I think I did, deep down. I always knew I wasn't supposed to be alone."

Kev gave him a dour look. "This changes nothing. I'm not your family. There's no tie between us."

"Blood counts for something," Cam replied affably. "And since the rest of my tribe has disappeared, you're all I have, *phral*. Just try and get rid of me."

Chapter Eleven

Win descended the main staircase of the hotel while one of the Hathaways' footmen, Charles, followed closely. "Careful, Miss Hathaway," he cautioned. "One slip and you could break your neck on these stairs."

"Thank you, Charles," she said without moderating her speed. "But there's no need to worry." She was quite adept at stairs, having gone up and down long staircases at the clinic in France as part of her daily exercise. "I should warn you, Charles, that I will proceed at a vigorous pace."

"Yes, miss," he said, sounding disgruntled. Charles was somewhat stout, and not fond of walking.

Win bit back a smile. "Just to Hyde Park and back, Charles."

As they neared the entrance to the hotel, Win saw a tall, dark form moving through the lobby. It was Kev, looking moody and distracted as he walked with his gaze focused downward. She couldn't suppress the pleasure that went through her at the sight of him. He approached the stairs, glancing upward, and his expression changed as he saw her. There was a flash of hunger in his eyes before he managed to extinguish it. But that brief, bright flare caused Win's spirits to lift.

After the scene that morning, and Kev's display of jealous rage, Win had apologized to Julian. The doctor had been amused rather than disconcerted. "He's exactly as you described," Julian had said, adding ruefully, "only more."

"More" was a fitting word to apply to Kev, she thought. There was nothing understated about him.

The discreet glances Kev was attracting from a group of ladies in the lobby made it evident that Win was not the only one who found him mesmerizing. He wore the well-tailored clothes without a trace of self-consciousness, as if he couldn't have cared less whether he was dressed like a gentleman or a dock laborer. And knowing Kev, he didn't.

Win stopped and waited, smiling, as he came to her. His gaze swept over her, not missing a detail of the simple pink walking gown and matching jacket.

"You're dressed now," Kev remarked, as if he were surprised that she wasn't parading naked through the lobby.

"This is a walking dress," she said. "As you can see, I'm going out for some air."

"Who's escorting you?" he asked, even though he could see the footman standing a few feet away.

"Charles," she replied.

"*Only* Charles?" Kev looked outraged. "You need more protection than that."

"We're only walking to Marble Arch," she said, amused.

"Are you out of your mind, woman? Do you have any idea what could happen to you at Hyde Park? There are pickpockets, cutpurses, confidence tricksters, and gangs, all ready for a little pigeon like you to pluck."

Rather than take offense, Charles said eagerly, "Perhaps Mr. Merripen has a point, Miss Hathaway. It *is* rather far . . . and one never knows . . ."

"Are you offering to go in his stead?" Win asked Kev.

As she had expected, he put on a show of grumbling reluctance. "I suppose so, if the alternative is to see you traipsing through the streets of London and tempting every criminal in sight." He frowned at Charles. "You needn't go with us. I'd rather not have to look after you, too."

"Yes, sir," came the footman's grateful reply, and he went back up the stairs with considerably more enthusiasm than he had shown while descending them.

Win slipped her hand through Kev's arm and felt the fierce tension in his muscles. Something had upset him deeply, she realized. Something far more than her exercise costume or the prospective walk to Hyde Park.

They left the hotel, Kev's long strides easily keeping measure with her brisk ones. Win kept her tone casual and cheerful. "How cool and bracing the air is today."

"It's polluted with coal smoke," he said, steering her around a puddle as if it might cause mortal harm to get her feet wet.

"Actually, I detect a strong scent of smoke from your coat. Not tobacco smoke, either. Where did you and Cam go this morning?"

"To a Romany camp."

"For what reason?" Win persisted.

"Rohan thought we might find someone there from my tribe."

"And did you?" she asked softly, knowing the subject was a sensitive one.

"No."

"Yes, you did. I can tell you're brooding."

As Kev saw how closely she was studying him, he sighed and said, "In my tribe, there was a girl named Shuri . . ."

Win felt a pang of jealousy. A girl he had known and never mentioned. Perhaps he had cared for her.

"We found her today in the camp," Kev continued. "She

hardly looks the same. She was once very beautiful, but now she appears much older than her years."

"Oh, that's too bad," Win said, trying to sound sincere.

"Her husband, the *rom baro,* was my uncle. He was . . . not a good man."

Win was filled with compassion and tenderness. She wished they were in some private place where she could coax Kev to tell her everything. She wished she could embrace him, not as a lover, but as a loving friend. No doubt many people would think it ludicrous that she should feel so protective of such an invulnerable-seeming man. But beneath that hard and impervious facade, Kev possessed a rare depth of feeling. She knew that about him. She also knew that he would deny it to the death.

"Did Cam tell Shuri about his tattoo?" Win asked. "That it was identical to yours?"

"Yes."

"And what did Shuri say about it?"

"Nothing." His reply was a shade too quick.

A pair of street sellers, one bearing bundles of watercress, the other carrying umbrellas, approached them hopefully. But one glower from Kev caused them to retreat, braving the traffic of carriages, carts, and horses to go to the other side of the street.

Win didn't say anything for a minute or two, just held Kev's arm as he guided her along with exasperating bossiness, muttering "Don't step there," or "Come this way," or "Tread carefully here," as if stepping on broken or uneven pavement might result in severe injury.

"Kev," she finally protested, "I'm not fragile."

"I know that."

"Then please don't treat me as if I'll break at the first misstep."

Kev grumbled a little, something about the street not being good enough for her. It was too rough. Too dirty.

Win couldn't help chuckling. "For heaven's sake. If this street was paved with gold and angels were sweeping it, you would still say it was too rough and dirty for me. You must rid yourself of this habit of protecting me."

"Not while I live."

Win was quiet, gripping his arm more tightly. The passion buried beneath the rough, simple words filled her with an almost indecent pleasure. So easily he could reach down to the deepest region of her heart.

"I'd rather not be put on a pedestal," she finally said.

"You're not on a pedestal. You're—" But he checked the words, and he shook his head a little, as if he was vaguely surprised he'd said them. Whatever had happened that day, it had shaken his self-control badly.

Win pondered what possible things Shuri might have said. Something about the connection between Cam and Kev . . .

"Kev." Win eased her pace, forcing him to go more slowly as well. "Even before I left for France, I had the idea that those tattoos were evidence of a close link between you and Cam. Being so ill, I had little to do except observe the people in my sphere. I noticed things that no one else did. Especially about you." Taking in his expression with a quick sidelong glance, Win saw that he didn't like that. "And when I met Cam," she continued casually, "I was struck by many similarities between the two of you. The tilt of his head, that half smile he has . . . the way he gestures with his hands . . . all things I had seen you do. And I thought to myself, I wouldn't be surprised to learn someday that the two of them are . . . brothers."

Kev stopped completely. He turned to face her, standing right there on the street while other pedestrians were forced to go around them, muttering about how inconsiderate it was for people to block a public footpath. Win looked up into his dark eyes and gave an innocent shrug. And she waited for his response.

"Improbable," he said gruffly.

"Improbable things happen all the time," Win said. "Especially to our family." She continued to stare at him, reading him. "It's true, isn't it?" she asked in wonder. "He's your brother?"

Kev hesitated. His whisper was so soft she could barely hear it. "Younger brother."

"I'm glad for you. For both of you." She smiled up at him steadily, until his mouth took on a wry, answering curve.

"I'm not."

"Someday you will be."

After a moment he pulled her arm through his and they began walking again.

"If you and Cam are brothers," Win said, "then you're half-*gadjo*. Just like he is. Are you sorry about that?"

"No, I . . ." He paused to mull over the discovery. "I wasn't as surprised as I should have been. I've always felt I was Romany and . . . something other."

And Win understood what he didn't say. Unlike Cam, he wasn't eager to face this entire other identity, this vast part of himself that was so far unrealized. "Are you going to talk about it with the family?" she asked softly. Knowing Kev, he would want to keep the information private until he'd sorted through all its implications.

He shook his head. "There are questions that must be answered first. Including why the *gadjo* who fathered us wanted to kill us."

"He did? Good heavens, why?"

"My guess is that it was probably some question of inheritance. With *gadjos*, it usually comes down to money."

"So bitter," Win said, clinging more tightly to his arm.

"I have reason."

"You have reason to be happy as well. You found a brother today. And you found out that you're half-Irish."

That actually drew a rumble of amusement from him. "*That* should make me happy?"

"The Irish are a remarkable race. And I see it in you: your love of land, your tenacity . . ."

"My love of brawling."

"Yes. Well, perhaps you should continue to suppress that part."

"Being part-Irish," he said, "I should be a more proficient drinker."

"And a far more glib conversationalist."

"I prefer to talk only when I have something to say." But he was smiling now, and Win felt a warm ripple of delight spread through all her limbs.

"That's the first real smile I've seen from you since I came back," she said. "You should smile more, Kev."

"Should I?" he asked softly.

"Oh yes. It's beneficial for your health. Dr. Harrow says his cheerful patients tend to recover far more quickly than the sour ones."

The mention of Dr. Harrow caused Kev's elusive smile to vanish. "Lord Ramsay says you've become close with him."

"Dr. Harrow is a friend."

"Only a friend?"

"So far. Would you object if he wished to court me?"

"Of course not," Kev muttered. "What right would I have to object?"

"None at all. Unless you'd staked some prior claim, which you certainly have not."

She sensed Kev's inner struggle to let the matter drop. A struggle he lost, for he said abruptly, "Far be it from me to deny you a diet of pabulum, if that's what your appetite demands."

Win fought to hold back a satisfied grin. The small display of jealousy was a balm to her spirits. "I assure you, he's not at all bland. He is a man of substance and character."

"He's a watery-eyed, pale-faced *gadjo*."

"He's very attractive. And his eyes are not at all watery."

"Have you let him kiss you?"

"Kev, we're on a public thoroughfare—"

"Have you?"

"Once," she admitted, and waited as he digested the information. He scowled ferociously at the pavement before them. When it became apparent he wasn't going to say anything, Win volunteered, "It wasn't like your kisses."

Still no response.

Stubborn ox, she thought in annoyance, and felt a blush rising as she added, "We've never done anything similar to what you and I . . . the other night . . ."

"We're not going to discuss that."

"Why can we discuss Dr. Harrow's kisses but not yours?"

"Because my kisses aren't going to lead to courtship."

That hurt. It also puzzled and frustrated her. Before all was said and done, Win intended to make Kev admit just why he wouldn't pursue her. But not here, and not now.

"Well, I do have a chance of courtship with Dr. Harrow," she said, attempting a pragmatic tone. "And at my age, I must consider any marriage prospect quite seriously."

"Your age?" he scoffed. "You're only twenty-five."

"Twenty-six. And even at twenty-five, I'd be considered long in the tooth. I lost several years—my best ones perhaps—because of my illness."

"You're more beautiful now than you ever were. Any man

would be mad or blind not to want you." The compliment was not given smoothly, but with a sincerity that heightened her blush.

"Thank you, Kev."

He slid her a guarded look. "You want to marry?"

Win's willful, treacherous heart gave a few painfully excited thuds, because at first she thought he'd asked, "You want to marry *me*?" But no, he was merely asking her opinion of marriage as . . . well, as her scholarly father would have said, as a "conceptual structure with a potential for realization."

"Yes, of course," she said. "I want children to love. I want a husband to grow old with. I want a family of my own."

"And Harrow says all of that is possible now?"

Win hesitated a bit too long. "Yes, completely possible."

But Kev knew her too well. "What are you not telling me?"

"I am well enough to do anything I choose now," she said firmly.

"What does he—"

"I don't wish to discuss it. You have your forbidden topics; I have mine."

"You know I'll find out," he said quietly.

Win ignored that, casting her gaze to the park before them. Her eyes widened as she saw something that had not been there when she had left for France . . . a huge, magnificent structure of glass and iron. "Is that the Crystal Palace? It's so beautiful—even more so than the engravings I've seen." The building, which covered an area of more than nine acres, housed an international show of art and science called the Great Exhibition. Her steps quickened as they headed toward the glittering building. "How long since it was completed?" she asked.

"Not quite a month."

"Have you been inside? Have you seen the exhibits?"

"I've visited once," Kev said, smiling at her eagerness.

"And I saw a few of the exhibits, but not all. It would take three days or more to look at everything."

"Which part did you go to?"

"The machinery court, mostly."

"I do wish I could see even a small part of it," she said wistfully, watching the throngs of visitors exiting and entering the remarkable building. "Won't you take me?"

"You wouldn't have time to see anything. It's already afternoon. I'll bring you tomorrow."

"Now. *Please*." She tugged impatiently on his arm. "Oh, Kev, don't say no."

As Kev looked down at her, he was so handsome that it caused a pleasant pang at the pit of her stomach. "How could I say no to you?" he asked softly.

He took her to the towering arched entrance of the Crystal Palace and paid a shilling each for their admission, while Win gazed at their surroundings in awe. Prince Albert, a man of vision and wisdom, had been the driving force behind the exhibition of industrial design. According to the tiny printed map that was given out with the tickets, the building itself was constructed of over a thousand iron columns and three hundred thousand panes of glass. Parts of it were tall enough to encompass full-grown elm trees. All totaled, there were one hundred thousand exhibits from around the world.

People of all manner of dress and appearance crowded inside the building. The exhibition provided a rare opportunity for all classes, high and low, to mingle freely beneath one roof.

Kev handed Win the little map.

After scrutinizing the list of courts and displays, she said decisively, "Let's start at fabrics and textiles."

They went through a crowded glass hallway into a room of astonishing size and breadth. The air chattered with the sounds of looms and textile machinery, with carpet bales arranged around the room and down the center. Scents of wool and dye made the atmosphere acrid and lightly pungent. Goods from Kidderminster, America, Spain, France, and the Orient filled the room with a rainbow of hues and textures.

Win removed her gloves and ran her hands over the gorgeous offerings. "Kev, look at this!" she exclaimed. "It's a Wilton carpet. Similar to Brussels, but the pile is sheared. It feels like velvet, doesn't it?"

The manufacturer's representative, who was standing nearby, said, "Wilton is much more affordable now that we are able to produce it on steam-powered looms."

"Where is the factory located?" Kev asked, running a bare hand over the soft carpet pile. "Kidderminster, I assume?"

"There, and another in Glasgow."

As the men conversed, Win wandered along a row of machines, some made to weave fabrics, some to print patterns, some to spin tufts of wool into yarn and worsted. One was used in a demonstration of how stuffing mattresses and pillows would someday be mechanized.

Watching in fascination, Win was aware of Kev coming to stand beside her. "It seems as if everything in the world will eventually be done by machine," she said.

He smiled slightly. "If we had time, I'd take you to the agricultural exhibits. A man can grow twice as much food with a fraction of the time and labor it takes to do by hand. We've already acquired a threshing machine for the Ramsay estate tenants. I'll show it to you when we go there."

"You approve of these technological advances?" Win asked with a touch of surprise.

"Yes, why wouldn't I?"

"What about the men who'll lose their livelihoods when machines take their places?"

"New jobs are being created. Why put a man to work doing

mindless tasks instead of educating him to do something more?"

Win smiled. "You speak like a reformist," she whispered impishly.

"Economic change is always accompanied by social change. No one can stop that."

What an adept mind he had, Win thought with pride. Her father would have been pleased.

She was about to ask something else when she was interrupted by an explosive *puff* and a few cries of surprise from the visitors around them. The pillow-stuffing machine had malfunctioned, sending eddies of feathers and down over everyone in sight.

Reacting swiftly, Kev stripped off his coat, and pulled it over Win, and clamped a handkerchief over her mouth and nose. "Breathe through this," he muttered, and hauled her through the room. The crowd was scattering, people coughing, swearing, or laughing as great volumes of fluffy white down settled over the scene. There were cries of delight from children who had come from the next room, dancing and hopping to try to catch the floating clumps.

Kev didn't stop until they had reached another nave that housed a fabric court. Enormous wood and glass cases had been built for displays of fabric that flowed like rivers. The walls were hung with velvets, brocades, silks, cotton, muslin, wool, every imaginable substance created for clothing, upholstery, or drapery. Towering bolts of fabric were arranged in vertical rolls affixed to more display walls that formed deep corridors within the court.

Emerging from beneath Kev's coat, Win took one look at him and began to gasp with laughter. White down had covered his black hair and clung to his clothes like new-fallen snow.

Kev's expression of concern changed to a scowl. "I was going to ask if you had breathed in any of the feather dust," he said. "But judging from all the noise you're making, your lungs seem quite clear."

Win couldn't reply; she was laughing too hard.

As Kev raked his hand through the midnight locks of his hair, the down became even more enmeshed.

"Don't," Win managed, struggling to restrain her amusement. "Let me help you. You're making it worse . . . and you s-said *I* was a pigeon to be plucked . . ." Still chortling, she snatched his hand and tugged him into one of the fabric corridors, where they were partially hidden from view. They went beyond the half-light and into the shadows. "Here, before anyone sees us." She urged him to the floor with her, where he lowered to his haunches. Win knelt amid the mass of her skirts. After untying her bonnet, she tossed it aside and went to work, brushing at Kev's shoulders and hair.

"You can't be enjoying this," he said.

"Silly man. You're covered in feathers—of *course* I'm enjoying it." And she was. He looked so . . . well, adorable, kneeling and frowning and holding still while she defeathered him. And it was lovely to play with the thick, shiny layers of his hair, which he never would have allowed in other circumstances. Her giggles kept frothing up, impossible to suppress.

But as a minute passed, and then another, a dreamlike feeling came over her as she continued to pull the fluff from his hair. The sound of the crowds was muffled by the velvet draped all around them, hanging like curtains of night and clouds and mist.

"Almost done," she whispered, although she was already finished. Her fingers sifted gently through his hair.

Her breath caught as he moved. At first she thought he was

rising to his feet, but he tugged her closer and took her head in his hands. His mouth was so close, his exhalations like steam against her lips.

"I have nothing to offer you," he finally said in a guttural voice. "Nothing."

Win's lips had turned dry. She moistened them, and tried to speak through a thrill of anxious trembling. "You have yourself," she whispered.

"You don't know me. You think you do, but you don't. The things I've done, the things I'm capable of—you and your family, all you know of life comes from books. If you understood anything—"

"*Make* me understand. Tell me why you have to keep pushing me away."

He shook his head.

"Then stop torturing the both of us," she said unsteadily. "Leave me, or let me go."

"I can't," he snapped. Before she could make a sound, he kissed her.

Her heart thundered, and she opened to him with a low, despairing moan. Her nostrils were filled with the fragrance of smoke, and man, and the earthy autumn spice of him. His mouth shaped to hers with primitive hunger, his tongue stabbing deep, searching hungrily. They knelt together more tightly as Win rose to press her torso against his, closer, harder.

The desire flared high and wild, leaving no room for sanity. If only he would press her back among all this velvet, here and now, and have his way with her. His mouth searched her throat, and her head tipped back to give him free access. He found the throb of her pulse, his tongue stroking the vulnerable spot until she gasped.

Reaching up to his face, she shaped her fingers over his jaw, the heavy grain of shaven beard scraping deliciously against her delicate palms. "Kev," she whispered in between kisses, "I've loved you for so—"

He crushed her mouth with his desperately, as if he could smother not only the words but the emotion itself. He stole as deep a taste of her as possible, determined to leave nothing unclaimed. She clung to him, her body racked with sustained shivers, her nerves singing with incandescent heat. He was all she'd ever wanted, all she would ever need.

But a sharp breath was torn from her throat as he pushed her back, breaking the contact between their bodies.

For a long moment neither of them moved, both striving to recover equilibrium. As the glow of desire faded, Win heard Kev say roughly, "I can't be alone with you. This can't happen again."

It was an impossible situation. Kev refused to acknowledge his feelings for her and wouldn't explain why. Surely she deserved more from him than that.

"Very well," she said stiffly, struggling to her feet. As Kev stood and reached for her, she pushed impatiently at his hand. "No, I don't want help." She began to shake out her skirts. "You're absolutely right, Kev. We shouldn't be alone together, since the result is always a foregone conclusion: you make an advance, I respond, and then you push me away. I'm no child's toy to be pulled back and forth on a string."

He found her bonnet and handed it to her. "I know you're not—"

"You say I don't know you," she continued. "Apparently it hasn't occurred to you that you don't know me, either. I've changed during the past two years. You might at least make an effort to find out who I've become." She went to the end of the fabric corridor, peeked out to make certain the coast was clear, and stepped out into the main part of the court.

Kev followed. "Where are you going?"

Glancing at him, Win was satisfied to see that he looked

as rumpled and exasperated as she felt. "I'm leaving. I'm too cross to enjoy any of the displays now."

"Go the other direction."

Win was silent as Kev led her from the Crystal Palace. It annoyed her that he kept pace so easily with her brisk, ground-digging strides, and that when she had begun to breathe hard from exertion, he barely seemed affected by the exercise.

Only when they approached the Rutledge did Win break the silence. "I'll abide by your wishes, Kev. From now on, our relationship will be platonic and friendly. Nothing more." She paused at the first step and looked up at him solemnly. "I've been given a rare opportunity . . . a second chance at life. And I intend to make the most of it. I'm not going to waste my love on a man who doesn't want or need it. I won't bother you again."

When Cam entered the bedroom of their suite, he found Amelia standing before a towering pile of parcels and boxes overflowing with ribbons and silk and feminine adornments. She turned with a sheepish smile as he closed the door, her heart tripping a little at the sight of him. His collarless shirt was open at the throat, his body almost feline in its lithe muscularity, his face riveting in its sensuous male beauty. Not long ago, she would never have envisioned being married at all, much less to such a magnificent man.

His gaze chased lightly over her, the pink velvet dressing gown open to reveal her chemise and naked thighs. "I see the shopping expedition was a success."

"I don't know what came over me," Amelia replied a touch apologetically. "You know I'm never extravagant. I only meant to purchase some handkerchiefs and some stockings. But . . ." She gestured lamely to the piles of fripperies. "I seem to have been in an acquisitive mood today."

A smile flashed across his face. "As I've told you before,

love, spend as much as you like. You couldn't beggar me if you tried."

"I bought some things for you, too," she said, rummaging through the pile. "Some cravats, and books, and French shaving soap . . . although I've been meaning to discuss that with you . . ."

"Discuss what?" Cam approached her from behind, kissing the side of her throat.

Amelia drew in a breath at the hot imprint of his mouth and nearly forgot what she had been saying. "Your shaving," she said vaguely. "Beards are becoming quite fashionable of late. I think you should try a goatee. You would look very dashing, and . . ." Her voice faded as he worked his way down her neck.

"It might tickle," Cam murmured, and laughed as she shivered.

Gently turning her to face him, he stared into her eyes. There was something different about him, she thought. A curious vulnerability she had never seen before.

"Cam," she said carefully, "how did your errand with Merripen go?"

The amber eyes were soft and alive with excitement. "Quite well. I have a secret, *monisha*. Shall I tell you?" He drew her against him, wrapping his arms around her, and he whispered into her ear.

Chapter Twelve

Kev was in a devil of a temper that evening for a variety of reasons. The uppermost being that Win was carrying out her threat. She was being *friendly* to him. Polite, courteous, damnably nice. He was in no position to object, since this was precisely what he'd wanted. But he hadn't expected there was one thing even worse than having Win glance at him with longing: indifference.

To Kev, she was affectionate in the same way she was with Leo or Cam. She treated him as if he were a brother. He could hardly bear it.

The Hathaways gathered in the eating area of their suite, laughing and joking about the close quarters as they sat at the table. It was the first time in years that they'd all been able to dine together: Kev, Leo, Amelia, Win, Poppy, and Beatrix, with the additions of Cam, Miss Marks, and Dr. Harrow.

Although Miss Marks had tried to demur, they'd insisted that she dine with the family. "After all," Poppy had said, laughing, "how else will we know how to behave? Someone has to save us from ourselves."

Miss Marks had relented, although it was clear that she would have preferred to be elsewhere. She took up as small a space as possible, a narrow, colorless figure wedged between Beatrix and Dr. Harrow. She rarely looked up from her plate except when Leo was speaking. Although her eyes were partially concealed by the spectacles, Kev suspected they held nothing but dislike for the Hathaways' brother.

It seemed Miss Marks and Leo had found in each other the personification of everything they disliked most. Leo couldn't stand humorless people, or judgmental ones, and he had immediately taken to referring to the governess as "Lucifer in petticoats." And Miss Marks, for her part, despised rakes. The more charming they were, the deeper her loathing.

Most of the dinner conversation centered on the subject of Harrow's clinic. The women fawned on Harrow to a nauseating degree, delighting in his commonplace remarks, admiring him openly.

Kev had an instinctive aversion to Harrow, although he wasn't certain if that was because of the doctor himself, or because Win's affections were at stake.

It was tempting to disdain Harrow for all his smooth-faced perfection. But a roguish good humor lurked in his smile, and he displayed a lively interest in the conversation around him, and he seemed never to take himself too seriously. Harrow was obviously a man who shouldered heavy responsibility—that of life and death itself—and yet he carried it lightly. He was the kind of person who always seemed to fit in no matter what the circumstances.

While the family ate and conversed, Kev remained quiet except when called upon to answer some question about the Ramsay estate. He watched Win covertly, unable to discern exactly what her feelings for Harrow were. She reacted to the doctor with her usual composure, her face giving away nothing. But when their gazes met, there was an unmistakable connection, a sense of shared history. And worst of all,

Kev recognized something in the doctor's expression . . . a haunting echo of his own fascination for Win.

Midway through the gruesomely cheerful dinner, Kev became aware that Amelia, who was seated at the end of the table, was unusually quiet. He looked at her closely, realizing her color was off and her cheeks were sweaty. Since he was seated at her immediate left, Kev leaned close to whisper, "What is it?"

Amelia gave him a distracted glance. "Ill," she whispered back, swallowing weakly. "I feel so . . . oh, Merripen, do help me away from the table."

Without another word, Kev pushed his chair back and helped her up.

Cam, who was at the other end of the long table, looked at them sharply. "Amelia?"

"She's ill," Kev said.

Cam reached them in a flash, his face taut with anxiety. As he gathered Amelia in his arms and carried her, protesting, from the room, one would think she'd suffered a severe injury rather than a probable case of indigestion.

"Perhaps I might be of service," Harrow said with quiet concern, laying his napkin on the table as he made to follow them.

"Thank you," Win told him gratefully. "I'm so glad you're here."

Kev barely restrained himself from gnashing his teeth in jealousy as Harrow left the room.

The rest of the meal was largely neglected, the family going to the main receiving room to wait for a report on Amelia. It took an unnervingly long time for anyone to appear.

"What could be the matter?" Beatrix asked plaintively. "Amelia's never ill."

"She'll be fine," Win soothed. "Dr. Harrow will take excellent care of her."

"Perhaps I should go to their room," Poppy suggested, "and ask how she is."

But before anyone could offer an opinion, Cam appeared in the doorway of the receiving room. He looked bemused, his hazel eyes vivid as he glanced at the assorted family members around him. He appeared to search for words. A dazzling smile appeared. "No doubt *gadje* have a more civilized way to put this," he said, "but Amelia is with child."

A chorus of happy exclamations greeted the revelation.

"What did Amelia say about it?" Leo asked.

Cam's smile turned wry. "Something to the effect that this wouldn't be convenient."

Leo grinned. "She'll adore having someone new to manage."

Kev watched Win from across the room. He was fascinated by the momentary wistfulness that hazed her expression. If he had ever doubted how much she wanted children of her own, it was clear to him then. As he stared at her, a flush of warmth rose in him, strengthening and thickening until he realized what it was. He was aroused, his body yearning to give her what she wanted. He longed to hold her, love her, fill her with his seed. The reaction was so inappropriate that it mortified him.

Seeming to feel his gaze, Win glanced in his direction. She gave him an arrested stare, as if she could see down to all the raw heat inside him. And then she looked away from him in swift rejection.

EXCUSING HIMSELF FROM THE RECEIVING ROOM, CAM WENT back to Amelia, who was sitting on the edge of the bed. Dr. Harrow had left the bedchamber to allow them privacy.

Cam closed the door and leaned back against it, letting his caressing gaze fall on the small, tense form of his wife. He knew little of these matters. Pregnancy and childbirth were a strictly female domain. But he did know that his wife was uneasy in situations she had no control over. He also knew that women in her condition needed reassurance and tenderness. And he had an inexhaustible supply of both for her.

"Nervous?" Cam asked softly, approaching her.

"Oh no, not in the slightest; it's an ordinary circumstance, and only to be expected after—" Amelia broke off with a little gasp as he sat beside her and pulled her into his arms. "Yes, I'm a bit nervous. I wish . . . I wish I could talk to my mother. I'm not exactly certain how to do this."

Of course. Amelia liked to manage everything, to be authoritative and competent no matter what she did. But the entire process of childbearing would be one of increasing dependence and helplessness until the final stage, when nature took over entirely.

Cam pressed his lips into her gleaming dark hair and began to rub her back in the way he knew she liked best. "We'll find some experienced women for you to talk to. Lady Westcliff, perhaps. And you'll let me take care of you, and spoil you, and give you anything you want." He felt her relax a little. "Amelia, love," he murmured, "I've hoped for this."

"Have you?" She smiled and snuggled against him. "So have I. Although I would have preferred it to happen at a more convenient time, when Ramsay House was finished, and Poppy was betrothed, and the family was settled—"

"Trust me, with your family there'll never be a convenient time." Cam eased her back to lie on the bed with him. "What a pretty little mother you'll be," he whispered, cuddling her. "With your blue eyes, and your pink cheeks, and your belly all round with my child . . ."

"When I grow large, I hope you won't strut and swagger and point to me as an example of your virility."

"I do that already, *monisha*."

Amelia looked up into his smiling eyes. "I can't imagine how this happened."

"Didn't I explain that on our wedding night?"

She chuckled and put her arms around his neck. "I was referring to the fact that I've been taking preventative measures. All those cups of nasty-tasting tea. And I *still* ended up conceiving."

"Rom," he said by way of explanation, and kissed her passionately.

WHEN AMELIA FELT WELL ENOUGH TO JOIN THE OTHER women for tea in the receiving room, the men went downstairs to the Rutledge's gentlemen's room. Although the room was ostensibly for the use of hotel guests, it had become a favorite haunt of the peerage, who wished to share the company of the Rutledge's many notable foreign visitors.

The ceilings were comfortably dark and low, paneled in glowing rosewood, the floors covered in thick Wilton carpeting. The gentlemen's room was cornered with large, deep apses that provided private spaces for reading, drinking, and conversing. The main space was furnished with velvet-upholstered chairs, and tables laden with cigar boxes and newspapers. Servants moved unobtrusively through the room, bringing snifters of warmed brandy and glasses of port.

Settling in one of the unoccupied octagonal apses, Kev requested brandy for the table. "Yes, Mr. Merripen," the servant said, hastening to comply.

"What well-trained staff," Harrow remarked. "I find it commendable that they give impartial service to all the guests."

Kev slanted him a questioning glance. "Why wouldn't they?"

"I imagine a man of your origins doesn't receive service at every establishment you frequent." Harrow looked uncomfortable. "My apologies. I'm not usually so tactless, Merripen."

Kev gave him a short nod to indicate no offense had been taken.

Harrow turned to Cam, seeking to change the subject. "I hope you'll allow me to recommend a colleague to attend Mrs. Rohan during the remainder of your stay in London. I'm acquainted with many excellent physicians here."

"I'd appreciate that," Cam said, accepting a brandy from a servant. "Although I suspect we won't remain in London much longer."

"Miss Winnifred is fond of children," Harrow mused. "In light of her condition, it's fortunate she'll have nieces and nephews to dote on."

The other three men looked at him sharply. Cam had paused in the act of lifting the brandy to his lips. "Condition?" he asked.

"Her inability to have children of her own," Harrow clarified.

"What the devil do you mean, Harrow?" Leo asked. "Haven't we all been trumpeting my sister's miraculous recovery due to your efforts?"

"She has indeed recovered, my lord." Harrow frowned thoughtfully as he stared into his brandy snifter. "But she'll always be somewhat fragile. In my opinion, she should never try to conceive. In all likelihood the process would result in her death."

A heavy silence followed this pronouncement. Even Leo, who usually affected an air of insouciance, couldn't manage to conceal his reaction. "Have you made my sister aware of this?" he asked. "Because she's given me the impression she fully expects to marry and have her own family someday."

"I've discussed it with her, of course," Harrow replied. "I told her that if she marries, her husband would have to agree that it would be a childless union." He paused. "However,

Miss Hathaway isn't yet ready to accept the idea. In time, I hope to persuade her to adjust her expectations."

Cam stared at him intently. "My sister-in-law will find it a disappointment, to say the least."

"Yes. But she'll live longer and enjoy a higher quality of life as a childless woman. And she'll learn to accept her altered circumstances. That is her strength." He swallowed some brandy before continuing quietly, "Miss Hathaway was never destined for childbearing, even before the scarlet fever. Such a narrow frame. Elegant, but hardly ideal for breeding purposes."

Kev tossed back his brandy, letting the amber fire wash down his throat. He pushed back from the table and stood, unable to bear another moment of the bastard's proximity. The mention of Win's "narrow frame" had been the last straw. Excusing himself with a rough mutter, he walked out of the hotel and into the night. His senses drew in the cool air, the foul, sharp city smells, the stirrings of the London night coming to life. Christ, he wanted to be away from this place.

He wanted to take Win to the country with him, away from the gleaming Dr. Harrow, whose clean, fastidious perfection filled him with dread. Every instinct warned that Win wasn't safe from Harrow.

But she wasn't safe from Kev, either.

His own mother had died giving birth. The thought of killing Win with his own body, his child swelling inside her until—

His entire being shied at the thought. His deepest terror was harming her. Losing her.

Kev wanted to talk to her, to listen to her, to help her some-how to come to terms with the limitations she'd been given. But he'd put a barrier between them, and he didn't dare cross it. Because if Harrow's flaw was a lack of empathy, Kev's was just the opposite. Too much feeling, too much need.

Enough to kill her.

LATER THAT EVENING CAM CAME TO KEV'S ROOM.

Kev had just returned from his walk, a glaze of evening mist still clinging to his coat and hair. Answering the knock at the door, he stood at the threshold and scowled. "What is it?"

"I talked privately with Harrow," Cam said, his face expressionless.

"And?"

"He wants to marry Win. But he intends the marriage to be in name only. She doesn't know it yet."

"Bloody hell," Kev muttered. "She'll be the latest addition to his collection of fine objects. She'll stay chaste while he has his affairs—"

"I don't know her well," Cam murmured, "but I don't think she'd ever agree to such an arrangement. Especially if you offered her an alternative, *phral*."

"That's not possible."

"Why not?"

Kev felt his face burn. "I couldn't stay celibate with her. I could never hold to it."

"There are ways to prevent conception."

That elicited a contemptuous snort from Kev. "That worked well for you, didn't it?" He rubbed his face wearily. "You know the other reasons I can't offer for her."

"I know the way you once lived," Cam said, choosing his words with obvious care. "I understand your fear of harming her. But in spite of all that, I find it hard to believe you'd really let her go to another man."

"I would if it were best for her."

"Can you actually say that the best Win deserves is someone like Harrow?"

"Better him," Kev managed to say, "than someone like me."

ALTHOUGH THE LONDON SEASON WASN'T YET OVER, THE family agreed to return to Hampshire. There was Amelia's condition to consider—she'd be better off in the healthful surroundings—and Win and Leo wanted to see the Ramsay estate. The only question was the fairness of depriving Poppy and Beatrix of the remainder of the season, but they both claimed to be quite happy to leave London.

This attitude was hardly unexpected coming from Beatrix, who still seemed far more interested in books and animals and romping through the countryside like a wild creature. But Leo was surprised that Poppy, who was candid about wanting to find a husband, would be so willing to depart.

"I've seen all this season's prospects," Poppy told Leo grimly as they rode through Hyde Park in an open carriage. "Not one of them is worth staying in town for."

Beatrix sat in the opposite seat with Dodger the ferret curled in her lap. Miss Marks had wedged herself in the corner, her bespectacled gaze fixed on the scenery.

Leo had rarely encountered such an off-putting female. Abrasive, pale, her form an accumulation of pointy elbows and angular bones. The only people Catherine Marks seemed to unbend with were Poppy and Beatrix, who'd reported that she could be very witty at times, and had a lovely smile.

Leo had a difficult time imagining the tight little seam of Miss Marks's mouth curving in a smile.

"She'll ruin the view," he'd complained that morning when Poppy and Beatrix had told him they were bringing him on their drive. "I won't enjoy the scenery with the Grim Reaper casting her shadow over it."

"Don't call her horrid names, Leo," Beatrix had protested. "I like her very much. And she's very nice when you're not around."

"I believe she was treated wrongly by a man in her past," Poppy had said sotto voce. "In fact, I've heard a rumor or two that Miss Marks became a governess because she was involved in a scandal."

Leo was interested despite himself. "What kind of scandal?"

Poppy had lowered her voice to a whisper. "They say she *squandered her favors.*"

Now, as the carriage passed Marble Arch and proceeded to Park Lane, Leo glanced covertly at Miss Marks. She had a decent profile—a sweet little tip of a nose supporting the spectacles, a gently rounded chin. Too bad the clenched mouth and frowning forehead ruined the rest of it.

He turned his attention back to Poppy, pondering her lack of desire to stay in London. Surely any other girl her age would have been begging to finish the season and enjoy all the balls and parties.

"Tell me about this season's prospects," he said to Poppy. "None of them holds any interest for you?"

She shook her head. "Not one. I've met a few I do like, such as Lord Bromley, or—"

"Bromley?" Leo repeated, his brows lifting. "Are there any younger ones you might consider? Someone born in this century, perhaps?"

"Well, there's Mr. Radstock, but . . . he's a rabbit."

"Curious and cuddly?" Beatrix asked, having a high opinion of rabbits.

Poppy smiled. "No, I meant colorless and . . . oh, just

rabbity. Which is a fine thing in a pet, but not a husband." She made a project of neatening the bonnet ribbons tied beneath her chin. "You'll probably advise me to lower my expectations, Leo, but I've already done that. A worm couldn't squeeze itself beneath my expectations. The London season has been a grave disappointment."

"I'm sorry, Poppy," Leo said gently. "I wish I knew a fellow to recommend to you, but the only ones I know are ne'er-do-wells and drunkards. Excellent friends, but I'd rather shoot one of them than have him as a brother-in-law."

"That leads to something I've wanted to ask you."

"Oh?" He looked into her sweet, serious face, his perfectly lovely sister who aspired so desperately to have a calm and ordinary life.

"Now that I've been out in society," Poppy said, "I've heard rumors . . ."

Leo's smile turned rueful as he understood what she wanted to know. "About me."

"Yes. Are you really as wicked as some people say?"

Despite the private nature of the query, Leo was aware of both Miss Marks and Beatrix turning their full attention to him.

"I'm afraid so, darling," he said, while a sordid parade of his past sins swept through his mind.

"Why?" Poppy asked with a frankness he ordinarily would have found endearing. But not with Miss Marks's sanctimonious gaze fastened on him.

"It's much easier to be wicked," he said. "Especially if one has no reason to be good."

"What about earning a place in heaven?" Miss Marks asked. He would have thought she had a pretty voice if it hadn't come from such an unappealing source. "Isn't that reason enough to conduct yourself with some modicum of decency?"

"That depends," he said sardonically. "What is heaven to you, Miss Marks?"

She considered the question with more care than he would have expected. "Peace. Serenity. A place where there is neither sin, nor gossip, nor conflict."

"Well, Miss Marks, I'm afraid your idea of heaven is my idea of hell. Therefore my wicked ways shall happily continue." Turning back to Poppy, he spoke far more kindly. "Don't lose hope, sis. There's someone out there, waiting for you. Someday you'll find him, and he'll be everything you were hoping for."

"Do you really think so?" Poppy asked.

"No. But I've always thought that was a nice thing to say to someone in your circumstances."

Poppy snickered and poked Leo in the side, while Miss Marks gave him a stare of pure disgust.

Chapter Thirteen

On their last evening in London, the family attended a private ball given at the home of Mr. and Mrs. Simon Hunt in Mayfair. Mr. Hunt, a railway entrepreneur and part owner of a British locomotive works, was a self-made man, the son of a London butcher. He was part of a new and growing class of investors, businessmen, and managers who were unsettling the long-held traditions and authority of the peerage itself.

Just before the Hathaways arrived at the Hunt mansion, Miss Marks whispered a few last-minute reminders to her charges, telling them not to fill their dance cards too quickly in case a prepossessing gentleman might arrive later at the ball, and never to be seen without their gloves, and never to refuse a gentleman who asked them to dance unless they were already engaged to dance with another. But by all means, they must never allow one gentleman more than three dances—such excessive familiarity would cause gossip.

Win was ruefully aware that her own knowledge of social etiquette was lacking. "I hope I won't embarrass any of you," she said. "I hope you'll undertake to teach me as well, Miss Marks."

The governess smiled. "You have such a natural sense of propriety," she told Win, "I can't imagine you being anything less than a perfect lady."

"Oh, Win never does anything wrong," Beatrix told Miss Marks.

"Win is a saint," Poppy agreed. "It's very trying. But we do our best to tolerate her."

As guests entered the mansion, domestics came to take the cloaks and shawls, and the gentlemen's hats and coats. Win smiled as she saw Cam and Kev shrugging off their coats with the same deft gestures. Their kinship was obvious to her, even though they weren't identical. They had the same wavy dark hair, although Cam's was longer and Kev kept his neatly cropped. The same long, athletic build, although Cam was slimmer and more supple, whereas Kev had the sturdier, more muscular form of a boxer.

Dr. Harrow joined the Hathaways as they approached Mr. and Mrs. Hunt, who were greeting guests near the ballroom entrance.

Mrs. Hunt, a renowned beauty with golden-brown hair and a vivacious disposition, smiled as she saw the family. "The mysterious missing Hathaway sister," she exclaimed, taking both Win's hands in her gloved ones. "What a delight to meet you at last."

Poppy murmured to Win, "Mrs. Hunt always asks after your health."

"Thank you, Mrs. Hunt," Win said shyly. "I'm quite well now, and honored to be a guest at your lovely home."

Mrs. Hunt turned to Cam and Amelia. "I have no doubt Miss Hathaway will easily attain the popularity of her sisters."

"Next year, I'm afraid," Cam said easily. "This ball marks the end of the season for us. We're all traveling to Hampshire within the week."

"So soon? I suppose it's only to be expected. Lord Ramsay will want to see his estate."

"Naturally," Leo said. "I adore country scenery. One can never view too many sheep."

Mrs. Hunt laughed.

Mr. Hunt joined the conversation, having just finished speaking with another guest. "Welcome," he said with a precise bow, his friendly gaze traveling over the Hathaways.

"Mr. Hunt," Leo said, "I'd like to introduce Dr. Harrow, the physician who helped my sister to recover her health."

"A pleasure, sir," Dr. Harrow said.

"Likewise." But Hunt gave the doctor an odd, speculative look. "You are the Harrow who runs a clinic in France?"

"I am."

"I believe I'm acquainted with the family of your late wife," Hunt said.

After a quick double blink, Harrow said, "The Lanhams. Estimable people. I haven't seen them for years. The memories, you understand."

"Indeed," Hunt said quietly.

Win was puzzled by the awkward pause that followed, and the sense of discord between the two men.

"Well, darling," Mrs. Hunt said brightly to her husband, "are we going to shock everyone by dancing together? They're going to play a waltz quite soon."

Hunt's attention was immediately distracted by the flirtatious note in his wife's voice. He smiled at her. "Anything for you, love."

Harrow glanced at Win. "I haven't waltzed in far too long," he said. "Might you save a place for me on your dance card?"

"Your name's already there," she replied, and placed a light hand on his arm. They followed the Hunts to the drawing room.

Poppy and Beatrix were already being approached by prospective partners, while Cam closed his gloved fingers over Amelia's. "I'll be damned if Hunt's the only one who's allowed to be shocking. Come dance with me."

After the pair had left, Leo spoke quietly to Kev. "I wonder what Hunt knows about Harrow?"

"I'll find out," Kev said grimly.

IT WAS A LOVELY BALL, WIN THOUGHT, OR WOULD HAVE BEEN, if Kev had behaved like a reasonable human being. He watched her constantly, hardly bothering to be discreet about it. While she stood in one group or another and he conversed with a group of men that included Mr. Hunt, Kev's gaze never strayed far from Win.

At least three times Win was approached by various men with whom she had engaged to dance, and each time Kev appeared at her side and glowered at the would-be dance partner until he slunk away.

Kev was frightening off suitors right and left.

Even Miss Marks was unable to deter him. The governess had told him most firmly that his chaperonage was unnecessary, as she had the situation well in hand. But he'd replied obstinately that if she were to act as chaperone, she had better do a better job of keeping undesirable men away from her charge.

"What do you think you're doing?" Win whispered to him furiously, as he sent off yet another abashed gentleman. "I wanted to dance with him! I'd promised I would!"

"You're not going to dance with scum like him," Kev muttered.

Win shook her head in bewilderment. "He's a viscount from a respected family. What could you possibly object to?"

"He's a friend of Leo's. That's reason enough."

Win glared up at Kev. She'd always found it so easy to conceal her emotions beneath a serene facade, but lately she was finding it more and more difficult. "If you're trying to ruin my evening," she said, "you're doing a splendid job. I want to dance, and you're scaring away everyone who approaches me. Leave me alone." She turned her back to him, and sighed with relief as Julian Harrow came to them.

"Miss Hathaway," he said, "will you do me the honor—"

"Yes," she said before he could even finish the sentence. Taking his arm, she let him lead her into the mass of swirling, waltzing couples. Glancing over her shoulder, she saw Kev scowling after her. He was a dog in the manger, refusing to have a relationship with her but not allowing her to be with anyone else. And knowing his capacity for endurance, it would probably go on for years. Forever. She couldn't live like this.

"Winnifred," Julian Harrow said, his gray eyes concerned. "This is far too lovely a night for you to be distressed. What were you arguing about?"

"Nothing important," she said. "Just a squabble."

She curtseyed, and Julian bowed, and he took her in his arms. His hand was firm on her back, guiding her easily as they danced.

Julian's touch reawakened memories of the clinic, the way he had encouraged and helped her, the times he had been stern when she had needed it, and the times they had celebrated when she had reached another milestone in her progress. He was a good, kind, high-minded man. A handsome man. Win was hardly oblivious to the admiring feminine gazes he attracted. Most of the unmarried girls in this room would have given anything to have such a splendid suitor.

I could marry him, she thought. He'd made it clear that all it would take was a bit of encouragement on her part. She could become a doctor's wife and live in the south of France, and perhaps help somehow in his work at the clinic. To help other people who were suffering the way she had . . . to do something positive and worthwhile with her life . . . wouldn't that have been better than this?

Anything was preferable to the pain of loving a man she couldn't have. And, God help her, living in close proximity to him. She would become bitter and frustrated. She might even come to hate Kev.

She felt herself relaxing in Julian's arms. The bleak, angry feeling faded, soothed by the music and the waltz rhythm. Julian swept her around the drawing room, guiding her carefully among the dancing couples.

"This is what I dreamed of," Win told him. "Being able to do this . . . just like everyone else."

His hand tightened on her waist. "And so you are. But you're not like everyone else. You're the most beautiful woman here."

"No," she said, laughing.

"Yes. Like an angel in an Old Master's work." Julian laughed quietly as he saw her heightened color. "Have I embarrassed you? I'm sorry."

"I don't think you are. I think you meant to disconcert me." It was a new experience, flirting with Julian.

"You're right. I want to set you a bit off-balance."

"Why?"

"Because I'd like for you to see me as someone other than predictable, tedious old Dr. Harrow."

"You're none of those things," she said, laughing.

"Good." The waltz ended, and gentlemen began to lead their partners out of the dancing area, while others took their places. "It's warm in here, and far too crowded," he said. "Would you like to be scandalous and slip away with me for a moment?"

"I'd love to."

Julian took her to a corner partially screened by some massive potted plants. At an opportune moment, he led her out of the drawing room and into a huge glass conservatory. The space was filled with paths, and indoor trees and flowers, and secluded little benches. Beyond the conservatory, a wide terrace overlooked the fenced gardens and the other mansions of Mayfair.

They sat on a bench, Win's skirts billowing around them. Julian turned to face her. "Winnifred," he murmured, and the timbre of his voice was low and intimate. He removed one of her gloves with exquisite care. Lifting her slender hand to his lips, he kissed the backs of her fingers, and held her hand like a half-open flower against his face. His tenderness disarmed her. "You know why I've come to England," he said softly. "I want to know you much better, my dear, in a way that wasn't possible at the clinic. I want—"

But a sound from nearby caused Julian to break off, his head lifting.

Together, he and Win stared at the intruder.

It was Kev, striding purposefully toward them.

Win's jaw sagged in disbelief. He'd followed her out here? For heaven's sake, was there no place she could evade his outrageous stalking?

"*Go . . . away,*" she said, enunciating each word with scornful precision. "You're not my chaperone."

"You shouldn't be out here with him."

Win had never found it so difficult to master her emotions. She shoved them back, closing them behind an expressionless face. Her voice shook only a little as she turned to Julian. "Would you be so kind as to leave us, Dr. Harrow? There's something I must settle with Merripen."

Julian glanced from Kev's set face to hers. "I'm not sure I should," he said slowly.

"He's been plaguing me all evening," Win said. "I'm the

only one who can put a stop to it. Please allow me a moment with him."

"Very well." Julian stood from the bench. "Where shall I wait for you?"

"Back in the drawing room."

"Very well."

Win was so focused on Kev, she was barely aware of Julian's departure. "You're driving me mad!" she exclaimed. "I want you to stop this, Kev! Do you have any idea how ridiculous you're being? How badly you've behaved tonight?"

"*I've* behaved badly? You were about to let yourself be compromised."

"Perhaps I want to be. For years I've had to watch everyone around me enjoying their lives. I've had enough safety to last a lifetime, Kev. And if what you want is for me to continue being alone and unloved, then you can go to the devil."

"You were never alone. You've never been unloved."

"I want to be loved as a *woman*. Not as a child, or a sister, or an invalid—"

"That's not how I—"

"Perhaps you're not even capable of such love." In her blazing frustration, Win experienced something she had never felt before. The desire to hurt someone. "You don't have it in you."

Kev moved through a shaft of moonlight that had slipped through the conservatory glass, and Win felt a little shock as she saw his murderous expression. In just a few words she had managed to cut him deeply, enough to open a vein of dark and furious feeling. She fell back a step, alarmed as he seized her in a brutal grip.

He jerked her upward. "All the fires of hell could burn for a thousand years and it wouldn't equal what I feel for you in one minute of the day. I love you so much there's no pleasure in it. Nothing but torment. Because if I could dilute what I feel for you to the millionth part, it would still be enough to kill you. And even if it drives me mad, I'd rather see you live in the arms of that cold, soulless bastard than die in mine."

Before Win could begin to comprehend what he'd said, he took her mouth with his. For a full minute, perhaps two, she couldn't even move, could only stand there helplessly, falling apart, every rational thought dissolving. Her hand fluttered to the back of his neck, the muscles rigid above the crisp edge of his collar, the locks of his hair like raw silk.

Her fingers unconsciously caressed his nape, trying to soothe his hard-breathing fervor. His mouth slanted deeper over hers, sucking and teasing, his taste drugging and sweet. And then something quieted his frenzy, and he became gentle. His hand trembled as he touched her face, his fingers smoothing over her cheek, his palm cradling her jaw. The hungry pressure of his mouth lifted from hers, and he kissed her eyelids and nose and forehead.

In his drive to press close, he had urged her back against the conservatory wall. She gasped as her bare upper shoulders were flattened on a pane of glass, causing gooseflesh to rise. Cold glass . . . but his mouth was so warm as he kissed his way down her throat to the upper curves of her breasts. He slipped two fingers inside her bodice, stroking the cool cushion of her breast. It wasn't enough. He tugged impatiently at the edge of the bodice, and Win closed her eyes, offering not so much as a word of protest.

Kev gave a soft grunt of satisfaction as her breast was revealed. He lifted her higher against the glass and closed his mouth over the tip of her breast.

Win bit her lip to keep from crying out. Each swirling lick of his tongue sent darts of heat down to her toes. When her nipple was taut and throbbing, he moved back up to kiss her mouth again, while he took the hard peak of her breast in his fingers.

Then it all ended with cruel suddenness. He froze inexplicably and jerked her away from the window, pulling the front of her body into his. As if he was trying to hide her from something. A quiet curse escaped him.

"What . . ." Win found it difficult to speak. She was as dazed as if she'd just emerged from a deep sleep. "What is it?"

"I saw movement on the terrace. Someone may have seen us."

That startled Win back into a semblance of normalcy. She turned from him, clumsily pulling her bodice back into place. "My glove," she whispered, seeing it lying by the bench like a tiny abandoned flag of truce.

Kev went to retrieve it for her.

"I . . . I'm going to the ladies' dressing room," she said shakily. "I'll put myself to rights and return to the drawing room as soon as I'm able."

She wasn't altogether certain what had just happened, what it had meant. Kev had admitted he loved her. He had finally said it. But she had always imagined it as a joyful confession, not an angry and bitter one. Everything seemed so terribly wrong.

If only she could go back to the hotel, now, and be alone in her room. She needed privacy in which to think. What was it he had said? . . . *I'd rather see you live in the arms of that cold, soulless bastard than die in mine.* But that made no sense. Why had he said such a thing?

She wanted to confront him, but this wasn't the time or place.

"We must talk later, Kev," she said.

He gave a short nod, his shoulders and neck set as if he were carrying an unbearable burden.

WIN WENT TO THE LADIES' DRESSING ROOM UPSTAIRS, WHERE maids were busy repairing torn flounces, helping to blot the shine from perspiring faces, and anchoring coiffures with extra hairpins. She sat before a looking glass and inspected her reflection. Her cheeks were flushed and her lips were red and swollen.

A maid came to blot Win's face and dust it with rice powder, and she murmured her thanks. She took several calming breaths—as deep as the corset would allow—and tried inconspicuously to make certain her bodice was fully covering her breasts.

By the time Win felt ready to go downstairs once more, approximately thirty minutes had passed. She smiled as Poppy entered the ladies' dressing room and came to her.

"Hello, dear," Win said, standing from the chair. "Here, take my chair. Do you need hairpins? Powder?"

"No, thank you." Poppy's expression was tense and anxious.

"Are you enjoying yourself?" Win asked with a touch of concern.

"Not really." Poppy drew her to the corner to keep from being overheard. "I was hoping to meet someone other than the usual crowd of stuffy old peers, or worse, the stuffy young ones, but it's always the same."

"And Beatrix? How is she faring?"

"She's quite popular, actually. She goes around saying outrageous things, and people laugh and think she's being witty when they don't realize she's perfectly serious."

Win smiled. "Shall we go downstairs and find her?"

"Not yet." Poppy reached out to take her hand, and gripped it tightly. "Win, dear . . . I've come to find you because . . . there's trouble brewing downstairs. And . . . it involves you."

Win shook her head, feeling cold in the marrow of her bones. Her stomach gave a sick plunge. "I don't understand."

"You were seen in the conservatory in a compromising position. A *very* compromising one."

Win felt her face turn white. "It's only been thirty minutes," she whispered.

A pair of young women entered the dressing room, saw Win, and immediately whispered to each other.

Win's stricken gaze met Poppy's. "There's going to be a scandal, isn't there?" she asked faintly.

"Not if it's managed quickly." Poppy squeezed her hand. "I'm to take you to the library, dear. Amelia and Mr. Rohan are there—we're going to meet them, and put our heads together, and decide what to do."

Win almost wished she could go back to being an invalid with frequent fainting spells. Because at the moment, a good, long swoon sounded quite appealing. "Oh, what have I done?" she whispered.

That elicited a faint smile from Poppy. "That seems to be the question on everyone's mind."

Chapter Fourteen

The Hunts' library was a handsome room lined with mahogany bookcases with fronts of glazed glass. Cam and Simon Hunt were standing beside a large inlaid sideboard laden with glittering spirit decanters. Holding a glass half-filled with amber liquid, Hunt gave Win an inscrutable glance as she entered the library. Amelia, Mrs. Hunt, and Dr. Harrow were also there. Win had the curious feeling that it couldn't really be happening. She had never been involved in a scandal before, and it wasn't nearly as exciting or interesting as she had imagined while lying in her sickbed. It was frightening.

Because in spite of her earlier words to Kev about wanting to be compromised, she hadn't meant any of it. No sane woman would wish for such a thing. Causing a scandal meant ruining not only Win's prospects, but those of her younger sisters. It would cast a shadow over the entire family. Her carelessness was going to harm all the people she loved.

"Win." Amelia came to her at once. "It's all right, dear. We'll manage this."

Had Win not been so distressed, she would have smiled. Her older sister was famous for her confidence in her ability to manage anything, including natural disasters, foreign invasions, and stampeding wildlife. None of those, however, could come close to the havoc of a London society scandal.

"Where is Miss Marks?" Win asked in a muffled voice.

"In the drawing room with Beatrix. We're trying to keep appearances normal." Amelia sent a tense, rueful smile to the Hunts. "But our family has never been especially good at that."

Win stiffened as she saw Leo and Kev enter the room. Leo came straight to her, while Kev went to lurk in the corner as usual. He wouldn't meet her gaze. The room was filled with a charged silence that caused the down on the back of her neck to rise.

She hadn't gotten herself into this all alone, Win thought with a flare of anger.

Kev would have to help her now. He would have to protect her with any means at his disposal. Including his name.

Her heart began to pound so heavily that it almost hurt.

"It appears you've been making up for lost time, sis," Leo said flippantly, but there was a flicker of concern in his light eyes. "We have to be quick about this. Tongues are wagging so fast, they've created a strong breeze in the drawing room."

Mrs. Hunt approached Amelia and Win. "Winnifred." Her voice was very gentle. "If this rumor is not true, I'll take action at once to deny it on your behalf."

Win drew in a trembling breath. "It is true," she said.

Mrs. Hunt gave her a reassuring glance. "Trust me, you're not the first nor will you be the last to find yourself in this predicament."

"In fact," came Mr. Hunt's lazy drawl, "Mrs. Hunt has firsthand experience in just such a—"

"Mr. Hunt," his wife said indignantly, and he grinned. Turning back to Win, Mrs. Hunt asked, "Winnifred, may I ask the name of the gentleman you were seen with?"

Win couldn't answer. She let her gaze fall to the carpet, and she studied the pattern of medallions and flowers dazedly as she waited for Kev to speak. The silence only lasted a matter of seconds, but it seemed like hours. *Say something,* she thought desperately. *Tell them it was you!*

He parted his lips and began to move forward—

—but Julian Harrow beat him to it. "I'm the gentleman in question," he said quietly.

Win's head jerked up. She gave him an astonished glance as he took her hand.

"I apologize to all of you," Julian continued, "and especially to Miss Hathaway. I didn't intend to expose her to gossip or censure. But this precipitates something I'd already resolved to do, which is to ask for Miss Hathaway's hand in marriage."

Win stopped breathing. She looked directly at Kev, and a silent cry of anguish seared through her heart. His hard face and coal-black eyes revealed nothing.

He'd compromised her and now he was letting someone else rescue her.

What choice did she have but to accept Julian? It was either that or allow herself and her sisters to be ruined. Win hated him. She would hate him until her dying day and beyond. She felt her face drain of all color, but she summoned a paper-thin smile as she glanced at her brother.

"Well, my lord?" she asked Leo. "Should we ask your permission first?"

"You have my blessing," her brother said dryly. "After all, I certainly don't want my pristine reputation to be marred by your scandals."

She turned to face Julian. "Then yes, Dr. Harrow," she said in a steady voice. "I will marry you."

A frown notched between Mrs. Hunt's fine dark brows as she stared at Win. She nodded in a businesslike manner.

"I will go out and explain quietly to the appropriate parties that what they saw was a betrothed couple embracing . . . a bit intemperate perhaps, but quite forgivable in light of a betrothal."

"I'll go with you," Mr. Hunt said, coming to his wife's side. He extended a hand to Dr. Harrow and shook it. "My congratulations, sir." His tone was cordial but far from enthusiastic. "You're most fortunate to have won Miss Hathaway's hand."

As the Hunts left, Cam approached Win. She forced herself to stare directly into his perceptive hazel eyes, though it cost her.

"Is this what you want, little sister?" he asked softly.

His sympathy nearly undid her. "Oh yes." She set her jaw against a wretched quiver and managed to smile. "I'm the luckiest woman in the world."

And when she brought herself to look at Kev, she saw that he was gone.

"What a ghastly evening," Amelia muttered after everyone had left the library.

"Yes." Cam led her into the hallway.

"Where are we going?"

"Back to the drawing room. Try to look pleased and confident."

"Oh, good God." Amelia pulled away from him and strode to a large arched wall niche, where a Palladian window revealed a view of the street below. She pressed her forehead against the glass and sighed heavily. A repeated tapping noise echoed through the hallway.

Serious as the situation was, Cam couldn't prevent a quick grin. Whenever Amelia was worried or angry, her nervous habit asserted itself. As he had once told her, she reminded him of a hummingbird tamping down her nest with one foot.

Cam went to her and rested his warm palms on the cool slopes of her shoulders. He felt her shiver at his touch. "Hummingbird," he whispered, and slid his hands up to the back of her neck to knead the tight muscles. As her tension ebbed, the foot tapping gradually died away. Finally Amelia relaxed enough to tell him her thoughts.

"Everyone in that library was aware that Merripen was the one who compromised her," she said curtly. "I can't believe it. After all Win's gone through, it comes to this? She'll marry a man she doesn't love and go to France, and Merripen simply lets it happen? What's the *matter* with him?"

"More than can be explained here and now. Calm yourself, love. It won't help Win for you to appear distressed."

"I can't help it. This is all wrong. Oh, the look on my sister's face . . ."

"We have time to sort it out," Cam murmured. "A betrothal isn't the same as marriage."

"But a betrothal is binding," Amelia said with miserable impatience. "You know people think of it as a contract that can't be broken easily."

"Semi-binding," he allowed.

"Oh, Cam." Her shoulders drooped. "You'd never let anything come between us, would you? You'd never let us be parted?"

The question was so patently ridiculous that Cam hardly knew what to say. He turned Amelia to face him and saw with a jolt of surprise that his practical, sensible wife was close to tears. The glitter of moisture in her eyes sent a rush of fierce tenderness through him. He curved a protective arm around her, holding her close.

"You're the reason I live," he said in a low voice. "You're everything to me. Nothing could ever make me leave you. And if anyone ever tried to separate us, I'd kill them." He covered her mouth with his and kissed her with devastating sensuality, not stopping until she was weak and flushed and leaning hard against him. "Now," he said, only half-joking, "where is that conservatory?"

That provoked a watery chuckle from her. "I think there's been enough gossip fodder for one night. Are you going to talk to Merripen?"

"Of course. He won't listen, but that's never stopped me before."

"Do you think he—" Amelia broke off as she heard footsteps coming along the hallway, as well as the crisp, abundant rustling of heavy skirts. She shrank farther into the niche with Cam, burrowing into his arms. She felt him smile against her hair. They held still as they listened to a pair of ladies chattering.

". . . in heaven's name did the Hunts invite them?" one of them was asking indignantly.

Amelia thought she recognized the voice—it belonged to one of the prune-faced chaperones who had been sitting at the side of the drawing room. Someone's maiden aunt, relegated to spinster status.

"Because they're monstrously wealthy?" her companion suggested.

"I suspect it is more because Lord Ramsay is a viscount. But all the same . . . *Gypsies* in the family! The very thought of it! One can never expect them to behave in a civilized manner—they live by their animal instincts. And we're expected to hobnob with such people as if they're our equals."

"The Hunts are *bourgeois* themselves, you know. No matter that Hunt owns half of London by now, he's still a butcher's son."

"They and many of the guests here are not at all suitable for us to associate with. I have no doubt at least a half a dozen other scandals will erupt before the night is out."

"Dreadful, I agree." A pause, and then the second woman

added wistfully, "I do hope we'll be invited back next year . . ."

As the voices faded, Cam looked down at his wife with a frown. He didn't give a damn what anyone said—by now he'd heard everything that could be said about "Gypsies." But he hated that the arrows were sometimes directed at Amelia.

To his surprise, she was smiling up at him steadily, her eyes midnight blue.

His expression turned quizzical. "What's so amusing?"

Amelia toyed with a button on his coat. "I was just thinking . . . tonight those two old hens will probably go to their beds cold and alone." An impish grin curved her lips. "Whereas *I* will be with a wicked, handsome Rom who will keep me warm all night."

KEV WATCHED AND WAITED UNTIL HE FOUND AN OPPORTUnity to approach Simon Hunt, who had just managed to extricate himself from a conversation with a pair of giggling women. "May I have a word with you?" Kev asked quietly.

Hunt didn't appear at all surprised. "Let's go to the back terrace."

They made their way to a side door of the drawing room, which opened directly onto the terrace. A group of gentlemen were enjoying cigars. The rich scent of tobacco drifted on the cool breeze.

Hunt smiled pleasantly and shook his head as the men beckoned for him and Kev to join them. "We have some business to discuss," he told them. "Perhaps later."

Leaning casually against the iron balustrade, Hunt regarded Kev with assessing dark eyes.

On the few occasions they had met in Hampshire at Stony Cross Park, the estate that bordered the Ramsay lands, Kev had liked Hunt. He was a man's man who spoke in a straightforward manner.

"I assume you're going to ask what I know about Harrow," Hunt said.

"Yes."

"In light of recent events, this seems a bit like shutting the door after the house is robbed. I should add that I have no proof of wrongdoing. But the accusations the Lanhams have made against Harrow are sufficiently serious to merit consideration."

"What accusations?" Kev growled.

"Before Harrow built the clinic in France, he married the Lanhams' eldest daughter, Louise. She was said to be an unusually beautiful girl, with a large dowry and a well-connected family." Reaching into his coat, Hunt extracted a slender silver cigar case. "Care for one?" Kev shook his head. Hunt pulled out a cigar, deftly bit off the tip, and lit it. The end of the cigar glowed as Hunt drew on it.

"According to the Lanhams," Hunt continued, exhaling a stream of aromatic smoke, "a year into the marriage, Louise changed. She became quite docile and distant, and seemed to have lost interest in her former pursuits. When the Lanhams approached Harrow with their concerns, he claimed the changes in her were simply evidence of maturity and marital contentment."

"But they didn't believe that?"

"No. When they questioned Louise, however, she claimed to be happy and asked them not to interfere." Hunt raised the cigar to his lips again and stared thoughtfully at the lights of London winking through the night haze. "Sometime during the second year, Louise went into a decline."

Kev felt a discomforting chill at the word "decline," commonly used for any illness a doctor couldn't diagnose or comprehend.

"She became bedridden. No one could do anything for her. The Lanhams brought their own doctor to examine her, but he could find no cause for illness. Louise's condition deteriorated over a month or so, and then she died. The family blamed Harrow for her demise. Before the marriage, Louise had been a healthy, high-spirited girl, and not quite two years later, she was gone."

"Sometimes declines happen," Kev remarked, feeling the need to play devil's advocate. "It wasn't necessarily Harrow's doing."

"No. But it was Harrow's reaction that convinced the family that he was responsible in some way for Louise's death. He was too composed. Dispassionate. A few crocodile tears for appearance's sake, and that was it."

"And after that he went to France with the dowry money?"

"Yes." Hunt's broad shoulders lifted in a shrug. "I despise gossip, Merripen. I rarely choose to pass it along. But the Lanhams are respectable people and not given to dramatics." Frowning, he tapped the ash from his cigar over the edge of the balustrade. "And despite all the good Harrow has reportedly done for his patients . . . I can't help but feel there's something amiss with him. It's nothing I can put into words."

Kev felt an ineffable relief to have his own thoughts echoed by a man like Hunt. "I've had the same feeling about Harrow ever since I first met him," he said. "But everyone else seems to revere him."

There was a wry glint in Hunt's black eyes. "Yes, well . . . this wouldn't be the first time I didn't agree with popular opinion. But I think anyone who cares for Miss Hathaway should be concerned for her sake."

Chapter Fifteen

Kev was gone by morning. He had checked out of the Rutledge and had left word that he would be traveling alone to the Ramsay estate.

Win had awoken with memories rising to the forefront of her bewildered mind. She felt heavy and weary. Kev had been a part of her for too long. She had carried him in her heart, had absorbed him into the marrow of her bones. To let go of him now would feel like amputating part of herself. And yet it had to be done. Kev himself had made it impossible for her to choose otherwise.

She washed and dressed with the help of a maid, and arranged her hair in a plaited chignon. There would be no meaningful talks with anyone in her family, she decided numbly. There would be no weeping or regrets. She was going to marry Dr. Julian Harrow and live far away from Hampshire.

"I want to be married as quickly as possible," she told Julian later that morning, as they had tea in the family suite. "I miss France. I want to go back without delay. As your wife."

Julian smiled and touched the curve of her cheek with

smooth, tapered fingertips. "Very well, my dear." He took her hand in his, brushing across her knuckles with his thumb. "I have some business in London to take care of, and I'll join you in Hampshire in a few days. We'll make our plans there. We can marry at the estate chapel, if you like."

The chapel Kev had rebuilt. "Perfect," Win said evenly.

"I'll buy a ring for you today," Julian said. "What kind of stone would you like? A sapphire to match your eyes?"

"Anything you choose will be lovely." Win let her hand remain in his as they both fell silent. "Julian . . . you haven't yet asked what . . . what happened between Merripen and me last night."

"There's no need," Julian replied. "I'm far too pleased by the result."

"I . . . I want you to understand that I'll be a good wife to you," Win said earnestly. "I . . . my former attachment to Merripen . . ."

"That will fade in time," Julian said gently.

"Yes."

"And I warn you, Winnifred, I'll launch quite a battle for your affection. I'll prove such a devoted and generous husband, there'll be no room in your heart for anyone else."

She thought about bringing up the subject of children, asking if perhaps he would relent someday if her health improved even more. But from what she did know about Julian, he wouldn't reverse his decisions easily. And it didn't really matter: she was trapped.

Whatever life held in store for her now, she would have to make the best of it.

AFTER TWO DAYS OF PACKING, THE FAMILY WAS ON ITS WAY to Hampshire. Cam, Amelia, Poppy, and Beatrix were in the first carriage, while Leo, Win, and Miss Marks were in the second.

Cam was both touched and amused that Poppy and Beatrix were trying to convince him that Merripen should marry Win. Naively the girls had assumed the only thing standing in the way was Merripen's lack of fortune.

"—so if you could give him some of your money—" Beatrix was saying eagerly.

"—or give him part of Leo's fortune," Poppy said. "Leo would only waste it."

"Make Merripen understand that it would be Win's dowry," Beatrix said, "so it wouldn't hurt his pride—"

"—and they wouldn't need very much," Poppy said. "Neither of them gives a fig for mansions or fine carriages or—"

"Wait, both of you," Cam said, lifting his hands in a defensive gesture. "The problem is more complex than a matter of money, and—no, stop chirping for a moment and hear me out." He smiled into the two pairs of blue eyes regarding him so anxiously. "Merripen has ample means to offer for Win. What he earns as the Ramsay estate manager is a handsome living in itself, and he also has unlimited access to the Ramsay accounts."

"Then why is Win going to marry Dr. Harrow and not Merripen?" Beatrix demanded.

"For reasons Merripen wants to be kept private, he believes he wouldn't be an appropriate husband for her."

"But he loves her!"

"Love doesn't solve every problem, Bea," Amelia said gently.

"That sounds like something Mother would have said," Poppy remarked with a slight smile, while Beatrix looked disgruntled.

"What would your father have said?" Cam asked.

"He would have led us all into some lengthy philosophical exploration of the nature of love, and it would have accomplished nothing whatsoever," Amelia said. "But it would have been fascinating."

"I don't care how complicated everyone says it is," Beatrix said. "Win should marry Merripen. Don't you agree, Amelia?"

"It's not our choice," Amelia replied. "And it's not Win's, either, unless the big dunderhead offers her an alternative. There's nothing Win can do if he won't propose to her."

"Wouldn't it be nice if ladies could propose to gentlemen?" Beatrix mused.

"Heavens, no," Amelia said promptly. "That would make it far too easy for the gentlemen."

"In the animal kingdom," Beatrix commented, "males and females enjoy equal status. A female may do anything she wishes."

"The animal kingdom allows many behaviors that we humans cannot emulate, dear. Scratching in public, for example. Regurgitating food. Flaunting themselves to attract a mate. Not to mention . . . well, I needn't go on."

"I wish you would," Cam said with a grin. He settled Amelia more comfortably against his side and spoke to Beatrix and Poppy. "Listen, you two. Neither of you is to bedevil Merripen about the situation. I know you want to help, but all you'll succeed in doing is provoking him."

They both grumbled, and nodded reluctantly, and snuggled in their respective corners. It was still dark outside, and the rocking motion of the carriage was soothing. In a matter of minutes, both sisters were drowsing.

Glancing at Amelia, Cam saw that she was still awake. He stroked the fine-grained skin of her face and throat, looking down into her pure blue eyes.

"Why didn't he step forward, Cam?" she whispered. "Why did he give Win to Dr. Harrow?"

Cam took his time about answering. "He's afraid."

"Of what?"

"What he might do to her."

Amelia frowned in bewilderment. "That makes no sense. Merripen would never hurt her."

"Not intentionally."

"You're referring to the danger of conceiving a child?"

"It's not just that." Cam sighed and settled her more closely against him. "Did Merripen ever tell you that he was *asharibe*?"

"No, what does that mean?"

"It's a word used to describe a bare-knuckle fighter. In a few tribes, boys are trained to fight with no rules or time limits. The goal is to inflict the worst damage as quickly as possible until someone drops. They fight with fractured wrists and broken ribs if necessary." Absently Cam smoothed Amelia's hair as he added, "Most Roma aren't like that. There were none in our tribe. Our leader decided it was too cruel. We learned to fight, of course, but it was never a way of life for us."

"Merripen . . . ," ? Amelia whispered.

"From what I can tell, it was even worse than that for him. The man who raised him . . ." Cam, always so articulate, found it difficult to go on.

"His uncle?" Amelia prompted.

"Our uncle." Cam had already told her that he and Merripen were brothers. But he hadn't yet confided the rest of what Shuri had said. "Apparently he raised Merripen to be as vicious as a pit animal. He was badly abused, and conditioned to fight anyone under any circumstances."

"Poor boy," Amelia murmured. "That explains much about the way he was when he first came to us. But . . . that was all a long time ago. His life has been very different since then. And having once suffered so terribly, doesn't he want to be loved now? Doesn't he want to be happy?"

"It doesn't work that way, sweetheart." Cam smiled into her puzzled face. It was no surprise that Amelia, who had been brought up in a large and affectionate family, should find it difficult to understand a man who feared his own needs as if they were his worst enemy. "What if you were taught all during your childhood that the only reason for your existence was to inflict pain on others? That violence was all you were good for? How do you unlearn such a thing? You can't. So you cover it as best you can, always aware of what lies beneath the veneer."

"But . . . obviously Merripen has changed. He's a man with many fine qualities."

"He wouldn't agree."

"Well, Win has made it clear that she'd have him regardless."

"That doesn't matter to him. He's determined to protect her from himself."

Amelia hated being confronted with problems that had no definite solution. "Then what can we do?"

Cam lowered his head to kiss the tip of her nose. "I know how you hate to hear this, love . . . but it's in their hands."

THE LAST TIME WIN AND LEO HAD SEEN RAMSAY HOUSE IT had been dilapidated and half-burned, the grounds barren except for weeds and rubble. And unlike the rest of the family, they had not seen the stages of its progress as it was being rebuilt.

The affluent southern county of Hampshire encompassed coastal land, heathland, and ancient forests filled with abundant wildlife. Hampshire had a milder, sunnier climate that most other parts of England, owing to the stabilizing effect of its location. Although Win hadn't lived in Hampshire for very long before she had gone to Dr. Harrow's clinic, she had the feeling of coming home. It was a welcoming, friendly place, with the lively market town of Stony Cross just within walking distance of the Ramsay estate.

It seemed the Hampshire weather had decided to present the estate to its best effect, with profuse sunshine and a few picturesque clouds in the distance.

The carriage passed the gatekeeper's lodge, constructed of grayish blue bricks with cream stone detailing.

"How lovely!" Win exclaimed. "I've never seen bricks that color in Hampshire before."

"Staffordshire blue brick," Leo said, craning his neck to see the other side of the house. "Now that they're able to bring brick from other places on the railway, there's no need for the builder to make them on-site."

They went along the lengthy drive toward the house, which was surrounded by velvety green lawn, and white-graveled walking paths, and young hedges and rosebushes. "My God," Leo murmured as they approached the house itself. It was a multigabled cream stone structure with cheerful dormers. The blue slate roof featured hips and bays outlined with contrasting terra-cotta ridge tiles. Although the place was similar to the old house, it had been much improved. And what remained of the original structure had been so lovingly restored that one could hardly tell the old sections from the new.

People were working everywhere: carters, stockmen, sawyers, and masons, gardeners clipping hedges, stable boys and footmen coming out to the arriving carriages. The estate had not only come to life; it was thriving.

Watching her brother's intent profile, Win felt a surge of gratitude toward Merripen, who had made all this happen. It was good for Leo to come home to this. It was an auspicious beginning to a new life.

After the carriage had stopped at the entrance, Win descended from the carriage with a footman's help. As soon as Win reached the front doors, they opened to reveal a middle-aged woman with ginger hair and a fair, freckled complexion. "Welcome, Miss Hathaway," she said warmly. "I'm Mrs. Barnstable, the housekeeper." She showed Win into the entrance hall, bright and airy with cream-painted paneling. A gray stone staircase was set in the back of the hall, its iron balustrades gleaming black and spotless. Everywhere smelled of soap and fresh wax.

"It's not the same place at all," Win said in wonder.

Leo came up beside her. "It's a bloody miracle," he said. "I'm astonished." He turned to the housekeeper. "Where's Merripen, Mrs. Barnstable?"

"Out at the estate timber, my lord. He's helping to unload a wagon."

"We have a timber yard?" Leo asked.

Miss Marks replied, "Mr. Merripen is building houses for the new tenant farmers."

"This is the first I've heard of it. Why are we providing houses for them?" Leo's tone was not at all censuring, merely interested. But Miss Marks's lips thinned, as if she'd interpreted his question as a complaint.

"Other local estates, such as Stony Cross Park, are building homes for their tenants and laborers. If you disapprove—"

"It's all right," Leo interrupted. "No need to be defensive, Marks." He glanced at the housekeeper. "If you'll point the way, Mrs. Barnstable, I'll find Merripen. Perhaps I might help to unload the timber wagon."

"A footman will show you the way," the housekeeper said at once. "But the work is hazardous, my lord, and not fitting for a man of your station."

Miss Marks added in a light but caustic tone, "Besides, it's doubtful you could be of any help."

The housekeeper's mouth fell open.

Win had to bite back a grin. Miss Marks had spoken as if

Leo were a small weed of a man instead of a strapping six-footer.

Leo gave the governess a sardonic smile. "I'm more physically capable than you might expect, Marks. You have no idea what lurks beneath this coat."

"I'm profoundly grateful for that."

"Miss Hathaway," the housekeeper broke in, "may I show you to your room?"

"Yes, thank you." Hearing her sisters' voices, Win turned to see them entering the hall along with Cam.

"Well?" Amelia asked with a grin, spreading her hands to indicate their surroundings.

"Beautiful beyond words," Win replied.

"Let's freshen ourselves and brush off the travel dust, and I'll take you around."

"I'll only be a few minutes."

Win went to the staircase with the housekeeper. "How long have you worked here, Mrs. Barnstable?" she asked as they ascended to the second floor.

"A year, more or less. I was previously employed in London, but the old master passed on to his reward, and the new master dismissed most of the staff and replaced them with his own. I was in desperate need of a position."

"I'm sorry to hear that, but very pleased for the Hathaways' sake."

"It's been a challenge," the housekeeper said, "putting together a new staff and training them all. But Mr. Merripen was very persuasive."

"Yes," Win said absently, "it's difficult to say no to him."

"He's a steady one, our Mr. Merripen. I've marveled to see him in the center of a dozen undertakings—the carpenters, the painters, the blacksmith, the head groomsman, all clamoring for his attention. And he always keeps a cool head. We can't do without him."

Win nodded morosely and followed as Mrs. Barnstable led her to a beautiful room with windows overlooking the gardens. "This is yours," the housekeeper said. "No one's occupied it." The bed was made of light blue upholstered panels, tufted with fabric covered buttons. There was a pretty writing desk in the corner, and a satin maple wardrobe with a looking glass set in the door.

"Mr. Merripen personally selected the wallpaper," Mrs. Barnstable told her. "He nearly drove the interior architect mad with his insistence on seeing hundreds of samples until he found this pattern."

The wallpaper was white, with a delicate pattern of flowering branches. And at sparse intervals, there was the motif of a little robin perched on one of the twigs.

Slowly Win went to one of the walls and touched one of the birds with her fingertips. Her vision blurred.

During her long recuperation from the scarlet fever, when she'd grown tired of holding a book in her hands and there had been no one to read to her, she'd stared out the window at a robin's nest in a nearby maple tree. She'd watched the fledglings hatch from their blue eggs, their bodies pink and veined and fuzzy. She'd watched their feathers grow in, and later she'd seen the mother robin working to fill their ravenous beaks. And eventually, one by one, they'd flown from the nest while Win had remained in bed.

Merripen, despite his fear of heights, had often climbed a ladder to wash the second-floor window for her. He'd wanted her view of the outside world to be clear.

He'd said the sky should always be blue for her.

"You're fond of birds, Miss Hathaway?" the housekeeper asked.

Win nodded without looking around, afraid that her face was red with unexpressed emotion. "Robins especially," she half whispered.

"A footman will bring your trunks up soon, and one of the maids will unpack them. There's fresh water at the wash-stand if you should need it."

"Thank you." Win went to the porcelain pitcher and basin and sluiced clumsy handfuls of cooling water on her face and throat, heedless of the drips that fell onto her bodice. As she blotted her face with a soft cloth, she heard the creak of a floorboard and turned sharply.

Kev was at the threshold, watching her. The damnable flush wouldn't stop. She wanted to be on the other side of the world from him. She wanted never to see him again. And at the same time her gaze drank in the sight of him in an open-throated shirt, white linen clinging to his sweat-dampened skin.

"How was the journey from London?" he asked, his face expressionless.

"I'm not going to make polite conversation with you." Win went to the window and focused blindly on the dark wood-land in the distance.

"Is the room to your liking?"

She nodded without looking at him.

"If there's anything you need—"

"I have everything I need," she interrupted. "Thank you."

"I want to talk to you about the other—"

"That's quite all right," she said. "You don't need to come up with excuses about why you didn't offer for me."

"I want you to understand—"

"I do understand. And I've already forgiven you."

"I don't want your forgiveness," he said curtly.

"Fine, you're not forgiven. Whatever pleases you." She couldn't bear to be alone with him for another moment. Her heart was breaking; she could feel it fracturing. Putting her head down, she began to walk past his motionless form.

Win didn't intend to stop. But before she crossed the

threshold, she halted within arm's length of him. There was one thing she wanted to say. The words would not be contained.

"Incidentally," she heard herself say, "I went to visit a London doctor yesterday. A highly respected one." Aware of the intensity of Kev's gaze, Win continued evenly. "In his professional opinion, there's no reason I shouldn't have children if I want them. He said there's no guarantee for any woman that childbirth will be free of risk. But I will lead a full life. I'll have marital relations with my husband, and God willing, I'll become a mother someday." She paused, and added in a bitter voice that didn't sound at all like her own, "Julian will be so pleased when I tell him, don't you think?"

If the jab had pierced through Kev's guard, there was no sign of it. "There's something you need to know about him," he said quietly. "His first wife's family—the Lanhams—suspect he had something to do with her death."

Win glanced at him sharply. "I can't believe you would sink so low. Julian told me all about it. He loved her. He did everything he could to bring her through the illness. When she died, he was devastated, and then he was victimized further by her family. In their grief, they needed someone to blame. Julian was a convenient scapegoat."

"The Lanhams claim he behaved suspiciously after her death. He didn't fit anyone's idea of a bereaved husband."

"Not all people show their grief in the same way," she said. "Julian is a doctor—he has trained himself to be impassive in the course of his work because that is best for his patients. Naturally he wouldn't let himself fall apart, no matter how deep his sorrow. How dare you judge him?"

"Don't you realize you may be in danger?"

"From *Julian*? The man who made me well?" Win shook her head with a disbelieving laugh. "For the sake of our friendship, I'm going to forget you said anything about this,

Kev. But remember in the future that I won't tolerate any insult to Julian. He stood by me when you didn't."

She brushed by him without waiting for his reaction and saw her older sister coming along the hallway. "Amelia," she said brightly. "Shall we begin the tour now? I want to see everything."

Chapter Sixteen

Although Merripen had made it clear to the Ramsay household that Leo, not he, was master, the servants and laborers still considered him the authority. Merripen was the one they first approached with all concerns. And Leo was content to let it remain so while he familiarized himself with the reinvigorated estate and its inhabitants.

"I'm not a complete idiot, despite appearances to the contrary," he told Merripen dryly as they rode out to the east corner of the estate one morning. "The arrangements you've made are obviously working. I don't intend to foul things up in an effort to prove I'm lord of the manor. That being said . . . I do have a few improvements to suggest regarding the tenant housing."

"Oh?"

"A few inexpensive alterations in design would make the cottages more comfortable and attractive. And if the idea is to establish a hamlet of sorts on the estate, it might behoove us to come up with a set of plans for a model village."

"You want to work on plans and elevations?" Merripen asked, surprised at the show of interest from the usually indolent lord.

"If you have no objections."

"Of course not. It's your estate." Merripen regarded him speculatively. "Are you considering returning to your former profession?"

"Yes, actually. I might start as a jobbing architect. We'll see where some earnest dabbling might lead. And it makes sense to cut my teeth on my own tenants' houses." He grinned. "One can only hope they'll be less likely than outsiders to sue me."

On an estate with a crowded wood like the Ramsey lands, it was necessary to thin the forest every ten years. By Merripen's calculation, the estate had missed at least two previous cycles, which meant there was a good thirty years' worth of dead, sickly, or suppressed-growth trees to be cleared from the Ramsay forests.

To Leo's dismay, Merripen insisted on dragging him through the entire process, until Leo knew far more than he'd ever wanted to know about trees.

"Correct thinning helps nature," Merripen said in response to Leo's grumbling. "The estate wood will have healthier timber and far more value if the right trees are removed to help the others grow."

"Can't the trees settle it among themselves?" Leo asked, but Merripen ignored him.

To educate Leo further, Merripen arranged a meeting with the estate woodmen. They went out to examine some targeted standing trees, while the woodmen explained how to measure the length and mean transverse area of a tree to determine its cubic contents. Using a girthing tape, a twenty-foot rod, and a ladder, they made some preliminary assessments.

Before Leo quite knew how it had happened, he had found himself high up on a ladder, helping in the measurements.

"May I ask why," he called down to Merripen, "you happen

to be standing down there while I'm up here risking my neck?"

"Your tree," Merripen pointed out succinctly.

"Also my neck!"

As they went over other items on a daily list that only seemed to lengthen as the week progressed, Leo began to comprehend just how overwhelming a job Merripen had undertaken for the past three years. Most estate managers had undergone apprenticeships, and most sons of the peerage had been educated from a young age in the various concerns of the estates they would someday inherit.

Merripen, on the other hand, had learned all of this—livestock management, farming, forestry, construction, land improvement, wages, profits, and rents—with no preparation and no time. But the man was ideally suited for it. He had a keen memory, an appetite for hard work, and a tireless interest in details.

"Just admit one thing," Leo had said after a particularly stultifying conversation on farming. "You do find this tedious on occasion, don't you? You must be bored out of your skull after an hour of discussion on how intensive the crop rotation should be, and how much arable land should be allocated to corn and beans."

Merripen had considered the question carefully. "Not if it needs to be done."

That was when Leo had finally understood. If Merripen had decided on a goal, no detail was too small, no task beneath him. No amount of adversity would deter him. The workmanlike quality that Leo had derided in the past had found its perfect outlet. God or the devil help anyone who got in Merripen's way.

But Merripen had a weakness.

By now everyone in the family had become aware of the attachment between Merripen and Win. And they all knew that to mention it would earn nothing but trouble. Leo had never seen two people battle their mutual attraction so desperately.

But after having watched his sister's struggle to get well, and the grace of character that had never faltered, Leo thought it a damned shame she couldn't have the husband she wanted.

On the third morning after their arrival in Hampshire, Amelia and Win went for a walk on a circular route that eventually led back to Ramsay House. It was a fresh, clear day, the path a bit muddy in places, the meadows covered with such a wealth of white oxeye daisies that at first glance it looked like new-fallen snow.

Amelia, who had always loved walking, matched Win's brisk pace easily.

"I love Stony Cross," Win said, relishing the sweet, cool air. "It feels like home even more than Primrose Place, even though I've never lived here for long."

"Yes. There is something special about Hampshire. Whenever we return from London, I find it an indescribable relief." Removing her bonnet, Amelia held it by the ribbons and swung it lightly as they walked. She seemed absorbed in the scenery, the tumbles of flowers everywhere, the clicks and drones of insects busy among the trees, the scents released by sun-warmed grasses and peppery watercress. "Win," she said eventually, her voice pensive, "you don't have to leave Hampshire, you know."

"Yes, I do."

"Our family can weather any scandal. Look at Leo. We survived all of his—"

"In terms of scandal," Win interrupted wryly, "I think I've actually managed to do something worse than Leo."

"I don't think that's possible, dear."

"You know as well as I that the loss of a woman's virtue can ruin a family far more effectively than the loss of a man's honor. It's not fair, but there you have it."

"You didn't lose your virtue," Amelia said indignantly.

"Not for lack of trying. Believe me, I wanted to." Glancing at her older sister, Win saw that she had shocked her. She smiled faintly. "Did you think I was above feeling that way, Amelia?"

"Well . . . yes, I suppose I did. You were never one to moon over handsome boys, or talk about balls and parties, or dream about your future husband."

"That was because of Merripen," Win admitted. "He was all I ever wanted."

"Oh, Win," Amelia whispered. "I'm so sorry."

Win stepped up onto a stile leading through a narrow gap in a stone fence, and Amelia followed. They walked along a grassy footpath that led to a forest trail and continued to a footbridge that crossed a stream.

Amelia linked her arm with Win's. "In light of what you just said, I feel even more strongly that you should not marry Harrow. What I mean is, you should marry Harrow if you wish, but not out of fear over a scandal."

"I want to. I like him. I believe he's a good man. And if I stay here, it would result in endless misery for me and Merripen. One of us has to leave."

"Why does it have to be you?"

"Merripen is needed here. He belongs here. And it truly doesn't matter to me where I am. In fact, I think it would be better for me to make a new beginning elsewhere."

"Cam's going to talk to him," Amelia said.

"Oh no, he mustn't! Not on my behalf." Win's pride bristled, and she turned to face Amelia. "Don't let him. *Please.*"

"I couldn't stop Cam no matter how I tried. He's not talking to Merripen for your sake, Win. It's for Merripen's own sake. We very much fear what will become of him once he's lost you for good."

"He's already lost me," Win said flatly. "And after I leave, he'll be no different than he has always been. He'll never allow softness in himself. In fact, I think he despises the things that give him pleasure." All the tiny muscles of her face felt frozen. Win reached up to massage her tense, pinching forehead. "The more he cares for me, the more determined it makes him to push me away."

"Men," Amelia grumbled, crossing the footbridge.

"Merripen is convinced he has nothing to give me. There's a kind of arrogance in that, don't you think? Deciding what I need. Disregarding my feelings. Setting me so high on the pedestal that it absolves him of any responsibility."

"Not arrogance," Amelia said softly. "Fear."

"Well, I won't live that way. I won't be bound by my fears, or his." Win felt herself relaxing slightly, calmness stealing over her as she admitted the truth. "I love him, but I don't want him if he has to be trapped into marriage. I want a willing partner."

They pushed on through the damp, warm landscape. As they eventually approached Ramsay House, they saw a carriage coming to a stop before the entrance. "It's Julian," Win said. "So early! He must have left London well before first light." She quickened her pace and reached him just as he stepped from the carriage.

"Welcome to Hampshire," she exclaimed, smiling.

"Thank you, my dear. Have you been out walking?"

"Briskly," she assured him, smiling.

"Very good. Here, I have something for you." He reached in his pocket and withdrew a small object. Win felt him slide a ring onto her finger. She looked down at a ruby the shade of red known as pigeon's blood, set in gold and diamonds.

"It's said," Julian told her, "that to own a ruby is to have contentment and peace."

"Thank you, it's lovely," Win murmured, leaning forward. Her eyes closed as she felt his lips press gently against her forehead. Contentment and peace . . . God willing, perhaps someday she would have those things.

CAM DOUBTED HIS OWN SANITY, APPROACHING MERRIPEN when he was working in the timber yard. He watched for a moment as Merripen helped a trio of woodmen to unload massive logs from the wagon. It was a dangerous job, with one mistake resulting in the possibility of severe injury or death.

With the use of sloping planks and long levers, the men rolled the logs inch by inch to the ground. Grunting with effort, muscles straining, they fought to control the descending weight. Merripen, as the largest and strongest of the group, had taken the center position, making him the least likely to escape if anything went wrong.

Concerned, Cam started forward to help.

"*Get back,*" Merripen barked, seeing Cam out of the corner of his eye.

Cam stopped at once. The woodmen had worked out a method, he realized. Anyone who didn't know their procedures might inadvertently cause harm to them all.

He waited and watched as the logs were eased safely to the ground. The woodmen breathed heavily, leaning over and bracing their hands on their knees as they sought to recover from the dizzying effort. All except Merripen, who sank the tip of a deadly sharp hand hook into one of the logs. He turned to face Cam while still holding a pair of tongs.

Merripen's face was smudged and sweat-streaked, his eyes bright with hellfire. Although Cam had come to know him well over the past three years, he had never seen Merripen like this. He looked like a damned soul with no hope or desire for redemption.

God help me, Cam thought. Once Win was married to Dr. Harrow, Merripen might career out of control. Remembering all the trouble they'd had with Leo, Cam groaned inwardly.

He was tempted to wash his hands of the entire damned mess, reasoning that he had far better things to do than fight for his brother's sanity. Let Merripen deal with the consequences of his own choices.

But then Cam considered how he himself would behave if anyone or anything threatened to take Amelia away from him. Not any better, surely. Reluctant compassion stirred inside him.

"What do you want?" Merripen asked curtly, setting the tongs aside.

Cam approached slowly. "Harrow's here."

"I saw."

"Are you going inside to welcome him?"

Merripen gave Cam a contemptuous glance. "Leo's the master of the household. He can welcome the bastard."

"While you hide out here in the timber yard?"

The coffee-black eyes narrowed. "I'm not hiding. I'm working. And you're in the way."

"I want to talk to you, *phral.*"

"Don't call me that. And I don't need your interference."

"Someone has to try and talk some sense into you," Cam said softly. "Look at you, Kev. You're behaving exactly like the brute the *rom baro* tried to make you into."

"Shut up," Merripen said hoarsely.

"You're letting him decide the rest of your life for you," Cam insisted. "You're clutching those damned chains around you with all your strength."

"If you don't close your mouth—"

"If you were only hurting yourself, I wouldn't say a word. But you're hurting her as well, and you don't seem to give a d—"

Cam was interrupted as Merripen launched toward him, attacking him with a bloodthirsty force that sent them both to the ground. The impact was hard, even on the muddy ground. They rolled twice, thrice, each striving to gain the dominant position. Merripen was as heavy as hell.

Realizing that being pinned was going to result in some serious damage to himself, Cam twisted free and sprang to his feet. Raising his guard, he blocked and sidestepped as Merripen leaped up like a striking tiger.

The woodmen all rushed forward, two of them grabbing Merripen and hauling him back, the other one pouncing on Cam.

"You're such an idiot," Cam snapped, glaring at Merripen. He shook free of the man who was trying to restrain him. "You're determined to foul things up for yourself no matter what, aren't you?"

Merripen lunged, his face murderous, while the woodmen fought to hold him back.

Cam shook his head in disgust. "I'd hoped for a minute or two of rational conversation, but apparently that's beyond you." He glanced at the woodmen. "Let him go! I can handle him. It's easy to win against a man who lets his emotions get the better of him."

At that, Merripen made a visible effort to control his rage, going still, the wildness in his eyes diminishing to a glint of cold hatred. Gradually, with the same care they had used to manage the heavy crushing logs, the woodmen released his arms.

"You've made your point," Cam told Merripen. "And it seems you'll keep on making it until you've proven it to everyone. So let me spare you the effort: I agree with you. You aren't fit for her."

And he left the timber yard while Merripen glared after him.

MERRIPEN'S ABSENCE CAST A SHADOW OVER DINNER THAT night, no matter how they all tried to behave naturally. The odd thing was, Merripen had never been one to dominate a conversation or take the central role of the gathering, and yet removing his unobtrusive presence was the same as taking off the leg of a chair. Everything was off-balance when he was gone.

Julian filled the gap with charm and lightness, relaying amusing stories about his acquaintances in London, discussing his clinic, revealing the origins of the therapies that served his patients to such good effect.

Win listened and smiled. She was calm on the surface, but underneath she was nothing but writhing emotion.

Midway through the dinner, between the fish and carvery courses, a footman went to the head of the table with a tiny silver tray. He gave a note to Leo.

The entire table fell silent as everyone watched Leo read the note. Casually he tucked the slip of paper into his coat and murmured something to the footman about readying his horse.

A smile touched Leo's lips as he saw their gazes fastened on him. "My apologies, all," he said calmly, and stood from the table. "I'm needed for a bit of business that can't wait."

Win was gripped with worry. She knew this had something to do with Merripen; she felt it in her bones. "My lord," she said in a suffocated voice. "Is it—"

"All is well," he said at once.

"Shall I go?" Cam asked, staring hard at Leo.

It was a new concept for all of them, Leo as a problem-solver.

"Not a chance," Leo replied. "I wouldn't be deprived of this for the world."

THE STONY CROSS GAOL WAS LOCATED ON FISHMONGER LANE. Locals referred to the two-room lockup as "the pinfold." The antique word referred to a pen where stray animals were kept, hearkening back to medieval times when the open field system had still been practiced. The owner of a lost cow, sheep, or goat had usually been able to find it at the pinfold, where he could claim it for a fee. Nowadays, drunkards and minor lawbreakers were claimed by their relatives in much the same way.

Leo had spent more than a few nights in the pinfold himself. But to his knowledge, Merripen had never run afoul of the law and had certainly never been guilty of drunkenness, public or private. Until now.

It was rather perplexing, this reversal of their situations. Merripen had always been the one to collect Leo from whatever gaol or strong room he had managed to land himself in.

Leo met briefly with the parish constable, who seemed similarly struck by the arse-about of it all.

"May I ask the nature of the crime?" Leo inquired diffidently.

"Got himself good and pickled at the tavern," the constable replied, "and went into a real Tom-'n'-Jerry with a local."

"What were they fighting over?"

"The local made some remark about Gypsies and drink, and that set Merripen off like a Roman candle." Scratching his head through his wiry hair, the constable said reflectively, "Merripen had plenty of men jumping to defend him—he's well-liked among folk here—but he fought them, too. And even then they tried to pay his bail. They said it wasn't like him, drinking and brawling. From what I know of Merripen, he's a quiet sort. But I said no, I wasn't taking bail money until he'd cooled his heels for a bit. Those fists are the size of Hampshire hams. I'm not releasing him until he's more than half-sober."

"May I speak to him?"

"Yes, my lord. He's in the first room. I'll take you there."

"You needn't trouble yourself," Leo said pleasantly. "I know the way."

The constable grinned at that. "I suppose you do, my lord."

The cell was unfurnished except for a short-legged stool, an empty bucket, and a straw pallet. Merripen was sitting on the pallet, leaning his back against a timbered wall. One knee was propped up, his arm half curled around it. His black head was lowered in a posture of utter defeat.

Merripen looked up as Leo approached the row of iron bars that separated them. His face was drawn and saturnine. He looked as if he hated the world and everyone in it.

Leo was certainly familiar with that feeling. "Well, this is a change," he remarked cheerfully. "Usually you're on this side and I'm on that side."

"Sod off," Merripen growled.

"And that's what *I* usually say," Leo marveled.

"I'm going to kill you," Merripen said with guttural sincerity.

"That doesn't provide much incentive for me to get you out, does it?" Leo folded his arms across his chest and gave him an assessing glance. Merripen was no longer drunk. Only mean as the devil. "Nevertheless," Leo said, "I'll have you set free, since you've done the same for me on so many occasions."

"Then do it."

"Soon. But I have a few things to say. And it's obvious that if I let you out first, you'll bolt like a hare at a coursing, and then I won't have the chance."

"Say what you like. I'm not listening."

"Look at you. You're a filthy mess and you're locked up in the pinfold. And you're about to receive a lecture on behavior from me, which is obviously as low as a man can sink."

From all appearances, the words fell on deaf ears. Leo continued undaunted. "You're not suited for this, Merripen. You can't hold your liquor worth a damn. And unlike people such as me, who become quite amicable while drinking, you turn into a vile-tempered troll." Leo paused, understanding the situation more than the bastard would have believed or wanted to believe. Perhaps Leo didn't know the whole mysterious tangle of Merripen's past, or the complex twists and turns of character that made him unable to have the woman he loved. But Leo knew one simple truth that superseded all others.

Life was too bloody short.

Leo paced back and forth. He had the sense that he was somehow standing between Merripen and annihilation, and some brace of essential words, a crucial argument, had to be set forth.

"If you weren't such a stubborn ass," Leo muttered, "I wouldn't have to do this."

No response from Merripen. Not even a glance.

Leo turned to the side, and rubbed the back of his neck, and dug his fingers into his own rigid muscles. "You know I never speak of Laura Dillard. In fact, this may be the first time I've said her full name since she died. But I am going to say something about her, because not only do I owe you for what you've done for the Ramsay estate, but—"

"Don't, Leo." The words were hard and cold. "You're embarrassing yourself."

"Well, I'm good at that. And you've left me no bloody choice. Do you understand what you are in, Merripen? A prison of your making. And even after you're out of here, you'll still be trapped. Your entire life will be a prison." Leo thought of Laura, the physical details of her no longer precise in his mind. But she lingered inside him like the memory of sunlight in a world that had been bitterly cold since her death.

Hell was not a pit of fire and brimstone. Hell was waking up alone, the sheets wet with your tears and your seed, knowing the woman you had dreamed of would never come back to you.

"Since I lost Laura," Leo said, "everything I do is merely a way of passing the time. It's hard to give a damn about much of anything. But at least I can live with the knowledge that I fought for her. At least I took every bloody minute with her that was possible to have. She died knowing I loved her." He stopped pacing and stared at Merripen contemptuously. "But you're throwing everything away—and breaking my sister's heart—because you're a damned coward. Either that or a fool. How can you—" He broke off as Merripen hurled himself at the bars, shaking them like a lunatic.

"Shut up, damn it."

"What will either of you have once Win has gone with Harrow?" Leo persisted. "You'll stay in your self-made prison, that's obvious. But Win will be worse off. She'll be alone. Away from her family. Married to a man who regards her as nothing more than a decorative object to keep on a bloody shelf. And what happens when her beauty fades and she loses her value to him? How will he treat her then?"

Merripen went motionless, his expression contorted, murder in his eyes.

"She's a strong woman," Leo said. "I spent two years with Win, watching as she met one challenge after another. After all the struggles she's faced, she's bloody well entitled to make her own decisions. If she wants to risk having a child—if she feels strong enough—that's her right. And if you're the man she wants, don't be a sodding idiot by turning her away." Leo rubbed his forehead wearily. "Neither you nor I are worth a damn," he muttered. "Oh, you can work the estate and show me how to balance account books and manage the tenants and inventory the stinking larder. I suppose we'll keep it running well enough. But neither of us will ever be more than half-alive like most men, and the only difference is, we know it."

Leo averted his gaze as he continued. "Amelia told me once that when Win and I had fallen ill with scarlet fever and you made the deadly nightshade syrup, you'd concocted far more than was necessary. And you'd kept a cup of it on Win's nightstand, like some sort of macabre nightcap. Amelia said that if Win had died, she thought you would have taken the rest of that poison. I've always hated you for that. Because you forced me to stay alive without the woman I loved, while you had no bloody intention of doing the same."

Merripen didn't answer, gave no sign that he registered Leo's words.

"Christ, man," Leo said huskily. "If you had the bollocks to die with her, don't you think you could work up enough courage to *live* with her?"

There was nothing but silence as Leo walked away from the cell. He wondered what the hell he had done, what effect it would have.

Leo went to the parish constable's office and told him to let Merripen out. "Wait another five minutes, however," he added. "I need a running start."

AFTER LEO HAD LEFT, THE TALK AT THE DINNER TABLE HAD taken on a tone of determined cheerfulness. No one wanted to speculate aloud on the reason for Kev's absence, or why Leo had gone on a mysterious errand . . . but it seemed likely the two were connected.

Win worried silently and told herself sternly that it was not her place, nor her right, to worry about Kev. And then she worried some more. As she forced a few bites of dinner down, she felt the food stick in her clenched throat.

She had gone to bed early, pleading a headache, and had left the others playing games in the parlor. After Julian had escorted her to the main staircase, she had let him kiss her. It was a lingering kiss, turning damp as he had searched just inside her lips. The patient sweetness of his mouth on hers had been—if not earth-shattering—very pleasant.

Win thought that Julian would be a skilled and sensitive partner when she finally did manage to coax him into making love to her. But he didn't seem terribly driven in that regard. Had he ever looked at her with a fraction of the hunger, the need, that Kev did, perhaps it might have awakened a response in her.

But Julian's feelings didn't begin to approach the all-encompassing intensity of Kev's. And she found it difficult to imagine Julian losing his composure even during that most intimate of acts.

Filled with melancholy, Win bathed, and donned a white nightgown, and sat in bed reading for a while. Eventually she turned out the lamp and tried to sleep. Just as she began to drift off, however, she sensed that someone or something was in the room. Possibly Beatrix's ferret Dodger, who sometimes slipped past the door to collect objects that intrigued him.

Rubbing her eyes, Win began to sit up, when there was a movement beside the bed. A large shadow crossed over her. Before bewilderment could give way to fear, she heard a familiar murmur and felt warm fingers press across her lips.

"It's me."

Her lips moved soundlessly against his hand. *Kev.*

Win's stomach constricted with an ache of pleasure, and her heartbeat hammered in her throat. But she was still angry with him, she was *done* with him, and if he had come here for a midnight talk, he was sadly mistaken. She started to tell him so, but to her astonishment, she felt a thick piece of cloth descend over her mouth, and then he was tying it deftly behind her head. In a few more seconds, he had bound her wrists in front of her.

Win was rigid with shock. Kev would never do something like this. What did he want? What was going through his mind?

His breath was faster than usual as it brushed against her hair. He drew the ruby ring off her finger and set it on the bedside table. Taking her head in his hands, he stared into her wide eyes. He said only two words. But they explained everything he was doing, and everything he intended to do.

"You're mine."

He picked her up easily, draping her over one powerful shoulder, and he carried her from the room.

Win closed her eyes, yielding, trembling. She pressed a few sobs against the gag covering her mouth, not of unhappiness or fear, but of wild relief. This was not an impulsive act. This was ritual. She was going to be claimed.

Finally.

Chapter Seventeen

As far as "abductions" went, it was skillfully executed. One would have expected no less of Kev. Although Win had assumed he would carry her to his room, he surprised her by taking her outside, where his horse was waiting. Wrapping her in his coat, he held her against his chest and rode off with her. Not to the gatehouse, but alongside the woods, through night mist and dense blackness that daylight would soon filter.

Win stayed relaxed against him, trusting him, as he guided the horse expertly through a copse of oak and ash. A small white cottage appeared, ghost-colored in the darkness. Win wondered whom it belonged to. It was tidy and new-looking, with smoke curling from the chimney stack. It was lit, welcoming, as if it had been readied in anticipation of visitors.

Dismounting, Kev tugged Win down into his arms, and he carried her to the front step. "Don't move," he said. She stayed obediently still while he tethered the horse.

Kev closed his hand over her bound wrists and led her inside. Win followed easily, a willing captive. The cottage was sparely furnished, and it smelled of fresh wood and paint. Not only was it empty of current residents, but it seemed that no one had ever lived there.

Taking Win into the bedroom. Kev lifted her onto a bed covered with quilts and white linen. Her bare feet dangled over the edge of the mattress as she sat upright.

Kev stood before her, the light from the hearth gilding one side of his face. His gaze was locked on her. Slowly he removed his coat and dropped it to the floor, heedless of the fine fabric. As he pulled his open-necked shirt over his head, Win was startled by the powerful expanse of his torso, all muscle and brawn. His chest was hairless, the skin gleaming like satin, and Win's fingers twitched with the urge to touch it. She felt herself flush with anticipation, her face rouged with heat.

Kev's dark eyes took in her reaction. He removed his half boots, kicked them aside, and came to her. He touched the lace-edged collar of her nightgown, stroked downward, and caressed the shape of her breast. The light pressure drew a shiver from her, sensation gathering at the hardening tip. She wanted him to kiss her there. She wanted it so badly that she fidgeted, her toes curling, her lips parting with a gasp beneath the binding cloth.

To her relief, Kev reached around to the back of her head and untied the gag.

Red and trembling, Win managed an unsteady whisper. "You . . . you needn't have used that. I would have kept quiet."

Kev's tone was grave, but his lips curved slightly. "If I decide to do something, I do it properly."

"Yes." Her throat cinched around a sob of pleasure as his fingers slid into her hair and touched her scalp. "I know that."

Cradling her head in his hands, he bent to kiss her gently with hot, shallow laps into her mouth, and as she responded he went deeper, demanding more. The kiss went on and on, making her gasp and strain, her own small tongue darting greedily past the edges of his teeth. She was so absorbed in tasting him, so dazed by the current of arousal humming through her, that it took her a little while to realize she was lying back on the bed with him, her bound hands flung over her head.

His lips slid to her throat, savoring her with slow, open kisses.

"Wh-where are we?" she managed to ask, shivering as his mouth found a particularly sensitive place.

"Gamekeeper's cottage." He lingered on that vulnerable spot until she writhed.

"Where is the gamekeeper?"

Kev's voice was passion-thickened. "We don't have one yet."

Win rubbed her cheek and chin against the heavy locks of his hair, relishing the feel of him. "How is it that I've never seen this place?"

His head lifted. "It's far in the woods," he whispered, "away from noise." He toyed with her breast, softly thumbing the tip. "A gamekeeper needs peace and quiet to care for the birds."

Win was feeling anything but peace and quiet inside. She was dying to touch him, to hold him. "Kev, untie my arms."

He shook his head. The leisurely pass of his hand along her front caused her to arch.

"Oh, please," she gasped. "Kev—"

"Hush," he murmured. "Not yet." His mouth passed hungrily over hers. "I've wanted you for too long. I need you too much." His teeth caught at her lower lip with arousing delicacy. "One touch of your hands and I wouldn't last a second."

"But I want to hold you," she said plaintively.

The look on his face sent a thrill through her. "Before we're through, love, you're going to hold me with every part of your body." He covered her wild heartbeat with a gentle palm.

Lowering his head, he kissed her hot cheek and whispered, "Do you understand what I want to do, Win?"

She nodded.

"And it's what you want as well?" he asked softly.

"For years." She captured him with her looped arms and struggled upward to reach his mouth. He kissed her, pushing her back down, sliding one of his knees carefully between her thighs. Gently, farther and farther, until she felt an intimate pressure against the part of her that had begun to ache.

Night was dissolving into day, the silvery morning slanting into the room, the wood awakening with chirps and rustlings . . . redstarts, swallows. She thought briefly of everyone back at Ramsay House. Soon they would discover that she was gone. A chill went through her as she wondered if they would look for her. If she returned as a virgin, any future with Kev would be very much in peril.

"Kev," she whispered in agitation, "perhaps you should hurry."

"Why?" he asked against her throat.

"I'm afraid someone will stop us."

His head lifted, and he smiled in a way that made her lightheaded. "No one will stop us. An entire army could surround the cottage. Explosions. Lightning strikes. It's still going to happen."

"I still think you should go a bit faster."

A quiet laugh escaped him, and he covered her mouth with his.

He courted her mouth skillfully, distracting her with deep, fervid kisses. At the same time, he unfastened her nightgown with deft tugs. At the sight of her naked breasts, he made a low, needful sound and took the tip of her breast into his mouth. *So hot* . . . she flinched as if the contact had scalded her. When he lifted his head, the nipple was redder and tighter than it had ever been before.

His eyes were passion-drowsed as he kissed her other breast. His tongue provoked the soft peak into a stinging bud and soothed it with warm strokes. Win moaned as his strong hands traced over her body, gently charting every curve.

He parted her legs, but she resisted and blushed fiercely as she became aware of the unexpected wetness between her thighs.

"Wait," she said, mortified.

He stopped instantly, and unwound the length of silk from around her wrists. "What is it, love?"

"I . . . I need a handkerchief." She closed her eyes and turned to the side, her legs clamped together.

His hand caressed her hip, and then his fingertips wandered slowly down to the triangle of curls at her groin. "Is this what worries you?" he asked gently, insinuating a finger into the softness, finding a slick of moisture. "That you're wet here?"

She closed her eyes and nodded with a choked sound.

"No," he soothed, "this is good; this is how it's supposed to be. It helps me to go inside you, and . . ." His breathing roughened. "Oh, Win, you're so lovely, so sweet . . . let me touch you; let me have you . . ."

In an agony of modesty, Win let him roll her back and part her thighs. She tried to stay quiet and still, but her hips jerked as he stroked the place that had become almost painfully sensitive. He murmured softly, his fingers stroking her open, softly tickling and teasing around the stiff peak of her clitoris. More wetness, more heat, his touch skimming over and around, until a finger slid inside her. She stiffened and gasped, and the touch was immediately withdrawn.

"Did I hurt you?" he asked huskily.

Her lashes lifted. "No," she said in wonder, and gave a little sigh of relief. "Amelia said there's usually pain, but you didn't hurt me at all."

"Win . . ." He paused, looking uncomfortable and apologetic. "It probably will hurt when I do it with this." He nudged the hard, heavy length of his erection against her thigh.

"Oh." She pondered that for a moment. "What's the word for that?"

"Roma call it a *kori*. Thorn."

Win slid a bashful glance at the heavy protrusion straining behind his trousers. "Rather too substantial for a thorn. I should have thought they would use a more fitting word. But I suppose—" She inhaled sharply as his hand moved downward. "I suppose if one wants roses, one must"—his finger had slipped inside her again—"bear the occasional thorn."

He smiled against her cheek. "Very philosophical." He gently stroked and teased the clenching interior of her body.

Her toes curled into the quilt as wicked tension coiled low in her belly. "Kev, what should I do?"

"Nothing. Only let me please you."

All her life, she had hungered for this without quite knowing what it was, this slow, astonishing merging with him, this sweet dissolution of self. This mutual surrender. There was no doubt that he was in control, and yet he browsed over her with absolute wonder. She felt herself soaking up sensation, her body infused with sensation and heat.

Kev wouldn't let her hide any part of herself from him . . . He took what he wanted, turning and lifting her body, rolling her this way and that, always with care, and yet with passionate insistence. He kissed beneath her arms and along her sides and all over her, running his tongue along every curve and humid crease. Gradually the accumulating pleasure shaped into something dark and raw, and she moaned from the pain of acute need.

The drive of her heartbeat reverberated everywhere, in her breasts and limbs and stomach, even at the tips of her fingers and toes. It was too much, this wildness he had aroused. She begged him for a moment's respite.

"Not yet," he told her between ragged breaths, his tone rough with a triumph she didn't yet understand.

"*Please,* Kev—"

"You're so close, I can feel it. Oh God—" He took her head in his hands, kissed her ravenously, and said against her lips, "You don't want me to stop yet. Let me show you why."

A whimper escaped her as he slid low between her thighs, his head bending to the swollen place he had been tormenting with his fingers. He put his mouth on her, licking along the delicate salty strait, spreading her with his thumbs. She tried to sit bolt-upright, but fell back against the pillows as he found what he wanted, his tongue strong and wet.

She was spread beneath him like a pagan sacrifice, illuminated by the daylight that now flooded the room. Kev worshipped her with hot, glassy licks, savoring the taste of her pleasured flesh. Moaning, she closed her legs around his head, and he turned deliberately to nibble and lick at one pale inner thigh, then the other. Feasting on her. Wanting everything.

Win curled her fingers desperately in his hair, lost to shame as she guided him back, her body arching wordlessly . . . *Here, please, more, more, now* . . . and she groaned as he fastened his mouth over her with a fast, flicking rhythm. Pleasure seized her, wrenching an astonished cry from her, holding her stiff and paralyzed for excruciating seconds. Every measure and pulse of the universe had distilled to the compelling heat, riveted there on that crucial place, and then it all released, the feeling and tension shattering exquisitely, and she was racked with blissful shudders.

Win relaxed helplessly as the spasms faded. She was filled with glowing weariness, a sense of peace too pervasive to allow movement. Kev let go of her just long enough to undress completely. Naked and aroused, he came back to her. He gathered her up carefully, settling over her.

She lifted her arms to him with a drowsy murmur. His back was tough and sleek beneath her fingers, the muscles twitching eagerly at her touch. His head descended, his shaven cheek rasping against hers.

He pushed gently at first. The innocent flesh resisted, smarting at the intrusion. He thrust more strongly, and Win caught her breath at the burning pain of his entrance. Too much of him, too hard, too deep. She writhed in reaction, and he buried himself heavily and pinned her down, gasping for her to be still, telling her to wait, he wouldn't move, it would be better. They both stilled, breathing hard.

"Should I stop?" Kev whispered raggedly, his face taut.

Even now in this flash point of need, he was concerned for her. Understanding what it had cost him to ask, how much he needed her, Win was overwhelmed with love. "Don't even think of stopping now," she whispered back. Reaching down to his lean flanks, she stroked him in shy encouragement. He groaned and began to move, his entire body trembling as he pressed within her.

Although every thrust caused a sharp burn where they were joined, Win tried to pull him even deeper. The feeling of having him inside her went far beyond pain or pleasure. It was *necessary*.

Kev stared down at her, his eyes brilliant in his flushed face. He looked fierce and ravenous and even a bit disoriented, as if he were experiencing something beyond the scope of ordinary men. Only now did Win grasp the enormity of his passion for her, despite all his efforts to smother it. How hard he had fought against their fate for reasons she still didn't fully understand. But now he possessed her with a reverence that eclipsed all other feeling.

She took him, and took him, wrapping him in her slender

legs, burying her face in his throat and shoulder. She loved the sounds he made, the soft grunts and growls, the harsh flow of his breath. The power of him around her and inside her. Tenderly she stroked his back and sides and pressed kisses on his neck. He seemed electrified by her attentions, his movements quickening, his eyes closing tightly. And then he thrust upward and held, and shook all over as if he were dying.

"Win," he groaned, burying his face against her. "Win." The single syllable contained the faith and passion of a thousand prayers.

Minutes passed before either of them spoke. They stayed wrapped together, fused and damp and unwilling to part.

Win smiled as she felt Kev's lips drift over her face. When he reached her chin, he gave it a little nip. "Not a pedestal," he said gruffly.

"Hmm?" She stirred, raising her hand to the shaven bristle of his cheek. "What do you mean?"

"You said I put you on a pedestal . . . remember?"

"Yes."

"It was never that. I've always carried you in my heart. Always. I thought that would have to be enough."

Moved, Win kissed him gently. "What happened, Kev? Why did you change your mind?"

Chapter Eighteen

Kev didn't intend to answer that until he had taken care of her. He left the bed and went to the small kitchen, which had been fitted with a cookstove with a brass water reservoir and pipes leading through the firebox to provide hot water instantly. Filling a hot-water can, he brought it to the bedroom along with a clean tea towel.

He paused at the sight of Win lying on her side, the flowing curves draped in white linen, her hair spilling over her shoulders in rivers of silvery gold. And best of all, the sated softness of her face and the swollen rosiness of lips he had kissed and kissed. It was an image from his deepest dreams, seeing her in bed like that. Waiting for him.

He dampened the toweling with hot water and peeled back the sheet, enchanted by her beauty. He would have wanted her no matter what, virgin or not . . . but he privately acknowledged his satisfaction in having been her first lover. No one but he would touch her, pleasure her, see her . . . except . . .

"Win," he said, frowning as he washed her, pressing the steaming cloth between her thighs. "At the clinic, did you ever wear *less* than your exercise costume? That is, did Harrow ever look at you?"

Her face was composed, but there was a glitter of amusement in her rich blue eyes. "Are you asking if Julian ever saw me naked in a professional capacity?"

Kev was jealous, and they both knew it, but he couldn't stop from scowling. "Yes."

"No, he didn't," she said primly. "He was interested in my respiratory system, which, as you clearly know, is in a far different location than the reproductive organs."

"He's interested in more than your lungs," Kev said darkly.

She smiled. "If you're hoping to divert me from the question I asked earlier, it's not working. What happened to you last night, Kev?"

He rinsed the bloodstains from the towel, wrung it out, and pressed another warm pad between her thighs. "I was in the pinfold."

Her eyes widened. "The gaol? Is that where Leo went? To get you out?"

"Yes."

"Why in heaven's name were you behind bars?"

"I was in a fight at the tavern."

She clicked her tongue a few times. "That's not like you."

The statement was loaded with such unintended irony that Kev nearly laughed. In fact, a few huffs came from deep in his chest, and he was so amused and miserable that he couldn't speak. His expression must have been odd indeed, because Win stared at him intently and sat up. She removed the compress, and set it aside, and pulled the sheet up over her breasts. She ran a light, graceful hand across his bare shoulder, her touch soothing. And she continued to caress him, stroking his chest, his neck, his midriff, and each loving pass of her hand seemed to erode his self-restraint further.

"Until I came to your family," he said hoarsely, "it was

the only reason I existed. To fight. To hurt people. I was . . . cruel." Looking into Win's eyes, he saw nothing but concern.

"Tell me," she whispered.

He shook his head. A shiver chased across his back.

Her hand slipped around the nape of his neck. Slowly she drew his head down to her shoulder so that his face was half-hidden. "Tell me," she urged again.

Kev was lost, unable to withhold anything from her now. And he knew what he was about to confess would disgust and revolt her, but he found himself doing it anyway.

He revealed it all mercilessly, trying to make her understand the vicious bastard he had been. He told her about the boys he had beaten to a pulp, the ones he feared might have died later, but he'd never been certain. He told her how he had lived like an animal, eating scraps and stealing, and about the rage that had consumed him always. He had been a bully, a thief, a beggar. He revealed cruelties and humiliations that he should have had the pride and good sense to keep to himself.

Kev had kept the confessions inside forever, but now they were spilling out like garbage. And he was appalled to realize that he had lost all control, that whenever he tried to stop, all it took was a gentle touch and a murmur from Win and he was babbling like a criminal with a gallows priest.

"How could I touch you with these hands?" he asked, his tone shredded with anguish. "How could you stand to let me? God, if you knew all the things I've done—"

"I love your hands," she murmured.

"I'm not good enough for you. But no one is. And most men, good or bad, have limits to what they would do, even for someone they love. I have none. No God, no moral code, no faith in anything. Except you. You're my religion. I would do anything you asked. I would fight, steal, kill for you. I would—"

"Shhh. Hush. My goodness." She sounded breathless. "There's no need to break all the commandments, Kev."

"You don't understand," he said, drawing back to look at her. "If you believed anything I've told you—"

"I do understand." Her face was like an angel's, soft and compassionate. "And I believe what you've said . . . but I don't agree at all with the conclusions you seem to have drawn." Her hands lifted, molding against his lean cheeks. "You are a good man, a loving one. The *rom baro* tried to kill all that inside you, but he couldn't succeed. Because of your strength. Because of your heart."

She eased back onto the bed and drew him down to her. "Be at ease, Kev," she whispered. "Your uncle was an evil man, but what he did must be buried with him. Let the dead bury the dead—do you know what that means?"

He shook his head.

"To leave the past behind and look only to the journey ahead. Only then can you find a new way. A new life. It's a Christian saying . . . but it would make sense to anyone, I think."

It made more sense than Win perhaps even realized. Roma were superstitious regarding death and the dead, destroying all the possessions of those who had passed, mentioning the name of the deceased as seldom as possible. It was for the benefit of the dead, as well as the living, to keep them from returning to the living world as wretched ghosts. Let the dead bury the dead . . . but he wasn't certain he could.

"Hard to let go," he said thickly. "Hard to forget."

"Yes." Her arms tightened around him. "But we'll fill your mind with much better things to think about."

Kev was quiet for a long time, pressing his ear to Win's heart, listening to the even beat and the flow of her breathing.

"I knew when I first saw you what you would mean to me,"

Win murmured eventually. "I loved you at once. You felt it, too, didn't you?"

He nodded slightly, luxuriating in the feel of her. Her skin smelled sweet like plums, with an arousing hint of feminine musk.

"I wanted to tame you," she said. "Not all the way. Just enough that I could be close to you." She threaded her fingers through his hair. "Outrageous man. What possessed you to kidnap me when you knew I would have come willingly?"

"I was making a point," he said in a muffled voice.

She chuckled and stroked his scalp, the scrape of her oval fingernails nearly causing him to purr. "Your point was well-taken. Must we go back now?"

"Do you want to?"

Win shook her head. "Although . . . I wouldn't mind having something to eat."

"I brought food to the cottage before I went to get you."

She ran a flirtatious fingertip around the rim of his ear. "What an efficient villain you are. May we stay all day, then?"

"Yes."

Win wriggled with delight. "Will anyone come for us?"

"I doubt it." Kev drew the bed linens lower and nuzzled into the lush valley between her breasts. "And I would kill the first person who approached the threshold."

A quiet laugh caught in her throat.

"What is it?" he asked without moving.

"Oh, I was just thinking of all the years I spent trying to get out of bed to be with you. And when I came home, all I wanted was to climb back into bed. With you."

FOR BREAKFAST THEY HAD STRONG TEA AND RAREBIT—CHEESE melted on thick slices of buttered, toasted bread. Wrapped in Kev's shirt, Win perched on a low stool in the kitchen. She took pleasure in watching the play of muscles on his back as he poured steaming water into a portable hip bath. Smiling, she popped the last morsel of rarebit into her mouth.

There was a near-magical aura about this ordinary place, this small and quiet cottage. Win felt as if she had been caught in some enchanted spell. She was almost afraid she was dreaming, that she would wake alone in her chaste bed. But Kev's presence was too vital and real for it to be a dream. And the small aches and twinges in her body offered further proof that she had been taken. Possessed.

"They all know by now," Win said absently, thinking of everyone at Ramsay House. "Poor Julian. He must be furious."

"What about heartbroken?" Kev set the water can aside and came to her dressed only in trousers.

Win frowned thoughtfully. "He'll be disappointed, I think. And I believe he cares for me. But no, he won't be heartbroken." She leaned against Kev as he stroked her hair, and her cheek brushed the taut smoothness of his stomach. "He never wanted me the way you do."

"Any man who didn't would have to be a eunuch." There was a hitch in his breath as Win kissed the rim of his navel. "Did you tell him what the London doctor said? That you were healthy enough to bear children?"

Win nodded.

"What did Harrow say?"

"Julian told me that I could visit a legion of doctors and get any number of differing opinions to support the conclusion I wanted. But in Julian's view, I should remain childless."

Kev brought her to a standing position and looked down at her, his expression unfathomable. "I don't want to put you at risk. But neither do I trust Harrow or his opinions."

"Because you think of him as a rival?"

"That's part of it," he admitted. "But it's also instinct.

There's something . . . lacking in him. There's something false."

"Perhaps it's because he's a doctor," Win suggested, shivering as Kev drew his shirt away from her. "Men of his profession often seem aloof. Superior, even. But that's necessary, because—"

"It's not that." Kev guided her to the hip bath and helped to lower her in. Win gasped not only from the heat of the water, but also from being naked in front of him. The hip bath obliged one to straddle the tub and relax into the water with the legs held apart, which was wonderfully comfortable in private, but rather mortifying with someone else present. Her modesty was further violated as Kev knelt beside the tub and washed her. But his manner was not at all lascivious, only caring, and she couldn't help but relax under the ministrations of those strong, soothing hands.

"You still suspect Julian of having harmed his first wife, I know," Win said while Kev bathed her. "But he is a healer. He would never hurt anyone, least of all his own wife." She paused as she read Kev's expression. "You don't believe me. You're determined to think the worst of him."

"I think he feels entitled to play with life and death. Like the gods of those mythology stories you and your sisters are so fond of."

"You don't know Julian as I do."

Kev didn't reply, only continued to wash her.

She watched his dark face through the veil of steam, as beautiful and implacable as an ancient carving of a Babylonian warrior. "I shouldn't even bother to defend him," she said ruefully. "You'll never be disposed to think well of him, will you?"

"No," he admitted.

"And if you believed Julian was the better man?" she asked. "Would you have allowed him to marry me?"

She saw the muscles in his throat tense before he answered, "No." There was a touch of self-hatred in his response. "I'm too selfish for that. I could never have let it happen. If it came down to it, I would have carried you off on your wedding day."

Win wanted to tell him that she had no desire for him to be noble. She was happy—thrilled—to be loved in just this way, with a passion that left no room for anything else. But before she could say a word, Kev had taken up more soap, and his hand glided over the soreness between her thighs.

He touched her with love and tenderness. Her eyes half-closed. His finger eased inside her, and his free arm slid behind her back, and she leaned weakly into the cradle of his hard chest and shoulder. Even this small invasion hurt. Her flesh was still too newly broached, unused to being entered. But the hot water soothed her, and Kev was so gentle that her thighs relaxed, supported in the buoyant warmth.

She breathed in the morning air, luminous with steam, scented of soap and wood and hot copper. And the intoxicating fragrance of her lover. His warm fingers stroked like the idle sway of river reeds, quickly discovering where she most wanted them. He toyed with her, slowly investigating the cambered softness and the sensitive places within. Blindly she reached down to grip his strong wrist as he slid a finger inside her, his thumb gliding over her clitoris in tender circles.

The water sloshed in the tub as she began to push up rhythmically, urging herself into his hand. She felt herself clenching on him, her muscles tightening rhythmically around the gentle invasion, and an abbreviated cry left her lips at the first shock of release. She tried to stifle it, but another was torn from her, and another, and the bathwater rippled as she shuddered, the pleasure lingering until she was limp and panting.

Settling her against the high-backed tub, Kev left her for a few minutes. She soaked in the steaming water, too replete to ask or notice where he'd gone. He returned with a length of toweling and lifted her from the bath. She stood passively before him, letting him dry her, and looped her arms around his neck as he carried her back into the bedroom. After he settled her into a freshly made bed, she slid beneath the quilts and waited while he went to wash himself and empty the tub. She was steeped in a feeling she hadn't experienced in years . . . the kind of incandescent joy she had felt as a child waking on Christmas morning.

Win's eyes half-opened as she felt him climb into bed eventually. His weight depressed the mattress, and he pulled her into the crook of his arm and shoulder. She sighed deeply as his hand made a slow, lovely pattern over her back.

"Will we have a cottage like this someday?" she murmured.

Being Kev, he had already come up with a plan. "We'll live at Ramsay House for a year, more likely two, until the restoration is complete and Leo is on his feet. Then I'll find a suitable property to farm and build a house for you." His hand slid to her bottom, rubbing in slow circles. "It won't be an extravagant life, but it will be comfortable. You'll have a cookmaid and a footman and a driver. And we'll live near your family, so you can see them whenever you like."

"That sounds lovely," Win managed to say, so filled with happiness she could scarcely breathe. "It will be heaven." She had no doubt of his ability to take care of her, nor did she doubt she would make him happy.

His tone was sober. "If you marry me, you'll never be a lady of position."

"There's no better position for me than being your wife."

One of his big hands clasped over her skull, pressing her head against his shoulder.

They were quiet then, relishing the sensation of cuddling together. They had been close in so many ways before this . . . They had known each other so well, and yet not at all. Physical intimacy had created a new dimension to Win's feelings. She wondered how it was that people could engage in this act without love, how empty and pointless it must be by comparison.

Her bare foot explored the hairy surface of his leg, toes nudging against hard-sculpted muscle. "Did you think about me when you were with them?" she asked tentatively.

"Who?"

"The women you slept with."

She knew from the way Kev tensed that he didn't like the question. His reply was low and cautious. "No. I didn't think about anything when I was with them."

Win let her hand wander over his smooth chest, finding the small brown nipples, teasing them into points. Rising on her elbow, she said frankly, "When I imagine you doing this with someone else, I can hardly bear it."

His hand came over hers, securing it against his strong heartbeat. "It was always something to be done with as quickly as possible."

"You should have found someone you cared for, someone who cared for *you*."

"I couldn't."

"Couldn't what?"

"Care about anyone else. You took up too much room in my heart."

Win wondered what it said about her terrible selfishness that such an answer moved and pleased her.

"After you left," Kev said, "I thought I would go mad.

There was no place I could go to feel better. No one I wanted to be with. I wanted you to get well—I would have given my life for it. But at the same time I hated you for leaving. I hated my own heart for beating. I had only one reason to live, and that was to see you again."

"Did the women help?" she asked softly. "Did it ease you to lie with them?"

He shook his head. "It made it worse," came his soft reply. "Because they weren't you."

Win leaned farther over him, her hair falling in glinting light ribbons that went across his chest and throat and arms. She stared into eyes as black as sloe. "I want us to be faithful to each other," she said gravely. "From this day forward."

There was a brief silence, a hesitation born not of doubt, but awareness. As if their vows were being heard and witnessed by some unseen presence.

Kev's chest rose and fell in a long, deep breath. "I'll be faithful to you," he said. "Forever."

"So will I."

"Promise you'll never leave me again."

Win lifted her hand from the center of his chest and pressed a kiss there. "I promise."

She was entirely willing, eager, to seal their vows then, but he wouldn't. He wanted her to rest. When she objected, he quieted her with gentle kisses. "Sleep," he whispered, and she obeyed, sinking into the sweetest, darkest oblivion she had ever known.

DAYLIGHT CANTED IMPATIENTLY AGAINST THE UNLINED CURtains at the windows, turning them into butter-colored rectangles. Kev had held Win for hours. He had not slept at all in that time. The pleasure of staring at her eclipsed the need for rest. There had been other times in his life when he had watched over her like this, especially when she'd been ill. But it was different now that she belonged to him.

He had always been consumed with miserable longing, loving Win and knowing nothing would ever come of it. Now, holding her, he felt something unfamiliar, a bloom of euphoric heat. He let himself kiss her, unable to resist following the glinting arc of her eyebrow with his lips. He moved on to the rosy curve of her cheek. The tip of a nose so adorable it was worthy of an entire sonnet. He loved every part of her. It occurred to him that he hadn't yet kissed the spaces between her toes, an omission that desperately needed to be corrected.

Win slept with one of her legs hitched over him. Feeling the intimate brush of blond curls against his hip, he went erect, his flesh alive with a hard, precise throbbing he could feel against the linen sheet that covered him.

She stirred and moved her limbs in a trembling stretch, and her eyes half opened. He sensed her surprise at waking in his arms this way, and the slow dawning of satisfaction as she remembered what had gone before. Her hands crept over him, exploring softly. He was taut everywhere, aroused and unmoving, letting her discover him as she wished.

Win reconnoitered his body with an innocent abandon that seduced him utterly. Her lips brushed the taut skin of his chest and side, while one of her hands trailed over his thigh and wandered up to his groin. She cupped the weights of him below, then gripped the shaft lightly—too lightly. Kev would have begged her to do it harder had he been able to spare the breath. But he could only wait, gasping. Her head bent over him, her golden hair trapping him in a glimmering net. To his shock, he felt her lean down to kiss him. And she continued, working upward along the stiff length, while he groaned with pleasure.

Her beautiful mouth on him . . . he was dying, losing his sanity. She was too inexperienced to know how to proceed. She didn't take him deep, only licked the tip, but the sensation was almost too intense to bear. Kev let out an anguished groan as he felt a sweet, wet tug and heard the sound of her suckling. With an incoherent sound, he seized her hips and dragged them upward. He buried his face in her, his tongue working voraciously until she writhed like a captured mermaid.

Tasting her arousal, he sank his tongue deep, again and again. Her legs stiffened, as if she were about to come. But he had to be inside her when it happened, had to feel her grip and clench around him. So he moved her carefully, easing her to her front, and pushed a pillow beneath her hips.

She moaned and parted her knees wider. Needing no further invitation, he positioned himself, his cock slick with the moisture from her mouth. Reaching beneath her, he found the tiny swollen bud, and he massaged slowly while he fed his shaft into her, his fingers stroking faster with every hard inch that pushed forward. When he had finally buried his full length, she climaxed with a sobbing cry.

Kev could have found his own release then, but he had to prolong it. If it were possible, he would have gone on forever. He drew one hand along the pale, elegant curve of her back. She arched into the caress, sighing his name. He lay over her, changing the angle between them, still cupping her sex as he thrust. She shuddered as a few more spasms were teased out, passion splotches rising on her shoulders and back. He put his mouth to the patches of color, kissing every blushing place as he rocked slowly, working deeper in her, tighter, until he finally found his own wrenching release.

Rolling off her, Kev gathered Win against his ribs and struggled to catch his breath. His heartbeat hammered in his ears for some minutes, which was why he was slow to notice a knock at the door.

Win reached up to his cheeks and guided his face to hers. Her eyes were anxious. "Someone's here," she said.

Chapter Nineteen

Cursing beneath his breath, Kev dragged on his trousers and shirt and went barefoot to the door. Opening it, he saw Cam standing there nonchalantly, a valise in one hand and a covered basket in the other.

"Hello." Cam's hazel eyes danced with mischief. "I've brought you a few things."

"How did you find us?" Kev asked without heat.

"I knew you hadn't gone far. And since the front gatehouse was too obvious, this was the next place I thought of. Aren't you going to invite me in?"

"No," Kev said shortly, and Cam grinned.

"If our positions were reversed, *phral*, I suppose I'd be just as inhospitable. There's food in the basket and clothes for both of you in the valise."

"Thank you." Kev took the items and set them just inside the door. Straightening, he looked at his brother, searching for any sign of censure. There was none.

"*Ov yilo isi?*" Cam asked.

It was a Romany phrase, meaning "Is all well here?" But it was literally translated as "Is there heart here?"

"Yes," Kev said softly.

"There's nothing you need?"

"For the first time in my life," Kev admitted, "there's nothing I need."

Cam smiled. Nonchalantly tucking his hands in his coat pockets, he braced a shoulder against the door frame.

"What is the situation at Ramsay House?" Kev asked, half dreading the answer.

"There were a few moments of chaos this morning when it was discovered that you were both gone." A diplomatic pause. "Harrow's been insisting that Win was taken against her will. At one point he threatened to go to the parish constable. Harrow says if you don't return with Win by nightfall, he'll take drastic action."

"What would that be?" Kev inquired darkly.

"I don't know. But you might give a thought to the rest of us having to stay at Ramsay House with him while you're out here with his fiancée."

"She's my fiancée now. And I'll bring her back when I'm ready."

"Understood." Cam's lips twitched. "You intend to marry her soon, I hope."

"Immediately."

"Thank God. Even for the Hathaways, this is all a bit untoward." Cam glanced over Kev's disheveled form and smiled. "It's good to see you at ease finally, Merripen. If it were anyone but you, I'd say you actually looked happy."

It was not easy to shed the habit of privacy. But Kev was actually tempted to confide in his brother, things he wasn't even certain he had words for. Such as the discovery that the love of a woman could make the entire world seem new. Or his wonder that Win, who had always seemed so fragile and in need of protection, had emerged as an even stronger presence than he.

He scrubbed his hand through his hair and asked guardedly, "Are the Hathaways angry about what I've done?"

"You mean carrying Win off?"

"Yes."

"The only complaint I heard was that you took far too long."

"Do any of them know where we are?"

"Not that I'm aware." Cam's smile turned wry. "I can buy you a few more hours, *phral*. But have her back by nightfall, if for no other reason than to shut Harrow up." He frowned slightly. "He's an odd one, that *gadjo*."

Kev gave him an alert glance. "Why do you say that?"

Cam shrugged. "Most men in his position would have done something, *anything*, by now. Destroyed some furniture. Gone for someone's throat. By this time I would have turned all of Hampshire upside down to find my woman. But Harrow only talks. And talks."

"About what?"

"He's said quite a lot about what his rights are, what he's entitled to, his sense of betrayal . . . but so far it hasn't occurred to him to express any concern about Win's welfare, or consider what she wants. He acts like a child whose toy has been taken." Cam grimaced. "Damned embarrassing, even for a *gadjo*." He raised his voice and called to the unseen Win, "I'm leaving now. Good day, little sister."

"And to you, Cam!" her cheerful voice floated back.

THEY UNPACKED A FEAST FROM THE BASKET: COLD ROAST fowl, a variety of salads, fruit, and thick slices of seed cake. After devouring the lot, they sat before the hearth on a quilt. Dressed only in Kev's shirt, Win sat between his thighs while he brushed the tangles from her hair. He ran his fingers repeatedly through the length of silk, which gleamed like moonlight in his hands.

"Shall we go for a walk now that I have my clothes?" Win asked.

"If you like." Kev held her hair aside and kissed the nape of her neck. "And afterward, back to bed."

She shivered and made a sound of amusement. "I've never known you to spend so much time abed."

"Until now I've never had a good reason." Setting the brush aside, he pulled her into his lap and cradled her. He kissed her lazily. She pushed upward with increasing demand, making him smile and pull back. "Easy," he said, stroking her jaw. "We're not going to start that again."

"But you just said you wanted to go back to bed."

"I meant to rest."

"We aren't going to make love anymore?"

"Not today," he said gently. "You've had enough." He brushed his thumb over her kiss-swollen lips. "If I made love to you again, you wouldn't be able to walk tomorrow."

But as he was discovering, any challenge to Win's physical stamina was met with immediate resistance. "I'm quite well," she said stubbornly, sitting up in his lap. She spread kisses over his face and throat, everywhere she could reach. "Once more, before we go back. I need you, Kev. I need—"

He quieted her with his mouth and received such an ardently impatient response that he couldn't help chuckling against her lips. She drew back and demanded, "Are you laughing at me?"

"No. No. It's only . . . you please me so much. My eager little *gadji*." He kissed her again, trying to calm her. But she was insistent, stripping off his shirt, pulling his hands to her naked body.

"Why are you so anxious?" he whispered, lying back on the quilt with her. "No . . . wait . . . Win, talk to me."

She went still in his arms. "I'm afraid to go back," she

admitted. "I feel as if something bad will happen. It doesn't seem real that we can truly be together now."

"We can't hide here forever," Kev murmured, stroking her hair. "Nothing will happen, love. We've gone too far to turn back. You're mine now, and no one can change that. Are you afraid of Harrow? Is that it?"

"Not afraid, exactly. But I'm not looking forward to facing him."

"Of course not," Kev said quietly. "I'll help you through it. I'll talk to him first."

"I don't think that would be wise," she said uncertainly.

"I insist on it. I won't lose my temper. But I'm going to take responsibility for what I've done. I would hardly leave you to handle the consequences without me."

Win lowered her cheek to his shoulder. "Are you certain nothing will happen to change your mind about marrying me?"

"Nothing in the world could do that." Feeling the tension in her body, he ran his hands over her, lingering on her chest, where every heartbeat was a hard, anxious collision. He rubbed a circle to soothe her. "What can I do to make you feel better?" he asked tenderly.

"I already told you and you wouldn't," she said in a small, sullen voice, and that drew a smothered laugh from him.

"Then you'll have your way," he whispered. "But slowly, so I won't hurt you." He kissed the spaces behind her earlobes and moved down to the smooth whiteness of her shoulders, the pulse at the base of her throat.

More softly still he kissed the plump curves of her breasts. Her nipples were bright and stung-looking from all his previous attentions. He was careful with them, his mouth gentle as he covered a swollen peak.

Win made a little movement and gave a faint hiss, and he

guessed the nipple was smarting. But her hands came to his head, holding him there. He used his tongue to make languid circles, sucking only enough to keep the tender flesh inside the clamp of his lips. He spent a long time at her breasts, keeping his mouth soft, until she moaned and stirred her hips, needing more than the faint, feathery stimulation.

Dragging his lips down between her thighs, Kev rooted in the hot silk of her, finding the delicate blunt point of her clitoris, using the velvet flat of his tongue to paint and caress. She clutched his head more tightly and sobbed his name, the throaty sound exciting him.

When the responsive movements of her hips took on a regular rhythm, he pulled his mouth from her and pushed her knees wide and apart. He took an eternity to ease into the lush, clenching flesh. Fully seated, he wrapped his arms around her, securing her against his body.

She wriggled, urging him to thrust, but he held still and fast, and pressed his mouth to her ear, and whispered that he would make her come just like this, that he would stay hard inside her as long as it took. Her ear turned scarlet, and she tightened and throbbed around him. "Please move," she whispered, and he gently said no.

"Please move, please . . ."

No.

But after a while he began to flex his hips in a subtle rhythm. She whimpered and trembled as he drove into her, nudging deeper, relentless in his restraint. The climax broke over her finally, tearing low cries from her lips, bringing wild shudders to the surface. Kev was quiet, experiencing a release so acute and paralyzing that it robbed him of all sound. Her slender body pulled at him, milked him, enclosed him in delicate heat.

The pleasure was so great it shook him to his foundations. *Bloody hell,* Kev thought, realizing that something had changed in him, something that could never be put back. All his defenses had been reduced to the strength of one small woman.

THE SUN WAS DESCENDING INTO THE BASIN OF RICH WOODED valleys by the time they had both dressed. The fires were extinguished, leaving the cottage cold and dark.

Win clung to Kev's hand anxiously as he led her to the horse. "I wonder why happiness always seems so fragile," she said. "I think the things our family has experienced . . . losing our parents, Leo losing Laura, the fire, my illness . . . have made me aware of how easily the things we value can be snatched away. Life can change from one moment to the next."

"Not everything changes. Some things last forever."

Win stopped and turned to face him, wrapping her arms around his neck. He responded immediately, holding her secure and close, locking her against his powerful body. Win buried her face in his chest. "I hope so," she said after a moment. "Are you really mine now, Kev?"

"I've always been yours," he said against her ear.

BRACED FOR THE USUAL CLAMOR OF HER SISTERS, WIN WAS relieved when she and Kev returned to Ramsay House and found it serene and quiet. So unusually serene that it was clear everyone had agreed to behave as if nothing unusual had transpired. She found Amelia, Poppy, Miss Marks, and Beatrix in the upstairs parlor, the first three doing needlework while Beatrix read aloud.

As Win entered the room cautiously, Beatrix paused, and the women looked up with bright, curious gazes.

"Hello, dear," Amelia said warmly. "Did you have a nice outing with Merripen?" As if it had been nothing more than a picnic or carriage drive.

"Yes, thank you." Win smiled at Beatrix. "Do go on, Bea. Whatever you're reading sounds lovely."

"It's a sensation novel," Beatrix said. "*Very* exciting. There's a dark and gloomy mansion, and servants who behave oddly, and a secret door behind a tapestry." She lowered her voice dramatically. "Someone's about to be murdered."

While Beatrix continued, Win sat beside Amelia. Win felt her older sister's hand reach for hers. A small but capable hand. A comforting grip. So much was expressed in Amelia's loving clasp, and in the returning pressure of Win's fingers . . . concern, acceptance, reassurance.

"Where is he?" Amelia whispered.

Win felt a pang of worry, though she kept her expression serene. "He's gone to talk with Dr. Harrow."

Amelia's grip tightened. "Well," she returned wryly, "it should be a lively conversation. I have the impression your Dr. Harrow has been saving up quite a few things to say."

"You crude, stupid peasant." Julian Harrow was white-faced but controlled as he and Kev met in the library. "You have no idea what you've done. In your haste to grab what you want, you've given no heed to the consequences. And you won't until it's too late. Until you've killed her."

Having a fairly good idea of what Harrow was going to say, Kev had already decided how he would deal with him. For Win's sake, he would tolerate any number of insults or accusations. The doctor would have his say . . . and Kev would let it all roll off his back. He had won. Win was his now, and nothing else mattered.

It wasn't easy, however. Harrow was the perfect picture of an outraged romantic hero . . . slim, elegant, his face pale and indignant. He made Kev feel like an oafish villain by contrast. And those last words, *until you've killed her,* chilled him to the marrow.

So many vulnerable creatures had suffered at his hands. No one with Kev's past could ever deserve Win. And even though she had forgiven his history of brutality, he could never forget.

"No one's going to harm her," Kev said. "It's obvious that as your wife she would have been well-cared for, but it wasn't what she wanted. She's made her choice."

"Under duress!"

"I didn't force her."

"Of course you did," Harrow said with contempt. "You carried her off in a display of brute strength. And being a woman, of course she thought it thrilling and romantic. Women can be dominated and persuaded into accepting nearly anything. And in the future, as she's dying in childbirth, in grotesque pain, she won't blame you for it. But you'll know that you're responsible." A harsh laugh escaped him as he saw Kev's expression. "Are you really so simple-minded that you don't understand what I'm saying?"

"You believe she's too fragile to bear children," Kev said. "But she consulted another doctor in London, who—"

"Did Winnifred tell you the name of this doctor?" Harrow's eyes were frosty gray, his tone brittle with condescension.

Kev shook his head.

"I persisted in asking," Harrow said, "until she told me. And I knew at once it was an invented name. A sham. But just to make certain, I checked the registers of every legitimate physician in London. The doctor she named doesn't exist. She was lying, Merripen." Harrow raked his hands through his hair and paced back and forth. "Women are as devious as children when it comes to getting their way. My God, you're easily manipulated, aren't you?"

Kev couldn't answer. He had believed Win for the simple reason that she never lied. As far as he knew there was only

one time in her life she'd ever deceived him, and that had been
to trick him into taking morphine when he'd been suffering
from a burn wound. Later he'd understood why she'd done
it, and he had forgiven her at once. But if she had lied about
this . . . Anguish burned like acid in his blood.

Now he understood why Win had been so nervous about
returning.

Harrow paused at the library table and went to half sit, half
lean on it. "I still want her," he said quietly. "I'm still willing to have her. On condition that she hasn't conceived." He
broke off as Kev fastened a lethal glare on him. "Oh, you
may glower, but you can't deny the truth. Look at you—how
can you justify what you've done? You're a filthy Gypsy, attracted to pretty baubles like the rest of your ilk."

Harrow watched Kev closely as he continued. "I'm sure
you love her in your fashion. Not in a refined way, not in the
way she truly needs, but as much as someone of your kind
is capable. I find that somehow touching. And pitiable. No
doubt Winnifred feels the bonds of childhood kinship give
you a claim on her. But she's been too long sheltered from
the world. She has neither the wisdom nor the experience to
know her own needs. If she does marry you, it will only be
a matter of time before she tires of you and wants more than
you could ever offer. Do the right thing, Merripen. Give her
to me. It's not too late. She'll be safe with me."

Kev could barely hear his own rasping voice, his pulse
hammering with confusion and despair and fury. "Maybe I
should ask the Lanhams. Would they agree she'd be safer
with you?"

And without glancing to judge the effect of his words, Kev
strode from the library.

WIN'S SENSE OF UNEASE GREW AS EVENING SETTLED OVER THE
house. She stayed in the parlor with her sisters and Miss

Marks until Beatrix had tired of reading. The only relief from Win's growing tension was in watching the antics of Beatrix's ferret, Dodger, who seemed enamored of Miss Marks, despite—or perhaps because of—her obvious antipathy. He kept creeping up to the governess and trying to steal one of her knitting needles, while she watched him with narrowed eyes.

"Don't even consider it, you impudent rodent," Miss Marks told the hopeful ferret with chilling calm.

"Ferrets aren't rodents, actually," Beatrix said. "They're classified as *Mustelidae*. Weasels. So one might say the ferret is a distant cousin of the mouse."

"It's not a family I'd care to become closely acquainted with," Poppy said.

Dodger draped himself across the arm of the settee and pinned a lovestruck gaze on Miss Marks, who ignored him.

Win smiled and stretched. "I'm fatigued. I'll bid everyone good night now."

"I'm fatigued as well," Amelia said, covering a deep yawn.

"Perhaps we should all retire," Miss Marks suggested, deftly packing away her knitting in a little basket.

They all went to their rooms, while Win's nerves bristled in the ominous silence of the hallway. A lamp burned low in her room, its glow pushing feebly against the encroaching shadows. She blinked as she saw a motionless form in the corner . . . Kev, occupying a chair.

"Oh," she breathed in surprise.

His gaze tracked her as she came closer to him.

"Kev?" she asked hesitantly, while a chill slithered down her spine. The talk hadn't gone well. Something was wrong. "What is it?" she asked huskily.

Kev stood and towered over her, his expression unfathomable. "Who was the doctor you saw in London, Win? How did you find him?"

Then she understood. Her stomach dropped, and she took a few steadying breaths. "There was no doctor," she said. "I didn't see the need for it."

"You didn't see the need," he repeated slowly.

"No. Because—as Julian said later—I could go from doctor to doctor until I found one who would give me the answer I wanted."

Kev let out a breath that sounded like a scrape in his throat. He shook his head. "Jesus."

Win had never seen him look so devastated, beyond shouting or anger. She moved toward him with her hand outstretched. "Kev, please, let me—"

"Don't. Please." He was struggling visibly to control himself.

"I'm sorry," she said earnestly. "I wanted you so much, and I was going to have to marry Julian, and I thought if I told you about having seen another doctor, it would . . . well, push you a bit."

He turned away from her, his hands clenched.

"It makes no difference," Win said, trying to sound calm, trying to think above the desperate pounding of her heart. "It changes nothing, especially after today."

"It makes a difference if you lie to me," he said in a guttural tone.

She knew she'd broken Kev's trust at a time when he'd been particularly vulnerable. He had let down his guard, had let her inside. But how else could she have had him?

"I didn't feel I had a choice," she said. "You're impossibly stubborn when your mind is made up. I didn't know how to change it."

"Then you've just lied again. Because you're not sorry."

"I'm sorry that you're hurt and angry, and I understand how much you—"

She broke off as Kev moved with astonishing swiftness,

seizing her by the upper arms, bringing her up against the wall. His snarling face descended close to hers. "If you understood anything, you wouldn't expect me to give you a baby that will kill you."

Rigid and trembling, Win said stubbornly, "I'll see as many doctors as you like. We'll gather a full variety of opinions, and you can calculate the odds. But no one can predict with certainty what will happen. And none of it will change how I intend to spend the rest of my life. I will live it on my terms. And you . . . you can have all of me or nothing. I won't be an invalid any longer. Not even if it means losing you."

"I don't take ultimatums," he said.

Win's eyes went blurry, and she damned the rising tears. She wondered in furious despair why fate seemed determined to withhold from her the ordinary life that other people took for granted. "It's not your choice," she said, "it's mine. My body. My risk. And it may already be too late. I may have already conceived—"

"No." Kev gripped her head and pressed his forehead to hers, his breath striking her lips in bursts of heat. "I can't do this," he said raggedly. "I won't be forced into hurting you. I can't lose you."

"Just love me." Win wasn't aware that she was crying until she felt his mouth on her face, his throat vibrating with low growls as he licked at her tears. He kissed her desperately, savaging her mouth with a wildness that made her quiver from head to toe. As he crushed his body against hers, she felt the prodding of his arousal even through the bunched layers of their clothes. It sent a shock of response through all her veins, and she felt her intimate flesh prickling, turning wet. She wanted him inside her, to pull him deep and close, to pleasure him until his ferocity was soothed.

She reached down to the stiff length of him, kneading and gripping until he groaned into her mouth.

"Take me to bed, Kev," she whispered. "Take me . . ."

But he shoved away from her with a vicious curse.

"Kev—"

A scalding glance and he left the room, the door trembling on its hinges from the abrupt slam.

Chapter Twenty

The early morning air was fresh and heavy with the promise of rain, a cool breeze sweeping through the half-open window of Cam and Amelia's room. Cam awakened slowly as he felt his wife's voluptuous body snuggling close to his. She always slept in a nightgown made of modest white cambric, with infinite numbers of tucks and tiny ruffles. It never failed to stir him, knowing what splendid curves were concealed beneath the demure garment.

The nightgown had ridden up to her knees during the night. One of her bare legs was hooked over his, her knee resting near his groin. The slight roundness of her stomach pressed against his side. Pregnancy had made her feminine form more ample and delicious. There was a glow about her these days, a burgeoning vulnerability that filled him with an overwhelming urge to protect her. And knowing that the changes in her were caused by his seed, a part of him growing inside her . . . that was undeniably arousing.

As he patted her hip drowsily, the urge to make love to her was too much to resist. He inched her gown upward and caressed her bare bottom. He kissed her lips, her chin, savoring the fine texture of her skin.

Amelia stirred. "Cam," she murmured sleepily. Her legs parted, inviting more of the gentle exploration.

Cam smiled against her cheek. "What a good little wife you are," he whispered in Romany. She stretched and gave a pleasured sigh as his hands slipped over her warm body. He arranged her limbs carefully, stroking and praising her, kissing her breasts. His fingers played between her thighs, teasing wickedly until she began to breathe in quiet moans. Her hands clutched at his back as he mounted her, his body hungry for the warm, wet welcome of her—

A tap at the door. A muffled voice. "Amelia?"

They both froze.

The soft feminine voice tried again. "Amelia?"

"One of my sisters," Amelia whispered.

Cam muttered a curse that explicitly described what he had been about to do, and was apparently not going to be able to finish. "Your family—" he began in a dark tone.

"I know." She flipped back the bedclothes. "I'm sorry. I—" She broke off as she saw the extent of his arousal and said weakly, "Oh dear."

Although he was usually tolerant when it came to the Hathaways' multitude of quirks and issues, Cam was currently in no mood to be understanding.

"Get rid of whoever it is," he said, "and come back here."

"Yes. I'll try." She pulled a dressing robe over her nightgown and hastily fastened the top three buttons. As she hurried into the adjoining sitting room, the thin white dressing robe flapped behind her like the mainsail of a schooner.

Cam remained on his side, listening intently. There was the sound of the door to the hallway opening and someone coming into the little sitting room. There was also the calm lilt of Amelia's questioning voice, and the anxious response of one of her sisters. Win, he guessed, since Poppy and Beatrix would only awaken this early in the event of some major catastrophe.

One of the things Cam adored about Amelia was her tender and unflagging interest in all the concerns, large and small, of her siblings. She was a little mother hen, valuing family as much as any Romany wife. That felt good to him. It hearkened back to his early childhood, when he'd still been allowed to live with the tribe. But it also meant having to share Amelia, which, at times like this, was damned annoying.

After a few minutes, the sisterly chatter still hadn't stopped. Gathering that Amelia wasn't going to return to bed anytime soon, Cam sighed and left the bed.

He dragged on some clothes, went into the sitting room, and saw Amelia on a small settee with Win. Who looked wretched.

They were so intent on their conversation that, Cam listened until he comprehended that Win had lied to Merripen about having seen a doctor, that Merripen had been furious, and that the relationship between the two was a wreck.

Amelia turned to Cam, her forehead puckered with concern. "Perhaps Win shouldn't have deceived him, but it is her right to make this decision for herself." Amelia retained Win's hand in hers as she spoke. "You know that I would love nothing better than to keep Win safe from harm, always . . . but even I have to acknowledge that it isn't possible. Merripen must accept that Win wants to have a normal married life with him."

Cam rubbed his face and stifled a yawn. "Yes. But the way to help him accept that is *not* to manipulate him." He looked at Win directly. "Or give ultimatums."

"I didn't tell him what to do," Win protested miserably. "I just told him—"

"That it didn't matter what he thought or felt," Cam murmured. "That you intend to live your life on your own terms, no matter what."

"Yes," she said faintly. "But I didn't mean to imply that I didn't care about his feelings."

Cam smiled ruefully. "I admire your fortitude, little sister. I even happen to agree with your position. But even your sister, who isn't generally known for her diplomacy, knows better than to approach me in such an uncompromising way."

"I am *quite* diplomatic when I wish to be," Amelia protested, frowning, and he gave her a brief grin. Turning to Win, she admitted reluctantly, "Cam is right, however."

Win was quiet for a moment, absorbing that. "What should I do now? How can things be made right?"

Both women looked at Cam.

The last thing he wanted was to involve himself in Win and Merripen's problems. And God knew Merripen would probably be as charming as a baited bear this morning. All Cam wanted was to go back to bed and plow his wife. And perhaps sleep a bit longer. But as the sisters stared at him with entreating blue eyes, he sighed. "I'll talk to him," he muttered.

"He's most likely awake now," Amelia said hopefully. "Merripen always rises early."

Cam gave her a glum nod, hardly relishing the prospect of talking to his surly brother about womanish matters. "He's going to beat me like a dusty parlor rug," Cam said. "And I won't blame him a bit."

AFTER DRESSING AND WASHING, CAM WENT DOWNSTAIRS to the morning room, where Merripen always took breakfast. Passing the sideboard, Cam saw toad-in-the-hole, a casserole of sausages covered in batter and roasted, platters of bacon and eggs, sole fillets, and fried bread.

A chair had been pushed back from one of the round tables. There was an empty cup and saucer, and a small steaming silver pot next to it. The scent of strong black coffee lingered in the air.

Cam glanced at the glass doors that led to a back terrace and saw Merripen's lean, dark form. He appeared to be staring at the fruit orchard beyond the structured formal garden. The set of his shoulders and head conveyed both irritability and moroseness.

Hell. Cam had no idea what he was going to say to his brother. They had far to go before they approached a basic level of trust. Any advice he tried to give Merripen would probably be thrown back into his face.

Picking up a slice of fried bread, Cam ladled a spoonful of orange marmalade on it, and wandered out to the terrace.

Merripen gave Cam a cursory glance and returned his attention to the landscape: the flourishing fields beyond the manor grounds, the heavy forests nourished by the thick artery of the river. A few gentle streams of smoke arose from the distant riverbank, one of the places where Roma were wont to camp as they traveled through Hampshire. Cam had personally carved identifying marks on the trees to indicate that this was a friendly place. Every time a new tribe came, Cam went to visit them on the off-chance that someone from his long-ago family might be there.

"Another *kumpania* passing through," he remarked casually, joining Merripen at the balcony. "Why don't you come with me to visit them this morning?"

Merripen's tone was distant and unfriendly. "The workmen are casting new plasterwork moldings for the east wing. And after the way they fouled it up last time, I have to be there."

"Last time, the screeds they nailed up weren't properly aligned," Cam said.

"I know that," Merripen snapped.

"Fine." Feeling sleepy and annoyed, Cam rubbed his face. "Look, I have no desire to stick my nose in your affairs, but—"

"Then don't."

"It's not going to hurt you to hear an outside perspective."

"I don't give a damn about your perspective."

"If you weren't so bloody self-absorbed," Cam said acidly, "it might occur to you that you're not the only one who's got something to worry about. Do you think I'm not worried about what might happen to Amelia now that she's conceived?"

"Nothing will happen to Amelia," Merripen said dismissively.

Cam scowled. "Everyone in this family chooses to think of Amelia as indestructible. Amelia herself thinks it. But she's subject to all the usual problems and frailties of any other woman in her condition. The truth is that it's always a risk."

Merripen's dark eyes simmered with hostility. "More so for Win."

"Probably. But if she wants to assume that risk, it's her decision."

"That's where we differ."

"Because you don't take risks on anyone, do you? It's too bad you've fallen in love with a woman who won't be kept on a shelf, *phral*."

"If you call me that again," Merripen growled, "I'll take your bloody head off."

"Go ahead and try."

Merripen would probably have launched at Cam then, if not for the glass doors opening and another figure stepping out on the terrace. Glancing in the direction of the intruder, Cam groaned inwardly.

It was Harrow, looking controlled and capable. He approached Cam and ignored Merripen. "Good morning, Rohan. I've just come to tell you that I'll be leaving Hampshire later in the day. If I can't persuade Miss Hathaway to come to her senses, that is."

"Of course," Cam said pleasantly. "Please let me know if there is anything we can do to facilitate your departure."

"I only want what's best for her," the doctor murmured, still not looking at Merripen. "I'll continue to believe that going to France with me is the wisest choice for all concerned. But it's Miss Hathaway's decision." He paused, his gray eyes somber. "I hope you'll exert any influence you have to make certain *all* parties concerned understand what is at stake."

"I think we all grasp the situation," Cam said with a gentleness that masked the sting of sarcasm.

Harrow stared at him suspiciously and gave a short nod. "I'll leave the two of you to your *discussion*, then." He placed a subtle, skeptical emphasis on the word "discussion," as if he was aware that they'd been on the verge of an outright brawl. He left the terrace, closing the glass door behind him.

"I hate that bastard," Merripen said beneath his breath.

"He's not my favorite, either," Cam admitted. Wearily he gripped the back of his own neck, trying to ease the stiffness of the pinching muscles. "I'm going down to the campsite. If you don't mind, I'll take a cup of that evil brew you drink. I despise the stuff, but I need something to help me stay awake."

"Have whatever's left in the pot," Merripen muttered. "I'm more awake than I'd like to be."

Cam nodded and went to the French doors. But he paused at the threshold, and smoothed the hair at the back of his neck, and spoke quietly. "The worst part about loving someone, Merripen, is that there will always be things you can't protect her from. Things beyond your control. You finally realize there's something worse than dying . . . and that's having something happen to her. You have to live with that fear always. But you have to take the bad part if you want the good part."

Merripen looked at him bleakly. "What's the good part?"

A smile touched Cam's lips. "All the rest of it is the good part," he said, and went inside.

"I've been warned on pain of death not to say anything," was Leo's first comment as he joined Kev in one of the east wing rooms. There were two plasterers in the corner measuring and marking on the walls, and another was repairing scaffolding that would support a man close to the ceiling.

"Good advice," Kev said. "You should take it."

"I never take advice, good or bad. That would only encourage more of it."

Despite Kev's brooding thoughts, he felt an unwilling smile tug at his lips. He gestured to a nearby bucket filled with light gray ooze. "Why don't you pick up a stick and stir the lumps out of that?"

"What is it?"

"A lime plaster and hairy clay mix."

"Hairy clay. Lovely." But Leo obediently picked up a discarded stick and began to poke around in the bucket of plaster. "The women are gone for the morning," he remarked. "They went to Stony Cross Manor to visit Lady Westcliff. Beatrix warned me to be on the lookout for her ferret, which seems to be missing. And Miss Marks stayed here." A reflective pause. "An odd little creature, wouldn't you say?"

"The ferret or Miss Marks?" Kev carefully positioned a strip of wood on the wall and nailed it in place.

"Marks. I've been wondering . . . Is she a misandrist, or does she hate everyone in general?"

"What's a misandrist?"

"A man-hater."

"She doesn't hate men. She's always been pleasant to me and Rohan."

Leo looked genuinely puzzled. "Then . . . she merely hates me?"

"It would seem so."

"But she has no reason!"

"What about your being arrogant and dismissive?"

"That's part of my aristocratic charm," Leo protested.

"It would appear your aristocratic charm is lost on Miss Marks." Kev arched a brow as he saw Leo's scowl. "Why should it matter? You have no personal interest in her, do you?"

"Of course not," Leo said indignantly. "I'd sooner climb into bed with Bea's pet hedgehog. Imagine those pointy little elbows and knees. All those sharp angles. A man could do fatal harm to himself, tangling with Marks . . ." He stirred the plaster with new vigor, evidently preoccupied with the myriad dangers in bedding the governess.

A bit too preoccupied, Kev thought.

IT WAS A SHAME, CAM MUSED AS HE WALKED THROUGH A green meadow with his hands tucked in his pockets, that being part of a close-knit family meant one could never enjoy his own good fortune when someone else was having problems.

There was much for Cam to take pleasure in at the moment . . . the benediction of sunshine on the spring-roughened landscape, and all the waking, droning, vibrant activity of plants pushing from the damp earth. The promising tang of smoke from a Romany campfire floated on a breeze. Perhaps today he might finally find someone from his old tribe. On a day like this, anything seemed possible.

He had a beautiful wife who was carrying his child. He loved Amelia more than life. And he had so much to lose. But Cam wouldn't let fear cripple him or prevent him from loving her with all his soul. Fear . . . He slowed his pace, perplexed by the sudden rapid escalation of his heartbeat. As if he'd been running for miles without stopping. Glancing across the field, he saw that the grass was unnaturally green.

The thump of his heart became painful, as if someone were kicking him repeatedly. Bewildered, Cam tensed like a man held at knifepoint, putting a hand to his chest. Jesus, the sun was bright, boring through his eyes until they watered. He blotted the moisture with his sleeve, and was abruptly surprised to find himself on the ground, on his knees.

He waited for the pain to subside, for his heart to slow as it surely must, but it only got worse. He struggled to breathe, tried to stand. His body would not obey. A slow, boneless collapse, the green grass stabbing harshly into his cheek. More pain, and more, his heart threatening to explode from the extraordinary force of its beats.

Cam realized with a kind of wonder that he was dying. He couldn't think why it was happening or how, only that no one would take care of Amelia and she needed him, he couldn't leave her. Someone had to watch over her; she needed someone to rub her feet when she was tired. So tired. He couldn't lift his head or arms or move his legs, but muscles in his body were jumping independently, tremors jerking him like a puppet on strings. *Amelia. I don't want to go away from you. God, don't let me die; it's too soon.* And yet the pain kept pouring over him, drowning him, smothering every breath and heartbeat.

Amelia. He wanted to say her name, and he couldn't. It was an unfathomable cruelty that he couldn't leave the world with those last precious syllables on his lips.

AFTER AN HOUR OF NAILING UP SCREEDS AND TESTING VARIous mixtures of lime, gypsum, and hairy clay, Kev and Leo and the workmen had settled on the right proportions.

Leo had taken an unexpected interest in the process, even devising an improvement on the three-coat plasterwork by improving the base layer, or scratch coat. "Put more hair in this layer," he had suggested, "and rough it up with a darby tool, and that will give more of a clinch to the next coat."

It was clear to Kev that although Leo had little interest in the financial aspects of running the estate, his love of architecture and all related matters of construction was more keenly developed than ever.

As Leo was climbing down from the scaffolding, the housekeeper, Mrs. Barnstable, came to the doorway with a boy in tow. Kev regarded him with sharp interest. The boy, a Rom, appeared to be about eleven or twelve years of age.

"Sir," the housekeeper said to Kev apologetically, "I beg your pardon for interrupting your work. But this lad came to the doorstep speaking gibberish, and he refuses to be chased away. We thought you might be able to understand him."

The "gibberish" turned out to be perfectly articulate Romany.

"*Droboy tume Romale*," the boy said politely.

Kev acknowledged the greeting with a nod and continued the conversation in Romany. "Are you from the *vitsa* by the river?"

"Yes, *kako*. I was sent by the *rom phuro* to tell you that we found a Rom lying in the field. He's dressed like a *gadjo*. We thought he might belong to someone here."

"Lying in the field," Kev repeated, while a cold, biting

urgency rose inside him. He knew at once that something very bad had happened. With an effort, he kept his tone patient. "Was he resting?"

The boy shook his head. "He's ill and out of his head. And he shakes like this—" He mimicked a tremor with his hands.

"Did he tell you his name?" Kev asked. "Did he say anything?" Although they were still speaking in Romany, Leo and Mrs. Barnstable stared at Kev intently, gathering that some emergency was taking place.

"What is it?" Leo asked, frowning.

The boy answered Kev, "No, *kako,* he can't say much of anything. And his heart—" The boy hit his own chest with a small fist in a few emphatic thumps.

"Take me to him." There was no doubt in Kev's mind that the situation was dire. Cam was never ill, and he was in superb physical condition. Whatever had befallen him, it was outside the category of ordinary maladies.

Switching to English, Kev spoke to Leo and the housekeeper. "Rohan has been taken ill. He's at the Romany campsite. My lord, I suggest you send a footman and driver to Stony Cross Manor to collect Amelia at once. Mrs. Barnstable, send for the doctor. I'll bring Rohan here as soon as I can."

"Sir," the housekeeper asked in bewilderment, "are you referring to Dr. Harrow?"

"No," Kev said instantly. All his instincts warned him to keep Harrow out of this. "In fact, don't let him know what's going on. For the time being, keep this as quiet as possible."

"Yes, sir." Although the housekeeper didn't understand Kev's reasons, she was too well-trained to question his authority. "Mr. Rohan seemed perfectly well earlier this morning. What could have happened to him?"

"We'll find out." Without waiting for further questions or

reactions, Kev gripped the boy's shoulder and steered him toward the doorway. "Let's go."

THE *VITSA* APPEARED TO BE A SMALL AND PROSPEROUS FAMILY tribe. They had set up a well-organized camp, with two *vardos* and some healthy-looking horses and donkeys. The leader of the tribe, whom the boy identified as the *rom phuro*, was an attractive man with long black hair and warm dark eyes. Although he was not tall, he was fit and lean, with an air of steady authority. Kev was surprised by the leader's relative youth. The word *phuro* usually referred to a man of advanced age and wisdom. For a man who appeared to be in his late thirties, it signified that he was an unusually respected leader.

They exchanged cursory greetings, and the *rom phuro* led Kev to his own *vardo*. "Is he your friend?" the leader asked with obvious concern.

"My brother." For some reason Kev's comment earned an arrested glance.

"It is good that you're here. It may be your last chance to see him this side of the veil."

Kev was astonished by his own visceral reaction to the comment, the rush of outrage and grief. "He's not going to die," he said harshly, quickening his stride and fairly leaping into the *vardo*.

The interior of the vehicle was approximately twelve feet long and six feet broad, with the typical stove and metal chimney pipe located to the side of the door. A pair of transverse berths was located at the other end of the *vardo*, one upper and one lower. Cam's long body was stretched out on the lower berth, his booted feet dangling over the end. He was twitching and juddering, his head rolling ceaselessly on the pillow.

"Holy hell," Kev said thickly, unable to believe such a

change had been wrought in the man in such a short amount of time. The healthy color had been leeched out of Cam's face until it was as white as paper, and his lips were cracked and gray. He moaned in pain, panting like a dog.

Kev sat on the edge of the berth and put his hand on his brother's icy forehead. "Cam," he said urgently. "It's Merripen. Open your eyes. Tell me what happened."

Cam struggled to control the tremors, to focus his gaze, but it was clearly impossible. He tried to form a word, but all he could produce was an incoherent sound.

Flattening a hand on Cam's chest, Kev felt a ferocious and irregular heartbeat. He swore, recognizing that no man's heart, no matter how strong, could go on at that manic pace for long.

"He must have eaten some herb without knowing it was harmful," the *rom phuro* commented, looking troubled.

Kev shook his head. "My brother is familiar with medicinal plants. He'd never make that kind of mistake." Staring down at Cam's drawn face, Kev felt a mixture of fury and fear. He wished his own heart could take over the work for his brother's. "Someone poisoned him."

"Tell me what I can do," the tribe leader said quietly.

"First we need to get rid of as much of the poison as possible."

"His stomach emptied before we brought him into the *vardo*."

That was good. But for the reaction to be this bad even after expelling the poison meant it was a highly toxic substance. The heart beneath Kev's hand seemed ready to burst from Cam's chest. He would go into convulsions soon. "Something must be done to slow his pulse and ease the tremors," Kev said curtly. "Do you have laudanum?"

"No, but we have raw opium."

"Even better. Bring it quickly."

The *rom phuro* spoke to a pair of women who had come to the entrance of the *vardo*. In less than a minute, they'd produced a tiny jar of thick brown paste. It was the dried fluid of the unripened poppy pod. Scraping up some of the paste with the tip of a spoon, Kev tried to feed it to Cam.

Cam's teeth clattered violently against the metal, his head jerking until the spoon was dislodged. Doggedly Kev slid his arm beneath his brother's neck and lifted him upward. "Cam. It's me. I've come to help you. Take this for me. Take it now." He shoved the spoon back into Cam's mouth and held it there while he choked and shook in Kev's grip. "That's it," Kev murmured, withdrawing the spoon after a moment. He laid a warm hand on his brother's throat, rubbing gently. "Swallow. Yes, *phral,* that's it."

The opium worked with miraculous speed. Soon the tremors began to subside, and the frantic gasping eased. Kev wasn't aware of holding his breath until he let it out in a relieved sigh. He put his palm over Cam's heart, feeling the jerking rhythm slow.

"Try giving him some water," the tribe leader suggested, handing a carved wooden cup to Kev. He pressed the edge of the cup against Cam's lips and coaxed him to take a sip.

The heavy lashes lifted, and Cam focused on him with effort. "Kev . . ."

"I'm here, little brother."

Cam stared and blinked. He reached up and clutched the placket of Kev's open-necked shirt like a drowning man. "Blue," he whispered raggedly. "Everything . . . blue."

Kev slid his arm around Cam's back and gripped him firmly. He glanced at the *rom phuro* and tried desperately to think. He'd heard of such a symptom before, a blue haze over the vision. It was caused by taking too much of a potent heart medicine. "It could be digitalis," he murmured. "But I don't know what plant that comes from."

"Foxglove," the *rom phuro* said. His tone was matter-of-fact, but his face was taut with anxiety. "Quite lethal. Kills livestock."

"What's the antidote?" Kev asked sharply.

The leader's reply was soft. "I don't know. I don't even know if there is one."

Chapter Twenty-one

After dispatching a footman for the village doctor, Leo decided to go to the Romany camp and see how Cam was faring. Leo couldn't stand the inactivity or suspense of waiting. And he was deeply troubled by the thought of anything happening to Cam.

Rapidly navigating his way down the grand staircase, Leo had just reached the entrance hall when he was approached by Miss Marks. She had a housemaid in tow and was holding the hapless girl by the wrist. The maid was pale and red-eyed.

"My lord," Miss Marks said tersely, "I bid you to come with us to the parlor immediately."

"In your supposed knowledge of etiquette, Marks, you should know that no one *bids* the master of the house to do anything."

The governess's stern mouth twisted impatiently. "Devil take etiquette. This is important."

"Very well. Apparently you must be humored. But tell me here and now, as I've no time for chitchat."

"Come to the parlor," she insisted.

After a brief glance heavenward, Leo followed the governess and housemaid through the entrance hall. "I warn you, if this is about some trivial household matter, I'll have your head. I've got a pressing issue to deal with right now, and—"

"Yes," Miss Marks cut him off as they walked swiftly to the parlor. "I know about that."

"You do? Hang it all, Mrs. Barnstable wasn't supposed to tell anyone."

"Secrets are rarely kept belowstairs, my lord."

As they went into the parlor, Leo stared at the governess's straight spine and experienced the same sting of irritation he always felt in her presence. She was like one of those unreachable itches on one's back. It had something to do with the coil of light brown hair pinned so tightly at her nape. And the narrow torso and tiny corseted waist, and the dry, pristine paleness of her skin. He couldn't help thinking about what it would be like to unlace, unpin, and unloosen her. Remove her spectacles. Do things that would make her all pink and steamy and profoundly bothered.

Yes, that was it. He wanted to bother her.

Repeatedly.

Good God, what was wrong with him?

Once they were in the parlor, Miss Marks closed the door and patted the housemaid's arm with a slender white hand. "This is Sylvia," she told Leo. "She saw something untoward this morning and was afraid to tell anyone. But after learning of Mr. Rohan's illness, she came to me with this information."

"Why wait until now?" Leo asked impatiently. "Surely anything untoward should be reported at once."

Miss Marks answered with annoying calmness, "There are no protections for a servant who inadvertently sees something she shouldn't. And being a sensible girl, Sylvia doesn't want to be made a scapegoat. Do we have your assurance that she will suffer no ill consequences from what she's about to divulge?"

"You have my word," Leo said. "No matter what it is. Tell me, Sylvia."

The housemaid nodded and leaned against Miss Marks for support. Sylvia was so much heavier than the frail governess, it was a wonder they didn't both topple over. "My lord," the maid faltered, "I polished the fish forks this morning and brought them to the breakfast sideboard, for the sole fillets. But as I came into the morning room, I saw Mr. Merripen and Mr. Rohan out on the terrace, talking. And Dr. Harrow was in the room, watching them . . ."

"And?" Leo prompted as the girl's lips trembled.

"And I thought I saw Dr. Harrow put something into Mr. Merripen's coffeepot. He reached for something in his pocket—it looked like one of those queer little glass tubes at the apothecary's. But it was so fast, I couldn't be sure what he'd done. And then he turned around and looked at me as I came into the room. I pretended not to see anything, my lord. I didn't want to make trouble."

"We think Mr. Rohan drank the adulterated beverage," the governess said.

Leo shook his head. "Rohan doesn't like coffee."

"Isn't it possible that he might have made an exception this morning?"

The edge of sarcasm in her voice was unbearably annoying.

"It's possible. But it wouldn't be in character." Leo let out a harsh sigh. "Damn it all. I'll try to find out what, if anything, Harrow did. Thank you, Sylvia."

"Yes, my lord." The housemaid looked relieved.

As Leo strode from the room, he was exasperated to discover that Miss Marks was at his heels. "Do *not* come with me, Marks."

"You need me."

"Go somewhere and knit something. Conjugate a verb. Whatever it is governesses do."

"I would," she said acerbically, "had I any confidence in your ability to handle the situation. But from what I've seen of your skills, I doubt you'll accomplish anything without my help."

Leo wondered if other governesses dared to talk to the master this way. He didn't think so. Why the devil couldn't his sisters have chosen a quiet, pleasant woman instead of this little wasp? "I have skills you'll never be fortunate enough to see or experience, Marks."

She made a scornful *humph* and continued to follow him.

Reaching Harrow's room, Leo gave a perfunctory knock and went inside. The wardrobe was empty and there was an open trunk by the bed. "Do excuse the intrusion, Harrow," Leo said with only the shallowest pretense of politeness. "But a situation has arisen."

"Oh?" The doctor looked remarkably incurious.

"Someone has been taken ill."

"How unfortunate. I wish I could be of assistance, but if I'm to reach London before midnight, I must leave shortly."

"Surely you have an ethical obligation to help someone who needs it," Miss Marks said incredulously. "What about the oath of Hippocrates?"

"The oath is not obligatory. And in light of recent events, I have every right to decline. You will have to find another doctor to treat him."

Him.

Leo didn't have to look at Miss Marks to know that she, too, had caught the slip. He decided to keep Harrow talking. "Merripen won my sister fairly, old fellow. And what brought them together was set in motion long before you entered the scene. It's not sporting to blame them."

"I don't blame them," Harrow said curtly. "I blame you."

"*Me?*" Leo was indignant. "What for? I had nothing to do with this."

"You have so little regard for your sisters that you'd allow not one but *two* Gypsies to be brought into your family."

Out of the corner of his eye, Leo saw Dodger the ferret creeping across the carpeted floor. The inquisitive creature reached a chair over which a dark coat had been draped. Standing on his hind legs, he rummaged in the coat pockets.

Miss Marks was speaking crisply. "Mr. Merripen and Mr. Rohan are men of excellent character, Dr. Harrow. One may fault Lord Ramsay for many other things, but not for that."

"They're *Gypsies*," Harrow said scornfully.

Leo began to speak, but he was cut off as Miss Marks continued her lecture. "A man must be judged by his character, Dr. Harrow. By how he treats others, and what he makes of himself. Having lived in proximity to Mr. Merripen and Mr. Rohan, I can state with certainty that they are both fine, honorable men."

Dodger extracted an object from the coat pocket and wriggled in triumph. He began to lope slowly around the edge of the room, watching Harrow warily.

"Forgive me if I don't accept assurances of character from a woman such as you," Harrow said to Miss Marks. "But according to rumor, you've been in rather *too much* proximity with certain gentlemen in your past."

The governess turned white with outrage. "How dare you!"

"I find that remark entirely inappropriate," Leo said to Harrow. "It's obvious no sane man would ever attempt something scandalous with Marks." Seeing that Dodger had made it to the doorway, Leo reached for the governess's rigid arm. "Come, Marks. Let's leave the doctor to his packing."

At the same moment, Harrow caught sight of the ferret, who was carrying a slim glass vial in his mouth. Harrow's eyes bulged, and he went pale. "Give that to me!" he cried, and launched toward the ferret. "That's mine!"

Leo leaped on the doctor and brought him to the floor. Harrow surprised him with a sharp right hook, but Leo's jaw had been hardened from many a tavern fight. He traded blow for blow, rolling across the floor with the doctor as they struggled for supremacy.

"What the devil"—Leo grunted—"did you put into that coffee?"

"Nothing." The doctor's strong hands clamped on his throat. "Don't know what you're talking about—"

Leo bashed him in the side with a closed fist until the doctor's grip weakened. "The hell you don't," Leo gasped, and kneed him in the groin. It was a dirty trick he'd picked up from one of his more colorful escapades in London.

Harrow collapsed to his side, groaning. "Gentleman . . . wouldn't . . . do that . . ."

"Gentlemen don't poison people, either." Leo seized him. "Tell me what it was, damn you!"

Despite his pain, Harrow's lips curved in an evil grin. "Merripen will have no help from me."

"Merripen didn't drink the filthy stuff, you idiot! Rohan did. Now tell me what you put in that coffee or I'll rip your throat out."

The doctor looked stunned. He clamped his mouth shut and refused to speak. Leo struck him with a right and then a left, but the bastard remained silent.

Miss Marks's voice broke through the boiling fury. "My lord, stop it. *This instant.* I need your assistance in retrieving the vial."

Hauling Harrow upward, Leo dragged him to the empty wardrobe and closed him inside. Leo locked the door and turned to face Miss Marks, his face sweating and his chest heaving.

Their gazes locked for a split second. Her eyes turned as round as her spectacle lenses. But the peculiar awareness between them was immediately punctured by Dodger's triumphant chatter.

The blasted ferret waited at the threshold, doing a happy war dance that consisted of a series of sideways hops. Obviously he was delighted by his new acquisition, and even more by the fact that Miss Marks seemed to want it.

"Let me out!" Harrow cried in a smothered voice, and there was a violent pounding from inside the wardrobe.

"That blasted weasel," Miss Marks muttered. "This is a game to him. He'll spend hours teasing us with that vial and keeping it just out of reach."

Staring at the ferret, Leo sat on the carpet and relaxed his voice. "Come here, you flea-ridden hair wad. You'll have all the sugar biscuits you want if you'll give your new toy to me." He whistled softly and clicked.

But the blandishments did not work. Dodger merely regarded him with bright eyes and stayed at the threshold, clutching the vial in his tiny paws.

"Give him one of your garters," Leo said, still staring at the ferret.

"I beg your pardon?" Miss Marks asked frostily.

"You heard me. Take off a garter and offer it to him as a trade. Otherwise we'll be chasing this damned animal all through the house. And I doubt Rohan will appreciate the delay."

The governess gave Leo a long-suffering glance. "Only for Mr. Rohan's sake would I consent to this. Turn your back."

"For God's sake, Marks, do you think anyone really wants a glance at those dried-up matchsticks you call legs?" But Leo complied, facing the opposite direction. He heard a great deal of rustling as Miss Marks sat on a bedroom chair and lifted her skirts.

It just so happened that Leo was positioned near a full-length looking glass, the oval cheval style that tilted up or down to adjust one's reflection. And he had an excellent view of Miss Marks in the chair. And the oddest thing happened—he got a flash of an astonishingly pretty leg. He blinked in bemusement, and then the skirts were dropped.

"Here," Miss Marks said gruffly, and tossed it in Leo's direction. Turning, he managed to catch it in midair.

Dodger surveyed them both with beady-eyed interest.

Leo twirled the garter enticingly on his finger. "Have a look, Dodger. Blue silk with lace trim. Do all governesses anchor their stockings in such a delightful fashion? Perhaps those rumors about your unseemly past are true, Marks."

"I'll thank you to keep a civil tongue in your head, my lord."

Dodger's little head bobbed as it followed every movement of the garter. Fitting the vial in his mouth, the ferret carried it like a miniature dog, loping up to Leo with maddening slowness.

"This is a trade, old fellow," Leo told him. "You can't have something for nothing."

Carefully Dodger set down the vial and reached for the garter. Leo simultaneously gave him the frilly circlet and snatched the vial. It was half-filled with a fine, dull green powder. He stared down at it intently, rolling it in his fingers.

Miss Marks was at his side in an instant, crouching on her hands and knees. "Is it labeled?" she asked breathlessly.

"No. Damn it all." Leo was gripped with volcanic fury.

"Let me have it," Miss Marks said, prying the vial from him.

Leo jumped to his feet immediately, hurling himself at the wardrobe. He slammed it with both his fists. "Damn you, Harrow, what is it? What is this stuff? Tell me, or you'll stay in there until you rot."

There was nothing but silence from the wardrobe.

"By God, I'm going to—" Leo began, but Miss Marks interrupted.

"It's digitalin powder."

Leo threw her a distracted glance. She had opened the vial and was sniffing it cautiously. "How do you know?"

"My grandmother used to take it for her heart. The scent is like tea, and the color is unmistakable."

"What's the antidote?"

"I have no idea," Miss Marks said, looking more distressed by the moment. "But it's a powerful substance. A large dose could very well stop a man's heart."

Leo turned back to the wardrobe. "Harrow," he bit out, "if you want to live, you'll tell me the antidote now."

"Let me out first," came the muffled reply.

"No negotiating! Tell me what counteracts the poison, damn you!"

"*Never.*"

"Leo?" A new voice entered the fray. He turned swiftly to see Amelia, Win, and Beatrix at the threshold. They were staring at him as if he'd gone mad.

Amelia spoke with admirable composure. "I have two questions, Leo: Why did you send for me, and why are you having an argument with the wardrobe?"

"Harrow's in there," he told her.

Her expression changed. "Why?"

"I'm trying to make him tell me how to counteract an overdose of digitalin powder." He glared vengefully at the wardrobe. "And I'll *kill* him if he doesn't."

"Who's taken an overdose?" Amelia demanded, her face draining of color. "Is someone ill? Who is it?"

"It was meant for Merripen," Leo said in a low voice, reaching out to steady her before he continued. "But Cam took it by mistake."

A strangled cry escaped her. "Oh God. Where is he?"

"The Romany campsite. Merripen's with him."

Tears sprang to Amelia's eyes. "I must go to him."

"You won't do him any good without the antidote."

Win brushed by them, striding to the bedside table. Moving with swift deliberation, she picked up an oil lamp and a tin matchbox and brought them to the wardrobe.

"What are you doing?" Leo demanded, wondering if she had lost her wits entirely. "He doesn't need a lamp, Win."

Ignoring him, Win removed the glass fount and tossed it to the bed. She did the same with the brass wick burner, exposing the oil reservoir. Without hesitation, she poured the lamp oil over the front of the wardrobe. The pungent odor of highly flammable paraffin spread through the room.

"Have you lost your mind?" Leo demanded, astonished not only by her actions, but also by her calm demeanor.

"I have a matchbox, Julian," she said. "Tell me what to give Cam, or I'll set the wardrobe on fire."

"You wouldn't dare," Harrow cried.

"Win," Leo said, "you'll burn the entire damned house down just after it's been rebuilt. Give me the bloody matchbox."

She shook her head resolutely.

"Are we starting a new springtime ritual?" Leo demanded. "The annual burning-of-the-manse? Come to your senses, Win."

Win turned from him and glared at the wardrobe door. "I was told, Julian, that you killed your first wife. Possibly by poison. And now knowing what you've done to my brother-in-law, I believe it. And if you don't help us, I'm going to roast you like Welsh rarebit." She opened the matchbox.

Realizing she couldn't possibly be serious, Leo decided to back her bluff. "I'm begging you, Win," he said theatrically, "don't do this. There's no need to—*Christ!*" He broke off, aghast, as Win struck a match and set the wardrobe on fire.

It wasn't a bluff, he thought dazedly. She actually intended to broil the bastard.

At the first bright, curling blossom of flame, there was a terrified cry from inside the wardrobe. "All right! Let me out! *Let me out!* It's tannic acid. *Tannic acid.* It's in my medical case—let me *out!*"

"Very well, Leo," Win said, a bit breathless. "You may extinguish the fire."

In spite of the panic that raced through his veins, Leo couldn't suppress a choked laugh. She spoke as if she'd asked him to snuff a candle, not put out a large flaming piece of furniture. Tearing off his coat, he rushed forward and beat wildly at the wardrobe door. "You're a madwoman," he told Win as he passed her.

"He wouldn't have told us otherwise," Win said.

Alerted by the commotion, a few servants appeared, one of them a footman who removed his own coat and hastened to assist Leo. Meanwhile, the women were rummaging for Harrow's black leather medical case.

"Isn't tannic acid the same as tea?" Amelia asked, her hands shaking as she fumbled with the latch.

"No, Mrs. Rohan," the governess said. "I believe the doctor was referring to tannic acid from oak leaves, not the tannins from tea." She reached out quickly as Amelia nearly overturned the case. "Careful, don't knock it over. He doesn't label his vials." Opening the hard-sided case, they found rows of neatly arranged glass tubes containing powders and liquids. Although the vials themselves were not marked, the slots they fit in had been identified with inked letters. Poring over the vials, Miss Marks extracted one filled with pale yellow-brown powder. "This one."

Win took it from her. "Let me take it to them," she said. "I know where the campsite is. And Leo's busy putting out the wardrobe."

"I'll take the vial to Cam," Amelia said vehemently. "He's my husband."

"Yes. And you're carrying his child. If you fell while riding at a breakneck pace, he'd never forgive you for risking the baby."

Amelia gave her an anguished glance, her mouth trembling. She nodded and croaked, "*Hurry*, Win."

"CAN YOU MAKE A SLING WITH CANVAS AND POLES?" KEV asked the *rom phuro*. "I must get him back to Ramsay House."

The tribe leader nodded at once. He called out to a small group waiting near the entrance of the *vardo*, gave a few instructions, and they disappeared instantly. Turning back to Kev, he murmured, "We'll have something put together in a few minutes."

Kev nodded, staring down at Cam's ashen face. He wasn't well by any means, but at least the threat of convulsions and heart failure had been temporarily staved off. Robbed of his usual expressiveness, Cam looked young and defenseless.

It was peculiar to think they were brothers but had never known about each other. *I always knew I wasn't supposed to be alone,* Cam had told him on the day they discovered their blood ties. Kev had felt the same. He just hadn't been able to say it.

Taking up a cloth, he blotted the film of sweat from Cam's face. A quiet whimper escaped Cam's lips, as if he were a child having a nightmare.

"It's all right, *phral*," Kev murmured, putting a hand on Cam's chest, testing the slow and lurching heartbeat. "You'll be well soon. I won't leave you."

"You're close to your brother," the *rom phuro* said softly. "That's good. Do you have other family?"

"We live with *gadje*," Kev said, his gaze daring the man to disapprove. The tribe leader's expression remained friendly and interested. "One of them is his wife."

Kev glanced down at Cam again, thinking he was starting to look worse. "If they need help making the sling to carry him—"

"No, my men are fast. They'll be finished soon. But it must be made well and strong to carry a man of his size."

Cam's hands were twitching, his long fingers plucking fitfully at the blanket they had put over him. Kev took the cold hand and gripped it firmly, trying to warm and reassure him.

The *rom phuro* stared at the visible tattoo on Cam's forearm, the striking lines of the winged black horse.

"When did you meet Rohan?" he asked quietly.

Kev gave him a startled glance, his protective grasp tightening on Cam's hand. "How do you know his name?"

The tribe leader smiled, his eyes warm. "I know other things as well. You and your brother were separated for a long time." He touched the tattoo with his forefinger. "This mark . . . you have one, too."

Kev stared at him without blinking.

The sounds of a minor to-do filtered in from outside, and someone came pushing through the doorway. A woman. With surprise and concern, Kev saw the gleam of white-blond hair. "Win!" he exclaimed, carefully setting Cam's hand down and coming to his feet. Unfortunately, he couldn't stand fully upright in the low-ceilinged vehicle. "Did you come alone? It's not safe."

"I'm trying to help," she said, and hurried into the *vardo*. One of her hands was ungloved, and she was holding something in it. She didn't spare a glance for the *rom phuro,* she was so intent on reaching Kev. "Here. *Here.*" She was breathing hard from riding at a breakneck pace, her cheeks flushed.

"What is it?" Kev took the object from her, his free hand coming to her back. He looked down at a small vial filled with powder.

"The antidote," she said. "Give it to him quickly."

"How do you know it's the right medicine?"

"I made Dr. Harrow tell me."

"He might have been lying."

"No. I'm sure he wasn't, because at that moment he was nearly on f—I mean, he was under duress."

Waiting for another doctor wasn't an option. From the look of it, Cam didn't have time to spare.

Kev proceeded to dissolve ten grains in a small quantity of water, reasoning it was better to start with a weak solution rather than overdose Cam with yet another poison. He eased Cam to a sitting position, supporting him against his chest.

Delirious and unsteady, Cam made a protesting noise as the movement sent new pain through his cramping muscles.

Win reached out to grip Cam's jaw, rubbing the frozen muscles and prying his mouth open. After tilting the liquid from a spoon into his mouth, she stroked his throat and coaxed him to swallow. Cam downed the medicine and shuddered, and rested heavily against Kev.

"Thank you," Win whispered, stroking back Cam's damp hair, flattening her palm against the side of his cold face. "You'll be better now. Lie easy and let it take effect." Kev thought she had never looked as lovely as she did at that moment, her tender and grave. After a few minutes Win said quietly, "His color is improving."

And so was his breathing, the jagged rhythm lengthening and slowing. Kev felt Cam's body relax, the clenched muscles softening as the active principles of the digitalis were neutralized.

Cam stirred as if he were waking from a long sleep. "Amelia," he said in an opium-slurred voice.

Win took one of his hands in hers. "She's quite well and waiting for you at home, dear."

"Home," he repeated with an exhausted nod.

Kev lowered Cam carefully to the berth and looked over him in sharp assessment. The masklike pallor was vanishing second by second, healthy color returning to his face. The rapidity of the transformation was no less than astonishing.

The amber eyes cracked open, and Cam focused on Kev. "Merripen," he said in a tone so lucid that Kev was overcome with relief.

"Yes, *phral*?"

"Am I dead?"

"No."

"I must be."

"Why?" Kev asked, amused.

"Because . . ." Cam paused to moisten his dry lips. "Because you're *smiling* . . . and I just saw my cousin Noah over there."

Chapter Twenty-two

The *rom phuro* came forward and knelt beside the berth. "Hello, Camlo," he murmured.

Cam regarded him with puzzled wonder. "Noah. You're older."

His cousin chuckled. "The last time I saw you, you barely came up to my chest. And now you look as if you could be a head taller than me."

"You never came back for me."

Kev broke in tautly. "And you never told him he had a brother."

Noah's smile turned regretful. "I couldn't do either of those things. For your own protection." His gaze swerved in Kev's direction. "We were told you were dead, Kev. I'm glad to find out we were wrong. How did you survive? Where have you been living?"

Kev scowled at him. "Never mind about that. Cam has spent *years* looking for you. Looking for answers. You tell him the truth now, about why he was sent away from the tribe, and what that cursed tattoo means. And don't leave anything out."

Noah looked mildly taken aback by Kev's autocratic manner. As the leader of the *vitsa,* he wasn't used to taking orders from anyone.

"He's always like this," Cam told Noah. "You get used to it."

Reaching beneath the berth, Noah pulled out a wooden box and began to rummage through its contents.

"What do you know about our Irish blood?" Kev demanded. "What was our father's name?"

"There is much I don't know," Noah admitted. Finding what he had evidently been looking for, he pulled it from the box and looked at Cam. "But our grandmother told me as much as she could on her deathbed. And she gave me this—"

He raised a tarnished silver knife.

In a lightning-swift reflex, Kev seized his cousin's wrist in a crushing grip. Win gave a startled cry, while Cam tried unsuccessfully to lift up on his elbows.

Noah stared hard into Kev's eyes. "Peace, cousin. I would never harm Camlo." He let his hand open. "Take it from me. It belongs to you; it was your father's. His name was Brian Cole."

Kev took the knife and slowly released Noah's wrist. He stared at the object, a boot knife with a double-edged fixed blade approximately four inches long. The handle was silver, with engraving on the bolsters. It looked old and costly. But what amazed Kev was the engraving on the flat of the handle . . . a perfect stylized symbol of the Irish *pooka.*

He showed it to Cam, who stopped breathing for a moment.

"You are Cameron and Kevin Cole," Noah said. "That horse symbol was the mark of your family . . . it was in their crest. When we separated the two of you, it was decided to put the mark on both of you. Not only to identify you, but also as an appeal to the second son of Moshto, to preserve and protect you."

"Who is Moshto?" Win asked softly.

"The god of all things good," Kev said, hearing his own dazed voice as if it belonged to someone else.

"I looked . . ." Cam began, still staring at the knife, and shook his head as if the effort to explain was too much.

Kev spoke for him. "My brother hired heraldic experts and researchers to go through books of Irish family crests, and they never found this symbol."

"I believe the Coles removed the *pooka* from the crest about three hundred years ago, when the English king declared himself the head of the Church of Ireland. The *pooka* was a pagan symbol. No doubt they thought it might threaten their standing in the reformed church. But the Coles still had a fondness for it. I remember your father wore a big silver ring engraved with the *pooka*."

Glancing at his brother, Kev sensed that Cam felt just as he did, that it was like having been in a closed room all his life and suddenly having a door opened.

"Your father, Brian," Noah continued, "was the son of Lord Cavan, an Irish representative peer in the British House of Lords. Brian was his only heir. But your father made a mistake—he fell in love with a Romany girl named Sonya. Quite beautiful. He married her in defiance of his family and hers. They lived away from everyone long enough for Sonya to have two sons. She died in childbed when Cam was born."

"I always thought my mother died having me," Kev said softly. "I never knew about a younger brother."

"It was after the second son that she went to God." Noah looked pensive. "I was old enough to remember the day Cole brought the two of you to our grandmother. He told *Mami* it had been a misery trying to live in both worlds, and he wanted to go back where he belonged. So he left his children with the tribe and never returned."

"Why did you separate us?" Cam asked, still looking exhausted but far more like his usual self.

Noah stood in an easy movement and went to the corner near the stove. As he replied, he made tea with deft assurance, measuring out dried leaves into a little pot of steaming water. "After a few years, your father remarried. And then other *vitsas* told us that some *gadjos* had come looking for the boys, offering money for information and doing violence when Roma wouldn't tell them anything. We realized your father wanted to get rid of his half-breed sons, who were the legitimate heirs to the title. He had a new wife who would bear him white children."

"And we were in the way," Kev said grimly.

"Yes." Noah strained the tea into a pot. He poured a cup, added sugar, and brought it to Cam. "Have some, Camlo. You need to wash the poison out."

Cam sat up and leaned his back against the wall. He took the cup in a wobbling grip and sipped the hot brew carefully. "So to reduce the chances of both of us being found," he said, "you kept me and gave Kev to our uncle."

"Yes, to Uncle Pov." Noah frowned and averted his gaze from Kev. "Sonya was his favorite sister. We thought he would be a good protector. No one expected him to blame her children for her death."

"He hated *gadje*," Kev said in a low voice. "That was something else he held against me."

"After we heard that you'd died," Noah continued, "we thought it too dangerous to keep Cam. So I brought him to London and helped him find work."

"In a gaming club?" Cam asked, a note of skepticism in his voice.

"Sometimes the best hiding places are in plain sight," came Noah's prosaic reply.

Cam was shaking his head ruefully. "I'll bet half of London has seen my tattoo. It's a wonder Lord Cavan never caught wind of it."

Noah frowned. "I told you to keep it covered."

"No, you didn't."

"I did," Noah insisted, and put his hand on his forehead. "Ah, Moshto, you were never good at listening."

WIN SAT QUIETLY BESIDE KEV. SHE LISTENED AS THE MEN talked, but she was also busy taking in her surroundings. The *vardo* was old but scrupulously maintained, the interior clean and tidy. A faint, crisp scent of smoke seemed to emanate from the walls, the boards seasoned by thousands of meals that had been prepared in the vehicle. Children played outside, laughing and quarreling. It was odd to think that this caravan was a family's only refuge from the outside world. The lack of sheltered space compelled the tribe to live mostly out-of-doors. As foreign as that idea was, there was a kind of freedom in it.

Win wondered how Kev felt at having his past finally uncovered, the mysteries explained. He seemed perfectly calm and controlled, but it would be unsettling for anyone to experience this.

". . . with all the time that has passed," Cam was saying, "I wonder if there's still danger to us? And is our father still alive?"

"It would be easy enough to find out," Kev replied, and added darkly, "He probably wouldn't be happy to find out that *we* were still alive."

"You're more or less safe as long as you remain Roma," Noah said. "But if Kev reveals himself as the Cavan heir and tries to claim the title, there could be trouble."

Kev looked scornful. "Why would I do that?"

Noah shrugged. "No Rom would. But you're half-*gadjo*."

"I don't want the title or what comes with it," Kev said firmly. "And I want nothing to do with the Coles, Lord Cavan, or anything Irish."

"And ignore half of yourself?" Cam asked.

"I've spent most of life not knowing about my Irish half. It will be no problem to ignore it now."

A Romany boy came to the *vardo* to let them know that the sling had been finished.

"Good," Kev said decisively. "I'll help him outside, and he—"

"Oh no," Cam said, scowling. "I'm not going to let myself be carried in a sling to Ramsay House."

Kev gave him a sardonic glance. "How are you planning to get there?"

"I'll ride."

Kev's brows lowered. "You're in no condition to ride. You'll fall and break your neck."

"I can do it," Cam insisted stubbornly. "It's not far."

"You'll fall off the horse!"

"I'm not going in the bloody sling. It would frighten Amelia."

"You're not worried about Amelia nearly so much as your pride. You'll be carried, and that's final."

"Bugger you," Cam snapped.

Win and Noah exchanged a worried glance. The brothers seemed ready to come to blows.

"As the tribe leader, I may be able to help settle the dispute—" Noah began diplomatically.

Kev and Cam answered at the same time. "*No.*"

"Kev," Win murmured, "could he ride with me? He could sit behind me and hold on to me for balance."

"All right," Cam said immediately. "We'll do that."

Kev scowled at them both.

"I'll go as well," Noah said with a slight smile. "On my own horse. I'll tell my son to saddle him." He paused. "Can you stay a few minutes more? You have many cousins to meet. And I have a wife and children I want to show to you, and—"

"Later," Kev said. "I need to take my brother to his wife without delay."

"Very well."

After Noah had gone outside, Cam stared absently into the dregs of his tea.

"What are you thinking?" Kev asked.

"I'm wondering if our father had children by his second wife. And if so, how many? Are there half brothers and half sisters we don't know about?"

Kev's eyes narrowed. "What does it matter?"

"They're our family."

Kev smacked his forehead with his hand in an uncharacteristically dramatic gesture. "We have the Hathaways, and we have more than a dozen Roma running around outside who are all cousins. How much more damn family do you want?"

Cam only smiled.

Not surprisingly, Ramsay House was in an uproar. The Hathaways, Miss Marks, the servants, the parish constable, and a doctor were crowded in the entrance hall. Since the short ride had depleted Cam's strength, he was forced to lean on Kev as they went inside.

They were immediately surrounded by the family, with Amelia pushing her way to Cam. She gave a sob of relief as she reached him, fighting tears as she ran frantic hands over his chest and face. Letting go of Kev, Cam wrapped his arms around Amelia, his head lowering nearly to her shoulder. They were quiet amid the tumult, breathing in measured sighs. One of her hands crept up to his hair, fingers closing in the dark layers. Cam murmured something against her ear, some soft and private reassurance. And he swayed, causing Amelia to grip him more tightly, while Kev took his shoulders to steady him.

Cam lifted his head and looked down at his wife. "I drank some coffee this morning," he told her. "It didn't sit well."

"So I heard," Amelia said, smoothing her hand across his chest. She threw a worried glance at Kev. "His gaze isn't focused."

"He's higher than a jackdaw," Kev said. "We gave him raw opium to calm his heart before Win brought the antidote."

"Let's take him upstairs," Amelia said, using the edge of her sleeve to scrub her wet eyes. Raising her voice, she spoke to the elderly bearded man who stood outside the group. "Dr. Martin, please accompany us upstairs and you will be able to evaluate my husband's condition in private."

"I don't need a doctor," Cam protested.

"I wouldn't complain if I were you," Amelia told him. "I'm tempted to send for at least a half a dozen doctors, not to mention specialists from London." She paused long enough to glance at Noah. "Are you the gentleman who helped Cam? We're indebted to you, sir."

"Anything for my cousin," Noah replied.

"Cousin?" Amelia repeated, her eyes widening.

"I'll explain upstairs," Cam said, lurching forward. Immediately Noah took one side and Kev the other, and they half dragged, half carried Cam up the grand staircase. The family followed, exclaiming and talking excitedly.

"These are the noisiest *gadje* I've ever met," Noah remarked.

"This is nothing," Cam said, panting with effort as they ascended. "They're usually much worse."

"*Moshto!*" Noah exclaimed, shaking his head.

Cam's privacy was marginal at best as he was deposited on the bed and Dr. Martin began to examine him. Amelia made a few attempts to shoo family and relatives from the room, but they kept pushing back in to see what was happening. After Dr. Martin tested Cam's pulse, pupil size, lung sounds, skin moisture and color, and reflexes, he pronounced that in his opinion, the patient would make a full recovery. If there were any troublesome symptoms during the night, such as heart palpitations, they could be soothed by imbibing a drop of laudanum in a glass of water.

The doctor also said that Cam should be given clear liquids and bland foods and that he should rest for the next two or three days. He would probably experience a loss of appetite and almost certainly some headaches, but when he was fully rid of the last traces of digitalis, everything would be back to normal.

Satisfied that his brother was in good condition, Kev went to Leo in the corner of the room and asked softly, "Where is Harrow?"

"Out of your reach," Leo said. "They took him off to the jail just before you returned. And don't bother trying to reach him. I've already told the constable not to let you within a hundred yards of the pinfold."

"I would think you'd like to reach him first," Kev said. "You despise him as much as I do."

"True. But I believe in letting due process take its course. And I don't want Beatrix to be disappointed. She's hoping for a trial."

"Why?"

"She wants to present Dodger as a witness."

Lifting his gaze heavenward, Kev went to the corner of the room and leaned his back against the wall. He listened as the Hathaways exchanged their versions of the day's events, and the constable asked questions and even Noah became involved, which then led to the revelation of Kev's and Cam's pasts, and so forth. Information flew in animated volleys. It was never going to end.

Cam, in the meantime, seemed more than content to lie on the bed while Amelia fussed over him. She smoothed his hair, gave him water, straightened the covers, and caressed him repeatedly. He yawned and struggled to keep his eyes open, and turned his cheek into the pillow.

Kev turned his attention to Win, who was sitting in a chair near the bed, her back straight as always. She looked serene and proper, except for the loose strands of hair that had slipped from their pins. One would never guess that she was capable of setting a wardrobe on fire. With Harrow in it. As Leo had put it, the deed may not have reflected well on her intelligence, but one had to give her points for ruthlessness. And it had gotten the job done.

Kev had been rather sorry to hear that Leo had pulled Harrow out, smoky but unharmed.

Eventually Amelia announced that the visit must soon come to an end, as Cam needed to rest. The constable departed, as did Noah and the servants, until the only ones left were immediate family.

"I think Dodger's under the bed." Beatrix dropped to the floor and peered under it.

"I want my garter back," Miss Marks said darkly, lowering to the carpet beside Beatrix. Leo regarded Miss Marks with covert interest.

Meanwhile, Kev wondered what to do about Win.

It seemed that love was working through him inexorably, more pervasive than oxygen from air. He was so damn tired of trying to resist it.

Cam had been right. He could never predict what would happen. All he could do was love her.

Very well.

He would give in to it, to her, without trying to qualify or control anything. He would surrender. He would come out of the shadows for good. He took a long, slow breath and let it out.

I love you, he thought, looking at Win. *I love every part of you, every thought and word . . . the entire complex, fascinating bundle of all the things you are. I want you with ten different kinds of need at once. I love all the seasons of you, the way you are now, the thought of how much more beautiful you'll be in the decades to come. I love you for being the answer to every question my heart could ask.*

And it seemed so easy once he capitulated. It seemed natural and right.

Kev wasn't certain if he was surrendering to Win or to his own passion for her. Only that there was no more holding back. He would take her. And he would give her everything he had, every part of his soul, even the broken pieces.

He stared at her without blinking, half fearing that the slightest movement on his part might precipitate actions he wouldn't be able to control. He might simply launch toward her and drag her from the room. The anticipation was delicious, knowing he was going to have her soon.

Drawn by his gaze, Win glanced at him. Whatever she saw in his face caused her to blink and color. Her fingers fluttered to her throat as if to soothe her own racing pulse. That made it worse, his desperate need to hold her. He wanted to taste the blush on her skin, absorb the heat with his lips and tongue. His most primitive impulses began firing, and he stared intently at her, willing her to move.

"Excuse me," Win murmured, standing in a graceful motion that impassioned him beyond sanity. Her fingers made that little flutter again, this time near her hip, as if her nerves were jumping, and he wanted to seize her hand and bring it to his mouth. "I will leave you to rest, dear Cam," she said unsteadily.

"Thank you," Cam mumbled from the bed. "Little sister . . . thank you for . . ."

As he hesitated, Win said with a quick little grin, "I understand. Sleep well."

The grin faded as she risked a glance at Kev. Seemingly inspired by a healthy sense of self-preservation, she left the room hastily.

Before another second had passed, Kev was at her heels.

"Where are they going in such a hurry?" Beatrix asked from beneath the bed.

"Backgammon," Miss Marks said hastily. "I'm sure I heard them planning to play a round or two of backgammon."

"So did I," Leo commented.

"It must be fun to play backgammon in bed," Beatrix said innocently, and snickered.

IT IMMEDIATELY BECAME CLEAR THAT IT WOULD NOT BE AN arbitration of words, but of something far more primal. Win went swiftly and silently toward her room, not daring to look back, though she had to be aware that he was following closely. The carpeted floor absorbed the sound of their footsteps, one set hurried, the other predatory.

Still without looking at him, Win stopped at her closed door, her fingers curling around the handle. "My terms," she said softly. "As I told them to you before."

Kev understood. And he loved her for her stubborn strength. He shouldered the door open, nudged her into the room, and closed them both inside. He turned the key in the lock.

Before she could take another breath, he had secured her head in his hands and he was kissing her, opening her mouth with his. The taste of her inflamed him, but he went slowly, letting the kiss become a deep, luscious gnawing, sucking to draw her tongue into his mouth. He felt her body mold against his, or at least as much as her heavy skirts would allow.

"Don't lie to me again," he said gruffly.

"I won't. I promise." Her blue eyes were brilliant with love.

He wanted to touch the soft flesh beneath the layers of cloth and lace. Urgently he began to pull at the back of her gown, unfastening the ornate buttons, tearing off the resistant ones, tugging his way down until the whole mass of it loosened and she was gasping. Crushing the billows with his feet, he stood with her in the deep folds of the ruined gown as if they were at the heart of some gigantic flower. He reached for her undergarments, untying the ribbon at the neckline of her chemise and the tapes of her drawers. She moved to help him, her slender arms and legs emerging from the crumpled linen.

Her pink-and-white nakedness was breathtaking. The slim, strong calves were sheathed in white stockings tied with plain garters. It was unbearably erotic, the contrast of luxurious warm flesh and prim cotton. Intending to unfasten the garters, he knelt in the soft heaps of pink muslin. She crooked one of her knees to help him, the shy offering distracting him insanely. He bent to kiss her knees, the silken inner thighs, and when she murmured and tried to evade him, he gripped her hips and kept her still. He nuzzled gently into the pale curls, into the fragrance and softness of her, and stroked with his tongue. Her moan was soft and pleading.

"My knees are shaking," she whispered. "I'll fall."

Kev ignored her, searching deeper. He lapped and sucked

and ate her, his hunger surging. She pulsed around him as he thrust his tongue deeply, and he felt the response resonating through her. Breathing into the plush folds, he licked one side of her, then the other, then straight between to the place where her pleasure centered. Entranced, he stroked her over and over, until her hands were gripped in his hair and her hips urged forward in tight undulations.

He took his mouth from her and came to his feet. Her face was dazed, her gaze distant, as if she didn't quite see him. She was trembling from head to toe. His arms slid around her, gathering her naked body against his clothed one. Lowering his mouth to the tender crook of her neck and shoulder, he kissed her skin and touched his tongue to it. At the same time, he reached for the fastenings of his trousers and undid them.

She clung to him as he lifted her and pressed her against the wall, one of his arms protecting her back from abrasion. Her body was supple and surprisingly light, her spine tensing as he eased her weight down and she realized what he meant to do. He settled her fully, watching her mouth draw into a soft *O* of surprise as she was impaled in a slow, sure glide.

The stockinged legs clamped around his waist, and she held on to him desperately, as if they were on the tossing deck of a storm-ravaged ship. But Kev kept her pinned and secure, letting his hips do the work. The band of his trousers slipped free of the anchoring clips of his braces, and the garment slid to his knees. He averted his face to hide a brief grin, momentarily considering the idea of stopping to take his clothes off . . . but it felt too good, the lust rising until it eclipsed every trace of amusement.

Win let out a little breath with each wet, rolling drive. He paused to kiss her hungrily while he reached down with gentle fingers and teased the swollen lips apart. When the rhythm resumed, his thrusts grazed the little peak with each firm inward plunge. Her eyes closed as if in sleep, her intimate flesh working on him in frantic pulses.

In and in, rooting deeper, driving her further to the edge. Her legs went tight around his waist. She stiffened and cried out against his mouth, and he sealed the kiss to keep her quiet. But little moans slipped through, her pleasure shuddering and overrunning. As Kev buried himself in the lovely milking softness, ecstasy shot through him, spilling hotly, gradually easing into helpless throbs.

Gasping, Kev lowered her legs to the floor. They stood, their bodies moistly locked, their mouths rubbing in soothing kisses and sighs. Win's hands slipped beneath his shirt and moved over his sides and back in gentle benediction. He withdrew from her carefully and stripped the clothes from his steaming body.

Somehow they made it to the bed. Kev dragged them both into the cocoon of wool and linen and nestled Win against him. The scents of her, of both of them, rose in a light saline perfume to his nose. He breathed it in, stirred by the mingled fragrance.

"*Me voliv tu,*" he whispered, and brushed her smiling lips with his. "When a Rom tells his woman 'I love you,' the meaning of the word is never chaste. It expresses desire as well."

That pleased Win. "*Me voliv tu,*" she whispered back. "Kev . . ."

"Yes, love?"

"How does one marry the Romany way?"

"Join hands in front of witnesses and make a vow. But we'll do it the way of the *gadje,* too. And every other way I can think of." He took off her garters, and unrolled her stockings one by one, and wiggled her toes individually until she made a little purring sound.

Reaching for him, she guided his head to her breasts, arching upward invitingly. He obliged her, taking a pink tip into his mouth and circling it with his tongue until it contracted into a tender-hard bud.

"I don't know what to do now," Win said, her voice languid.

"Just lie there. I'll take care of the rest."

She chuckled. "No, what I meant was, what do people do when they finally reach their happy ever after?"

"They make it a long one." He fondled her other breast, gently shaping the roundness with his fingers.

"Do you believe in happy ever after?" she persisted, gasping a little as he gave her a playful nip.

"As in the children's tales? No."

"You don't?"

He shook his head. "I believe in two people loving each other." A smile curved his lips. "Finding pleasure in ordinary moments. Walking together. Arguing over things like the timing of an egg, or how to manage the servants, or the size of the butcher's bill. Going to bed each night and waking up together each morning." Lifting his head, he cradled the side of her face in his hand. "I've always started every day by going to the window for a glimpse of the sky. But now I won't have to."

"Why not?" she asked softly.

"Because I'll see the blue of your eyes instead."

"How romantic you are," she murmured with a grin, kissing him gently. "But don't worry. I won't tell anyone."

Kev began to make love to her again, so engrossed that he didn't seem to notice the slight rattle of the door lock.

Peeking over his shoulder, Win saw the long, skinny body of Beatrix's ferret stretching upward to pluck the key from the lock. Her lips parted to say something, but then Kev kissed her and spread her thighs. *Later,* she thought giddily, ignoring the sight of Dodger squeezing beneath the door with the key in his mouth. Perhaps later would be a better time to mention it.

And soon she forgot all about the key.

Chapter Twenty-three

Although the *pliashka,* or betrothal ceremony, tradition-
ally went on for several days, Kev had decided it would
last for only one night, especially when he saw the crowd of
high-spirited Roma pouring into the house.

In Kev's opinion, Cam was enjoying the betrothal process a bit too much. A few days earlier he had made a show
of presenting himself as Kev's representative to negotiate a
bride-price with Leo. The two of them had mock-debated
the respective merits of groom and bride, and how much
the groom's family should pay for the privilege of acquir-
ing a treasure such as Win. Both sides had concluded, with
great hilarity, that it was worth a fortune to find a woman
who would tolerate Kev. All this while Kev sat and scowled
at them, which seemed to amuse the addlepates even more.

With that formality concluded, the *pliashka* had been
quickly planned and enthusiastically undertaken. A huge feast
would be served after the betrothal ceremony, featuring roast
pig and beef joints, all manner of fowl, and platters of pota-
toes fried with herbs and garlic

Music from guitars and violins filled the ballroom while
the guests gathered in a circle. Dressed in a loose white shirt,

leather breeches and boots, and a red sash knotted at the side of his waist, Cam went to the center of the circle. He held a bottle wrapped in bright silk, the neck of it wrapped with a string of gold coins. He gestured for everyone to be quiet, and the music obligingly settled into a lull.

Enjoying the tumult of the gathering, Win stood beside Kev and listened as Cam made several remarks in Romany. Unlike his brother, Kev wore *gadjo* attire, except that he'd left off a cravat and collar. The glimpses of his smooth brown throat beguiled Win. She wanted to put her lips to the spot where a steady pulse lurked. Instead, she contented herself with the discreet brush of his fingers against hers. Kev was rarely given to public demonstrations. In private, however . . .

She felt his hand wrap slowly around hers, his thumb stroking the tender flesh just above her palm.

Finishing the short speech, Cam came to Win. Deftly he removed the coins from the bottle and placed them around her neck. They were heavy and cool against her skin, settling in a jubilant clatter. The necklace advertised that she was now betrothed, and any man other than Kev would now approach her at his own peril.

Smiling, Cam embraced Win firmly, murmured something affectionate in her ear, and gave her the bottle to drink from. She took a cautious sip of strong red wine and gave the bottle to Kev, who drank after her. Meanwhile, wine in liberally filled goblets was given to all the guests. There were various cries of "*Sastimos,*" or good health, as they drank in honor of the betrothed couple.

The celebration began in earnest. Music flared to life, and the goblets were quickly drained.

"Dance with me," Kev surprised her by murmuring.

Win shook her head with a little laugh, watching couples twirl and move sinuously around each other. Women used their hands in shimmering motions around their bodies, while men stomped with their heels and clapped their hands, and they circled each other, holding each other's gaze as long as possible.

"I don't know how," Win said.

Kev stood behind her and crossed his arm around her front, drawing her back against him. Another surprise. She had never known him to touch her so openly. But amid the goings-on, it seemed no one noticed or cared.

His voice was hot and soft in her ear. "Watch for a moment. You see how little space is needed? How they circle each other? When Roma dance they lift their hands to the sky, but they stomp their feet to express connection to the earth. And to earthly passions." He smiled against her cheek and gently turned her to face him. "Come," he murmured, and hooked his hand around her waist to urge her forward.

Win followed him shyly, fascinated by a side of him she hadn't seen before. She wouldn't have expected him to be this self-assured, drawing her into the dance with animal grace, watching her with a wicked gleam in his eyes. He coaxed her to raise her arms, to snap her fingers, even to swish her skirts at him as he moved around her. She couldn't stop giggling. They were dancing, and he was so good at it, turning it into a cat-and-mouse game.

She twirled in a circle, and he caught her around the waist, pulling her close for one scalding moment. The scent of his skin, the movement of his chest against hers, filled her with intense desire. Leaning his forehead against hers, Kev stared at her until she was drowning in the depths of his eyes, as dark and bright as hellfire.

"Kiss me," she whispered unevenly, not caring where they were or who might see them.

A smile touched his lips. "If I start now, I won't be able to stop."

The spell was broken by an apologetic throat clearing from nearby.

Kev glanced to the side where Cam was standing.

Cam's face was carefully blank. "My apologies for interrupting. But Mrs. Barnstable just came to me with the news that an unexpected guest has arrived."

"More family?"

"Yes. But not from the Romany side."

Kev shook his head, perplexed. "Who is it?"

Cam swallowed visibly. "Lord Cavan. Our grandfather."

IT WAS DECIDED THAT CAM AND KEV WOULD MEET CAVAN with no other family members present. While the *pliashka* continued in full vigor, the brothers withdrew to the library and waited. Two footmen dashed back and forth, bringing in objects from a carriage outside: cushions, a velvet-covered footstool, a lap blanket, a foot warmer, a silver tray bearing a cup. After a multitude of preparations was made, Cavan was announced by one of the footmen, and he entered the room.

The old Irish earl was physically unimposing, old and small and slight. But Cavan had the presence of a deposed monarch, a faded grandeur textured with weary pride. A frill of white hair had been cut to lie against his ruddy scalp, and a goatee framed his chin like a lion's whiskers. His shrewd brown eyes assessed the young men dispassionately.

"You are Kevin and Cameron Cole," he said rather than asked in a flowing Anglo-Irish accent, the syllables graceful and lightly arid.

Neither of them replied.

"Who is the elder?" Cavan asked, seating himself in an upholstered chair. A footman immediately arranged a footstool beneath his heels.

"He is," Cam said, helpfully pointing at Kev, while Kev

gave him a sideways glare. Ignoring the look, Cam asked casually, "How did you find us, my lord?"

"A heraldic master recently approached me in London with the information that you had hired him to research a particular design. He had identified it as the Coles' ancient mark. When he showed me the sketch he'd made of the tattoo on your arm, I knew at once who you were and why you wanted the design researched."

"And why is that?" Cam asked softly.

"You want social and financial gain. You wish to be recognized as a Cole."

Cam smiled without amusement. "Believe me, my lord, I wish for neither gain nor recognition. I merely wanted to know who I was." His eyes flashed with annoyance. "And I paid that bloody researcher to give the information to *me*, not to take it to you first. I'll take a strip out of his hide for that."

"Why do you want to see us?" Kev asked brusquely. "We want nothing from you, and you'll get nothing from us."

"First, it may interest you to learn that your father is dead. He expired a matter of weeks ago as a result of a riding accident. He was always inept with horses. It eventually proved the death of him."

"Our condolences," Cam said flatly.

Kev merely shrugged.

"*This* is how you receive the death of your sire?" Cavan demanded.

"I'm afraid we didn't know our sire well enough to display a more satisfying reaction," Kev said sardonically. "Pardon the lack of tears."

"I want something other than tears from you."

"Why am I alarmed?" Cam wondered aloud.

"My son left behind a wife and three daughters. No sons, except for you." The earl made a temple of his pale, knotty fingers. "The lands are entailed to male issue only, and there are none to be found in the Cole line in any of its branches. As things stand at present, the Cavan title and all that is attached to it will become extinct upon my death." His jaw hardened. "I will not let the patrimony be lost forever merely because of your father's inability to reproduce."

Kev arched a brow. "I'd hardly call two sons and three daughters an inability to reproduce."

"Daughters are of no consequence. And the two of you are half-breeds. One can hardly claim that your father succeeded in furthering the family's interests. But no matter. The situation must be tolerated. You are, after all, legitimate issue." An acrid pause. "You're my only heirs."

The vast cultural chasm between them couldn't have been clearer. Had Lord Cavan bestowed such bounty on any other kind of man, it would have been received with nothing short of ecstasy. But presenting a pair of Roma with the prospect of lofty social status and vast material riches hadn't elicited the kind of reaction Cavan had anticipated.

Instead, they were both singularly—rather maddeningly—unimpressed.

Cavan spoke irritably to Kev. "You are Viscount Mornington, inheritor of the Mornington estate in County Meath. Upon my death you will also receive Knotford Castle in Hillsborough, the Fairwall estate in County Down, and Watford Park in Hertfordshire. Does that mean anything to you?"

"Not really."

"You're the last in line," Cavan persisted, his voice sharpening, "to a family that traces its origins to a thane created by Athelstan in the year 936. Moreover, you're the heir to an earldom of more distinguished lineage than three-quarters of all the peerages of the Crown. Have you *nothing* to say? Do you even understand the remarkable good fortune that has befallen you?"

Kev understood all of that. He also understood that an imperious old bastard who had once wanted him dead now expected him to fall over himself because of an unasked-for inheritance. "Weren't you once searching for us with the intention of dispatching us like a pair of unwanted pups?"

Cavan scowled. "That question has no relevance to the matter at hand."

"That means yes," Cam told Kev.

"Circumstances have altered," Cavan said. "You've become more useful to me alive than dead. A fact for which you should be appreciative."

Kev was about to tell Cavan where he could shove his estates and titles when Cam shouldered Kev roughly aside.

"Excuse us," Cam said over his shoulder to Cavan, "while we have a brotherly chat."

"I don't want to chat," Kev muttered.

"For once would you listen to me?" Cam asked, his tone mild, his eyes narrowed. "*Just* once?"

Folding his arms over his chest, Kev inclined his head.

"Before you toss him out on his withered old arse," Cam said softly, "you may want to consider a few points. First, he's not going to live long. Second, the tenants on the Cavan lands are probably in desperate need of management and help. There's much you could do for them, even if you choose to reside in England and oversee the entailment from afar. Third, think about Win. She would have wealth and position. No one would dare slight a countess. Fourth, we apparently have a stepmother and three half sisters with no one to care for them after the old man turns up his toes. Fifth—"

"There's no need for a fifth," Kev said. "I'll do it."

"What?" Cam raised his brows. "You agree with me?"

"Yes."

The old man regarded Kev with a sour expression. "You

seem to be under the misapprehension that I was giving you a choice. I wasn't *asking* for anything. I was *informing* you of your good fortune and your duty. Furthermore—"

"Well, it's all settled," Cam interrupted hastily. "Lord Cavan, you now have an heir and a spare. I propose that we all take leave of each other to contemplate our new circumstances. If it pleases you, my lord, we'll meet again on the morrow to discuss the particulars."

"Agreed."

"May we offer you and your servants lodging for the night?"

"I've already arranged to bestow my company on Lord and Lady Westcliff. No doubt you have heard of the earl. A most distinguished gentleman. I was acquainted with his father."

"Yes," Cam said gravely. "We've heard of Westcliff."

Cavan's lips thinned. "I suppose it will fall to me to introduce you to him someday." He slid a disdainful glance over both of them and snapped his fingers. The two footmen swiftly collected the items they had brought in. Rising from the chair, Cavan allowed his coat to be draped over his narrow shoulders. With a morose shake of his head, he looked at Kev and muttered, "As I frequently remind myself, you're better than nothing. Until tomorrow."

The moment Cavan left the parlor, Cam went to the sideboard and poured two brandies. Looking bemused, he gave one to Kev. "What are you thinking?" he asked.

"He seems like the kind of grandfather we'd have," Kev said, and Cam nearly choked on his liquor as he laughed.

MUCH LATER THAT EVENING WIN LAY DRAPED ACROSS KEV'S chest, her hair streaming over him like trickles of moonlight. She was naked except for the coin necklace. Gently disentangling it from her hair, Kev pulled the necklace off and set it on the nightstand.

"Don't," she protested.

"Why?"

"I like wearing it. It reminds me that I'm betrothed."

"I'll remind you," he murmured, rolling until she lay in the crook of his arm. "As often as you need."

She smiled up at him, touching the edges of his lips with exploring fingertips. "Are you sorry that Lord Cavan found you?"

He kissed the delicate pads of her fingers as he pondered the question. "No," he said eventually. "He's a bitter old cretin, and I wouldn't care to spend a great deal of time in his company. But now I have the answers to things I wondered about for my entire life. And . . ." He hesitated before admitting sheepishly, "I wouldn't mind being the Earl of Cavan someday."

"You wouldn't?" She regarded him with a quizzical grin.

Kev nodded. "I think I might be good at it," he confessed.

"So do I," Win said in a conspiratorial whisper. "In fact, I think a great many people will be surprised by your absolute brilliance at telling them what to do."

Kev grinned and kissed her forehead. "Did I tell you the last thing Cavan said before he left this evening? He said he frequently reminds himself that I'm better than nothing."

"What a silly old windbag," Win said, slipping her hand behind Kev's neck. "And he's utterly wrong," she added, just before their lips met. "Because, my love, you're better than *everything*."

For a long time afterward, there were no words.

Epilogue

According to the doctor, it had been the first delivery during which he had more concerns for the expectant father than the mother and infant.

Kev had conducted himself quite well during the majority of Win's confinement, though he had tended to overreact at times. The commonplace aches and twinges of pregnancy had caused nothing short of alarm, and there had been many a time that he had insisted on sending for the doctor for no good reason at all, despite Win's exasperated refusal.

But parts of it had been marvelous. The quiet evenings when Kev had rested beside her with his hands flattened on her stomach to feel the baby kicking. The summer afternoons when they had walked through Hampshire, feeling at one with nature and the life teeming everywhere. The unexpected discovery that marriage, rather than weighting their relationship with seriousness, had somehow given life a sense of lightness, of buoyancy.

Kev laughed often now. He was far more apt to tease, to play, to show his affection openly. He seemed to adore Cam and Amelia's son, Rye, and readily joined in the family's general spoiling of the dark-haired infant.

However, during the last few weeks of Win's pregnancy, Kev hadn't been able to conceal his growing dread. And when Win's labor had begun in the middle of the night, he had gone into a state of subdued terror that nothing would soothe. Every birthing pain, every sharp gasp she took, had caused Kev to turn ashen, until Win had realized she was faring far better than he.

"Please," Win had whispered to Amelia privately, "do something with him."

And so Cam and Leo had dragged Kev from the bedroom down to the library, plying him with good Irish whiskey for most of the day.

When the future Earl of Cavan was born, the doctor said he was perfectly healthy, and that he wished all births could go so well. Amelia and Poppy bathed Win and dressed her in a fresh nightgown, and cleaned and swaddled the baby in soft cotton. Only then was Kev allowed to come up to see them. After ascertaining for himself that his wife and child were both in good condition, Kev wept in unashamed relief and promptly fell asleep on the bed beside Win.

She glanced from her handsome, slumbering husband to the baby in her arms. Her son was small but perfectly formed, fair-skinned, with a remarkable quantity of black hair. His eye color was indeterminate at the moment, but Win thought his eyes would eventually turn out to be blue. She lifted him higher against her chest until her lips were close to his miniature ear. And in accordance with Romany tradition, she told him his secret name.

"You are Andrei," she whispered. It was a name for a warrior. A son of Kev could be no less. "Your *gadjo* name is Jason Cole. And your tribal name . . ." She paused thoughtfully.

"Jado," came her husband's drowsy voice from beside her.

Win looked down at Kev and reached out to stroke his thick,

dark hair. The lines on his face were gone, and he looked relaxed and content.

"That's perfect." She let her hand linger in his hair. "*Ov yilo isi?*" she asked him gently.

"Yes," Kev said, answering in English. "There is heart here."

And Win smiled as he sat up to kiss her.

Tempt Me
at Twilight

Chapter One

Her chances of a decent marriage were about to be dashed—and all because of a ferret.

Unfortunately Poppy Hathaway had pursued Dodger halfway through the Rutledge Hotel before she recalled an important fact: to a ferret, a straight line included six zigs and seven zags.

"Dodger," Poppy said desperately. "Come back. I'll give you a biscuit, any of my hair ribbons, *anything!* Oh, I'm going to make a *scarf* out of you . . ."

As soon as she caught her sister's pet, Poppy swore she was going to alert the management of the Rutledge that Beatrix was harboring wild creatures in their family suite, which was definitely against hotel policy. Of course, that might cause the entire Hathaway clan to be forcibly removed from the premises.

At the moment, Poppy didn't care.

Dodger had stolen a love letter that had been sent to her from Michael Bayning, and nothing in the world mattered except retrieving it. All the situation needed was for Dodger to hide the blasted thing in some public place where it would be discovered. And then Poppy's chances of marrying a respectable and perfectly wonderful young man would be forever lost.

Dodger hurried through the luxurious hallways of the Rutledge Hotel in a sinuous lope, staying just out of reach. The letter was clamped in his long front teeth.

As she dashed after him, Poppy prayed that she would not be seen. No matter how reputable the hotel, a respectable young woman should never have left her suite unescorted. However, Miss Marks, her companion, was still abed. And Beatrix had gone for an early morning ride with their sister, Amelia.

"You're going to pay for this, Dodger!"

The mischievous creature thought everything in the world was for his own amusement. No basket or container would go without being overturned or investigated, no stocking or comb or handkerchief could be left alone. Dodger stole personal items and left them in heaps beneath chairs and sofas, and he took naps in drawers of clean clothes, and worst of all, he was so entertaining in his naughtiness that the entire Hathaway family was inclined to overlook his behavior.

Whenever Poppy objected to the ferret's outrageous antics, Beatrix was always apologetic and promised that Dodger would never do it again, and she seemed genuinely surprised when Dodger didn't heed her earnest lectures. And because Poppy loved her younger sister, she had tried to endure living with the obnoxious pet.

This time, however, Dodger had gone too far.

The ferret paused at a corner, checked to make certain he was still being chased, and in his happy excitement, he did a little war dance, a series of sideways hops that expressed pure delight. Even now, when Poppy wanted to murder him, she couldn't help but acknowledge that he was adorable. "You're still going to die," she told him, approaching him in as unthreatening a manner as possible. "Give me the letter, Dodger."

The ferret streaked past a colonnaded lightwell that admitted sunshine from overhead and sent it down three floors to the mezzanine level. Grimly, Poppy wondered how far she was going to have to chase him. He could cover quite a lot of territory, and the Rutledge was massive, occupying five full blocks in the theater district.

"This," she muttered beneath her breath, "is what happens when you're a Hathaway. Misadventures . . . wild animals . . . house fires . . . curses . . . scandals . . ."

Poppy loved her family dearly, but she longed for the kind of quiet, normal life that didn't seem possible for a Hathaway. She wanted peace. Predictability.

Dodger ran through the doorway of the third-floor steward's offices, which belonged to Mr. Brimbley. The steward was an elderly man with a full white mustache, the ends neatly waxed into points. As the Hathaways had stayed at the Rutledge many times in the past, Poppy knew that Brimbley reported every detail of what occurred on his floor to his superiors. If the steward found out what she was after, the letter would be confiscated, and Poppy's relationship with Michael would be exposed. And Michael's father, Lord Andover, would never approve of the match if there were even one whiff of impropriety attached to it.

Poppy caught her breath and backed up against the wall as Brimbley exited his offices with two of the Rutledge staff. ". . . go to the front office at once, Harkins," the steward was saying. "I want you to investigate the matter of Mr. W's room charges. He has a history of claiming that charges are incorrect when they are, in fact, accurate. From now on, I think it best to have him sign a receipt whenever a charge is made."

"Yes, Mr. Brimbley." The three men proceeded along the hallway, away from Poppy.

Cautiously, she crept to the doorway of the offices and peeked around the jamb. The two connected rooms appeared to be unoccupied. *"Dodger,"* she whispered urgently, and saw him scurry beneath a chair. "Dodger, do come here!"

Which, of course, produced more excited hopping and dancing.

Biting her lower lip, Poppy went across the threshold. The main office room was generously sized, furnished with a massive desk piled high with ledgers and papers. An armchair upholstered in burgundy leather had been pushed up against the desk, while another was positioned near an empty fireplace with a marble mantel.

Dodger waited beside the desk, regarding Poppy with bright eyes. His whiskers twitched above the coveted letter. He held very still, holding Poppy's gaze as she inched toward him.

"That's right," she soothed, extending her hand slowly. "What a good boy, a lovely boy . . . wait right there, and I'll take the letter and carry you back to our suite, and give you—*Drat!*"

Just before she could grasp the letter, Dodger had slithered beneath the desk with it.

Red with fury, Poppy glanced around the room in search of something, *anything,* she could use to poke Dodger from his hiding place. Spying a candlestick in a silver holder on the mantel, she tried to pull it down. But the candle wouldn't budge. The silver holder had been affixed to the mantel.

Before Poppy's astonished eyes, the entire back of the fireplace rotated noiselessly. She gasped at the mechanical wizardry of the door as it revolved with a smooth automated motion. What had appeared to be solid brick was nothing but a textured façade.

Gleefully, Dodger darted from the desk and went through the opening.

"Bother," Poppy said breathlessly. "Dodger, don't you dare!"

But the ferret paid no heed. And to make matters worse, she could hear the rumble of Mr. Brimbley's voice as he returned to the room. ". . . of course Mr. Rutledge must be informed. Put it in the report. And by all means don't forget—"

With no time to consider her options or the consequences, Poppy dashed through the fireplace, and the door closed behind her.

She was engulfed in near darkness as she waited, straining to hear what was happening inside the office. Apparently she had not been detected. Mr. Brimbley continued his conversation, something about reports and housekeeping concerns.

It occurred to Poppy that she might have to wait for a long time before the steward left the office again. Or she would have to find another way out. Of course, she could simply go back through the fireplace and announce her presence to Mr. Brimbley. However, she couldn't begin to imagine how much explaining she would have to do, and how embarrassing it would be.

Turning, Poppy discerned that she was in a long passageway, with a source of diffused light coming from somewhere overhead. She looked upward. The passage was illuminated by a daylight shaft, similar to the ones that ancient Egyptians had used to determine the positioning of stars and planets.

She could hear the ferret creeping somewhere nearby. "Well, Dodger," she muttered, "you got us into this. Why don't you help me find a door?"

Obligingly Dodger advanced along the passageway and disappeared into the shadows. Poppy heaved a sigh and followed. She refused to panic, having learned during the Hathaways' many brushes with calamity that losing one's head never helped a situation.

As Poppy made her way through the darkness, she kept her fingertips against the wall to maintain her bearings. She had gone only a few yards when she heard a scraping noise. Freezing in place, Poppy waited and listened intently.

All was quiet.

But her nerves prickled with awareness and her heart began to drum as she saw the glow of yellow lamplight ahead. And then it was extinguished.

She was not alone in the passageway.

The footsteps came closer, closer, with the swift purpose of a predator. Someone was heading right for her.

Now, Poppy decided, was the appropriate time to panic. Whirling around in full-scale alarm, she dashed back the way she had come. Being chased by unknown people in dark corridors was a novel experience even for a Hathaway. She cursed her heavy skirts, grabbing them up in frantic handfuls as she tried to run. But the person who chased her was much too fast to be eluded.

A cry escaped her as she was caught up in a brutal, expert grip. It was a man—a large one—and he seized her in a way that arched her back against his chest. One of his hands pressed her head sharply to the side.

"You should know," came a low, chilling voice close to her ear, "that with just a bit more pressure than this, I could snap your neck. Tell me your name, and what you're doing in here."

Chapter Two

Poppy could scarcely think above the blood rushing in her ears and the pain of his tight grasp. The stranger's chest was very hard behind her. "This is a mistake," she managed to say. "Please—"

He forced her head farther to the side until she felt a cruel pinch of the nerves in the joint between her neck and shoulder. "Your name," he insisted gently.

"Poppy Hathaway," she gasped. "I'm so sorry. I didn't mean to—"

"Poppy?" His hold loosened.

"Yes." Why had he said her name as if he knew her? "Are you . . . you must be one of the hotel staff?"

He ignored the question. One of his hands coasted lightly over her arms and her front as if he were searching for something. Her heart threshed like the wing beats of a small bird.

"Don't," she gasped between fragmented breaths, arching away from his touch.

"Why are you in here?" He turned her to face him. No one of Poppy's acquaintance had ever handled her so familiarly. They were close enough to the overhead lightwell that Poppy could see the outline of hard, lean features and the glitter of deep-set eyes.

Fighting to catch her breath, Poppy winced at the sharp ache in her neck. She reached for it and tried to soothe the pain as she spoke. "I was . . . I was chasing a ferret, and the fireplace in Mr. Brimbley's office opened, and we went through it and then I tried to find another way out."

Nonsensical as the explanation was, the stranger sorted through it efficiently. "A ferret? One of your sister's pets?"

"Yes," she said, bewildered. She rubbed her neck and winced. "But how did you know . . . have we met before? No, please don't touch me, I . . . *ouch*!"

He had turned her around and had put his hand on the side of her neck. "Be still." His touch was deft and sure as he massaged the tender nerve. "Let me help."

Quivering, Poppy endured his kneading, probing fingers and wondered if she were at the mercy of a madman. He pressed harder, exacting a sensation that was neither pleasure nor pain but some unfamiliar mingling of the two. She made a sound of distress, writhing helplessly. To her surprise, the burn of the pinched nerve eased, and her rigid muscles went lax with relief. She went still and let out a long breath, her head dropping.

"Better?" he asked, using both hands now, his thumbs stroking the back of her neck.

Thoroughly unnerved, Poppy tried to step away from him, but his hands clamped on her shoulders instantly. She cleared her throat and attempted a dignified tone. "Sir, I—I would appreciate it if you would guide me out of here. My family will reward you. No questions will be—"

"Of course." He released her slowly. "No one ever uses this passageway without my permission. I assumed anyone in here was up to no good."

The comments resembled an apology, although his tone wasn't regretful in the least.

"I assure you, I had no intention of doing anything other than retrieving this atrocious animal." She felt Dodger rustling near the hem of her skirts.

The stranger bent and scooped up the ferret. Holding Dodger by the scruff of his neck, he handed him to Poppy.

"Thank you." The ferret's supple body went limp and compliant in Poppy's grasp. As she might have expected, the letter was gone. "Dodger, you blasted thief—where is it? What have you done with it?"

"What are you looking for?"

"A letter," Poppy said tensely. "Dodger stole it and carried it in here . . . it must be somewhere nearby."

"It will be found later."

"But it's important."

"Obviously, if you've gone to such trouble to recover it. Come with me."

Reluctantly Poppy murmured her assent and allowed him to take her elbow. "Where are we going?"

There was no reply.

"I would prefer this to be kept private," Poppy ventured.

"I'm sure you would."

"May I rely on your discretion, sir? I must avoid scandal at all cost."

"Young women who wish to avoid scandal should probably stay in their hotel suites," he pointed out unhelpfully.

"I was perfectly content to stay in my room," Poppy protested. "It was only because of Dodger that I had to leave. I must have my letter back. And I'm certain my family will compensate you for your trouble, if you would—"

"No need."

He found his way through the shadow-tricked passageway

with no difficulty at all, his grip on Poppy's elbow gentle but inexorable.

Finally the stranger stopped and turned to a place in the wall, and pushed a door open. "Go in."

Hesitantly Poppy preceded him into a well-lit room, a sort of parlor, with a row of Palladian windows overlooking the street. A heavy oak drafting table occupied one side of the room, and bookshelves lined nearly every inch of wall space. There was a pleasant mixture of scents in the air— candle wax and vellum and ink and book dust—it smelled like her father's old study.

Poppy turned toward the stranger, who had come into the room and closed the concealed door.

It was difficult to ascertain his age—he appeared to be on the early side of his thirties, but there was an air of hard-bitten worldliness about him, a sense that he had seen enough of life to cease being surprised by anything. He had heavy, well-cut hair, black as midnight, and a fair complexion with dark brows that stood out in striking contrast. He was as handsome as Lucifer, his features straight and defined, the mouth brooding. But he looked like a man who perhaps took everything—including himself—a bit too seriously.

Poppy felt herself flush as she stared into a pair of remark- able eyes . . . intense cool green with dark rims, shadowed by bristly black lashes. His gaze seemed to take her in, consum- ing every detail. She noticed faint shadows beneath his eyes, but they did nothing to impair his hard-faced good looks.

A gentleman would have uttered some pleasantry, some- thing reassuring, but the stranger remained silent.

She had to say something, anything, to break the tension. "The smell of books and candle wax," she remarked inanely, "it reminds me of my father's study."

The man stepped toward her, and Poppy shrank back

reflexively. They both went still. It seemed that questions filled the air between them as if they had been written in invisible ink.

"Your father passed away some time ago, I believe." His voice matched the rest of him, polished, dark, inflexible. He had an interesting accent, not fully British, the vowels flat and open, the *r*'s heavy.

Poppy gave a bewildered nod.

"And your mother soon after," he added.

"How . . . how do you know that?"

"It's my business to know as much about the hotel guests as possible."

Dodger wriggled in her grasp. Poppy bent to set him down. The ferret pranced to an oversized chair near a small hearth, and settled deep into the velvet upholstery.

Poppy brought herself to look at the stranger again. He was dressed in beautiful dark clothes, tailored with sophisticated looseness. Fine garments, but he wore a simple black cravat with no pins, and there were no gold buttons on his shirt, or any other ornamentation that would proclaim him as a gentleman of means. Only a plain watch chain at the front of his gray waistcoat.

"You sound like an American," she said.

"Buffalo, New York," he replied. "But I've lived here for a while."

"Are you employed by Mr. Rutledge?" she asked cautiously.

A single nod was her answer.

"You are one of his managers, I suppose?"

His face was inscrutable. "Something like that."

She began to inch toward the door. "Then I will leave you to your labors, Mister . . ."

"You'll need a proper companion to walk back with you."

Poppy considered that. Should she ask him to send for her companion? No . . . Miss Marks was probably still sleeping. It had been a difficult night for her. Miss Marks was sometimes prone to nightmares that left her shaky and exhausted the next day. It didn't happen often, but when it did, Poppy and Beatrix tried to let her rest as much as possible afterward.

The stranger contemplated her for a moment. "Shall I send for a housemaid to accompany you?"

Poppy's first inclination was to agree. But she didn't want to wait here with him, even for a few minutes. She didn't trust him in the least.

As he saw her indecision, his mouth twisted sardonically. "If I were going to molest you," he pointed out, "I would have done so by now."

Her flush deepened at his bluntness. "So you say. But for all I know, you could be a very *slow* molester."

He looked away for a moment, and when he glanced back at her, his eyes were bright with amusement. "You're safe, Miss Hathaway." His voice was rich with unspent laughter. "Really. Let me send for a maid."

The glow of humor changed his face, imparting such warmth and charm that Poppy was almost startled. She felt her heart begin to pump some new and agreeable feeling through her body.

As she watched him go to the bellpull, Poppy recalled the problem of the missing letter. "Sir, while we wait, would you be so kind as to look for the letter that was lost in the passageway? I must have it back."

"Why?" he asked, returning to her.

"Personal reasons," Poppy said shortly.

"Is it from a man?"

She did her best to deliver the kind of withering glance she had seen Miss Marks give to importunate gentlemen. "That is none of your concern."

"Everything that occurs in this hotel is my concern." He paused, studying her. "It is from a man, or you would have said otherwise."

Frowning, Poppy turned her back to him. She went to look more closely at one of the many shelves lined with peculiar objects.

She discovered a gilded, enameled samovar, a large knife in a beaded sheath, collections of primitive stone carvings and pottery vessels, an Egyptian headrest, exotic coins, boxes made of every conceivable material, what looked like an iron sword with a rusted blade, and a Venetian glass reading stone.

"What room is this?" Poppy couldn't help asking.

"Mr. Rutledge's curiosities room. He collected many of the objects, others are gifts from foreign visitors. Have a look if you like."

Poppy was intrigued, reflecting on the large contingent of foreigners among the hotel guests, including European royalty, nobility, and members of the *corps diplomatique*. No doubt some unusual gifts had been presented to Mr. Rutledge.

Browsing among the shelves, Poppy paused to examine a jeweled silver figurine of a horse, its hooves extended in mid-gallop. "How lovely."

"A gift from the Crown Prince Yizhu of China," the man behind her said. "A Celestial horse."

Fascinated, Poppy ran a fingertip along the figure's back. "Now the prince has been crowned as the Emperor Xianfeng," she said. "A rather ironic ruling name, isn't it?"

Coming to stand beside her, the stranger glanced at her alertly. "Why do you say that?"

"Because it means 'universal prosperity.' And that is certainly not the case, considering the internal rebellions he is facing."

"I'd say the challenges from Europe are an even greater danger to him, at present."

"Yes," Poppy said ruefully, nudging the figurine back into place. "One wonders how long Chinese sovereignty can last against such an onslaught."

Her companion was standing close enough that she could detect the scents of pressed linen and shaving soap. He stared at her intently. "I know very few women who can discuss international politics."

She felt color rise in her cheeks. "My family has rather unusual conversations around the supper table. At least, they're unusual in that my sisters and I always take part. My companion says it's perfectly all right to do that at home, but she has advised me not to appear too learned when I'm out in society. It tends to drive away suitors."

"You'll have to be careful, then," he said softly, smiling. "It would be a shame for some intelligent comment to slip out at the wrong moment."

Poppy was relieved when she heard a discreet tap at the door. The maid had come sooner than she had expected. The stranger went to answer. Opening the door a crack, he murmured something to the maid, who bobbed a curtsey and disappeared.

"Where is she going?" Poppy asked, nonplussed. "She was supposed to escort me to my suite."

"I sent her to fetch a tea tray."

Poppy was momentarily speechless. "Sir, I can't have tea with you."

"It won't take long. They'll send it up on one of the food lifts."

"That doesn't matter. Because even if I did have the time, I *can't*! I'm sure you are well aware of how improper it would be."

"Nearly as improper as sneaking through the hotel unescorted," he agreed smoothly, and she scowled.

"I was not sneaking, I was chasing a ferret." Hearing herself make such a ridiculous statement, she felt her color rise. She attempted a dignified tone. "The situation was not at all of my making. And I will be in *very . . . serious . . . trouble . . .* if I am not returned to my room soon. If we wait much longer, you may find yourself involved in a scandal, which I am certain Mr. Rutledge would not approve of."

"True."

"Then please call the maid back."

"Too late. We'll have to wait until she comes with the tea."

Poppy heaved a sigh. "This has been a *most* difficult morning." Glancing at the ferret, she saw bits of fluff and clumps of horsehair being tossed in the air, and she blanched. "*No,* Dodger!"

"What is it?" the man asked, following as Poppy raced toward the busy ferret.

"He's eating your chair," she said miserably, scooping up the ferret. "Or rather, Mr. Rutledge's chair. He's trying to make a nest for himself. I'm so sorry." She stared at the gaping hole in the thick, luxurious velvet upholstery. "I promise you, my family will pay for the damage."

"It's all right," the man said. "There's a monthly allotment in the hotel budget for repairs."

Lowering to her haunches—not an easy feat when one was wearing stay laces and stiffened petticoats—Poppy grabbed bits of fluff and tried to stuff them back into the hole. "If necessary, I will provide a written statement to explain how this happened."

"What about your reputation?" the stranger asked gently, reaching down to pull her to a standing position.

"My reputation is nothing compared to a man's livelihood.

You might be sacked for this. You undoubtedly have a family to support—a wife and children—and whereas I could survive the disgrace, you might not be able to secure a new position."

"That is very kind of you," he said, taking the ferret from Poppy's grasp and depositing him back on the chair. "But I have no family. And I can't be sacked."

"Dodger," Poppy said anxiously, as bits of fluff went flying again. Clearly the ferret was having a grand time.

"The chair is already ruined. Let him have at it."

Poppy was bemused by the stranger's easy consignment of an expensive piece of hotel furniture to a ferret's mischief. "You," she said distinctly, "are a bit different from the other managers here."

"You're a bit different yourself."

That elicited a wry smile from her. "So I've been told."

The sky had turned the color of pewter. A heavy drizzle fell to the gravel-covered paving blocks of the street, tamping down the pungent dust that had been stirred by passing vehicles.

Taking care not to be seen from the street, Poppy went to the side of one window and watched pedestrians scatter. Some methodically unfolded umbrellas and continued walking.

Costermongers crowded the thoroughfare, hawking their wares with impatient cries. They sold everything imaginable: ropes of onions and braces of dead game, teapots, flowers, matches, and caged larks and nightingales. This last presented frequent problems to the Hathaways, as Beatrix was determined to rescue every living creature she saw. Many a bird had been reluctantly purchased by their brother-in-law, Mr. Rohan, and set free at their country estate. Rohan swore that by now he had purchased half the avian population in Hampshire.

Turning from the window, Poppy saw that the stranger

had settled his shoulder against one of the bookshelves and folded his arms across his chest. He was watching her as if puzzling what to make of her. Despite his relaxed posture, Poppy had the unnerving sense that if she tried to bolt, he would catch her in an instant.

"Why aren't you betrothed to anyone?" he asked with startling directness. "You've been out in society for two, three years?"

"Three," Poppy said, feeling more than a little defensive.

"Your family is one of means—one would assume you have a generous dowry on the table. Your brother is a viscount—another advantage. Why haven't you married?"

"Do you always ask such personal questions of people you've just met?" Poppy asked in amazement.

"Not always. But I find you . . . interesting."

She considered the question he had put to her, and shrugged. "I wouldn't want any of the gentlemen I've met during the past three years. None of them are remotely appealing."

"What kind of man appeals to you?"

"Someone with whom I could share a quiet, ordinary life."

"Most young women dream of excitement and romance."

She smiled wryly. "I suppose I have a great appreciation for the mundane."

"Has it occurred to you that London is the wrong place to seek a quiet, ordinary life?"

"Of course. But I'm not in a position to look in the right places." She should have stopped there. There was no need to explain more. But it was one of Poppy's failings that she loved conversation, and like Dodger facing a drawer full of garters, she couldn't resist indulging. "The problem began when my brother, Lord Ramsay, inherited the title."

The stranger's brows lifted. "That was a problem?"

"Oh, yes," Poppy said earnestly. "You see, none of the

Hathaways were prepared for it. We were distant cousins of the previous Lord Ramsay. The title only came to Leo because of a series of untimely deaths. The Hathaways had no knowledge of etiquette—we knew nothing of the ways of the upper classes. We were happy in Primrose Place."

She paused to sort through the comforting memories of her childhood: the cheerful cottage with its thatched roof, the flower garden where her father had tended his prized Apothecary's Roses, the pair of lop-eared Belgian rabbits who had lived in a hutch near the back doorstep, the piles of books in every corner. Now the abandoned cottage was in ruins and the garden lay fallow.

"But there's never any going back, is there," she said rather than asked. She bent to regard an object on a lower shelf. "What is this? Oh. An astrolabe." She picked up an intricate brass disk that contained engraved plates, the rim notched with degrees of arc.

"You know what an astrolabe is?" the stranger asked, following her.

"Yes, of course. A tool used by astronomers and navigators. Also astrologers." Poppy inspected the tiny star chart etched in one of the disks. "This is Persian. I would estimate it to be about five hundred years old."

"Five hundred and twelve," he said slowly.

Poppy couldn't repress a satisfied grin. "My father was a medieval scholar. He had a collection of these. He even taught me how to make one out of wood, string, and a nail." She dialed the disks carefully. "What is the date of your birth?"

The stranger hesitated before replying, as if he disliked having to give information about himself. "November the first."

"Then you were born under Scorpius's reign," she said, turning the astrolabe over in her hands.

"You believe in astrology?" he asked, his tone edged with derision.

"Why shouldn't I?"

"It has no scientific basis."

"My father always encouraged me to be open-minded about such matters." She played a fingertip across the star chart, and looked up at him with a sly smile. "Scorpions are quite ruthless, you know. That is why Artemis bid one of them to kill her foe Orion. And as a reward, she set the scorpion up in the sky."

"I'm not ruthless. I merely do whatever it takes to achieve my goals."

"That's not ruthless?" Poppy asked, laughing.

"The word implies cruelty."

"And you're not cruel?"

"Only when necessary."

Poppy's amusement dissolved. "Cruelty is never necessary."

"You haven't seen much of the world, if you can say that."

Deciding not to pursue the subject, Poppy stood on her toes to view the contents of another shelf. It featured an intriguing collection of what looked like tinplate toys. "What are these?"

"Automata."

"What are they for?"

He reached up, lifted one of the painted metal objects, and gave it to her.

Holding the machine by its circular base, Poppy examined it carefully. There were a group of tiny racehorses, each on its own track. Seeing the end of a pull cord on the side of the base, Poppy tugged it gently. That set off a series of inner mechanisms, including a flywheel, which sent the little horses spinning around the track as if they were racing.

Poppy laughed in delight. "How clever! I wish my sister Beatrix could see this. Where did it come from?"

"Mr. Rutledge fashions them in his spare time, as a means of relaxing."

"May I see another?" Poppy was enchanted by the objects, which were not toys so much as miniature feats of engineering. There was Admiral Nelson on a little tossing ship, a monkey climbing a banana tree, a cat playing with mice, and a lion tamer who cracked his whip while the lion shook his head repeatedly.

Seeming to enjoy Poppy's interest, the stranger showed her a picture on the wall, a tableau of couples waltzing at a ball. Before her wide eyes, the picture seemed to come to life, gentlemen guiding their partners smoothly across the floor. "Good heavens," Poppy said in wonder. "How is it done?"

"A clockwork mechanism." He removed the picture from the wall and displayed the open back. "There it is, attached to a flywheel by that drive band. And the pins work these wire levers . . . here . . . which in turn activate the other levers."

"Remarkable!" In her enthusiasm, Poppy forgot to be guarded or cautious. "Obviously Mr. Rutledge is mechanically gifted. This brings to mind a biography I read recently, about Roger Bacon, a Franciscan friar of the Middle Ages. My father was a great admirer of his work. Friar Bacon did a great deal of mechanical experimentation, which of course led some people to accuse him of sorcery. It was said that he once built a mechanical bronze head, which—" Poppy stopped abruptly, realizing she had been chattering. "There, you see? *This* is what I do at balls and soirées. It's one of the reasons I'm not sought after."

He had begun to smile. "I thought talking was encouraged at such affairs."

"Not my sort of talking."

Tap. Tap. Tap.

They both turned at the sound. The maid had arrived.

"I must go," Poppy said uneasily. "My companion will be very distressed if she wakes to find me missing."

The dark-haired stranger contemplated her for what seemed a very long time. "I'm not finished with you yet," he said with stunning casualness. As if no one ever refused him anything. As if he planned to keep her with him for as long as he wished.

Poppy took a deep breath. "Nevertheless, I am leaving," she said calmly, and went to the door.

He reached it at the same time she did, one hand flattening against the door panel.

Alarm jolted through her, and she turned to face him. A swift, frantic throbbing awakened in her throat and wrists and the backs of her knees. He was standing much too close, his long, hard body nearly touching hers. She shrank against the wall.

"Before you go," he said softly, "a word of advice: It's not safe for a young woman to wander alone through the hotel. Don't take such a risk again."

Poppy stiffened. "It's a reputable hotel," she said. "I have nothing to fear."

"You might." A flirtatious glint had entered his eye. "You could be kissed by a stranger."

Poppy gave him a questioning glance.

Slowly he bent over her, giving her time to object. She surprised herself by holding still, her pulse racing with excitement as his mouth came gently to hers. The kiss was so subtle in its demand that she wasn't aware of the moment her own lips parted. His hands came to her jaw, cradling, angling her face upward.

One arm slid around her, bringing her body fully against his, and the feel of him was hard and richly stimulating. With every breath, she drew in an enticing scent, an incense of amber and musk, starched linen and male skin. His mouth was so tenderly persuasive, erotic, imparting messages of peril and promise. His lips slid to her throat and he hunted for her pulse, working his way downward, layering sensations like silken gauze until she shivered and arched away from him.

The stranger held her chin carefully, forcing her to look at him. They both went still. As Poppy met his searching gaze, she saw a hint of uncertainty, as if he had just made some unwelcome discovery.

He let go of her with great care and opened the door. "Bring it in," he told the maid, who waited at the threshold with a large silver tea tray.

The servant obeyed quickly, too well trained to evince curiosity about Poppy's presence in the room.

The man went to retrieve Dodger, who had fallen asleep in his chair. Returning with the drowsy ferret, he gave it to Poppy. She took Dodger with an inarticulate murmur, cradling him against her midriff. The ferret's eyes remained closed, lids completely concealed in the black mask that crossed his face. She felt the tapping of his tiny heartbeat beneath her fingertips, the silkiness of the white undercoat beneath the overlying guard hairs.

"Will there be anything else, sir?" the maid asked.

"Yes. I want you to accompany this lady to her suite. And inform me when she is safely returned."

"Yes, Mr. Rutledge."

Mr. Rutledge?

Poppy felt her heart stop. She looked back at the stranger. Deviltry glittered in his green eyes. He seemed to relish her open astonishment.

Harry Rutledge . . . the mysterious and reclusive owner of the hotel. Who was nothing at all as she had imagined him to be.

Bewildered and mortified, Poppy turned from him. She crossed the threshold and heard the door close, the latch clicking smoothly shut. How wicked he was, to have amused himself at her expense! She consoled herself with the knowledge that she would never see him again.

And she went down the hallway with the housemaid . . . never suspecting that the course of her entire life had just changed.

Chapter Three

Harry went to stare at the fire in the hearth.

"Poppy Hathaway," he whispered as if it were a magical incantation.

He had seen her from a distance on two occasions, once when she had been entering a carriage at the front of the hotel, and once at a ball held at the Rutledge. Harry hadn't attended the event, but he had watched for a few minutes from a vantage point at an upper floor balcony. Despite her finespun beauty and mahogany hair, he hadn't spared her a second thought.

Meeting her in person, however, had been a revelation.

Harry began to lower himself into a chair and noted the shredded velvet and clumps of stuffing left by the ferret.

A reluctant smile curved his lips as he moved to take the other chair.

Poppy. How artless she had been, chatting casually about astrolabes and Franciscan monks as she had browsed among his treasures. She had thrown out words in bright clusters, as if she were scattering confetti. She had radiated a kind of cheery astuteness that should have been annoying, but instead it had given him unexpected pleasure. There was something about her, something . . . it was what the French called *esprit,* a liveliness of mind and spirit. And that face . . . innocent and knowing, and open.

He wanted her.

Usually Jay Harry Rutledge was given something before it ever occurred to him to want it. In his busy, well-regulated life, meals arrived before he was hungry, cravats were replaced before they had shown any signs of wear, reports were placed on his desk before he asked for them. And women were everywhere, and always available, and every last one of them told him what she assumed he wanted to hear.

Harry was aware that it was high time to marry. At least, most of his acquaintances assured him that it was high time, although he suspected it was because they had all put that particular noose around their own necks and wanted him to do the same. He had considered it without enthusiasm. But Poppy Hathaway was too compelling to resist.

Reaching into his left coat sleeve, Harry tugged out Poppy's letter. It was addressed to her from the Honourable Michael Bayning. He considered what he knew of the young man. Bayning had attended Winchester, where his studious nature had acquitted him well. Unlike other young men at university, Bayning had never gotten into debt, and there had been no scandals. More than a few women were attracted by his good looks and even more by the title and fortune he would inherit someday.

Frowning, Harry began to read.

Dearest love,

As I reflected on our last conversation, I kissed the place on my wrist where your tears fell. How can you not believe that I weep the same tears every day and night that we're apart? You have made it impossible for me to think of anyone or anything but you. I am mad with ardor for you, don't doubt it in the least.

If you will be patient only a bit longer, I will soon find the opportunity to approach my father. Once he understands how utterly and completely I adore you, I know he will give his approval to our union. We have a close bond, Father and I, and he has indicated that he wishes to see me as happy in my marriage as he was with my mother, God rest her soul. How she would have enjoyed you, Poppy . . . your sensible, happy nature, your love of family and home. If only she were here to help persuade my father that there could be no better wife for me than you.

Wait for me, Poppy, as I am waiting for you.

I am, as always, forever under your spell,

—M

A quiet, scoffing breath escaped him. Harry stared into the hearth, his face still, his mind busy with schemes. A log broke, part of it falling from the grate with a plush *pop*, sending out fresh heat and white sparks. Bayning wanted Poppy to wait? Unfathomable, when every cell in Harry's body was charged with impatient desire.

Closing the note with the care of a man handling valuable currency, Harry slipped it into his coat pocket.

ONCE POPPY WAS SAFELY INSIDE THE FAMILY SUITE, SHE settled Dodger into his favorite sleeping place, a basket that her sister Beatrix had lined with soft cloth. The ferret remained asleep, as limp as a rag.

Standing, Poppy leaned back against the wall and closed her eyes. A sigh slid upward from her lungs.

Why had he done it?

More importantly, why had she allowed it?

It was not the way a man should have kissed an innocent girl. Poppy was mortified that she had landed herself in such a position, and even more that she had behaved in a way she would have judged harshly in someone else. She felt very certain of her feelings for Michael.

Why, then, had she responded to Harry Rutledge in such a way?

Poppy wished she could ask someone, but her instincts warned that it was a matter best forgotten.

Clearing the worried grimace from her face, Poppy tapped at her companion's door. "Miss Marks?"

"I'm awake," came a wan voice.

Poppy entered the small bedroom and found Miss Marks in her nightgown, standing at the washstand.

Miss Marks looked dreadful, her complexion ashen, her quiet blue eyes shadowed the color of bruises. Her light brown hair, usually braided and pinned in a scrupulous knot, was loose and tangled. After tilting a paper of medicinal powder to the back of her tongue, she took an unsteady gulp of water.

"Oh, dear," Poppy said softly. "What can I do?"

Miss Marks shook her head and then winced. "Nothing, Poppy. Thank you, you're very kind to ask."

"More nightmares?" Poppy watched in concern as she went to a dresser and rummaged for stockings and garters and undergarments.

"Yes. I shouldn't have slept so late. Forgive me."

"There's nothing to forgive. I only wish your dreams were more pleasant."

"They are, most of the time." Miss Marks smiled faintly. "My best dreams are of being back at Ramsay House, with the elders in bloom and the nuthatches nesting in the hedgerow. Everything peaceful and safe. How I miss it all."

Poppy missed Ramsay House, too. London, with all its sophisticated delights and entertainments, could not hold a candle to Hampshire. And she was eager to see her older sister Win, whose husband, Merripen, was managing the Ramsay estate. "The season's almost over," Poppy said. "We'll be back there soon."

"If I live that long," Miss Marks muttered.

Poppy smiled sympathetically. "Why don't you return to bed? I'll fetch a cool cloth for your head."

"No, I can't give in to it. I'm going to dress and have a cup of strong tea."

"That's what I thought you'd say," Poppy commented wryly.

Miss Marks had been steeped in the classic British temperament, possessing a deep suspicion of all things sentimental or carnal. She was a young woman, barely older than Poppy, with a preternatural composure that would have allowed her to face any disaster, whether divine or man-made, without blinking an eye. The only time Poppy had ever seen her ruffled was when she was in the company of Leo, the Hathaways' brother, whose sarcastic wit seemed to annoy Miss Marks beyond endurance.

Two years earlier, Miss Marks had been hired as a governess, not to supplement the girls' academic learning, but to teach them the infinite variety of rules for young ladies who wished to navigate the hazards of upper society. Now her position was that of paid companion and chaperone.

In the beginning, Poppy and Beatrix had been daunted by the challenge of learning so many social rules. "We'll make a game of it," Miss Marks had declared, and she had written a series of poems for the girls to memorize.

For example:

> *If a lady you wish to be,*
> *Behave with all formality.*
> *At supper when you sit to eat,*
> *Don't refer to beef as "meat."*
> *Never gesture with your spoon,*
> *Or use your fork as a harpoon.*
> *Please don't play with your food,*
> *And try to keep your voice subdued.*

When it came to taking public walks:

> *Don't go running in the street,*
> *And if a stranger you should meet,*
> *Do not acknowledge him or her,*
> *But to your chaperone defer.*
> *When crossing mud, I beg,*
> *Don't raise your skirts and show your leg.*
> *Instead draw them slightly up and to the right,*
> *Keeping ankles out of sight.*

For Beatrix, there were also special codas:

> *When paying calls, wear gloves and hat,*
> *And never bring a squirrel, or rat,*
> *Or any four-legged creatures who*
> *Do not belong indoors with you.*

The unconventional approach had worked, giving Poppy and Beatrix enough confidence to participate in the season without disgracing themselves. The family had praised Miss Mark for her cleverness. All except for Leo, who had told her sardonically that Elizabeth Barrett Browning had nothing to fear. And Miss Marks had replied that she doubted Leo had sufficient mental aptitude to judge the merits of any kind of poetry at all.

Poppy had no idea why her brother and Miss Marks displayed such antagonism toward each other.

"I think they secretly like each other," Beatrix had said mildly.

Poppy had been so astonished by the idea, she had laughed. "They *war* with each other whenever they're in the same room, which, thank heavens, isn't often. Why would you suggest such a thing?"

"Well, if you consider the mating habits of certain animals—ferrets, for example—it can be quite a rough-and-tumble business—"

"Bea, please don't talk about mating habits," Poppy said, trying to suppress a grin. Her nineteen-year-old sister had a perpetual and cheerful disregard for propriety. "I'm sure it's vulgar, and . . . how do you know about mating habits?"

"Veterinary books, mostly. But also from occasional glimpses. Animals aren't very discreet, are they?"

"I suppose not. But do keep such thoughts to yourself, Bea. If Miss Marks heard you, she would write another poem for us to memorize."

Bea looked at her for a moment, her blue eyes innocent. "Young ladies never contemplate . . . the ways that creatures procreate . . ."

"Or their companion will be irate," Poppy finished for her.

Beatrix had grinned. "Well, I don't see why they shouldn't be attracted to each other. Leo is a viscount, and he's quite handsome, and Miss Marks is intelligent and pretty."

"I've never heard Leo aspire to marry an intelligent woman," Poppy had said. "But I agree—Miss Marks is very pretty. Especially of late. She used to be so dreadfully thin and white, I didn't think much of her looks. But now she's filled out a bit."

"At least a stone," Beatrix had confirmed. "And she seems much happier. When we first met her, I think she had been through some dreadful experience."

"I thought so, too. I wonder if we'll ever find out what it was?"

Poppy hadn't been certain of the answer. But as she glanced at Miss Marks's weary face this morning, she thought there was a good chance that her recurrent nightmares had something to do with her mysterious past.

Going to the wardrobe, Poppy viewed the row of tidy, neatly pressed dresses made up with quiet colors and prim white collars and cuffs. "Which dress shall I find for you?" she asked softly.

"Any of them. It doesn't matter."

Poppy chose a dark blue wool twill, and laid the dress out on the rumpled bed. Tactfully she looked away as her companion removed her nightgown and donned a chemise and drawers and stockings.

The last thing Poppy wanted to do was trouble Miss Marks when her head was aching. However, the events of the morning had to be confessed. If any hint of her misadventure involving Harry Rutledge ever got out, it was far better for her companion to be prepared.

"Miss Marks," she said carefully, "I don't wish to make your headache worse but I have something to tell you . . ." Her voice trailed away as Miss Marks shot her a brief, pained glance.

"What is it, Poppy?"

Now was not a good time, Poppy decided. In fact . . . was there any obligation to say anything ever? In all likelihood, she would never see Harry Rutledge again. He certainly didn't attend the same social events the Hathaways did. And really, why would he bother causing trouble for a girl who was so far beneath his notice? He had nothing to do with her world, nor she with his.

"I dropped a bit of something-or-other on the bodice of my pink muslin frock the other evening at supper," Poppy improvised. "And now there's a grease stain on it."

"Oh, dear." Miss Marks paused in the middle of hooking up the front of her corset. "We'll mix a solution of hartshorn powder and water and sponge the stain. Hopefully that will take it out."

"I think that's an excellent idea."

Feeling only the tiniest bit guilty, Poppy picked up Miss Marks's discarded nightgown and folded it.

Chapter Four

Jake Valentine had been born a *filius nullius,* the Latin term for "son of nobody." His mother Edith had been a maid-servant for a well-to-do barrister in Oxford, and his father the selfsame barrister. Contriving to rid himself of mother and son in one fell swoop, the barrister had bribed a loutish farmer to marry Edith. At the age of ten, having had enough of the farmer's bullying and beatings, Jake had left home for good and struck out for London.

He had labored in a blacksmith's forge for ten years, gaining significant size and strength, as well as a reputation for hard work and trustworthiness. It had never occurred to Jake to want more for himself. He had been employed, and his belly had been full, and the world outside London held no interest for him.

One day, however, a dark-haired man came to the blacksmith's shop and asked to speak to Jake. Intimidated by the gentleman's fine clothes and sophisticated bearing, Jake mumbled answers to a multitude of questions about his personal history and his work experience. And then the man astonished Jake by offering employment as his own valet, with many times the wages he was now getting.

Suspiciously, Jake had asked why the man would hire a novice, largely uneducated and roughcast in nature and appearance. "You could have your pick of the finest valets in London," Jake had pointed out. "Why someone like me?"

"Because those valets are notorious gossips, and they're acquainted with the servants of leading families across England and the continent. You have a reputation for keeping your mouth shut, which I value far more than experience. Also, you look as though you could give a good account of yourself in a dustup."

Jake's eyes had narrowed. "Why would a valet need to fight?"

The man had smiled. "You'll be doing errands for me. Some of them will be easy, some of them less so. Come, are you in or not?"

And that was how Jake had come to work for Jay Harry Rutledge, first as a valet, and then as an assistant.

Jake had never known anyone like Rutledge—eccentric, driven, manipulative, demanding. Rutledge had a shrewder understanding of human nature than anyone Jake had ever met. Within a few minutes of meeting someone, he sized them up with complete accuracy. He knew how to make people do what he wanted, and he nearly always got his way.

It seemed to Jake that Rutledge's brain never stopped, not even for the necessary act of sleeping. He was constantly active. Jake had seen him work out some problem in his head while simultaneously writing a letter and carrying on a fully coherent conversation. His appetite for information was voracious, and he possessed a singular gift for recall. Once Rutledge saw or read or heard something, it was in his brain forever. People could never lie to him, and if they were foolish enough to try, he decimated them.

Rutledge was not above gestures of kindness or consideration, and he rarely lost his temper. But Jake had never been certain how much, if at all, Rutledge cared for his fellow men. At his core, he was cold as a glacier. And as many things as Jake knew about Harry Rutledge, they were still essentially strangers.

No matter. Jake would have died for the man. The hotelier had secured the loyalty of all his servants, who were made to work hard but were given fair treatment and generous salaries. In return, they safeguarded his privacy zealously. Rutledge was acquainted with a great many people, but these friendships were rarely discussed. And he was highly selective about whom he admitted into his inner circle.

Rutledge was besieged by women, of course—his rampaging energy often found outlet in the arms of some beauty or another. But at the first indication that a woman felt the merest flicker of affection, Jake was dispatched to her residence to deliver a letter that broke off all future communications. In other words, Jake was required to endure the tears, anger, or other messy emotions that Rutledge could not tolerate. And Jake would have felt sorry for the women, except that along with each letter, Rutledge usually included some monstrously expensive piece of jewelry that served to mollify any hurt feelings.

There were certain areas of Rutledge's life where women were never allowed. He did not allow them to stay in his private apartments, nor did he let any of them into his curiosities room. It was there that Rutledge went to dwell on his most difficult problems. And on the many nights when Rutledge was unable to sleep, he would go to the drafting table to occupy himself with automata, working with watch parts and bits of paper and wire until he had settled his overactive brain.

So when Jake was discreetly told by a housemaid that a young woman had been with Rutledge in the curiosities room, he knew something significant had occurred.

Jake finished his breakfast in the hotel kitchens with dispatch, hurrying over a plate of creamed eggs scattered with crisp curls of fried bacon. Ordinarily, he would have taken the time to savor the fare. However, he couldn't be late for his morning meeting with Rutledge.

"Not so fast," said Andre Broussard, a chef whom Rutledge had lured away from the French ambassador two years earlier. Broussard was the only employee in the hotel who possibly slept less than Rutledge. The young chef had been known to rise at three in the morning to begin preparing for a day's work, going to the morning markets to personally select the best produce. He was fair-haired and slight of build, but he possessed the discipline and will of an army commander.

Pausing in the act of whisking a sauce, Broussard regarded Jake with amusement. "You might try chewing, Valentine."

"I don't have time to chew," Jake replied, setting aside his napkin. "I'm due to get the morning list from Mr. Rutledge in"—he paused to consult his pocket watch—"two and a half minutes."

"Ah, yes, the morning list." The chef proceeded to mimic his employer. " 'Valentine, I want you to arrange for a soirée in honor of the Portuguese ambassador to be held here on Tuesday with a pyrotechnic display at the conclusion. Afterward, run to the patent office with the drawings for my latest invention. And on the way back, stop by Regent Street and purchase six French cambric handkerchiefs, plain not patterned, and God help me no lace—' "

"Enough, Broussard," Jake said, trying not to smile.

The chef returned his attention to the sauce. "By the way, Valentine . . . when you find out who the girl was, come back and tell me. And in return I'll let you have your pick of the pastry tray before I send it to the dining room."

Jake shot him a sharp look, his brown eyes narrowing. "What girl?"

"You know very well what girl. The one Mr. Rutledge was seen with this morning."

Jake frowned. "Who told you about that?"

"At least three people mentioned it to me in the past half hour. Everyone's talking about it."

"The Rutledge employees are forbidden to gossip," Jake said sternly.

Broussard rolled his eyes. "To outsiders, yes. But Mr. Rutledge never said we couldn't gossip amongst ourselves."

"I don't know why the presence of a girl in the curiosities room should be so interesting."

"Hmmm . . . could it be because Rutledge *never* allows anyone in there? Could it be because everyone who works here is praying that Rutledge will soon find a wife to distract him from his constant meddling?"

Jake shook his head ruefully. "I doubt he'll ever marry. The hotel is his mistress."

The chef gave him a patronizing glance. "That's how much you know. Mr. Rutledge will marry, once he finds the right woman. As my countrymen say, 'A wife and a melon are hard to choose.'" He watched as Jake buttoned his coat and straightened his cravat. "Bring back information, *mon ami*."

"You know I would never reveal one detail of Rutledge's private affairs."

Broussard sighed. "Loyal to a fault. I suppose if Rutledge told you to murder someone, you'd do it?"

Although the question was asked in a light vein, the chef's gray eyes were alert. Because no one, not even Jake, was entirely certain what Harry Rutledge was capable of, or how far Jake's allegiance would go.

"He hasn't asked that of me," Jake replied, and paused to add with a flash of humor, "yet."

As Jake hurried to the private suite of unnumbered rooms on the third floor, he passed many employees on the back stairs. These stairs, and the entrances at the back of the hotel, were used by servants and deliverymen as they went about their daily tasks. A few people tried to stop Jake with questions or concerns, but he shook his head and quickened his pace. Jake took care never to be late for his morning meetings with Rutledge. These consultations were usually brief, no more than a quarter hour, but Rutledge demanded punctuality.

Jake paused before the entrance of the suite, tucked at the back of a small private lobby lined with marble and priceless artwork. A secure inner hallway led to a discreet staircase and side door of the hotel, so that Rutledge never had to use the main hallways for his comings and goings. Rutledge, who liked to keep track of everyone else, did not allow anyone to do the same to him. He took most of his meals in private, and came and went as he pleased, sometimes with no indication of when he would return.

Jake knocked at the door and waited until he heard a muffled assent to enter.

He went into the suite, a series of four connected rooms that could be expanded into as large an apartment as one desired, up to fifteen rooms. "Good morning, Mr. Rutledge," he said, entering the study.

The hotelier sat at a massive mahogany desk fitted with a cupboard filled with drawers and cubbies. As usual, the desk was covered with folios, papers, books, correspondence, calling cards, a stamp box, and an array of writing implements. Rutledge was closing a letter, applying a seal precisely into a little pool of hot wax.

"Good morning, Valentine. How did the staff meeting go?"

Jake handed him the daily sheaf of manager reports. "Everything is going smoothly, for the most part. There have been few issues with the diplomatic contingent from Naga-raja."

"Oh?"

The tiny kingdom of Nagaraja, wedged between Burma and Siam, had just become a British ally. After offering to help the Nagarajans drive out the encroaching Siamese, Britain had now made the country one of its protectorates. Which was akin to being pinned beneath a lion's paw and being informed by the lion that you were perfectly safe. Since the British were currently fighting the Burmese and annexing provinces right and left, the Nagarajans hoped desperately to remain self-governing. Toward that end, the kingdom had sent a trio of high-level envoys on a diplomatic mission to England, bearing costly gifts in tribute to Queen Victoria.

"The reception manager," Jake said, "had to change their rooms three times when they first arrived yesterday afternoon."

Rutledge's brows rose. "There was a problem with the rooms?"

"Not the rooms themselves . . . the room *numbers,* which according to Nagarajan superstition were not auspicious. We finally settled them into suite 218. However, not long afterward, the second-floor manager detected the odor of smoke coming from the suite. It seems they were conducting an arrival-in-a-new-land ceremony, which involved starting a small fire on a bronze plate. Unfortunately the fire got out of hand, and the carpet was scorched."

A smile curved Rutledge's mouth. "As I recall, Nagarajans have ceremonies for nearly everything. See that an appropriate location is found for them to start as many sacred fires as they like without burning the hotel down."

"Yes, sir."

Rutledge riffled through the managers' reports. "What's our current occupancy rate?" he asked without looking up.

"Ninety-five percent."

"Excellent." Rutledge continued to peruse the reports.

In the silence that followed, Jake let his gaze wander over the desk. He saw a letter addressed to Miss Poppy Hathaway, from the Honourable Michael Bayning.

He wondered why it was in Rutledge's possession. Poppy Hathaway . . . one of the sisters of a family that stayed at the Rutledge during the London season. Like other families of the peerage who didn't own a residence in town, they were obligated either to let a furnished house or stay in a private hotel. The Hathaways had been loyal customers of the Rutledge for three years. Was it possible that Poppy was the girl Rutledge had been seen with that morning?

"Valentine," the hotelier said in an offhand manner, "one of the chairs in my curiosities room needs to be reupholstered. There was a slight mishap this morning."

Jake usually knew better than to ask questions, but he couldn't resist. "What kind of mishap, sir?"

"It was a ferret. I believe he was trying to make a nest in the cushions."

A *ferret?*

The Hathaways were definitely involved.

"Is the creature still at large?" Jake asked.

"No, it was retrieved."

"By one of the Hathaway sisters?" Jake guessed.

A warning glint appeared in the cool green eyes. "Yes, as a matter of fact." Setting the reports aside, Rutledge leaned back in his chair. The position of ease was belied by the repeated tapping of his fingers as he rested his hand on the desk. "I have a few errands for you, Valentine. First, go to the residence of Lord Andover in Upper Brook Street. Arrange for a private meeting between myself and Andover within the next two days. Make it clear that no one is to know about it, and impress upon Andover the matter is one of great importance."

"Yes, sir." Jake didn't think there would be any difficulty in making the arrangements. Whenever Harry Rutledge wanted to meet with someone, they complied without delay. "Lord Andover is the father of Mr. Michael Bayning, isn't he?"

"He is."

What the devil was going on?

Before Jake could respond, Rutledge went on with the list. "Next, take this"—he handed Jake a narrow-bound folio tied with leather cord—"to Sir Gerald at the War Office. Place it directly into his hands. After that, go to Watherston & Son, and buy a necklace or bracelet on my credit. Something nice, Valentine. And deliver it to Mrs. Rawlings at her residence."

"With your compliments?" Jake asked hopefully.

"No, with this note." Rutledge gave him a sealed letter. "I'm breaking it off."

Jake's face fell. God. Another scene. "Sir, I'd rather go on an errand in east London and be pummeled by street thieves."

Rutledge smiled. "That will probably happen later in the week."

Jake gave his employer a speaking glance and left.

Poppy was well aware that in terms of marriageability, she had good points and bad points.

In her favor: Her family was wealthy, which meant she would have a handsome dowry.

Not in her favor: The Hathaways were neither a distinguished family nor blue-blooded, in spite of Leo's title.

In her favor: She was attractive.

Not in her favor: She was chatty and awkward, often at

the same time, and when she was nervous, both problems worsened.

In her favor: The aristocracy could not afford to be as particular as they once had been. While the peerage's power slowly diminished, a class of industrialists and merchants was swiftly rising. Therefore, marriages between moneyed commoners and impoverished nobility occurred with increasing frequency. More and more often, the peerage had to figuratively hold its nose and mingle with those of low origins.

Not in her favor: Michael Bayning's father, the viscount, was a man of high standards, especially where his son was concerned.

"The viscount will certainly have to consider the match," Miss Marks had told her. "He may have impeccable lineage, but from all accounts, his fortune is waning. His son will have to marry a girl from a family of means. It may as well be a Hathaway."

"I hope you're right," Poppy had replied feelingly.

Poppy had no doubt that she would be happy as Michael Bayning's wife. He was intelligent, affectionate, quick to laugh . . . a born and bred gentleman. She loved him, not in a bonfire of passion, but in a warm, steady flame. She loved his temperament, the confidence that superseded any hint of arrogance. And she loved his looks, as unladylike as it was to admit such a thing. But he had thick chestnut hair and warm brown eyes, and his form was tall and well exercised.

Once Poppy had met Michael, it had seemed almost too easy . . . in no time at all she had fallen in love with him.

"I hope you're not trifling with me," Michael had told her one evening as they browsed along the art gallery of a London mansion during a soirée. "That is, I hope I haven't mistaken what might be mere politeness on your part for something more meaningful." He had stopped with her in front of a large landscape done in oils. "The truth is, Miss

Hathaway . . . Poppy . . . every minute I spend in your company gives me such pleasure that I can scarcely bear to be apart from you."

And she had stared up at him in wonder. "Could it be possible?" she whispered.

"That I love you?" Michael had whispered back, a wry smile touching his lips. "Poppy Hathaway, it is impossible *not* to love you."

She had taken an unsteady breath, her entire being filled with joy. "Miss Marks never told me what a lady is supposed to do in this situation."

Michael had grinned and leaned a bit closer, as if imparting a highly confidential secret. "You're supposed to give me discreet encouragement."

"I love you, too."

"That's not discreet." His brown eyes sparkled. "But it's very nice to hear."

The courtship had been beyond circumspect. Michael's father, Viscount Andover, was protective of his son. A good man, Michael had said, but stern. And Michael had asked for sufficient time to approach the viscount and convince him of the rightness of the match. Poppy was entirely willing to give Michael however much time he needed.

The rest of the Hathaways, however, were not quite as amenable. To them, Poppy was a treasure, and she deserved to be courted openly and with pride.

"Shall I go and discuss the situation with Andover?" Cam Rohan had suggested as the family relaxed in the parlor of their hotel suite after supper. He lounged on the settee next to Amelia, who was holding their six-month-old baby. When the baby grew up, his *gadjo* name—*gadjo* being the word Roma used for outsiders—would be Ronan Cole, but among the family he was called by his Romany name, Rye.

Poppy and Miss Marks occupied the other settee, while Beatrix lounged on the floor by the hearth, playing idly with a pet hedgehog named Medusa. Dodger sulked nearby in his basket, having learned through hard experience that it was unwise to tangle with Medusa and her quills.

Frowning contemplatively, Poppy looked up from her needlework. "I don't think that would help," she told her brother-in-law regretfully. "I know how persuasive you are . . . but Michael is very firm on how to handle his father."

Cam appeared to be thinking the matter over. With his black hair worn a trifle too long, his rich brown complexion, and a diamond stud sparkling at one ear, Rohan looked far more like a prince than a businessman who had garnered a fortune in manufacturing investments. Ever since he had married Amelia, Rohan had been the *de facto* head of the Hathaway family. No man alive would have been able to manage the unruly lot as adeptly as he did. His tribe, he called them.

"Little sister," he said to Poppy, sounding relaxed even though his gaze was intent, "as Roma say, 'the tree without sunlight will bear no fruit.' I see no reason why Bayning should not ask for permission to court you, and go about it openly in the usual way."

"Cam," Poppy said carefully, "I know Roma have a more straightforward approach to courtship—"

Amelia smothered a laugh at the understatement. Cam pointedly ignored her.

"But you know as well as any of us," Poppy continued, "that it is a far more delicate process for the British peerage."

"Actually," Amelia said dryly, "from what I've seen, the British peerage negotiates marriages with all the romantic delicacy of a bank transaction."

Poppy scowled at her older sister. "Amelia, whose side are you on?"

"For me, there's no side but yours." Amelia's blue eyes were filled with concern. "And that is why I don't care for this kind of covert courtship . . . arriving separately at events, never coming to take you and Miss Marks on a carriage drive . . . it bears the odor of shame. Embarrassment. As if you were some guilty secret."

"Are you saying you doubt Mr. Bayning's intentions?"

"Not at all. But I don't like his methods."

Poppy sighed shortly. "I'm an unconventional choice for a peer's son. And therefore Mr. Bayning must proceed with caution."

"You're the most conventional person in the entire family," Amelia protested.

Poppy gave her a dark glance. "Being the most conventional Hathaway is hardly something to boast about."

Looking annoyed, Amelia glanced at her companion. "Miss Marks, my sister seems to believe that her family is so outlandish, so completely out of the ordinary, that Mr. Bayning must go through these exertions—sneaking about and so forth—instead of going to the viscount in an upstanding manner and saying 'Father, I intend to marry Poppy Hathaway and I would like your blessing.' Can you tell me *why* there is a need for such excessive caution on Mr. Bayning's part?"

For once, Miss Marks seemed at a loss for words.

"Don't put her on the spot," Poppy said. "Here are the facts, Amelia: You and Win are married to Roma, Leo is a notorious rake, Beatrix has more pets than the Royal Zoological Society, and I am socially awkward and can't carry on a proper conversation to save my life. Is it so difficult to understand why Mr. Bayning has to break the news to his father gently?"

Amelia looked as though she wanted to argue, but instead she muttered, "Proper conversations are very dull, in my opinion."

"Mine, too," Poppy said glumly. "That's the problem."

Beatrix looked up from the hedgehog, who had curled up in a ball in her hands. "Does Mr. Bayning make interesting conversation?"

"You wouldn't need to ask," Amelia said, "if he dared to come here for a visit."

"I suggest," Miss Marks said hastily, before Poppy could retort, "that as a family, we invite Mr. Bayning to accompany us to the Chelsea flower show, the day after next. That will allow us to spend the afternoon with Mr. Bayning—and perhaps we will gain some reassurance about his intentions."

"I think that's a lovely idea," Poppy exclaimed. Attending a flower show together was far more innocuous and discreet than Michael having to call on them at the Rutledge. "I'm sure that talking to Mr. Bayning will ease your worries, Amelia."

"I hope so," her sister replied, sounding unconvinced. A tiny frown pleated the space between her sister's slim brows. She turned her attention to Miss Marks. "As Poppy's chaperone, you have seen far more of this furtive suitor than I have. What is your opinion of him?"

"From what I have observed," the companion said carefully, "Mr. Bayning is well regarded and honorable. He has an excellent reputation, with no history of seducing women, spending beyond his means, or brawling in public venues. In short, he is the complete opposite of Lord Ramsay."

"That speaks well of him," Cam said gravely. His golden hazel eyes twinkled as he glanced down at his wife. A moment of silent communication passed between them before he murmured softly, "Why don't you send him an invitation, *monisha*?"

A sardonic smile flitted across Amelia's soft lips. "*You* would voluntarily attend a flower show?"

"I like flowers," Cam said innocently.

"Yes, scattered across meadows and marshes. But you hate seeing them organized in raised beds and neat little boxes."

"I can tolerate it for an afternoon," Cam assured her. Idly he toyed with a loose lock of hair that had fallen on her neck. "I suppose it's worth the effort to gain an in-law like Bayning." He smiled as he added, "We need at least one respectable man in the family, don't we?"

Chapter Five

An invitation was sent to Michael Bayning the next day, and to Poppy's elation, it was accepted immediately. "It's only a matter of time now," she told Beatrix, barely restraining herself from hopping in excitement the way Dodger did. "I'm going to be Mrs. Michael Bayning, and I love him, I love everyone and everything . . . . I even love your smelly old ferret, Bea!"

Late in the morning, Poppy and Beatrix dressed for a walk. It was a clear, warm day, and the hotel gardens, intercut with neatly graveled paths, were a symphony of blooms.

"I can hardly wait to go out," Poppy said, standing at the window and staring down at the extensive gardens. "It almost reminds me of Hampshire, the flowers are so beautiful."

"It doesn't remind me at all of Hampshire," Beatrix said, "It's too orderly. But I do like walking through the Rutledge rose garden. The air smells so sweet. Do you know, I spoke with the master gardener a few mornings ago, when Cam and Amelia and I went out, and he told me his secret recipe for making the roses so large and healthy."

"What is it?"

"Fish broth, vinegar, and a dash of sugar. He sprinkles them with it right before they bloom. And they love it."

Poppy wrinkled her nose. "What a dreadful concoction."

"The master gardener said that old Mr. Rutledge is especially fond of roses, and people have brought him some of the exotic varieties you see in the garden. The lavender roses are from China, for example, and the Maiden's Blush variety comes from France, and—"

"*Old* Mr. Rutledge?"

"Well, he didn't actually say Mr. Rutledge was old. I just can't help thinking of him that way."

"Why?"

"Well, he's so awfully mysterious, and no one ever sees him. It reminds me of the stories of mad old King George, locked away in his apartments at Windsor Castle." Beatrix grinned. "Perhaps they keep Mr. Rutledge up in the attic."

"Bea," Poppy whispered urgently, filled with an overwhelming urge to confide in her, "There's something I'm bursting to tell you, but it must remain a secret."

Her sister's eyes lit with interest. "What is it?"

"First promise you won't tell anyone."

"I *promise* promise."

"Swear on something."

"I swear on St. Francis, the patron saint of all animals." Seeing Poppy's hesitation, Beatrix added enthusiastically, "If a band of pirates kidnapped me and took me to their ship and threatened to make me walk the plank over a shiver of starving sharks unless I told them your secret, I *still* wouldn't tell it. If I were tied up by a villain and thrown before a herd of stampeding horses all shod in iron, and the *only way* to keep from being trampled was to tell the villain your secret, I—"

"All right, you've convinced me," Poppy said with a grin.

Dragging her sister to the corner, she said softly, "I have met Mr. Rutledge."

Beatrix's blue eyes turned huge. "You have? When?"

"Yesterday morning." And Poppy told her the entire story, describing the passageway, the curiosities room, and Mr. Rutledge himself. The only thing she left out was the kiss, which, as far as she was concerned, had never happened.

"I'm so terribly sorry about Dodger," Beatrix said earnestly. "I apologize on his behalf."

"It's all right, Bea. Only . . . I do wish he hadn't lost the letter. So long as no one finds it, I suppose there's no problem."

"Then Mr. Rutledge is not a decrepit madman?" Beatrix asked, sounding disappointed.

"Heavens, no."

"What does he look like?"

"Quite handsome, actually. He's very tall, and—"

"As tall as Merripen?"

Kev Merripen had come to live with the Hathaways after his tribe had been attacked by a group of landowners bent on destroying a Romany encampment. The boy had been left for dead, but the Hathaways had taken him in, and he had stayed for good. Recently he had married the second oldest sister, Winnifred. Merripen had undertaken the monumental task of running the Ramsay estate in Leo's absence. The newlyweds were both quite happy to stay in Hampshire during the season, enjoying the beauty and relative privacy of Ramsay House.

"No one's as tall as Merripen," Poppy said. "But Mr. Rutledge is tall nonetheless, and he has dark hair and piercing green eyes . . ." Her stomach gave an unexpected little leap as she remembered.

"Did you like him?"

Poppy hesitated. "Mr. Rutledge is . . . unsettling. He's

charming, but one has the feeling he's capable of nearly anything. He's like some wicked angel from a William Blake poem."

"I wish I could have met him," Beatrix said wistfully. "And I wish even more that I could visit the curiosities room. I envy you, Poppy. It's been so long since anything interesting has happened to me."

Poppy laughed quietly. "What, when we've just gone through nearly the entire London season?"

Beatrix rolled her eyes. "The London season is about as interesting as a snail race. In January. With dead snails."

"Girls, I'm ready," came Miss Marks's cheerful summons, and she entered the room. "Make certain to fetch your parasols—you don't want to become sunbrowned." The trio left the suite and proceeded at a dignified pace along the hallway. Before they turned the corner to approach the grand staircase, they became aware of an unusual disturbance in the decorous hotel.

Men's voices tangled in the air, some agitated, at least one of them angry, and there was the sound of foreign accents, and heavy thumping, and a queer metallic rattling.

"What the devil . . ." Miss Marks said under her breath.

Rounding the corner, the three women stopped abruptly at the sight of a half dozen men clustered near the food lift. A shriek rent the air.

"Is it a woman?" Poppy asked, turning pale. "A child?"

"Stay here," Miss Marks said tensely. "I'll undertake to find out—"

The three of them flinched at a series of screams, the sounds blistered with panic.

"It is a child," Poppy said, striding forward despite Miss Marks's command to stay. "We must do something to help."

Beatrix had already run ahead of her. "It's not a child," she said over her shoulder. "It's a monkey!"

Chapter Six

There were few activities Harry enjoyed as much as fencing, even more so because it had become an obsolete art. Swords were no longer necessary as weapons or fashion accessories, and its practitioners were now mainly military officers and a handful of amateur enthusiasts. But Harry liked the elegance of it, the precision that required both physical and mental discipline. A fencer had to plan several moves in advance, something that came naturally to Harry.

A year earlier, he had joined a fencing club consisting of approximately a hundred members, including peers, bankers, actors, politicians, and soldiers from various ranks of the military. Thrice weekly, Harry and a few trusted friends met at the club, practicing with both foils and quarterstaffs beneath the watchful eye of a fencing master. Although the club had a changing room and shower baths, there was often a queue, so Harry usually left directly from practice.

This morning's practice had been especially vigorous, as the fencing master had taught them techniques for fighting off two opponents simultaneously. Although it had been invigorating, it was also challenging, and they had all been left bruised and tired. Harry had gotten a few hard strikes on his chest and bicep, and he was soaked in sweat.

When he returned to the hotel, he was still in his fencing whites, although he had removed the protective leather padding. He was looking forward to a shower bath, but it quickly became evident that the shower bath would have to wait.

One of his managers, a bespectacled young man named William Cullip, met him as he entered the back of the hotel. Cullip's face was drawn with anxiety. "Mr. Rutledge," he said apologetically, "I was told by Mr. Valentine to tell you immediately upon your return that we are having a . . . well, a difficulty . . ."

Harry stared at him and remained silent, waiting with forced patience. One could not rush Cullip, or the information would take forever to emerge.

"It involves the Nagarajan diplomats," the manager continued.

"Another fire?"

"No, sir. It has to do with one of the articles of tribute the Nagarajans had planned to present to the Queen tomorrow. It has disappeared."

Harry frowned, reflecting on the collection of priceless gemstones, artwork, and textiles the Nagarajans had brought. "Their possessions are stored in a locked basement room. How could something go missing?"

Cullip let out a ragged breath. "Well, sir, it has apparently left on its own."

Harry's brows lifted. "What?"

"Among the items the Nagarajans brought for the Queen are a pair of rare animals . . . blue macaques . . . which are found only in the Nagarajan teak forest. They are to be housed at the zoological gardens at Regent's Park. Evidently each macaque was kept in its own crate, but somehow one of them learned to pick a lock, and—"

"The devil you say!" Incredulity was rapidly crushed by outrage. Yet somehow Harry managed to keep his voice quiet. "May I ask why no one bothered to inform me that we're harboring a pair of *monkeys* in my hotel?"

"There seems to be some confusion on that point, sir. You see, Mr. Lufton in reception is certain that he included it in his report, but Mr. Valentine says he never read anything about it, and he lost his temper and frightened a housemaid and two stewards, and now everyone is searching while at the same time making certain not to alert the guests—"

"Cullip." Harry gritted his teeth with the effort to stay calm. "How long has the macaque been missing?"

"We estimate at least forty-five minutes."

"Where is Valentine?"

"The last I heard, he had gone up to the third floor. One of the housemaids discovered what she thought might be droppings near the food lift."

"Monkey droppings near the food lift," Harry repeated, disbelieving his own ears. *Christ*. All the situation needed was for one of his elderly guests to be frightened into apoplexy from having a wild animal spring out from nowhere, or to have a woman or child bitten, or some other outrageous scenario.

It would be impossible to find the damned creature. The hotel was a virtual maze, riddled with hallways and concealed doors and passages. It could take days, during which the Rutledge would be in an uproar. He would lose business. And worst of all, he would be the butt of jokes for *years*. By the time the humorists got through with him . . .

"By God, heads are going to roll," Harry said with a lethal softness that caused Cullip to flinch. "Go to my apartments, Cullip, and get the Dreyse from the mahogany cabinet in my private office."

The young manager looked perplexed. "The Dreyse, sir?"

"A shotgun. It's the only percussion cap breechloader in the cabinet."

"A percussion . . ."

"The brown one," Harry said gently. "With a large bolt sticking out of the side."

"Yes, sir!"

"And for God's sake, don't point it at anyone. It's loaded."

Still gripping the foil, Harry raced up the back stairs. He took them two at a time, swiftly passing a pair of startled housemaids carrying baskets of linens.

Reaching the third floor, he headed to the food lift, where he found Valentine, all three of the Nagarajan diplomats, and Brimbley, the floor steward. A wood and metal crate had been positioned nearby. The men had gathered around the opening to the food lift, and were looking inside.

"Valentine," Harry said curtly, striding up to his right-hand man, "have you found it?"

Jake Valentine threw him a harassed glance. "He climbed up the rope pulley in the food lift. Now he's sitting on top of the movable frame. Every time we try to lower it, he hangs onto the rope and dangles above us."

"Is he close enough for me to reach him?"

Valentine's gaze flickered to the foil in his employer's grasp. His dark eyes widened as he understood that Harry intended to skewer the creature rather than let it roam freely through the hotel.

"It wouldn't be easy," Valentine said. "You'd probably only end up agitating him."

"Have you tried to lure it with food?"

"He won't take the bait. I reached up in the shaft with an apple, and he tried to bite my hand." Valentine cast a distracted glance at the food lift, where the other men were whistling and cooing to the obstinate monkey.

One of the Nagarajans, a slim middle-aged man dressed

in a light suit with a richly patterned cloth draped over both shoulders, stepped forward. His expression was fraught with distress. "You are Mr. Rutledge? Good, yes, I thank you for coming to help retrieve this most important gift for Her Majesty. Very rare macaque. Very special. It must not be harmed."

"Your name?" Harry asked brusquely.

"Niran," the diplomat supplied.

"Mr. Niran, while I understand your concern for the animal, I have a responsibility to protect my guests."

The Nagarajan glowered. "If you damage our gift to the Queen, I fear it will not go well for you."

Leveling a hard stare at the diplomat, Harry said evenly, "If you don't find a way to get that animal out of my food lift and into that crate in five minutes, Niran, I'm going to make a kabob out of him."

This statement produced a stare of purest indignation, and the Nagarajan rushed to the opening of the food lift. The monkey gave an excited hoot, followed by a series of grunts.

"I have no idea what a kabob is," Valentine said to no one in particular, "but I don't think the monkey's going to like it."

Before Harry could reply, Valentine caught sight of something behind him, and he groaned. "Guests," the assistant muttered.

"Damn it," Harry said beneath his breath, and turned to face the approaching guests, wondering what he was going to say to them.

A trio of women rushed toward him, two of them in pursuit of a dark-haired girl. A small shock of recognition went through Harry as he recognized Catherine Marks and Poppy Hathaway. He guessed the third was Beatrix, who seemed determined to plow through him in her haste to reach the food lift.

Harry moved to block her way. "Good morning, miss. I'm afraid you can't go over there. Nor would you want to."

She stopped immediately, staring at him with eyes the same rich blue as her sister's. Catherine Marks regarded him with flinty composure, while Poppy took an extra breath, her cheeks infused with color.

"You don't know my sister, sir," Poppy said. "If there is a wild creature in the vicinity, she most definitely wants to see it."

"What makes you think there's a wild creature in my hotel?" Harry asked, as if the idea were inconceivable.

The macaque chose that moment to utter an enthusiastic screech.

Holding his gaze, Poppy grinned. Despite his annoyance at the situation and his lack of control over it, Harry couldn't help smiling back. She was even more exquisite than he had remembered, her eyes a dark, lucid blue. There were many beautiful women in London, but not one of them possessed her combination of intelligence and subtly off-kilter charm. He wanted to sweep her away somewhere, that very minute, and have her all to himself.

Schooling his expression, Harry recalled that although they had met the previous day, they weren't supposed to know each other. He bowed with impeccable politeness. "Harry Rutledge, at your service."

"I'm Beatrix Hathaway," the younger girl said, "and this is my sister Poppy and my companion, Miss Marks. There's a monkey in the food lift, isn't there?" She seemed remarkably prosaic, as if discovering exotic animals in one's residence occurred all the time.

"Yes, but—"

"You'll never catch him that way," Beatrix interrupted.

Harry, who was never interrupted by anyone, found himself biting back another smile. "I assure you, we have the situation well in hand, Miss—"

"You need help," Beatrix told him. "I'll return directly.

Don't do anything to upset the monkey. And don't try to poke him out with that sword—you may accidentally pierce him." With no further ado, she dashed back in the direction she had come from.

"It wouldn't be accidental," Harry muttered.

Miss Marks looked from Harry to her retreating charge, her mouth falling open. "Beatrix, do *not* run through the hotel like that. Stop at once!"

"I think she has a plan," Poppy remarked. "You'd better go after her, Miss Marks."

The companion threw her a beseeching glance. "Come with me."

But Poppy didn't move, only said innocently, "I'll wait here, Miss Marks."

"But it's not proper—" The companion looked from Beatrix's fast-disappearing form to Poppy's unmoving one. Deciding in a flash that Beatrix posed the greater problem, she turned with an unladylike curse and ran after her charge.

Harry found himself left with Poppy, who, like her sister, seemed remarkably unperturbed by the macaque's antics. They faced each other, he with his foil, she with her parasol.

Poppy's gaze traveled over his fencing whites, and rather than staying demurely silent or displaying the appropriate nervousness of a young lady with no companion to protect her . . . she launched into conversation. "My father called fencing 'physical chess,'" she said. "He very much admired the sport."

"I'm still a novice," Harry said.

"According to my father, the trick of it is to hold the foil as if it were a bird in your hand—close enough to prevent its escape, but not tight enough to crush it."

"He gave you lessons?"

"Oh, yes, my father encouraged all his daughters to try it.

He said he knew of no other sport that would fall so directly in a woman's line."

"Of course. Women are agile and fast."

Poppy smiled ruefully. "Not enough to elude you, it seems."

The single comment managed, with wry humor, to gently mock herself and him.

Somehow they were standing closer together, although Harry wasn't certain who had stepped toward whom. A delicious scent clung to her, sweet skin and perfume and soap. Remembering how soft her mouth had been, he wanted to kiss her so badly that it was all he could do not to reach for her. He was stunned to realize that he was a bit breathless.

"Sir!" Valentine's voice recalled him from his thoughts. "The macaque is climbing up the rope."

"It has nowhere to go," Harry said curtly. "Try moving the lift upward and trapping it against the ceiling."

"You will injure the macaque!" the Nagarajan exclaimed.

"I can only hope so," Harry said, aggravated by the distraction. He didn't want to be bothered with the logistics of capturing an unruly macaque. He wanted to be alone with Poppy Hathaway.

William Cullip arrived, carrying the Dreyse with extreme care. "Mr. Rutledge, here it is!"

"Thank you." Harry began to reach for it, but at that second Poppy reared back in a startle reflex, her shoulders colliding with his chest. Harry caught her by the arms and felt the thrills of panic running through her. Carefully, he turned her to face him. Her face was bleached, her gaze not quite focused. "What is it?" he asked softly, holding her against him. "The shotgun? You're afraid of guns?"

She nodded, struggling to catch her breath.

Harry was shocked by the force of his own reaction to her, the tidal wave of protectiveness. She was trembling and winded, one hand pressing on the center of his chest. "It's all right," he murmured. He couldn't recall the last time anyone had sought comfort from him. Perhaps no one ever had. He wanted to draw her fully against him and soothe her. It seemed he had always wanted this, waited for it, without even knowing.

In the same quiet tone Harry murmured, "Cullip, the shotgun won't be needed. Take it back to the cabinet."

"Yes, Mr. Rutledge."

Poppy stayed in the shelter of his arms, her head downbent. Her exposed ear looked so tender. The fragrance of her perfume teased him. He wanted to explore every part of her, hold her until she relaxed against him. "It's all right," he murmured again, stroking a circle on her back with his palm. "It's gone. I'm sorry you were frightened."

"No, *I'm* sorry, I . . ." Poppy drew back, her white face now infused with color. "I'm not usually skittish, it was only the surprise. A long time ago—" She stopped herself and fidgeted, and muttered, "I'm *not* going to babble."

Harry didn't want her to stop. He found everything about her endlessly interesting, although he couldn't explain why. She simply *was*.

"Tell me," he said in a low voice.

Poppy made a helpless gesture and gave him a wry glance as if to convey that she had warned him. "When I was a child, one of my favorite people in the world was my Uncle Howard, my father's brother. He had no wife or children of his own, so he lavished all his attention on us."

A reminiscent smile touched her lips. "Uncle Howard was very patient with me. My chattering drove everyone else to distraction, but he always listened as if he had all the time in the world. One morning he came to visit us while Father went shooting with some of the village men. When they returned with a brace of birds, Uncle Howard and I went to the end of the lane to meet them. But someone's rifle discharged accidentally . . . I'm not certain if it was dropped, or if the man was carrying it incorrectly . . . I remember the sound if it, a boom like thunder, and there were a few hard pinches on my arm, and another on my shoulder. I turned to tell Uncle Howard, but he was crumpling very slowly to the ground. He'd been fatally wounded, and I had been hit by a few stray pellets."

Poppy hesitated, her eyes glittering. "There was blood all over him. I went to him and put my arms beneath his head, and asked him what I should do. And he whispered that I must always be a good girl, so that we could meet again in heaven someday." She cleared her throat and sighed shortly. "Forgive me. I talk excessively. I shouldn't—"

"No," Harry said, overwhelmed by a baffling and unfamiliar emotion, white-knuckled with it. "I could listen to you all day."

She blinked in surprise, jostled out of her melancholy. A shy grin rose to her lips. "Aside from my Uncle Howard, you're the first man ever to say that to me."

They were interrupted by exclamations from the men gathered around the rope lift, as the macaque climbed higher.

"Bloody hell," Harry muttered.

"Please wait just a moment more," Poppy said to him earnestly. "My sister is very good with animals. She'll have him out with no injury."

"She has experience with primates?" Harry asked sardonically.

Poppy considered that. "We've just been through the London season. Does that count?"

Harry chuckled, with a genuine amusement that didn't often occur, and both Valentine and Brimbley glanced at him with astonishment.

Beatrix hurried back to them, clutching something in her

arms. She paid no attention to Miss Marks, who was following and scolding. "Here we are," Beatrix said cheerfully.

"Our comfit jar?" Poppy asked.

"We've already offered him food, miss," Valentine said. "He won't take it."

"He'll take these." Beatrix strode confidently to the opening of the food lift. "Let's send the jar up to him."

"Have you adulterated the sweets?" Valentine asked hopefully.

All three of the Nagarajan envoys exclaimed anxiously to the effect that they did not want the macaque to be drugged or poisoned.

"No, no, no," Beatrix said. "He might fall down the shaft if I did that, and this precious animal must not be harmed."

The foreigners subsided at her reassurance.

"How may I help, Bea?" Poppy asked, approaching her.

Her younger sister handed her a length of heavy silk cord. "Tie this 'round the neck of the jar, please. Your knots are always much better than mine."

"A clove hitch?" Poppy suggested, taking the twine.

"Yes, perfect."

Jake Valentine regarded the two intent young women dubiously, and looked at Harry. "Mr. Rutledge—"

Harry gestured for him to be silent and allow the Hathaway sisters to proceed. Whether or not their attempt actually worked, he was enjoying this too much to stop them.

"Could you make some kind of loop for a handle at the other end?" Beatrix asked.

Poppy frowned. "An overhand knot, perhaps? I'm not sure I remember how."

"Allow me," Harry volunteered, stepping forward.

Poppy surrendered the end of the cord to him, her eyes twinkling.

Harry tied the end of the cord into an elaborate rope ball,

first wrapping it several times around his fingers, then passing the free end back and forth. Not above a bit of showmanship, he tightened the whole thing with a deft flourish.

"Nicely done," Poppy said. "What knot is that?"

"Ironically," Harry replied, "it is known as the 'Monkey's Fist.'"

Poppy smiled. "Is it really? No, you're teasing."

"I never tease about knots. A good knot is a thing of beauty." Harry gave the rope end to Beatrix, and watched as she placed the jar atop the frame of the food lift cab. Then he realized what her plan was. "Clever," he murmured.

"It may not work," Beatrix said. "It depends on whether the monkey is more intelligent than we are."

"I'm rather afraid of the answer," Harry replied dryly. Reaching inside the food lift shaft, he pulled the rope slowly, sending the jar up to the macaque, while Beatrix kept hold of the silk cord.

All was quiet. The group held their breath *en masse* as they waited.

Thump.

The monkey had descended to the top of the cab. A few inquiring hoots and grunts echoed through the shaft. A rattle, a silence, and then a sharp tug at the line. Offended screams filled the air, and heavy thumps shook the food lift.

"We caught him," Beatrix exclaimed.

Harry took the line from her, while Valentine lowered the cab. "Please stand back, Miss Hathaway."

"Let me do it," Beatrix urged. "The macaque is much more likely to spring at you than me. Animals trust me."

"Nevertheless, I can't risk one of my guests being injured."

Poppy and Miss Marks both drew Beatrix away from the food lift opening. They all gasped as a large, blue black macaque appeared, his eyes huge and bright above a hairless muzzle, his head comically tufted with a shock of fur.

The monkey was stocky and powerful in appearance, with hardly any tail to speak of. His expressive face contorted in fury, white teeth gleaming as it screeched.

One of the front paws appeared to be stuck in the comfit jar. The irate macaque tugged frantically to get it out, without success. His own clenched fist was the reason for his captivity—he refused to let go of the comfits even to remove his paw from the jar.

"Oh, isn't he beautiful!" Beatrix enthused.

"Perhaps to a female macaque," Poppy said dubiously.

Harry held the cord attached to the jar with one hand, his fencing foil with the other. The macaque was larger than he had expected, capable of inflicting considerable damage. And it was clearly considering whom to attack first.

"Come on, old fellow," Harry murmured, attempting to lead the monkey to the open crate.

Beatrix reached into her pocket, pulled out a few comfits, and went to toss them into the crate. "There you are, greedy boy," she said to the macaque. "Your treats are in there. Go on, and don't make such a fuss."

Miraculously, the monkey obeyed, dragging his jar with him. After casting a baleful glance at Harry, he entered his crate and scooped up the scattered comfits with his free paw.

"Give me the jar," Beatrix said patiently, tugging at the cord, and she pulled it out of the crate. She tossed a last handful of comfits to the monkey and closed the door. The Nagarajans hastened to lock it.

"I want it triple chained," Harry said to Valentine, "and the other monkey's crate chained as well. And then I want them delivered directly to Regent's Park."

"Yes, sir."

Poppy went to her sister, hugging her in an open display of affection. "Well done, Bea," she exclaimed. "How did you know the monkey wouldn't let go of the comfits in his hand?"

"Because it is a well-known fact that monkeys are nearly as greedy as people," Beatrix said, and Poppy laughed.

"Girls," Miss Marks said in a low voice, trying to hush them, draw them away. "This is unseemly. We must go."

"Yes, of course," Poppy said. "I'm sorry, Miss Marks. We'll go on with our walk."

However, the companion's attempt to urge the sisters to leave was foiled as the Nagarajans crowded around Beatrix.

"You have done us a *very* great service," the head diplomat, Niran, told the girl. "Very great indeed. You have the gratitude of our country and our king, and you shall be recommended to Her Majesty Queen Victoria for your brave assistance—"

"No, thank you," Miss Marks interceded firmly. "Miss Hathaway does not wish to be recommended. You will harm her reputation by exposing her publicly. If you are indeed grateful for her kindness, we beg you to repay her with silence."

This produced more discussion and vigorous nodding.

Beatrix sighed and watched as the macaque was carried away in his crate. "I wish I had a monkey of my own," she said wistfully.

Miss Marks gave Poppy a long-suffering glance. "One might wish she were as eager to acquire a husband."

Smothering a grin, Poppy tried to look sympathetic.

"Have the food lift cleaned," Harry told Valentine and Brimbley. "Every inch of it."

The men hastened to comply, the older man using the pulleys to send the food lift down, while Valentine departed in swift, controlled strides.

Harry glanced at all three of the women, lingering an

extra moment on Miss Marks's set face. "I thank you for your assistance, ladies."

"Not at all," Poppy said, her eyes dancing. "And if there are further problems with recalcitrant monkeys, do not hesitate to send for us."

Harry's blood quickened as lurid images filled his mind . . . her, against him, beneath him. That smiling mouth, his alone, her whispers curling into his ear. Her skin, soft and ivory pale in the darkness. Skin heated by skin, sensation emerging as he touched her.

She was worth anything, he thought, even giving up the last remnants of his soul.

"Good day," he heard himself say, his voice husky but polite. And he forced himself to walk away.

For now.

Chapter Seven

"Now I understand what you meant earlier," Beatrix said to Poppy, when Miss Marks had gone on some undisclosed errand. Poppy had settled in her bed, while Beatrix had washed Dodger and was now drying him with a towel before the hearth. "What you were trying to say about Mr. Rutledge," she continued. "No wonder you found him unsettling." She paused to grin at the happy ferret, who was wriggling on a warm towel. "Dodger, you do like to be clean, don't you? You smell so lovely after a good washing."

"You always say that, and he always smells the same." Poppy raised herself on an elbow and watched them, her hair spilling around her shoulders. She felt too restless to nap. "Then you found Mr. Rutledge unsettling, too?"

"No, but I understand why *you* do. He watches you like one of those ambushing sort of predators. The kind that lie in wait before they spring."

"How dramatic," Poppy said with a dismissive laugh. "He's not a predator, Bea. He's only a man."

Beatrix made no reply, only made a project of smoothing Dodger's fur. As she leaned over him, he strained upward and kissed her nose affectionately. "Poppy," she murmured, "no matter how Miss Marks tries to civilize me—and I do try to listen to her—I still have my own way of looking at the world. To me, people are scarcely different from animals. We're all God's creatures, aren't we? When I meet someone, I know immediately what animal they would be. When we first met Cam, for example, I knew he was a fox."

"I suppose Cam is somewhat fox-like," Poppy said, amused. "What is Merripen? A bear?"

"No, unquestionably a horse. And Amelia is a hen."

"I would say an owl."

"Yes, but don't you remember when one of our hens in Hampshire chased after a cow that had strayed too close to the nest? That's Amelia."

Poppy grinned. "You're right."

"And Win is a swan."

"Am I also a bird? A lark? A robin?"

"No, you're a rabbit."

"A *rabbit*?" Poppy made a face. "I don't like that. Why am I a rabbit?"

"Oh, rabbits are beautiful soft animals who love to be cuddled. They're very sociable, but they're happiest in pairs."

"But they're timid," Poppy protested.

"Not always. They're brave enough to be companions to many other creatures. Even cats and dogs."

"Well," Poppy said in resignation, "it's better than being a hedgehog, I suppose."

"Miss Marks is a hedgehog," Beatrix said in a matter-of-fact tone that made Poppy grin.

"And you're a ferret, aren't you, Bea?"

"Yes. But I was leading to a point."

"Sorry, go on."

"I was going to say that Mr. Rutledge is a cat. A solitary hunter. With an apparent taste for rabbit."

Poppy blinked in bewilderment. "You think he is interested in . . . oh, but Bea, I'm not at all . . . and I don't think I'll ever see him again . . ."

"I hope you're right."

Settling on her side, Poppy watched her sister in the flickering glow of the hearth, while a chill of uneasiness penetrated the very marrow of her bones.

Not because she feared Harry Rutledge.

Because she liked him.

CATHERINE MARKS KNEW THAT HARRY WAS UP TO SOMETHING. He was *always* up to something. He certainly had no intention of inquiring after her welfare—he didn't give a damn about her. He considered most people, including Catherine, a waste of his time.

Whatever mysterious mechanism sent Harry Rutledge's blood pumping through his veins, it wasn't a heart.

In the years of their acquaintance, Catherine had never asked anything of him. Once Harry did someone a favor, it went into the invisible ledger he carried around in that infernally clever brain, and it was only a matter of time until he demanded repayment with interest. People feared him for good reason. Harry had powerful friends and powerful enemies, and it was doubtful that even they knew what category they fell in.

The valet, or assistant, whatever he was, showed her into Harry's palatial apartment. Catherine thanked him with a frosty murmur. She sat in a receiving room with her hands resting in her lap. The receiving room had been designed to intimidate visitors, all of it done in slick, pale fabrics and cold marble and priceless Renaissance art.

Harry entered the room, large and breathtakingly self-assured. As always, he was elegantly dressed and meticulously groomed.

Stopping before her, he surveyed her with insolent green eyes. "Cat. You look well."

"Go to the devil," she said quietly.

His gaze dropped to the white plait of her fingers, and a lazy smile crossed his face. "I suppose to you, I *am* the devil." He nodded toward the other side of the settee she occupied. "May I?"

Catherine gave a short nod and waited until he had seated himself. "Why did you send for me?" Her voice was brittle.

"It was an amusing scene this morning, wasn't it? Your Hathaways were a delight. They're certainly not your run-of-the-mill society misses."

Slowly Catherine raised her gaze to his, trying not to flinch as she stared into the vivid depths of green. Harry excelled at hiding his thoughts . . . but this morning he had stared at Poppy with a hunger that he was usually too well disciplined to reveal. And Poppy had no idea of how to defend herself against a man like Harry.

Catherine strove to keep her voice even. "I will not discuss the Hathaways with you. And I warn you to stay away from them."

"You *warn* me?" Harry repeated softly, his eyes bright with mocking amusement.

"I won't let you hurt anyone in my family."

"*Your* family?" One of his dark brows lifted. "You have no family."

"I meant the family I work for," Catherine said with icy dignity. "I meant my charges. Especially Poppy. I saw the way you looked at her this morning. If you try to harm her in any way—"

"I have no intention of harming anyone."

"Regardless of your intentions, it happens, doesn't it?" Catherine felt a stab of satisfaction as she saw his eyes narrow.

"Poppy is far too good for you," she continued, "and she is out of your reach."

"Hardly anything is out of my reach, Cat." He said it without arrogance. It happened to be the truth. Which made Catherine all the more fearful.

"Poppy is practically betrothed," she replied sharply. "She is in love with someone."

"Michael Bayning."

Her heart began to hammer with alarm. "How do you know that?"

Harry ignored the question. "Do you really think that Viscount Andover, a man of notoriously exacting standards, would allow his son to marry a Hathaway?"

"I do. He loves his son, and therefore he will choose to overlook the fact that Poppy comes from an unconventional family. He could ask for no better mother for his future heirs."

"He's a peer. Bloodlines are everything to him. And while Poppy's bloodlines have led to an obviously charming result, they're far from pure."

"Her brother is a peer," Catherine snapped.

"Only by accident. The Hathaways are a twig on the farthest limb of the family tree. Ramsay may have inherited a title, but in terms of nobility, he's no more a peer than you or I. And Andover knows it."

"What a snob you are," Catherine observed in as calm a tone as she could manage.

"Not at all. I don't mind the Hathaways' common blood one bit. In fact, I like them all the better for it. All those anemic daughters of the peerage—none of them could hold a candle to the two girls I saw this morning." His smile became genuine for one dazzling moment. "What a pair. Catching a wild monkey with a comfit jar and string."

"Leave them alone," Catherine said. "You play with people as a cat does with mice. Entertain yourself with someone else, Harry. God knows you have no shortage of women who would do anything to please you."

"That's what makes them boring," he said gravely. "No, don't leave yet—there's something I want to ask. Has Poppy said anything to you about me?"

Mystified, Catherine shook her head. "Only that it was interesting to finally be able to put a face to the mysterious hotelier." She stared at him intently. "What else should she have told me?"

Harry adopted an innocent expression. "Nothing. I merely wondered if I had made an impression."

"I'm sure Poppy overlooked you entirely. Her affections are with Mr. Bayning, who, unlike you, is a good, honorable man."

"You wound me. Fortunately in matters of love, most women can be persuaded to choose a bad man over a good one."

"If you understood anything about love," Catherine said acidly, "you would know that Poppy would never choose *anyone* over the man she has already given her heart to."

"He can have her heart," came Harry's casual reply. "As long as I have the rest of her."

As Catherine spluttered in offended fury, Harry stood and went to the door. "Let me show you out. No doubt you'll want to go back and sound the alarms. For all the good it will do."

It had been a long time since Catherine had known such fathomless anxiety. Harry . . . Poppy . . . could he really have designs on her, or had he simply decided to torture Catherine with a cruel jest?

No, he had not been playacting. Of course Harry wanted Poppy, whose warmth and spontaneity and kindness was completely alien in his sophisticated world. He wanted a respite from his own inexhaustible needs, and once he was done with Poppy, he would have drained her of all the happiness and innocent charm that had attracted him in the first place.

Catherine didn't know what to do. She couldn't expose her own connection to Harry Rutledge, and he knew it.

The answer was to make certain that Poppy was betrothed to Michael Bayning, *publicly* betrothed, as soon as possible. Tomorrow Bayning would meet with the family and accompany them to the flower show. Afterward Catherine would find a way to hasten the courtship process. She would tell Cam and Amelia that they must press for the matter to be quickly resolved.

And if for some reason there was no betrothal—perish the thought—Catherine would suggest that she accompany Poppy on a trip abroad. Perhaps France or Italy. She would even tolerate the company of the galling Lord Ramsay, if he chose to go with them. Anything to keep Poppy safe from Harry Rutledge.

"Wake up, slugabed." Amelia strode into the bedroom wearing a dressing gown trimmed with cascades of soft lace, her dark hair gathered in a thick, neat braid over one shoulder. She had just come from feeding the baby. Having left him in the nursemaid's care, she was now set on the course of waking her husband.

Cam's natural preference was to stay up all hours of the night and rise late in the day. This habit was directly opposed to Amelia's early to bed, early to rise philosophy.

Going to one of the windows, she whisked open the curtains to admit the morning light, and was rewarded with a protesting groan from the bed. "Good morning," she said cheerfully. "The maid will be here soon to help me dress. You'd better put something on."

She busied herself at her dresser, sorting through a drawer of embroidered stockings. Out of the periphery of her vision she saw Cam stretch, his body lithe and powerful, his skin glowing like clover honey.

"Come here," Cam said in a sleep-darkened voice, drawing back the bed linens.

A laugh stirred in her throat. "Absolutely not. There is too much to be done. Everyone is busy except you."

"I intend to be busy. As soon as you come here. *Monisha,* don't make me chase you this early."

Amelia gave him a severe glance as she obeyed. "It's not early. In fact, if you don't wash and dress quickly, we'll be late to the flower show."

"How can you be late for flowers?" Cam shook his head and smiled, as he always did when she said something he considered to be nonsense. His gaze was hot and slumberous. "Come closer."

"Later." She gave a helpless gasp of laughter as he reached out with astonishing dexterity, snaring her wrist in his hand. "Cam, no."

"A good wife never refuses her husband," he teased.

"The maid—" she said breathlessly as she was pulled across the mattress, and clasped against all that warm golden skin.

"She can wait." He unbuttoned her robe, his hand slipping past the lace, fingertips exploring the sensitive curves of her breasts.

Amelia's giggles died away. He knew so much about her— too much—and he never hesitated to take ruthless advantage. She closed her eyes as she reached up to the nape of his neck. The clean, silky locks of his hair slipped through her fingers like liquid.

Cam kissed her tender throat, while one of his knees

nudged between hers. "It's either now," he murmured, "or behind the rhododendrons at the flower show. Your choice."

She writhed a little, not in protest but excitement as he trapped her arms in the confining sleeves of the dressing gown. "Cam," she managed to say as his head bent over her exposed breasts. "We're going to be so terribly late . . ."

He murmured his desire to her, speaking in Romany as he did whenever his mood turned amorous, and the liquid syllables fell hotly against her sensitive skin. And for the next several minutes he possessed her, consumed her, with a lack of inhibition that would have seemed outrageous had he not been so gentle.

"Cam," she said afterward, her arms clasped around his neck, "are you going to say something to Mr. Bayning today?"

"About pansies and primulas?"

"About his intentions toward my sister."

Cam smiled down at her as he fingered a loose lock of her hair. "Would you object if I did?"

"No, I want you to." A frown notched the space between her brows. "Poppy is adamant that no one should criticize Mr. Bayning for taking so long to speak to his father about courting her."

Gently Cam used the pad of his thumb to smooth away the little frown. "He's waited long enough. Roma say of a man like Bayning, 'he would like to eat fish, but he would not like to go into the water.'"

Amelia responded with a humorless chuckle. "It's very frustrating, to know that he's tiptoeing around the issue like this. I wish Bayning would simply go to his father and have it out."

Cam, who knew something about the aristocracy from his days as the manager of an exclusive gaming club, said dryly,

"A young man who stands to inherit as much as Bayning has to tread softly."

"I don't care. He's raised my sister's hopes very high. If it all comes to naught, she'll be devastated. And he kept her from being courted by other men, and wasted an entire season—"

"Shhh." Cam rolled to his side, taking her with him. "I agree with you, *monisha* . . . this shadow courtship must end. I'll make certain Bayning understands it's time to take action. And I'll speak to the viscount, if that will help."

"Thank you." Amelia tucked her cheek into one of the hard curves of his chest, seeking comfort. "I'll be so glad when this is resolved. Lately I haven't been able to rid myself of the feeling that things won't turn out well for Poppy and Mr. Bayning. I hope I'm wrong. I want so badly for Poppy to be happy, and . . . what will we do, if he breaks her heart?"

"We'll take care of her," he murmured, cuddling her. "And love her. That's what a family is for."

Chapter Eight

Poppy was light-headed with nerves and excitement. Michael would soon arrive to accompany the family to the flower show. After all their subterfuge, this was the first step toward an openly acknowledged courtship.

She had dressed with extra care in a yellow walking dress trimmed with black velvet cord. The layered skirts were caught up at intervals with black velvet bows. Beatrix wore a similar ensemble, only hers was blue trimmed in chocolate.

"Lovely," Miss Marks had pronounced, smiling as they entered the receiving room of the family suite. "You will be the two most elegant young ladies at the flower show." She reached up to Poppy's upswept curls and anchored a pin more securely. "And I predict that Mr. Bayning will not be able to take his gaze off you," she added.

"He's a bit late," Poppy said tensely. "It's not like him. I hope he hasn't met with some difficulty."

"He will arrive soon, I'm sure."

Cam and Amelia entered the room, the latter looking radiant in pink, her small waist cinched with a bronze leather belt that matched her walking boots.

"What a lovely day for an outing," Amelia said, her blue eyes twinkling. "Though I doubt you'll even notice the flowers, Poppy."

Putting a hand to her midriff, Poppy let out an unsteady sigh. "This is all so nerve-wracking."

"I know, dear." Amelia went to embrace her. "This makes me indescribably grateful that I never had to go through the London season. I would never have had your patience. Really, they should levy a tax on London bachelors until they marry. That would hasten the entire courtship process."

"I don't see why people have to marry at all," Beatrix said. "There was no one to marry Adam and Eve, was there? They lived together naturally. Why should any of us bother with a wedding if they didn't?"

Poppy gave a nervous laugh. "When Mr. Bayning is here," she said, "let's not bring up any outlandish debate topics, Bea. I'm afraid he's not used to our way of . . . well, our . . ."

"Colorful discussions," Miss Marks suggested.

Amelia grinned. "Don't worry, Poppy. We'll be absolute bores."

"Thank you," Poppy said fervently.

"Do I have to be boring, too?" Beatrix asked Miss Marks, who nodded emphatically.

With a sigh, Beatrix went to a table in the corner and began to empty her pockets.

Poppy's stomach flipped as she heard a knock at the door. "He's here," she said breathlessly.

"I will answer," Miss Marks said. She gave Poppy a quick smile. "Breathe, dear."

Poppy nodded and tried to calm herself. She saw Amelia and Cam exchange a glance she could not interpret. The understanding between the pair was so absolute, it seemed they could read each other's thoughts.

She was tempted to smile as she remembered Beatrix's

comment that rabbits were happiest in pairs. Beatrix had been right. Poppy wanted very much to be loved, to be part of a pair. And she had waited for so long, and she was still unwed when friends her age had already married and had two or three children. It seemed a common fate for Hathaways to find love later rather than sooner.

Poppy's thoughts were interrupted as Michael entered the room and bowed. A surge of gladness was tempered by the sight of his expression, more grim than she had ever imagined possible. His complexion was pale, his eyes reddened as if he'd had no sleep. He looked ill, as a matter of fact.

"Mr. Bayning," she said softly, her heart beating like a small animal fighting to free itself from a net. "Are you well? What is the matter?"

Michael's brown eyes, usually so warm, were bleak as he glanced at her family. "Forgive me," he said hoarsely. "I hardly know what to say." His breath seemed to shiver in his throat. "I am in some . . . some difficulty . . . it's impossible." His gaze settled on Poppy. "Miss Hathaway, I must speak with you. I don't know if it would be possible to have a moment alone . . ."

A difficult silence followed the request. Cam stared at the young man with an unfathomable expression, while Amelia gave a slight shake of her head as if to deny what was coming.

"I'm afraid that would not be proper, Mr. Bayning," Miss Marks murmured. "We have Miss Hathaway's reputation to consider."

"Of course." He passed a hand over his forehead, and Poppy realized that his fingers were trembling.

Something was very wrong indeed.

An icy calm settled over her. She spoke in a dazed voice that didn't sound quite like her own. "Amelia, perhaps you might stay in the room with us?"

"Yes, of course."

The rest of the family, including Miss Marks, left the room.

Poppy felt cold runnels of perspiration beneath her chemise, damp patches blossoming at the pits of her arms. She took a place on the settee and watched Michael with dilated eyes. "You may have a seat," she told him.

He hesitated and glanced at Amelia, who had gone to stand beside the window.

"Please do have a seat, Mr. Bayning," Amelia said, staring at the street outside. "I'm trying to pretend I'm not here. I'm so sorry you can't have more privacy than this, but I'm afraid Miss Marks is right. Poppy's reputation must be protected."

Although there was no trace of rebuke in her tone, Michael flinched visibly. Occupying the space next to Poppy, he took her hands and bent his head over them. His fingers were even colder than hers. "I had an unholy row with my father last night," he said, his voice muffled. "It seems one of the rumors reached him about my interest in you. About my intentions. He was . . . outraged."

"That must have been dreadful," Poppy said, knowing that Michael rarely, if ever, quarreled with his father. He held the viscount in awe, striving always to please him.

"Worse than dreadful." Michael took an unsteady breath. "I'll spare you the particulars. The result of a long, very ugly argument is that the viscount gave me an ultimatum. If I marry you, I will be cut off. He will no longer recognize me as his son, and I will be disinherited."

There was no sound in the room except for Amelia's swiftly indrawn breath.

Pain unfolded in Poppy's chest, crowding the breath from her lungs. "What reason did he give?" she managed to ask.

"Only that you do not fit the mold of a Bayning bride."

"If you allow time for his temper to cool . . . try to change his mind . . . I can wait, Michael. I'll wait forever."

Michael shook his head. "I cannot encourage you to wait. My father's refusal was absolute. It could take years to change his mind, if ever. And in the meantime, you deserve the chance to find happiness."

Poppy stared at him steadily. "I could only be happy with you."

Michael raised his head, his eyes dark and glittering. "I'm sorry, Poppy. Sorry for giving you any reason to hope, when it was never possible. My only excuse is that I thought I knew my father, when apparently I don't. I always believed I could convince him to accept the woman I loved, that my judgment would be enough. And I—" His voice cracked. He swallowed audibly. "I do love you. I . . . hell and damnation, I'll never forgive him for this." Releasing her hands, he reached into his coat pocket and extracted a packet of letters tied with cord. All the letters she had written to him. "I'm honor bound to return these."

"I won't give yours back," Poppy said, taking the letters in a shaking hand. "I want to keep them."

"That is your right, of course."

"Michael," Poppy said brokenly, "I love you."

"I . . . I can't give you any reason to hope."

They were both quiet and trembling, staring at each other in despair.

Amelia's voice pierced through the suffocating silence. She sounded blessedly rational. "The viscount's objections needn't stop you, Mr. Bayning. He can't prevent you from inheriting the title and entailed properties, can he?"

"No, but—"

"Take my sister to Gretna Green. We'll provide the carriage. My sister's dowry is large enough to secure a handsome annuity for you both. If you need more, my husband will increase it." Amelia leveled a steady, challenging gaze at him. "If you want my sister, Mr. Bayning, marry her. The Hathaways will help you weather what storms may come."

Poppy had never loved her sister more than she did at that moment. She stared at Amelia with a wobbly smile, her eyes brimming.

Her smile vanished, however, as Michael answered dully. "The title and real estate are entailed, but until my father dies, I would be abandoned to my own resources, which are nonexistent. And I can't live off the charity of my wife's family."

"It's not charity when it's family," Amelia countered.

"You don't understand how things are with the Baynings," Michael said. "This is a matter of honor. I'm the only son. I've been raised for one thing since I was born—to assume the responsibilities of my rank and title. It's all I've ever known. I can't live as an outcast, outside my father's sphere. I can't live with scandal and ostracism." He hung his head. "Sweet God, I'm weary of arguing. My brain's gone in circles all night."

Poppy saw the impatience on her sister's face, and she knew that Amelia was prepared to fight him on every point, for her sake. But she held Amelia's gaze and shook her head, sending the silent message, *It's no use*. Michael had already decided on his course. He would never defy his father. Arguing would only make him more miserable than he already was.

Amelia closed her mouth and turned to stare out the window again.

"I'm sorry," Michael said after a long silence, still gripping Poppy's hands. "I never meant to deceive you. Everything I told you about my feelings—every word was true. My only regret is that I wasted your time. Valuable time for a girl in your position."

Although he hadn't meant that as a slight, Poppy winced.

A girl in her position.

Twenty-three. Unmarried. On the shelf after her third season.

Carefully she drew her hands from Michael's. "Not a moment was wasted," she managed to say. "I am the better for having known you, Mr. Bayning. Please don't have any regrets. I don't."

"Poppy," he said in an aching voice that nearly undid her.

She was terrified that she might burst into tears. "Please go."

"If I could make you understand—"

"I understand. I do. And I will be perfectly—" She broke off and swallowed hard. "Please go. *Please.*"

She was aware of Amelia coming forward, murmuring something to Michael, efficiently shepherding him out of the suite before Poppy lost her composure. Dear Amelia, who did not hesitate to take charge of a man much larger than herself.

A hen chasing a cow, Poppy thought, and she let out a watery giggle even as hot tears began to slide from her eyes.

After closing the door firmly, Amelia sat beside Poppy and reached out to grasp her shoulders. She stared into Poppy's blurred eyes. "You are," she said, her voice ragged with emotion, "such a lady, Poppy. And much kinder than he deserved. I am so proud of you. I wonder if he understands how much he has lost."

"The situation wasn't his fault."

Amelia tugged a handkerchief from her sleeve and gave it to her. "Debatable. But I won't criticize him, since it won't help matters. However, I must say . . . the phrase 'I can't' comes rather too easily to his lips."

"He is an obedient son," Poppy said, mopping at her tears, then giving up and simply wadding the handkerchief against her flooding eyes.

"Yes, well . . . from now on, I advise you to look for a man with his own means of support."

Poppy shook her head, her face still buried in the handkerchief. "There's no one for me."

She felt her sister's arms go around her. "There is. There is, I *promise* you. He's waiting. He'll find you. And someday Michael Bayning will be nothing but a distant memory."

Poppy began to cry in earnest, wracking sobs that caused her ribs to ache. "God," she managed to gasp. "This hurts, Amelia. And it feels as if it will never end."

Carefully Amelia guided Poppy's head to her shoulder and kissed her wet cheek. "I know," she said. "I lived through it once. I remember what it was like. You'll cry, and then you'll be angry, and then despairing, and then angry again. But I know of a cure for heartbreak."

"What is it?" Poppy asked, letting out a shuddery sigh.

"Time . . . prayer . . . and most of all a family that loves you. You will always be loved, Poppy."

Poppy managed a wavering smile. "Thank God for sisters," she said, and wept against Amelia's shoulder.

MUCH LATER THAT NIGHT, THERE CAME A DETERMINED knock at the door of Harry Rutledge's private apartment. Jake Valentine paused in the act of laying out fresh clothes and polished black shoes for the morning. He went to answer the door and was confronted by a vaguely familiar–looking woman. She was small and slight, with light brown hair and blue gray eyes, and a pair of round spectacles perched on her nose. He considered her for a moment, trying to place her.

"May I help you?"

"I wish to see Mr. Rutledge."

"I'm afraid he's not at home."

Her mouth twisted at the well-worn phrase, used by servants when the master didn't wish to be disturbed. She spoke to him with scalding contempt. "Do you mean 'not at home' in the sense that he doesn't want to see me, or 'not at home' in the sense that he's actually gone?"

"Either way," Jake said implacably, "you won't see him tonight. But the truth is, he really isn't here. Is there a message I may convey to him?"

"Yes. Tell him that I hope he rots in hell for what he did to Poppy Hathaway. And then tell him that if he goes near her, I'll murder him."

Jake responded with a complete lack of alarm due to the fact that death threats against Harry were a more or less common occurrence. "And you are?"

"Just give him the message," she said curtly. "He'll know who it's from."

TWO DAYS AFTER MICHAEL BAYNING HAD VISITED THE HOTEL, the Hathaways' brother Leo, Lord Ramsay, came to call. Like other men-about-town, Leo leased a small Mayfair terrace during the season, and at the end of June retreated to his estate in the country. Although Leo could easily have chosen to live with the family at the Rutledge, he preferred privacy.

No one could deny that Leo was a handsome man, tall and broad shouldered, with dark brown hair and striking eyes. Unlike his sisters, his eyes were a light shade of blue, glacier colored with dark rims. Haunting. World-weary. He comported himself as a rake and did a thorough job of it, appearing never to care about anyone or anything. There were moments, however, when the mask was lifted just long enough to reveal a man of extraordinary feeling, and it was in those rare moments that Catherine was most apprehensive around him.

When they were in London, Leo was usually too busy to spend time with his family, for which Catherine was grateful. From the moment they had met, she had felt an intrinsic dislike for him, and he for her, flint and iron striking to create sparks of hatred. At times they competed to see who could say the most hurtful things to the other, each of them testing, prodding, trying to find places of vulnerability. They couldn't seem to help it, the constant urge to cut each other down to size.

Catherine answered the door of the family suite, and a jolt of reaction went through her as she was confronted by Leo's lanky, big-framed form. He was fashionably dressed in a dark coat with wide lapels, loose trousers with no creases, and a boldly patterned waistcoat with silver buttons.

He surveyed her with wintry eyes, an arrogant smile tilting the corners of his lips. "Good afternoon, Marks."

Catherine was stone-faced, her voice edged with scorn. "Lord Ramsay. I'm surprised you could tear yourself away from your amusements long enough to visit your sister."

Leo gave her a look of bemused mockery. "What have I done to earn a scolding? You know, Marks, if you ever learned to hold your tongue, your chances of attracting a man would rise exponentially."

Her eyes narrowed. "Why would I want to attract a man? I have yet to see anything they're good for."

"If for nothing else," Leo said, "you need us to help produce more women." He paused. "How is my sister?"

"Heartbroken."

Leo's mouth turned grim. "Let me in, Marks. I want to see her."

Catherine took a grudging step aside.

Leo went into the receiving room and found Poppy sitting alone with a book. He gave her an assessing glance. His normally bright-eyed sister was pale and drawn. She seemed unutterably weary, temporarily aged by grief.

Fury welled inside him. There were few people that mattered to him in the world, but Poppy was one of them.

It was unfair that the people who longed for love the most, searched the hardest for it, found it so elusive. And there seemed no good reason why Poppy, the prettiest girl in London, shouldn't have been married by now. But Leo had gone through lists of acquaintances in his mind, pondering whether any of them would do for his sister, and none of them was remotely suitable. If one had the right temperament, he was an idiot or in his dotage. And then there were the lechers, the spendthrifts, and the reprobates. God help him, the peerage was a deplorable collection of male specimens. And he included himself in that estimation.

"Hello, sis," Leo said gently, approaching her. "Where are the others?"

Poppy managed a wan smile. "Cam is out on business matters, and Amelia and Beatrix are at the park, pushing Rye in the perambulator." She moved her feet to make room for him on the settee. "How are you, Leo?"

"Never mind that. What about you?"

"Never better," she said bravely.

"Yes, I can see that." Leo sat and reached for Poppy, gathering her close. He held her, patting her back, until he heard her sniffle. "That bastard," he said quietly. "Shall I kill him for you?"

"No," she said in a congested voice, "it wasn't his fault. He sincerely wanted to marry me. His intentions were good."

He kissed the top of her head. "Don't ever trust men with good intentions. They'll always disappoint you."

Refusing to smile at his quip, Poppy drew back to look at him. "I want to go home, Leo," she said plaintively.

"Of course you do, darling. But you can't yet."

She blinked. "Why not?"

"Yes, why not?" Catherine Marks asked tartly, sitting in a nearby chair.

Leo paused to send a brief scowl in the companion's direction before returning his attention to Poppy. "Rumors are flying," he said bluntly. "Last night I went to a drum, given by the wife of the Spanish ambassador—one of those things you go to only to be able to say you went—and I couldn't count the number of times I was asked about you and Bayning. Everyone seems to think that you were in love with Bayning, and that he rejected you because his father thinks you're not good enough."

"That's the truth."

"Poppy, this is London society, where the truth can ruin everything. If you tell one truth, you'll have to tell another truth, and another, to keep covering up."

That elicited a genuine smile from her. "Are you trying to give me advice, Leo?"

"Yes, and although I always tell you to ignore my advice, this time you'd better take it. The last significant event of the season is a ball held by Lord and Lady Norbury next week—"

"We have just written our regrets," Catherine informed him. "Poppy does not wish to attend."

Leo glanced at her sharply. "Have the regrets been sent?"

"No, but—"

"Tear them up, then. That's an order." Leo saw her narrow frame stiffen, and he got a perverse pleasure from the sight.

"But, Leo," Poppy protested, "I don't want to go to a ball. People might be watching to see if I—"

"They will certainly be watching," Leo said. "Like a flock of vultures. Which is why you have to attend. Because if you don't, you'll be shredded by the gossips, and mocked without mercy when next season begins."

"I don't care," Poppy said. "I'll never go through another season again."

"You may change your mind. And I want you to have the choice. Which is why you're going to the ball, Poppy. You'll wear your prettiest dress, and blue ribbons in your hair, and show them all that you don't give a damn about Michael Bayning. You're going to dance and laugh, and hold your head high."

"Leo," Poppy groaned. "I don't know if I can."

"Of course you can. Your pride demands it."

"I don't have any reason to be proud."

"I don't either," Leo said. "But that doesn't stop me, does it?" He glanced from Poppy's reluctant expression to Catherine's unreadable one. "Tell her I'm right, damn it," he told her. "She has to go, doesn't she?"

Catherine hesitated uncomfortably. Much as it galled her to admit it, Leo was indeed right. A confident, smiling appearance by Poppy at the ball would do much to still the wagging tongues of London parlors. But her instincts urged that Poppy should be taken to the safety of Hampshire as soon as possible. As long as she remained in town, she was in Harry Rutledge's reach.

On the other hand . . . Harry never attended such events, where desperate matchmaking mothers with unclaimed daughters scrabbled to snare every last available bachelor. Harry would never lower himself to go to the Norbury ball, especially since his appearance there would turn it into a veritable circus.

"Please control your language," Catherine said. "Yes, you are right. However, it will be difficult for Poppy. And if she loses her composure at the ball—if she gives way to tears—it will give the gossips even more ammunition."

"I won't lose my composure," Poppy said, sounding drained. "I feel as if I've cried enough for a lifetime."

"Good girl," Leo said softly. He glanced at Catherine's troubled expression and smiled. "It appears we've finally agreed on something, Marks. But don't worry—I'm sure it won't happen again."

Chapter Nine

The Norbury ball was held in Belgravia, a district of calm and quietness in the heart of London. One could be overwhelmed by the bustle and roar of traffic and activity on Knightsbridge or Sloane Street, cross over to Belgrave Square, and find oneself in an oasis of soothing decorum. It was a place of large marble embassies and grand white terraces, of solemn mansions with tall powdered footmen and stout butlers, and carriages conveying languid young ladies and their tiny overfed dogs.

The surrounding districts of London held little interest for those fortunate enough to live in Belgravia. Conversations were largely about local matters—who had taken a particular house, or what nearby street needed repairs, or what events had taken place at a neighboring residence.

To Poppy's dismay, Cam and Amelia had agreed with Leo's assessment of the situation. A show of pride and unconcern was called for if Poppy wished to stem the tide of gossip concerning Michael Bayning's rejection. "The *gadje* has a long memory of these matters," Cam had said sardonically. "God knows why they attach such importance to things of no consequence. But they do."

"It's only one evening," Amelia had told Poppy in concern. "Do you think you could manage an appearance, dear?"

"Yes," Poppy had agreed dully. "If you are there, I can manage it."

However, as she ascended the front steps to the mansion's portico, Poppy was swamped with regret and dread. The glass of wine she'd had to bolster her courage had pooled like acid in her stomach, and her corset had been laced too tightly.

She wore a white dress, layers of draped satin and pale blue illusion. Her waist was cinched with a belt of satin folds, the bodice deep and scooped and trimmed with another delicate froth of blue. After arranging her hair in a mass of pinned-up curls, Amelia had threaded a thin blue ribbon through it.

Leo had arrived, as promised, to accompany the family to the ball. He held out his arm for Poppy and escorted her up the stairs, while the family followed *en masse*. They entered the overheated house, which was filled with flowers, music, and the din of hundreds of simultaneous conversations. Doors had been removed from their hinges to allow for the circulation of guests from the ballroom to the supper and card rooms.

The Hathaways waited in a receiving line in the entrance hall.

"Look how dignified and polite they all are," Leo said, observing the crowd. "I can't stay long. Someone might influence me."

"You promised you would stay until after the first set," Poppy reminded him.

Her brother sighed. "For you, I will. But I despise these affairs."

"As do I," Miss Marks surprised them all by saying grimly, surveying the gathering as if it were enemy territory.

"My God. Something else we agree on." Leo gave the companion a half-mocking, half-uneasy glance. "We have to stop doing this, Marks. My stomach is starting to turn."

"*Please* do not say that word," she snapped.

"Stomach? Why not?"

"It is indelicate to refer to your anatomy." She gave his tall form a disdainful glance. "And I assure you, no one has any interest in it."

"You think not? I'll have you know, Marks, that scores of women have remarked on my—"

"Ramsay," Cam interrupted, giving him a warning glance.

When they had made it through the entrance hall, the family dispersed to make the rounds. Leo and Cam went to the card rooms, while the women headed to the supper tables. Amelia was instantly captured by a small group of chattering matrons.

"I can't eat," Poppy commented, glancing with revulsion at the long buffet of cold joints, beef, ham, and lobster salads.

"I'm starved," Beatrix. said apologetically. "Do you mind if I have something?"

"Not at all, we'll wait with you."

"Have a spoonful of salad," Miss Marks murmured to Poppy. "For appearance's sake. And smile."

"Like this?" Poppy attempted to turn the corners of her mouth upward.

Beatrix regarded her doubtfully. "No, that's not pretty at all. You look like a salmon."

"I feel like a salmon," Poppy said. "One that's been boiled, shredded and potted."

As the guests queued at the buffet, footmen filled their plates and carried them to nearby tables.

Poppy was still waiting in line when she was approached by Lady Belinda Wallscourt, a pretty young woman she had befriended during the Season. As soon as Belinda had come out into society, she was pursued by several eligible gentlemen, and had quickly become betrothed.

"Poppy," Lady Belinda said warmly, "how nice to see you here. There was uncertainty as to whether you would come."

"The last ball of the Season?" Poppy said with a forced smile. "I wouldn't miss it."

"I'm so glad." Lady Belinda gave her a compassionate glance. Her voice lowered. "It's terrible, what happened to you. I'm dreadfully sorry."

"Oh, there's nothing to be sorry about," Poppy said brightly. "I'm perfectly fine!"

"You're very brave," Belinda replied. "And Poppy, remember that someday you will meet a frog who will turn into a handsome prince."

"Good," Beatrix said. "Because all she's met so far are princes who turn into frogs."

Looking perplexed, Belinda managed a smile and left them.

"Mr. Bayning is not a frog," Poppy protested.

"You're right," Beatrix said. "That was very unfair to frogs, who are lovely creatures."

As Poppy parted her lips to object, she heard Miss Marks snicker. And she began to laugh as well, until they attracted curious glances from the queue at the buffet.

After Beatrix had finished eating, they wandered to the ballroom. Music fluttered downward in continuous drifts from the orchestra playing in the upper gallery. The massive room glittered in the light of eight chandeliers, while the sweetness of abundant roses and greenery thickened the air.

Cinched in the unforgiving confines of her corset, Poppy

filled her lungs with strained breaths. "It's too warm in here," she said.

Miss Marks glanced at her perspiring face, quickly produced a handkerchief, and guided her into one of the many cane openwork chairs at the side of the room. "It is quite warm," she said. "In a moment, I will locate your brother or Mr. Rohan to escort you outside for some air. But first let me see to Beatrix."

"Yes, of course," Poppy managed, seeing that two men had already approached Beatrix in hopes of entering their names on her dance card. Her younger sister was at ease with men in a way that Poppy could never manage. They seemed to adore Beatrix because she treated them as she did her wild creatures, gently humoring, showing patient interest.

While Miss Marks supervised Beatrix's dance card, Poppy settled back in her chair and concentrated on breathing within the iron prison of her corset. It was unfortunate that in this particular chair, she was able to hear a conversation from the other side of a garlanded column.

A trio of young women spoke in low tones that oozed with smug satisfaction.

"Of course Bayning wouldn't have her," one of them said. "She's pretty, I'll allow, but so maladroit, in the social sense. A gentleman I know said that he tried to talk to her at the private art viewing at the Royal Academy, and she was prattling about some ridiculous topic . . . something about a long-ago French balloon experiment when they sent a sheep up into the air in front of King Louis something-or-other . . . can you *imagine*?"

"Louis the sixteenth," Poppy whispered.

"But what would you expect?" came another voice. "Such an odd family. The only one fit for society is Lord Ramsay, and he is quite wicked."

"A rogue," the other one agreed.

Poppy went from being overheated to chilled. She closed her eyes sickly, wishing she could disappear. It had been a mistake to come to the ball. She was trying to prove something to everyone . . . that she didn't care about Michael Bayning, when she did. That her heart wasn't broken, when it was. Everything in London was about appearances, pretenses . . . was it so unforgivable to be honest about one's feelings?

Apparently so.

She sat quietly, knitting her gloved fingers together until her thoughts were diverted by a stir near the main entrance of the ballroom. It seemed that some important person had arrived, perhaps royalty, or a military celebrity, or an influential politician.

"Who is he?" one of the young women asked.

"Someone new," the other said.

"And handsome."

"Divine," her companion agreed. "He must be a man of consequence—otherwise there wouldn't be such a to-do."

A light laugh. "And Lady Norbury wouldn't be fluttering so. See how she blushes!"

Curious despite herself, Poppy leaned forward to catch a glimpse of the newcomer. All she could make out was a dark head, taller than the others around him. He walked further into the ballroom, talking easily with his companions while the stout, bejeweled, and beaming Lady Norbury clung to his arm.

Recognizing him, Poppy sat back in her chair.

Harry Rutledge.

She couldn't fathom why he would be here, or why that made her smile.

Probably because she couldn't help recalling the last time she had seen him, dressed in fencing whites, trying to skewer a misbehaving monkey. Tonight Harry was forbiddingly handsome in full evening attire and a crisp white cravat. And he moved and conversed with the same charismatic ease that he appeared to do everything.

Miss Marks returned to Poppy, while Beatrix and a fair-haired man disappeared into the whirl of waltzing couples. "How do you—" she began, but stopped with a sharply indrawn breath. "Damn and blast," she whispered. "He's here."

It was the first time Poppy had ever heard her companion curse. Surprised by Miss Marks's reaction to Harry Rutledge's presence at the ball, Poppy frowned. "I noticed. But why do you—"

She broke off as she followed the direction of her companion's gaze.

Miss Marks wasn't looking at Harry Rutledge.

She was looking at Michael Bayning.

An explosion of pain filled Poppy's chest as she saw her former suitor across the room, slim and handsome, his gaze fixed on her. He had rejected her, exposed her to public mockery, and then he had come to a ball? Was he searching for a new girl to court now? Perhaps he had assumed that while he danced with eager young women in Belgravia, Poppy would be hiding in her hotel suite, weeping into her pillow.

Which was precisely what she wanted to be doing.

"Oh, God," Poppy whispered, staring into Miss Marks's concerned face. "Don't let him talk to me."

"He won't make a scene," her companion said softly. "Quite the opposite—a pleasantry or two will smooth the situation over for both of you."

"You don't understand," Poppy said hoarsely. "I can't *do* pleasantries right now. I can't face him. *Please,* Miss Marks—"

"I'll send him away," her companion said softly, squaring her narrow shoulders. "Don't worry. Collect yourself, dear." She moved in front of Poppy, blocking Michael's view, and went forward to speak to him.

"Thank you," Poppy whispered, even though Miss Marks couldn't hear. Horrified to feel the sting of desperate tears, she concentrated blindly on a section of floor in front of her. *Don't cry. Don't cry. Don't—*

"Miss Hathaway." Lady Norbury's jovial voice intruded on her frantic thoughts. "This gentleman has requested an introduction, you fortunate girl! It is my honor and delight to present Mr. Harry Rutledge, the hotelier."

A pair of highly polished black shoes came into her vision. Poppy glanced miserably up into his vivid green eyes.

Harry bowed, holding her gaze. "Miss Hathaway, how do you—"

"I'd love to waltz," Poppy said, practically leaping from her chair and seizing his arm. Her throat was so tight, she could hardly speak. "Let's go now."

Lady Norbury gave a disconcerted laugh. "What charming enthusiasm."

Poppy gripped Harry's arm as if it were a lifeline. His gaze dropped to the clench of her fingers on the fine black wool of his sleeve. He covered her fingers with the reassuring pressure of his free hand, his thumb smoothing over the edge of her wrist. And even through two layers of white gloves, she felt the comfort in his touch.

At that moment Miss Marks returned, having just dispatched Michael Bayning. Her brows lowered in a scowl as she looked up at Harry. "No," she said shortly.

"*No?*" His lips twitched with amusement. "I haven't asked for anything yet."

Miss Marks gave him a cold stare. "Obviously you wish to dance with Miss Hathaway."

"You have objections?" he asked innocently.

"Several," Miss Marks said, her manner so curt that both Lady Norbury and Poppy looked askance.

"Miss Marks," Lady Norbury said, "I can vouch for this gentleman's character."

The companion pressed her lips into a hyphen. She surveyed Poppy's glittering eyes and flushed face, seeming to understand how close she was to losing her composure. "When the dance is finished," she told Poppy grimly, "you will take his left arm, insist that he conduct you directly back to me, here, and then he will take his leave. Understood?"

"Yes," Poppy whispered, glancing over Harry's broad shoulder.

Michael was staring at her from across the room, his face ashen.

The situation was hideous. Poppy wanted to run from the ballroom. Instead, she would have to dance.

Harry led Poppy toward the crowd of waltzing couples and settled his gloved hand at her waist. She reached for him, one palm light and trembling at his shoulder, her other hand gripped securely in his. In one astute glance, Harry took in the entire scene: Poppy's unshed tears, Michael Bayning's set face, and the slew of curious gazes encompassing them.

"How can I help?" he asked gently.

"Take me away," she said. "As far as possible from here. Timbuktu."

Harry looked sympathetic and amused. "Would you settle for a tour around the ballroom?" He drew Poppy into the current of dancers, swift counter-clockwise turns in a clockwise pattern.

Poppy was profoundly grateful to have something to focus on besides Michael. As she might have expected, Harry Rutledge was an excellent dancer. Poppy relaxed into his smooth, strong lead. "Thank you," she said. "You're probably wondering why I—"

"No, I don't wonder. It was written on your face, and Bayning's, for everyone to see. You're not very good at subterfuge, are you?"

"I've never needed to be." To Poppy's horror, her throat clenched and her eyes stung. She was about to burst into tears in front of everyone. As she tried to take a steadying breath, the corset squeezed her lungs, and she felt dizzy. "Mr. Rutledge," she wheezed, "Could you take me out to the terrace for some air?"

"Certainly." His voice was reassuringly calm. "One more circuit around the room, and we'll slip out."

In other circumstances, Poppy might have taken pleasure in the surenccs of his lead, the music that gilded the air. She stared fixedly at the dark face of her unlikely rescuer. He was dazzling in the elegant clothes, his heavy dark hair brushed back in disciplined layers. But his eyes were underpinned by the ever-present hint of shadows. Windows to a restless soul. He didn't sleep enough, she thought, and wondered if anyone ever dared mention it to him.

Even through the haze of numb desolation, it occurred to Poppy that by asking her to dance, Harry Rutledge had singled her out in what could have been construed by many as a declaration of interest.

But that couldn't be true.

"Why?" she asked faintly, without thinking.

"Why what?"

"Why did you ask me to dance?"

Harry hesitated as if torn between the necessity of tact and the inclination toward honesty. He settled on the latter. "Because I wanted to hold you."

Thrown into confusion, Poppy focused on the simple knot

of his white cravat. At another time, in another situation, she would have been extraordinarily flattered. At the moment, however, she was too absorbed in her despair over Michael.

With sneak-thief adroitness, Harry extricated her from the aggregate of dancers and led her to the row of French doors opening onto the terrace. She followed blindly, hardly caring if they were seen or not.

The air outside was a brace of coolness, dry and sharp in her lungs. Poppy breathed in rapid gasps, grateful to have escaped the smothering atmosphere of the ballroom. Hot tears slid from her eyes.

"Here," Harry said, guiding her to the far side of the balcony, which extended nearly the full width of the mansion. The lawn below was a quiet ocean. Harry brought Poppy to a shadowed corner. Reaching inside his coat pocket, he found a pressed square of fine linen and gave it to her.

Poppy blotted her eyes. "I can't begin to tell you," she said unsteadily, "how very sorry I am. You were so kind in asking me to dance, and now you're k-keeping company with a w-watering pot."

Looking amused and sympathetic, Harry leaned an elbow on the balcony railing as he faced her. His quietness relieved her. He waited patiently, as if he understood that no words could be an adequate plaster for her bruised spirit.

Poppy let out a slow breath, feeling soothed by the coolness of the night and the blessed lack of noise. "Mr. Bayning was going to offer for me," she told Harry. She blew her nose with a childlike gust. "But he changed his mind."

Harry studied her, his eyes catlike in the darkness. "What reason did he give?"

"His father didn't approve of the match."

"And that surprises you?"

"Yes," she said defensively. "Because he made promises to me."

"Men in Bayning's position are rarely, if ever, allowed to marry whomever they want. There's far more to consider than their personal preferences."

"More important than love?" Poppy asked with bitter vehemence.

"Of course."

"When all is said and done, marriage is a union of two people made by the same God. Nothing more, nothing less. Does that sound naïve?"

"Yes," he said flatly.

Poppy's lips quirked, although she felt nothing close to actual amusement. "I'm sure I've read too many fairy tales. The prince is supposed to slay the dragon, defeat the villain, and marry the princess, and carry her off to his castle."

"Fairy tales are best read as entertainment," Harry said. "Not as a guide to life." He removed his gloves methodically and tucked them into one of his coat pockets. Resting both his forearms on the railing, he sent her a sideways glance. "What does the princess do when the prince disappoints her?"

"She goes home." Poppy's fingers tightened on the damp ball of the handkerchief. "I'm not suited for London and all its illusions. I want to return to Hampshire, where I can rusticate in peace."

"For how long?"

"Forever."

"And marry a farmer?" he asked skeptically.

"Perhaps." Poppy dried the residue of her tears. "I would make a wonderful farmwife. I'm good with cows. I know how to make hotchpotch. And I would appreciate the peace and quiet for my reading."

"Hotchpotch? What is that?" Harry seemed to have undue interest in the subject, his head inclined toward hers.

"A harvest vegetable broth."

"How did you learn to make it?"

"My mother." Poppy lowered her voice as if imparting highly confidential information. "The secret," she said wisely, "is a splash of ale."

They were standing too close. Poppy knew she should move away. But his nearness felt like shelter, and his scent was fresh and beguiling. The night air raised gooseflesh on her bare arms. How large and warm he was. She wanted to match herself against him and burrow inside the haven of his coat as if she were one of Beatrix's small pets.

"You're not meant to be a farmwife," Harry said.

Poppy gave him a rueful glance. "You think no farmer would have me?"

"I think," he said slowly, "you should marry a man who would appreciate you."

She made a face. "Those are in short supply."

He smiled. "You don't need a supply. You just need one." He grasped Poppy's shoulder, his hand curving over the illusion-trimmed sleeve of her gown until she felt its warmth through the fragile gauze. His thumb toyed with the filmy edge of fabric, brushing her skin in a way that made her stomach tighten. "Poppy," he said gently, "what if I asked for permission to court you?"

She went blank as astonishment swept through her.

Finally, someone had asked to court her.

And it wasn't Michael, or any of the diffident, superior aristocrats she had met during three failed seasons. It was Harry Rutledge, an elusive and enigmatic man she had known only a matter of days.

"Why me?" was all she could manage.

"Because you're interesting and beautiful. Because saying

your name makes me smile. Most of all because this may be my only hope of ever having hotchpotch."

"I'm sorry, but . . . no. It wouldn't be a good idea at all."

"I think it's the best idea I've ever had. Why can't we?"

Poppy's mind was spinning. She could hardly stammer out a reply. "I-I don't like courtship. It's very stressful. And disappointing."

His thumb found the soft ridge of her collarbone and traced it slowly. "It's arguable that you've ever had a real courtship. But if it pleases you, we'll dispense with it altogether. That would save time."

"I don't want to dispense with it," Poppy said, increasingly flustered. She trembled as she felt his fingertips glide along the side of her neck. "What I mean is . . . Mr. Rutledge, I've just been through a very difficult experience. This is too soon."

"You were courted by a boy, who had to do as he was told." His hot breath feathered against her lips as he whispered, "You should try it with a man, who needs no one's permission."

A man. Well, he certainly was that.

"I don't have the luxury of waiting," Harry continued. "Not when you're so hell-bent on going back to Hampshire. You're the reason I'm here tonight, Poppy. Believe me, I wouldn't have come otherwise."

"You don't like balls?"

"I do. But the ones I attend are given by a far different crowd."

Poppy couldn't imagine what crowd he was referring to, or what kind of people he usually associated with. Harry Rutledge was too much of a mystery. Too experienced, too overwhelming in every way. He could never offer the quiet, ordinary, sane life she longed for.

"Mr. Rutledge, please don't take this as an affront, but you don't have the qualities I seek in a husband."

"How do you know? I have some excellent qualities you haven't even seen yet."

Poppy gave a shaky laugh. "I think you could talk a fish out of its skin," she told him. "But still, I don't—" She broke off as he bent slowly and touched his lips to hers, as if her laughter were something he could taste. She felt the imprint of his mouth even after he drew back.

"Spend an afternoon with me," he urged. "Tomorrow."

"No, Mr. Rutledge. I'm—"

"Harry."

"Harry, I can't—"

"An hour?" he whispered. He bent to her again, and she lifted her face, her eyes half-closing. The pressure of his mouth was warm and gentle, caressing her lips before moving down to the edge of her jaw and along the vulnerable side of her neck.

No one had ever done such a thing, not even Michael. Who would have thought it would feel so delicious? Dazed, Poppy let her head fall back, her body accepting the steady support of his arms. He searched her throat with devastating care, touching his tongue to her pulse. His hand cradled her nape, the pad of his thumb tracing the satiny edge of her hairline. As her balance faltered, she reached around his neck.

He was so gentle, teasing color to the surface of her skin, chasing little shivers with his mouth. Blindly she followed, wanting the taste of him. As she angled her face toward his, her lips grazed the close-shaven surface of his jaw. His breath caught. "You should never cry over a man," he said against her cheek. His voice was soft, dark, like smoked honey. "No one is worth your tears." Before she could answer, he caught her mouth in a full, open kiss.

Poppy went weak, melting against him as he kissed her slowly. The tip of his tongue entered, played gently, and the feel of it was so strange and intimate and tantalizing that a wild tremor ran through her. His mouth lifted at once.

"I'm sorry. Did I frighten you?"

Poppy couldn't seem to think of an answer. It wasn't that he had frightened her, more that he had given her a glimpse of a vast erotic territory she had never encountered before. Even in her inexperience, she comprehended that this man had the power to turn her inside out with pleasure. And that was not something she had ever considered or bargained for.

She tried to swallow the heartbeat that had ascended in her throat. Her lips felt stung and swollen. Her body throbbed in unfamiliar places.

Harry framed her face in his hands, his thumbs stroking her crimson cheeks. "The waltz is over by now. Your companion is going to turn on me like a rat terrier for bringing you back late."

"She's very protective," Poppy managed to say.

"She should be." Harry lowered his hands, setting her free.

Poppy stumbled, her knees astonishingly weak. Harry grabbed her in a swift reflex, pulling her back against him. "Easy." She heard him laugh softly. "My fault. I shouldn't have kissed you like that."

"You're right," she said, her sense of humor tentatively reasserting itself. "I should give you a setdown . . . slap you or something . . . what is the usual response from ladies you've taken liberties with?"

"They encourage me to do it again?" Harry suggested in such a helpful manner that Poppy couldn't help smiling.

"No," she said. "I'm not going to encourage you."

They faced each other in darkness relieved only by the slivers of light shed by upper-floor windows. How capricious life was, Poppy thought. She should have been dancing with Michael tonight. But now she was Michael's castoff, and she was standing outside the ballroom, in the shadows with a stranger.

Interesting, that she could be so in love with one man and yet find another so compelling. But Harry Rutledge was one of the most fascinating people she had ever met, with so many layers of charm and drive and ruthlessness that she couldn't fathom what kind of man he really was. She wondered what he was like in his private moments.

She was almost sorry she would never find out.

"Give me a penance," Harry urged. "I'll do whatever you ask."

As their gazes caught and held in the shadows, Poppy realized that he actually meant it. "How large a penance?" she asked.

Harry tilted his head a little, studying her intently. "Ask for anything."

"What if I wanted a castle?"

"Done," he said promptly.

"Actually, I don't want a castle. Too drafty. What about a diamond tiara?"

"Certainly. A modest one suitable for daytime wear, or something more elaborate?"

Poppy began to smile, when a few minutes earlier she had thought she would never smile again. She felt a surge of liking and gratitude. She couldn't think of anyone else who would have been able to console her in these circumstances. But the smile turned bittersweet as she looked up at him once more.

"Thank you," she said. "But I'm afraid no one can give me the one thing I truly want."

Rising on her toes, she pressed her lips sweetly to his cheek. It was a friendly kiss.

A good-bye kiss.

Harry looked down at her intently. His gaze flicked to something beyond her, before his mouth came down over hers with smoldering demand. Confounded by his sudden aggression, thrown off balance, she reached out for him reflexively. It was the wrong reaction, the wrong time and place . . . wrong to feel a surge of pleasure as he tasted and sweetly delved inside her mouth . . . but, as she was discovering, there were some temptations impossible to resist. And his kisses seemed to wring a helpless response from every part of her, a bonfire of feeling. She couldn't catch up with her own pulse, her own breath. Her nerves lit with sparks of sensation, while stars cascaded all around her, little bursts of light striking the tiles of the terrace floor with the sound of breaking crystal . . .

Trying to ignore the harsh noise, Poppy leaned harder against him. But Harry eased her away with a quiet murmur, and guided her head to his chest as if he were trying to protect her.

Her lashes lifted, and she went cold and still as she saw that someone . . . *several* someones . . . had come out to the balcony.

Lady Norbury, who had dropped a glass of champagne in her surprise. And Lord Norbury, and another elderly couple.

And Michael, with a blond woman on his arm.

They all stared at Poppy and Harry in shock.

Had the angel of death appeared at that moment, complete with black wings and a gleaming scythe, Poppy would have run to him with open arms. Because being caught on the balcony kissing Harry Rutledge was not just a scandal . . . it would be the stuff of legend. She was ruined. Her life was ruined. Her family was ruined. Everyone in London would know by sunrise.

Dumbstruck by the sheer awfulness of the situation, Poppy looked helplessly up at Harry. And for one confusing moment, she thought she saw a flicker of predatory satisfaction in his eyes. But then his expression changed.

"This might be difficult for us to explain," he said.

Chapter Ten

As Leo made his way through the Norbury mansion, he was privately amused as he saw some of his friends— young lords whose debauchery had put even *his* past exploits to shame—now starched and buttoned up and impeccably mannered. Not for the first time, Leo reflected how unfair it was that men were held to far lower standards than women.

This business of manners, for example . . . he had seen his sisters struggling to remember hundreds of inane points of etiquette that were expected of upper-class society. Whereas Leo, as a man with a title, was unfailingly excused for nearly anything. Ladies at a supper party were criticized behind their backs if they used the wrong fork for the fish course, while a man could drink to excess or make some off-color remark, and everyone pretended not to notice.

Nonchalantly, Leo entered the ballroom and stood to the side of the triple-width doorway, surveying the scene. Dull, dull, dull. There was the ever-present row of virgins and their chaperones, and clusters of gossiping women that reminded him of nothing so much as a hen yard.

His attention was snared by the sight of Catherine Marks, standing in the corner and watching as Beatrix and her partner danced.

Marks looked tense as usual, her slender dark-clad figure as straight as a ramrod. She never missed an opportunity to disdain Leo and treat him as if he had all the intellectual prowess of an oyster. And she was resistant to any attempts at charm or humor. Like any sensible man, Leo did his best to avoid her.

But to his chagrin, Leo couldn't stop himself from wondering what Catherine Marks would look like after a good, thorough tupping. Her spectacles cast aside, her silky hair loose and tumbled, her pale body released from the contraption of stays and laces . . .

Suddenly nothing at the ball seemed quite so interesting as his sisters' companion.

Leo decided to go bother her.

He sauntered to her. "Hello, Marks. How is the—"

"*Where have you been?*" she whispered violently, her eyes flashing furiously behind her spectacles.

"In the card room. And then I had a plate of supper. Where else should I have been?"

"You were supposed to have been helping with Poppy."

"Helping with what? I promised I would dance with her, and here I am." Leo paused and glanced around them. "Where is she?"

"I don't know."

He frowned. "How can you not know? You mean to say you've lost her?"

"The last time I saw Poppy was approximately ten minutes ago, when she went to dance with Mr. Rutledge."

"The hotel owner? He never appears at these things."

"He did this evening," Miss Marks said grimly, keeping her tone low. "And now they've disappeared. *Together*. You

must find her, my lord. *Now.* She is in danger of being ruined."

"Why haven't you gone after her?"

"Someone has to keep an eye on Beatrix, or she'll disappear as well. Besides, I didn't want to draw attention to
Poppy's absence. Go find her, and be quick about it."

Leo scowled. "Marks, in case you hadn't noticed, other
servants don't snap out orders to their masters. So if you don't
mind—"

"You're not my master," she had the nerve to say, glaring
insolently at him.

Oh, I'd like to be, Leo thought in a quick flush of arousal,
every hair on his body standing erect. Along with a certain
feature of his anatomy. He decided to leave before her effect
on him became obvious. "All right, settle your feathers. I'll
find Poppy."

"Start looking in the places where you would take a
woman to compromise her. There can't be that many."

"Yes, there can. You'd be amazed at the variety of places
I've—"

"Please," she muttered. "I'm feeling nauseous enough at
the moment."

Casting an assessing glance around the ballroom, Leo
spied the row of French doors at the far end. He headed for
the balcony, trying to go as fast as possible without appearing to be in a hurry. It was his cursed luck to be snared in
two separate conversations on the way, one with a friend who
wanted his opinion of a certain lady, the other with a dowa-
ger who thought the punch was "off" and wanted to know if
he'd tried it.

Finally Leo made it to one of the doors and slipped outside.

His eyes widened as he beheld an astonishing tableau.

Poppy, clasped in the arms of a tall black-haired man . . . being watched by a small group of people who had come onto the balcony through another set of doors. And one of them was Michael Bayning, who looked sick with jealousy and outrage.

The black-haired man lifted his head, murmured something to Poppy, and leveled a cool glance at Michael Bayning.

A glance of triumph.

It only lasted a moment, but Leo saw it, and recognized it for what it was.

"Holy hell," Leo whispered.

His sister was in considerable trouble.

WHEN A HATHAWAY CAUSED A SCANDAL, THEY NEVER DID it by half measures.

By the time Leo steered Poppy back into the ballroom and collected Miss Marks and Beatrix, the scandal had started to spread. In no time at all, Cam and Amelia had found them, and the family drew together in a protective cluster around Poppy.

"What happened?" Cam asked, looking deceptively relaxed, his hazel eyes alert.

"Harry Rutledge happened," Leo muttered. "I'll explain everything shortly. For now, let's leave here as quickly as possible and meet Rutledge at the hotel."

Amelia leaned close to murmur into Poppy's scarlet ear. "It's all right, dear. Whatever it is, we'll fix it."

"You can't," Poppy whispered. "No one can."

Leo looked past his sisters and saw the subdued uproar of the crowd. Everyone was staring at them. "It's like watching an ocean wave," he remarked. "One can literally see the scandal sweep through the room."

Cam looked sardonic and resigned. "*Gadje*," he muttered.

"Leo, why don't you take your sisters and Miss Marks in your carriage? Amelia and I will make our farewells to the Norburys."

In a daze of wretchedness, Poppy allowed Leo to usher her outside to his carriage. All of them were silent until the vehicle had pulled away from the mansion with a sharp lurch.

Beatrix was the first to speak. "Have you been compromised, Poppy?" she asked with concern. "As Win was last year?"

"Yes, she has," Leo replied, while Poppy let out a little moan. "It's a bad habit our family's fallen into. Marks, you'd better write a poem about it."

"This disaster could have been avoided," the companion told him tersely, "had you found her sooner."

"It could also have been avoided if you hadn't lost her in the first place," Leo shot back.

"I'm responsible," Poppy broke in, her voice muffled against Leo's shoulder. "I went off with Mr. Rutledge. I had just seen Mr. Bayning in the ballroom, and I was distraught, and Mr. Rutledge asked me to dance but I needed air and we went out to the balcony—"

"No, *I'm* responsible," Miss Marks said, looking equally as upset. "I let you dance with him."

"It does no good to assign blame," Leo said. "What's done is done. But if anyone is responsible, it's Rutledge, who apparently came to the ball on a hunting expedition."

"What?" Poppy lifted her head and looked at him in bewilderment. "You think he . . . no, it was an accident, Leo. Mr. Rutledge didn't intend to compromise me."

"It was deliberate," Miss Marks said. "Harry Rutledge never is 'caught' doing anything. If he was seen in a compromising situation, it was because he wanted to be seen."

Leo looked at her alertly. "How do you know so much about Rutledge?"

The companion flushed. It seemed to require an effort for her to hold his gaze. "His reputation, of course."

Leo's attention was diverted as Poppy buried her face against his shoulder. "I'm going to die of humiliation," she said.

"No, you won't," Leo replied. "I'm an expert on humiliation, and if it were fatal, I'd have died a dozen times by now."

"You can't die a dozen times."

"You can if you're a Buddhist," Beatrix said helpfully.

Leo smoothed Poppy's shining hair. "I hope Harry Rutledge is," he said.

"Why?" Beatrix asked.

"Because there's nothing I'd rather do than kill him repeatedly."

HARRY RECEIVED LEO AND CAM ROHAN IN HIS PRIVATE library. Any other family in the situation would have been predictable . . . they would have demanded that he do the right thing, and terms of compensation would have been discussed, and arrangements would have been made. Because of Harry's vast fortune, most families would have accepted the results with good grace. He wasn't a peer, but he was a man of influence and means.

However, Harry knew better than to expect a predictable response to the situation from either Leo or Cam. They would have to be dealt with carefully. That being said, Harry wasn't worried in the least. He had complete confidence in his negotiating skills.

Pondering the events of the night, Harry was filled with immoral triumph. No, not triumph . . . elation. It was all turning out to be so much easier than he had expected, especially with Michael Bayning's unanticipated appearance at the Norbury ball. The idiot had practically handed Poppy to Harry on a silver platter. And when an opportunity presented itself, Harry took it.

Besides, any man who allowed scruples to get in the way of having a woman like Poppy was a fool. He recalled the way she had looked in the ballroom, pale and fragile and distraught. When Harry had approached her, there had been no mistaking the relief in her expression. She had turned to him, she had let him take her away.

And as Harry had brought her outside to the terrace, his satisfaction had been quickly supplanted by an entirely new sensation . . . the desire to ease someone else's pain. The fact that he had helped to bring about her heartbreak in the first place was regrettable. But the end justified the means. And once she was his, he would do more for her, take better care of her, than Michael Bayning ever could.

Now he had to deal with Poppy's family, who were understandably outraged that he had compromised her. That didn't worry him in the slightest. He had no doubt of his ability to persuade Poppy to marry him. And no matter how much the Hathaways objected, they would ultimately have to come to terms.

Marrying him was the only way to redeem Poppy's honor. Everyone knew it.

Keeping his expression neutral, Harry offered wine as Leo and Cam entered the library, but they refused.

Leo went to the fireplace mantel and leaned beside it with his arms folded across his chest. Cam went to a leather-upholstered chair and settled into it, stretching out his long legs and crossing them at the ankles.

Harry wasn't deceived by their comfortable postures.

Anger, masculine discord, permeated the room. Remaining relaxed, Harry waited for one of them to speak.

"You should know, Rutledge," Leo said in a pleasant tone, "that I had planned to kill you right away, but Rohan says we should talk for a few minutes first. Personally, I think he's trying to delay me so he can have the pleasure of killing you himself. And even if Rohan and I don't kill you, we probably won't be able to stop my brother-in-law Merripen from killing you."

Harry half sat on the edge of the heavy mahogany library table. "I suggest you wait until Poppy and I marry, so she can at least be made a respectable widow."

"Why do you assume," Cam asked, "that we would allow you to have Poppy?"

"If she doesn't marry me after this, she'll be ostracized. For that matter, I doubt any of the rest of your family would be welcome in London parlors."

"We're not welcome as it is," Cam replied, his hazel eyes narrowed.

"Rutledge," Leo added with deceptive casualness, "before I came into the title, the Hathaways lived outside London society for so many years that we couldn't give a monkey's arse as to whether we're received or not. Poppy doesn't have to marry anyone, for any reason, other than her own desire to do so. And she seems to believe you and she would never suit."

"Let me talk to your sister tomorrow," Harry said. "I'll convince her to make the best of the situation."

"Before you convince her," Cam said, "you're going to have to convince us. Because what little I know about you makes me damned uneasy."

Of course Cam Rohan would have some knowledge of him. Cam's former position at the gentlemen's gaming club would have made him privy to all kinds of private information. Harry was curious as to how much he had found out.

"Why don't you tell me what you know," Harry invited idly, "and I'll confirm if it's true."

The amber-shaded eyes regarded him without blinking. "You're originally from New York City, where your father was a hotelier of middling success."

"Buffalo, actually," Harry said.

"You didn't get on with him. But you found mentors. You apprenticed at an engineering works, where you became known for your abilities as a mechanic and draftsman. You patented several innovations in valves and boilers. At the age of twenty, you left America and came to England for undisclosed reasons."

Cam paused to observe the effects of his recitation.

Harry's ease had evaporated, the muscles of his shoulders drawing upward. He forced them back down and resisted the temptation to reach up and ease a cramp of tension at the back of his neck. "Go on," he invited softly.

Cam obliged. "You put together a group of private investors and bought a row of houses with very little capital of your own. You leased the houses for a short time, razed them and bought the rest of the street, and built the hotel as it now stands. You have no family, save your father in New York, with whom you have no communication. You have a handful of loyal friends and a host of enemies."

Harry reflected that Cam Rohan must have had impressive connections to have unearthed such information. "There are only three people in England who know that much about me," he muttered, wondering which one of them had talked.

"Now there are five," Leo said. "And Rohan forgot to mention the fascinating discovery that you've become a favorite with the War Office after designing some modifications to the standard issue army rifle. But lest we assume that you are only allied with the British government, you also seem to have dealings with foreigners, royalty and criminals alike. It rather gives one the impression that the only side you're ever on is your own."

Harry smiled coolly. "I've never lied about myself or my past. But I keep things private whenever possible. And I owe allegiance to no one." He went to the sideboard and poured a brandy. Holding the bowl in the palms of his hands to warm it, he glanced at both men. He'd bet his fortune that Cam knew more than he'd revealed. But this discussion, brief as it was, made it clear that there would be no helpful family coercion to make Poppy an honest woman. The Hathaways didn't give a damn about respectability, nor did they need his money or his influence.

Which meant that he would have to focus solely on Poppy.

"Whether you approve or not," he told Cam and Leo, "I'm going to propose to your sister. The choice is hers. And if she accepts, no power on earth will stop me from marrying her. I understand your concerns, so let me assure you that she will want for nothing. She'll be protected, cherished, even spoiled."

"You have no bloody idea how to make her happy," Cam said quietly.

"Rohan," Harry said with a faint smile, "I excel at making people happy—or at least making them think they are." He paused to survey their set faces. "Are you going to forbid me to speak to her?" he asked in a tone of polite interest.

"No," Leo said. "Poppy's not a child, nor a pet. If she wants to speak to you, she shall. But be aware that, whatever you say or do in the effort to convince her to marry you, it will be counterweighted by the opinions of her family."

"And there's one more thing to be aware of," Cam said,

with a wintry softness that disguised all hint of feeling. "If you succeed in marrying her, we're not losing a sister. You're gaining an entire family—who will protect her at any cost."

That was almost enough to give Harry pause.

Almost.

Chapter Eleven

M y brother and Mr. Rohan don't like you," Poppy told Harry the next morning, as they walked slowly through the rose garden behind the hotel. As the news of the scandal traveled through London like wildfire, it was necessary to do something about it with all expediency. Poppy knew that as a gentleman, Harry Rutledge was bound to offer for her, to save her from social disgrace. However, she wasn't certain if a lifetime of being married to the wrong man was any better than being a pariah. She didn't know Harry well enough to make any judgments about his character. And her family was emphatically *not* in favor of him.

"My companion doesn't like you," she continued, "and my sister Amelia says she doesn't know you well enough to decide, but she's inclined not to like you."

"What about Beatrix?" Harry asked, the sun striking glimmers in his dark hair as he looked down at her.

"She likes you. But then, she likes lizards and snakes."

"What about you?"

"I can't abide lizards or snakes."

A smile touched his lips. "Let's not fence today, Poppy. You know what I'm asking."

She responded with an unsteady nod.

It had been a hellish night. She had talked and cried and argued with her family until the early hours of the morning, and then she'd found it nearly impossible to sleep. And then more arguing and conversation this morning, until her chest was a cauldron of roiling emotions.

Her safe, familiar world had been turned upside down, and the peace of the garden was an unspeakable relief. Strangely, it made her feel better to be in Harry Rutledge's presence, even though he was partially responsible for the mess she was in. He was calm and self-assured, and there was something in his manner, sympathy woven with pragmatism, that soothed her.

They paused in a long arbor draped in sheets of roses. It was a tunnel of pink and white blossoms. Beatrix wandered along a nearby hedgerow. Poppy had insisted on taking her in lieu of Miss Marks or Amelia, both of whom would have made it impossible for her to have even marginal privacy with Harry.

"I like you," Poppy admitted bashfully. "But that's not enough to build a marriage on, is it?"

"It's more than many people start with." Harry studied her. "I'm sure your family has talked to you."

"At length," Poppy said. Her family had framed the prospect of marriage with Harry Rutledge in such dire terms that she had already decided to refuse him. She twisted her mouth in an apologetic grimace. "And after hearing what they had to say, I'm sorry to tell you that I—"

"Wait. Before you make a decision, I'd like to hear what *you* have to say. What your feelings are."

Well. That was a change. Poppy blinked in disconcertion as she reflected that her family and Miss Marks, well intentioned as they had been, had told her what they thought she should do. Her own thoughts and feelings hadn't received much attention.

"Well . . . you're a stranger," she said. "And I don't think I should make a decision about my future when I'm in love with Mr. Bayning."

"You still have hopes of marrying him?"

"Oh, no. All possibility of that is gone. But the feelings are still there, and until enough time passes for me to forget him, I don't trust my own judgment."

"That's very sensible of you. Except that some decisions can't be put off. And I'm afraid this is one of them." Harry paused before asking gently, "If you go back to Hampshire under the cloud of scandal, you know what to expect, don't you?"

"Yes. There will be . . . unpleasantness, to say the least." It was a mild word for the disdain, pity, and scorn she would receive as a fallen woman. "And my family won't be able to shield me from it," she added dully.

"But I could," Harry said, reaching for the braided coil at the top of her head, using a fingertip to nudge an anchoring pin further into place. "I could if you marry me. Otherwise, I'm powerless to do anything for you. No matter how anyone else advises you, Poppy, you're the one who will bear the brunt of the scandal."

Poppy tried, but couldn't quite manage, a weary smile. "So much for my dreams of a quiet, ordinary life. My choice is either to live as a social outcast or as the wife of a hotelier."

"Is the latter choice so unappealing?"

"It's not what I've always hoped for," she said frankly.

Harry absorbed that, considered it, while reaching out to skim his fingers over clusters of pink roses. "It wouldn't be a peaceful existence in a country cottage," he acknowledged.

"We would live at the hotel most of the year. But there are times we could go to the country. If you want a house in Hampshire as a wedding present, it's yours. Also a carriage of your own, and a team of four at your disposal."

Exactly what they said he'd do, Poppy thought, and sent him a wry glance. "Are you trying to bribe me, Harry?"

"Yes. Is it working?"

His hopeful tone made her smile. "No, although it was a very good effort." Hearing the rustling of foliage, Poppy called out, "Beatrix, are you there?"

"Two rows away," came her sister's cheerful reply. "Medusa found some worms!"

"Lovely."

Harry gave Poppy a bemused glance. "Who . . . or should I say *what* . . . is Medusa?"

"Hedgehog," she replied. "Medusa's getting a bit plump, and Beatrix is exercising her."

To Harry's credit, he remained composed as he remarked, "You know, I pay my staff a fortune to keep those *out* of the garden."

"Oh, have no fear. Medusa is merely a guest hedgehog. She would never run away from Beatrix."

"Guest hedgehog," Harry repeated, a smile working across his mouth. He paced a few impatient steps before turning to face her. A new urgency filtered through his voice. "Poppy. Tell me what your worries are, and I'll try to answer them. There must be some terms we can come to."

"You are persistent," she said. "They told me you would be."

"I'm everything they told you and worse," Harry said without hesitation. "But what they didn't tell you is that you are the most desirable and fascinating woman I've ever met, and I would do anything to have you."

It was insanely flattering to have a man like Harry Rutledge pursuing her, especially after the hurt inflicted by

Michael Bayning. Poppy flushed with cheek-stinging plea-sure, as if she'd been lying too long in the sun. She found herself thinking, *Perhaps I'll consider it, just for a moment, in a purely hypothetical sense. Harry Rutledge and me . . .*

"I have questions," she said.

"Ask away."

Poppy decided to be blunt. "Are you dangerous? Every-one says you are."

"To you? No."

"To others?"

Harry shrugged innocently. "I'm a hotelier. How danger-ous could I be?"

Poppy gave him a dubious glance, not at all deceived. "I may be gullible, Harry, but I'm not brainless. You know the rumors . . . you're well aware of your reputation. Are you as unscrupulous as you're made out to be?"

Harry was quiet for a long moment, his gaze fixed on a distant cluster of blossoms. The sun threw its light into the filter of branches, scattering leaf shadows over the pair in the arbor.

Eventually he lifted his head and looked at her directly, his eyes greener than the sunstruck rose leaves. "I'm not a gentleman," he said. "Not by birth, and not by character. Very few men can afford to be honorable while trying to make a success of themselves. I don't lie, but I rarely tell everything I know. I'm not a religious man, nor a spiritual one. I act in my own interests, and I make no secret of it. However, I always keep my side of a bargain, I don't cheat, and I pay my debts."

Pausing, Harry fished in his coat pocket, pulled out a penknife, and reached up to cut a rose in full bloom. After neatly severing the stem, he occupied himself with strip-ping the thorns with the sharp little blade. "I would never use physical force against a woman, or anyone weaker than myself. I don't smoke, take snuff, or chew tobacco. I always hold my liquor. I don't sleep well. And I can make a clock from scratch." Removing the last thorn, he handed the rose to her, and slipped the knife back into his pocket.

Poppy concentrated on the satiny pink rose, running her fingers along the top edges of the petals.

"My full name is Jay Harry Rutledge," she heard him say. "My mother is the only one who ever called me Jay, which is why I don't like it. She left my father and me when I was very young. I never saw her again."

Poppy looked at him with wide eyes, understanding that this was a sensitive subject he rarely, if ever, discussed. "I'm sorry," she said softly, although she kept her tone carefully devoid of pity.

He shrugged as if it was of no importance. "It was a long time ago. I barely remember her."

"Why did you come to England?"

Another pause. "I wanted to have a go at the hotel business. And whether I was a success or failure, I wanted to be far away from my father."

Poppy could only guess at the wealth of information buried beneath the spare words. "That's not the entire story," she said rather than asked.

The ghost of a smile touched his lips. "No."

She looked down at the rose again, feeling her cheeks color. "Do you . . . would you . . . want children?"

"Yes. Hopefully more than one. I didn't like being an only child."

"Would you want to raise them at the hotel?"

"Of course."

"Do you think it a suitable environment?"

"They would have the best of everything. Education. Travel. Lessons in anything that interested them."

Poppy tried to imagine bringing up children in a hotel. Could such a place ever feel like home? Cam had once told her that Roma believed the entire world was their home. As long as you were with your family, you were home. She looked at Harry, wondering what it would be like to live intimately with him. He seemed so self-contained and invulnerable. It was hard to think of him doing ordinary things such as shaving, or having his hair trimmed, or staying in bed with a head cold.

"Would you keep your wedding vows?" she asked.

Harry held her gaze. "I wouldn't make them otherwise."

Poppy decided that her family's worries about letting her talk to Harry had been entirely justified. Because he was so persuasive, and appealing, that she was beginning to consider the idea of marrying him, and seriously weigh the decision.

Fairy-tale dreams had to be set aside if she was to embark on marriage with a man she didn't love and hardly knew. But adults had to take responsibility for their actions. And then it occurred to Poppy that she was not the only one taking a risk. There was no guarantee for Harry that he would end up with the kind of wife he needed.

"It's not fair for me to ask all the questions," she told him. "You must have some as well."

"No, I've already decided that I want you."

Poppy couldn't prevent a bemused laugh. "Do you make all your decisions so impulsively?"

"Not usually. But I know when to trust my instincts."

It seemed Harry was about to add something else when he saw a movement on the ground from the periphery of his vision. Following his gaze, Poppy saw Medusa pushing her way through the rose arbor, waddling innocently across the path. The little brown and white hedgehog looked like a walking scrub brush. To Poppy's surprise, Harry lowered to his haunches to retrieve the creature.

"Don't touch her," Poppy warned. "She'll roll into a ball and sink her quills into you."

But Harry settled his hands on the ground, palms up, on either side of the inquisitive hedgehog. "Hello, Medusa." Gently he worked his hands beneath her. "Sorry to interrupt your exercise. But believe me, you don't want to run into any of my gardeners."

Poppy watched incredulously as Medusa relaxed and settled willingly into the warm masculine hands. Her spines flattened, and she let him lift and turn her so she was tummy upward. Harry stroked the soft white fur of her underbelly while Medusa's delicate snout lifted and she regarded him with her perpetual smile.

"I've never seen anyone except Beatrix handle her like that," Poppy said, standing beside him. "You have experience with hedgehogs?"

"No." He slanted a smile at her. "But I have some experience with prickly females."

"Excuse me," Beatrix's voice interrupted them, and she came into the tunnel of roses. She was disheveled, bits of leaves clinging to her dress, her hair straggling over her face. "I seem to have lost track of . . . oh, there you are, Medusa!" She broke into a grin as she saw Harry cradling the hedgehog in his hands. "Always trust a man who can handle a hedgehog, that's what I always say."

"Do you?" Poppy asked dryly. "I've never heard you say that."

"I only say it to Medusa."

Harry carefully transferred the pet to Beatrix's hands. "'The fox has many tricks,'" he quoted, "'the hedgehog only one.'" He smiled at Beatrix as he added, "But it's a good one."

"Archilochus," Beatrix said promptly. "You read Greek poetry, Mr. Rutledge?"

"Not usually. But I make an exception for Archilochus. He knew how to make a point."

"Father used to call him a 'raging iambic,'" Poppy said, and Harry laughed.

And in that moment, Poppy made her decision.

Because even though Harry Rutledge had his flaws, he admitted them freely. And a man who could charm a hedgehog and understand jokes about ancient Greek poets was a man worth taking a risk on.

She wouldn't be able to marry for love, but she could at least marry for hope.

"Bea," she murmured, "might you allow us a few moments alone?"

"Certainly. Medusa would love to grub about in the next row."

"Thank you, dear." Poppy turned back to Harry, who was dusting his hands. "May I ask one more question?"

He looked at her alertly and spread his hands as if to show he had nothing to hide.

"Would you say that you're a good man, Harry?"

He had to think about that. "No," he finally said. "In the fairy tale you mentioned last night, I would probably be the villain. But it's possible the villain would treat you far better than the prince would have."

Poppy wondered what was wrong with her, that she should be amused rather than frightened by his confession. "Harry. You're not supposed to court a girl by telling her you're the villain."

He gave her an innocent glance that didn't deceive her in the least. "I'm trying to be honest."

"Perhaps. But you're also making certain that whatever anyone says about you, you've already admitted it. Now you've made all criticism of you ineffectual."

Harry blinked as if she'd surprised him. "You think I'm *that* manipulative?"

She nodded.

Harry seemed stunned that she could see through him so easily. Instead of being annoyed, however, he stared at her with stark longing. "Poppy, I have to have you."

Reaching her in two steps, he took her into his arms. Her heart thumped with sudden force, and she let her head fall back naturally as she waited for the warm pressure of his mouth. When nothing happened, however, she opened her eyes and glanced at him quizzically.

"Aren't you going to kiss me?"

"No. I don't want your judgment clouded." But he brushed his lips against her forehead before he continued. "Here are your choices, as I see them. First, you could go to Hampshire in a cloud of social scorn, and content yourself with the knowledge that at least you didn't get trapped into a loveless marriage. Or you could marry a man who wants you beyond anything, and live like a queen." He paused. "And don't forget the country house and carriage."

Poppy could not contain a smile. "Bribery again."

"I'll throw in the castle and tiara," Harry said ruthlessly. "Gowns, furs, a yacht—"

"Hush," Poppy whispered, and touched his lips gently with her fingers, not knowing how else to make him stop. She took a deep breath, hardly able to believe what she was about to say. "I'll settle for a betrothal ring. A small, simple one."

Harry stared at her as if he were afraid to trust his own ears. "Will you?"

"Yes," Poppy said, her voice a bit suffocated. "Yes, I will marry you."

Chapter Twelve

This was the phrase of Poppy's wedding day: "It's not too late to change your mind."

She had heard it from every member of her family, or some variation thereof, since the early hours of the morning. That was, she'd heard it from everyone except Beatrix, who thankfully didn't share the Hathaways' general animosity toward Harry.

In fact, Poppy had asked Beatrix why she hadn't objected to the betrothal.

"I think it might turn out to be a good pairing," Beatrix said.

"You do? Why?"

"A rabbit and a cat can live together peaceably. But first the rabbit has to assert itself—charge the cat a time or two—and then they become friends."

"Thank you," Poppy said dryly. "I'll have to remember that. Although I daresay Harry will be surprised when I knock him over like a ninepin."

The wedding and the reception afterward would be as large and heavily attended as humanly possible, as if Harry intended for half of London to witness the ceremony. As a result, Poppy would spend most of her wedding day amidst a sea of strangers.

She had hoped that she and Harry might become better acquainted in the three weeks of their betrothal, but she had scarcely seen him except for the two occasions when he had come to take her on a drive. And Miss Marks, who had accompanied them, had glowered so fiercely that it had embarrassed and infuriated Poppy.

The day before the wedding, her sister Win and brother-in-law Merripen had arrived. To Poppy's relief, Win had elected to remain neutral on the controversy of the marriage. She and Poppy sat together in a richly appointed hotel suite, talking over the matter at length. And just as in the days of their childhood, Win assumed the role of peacemaker.

The light from a fringed lamp slid over Win's blond hair in a brilliant varnish. "If you like him, Poppy," she said gently, "if you've found things to esteem in him, then I'm sure I will, too."

"I wish Amelia felt that way. And Miss Marks, too, for that matter. They're both so . . . well, opinionated . . . that I can hardly discuss anything with either of them."

Win smiled. "Remember, Amelia has taken care of all of us for a very long time. And it's not easy for her to relinquish her role as our protector. But she will. Remember when Leo and I left for France, how difficult it was for her to see us off? How afraid she was for us?"

"I think she was more afraid for France."

"Well, France survived the Hathaways," Win said, smiling. "And you will survive becoming Harry Rutledge's wife on the morrow. Only . . . if I may say my piece . . . ?"

"Certainly. Everyone else has."

"The London season is like one of those Drury Lane melodramas in which marriage is always the ending. And no one ever seems to give any thought as to what happens after. But marriage isn't the end of the story, it's the beginning. And it demands the efforts of both partners to make a success of it. I hope Mr. Rutledge has given assurances that he will be the kind of husband that your happiness requires?"

"Well . . ." Poppy paused uncomfortably. "He told me I would live like a queen. Although that's not quite the same thing, is it?"

"No," Win said, her voice soft. "Be careful, dear, that you don't end up as the queen of a lonely kingdom."

Poppy nodded, stricken and uneasy, trying to hide it. In her gentle way, Win had offered more devastating advice than all the sharp warnings of the other Hathaways combined. "I'll consider that," she said, staring at the floor, at the tiny printed flowers of her dress, anywhere other than into her sister's perceptive gaze. She twisted her betrothal ring around her finger. Although the current fashion was for diamond clusters, or colored stones, Harry had bought her a single rose-cut diamond, shaped at the top with facets that mimicked the inner spiral of a rose.

"I asked for something small and simple," she had told Harry when he had given it to her.

"It's simple," he had countered.

"But not small."

"Poppy," he had told her with a smile, "I never do anything in a small way."

Spying the clock ticking busily on the mantel, Poppy brought her thoughts back to the present. "I won't change my mind, Win. I promised Harry that I would marry him, and so I shall. He has been kind to me. I would never repay him by jilting him at the altar."

"I understand." Win slid her hand over Poppy's, and pressed warmly. "Poppy . . . has Amelia had a 'certain talk' with you yet?"

"You mean the 'what to expect on my wedding night' talk?"

"Yes."

"She was planning to tell me later tonight, but I'd just as soon hear it from you." Poppy paused. "However, having spent so much time with Beatrix, I should tell you that I know the mating habits of at least twenty-three different species."

"Heavens," Win said with a grin. "Perhaps you should be leading the discussion, dear."

THE FASHIONABLE, THE POWERFUL, AND THE WEALTHY usually married at St. George's in Hanover Square, located in the middle of Mayfair. In fact, so many peers and virgins had been united in holy wedlock at St. George's that it was unofficially and quite vulgarly known as the "London Temple of Hymen."

A pediment with six massive columns fronted the impressive but relatively simple structure. St. George's had been designed with a deliberate lack of ornamentation so as not to detract from the beauty of the architecture. The interior was similarly austere, with a canopied pulpit built several feet higher than the box pews. But there was a magnificent work of stained glass above the front altar, depicting the Tree of Jesse and an assortment of biblical figures.

Surveying the crowd packed inside the church, Leo wore a carefully blank expression. So far he had given away two sisters in marriage. Neither of those weddings had begun to approach this kind of grandeur and visibility. But they had far eclipsed it in genuine happiness. Amelia and Win had both been in love with the men they had chosen to marry.

It was unfashionable to marry for love, a mark of the *bourgeoisie*. However, it was an ideal the Hathaways had always aspired to.

This wedding had nothing to do with love.

Dressed in a black morning coat with silver trousers and a white cravat, Leo stood beside the side door of the vestry room, where ceremonial and sacred objects were kept. Altar and choir robes hung in a row along one wall. This morning the vestry doubled as a waiting room for the bride.

Catherine Marks came to stand on the other side of the doorway as if she were a fellow sentinel guarding the castle gate. Leo glanced at her covertly. She was dressed in lavender, unlike her usual drab colors. Her mousy brown hair was pulled back into such a tight chignon as to make it difficult for her to blink. The spectacles sat oddly on her nose, one of the wire earpieces crimped. It gave her the appearance of a befuddled owl.

"What are you looking at?" she asked testily.

"Your spectacles are crooked," Leo said, trying not to smile.

She scowled. "I tried to fix them, but it only made them worse."

"Give them to me." Before she could object, he took them from her face and began to fiddle with the bent wire.

She spluttered in protest. "My lord, I didn't ask you to—if you damage them—"

"How did you bend the earpiece?" Leo asked, patiently straightening the wire.

"I dropped them on the floor, and as I was searching, I stepped on them."

"Nearsighted, are you?"

"Quite."

Having reshaped the earpiece, Leo scrutinized the spectacles carefully. "There." He began to give them to her and paused as he stared into her eyes, all blue, green, and gray, contained in distinct dark rims. Brilliant, warm, changeable. Like opals. Why had he never noticed them before?

Awareness chased over him, making his skin prickle as if exposed to a sudden change in temperature. She wasn't plain at all. She was beautiful, in a fine, subtle way, like winter moonlight, or the sharp linen smell of daisies. So cool and pale . . . delicious. For a moment, Leo couldn't move.

Marks was similarly still, locked with him in a moment of peculiar intimacy.

She snatched the spectacles from him and replaced them firmly on her nose. "This is a mistake," she said. "You shouldn't have let it happen."

Struggling through layers of bemusement and stimulation, Leo gathered that she was referring to his sister's wedding. He sent her an irritable glance. "What do you suggest I do, Marks? Send Poppy to a nunnery? She has the right to marry whomever she pleases."

"Even if it ends in disaster?"

"It won't end in disaster, it will end in estrangement. And I've told Poppy as much. But she's bound and determined to marry him. I always thought Poppy was too sensible to make this kind of mistake."

"She is sensible," Marks said. "But she's also lonely. And Rutledge took advantage of that."

"How could she be lonely? She's constantly surrounded by people."

"That can be the worst loneliness of all."

There was a disturbing note in her voice, a fragile sadness. Leo wanted to touch her . . . gather her close . . . pull her face into his neck . . . and that caused a twinge of something like panic. He had to do something, anything, to change the mood between them.

"Cheer up, Marks," he said briskly. "I'm sure that someday you, too, will find that one special person you can torment for the rest of your life."

He was relieved to see her familiar scowl reassert itself.

"I've yet to meet a man who could compete with a good strong cup of tea."

Leo was about to reply when he heard a noise from inside the vestry where Poppy was waiting.

A man's voice, taut with urgency.

Leo and Marks looked at each other.

"Isn't she supposed to be alone?" Leo asked.

The companion nodded uncertainly.

"Is it Rutledge?" Leo wondered aloud.

Marks shook her head. "I just saw him outside the church."

Without another word, Leo grasped the door handle and opened the portal, and Marks followed him inside the vestry.

Leo stopped so abruptly that the companion bumped into him from behind. His sister, clad in a high-necked white lace gown, was silhouetted against a row of black and purple robes. Poppy looked angelic, bathed in light from a narrow rectangular window, a veil cascading down her back from a neat coronet of white rosebuds.

And she was confronting Michael Bayning—who looked like a madman, his eyes wild, his clothes disheveled.

"Bayning," Leo said, closing the door with an efficient swipe of his foot. "I wasn't aware you'd been invited. The guests are being seated in the pews. I suggest you join them." He paused, his voice iced with quiet warning. "Or better yet, leave altogether."

Bayning shook his head, desperate fury gleaming in his eyes. "I can't. I must talk with Poppy before it's too late."

"It's already too late," Poppy said, her complexion nearly as white as her dress. "Everything's decided, Michael."

"You must know what I've found out." Michael threw a pleading glance at Leo. "Let me have just a moment alone with her."

Leo shook his head. He was not without sympathy for

Bayning, but he couldn't see that any good would come of this. "Sorry, old fellow, but someone has to think of appearances. This has the earmarks of a last tryst before the wedding. And while that would be scandalous enough between the bride and groom, it's even more objectionable between the bride and someone else." He was aware of Marks coming to stand beside him.

"Let him speak," the companion said.

Leo threw her an exasperated glance. "Blast it, Marks, do you ever tire of telling me what to do?"

"When you stop needing my advice," she said, "I'll stop giving it."

Poppy hadn't taken her gaze off Michael. It was like something from a dream, a nightmare, having him come to her when she was dressed in her wedding gown, minutes away from marrying another man. Dread filled her. She didn't want to hear what Michael had to say, but neither could she turn him away.

"Why are you here?" she managed to ask.

Michael looked anguished and imploring. He held out something . . . a letter. "Do you recognize this?"

Taking the letter in lace-gloved fingers, Poppy stared at it closely. "The love letter," she said, bewildered. "I lost it. Where . . . where did you find it?"

"My father. Harry Rutledge gave it to him." Michael raked a hand through his hair with distracted roughness. "That bastard went to my father and exposed our relationship. He put the worst possible light on it. Rutledge turned my father against us before I ever had a chance to explain our side of it."

Poppy turned even colder, and her mouth went dry, and her heart labored with slow, painful thumps. At the same time, her brain was working too fast, racing through a chain of conclusions, each more unpleasant than the last.

The door opened, and all of them turned to watch as someone else entered the vestry.

"Of course," Poppy heard Leo say dourly. "The drama only needed you to be complete."

Harry came into the small, overcrowded room, looking suave and astonishingly calm. He approached Poppy, his green eyes cool. He wore his self-control like impenetrable armor. "Hello, darling." He reached out to run a hand lightly over the transparent lace of her veil.

Even though he hadn't touched her directly, Poppy stiffened. "It's bad luck," she whispered through dry lips, "for you to see me before the ceremony."

"Fortunately," Harry said, "I'm not superstitious."

Poppy was filled with confusion, anger, and a dull ache of horror. Staring up into Harry's face, she saw no trace of remorse in his expression.

"*In the fairy tale*," he had told her, "*I would probably be the villain.*"

It was true.

And she was about to marry him.

"I told her what you did," Michael said to Harry. "How you made it impossible for us to marry."

"I didn't make it impossible," Harry said. "I merely made it difficult."

How young and noble and vulnerable Michael appeared, a wronged hero.

And how large and cruel and contemptuous Harry was. Poppy couldn't believe she had ever found him charming, that she had *liked* him, that she had thought some form of happiness would be possible with him.

"She was yours, if you'd truly wanted her," Harry continued, a pitiless smile touching his lips. "But I wanted her more."

Michael launched at him with a choked cry, his fist raised.

"No," Poppy gasped, and Leo started forward. Harry was faster, however, seizing Michael's arm and twisting it behind his back. Expertly he shoved him up against the door.

"Stop it!" Poppy said, rushing to them, hitting Harry's shoulder and back with her fist. "Let him go! Don't do this!"

Harry didn't seem to feel her blows. "Out with it, Bayning," he said coldly. "Did you come here merely to complain, or is there some point to all this?"

"I'm taking her away from here. Away from you!"

Harry gave a chilling smile. "I'll send you to hell first."

"*Let . . . him . . . go*," Poppy said in a voice she had never used before.

It was enough to make Harry listen. His gaze connected with hers in a flash of unholy green. Slowly he released Michael, who swung around, his chest heaving with the anguished force of his breaths.

"Come with me, Poppy," Michael pleaded. "We'll go to Gretna. I no longer give a damn about my father or my inheritance. I can't let you marry this monster."

"Because you love me?" she asked in a half whisper. "Or because you want to save me?"

"Both."

Harry watched her intently, taking in every nuance of her expression. "Go with him," he invited gently. "If that's what you want."

Poppy wasn't at all deceived. Harry would go to any lengths to get what he wanted, no matter what destruction or pain he caused. He would never let her go. He was merely testing her, curious to see what choice she would make.

One thing was clear: she and Michael would never be happy together. Because Michael's righteous fury would eventually wear off, and then all the reasons that had seemed so important before would regain their validity. He would come to regret having married her. He would lament the scandal and the disinheritance, and the lifelong disapproval of his father. And eventually Poppy would come to be the focus of his resentment.

She had to send Michael away—it was the best thing she could do for him.

As for her interests . . . all choices seemed equally bad.

"I suggest you get rid of both these idiots," Leo told her, "and let me take you home to Hampshire."

Poppy stared at her brother, her lips touched with a hopeless smile. "What kind of life would I have in Hampshire after this, Leo?"

His only reply was grim silence. Poppy turned her attention to Miss Marks, who looked anguished. In their shared gaze, Poppy saw that her companion understood her precarious situation more accurately than the men did. Women were judged and condemned far more harshly than men in these matters. Poppy's elusive dream of a simple, peaceful life had already vanished. If she didn't go through with the wedding, she would never marry, never have children, never have a place in society. The only thing left was to make the best of her situation.

She faced Michael with unyielding resolve. "You must go," she said.

His face contorted. "Poppy, I haven't lost you. You're not saying—"

"Go," she insisted. Her gaze switched to her brother. "Leo, please escort Miss Marks to her seat in the congregation. The wedding will start soon. And I need to speak to Mr. Rutledge alone."

Michael stared at her in disbelief. "Poppy, you can't marry him. Listen to me—"

"It's over, Bayning," Leo said quietly. "There's no undoing the part you've played in this bloody mess. Let my sister deal with it as she chooses."

"*Christ.*" Michael lurched toward the door like a drunken man.

Poppy longed to comfort him, to follow him, to reassure him of her love. Instead, she stayed in the vestry with Harry Rutledge.

After what seemed an eternity, the other three left, and Poppy and Harry faced each other.

It was clear he was indifferent to the fact that she now knew him for what he was. Harry wanted neither forgiveness nor redemption . . . he regretted nothing.

A lifetime, Poppy thought. *With a man I can never trust.*

To marry a villain, or never to marry at all. To be Harry Rutledge's wife, or live as an object of disgrace, to have mothers scold their children for speaking to her as if their innocence would be contaminated by her presence. To be propositioned by men who thought she was immoral or desperate. That was her future if she didn't become his wife.

"Well?" Harry asked quietly. "Will you go through with it or not?"

Poppy felt foolish standing there in her bridal finery, bedecked in flowers and a veil, all of it symbolizing hope and innocence when there was none left. She longed to tear off her betrothal ring and throw it at him. She wanted to crumple to the floor like a hat someone had stepped on. A brief thought came to her, that she wanted to send for Amelia, who would take charge of the situation and manage everything.

Except that Poppy was no longer a child whose life could be managed.

She stared into Harry's implacable face and hard eyes. He looked mocking, supremely confident that he'd won. No doubt he assumed he'd be able to run circles around her for the rest of their lives.

To be sure, she had underestimated him.

But he had underestimated her, too.

All of Poppy's sorrow and misery and helpless anger swirled together into some new bitter amalgam. She was surprised by the calmness of her own voice as she spoke to him. "I will never forget that you took away the man I loved and put yourself in his place. I'm not certain I can ever forgive you for that. The only thing I am absolutely certain of is that I will never love you. Do you still want to marry me?"

"Yes," Harry said without hesitation. "I've never wanted to be loved. And God knows no one's done it yet."

Chapter Thirteen

Poppy had forbidden Leo to tell the rest of the family about what had happened with Michael Bayning before the wedding. "You may tell them anything you wish after the breakfast," she had said. "But for my sake, please keep quiet until then. I won't be able to endure all those rituals—the breakfast, the wedding cake, the toasts—if I have to look into their eyes and know that *they* know."

Leo had looked angry. "You expect me to take you to the front of this church and give you to Rutledge for reasons I don't understand."

"You don't have to understand. Just help me through this."

"I don't want to help if it results in you becoming Mrs. Harry Rutledge."

But because she had asked it of him, Leo had played his part in the elaborate ceremony with grim-faced dignity. With a shake of his head, he had offered his arm, and they had followed Beatrix to the front of the church where Harry Rutledge was waiting.

The service was mercifully short and unemotional. There was only one moment when Poppy felt a sharp pang of unease, as the minister said, ". . . if any man can show any just cause why they may not lawfully be joined together, let him now speak; or else hereafter forever hold his peace." It seemed the whole world stilled for the two or three seconds that followed his pronouncement. Poppy's pulse quickened. She realized she expected, hoped, to hear Michael's vehement protest ring out through the church.

But there was only silence. Michael had gone.

The ceremony went on.

Harry's hand was warm as it closed around her cold one. They repeated their vows, and the minister gave the ring to Harry, who slid it firmly onto Poppy's finger.

Harry's voice was quiet and steady. "With this ring I thee wed, with my body I thee worship, and with all my worldly goods I thee endow."

Poppy didn't meet his gaze, but instead stared at the gleaming circlet on her finger. To her relief, there was no kiss to follow. The custom of kissing the bride was in bad taste, a plebeian practice that was never done at St. George's.

Finally bringing herself to look up at Harry, Poppy flinched at the satisfaction in his eyes. She took his arm, and they walked back down the aisle together, toward the future and a fate that seemed anything but benevolent.

HARRY KNEW THAT POPPY THOUGHT OF HIM AS A MONSTER. He acknowledged that his methods had been unfair, selfish, but there had been no other way to have Poppy as his wife. And he couldn't work up even a second's worth of regret for having taken her away from Bayning. Perhaps he was amoral, but it was the only way he knew to make his way in the world.

Poppy was his now, and he would make certain that she would not be sorry for marrying him. He would be as kind as she would allow. And in his experience, women would forgive anything if one offered the right incentives.

Harry was relaxed and in good spirits the rest of the day. A procession of "glass coaches," elaborate carriages with gold empire decorations and abundant windows, conveyed the wedding party to the Rutledge Hotel, where a huge formal breakfast was held in the hotel banquet room. The windows were crowded with onlookers, eager to catch a glimpse of the glittering scene. Greek pillars and arches had been placed all around the room, swathed in tulle and masses of flowers.

A regiment of servants brought out silver platters and trays of champagne, and the guests settled in their chairs to enjoy the repast. They were given individual servings of goose dressed with cream and herbs and covered with a steaming golden crust . . . bowls of melons and grapes, boiled quail eggs scattered lavishly on crisp green salad, baskets of hot muffins, toast, and scones, flitches of fried smoked bacon . . . plates of thinly sliced beefsteak, the pink strips littered with fragrant shavings of truffle. Three wedding cakes were brought out, thickly iced and stuffed with fruit.

As was the custom, Poppy was served first, and Harry could only guess at the effort it took for her to eat and smile. If anyone noticed that the bride was subdued, it was assumed that the event was overwhelming for her, or perhaps that, like all brides, she was nervously anticipating the wedding night.

Poppy's family regarded her with protective concern, especially Amelia, who seemed to sense that something was wrong. Harry was fascinated by the Hathaways, the mysterious connections between them, as if they shared some collective secret. One could almost see the wordless understanding that passed between them.

Although Harry knew a great deal about people, he knew nothing about being part of a family.

After Harry's mother had run off with one of her lovers,

his father had tried to get rid of every remaining trace of her existence. And he had done his best to forget that he even had a son, leaving Harry to the hotel staff and a succession of tutors.

Harry had few memories of his mother, only that she had been beautiful and had had golden hair. It seemed she had always been going out, away from him, forever elusive. He remembered crying for her once, clutching his hands in her velvet skirts, and she had tried to make him let go, laughing softly at his persistence.

In the wake of his parents' abandonment, Harry had taken his meals in the kitchen with the hotel employees. When he was sick, one or another of the maids had taken care of him. He saw families come and go, and he had learned to view them with the same detachment that the hotel staff did. Deep down Harry harbored a suspicion that the reason his mother had left, the reason his father never had anything to do with him, was because he was unlovable. And therefore he had no desire to be part of a family. Even if or when Poppy bore him children, Harry would never allow anyone close enough to form an attachment. He would never let himself be shackled that way. And yet he sometimes knew a fleeting envy for those who were capable of it, like the Hathaways.

The breakfast wore on, with endless rounds of toasting. When Harry saw the betraying droop of Poppy's shoulders, he deduced she'd had enough. He rose and made a short, gracious speech, offering his thanks for the honor of the guests' presence on such a significant day.

It was the signal for the bride to retire along with her bridesmaids. They would soon be followed by the general company, who would disperse to attend a variety of amusements for the rest of the day. Poppy paused at the doorway.

As if she could feel Harry's gaze on her, she turned to glance over her shoulder.

A warning flashed in her eyes, and it aroused him instantly. Poppy would not be a complacent bride, nor had he expected her to be. She would try to exact compensation for what he had done, and he would indulge her . . . up to a point. He wondered how she would react when he came to her that evening.

Harry tore his gaze away from his bride as he was approached by Kev Merripen, Poppy's brother-in-law, a black-haired Rom who managed to stay relatively inconspicuous despite his size and striking appearance.

"Merripen," Harry said pleasantly. "Did you enjoy the breakfast?"

The Rom was in no mood for small talk. He stared at Harry with a gaze promising death. "Something is wrong," he said. "If you've done something to harm Poppy, I will find you and rip your head from your—"

"Merripen!" came a cheerful exclamation as Leo suddenly appeared beside them. Harry didn't miss the way Leo jabbed a warning elbow against the man's ribs. "All charm and lightness, as usual. You're supposed to congratulate the bridegroom, *phral*. Not threaten to dismember him."

"It's not a threat," Merripen muttered. "It's a promise."

Harry met his gaze directly. "I appreciate your concern for her. I assure you, I'll do everything in my power to make her happy. Poppy will have anything she wants."

"I believe a divorce would top the list," Leo mused aloud.

Harry leveled a cool stare at Merripen. "I'd like to point out that your sister married me voluntarily. Michael Bayning should have had the bollocks to come to the church and carry her out bodily if necessary. But he didn't. And if he wasn't willing to fight for her, he didn't deserve her." He saw from Merripen's quick blink that he had scored a point. "Moreover, after going through these exertions to marry Poppy, the last thing I would do is mistreat her."

"What exertions?" the Rom asked suspiciously, and Harry realized that he hadn't yet been told the entire story.

"Never mind that," Leo told Merripen. "If I told you now, you'd only make an embarrassing scene at Poppy's wedding. And that's supposed to be my job."

They exchanged a glance, and Merripen muttered something in Romany.

Leo smiled faintly. "I have no idea what you just said. But I suspect it's something about battering Poppy's new husband into forest mulch." He paused. "Later, old fellow," he said. A look of grim understanding passed between them.

Merripen gave him a curt nod and left without another word to Harry.

"And that was one of his good moods," Leo remarked, staring after his brother-in-law with rueful affection. He returned his attention to Harry. Suddenly, his eyes were filled with a world-weariness that should have taken lifetimes to acquire. "I'm afraid no amount of discussion would ease Merripen's concern. He's lived with the family since he was a boy, and my sisters' welfare is everything to him."

"I will take care of Poppy," Harry said.

"I'm sure you'll try. And whether you believe it or not, I hope you succeed."

"Thank you."

Leo focused on him with an astute gaze that would have troubled a man with a conscience. "Incidentally, I'm not going with the family when they depart for Hampshire on the morrow."

"Business in London?" Harry asked politely.

"Yes, a few last parliamentary obligations. And a bit of

architectural dabbling—a hobby of mine. But mainly I'm staying for Poppy's sake. You see, I expect she'll want to leave you quite soon, and I intend to escort her home."

Harry smiled contemptuously, amused by his new brother-in-law's effrontery. Did Leo have any idea how many ways Harry could ruin him, and how easily it could be done? "Tread carefully," Harry said softly.

It was a sign of either naïveté or courage that Leo didn't flinch. He actually smiled, though there was no humor in it. "There's something you don't seem to understand, Rutledge. You've managed to acquire Poppy, but you don't have what it takes to keep her. Therefore, I won't be far away. I'll be there when she needs me. And if you harm her, your life won't be worth a bloody farthing. No man is untouchable—not even you."

AFTER A MAID HAD HELPED POPPY CHANGE FROM HER WEDding garments into a simple dressing gown, she brought a glass of iced champagne and tactfully left.

Grateful for the silence of the private apartments, Poppy sat at her dressing table and unpinned her hair slowly. Her mouth ached from smiling, and the tiny muscles of her forehead felt strained. She drank the champagne and made a project of brushing her hair in long strokes, letting it fall in mahogany waves. The boar bristles felt good against her scalp.

Harry had not yet come to the apartment. Poppy considered what she would say to him once he appeared, but nothing came to mind. With dreamlike slowness, she wandered through the rooms. Unlike the icy formality of the receiving area, the rest of the rooms had been decorated in plush fabrics and warm colors, with abundant places for sitting, reading, relaxing. Everything was immaculate, the window-panes polished to stunning clarity, the Turkish carpeting clean swept and scented of tea leaves. There were fireplaces with marble or carved wood mantels and tiled hearths, and many lamps and sconces to keep the rooms well lit in the evening.

An extra bedroom had been added for Poppy. Harry had told her that she could have as many rooms for her own use as she wished—the apartments had been designed so that connecting spaces could be opened up with ease. The counterpane on the bed was a soft shade of robin's egg blue, the fine linen sheets embroidered with tiny blue flowers. Pale blue satin and velvet curtains swathed the windows. It was a beautiful, feminine room, and Poppy would have taken great pleasure in it, had the circumstances been different.

She tried to decide if she was most angry with Harry, Michael, or herself. Perhaps equally with all three of them. And she was increasingly nervous, knowing it wouldn't be long until Harry arrived. Her gaze fell to the bed. She reassured herself with the thought that Harry would not force her to submit to him. His villainy would not lend itself to crude violence.

Her stomach dropped as she heard someone entering the apartments. She took a deep breath, and another, and waited until Harry's broad-shouldered form appeared in the doorway.

He paused, watching her, his features impassive. His cravat had been removed, the shirt opened to reveal the strong line of his throat. Poppy steeled herself not to move as Harry approached her. He reached out to touch her shining hair, letting it slide through his fingers like liquid fire. "I've never seen it down before," he said. He was close enough that she could smell a hint of shaving soap, and the tang of champagne on his breath. His fingers smoothed over her cheek, detecting the trembling within her stillness.

"Afraid?" he asked softly.

Poppy forced herself to meet his gaze. "No."

A smile touched his lips. "Good. As I told you, I intend to treat you very well."

Poppy was disoriented by the complex mixture of emotions he stirred in her, the antagonism and attraction and curiosity and resentment. Pulling away from him, she went to her dressing table and examined a small porcelain box with a gilded top.

"Why did you go through with it?" she heard him ask quietly.

"I thought it best for Michael."

Harry half sat on the bed, his posture informal. His gaze didn't stray from her. "Had there been a choice, I would have done all this the ordinary way. I would have courted you openly, won you fairly. But you'd already decided on Bayning. This was the only alternative."

"No, it wasn't. You could have let me be with Michael."

"It's doubtful he ever would have offered for you. He deceived you, and himself, by assuming he could persuade his father to accept the match. You should have seen the old man when I showed him the letter—he was mortally offended by the notion of his son taking a wife so far beneath him."

That hurt, as perhaps Harry had intended, and Poppy stiffened. "Then why didn't you let it all play out? Why not wait until Michael had abandoned me, and then come forward to pick up the pieces?"

"Because there was a chance Bayning might have dared to run off with you. I couldn't risk it. And I knew that sooner or later you'd realize that what you had with Bayning was nothing but infatuation."

Poppy gave him a glance of purest contempt. "What do you know of love?"

"I've seen how people in love behave. And what I witnessed in the vestry this morning was nothing close to it.

Had you truly wanted each other, no force in the world could have stopped you from walking out of that church together."

"You wouldn't have allowed it!" she shot back in outrage.

"True. But I would have respected the effort."

"Neither of us gives a damn about your respect."

The fact that she was speaking for Michael as well as herself . . . "us" . . . caused Harry's face to harden. "Whatever your feelings for Bayning are, you're my wife now. And he'll go on to marry some blue-blooded heiress as he should have done in the first place. Now all that's left to decide is how you and I will go on."

"I would prefer a marriage in name only."

"I don't blame you," Harry said calmly. "However, the marriage isn't legal until I bed you. And, unfortunately, I never leave loopholes."

He was going to insist on his rights, then. Nothing would dissuade him from getting what he wanted. Poppy's eyes and nose stung. But she would have rather died than cry in front of him. She shot him a look of revulsion, while her heart pounded until she felt its reverberations in her temples and wrists and ankles.

"I'm overwhelmed by such a poetic declaration. By all means, let's complete the contract." She began on the gilded buttons at the front of her dressing gown, her fingers stiff and shaking. Her breath trembled in her throat. "All I ask is that you make it quick."

Harry pushed away from the bed with graceful ease and came to her. One of his warm hands covered both of hers, and her fingers stilled. "Poppy." He waited until she could bring herself to look up at him. Amusement glinted in his eyes. "You make me feel like a vile ravisher," he said. "It's only fair to tell you that I've never forced myself on a woman. A simple refusal would be enough to deter me."

Damn him for toying with her like a cat with a mouse.

"Is that true?" she asked with offended dignity.

Harry gave her a guileless glance. "Refuse me, and we'll find out."

The fact that such a despicable human being could be so handsome was proof that the universe was vastly unfair, or at least very badly organized. "I'm not going to refuse you," she said, pushing his hand away. "I'm not going to entertain you with virginal theatrics." She continued to unfasten the buttons of her dressing gown. "And I'd like to have done with this so I won't have anything to dread."

Obligingly Harry removed his coat and went to drape it over a chair. Poppy dropped her dressing robe to the floor and kicked off her slippers. The cool air wafted beneath the hem of her thin cambric nightgown and lingered in icy curls around her ankles. She could scarcely think, her head filled with fears and worries. The future she had once hoped for was gone, and another was being created, one with infinite complications. Harry would know her in a way no one else ever had, or ever would. But it wouldn't be anything like her sisters' marriages . . . it would be a relationship built on something far different from love and trust.

Her sister Win's information on marital intimacy had been garnished with flowers and moonbeams, with the barest description of the physical act. Win's advice had been to trust one's husband, and to relax, and to understand that sexual closeness was a wonderful part of love. None of that had any relevance to the situation Poppy now found herself in.

The room was utterly silent. *This means nothing to me,* she thought, trying to make herself believe it. She felt as if she were in a stranger's body as she undid her nightgown and pulled it over her head and let it fall to the carpeting in a limp heap. Gooseflesh rose everywhere, the tips of her breasts contracting in the chill.

She went to the bed and turned back the covers and slipped in. Drawing the bed linens up to her breasts, she settled back against the pillows. Only then did she glance at Harry.

Her husband had paused in the act of unfastening a shoe, his foot propped on a chair. He had already removed his shirt and waistcoat, and the muscles of his long back were bunched and tense. He stared at her over his shoulder, his thick lashes half lowered. His color was high, as if sun flushed, and his lips were parted as if he'd forgotten something he'd been about to say. Letting out a breath that wasn't entirely steady, he turned back to his shoe.

His body was beautifully made, but Poppy took no pleasure in it. In fact, she resented it. She would have preferred a few signs of vulnerability, a touch of softness around the middle, a set of narrow shoulders, anything that would put him at a disadvantage. But he was lean and strong and powerfully proportioned. Still clad in his trousers, Harry came to stand beside the bed. Despite her efforts to appear indifferent, Poppy couldn't stop her fingers from curling into the embroidered sheets.

His hand went to her bare shoulder, his fingertips drifting to her throat and back again. He paused as he found a tiny, nearly invisible scar on her shoulder—the place a stray shotgun pellet had once lodged. "From the accident?" he asked huskily.

Poppy nodded, unable to speak. She realized he would become familiar with every small and unique detail of her body . . . she had given him that right. He found three more scars on her arm, stroking each one as if he could soothe those long-ago injuries. Slowly his hand went to a lock of hair that lay in a fine mahogany river over her chest, following it beneath the sheets and blankets.

She gasped as she felt his thumb brush over the bud of her nipple, circling, sending runners of heat to the pit of her stomach. His hand left her for a moment, and when he reached for her breast again, his thumb was damp from his own mouth. Another teasing, acute circle, moisture enhancing the caress. Her knees drew up slightly, her hips tilting as if her entire body had become a vessel to contain sensation. His other hand slid softly beneath her chin, tilting her face up to his.

He bent to kiss her, but Poppy turned her face away.

"I'm the same man who kissed you on the terrace," she heard him say. "You liked it well enough then."

Poppy could hardly speak with his hand cupping her breast. "Not anymore." A kiss meant more to her than a simple physical gesture. It was a gift of love, of affection, or at the very least liking, and she felt none of those things for him. He might have the right to her body, but not to her heart.

His hands left her, and she felt him nudge her gently to the side.

Poppy obeyed, her pulse racing as he joined her on the bed. He reclined on his side, his feet extending much farther than hers along the mattress. She forced her fingers to loosen from the covers as he drew them away from her.

Harry's gaze slid over her slim, exposed body, the curves of her breasts, the clamped seam of her thighs. Heat surfaced everywhere, a flush that deepened as he drew her against him. His chest was warm and hard, with a covering of dark hair that tickled her breasts.

Poppy shivered as his hand moved along her spine, pressing her close. The intimacy of being clasped against a half-naked man, breathing the scent of his skin, was almost more than her dazed mind could comprehend. He pressed her bare legs apart, the fabric of his trousers smooth and cool. And he held her like that, his hand roaming slowly over her back until the teeth-chattering shivers eased.

His mouth traced the taut side of her neck. He spent a long

time kissing her there, investigating the hollow behind her ear, the edge of her hairline, the front of her throat. His tongue found the hectic throb of her pulse, lingering until she gasped and tried to push him away. His arms tightened, one hand coming to the bare curve of her bottom, keeping her against him.

"Do you like that?" he asked against her throat.

"No," Poppy said, trying to work her arms between them.

Harry pressed her back to the mattress, his eyes flickering with amusement. "You're not going to admit to liking any of this, are you?"

She shook her head.

His hand cradled the side of her face, his thumb brushing her closed lips. "Poppy, if there's nothing else about me that pleases you, at least give this a chance."

"I can't. Not when I remember that I should be doing this with . . . him."

"Then I'll see if I can put him out of your thoughts." The bedclothes were pushed away gently, robbing her of any means of concealment. His hand curved beneath her breast, plumping it upward, and he bent until his breath fell against the peak in light, repeated shocks.

He traced the aureole with his tongue, caught it tenderly with his teeth, playing with the sensitive flesh. Delight fed into her veins with every swirl and lick and soft tug. Poppy's hands clenched into fists as she tried to keep them by her sides. It seemed important not to touch him voluntarily. But he was skilled and persistent, arousing deep and writhing impulses, and her body was apparently inclined to choose pleasure over principle.

She reached up to his head, the dark hair thick and soft between her fingers. Gasping, she guided him to her other breast. He complied with a hoarse murmur, his lips opening over the heat-stung bud. His hands glided over her body, charting the curves of her waist and hips. The tip of his middle finger circled the rim of her navel and wove in a teasing path across the flat of her stomach, along the valley where her legs pressed together . . . from her knees to the top of her thighs . . . back again.

Stroking gently, Harry whispered, "Will you open for me?"

Poppy was quiet, resisting, panting as if each breath were being torn from her throat. The pressure of tears rose behind her closed eyes. Experiencing any pleasure at all with Harry seemed like a betrayal.

And he knew it. His voice was soft against her ear as he said, "What happens in this bed is only between us. There's no sin in submitting to your husband, and nothing to gain by denying what enjoyment I might be able to give you. Let it happen, Poppy. You don't have to be virtuous with me."

"I'm not trying to be," she said unsteadily.

"Then let me touch you. Please."

At her silence, Harry pushed her resistless legs apart. His palm coursed along her inner thigh until his thumb brushed soft, private curls. The ragged rhythms of their breathing rustled through the quiet room. His thumb nestled into the curls, grazing against a place so sensitive that she jerked with a muffled protest.

He gathered her closer into hard muscle and smoothness and crisp hair. Reaching down again, he teased the yielding flesh apart. An irresistible urge came to press upward into his hand. But she forced herself to lay passive, even though the effort to hold still was exhausting.

Finding the entrance to her body, Harry stroked the softness until he had elicited a slick of hot serum. He fondled her, one of his fingers nudging inside. Startled, she stiffened and whimpered.

Harry kissed her throat. "Shhh . . . easy." He stroked within her, his finger gently crooking as if to urge her forward. Over and over, so patiently. The pleasure acquired a new tension, her limbs weighted with thickening layers of sensation. His finger withdrew, and he began to play with her idly.

Sounds climbed in her throat, but she swallowed them back. She wanted to move, to twist in the restless heat. She couldn't stop her hips from riding upward, her heels delving into the cool pliancy of the mattress. He slid along her front, kissing lower and lower, his mouth measuring tender distances across her body. When he nuzzled into the soft, private curls, however, she stiffened and tried to move away.

As she wriggled, his hands slid beneath her bottom, gripping her in place, and his tongue found her in wet, fluent strokes. Carefully he guided her into a deliberate rhythm, urging her upward, and again, while he stroked in voluptuous countermeasure. Wicked mouth, merciless tongue. Hot breath, flowing over her. The feeling built and built, until it came to a startling summit and flared in all directions. A cry escaped her, and another, as dense spasms rolled through her. There was no escaping, no holding back. And he stayed with her, prolonging the descent with soft licks, extorting a few last twitches of pleasure as she lay trembling beneath him.

Then came the worst part, when Harry took her into his arms to comfort her . . . and she let him.

She could hardly help but feel how aroused he was, his body taut and solid, his heartbeat swift beneath her ear. He ran his hand over the supple curve of her spine. With a pang of reluctant excitement, she wondered if he would take her now.

Her voice sounded strange and thick to her own ears. "You . . . you needn't stop."

"I'd rather wait until you're ready." Releasing her, he

rolled away. He drew the covers over her and paused. "Tell me, Poppy . . . did you think of him at all just now? Was his face, his name in your mind while I was touching you?"

Poppy shook her head, refusing to look at him.

"That's a start," he said softly. He extinguished the lamp and left.

Chapter Fourteen

Sleep was always difficult for Harry. Tonight it was impossible. His mind, accustomed to working on multiple problems simultaneously, now had a new and endlessly interesting subject to ponder.

His wife.

He had learned a great deal about Poppy in one day. She had shown that she was exceptionally strong under duress, not a woman to go to pieces in a difficult situation. And although she loved her family, she had not run to them for shelter.

Harry admired the way Poppy had dealt with her wedding day. Even more, he admired the way she had dealt with *him*. No virginal theatrics, as she had put it.

He thought of those blistering minutes before he had left her, when she had been sweet and yielding, her beautiful body blazing in response. Aroused and restless, Harry lay in his bedroom, on the other side of the apartment from hers. The thought of Poppy sleeping in the place where he lived was more than sufficient to keep him awake. No woman had ever stayed in his apartments before. He had always conducted his liaisons away from his residence, never spending a full night with anyone. It made him uncomfortable, the notion of actually sleeping in a bed with another person. Just why that seemed more intimate than the sexual act was not something Harry cared to ponder.

Harry was relieved when daybreak approached, the sky's low roof enameled with dull silver. He arose, washed, and dressed. He let in a housemaid, who stirred the grate and brought freshly ironed copies of the *Morning Chronicle,* the *Globe,* and the *Times.* As per their usual routine, the floor waiter would arrive with breakfast, and then Jake Valentine would deliver the managers' reports and take his morning list.

"Will Mrs. Rutledge want breakfast as well, sir?" the maid asked.

Harry wondered how long Poppy would sleep. "Tap on her door and ask."

"Yes, sir."

He saw the way the maid's gaze darted from the direction of his bedroom to Poppy's. Although it was common for upper-class couples to maintain separate bedrooms, the maid evinced a touch of surprise before she schooled her expression. Vaguely annoyed, Harry watched her leave the dining area.

He heard the housemaid's murmur, and Poppy's reply. The muffled sound of his wife's voice caused a pleasant ripple of awareness across his nerves.

The housemaid returned to the dining area. "I'll be bringing a tray for Mrs. Rutledge as well. Will there be anything else, sir?"

Harry shook his head, returning his attention to the papers as she left. He tried to read an article at least three times before finally giving up and staring in the direction of Poppy's room.

Finally she appeared, wearing a dressing gown made of blue taffeta, heavily embroidered with flowers. Her hair was loose, the brown locks shot with gleaming fire. Her expression was neutral, her eyes guarded. He wanted to peel the intricately stitched garment away from her, kiss her exposed body until she was flushed and panting.

"Good morning," Poppy murmured, not quite meeting his gaze.

Harry stood and waited until she came to the small table. It didn't escape him that she tried to avoid being touched by him as he seated her. *Patience,* he reminded himself. "Did you sleep well?" he asked.

"Yes, thank you." It was clear that politeness rather than concern motivated her to ask, "And you?"

"Well enough."

Poppy glanced at the variety of papers on the table. Picking one up, she held it so that any view of her face was obstructed as she read. Since it appeared that she was not inclined to converse, Harry occupied himself with another paper.

The silence was broken only by the rustling of flimsy news pages.

Breakfast was brought in, and two housemaids set out porcelain plates and flatware and crystal glasses.

Harry saw that Poppy had asked for crumpets, their flat, porous tops gently steaming. He began on his own breakfast of poached eggs on toast, cutting into the condensed yellow yolks and spreading the soft insides across the crisp bread.

"There's no need for you to awaken early if you don't wish," he said, sprinkling a pinch of salt over his eggs. "Many ladies of London sleep until noon."

"I like to rise when the day begins."

"Like a good farmwife," Harry said, casting her a brief smile.

But Poppy showed no reaction to the reminder, only applied herself to drizzling honey over the crumpets.

Harry paused with his fork held in midair, mesmerized by the sight of her slim fingers twirling the honey stick, meticulously filling each hole with thick amber liquid. Realizing that he was staring, Harry took a bite of his breakfast. Poppy replaced the honey stick in a small silver pot. Discovering a stray drop of sweetness on the tip of her thumb, she lifted it to her lips and sucked it clean.

Harry choked a little, reached for his tea, and took a swallow. The beverage scalded his tongue, causing him to flinch and curse.

Poppy gave him an odd look. "Is there anything the matter?"

Nothing. Except that watching his wife eating breakfast was the most erotic act he had ever seen. "Nothing at all," Harry said scratchily. "Tea's hot."

When he dared to look at Poppy again, she was consuming a fresh strawberry, holding it by the green stem. Her lips rounded in a luscious pucker as she bit neatly into the ripe flesh of the fruit. *Christ.* He moved uncomfortably in his chair, while all the unsatisfied desire of the previous night reawakened with a vengeance. Poppy ate two more strawberries, nibbling slowly, while Harry tried to ignore her. Heat collected beneath his clothing, and he used a napkin to blot his forehead.

Poppy lifted a bite of honey-soaked crumpet to her mouth, and gave him a perplexed glance. "Are you feeling well?"

"It's too warm in here," Harry said irritably, while lurid thoughts went through his mind. Thoughts involving honey, and soft feminine skin, and moist pink—

A knock came at the door.

"Come in," Harry said curtly, eager for any kind of distraction.

Jake Valentine entered the apartments more cautiously than usual, looking a bit surprised as he saw Poppy sitting at the breakfast table. Harry supposed the novelty of the situation would take a little getting used to on all sides.

"Good morning," Valentine said, uncertain whether to address only Harry or include Poppy.

She solved the dilemma by giving him an artless smile. "Good morning, Mr. Valentine. I hope there are no fugitive monkeys in the hotel today?"

Valentine grinned. "Not that I'm aware of, Mrs. Rutledge. But the day's still young."

Harry experienced a new sensation, a poisonous resentment that crept all through his body. Was it . . . jealousy? It had to be. He tried to suppress the feeling, but it lingered in the pit of his stomach. He wanted Poppy to smile at him like that. He wanted her playfulness, her charm, her attention.

Stirring a lump of sugar into his tea, Harry said coolly, "Tell me about the staff meeting."

"Nothing to report, really." Valentine handed him the sheaf of paper. "The sommelier asked that you approve a list of wines. And Mrs. Pennywhistle raised the problem of cutlery and flatware disappearing from trays when guests request food in their rooms."

Harry's eyes narrowed. "It's not an issue in the dining room?"

"No, sir. It seems that few guests are inclined to take the flatware straight from the dining room. But in the privacy of their own rooms . . . well, the other morning, an entire breakfast service went missing. As a result, Mrs. Pennywhistle proposed that we purchase a set of tinware to be used strictly for private dining."

"My guests, using tin knives and forks?" Harry shook his head emphatically. "No, we'll have to find some other way of discouraging petty thievery. We're not a damned coaching inn."

"That's what I thought you'd say." Valentine watched

Harry leaf through the top few pages. "Mrs. Pennywhistle said that whenever Mrs. Rutledge prefers, she would be honored to escort her around the hotel offices and kitchens, and introduce her to the staff."

"I don't think—" Harry began.

"That would be lovely," Poppy interrupted. "Please tell her I'll be ready after breakfast."

"There's no need," Harry said. "It's not as if you'll have a hand in running the place."

Poppy turned to him with a polite smile. "I would never dream of interfering. But since this is my new home, I'd like to become more familiar with it."

"It's not a home," Harry said.

Their gazes met.

"Of course it is," Poppy said. "People live here. Don't you consider it your home?"

Jake Valentine shifted his weight uncomfortably. "If you'll give me my morning list, Mr. Rutledge . . ."

Harry barely heard him. He continued to stare at his wife, wondering why the question seemed important to her. He tried to explain his reasoning. "The mere fact of people living here doesn't make it a home."

"You have no feelings of domestic affection for this place?" Poppy asked.

"Well," Valentine said awkwardly, "I'll go now."

Neither of them took notice of his hasty departure.

"It's a place I happen to own," Harry said. "I value it for practical reasons. But I attach no sentiment to it."

Her blue eyes searched his, curious and perceptive, oddly compassionate. No one had ever looked at him that way before. It made his nerves prickle defensively. "You've spent all your life in hotels, haven't you?" she murmured.

Harry was unable to fathom why any of that should signify. He brushed away the subject and tried to reassert his control.

"Let me be clear, Poppy . . . this is a business. And my employees are not to be treated as relations, or even as friends, or you'll create a management problem. Do you understand?"

"Yes," she said, still staring at him. "I'm beginning to."

This time it was Harry's turn to lift the newspaper, avoiding her gaze. Uneasiness stirred within him. He did not want any form of understanding from her.

"EVERYONE," MRS. PENNYWHISTLE, THE HEAD HOUSEKEEPER said emphatically, "from myself down to the laundry maids, is so *very* delighted that Mr. Rutledge has finally found a bride. And on behalf of the entire staff, we hope you will feel welcome here. You have three hundred people available to serve your every need."

Poppy was touched by the woman's obvious sincerity. The housekeeper was a tall, broad-shouldered woman with a ruddy complexion and an air of barely suppressed liveliness.

"I promise you," Poppy said with a smile, "I won't require the assistance of three hundred people. Although I will need your help in finding a lady's maid. I've never needed one before, but now without my sisters and my companion . . ."

"Certainly. We have a few girls among the staff who could be easily trained for such a purpose. You may interview them, and if none seems suitable, we will advertise."

"Thank you."

"I expect that from time to time you may wish to view the housekeeping accounts and ledgers, and the supply lists and inventory. I am at your disposal, of course."

"You are very kind," Poppy said. "I'm glad of the chance to meet some of the hotel staff. And to see some of the places I was never able to visit as a guest. The kitchens, especially."

"Our chef, Monsieur Broussard, is longing to show you his kitchen and boast of his achievements." She paused and added *sotto voce*, "Fortunately for us, his vanity is matched by his talent."

They began to descend the grand staircase. "How long have you been employed here, Mrs. Pennywhistle?" Poppy asked.

"Well nigh ten years . . . since the beginning." The housekeeper smiled at a distant memory. "Mr. Rutledge was so very young, lanky as a beanpole, with a sharp American accent and a habit of talking so fast, one could scarcely follow him. I worked in my father's tea shop in the Strand—I managed it for him—and Mr. Rutledge was a frequent customer. One day he came in and offered me the position I currently hold, although the hotel was still only a row of private houses. Nothing compared to what it is now. Of course I said yes."

"Why 'of course'? Didn't your father want you to stay at his shop?"

"Yes, but he had my sisters to help him. And there was something about Mr. Rutledge that I've never seen in any man before or since . . . an extraordinary force of character. He is very persuasive."

"I've noticed," Poppy said dryly.

"People want to follow him, or to be part of whatever it is he's involved in. It's why he was able to accomplish all this"—Mrs. Pennywhistle gestured at their surroundings—"at such an early age."

It occurred to Poppy that she could learn much about her husband from those who worked for him. She hoped at least a few of them would be as willing to talk as Mrs. Pennywhistle. "Is he a demanding master?"

The housekeeper chuckled. "Oh, yes. But fair, and always reasonable."

They went to the front office, where two men, one elderly, one in his middle years, were conferring over an enormous ledger, which lay open across an oak desk. "Gentlemen," the housekeeper said, "I am touring Mrs. Rutledge around the hotel. Mrs. Rutledge, may I present Mr. Myles, our general manager, and Mr. Lufton, the concierge."

They bowed respectfully, regarding Poppy as if she were a visiting monarch. The younger of the two, Mr. Myles, beamed and blushed until the top of his balding head was pink. "Mrs. Rutledge, it is a very great honor indeed! May we offer our sincere congratulations on your marriage—"

"*Most* sincere," Mr. Lufton chimed in. "You are the answer to our prayers. We wish you and Mr. Rutledge every happiness."

Slightly taken aback by their enthusiasm, Poppy smiled and nodded to each of them in turn. "Thank you, gentlemen."

They proceeded to show her the office, which housed a long row of arrival ledgers, managers' logs, books containing histories and customs of foreign countries, dictionaries for various languages, maps of all kinds, and floor plans of the hotel. The plans, tacked on a wall, were marked in pencil to indicate which rooms were vacant or under repair.

Two leather-bound books had been set apart from the rest, one red, one black.

"What are these volumes?" Poppy asked.

The men glanced at each other, and Mr. Lufton replied cautiously. "There are very rare occasions on which a guest has proved so . . . well, difficult—"

"Impossible," Mr. Myles chimed in.

"That regrettably we must enter them in the black book, which means they are no longer precisely welcome—"

"Undesirable," Mr. Myles added.

"And we are unable to allow them back."

"*Ever,*" Mr. Myles said emphatically.

Amused, Poppy nodded. "I see. And the purpose of the red book?"

Mr. Lufton proceeded to explain. "That is for certain guests who are a bit more demanding than usual."

"Problem guests," Mr. Myles clarified.

"Those who have special requests," Mr. Lufton continued, "or don't like their rooms cleaned at certain times; those who insist on bringing pets, things of that sort. We don't discourage them from staying, but we do make a note of their peculiarities."

"Hmmm." Poppy picked up the red book and cast a mischievous glance at the housekeeper. "I wouldn't be surprised if the Hathaways were mentioned a few times in this book."

Silence greeted her comment.

Seeing the frozen looks on their faces, Poppy began to laugh. "I knew it. Where is my family mentioned?" She opened the book and glanced over a few pages at random.

The two men were instantly distressed, hovering as if searching for an opportunity to seize the book. "Mrs. Rutledge, please, you mustn't—"

"I'm sure you're not in there," Mr. Myles said anxiously.

"I'm sure we are," Poppy countered with a grin. "In fact, we probably have our own chapter."

"Yes—I mean, *no*—Mrs. Rutledge, I beg of you—"

"Very well," Poppy said, surrendering the red book. The men sighed with relief. "However," she said, "I may borrow this book someday. I'm sure it would make excellent reading material."

"If you are done teasing these poor gentlemen, Mrs. Rutledge," the housekeeper said, her eyes twinkling, "I see that many of our employees have gathered outside the door to meet you."

"Lovely!" Poppy went to the reception area, where she was introduced to housemaids, floor managers, maintenance staff, and hotel valets. She repeated everyone's name, trying to memorize as many of them as possible, and asked questions about their duties. They responded eagerly to her interest, volunteering information about the various parts of England they had come from and how long they had worked at the Rutledge.

Poppy reflected that despite the many occasions she had stayed at the hotel as a guest, she had never given much thought to the employees. They had always been nameless and faceless, moving in the background with quiet efficiency. Now she felt immediate kinship with them. She was part of the hotel just as they were . . . all of them existing in Harry Rutledge's sphere.

AFTER THE FIRST WEEK OF LIVING WITH HARRY, IT WAS CLEAR to Poppy that her husband kept a schedule that would have killed a normal man. The only time she was sure to see him was in the mornings at breakfast; he was busy the rest of the day, often missing supper, and seldom retiring before midnight.

Harry liked to occupy himself with two or more things at once, making lists and plans, arranging meetings, reconciling arguments, doing favors. He was constantly approached by people who wanted him to apply his brilliant mind to some problem or other. People visited him at all hours, and it seemed a quarter hour couldn't pass without someone, usually Jake Valentine, tapping on the apartment door.

When Harry wasn't busy with his various intrigues, he meddled with the hotel and its staff. His demands for perfection and the highest quality of service were relentless. The employees were paid generously and treated well, but in return they were expected to work hard and, above all, to be loyal. If one of them were injured or ill, Harry sent for a doctor and paid for their treatments. If someone suggested a way to improve the hotel or its service, the idea was sent directly to Harry, and if he approved, he gave a handsome bonus. As a result, Harry's desk was always laden with piles of reports, letters, and notes.

It didn't seem to have occurred to Harry to suggest a honeymoon for himself and his new bride, and Poppy suspected he had no desire to leave the hotel. Certainly she had no desire for a honeymoon with a man who had betrayed her.

Since their wedding night, Poppy had been nervous around Harry, especially when they were alone. He made no secret of his desire for her, his interest in her, but so far there had been no more advances. In fact, he had gone out of his way to be polite and considerate. It seemed as if he were trying to get her accustomed to him, to the altered circumstances of her life. And she appreciated his patience, because it was all so very new. Ironically, however, his self-imposed restraint gave their occasional moments of contact—the touch of his hand on her arm, the press of his body when they stood close in a crowd—a charge of vibrant attraction.

Attraction without trust . . . not a comfortable thing to feel for one's own husband.

Poppy had no idea how long he would continue this conjugal reprieve. She was only grateful that Harry was so consumed with his hotel. Although . . . she couldn't help thinking that this sunrise-to-midnight agenda was not at all good for him. If someone Poppy cared for had been working so relentlessly, she would have urged him to ease his pace, to take some time to rest.

Simple compassion got the better of her one afternoon when Harry came into their apartment unexpectedly, carrying his coat in one hand. He had spent most of the day with the Chief Officer of the LFEE, the London Fire Engine Establishment. Together they had meticulously gone through the hotel to examine its safety procedures and equipment.

If, heaven forbid, a fire should ever break out at the Rutledge, the employees had been trained to help as many guests as possible leave the building expediently. Escape ladders were routinely counted and inspected, and floor plans and exit routes were examined. Firemarks had been mortared onto the outside of the building to designate it as one the LFEE had been paid to protect.

As Harry entered the apartment, Poppy saw that the day had been especially demanding. His face was etched with weariness.

He paused at the sight of Poppy curled in the corner of the settee, reading a book balanced on her drawn-up knees.

"How was the luncheon?" Harry asked.

Poppy had been invited to join a group of well-to-do young matrons, who held an annual charity bazaar. "It went nicely, thank you. They are a pleasant group. Although they do seem a bit too fond of forming committees. I've always thought a committee takes a month to accomplish something a single person could have done in ten minutes."

Harry smiled. "The goal of such groups isn't to be efficient. It's to have something to occupy their time."

Poppy took a closer look at him, and her eyes widened. "What happened to your clothes?"

Harry's white linen shirt and dark blue silk waistcoat had been streaked with soot. There were more black smudges on his hands, and one on the edge of his jaw.

"I was testing one of the safety ladders."

"You climbed down a ladder outside the building?" Poppy was amazed that he would have taken such an unnecessary risk. "Couldn't you have asked someone else to do it? Mr. Valentine, perhaps?"

"I'm sure he would have. But I wouldn't provide equipment for my employees without trying it myself. I still have concerns about the housemaids—their skirts would make their descent more difficult." He cast a rueful glance at his palms. "I have to wash and change before going back to work."

Poppy returned her attention to her book. But she was

intensely aware of the quiet sounds coming from the other room, the opening of drawers, the splash of water and soap, the thud of a discarded shoe. She thought of him being un-clothed, at that very moment, and a dart of warmth went through her stomach.

Harry came back into the room, clean and impeccable as before. Except . . .

"A smudge," Poppy said, conscious of a flutter of amuse-ment. "You missed a spot."

Harry glanced down over his front. "Where?"

"Your jaw. No, not that side." She picked up a napkin and gestured for him to come to her.

Harry leaned over the back of the settee, his face descend-ing toward hers. He held very still as she wiped the soot from his jaw. The scent of his skin drifted to her, fresh and clean, with a slight smoky tinge like cedarwood.

Wishing to prolong the moment, Poppy stared into his fathomless green eyes. They were shadowed from lack of sleep. Good heavens, did the man ever pause for even a mo-ment?

"Why don't you sit with me?" Poppy asked impulsively.

Harry blinked, clearly thrown off guard by the invitation. "Now?"

"Yes, now."

"I can't. There's too much to—"

"Have you eaten today? Aside from a few bites of break-fast?"

Harry shook his head. "I haven't had time."

Poppy pointed to the place on the settee beside her in wordless demand.

To her surprise, Harry actually obeyed. He came around the end of the settee and sat in the corner, staring at her. One of his dark brows arched questioningly.

Reaching for the tray beside her, Poppy lifted a plate laden with sandwiches. "The kitchen sent up far too much for one person. Have the rest."

"I'm really not—"

"Here," she insisted, pushing the plate into his hands.

Harry took a sandwich and began to consume it slowly. Taking her own teacup from the tray, Poppy poured fresh tea and added a spoonful of sugar. She gave it to Harry.

"What are you reading?" he asked, glancing at the book in her lap.

"A novel by a naturalist author. As of yet, I can't find anything resembling a plot, but the descriptions of the countryside are quite lyrical." She paused, watching him drain the teacup. "Do you like novels?"

He shook his head. "I usually read for information, not entertainment."

"You disapprove of reading for pleasure?"

"No, it's just that I can't seem to find the time for it."

"Perhaps that's why you don't sleep well. You need something relaxing to do before bedtime."

There was a dry, perfectly timed pause before Harry asked, "What would you suggest?"

Aware of his meaning, Poppy felt a bloom of color emerge from head to toe. Harry seemed to enjoy her discomfiture, not in a mocking way, but as if he found her charming.

"Everyone in my family loves novels," Poppy finally said, pushing the conversation back into line. "We gather in the parlor nearly every evening, and one of us reads aloud. Win is the best at it—she invents a different voice for each character."

"I'd like to hear you read," Harry said.

Poppy shook her head. "I'm not half as entertaining as Win. I put everyone to sleep."

"Yes," Harry said. "You have the voice of a scholar's daughter." Before she could take offense, he added, "Soothing. Never grates. Soft . . ."

He was extraordinarily tired, she realized. So much that even the effort to string words together was defeating him.

"I should go," he muttered, rubbing his eyes.

"Finish your sandwiches first," Poppy said authoritatively.

He picked up a sandwich obediently. While he ate, Poppy paged through the book until she found what she wanted . . . a description of walking through the countryside, under skies filled with fleecy clouds, past almond trees in blossom and white campion nestled beside quiet brooks. She read in a measured tone, occasionally stealing a glance at Harry while he polished off the entire plate of sandwiches. And then he settled deeper into the corner, more relaxed than she had ever seen him.

She read a few pages more, about walking past hedges and meadows, through a wood dressed with a counterpane of fallen leaves, while soft pale sunshine gave way to a quiet rain . . .

And when she finally reached the end of the chapter, she looked at Harry once more.

He was asleep.

His chest rose and fell in an even rhythm, his long lashes fanned against his skin. One hand was palm down against his chest, while the other lay half open at his side, the strong fingers partially curled.

"Never fails," Poppy murmured with a private grin. Her talent at putting people to sleep was too much even for Harry's relentless drive. Carefully she set the book aside.

This was the first time she'd ever been able to view Harry at her leisure. It was strange to see him so utterly disarmed. In sleep, the lines of his face were relaxed and almost innocent, at odds with his usual expression of command. His mouth, always so purposeful, looked as soft as velvet. He looked like a boy lost in a solitary dream. Poppy felt an urge to safeguard the sleep Harry so badly needed, to cover him with a blanket, and stroke the dark hair from his brow.

Several tranquil minutes passed, the silence disturbed only by distant sounds of activity in the hotel and from the street. This was something Poppy had not known she needed . . . time to contemplate the stranger who had taken utter possession of her life.

Trying to understand Harry Rutledge was like taking apart one of the intricate clockwork mechanisms he had constructed. One could examine every gear and ratchet wheel and lever, but that didn't mean one would ever comprehend what made it all work.

It seemed that Harry had spent his life wrestling with the world and trying to bend it to his will. And toward that end he had made a great deal of progress. But he was clearly dissatisfied, unable to enjoy what he had achieved, which made him very different from the other men in Poppy's life, especially Cam and Merripen.

Because of their Romany heritage, her brothers-in-law didn't view the world as something to be conquered, but rather something to roam through freely. And then there was Leo, who preferred to view life as an objective observer instead of as an active participant.

Harry was nothing short of a brigand, scheming to conquer everyone and everything in sight. How could such a man ever be restrained? How would he ever find peace?

Poppy was so lost in the peaceful stillness of the room that she started when she heard a tap at the door. Her nerves jangled unpleasantly. She made no response, wishing the blasted noise would go away. But there it was again.

Tap. Tap. Tap.

Harry awakened with an inarticulate murmur, blinking with the confusion of someone who had been too quickly roused from sleep. "Yes?" he said gruffly, struggling to sit up.

The door opened, and Jack Valentine entered. He looked apologetic as he saw Harry and Poppy together on the settee. Poppy could barely refrain from scowling, even though he was only doing his job. Valentine came to hand Harry a folded note, murmured a few cryptic words, and left the apartment.

Harry scanned the note with a bleary glance. Tucking it into his coat pocket, he smiled ruefully at Poppy. "I seem to have nodded off while you were reading." He stared at her, his eyes warmer than she had ever seen them. "Thank you," he said, and left before she could reply.

Chapter Fifteen

Only the wealthiest London ladies possessed their own carriages and horses, as it cost a fortune to maintain such a convenience. Women without their own stables, or those who lived alone, were compelled to "job" the horses, brougham, and coachman, hiring it all from a livery service or jobmaster whenever they needed to knock about London.

Harry had insisted that Poppy must have her own carriage and pair, and had sent for a designer from a carriage works to come to the hotel. After consulting with Poppy, the carriage maker was commissioned to build a vehicle specifically to her taste. Poppy was left rather bemused by the process, and even a bit nettled because her insistence on asking the prices of materials had caused a tiff. "You're not here to question how much any of this costs," Harry had told her. "Your only task is to choose what you like."

But in Poppy's experience, that had always been part of choosing something . . . viewing what was available and then comparing costs until one arrived at something that was neither the most expensive nor the least. Harry, however, seemed to view this approach as an affront, as if she were questioning his ability to provide for her.

Finally it was decided that the outside would be done in elegant black lacquer, the inside upholstered in green velvet and beige leather with brass bead trim, and the interior paneling would feature decorative paintwork. There would be green silk curtains and venetian blinds in lieu of mahogany shutters . . . morocco leather sleeping cushions . . . decorative welding on the outside steps, plated carriage lamps and matching door handles . . . it had never occurred to Poppy that there would be so much to decide.

She spent what was left of the afternoon in the kitchen with the chef, Monsieur Broussard, the pastry chef, Mr. Rupert, and Mrs. Pennywhistle. Broussard was involved in the creation of a new dessert . . . or more aptly, trying to re-create a dessert he had remembered from childhood.

"My great-aunt Albertine always made this with no recipe," Broussard explained ruefully as he pulled a bain-marie, or water bath, from the oven. Nestled inside were a half dozen perfect little steaming apple puddings. "I watched her every time. But it has all slipped from my mind. Fifteen times I have tried it, and still it's not perfect . . . but *quand on veut, on peut*."

"When one wants, one can?" Poppy translated.

"Exactement." Broussard carefully removed the dishes from the hot water.

Chef Rupert drizzled cream sauce over each pudding, and topped them with delicate pastry leaves. "Shall we?" he asked, handing out spoons.

Solemnly, Poppy, Mrs. Pennywhistle, and the two chefs each took a pudding and sampled it. Poppy's mouth was filled with cream, soft tart apple, and crisply imploding pastry. She closed her eyes to better enjoy the textures and flavors, and she heard satisfied sighs from Mrs. Pennywhistle and Chef Rupert.

"Still not right," Monsieur Broussard fretted, scowling at the dish of pudding as if it were deliberately being obstinate.

"I don't care if it's not right," the housekeeper said. "That is the best thing I've ever tasted in my life." She turned to Poppy. "Don't you agree, Mrs. Rutledge?"

"I think it's what angels must eat in heaven," Poppy said, digging into the pudding. Chef Rupert had already shoved another spoonful into his mouth.

"Maybe a touch more lemon and cinnamon . . ." Monsieur Broussard mused.

"Mrs. Rutledge."

Poppy twisted to see who had spoken her name. Her smile dimmed as she saw Jake Valentine entering the kitchen. It wasn't that she didn't like him. In fact, Valentine had been very personable and kind. However, he seemed to have been appointed as a watchdog, enforcing Harry's mandate that Poppy should refrain from keeping company with the employees.

Mr. Valentine looked no happier than Poppy as he spoke. "Mrs. Rutledge, I've been sent to remind you that you have an appointment at the dressmaker's."

"I do? Now?" Poppy looked at him blankly. "I don't recall having made an appointment."

"It was made for you. At Mr. Rutledge's request."

"Oh." Reluctantly Poppy set down her spoon. "When must I leave?"

"In a quarter hour."

That would give her just enough time to tidy her hair and fetch a walking cloak. "I have enough clothes," Poppy said. "I don't need more."

"A lady in your position," Mrs. Pennywhistle said wisely, "needs many dresses. I've heard it said that fashionable ladies never wear the same frock twice."

Poppy rolled her eyes. "I've heard that as well. And I think it's ridiculous. Why should it matter if a lady is seen in the same frock twice? Except to provide evidence that her husband is wealthy enough to buy her more clothes than a person needs."

The housekeeper smiled sympathetically. "Shall I walk with you to your apartments, Mrs. Rutledge?"

"No, thank you. I'll go along the servants' hallway. None of the guests will see me."

Valentine said, "You shouldn't go unescorted."

Poppy heaved an impatient sigh. "Mr. Valentine?"

"Yes?"

"I want to walk to my apartment by myself. If I can't even do that, this entire hotel will start to feel like a prison."

He nodded with reluctant understanding.

"Thank you." Murmuring good-bye to the chefs and the housekeeper, Poppy left the kitchen.

Jake Valentine shifted his weight uncomfortably as the other three glared at him. "I'm sorry," he muttered. "But Mr. Rutledge has decided that his wife shouldn't fraternize with the employees. He says it makes all of us less productive, and there are more suitable ways for her to occupy herself."

Although Mrs. Pennywhistle was usually disinclined to criticize the master, her face grew taut with annoyance. "Doing what?" she asked curtly. "Shopping for things she neither needs nor wants? Reading fashion periodicals by herself? Riding in the park with a footman in attendance? No doubt there are many fashion-plate wives who would be more than pleased by such a shallow existence. But that lonely young woman is from a close family, and she is accustomed to a great deal of affection. She needs someone to do things with . . . a companion . . . and she needs a husband."

"She has a husband," Jake protested.

The housekeeper's eyes narrowed. "Have you noticed *nothing* odd about their relationship, Valentine?"

"No, and it's not appropriate for us to discuss it."

Monsieur Broussard regarded Mrs. Pennywhistle with keen interest. "I'm French," he said. "I have no problem discussing it."

Mrs. Pennywhistle lowered her voice, mindful of the scullery maids who were washing pots in the adjoining room. "There is some doubt as to whether they've had conjugal relations yet."

"Now see here—" Jake began, outraged at this violation of his employer's privacy.

"Have some of this, *mon ami*," Broussard said, shoving a pastry plate at him. As Jake sat and picked up a spoon, the chef gave Mrs. Pennywhistle an encouraging glance. "What gives you the impression that he has not yet, er . . . sampled the watercress?"

"Watercress?" Jake repeated incredulously.

"*Cresson*." Broussard gave him a superior look. "A metaphor. And much nicer than the metaphors you English use for the same thing."

"I never use metaphors," Jake muttered.

"*Bien sur,* you have no imagination." The chef turned back to the housekeeper. "Why is there doubt about the relations between Monsieur and Madame Rutledge?"

"The sheets," she said succinctly.

Jake nearly choked on his pastry. "You have the housemaids *spying on them*?" he asked around a mouthful of custard and cream.

"Not at all," the housekeeper said defensively. "It's only that we have vigilant maids who tell me everything. And even if they didn't, one hardly needs great powers of observation to see they do not behave like a married couple."

The chef looked deeply concerned. "You think there's a problem with his carrot?"

"Watercress, carrot—is *everything* food to you?" Jake demanded.

The chef shrugged. *"Oui."*

"Well," Jake said testily, "there is a string of Rutledge's past mistresses who would undoubtedly testify there is nothing wrong with his carrot."

"Alors, he is a virile man . . . she is a beautiful woman . . . why are they not making salad together?"

Jake paused with the spoon raised halfway to his lips as he recalled the business with the letter from Bayning and the secret meeting between Harry Rutledge and Viscount Andover. "I think," he said uncomfortably, "that to win her hand in marriage, Mr. Rutledge may have . . . well, manipulated events to make things turn out the way he wanted. Without taking her feelings into consideration."

The other three looked at him blankly.

Chef Rupert was the first to speak. "But he does that to everyone."

"Apparently Mrs. Rutledge doesn't like it," Jake muttered.

Mrs. Pennywhistle leaned her chin on her hand and tapped her jaw thoughtfully. "I believe she would be a good influence on him, were she ever inclined to try."

"Nothing," Jake said decisively, "will ever change Harry Rutledge."

"Still," the housekeeper mused, "I think the two of them may need a bit of help."

"From whom?" Chef Rupert asked.

"From all of us," the housekeeper replied. "It's all to our benefit if the master is happy, isn't it?"

"No," Jake said firmly. "I've never known anyone more ill equipped for happiness. He wouldn't know what to do with it."

"All the more reason he should try it," Mrs. Pennywhistle declared.

Jake gave her a warning glance. "We are *not* going to meddle in Mr. Rutledge's personal life. I forbid it."

Chapter Sixteen

Sitting at her dressing table, Poppy brushed powder on her nose and applied rose-petal salve to her lips. That night she and Harry were to attend a supper given in one of the private dining rooms, a highly formal affair attended by foreign diplomats and government officials to honor the visiting monarch of Prussia, King Frederick William IV. Mrs. Pennywhistle had shown Poppy the menu, and Poppy had remarked wryly that with ten courses, she expected the supper would last half the night.

Poppy was dressed in her best gown, a violet silk that shimmered with tones of blue and pink as the light moved over it. The unique color had been achieved with a new synthetic dye, and it was so striking that little ornamentation was needed. The bodice was intricately wrapped, leaving the tops of her shoulders bare, and the full, layered skirts rustled softly as she moved.

Just as she set down the powder brush, Harry came to the doorway and surveyed her leisurely. "No woman will compare to you tonight," he murmured.

Poppy smiled and murmured her thanks. "You look very

fine," she said, although "fine" seemed an entirely inadequate word to describe her husband.

Harry was severely handsome in the formal scheme of black and white, his cravat crisp and snowy, his shoes highly polished. He wore the elegant clothes with unselfconscious ease, so debonair that it was easy to forget how calculating he was.

"Is it time to go downstairs yet?" Poppy asked.

Pulling a watch from his pocket, Harry consulted it. "Fourteen . . . no, thirteen minutes."

Her brows lifted as she saw how battered and scratched the watch was. "My goodness. You must have carried that for a long time."

He hesitated before showing it to her. Poppy took the object carefully. The watch was small but heavy in her palm, the gold casing warm from his body. Flipping it open, she saw that the scarred and scratched metal had not been inscribed or adorned in any way.

"Where did it come from?" she asked.

Harry tucked the watch into his pocket. His expression was inscrutable. "From my father, when I told him I was leaving for London. He said his father had given it to him years before, with the advice that when he became a success, he should celebrate by purchasing a much finer watch. And so my father passed it on to me with the same counsel."

"But you've never bought one for yourself?"

Harry shook his head.

A perplexed smile touched her lips. "I would say that you've had more than enough success to merit a new watch."

"Not yet."

She thought he must be joking, but there was no humor in his expression. Perturbed and fascinated, Poppy wondered how much more wealth he intended to gain, how much power he wanted to accrue, before he considered it enough.

Perhaps there was no such thing as "enough" for Harry Rutledge.

She was distracted from her thoughts as he pulled something from one of his coat pockets, a flat rectangular leather case.

"A present," Harry said, giving it to her.

Her eyes rounded with surprise. "You didn't need to give me anything. Thank you. I didn't expect . . . *oh*." This last as she opened the case and beheld a diamond necklace arranged on the velvet lining like a pool of glittering fire. It was a heavy garland of sparkling flowers and quatrefoil links.

"Do you like it?" Harry asked casually.

"Yes, of course, it's . . . breathtaking." Poppy had never imagined owning such jewelry. The only necklace she possessed was a single pearl on a chain. "Shall I . . . shall I wear it tonight?"

"I think it would be appropriate with that gown." Harry took the necklace from the case, stood behind Poppy, and fastened it gently around her neck. The cold weight of the diamonds and the warm brush of his fingers at her nape elicited a shiver. He remained behind her, his hands settling lightly on the curves of her neck, moving in a warm stroke to the tops of her shoulders. "Lovely," he murmured. "Although nothing is as beautiful as your bare skin."

Poppy stared into the looking glass, not at her flushed face, but at his hands on her skin. They were both still, watching their shared reflection as if they were two forms encased in ice.

His hands moved sensitively, as if he were touching a priceless work of art. With the tip of his middle finger, he traced the line of her collarbone to the hollow at the base of her throat.

Feeling agitated, Poppy pulled away from his hands and stood to face him, coming around the little chair. "Thank you," she managed to say. Cautiously she moved to embrace him, her arms sliding over his shoulders.

It was more than Poppy had intended to do, but there was something in Harry's expression that touched her. She had sometimes seen the same expression on Leo's face in childhood, when he had been caught in mischief and had gone to their mother with a bouquet of flowers or some little treasure.

Harry's arms went around her, pulling her farther up against him. He smelled delicious, and he was warm and hard beneath the layers of linen, silk and wool. The soft gust of his breath against her neck was ragged at the finish.

Closing her eyes, Poppy let herself lean against him. He kissed the side of her throat, working up to the juncture of her neck and jaw. She felt warm from the bottom of her feet to the top of her head. She found something surprising in the embrace, a sense of security. They fit nicely together, softness and hardness, pliancy and tension. It seemed that every curve of her was perfectly reconciled with his masculine contours. She wouldn't have minded standing against him, with him, for a while longer.

His hand went to the side of her head, easing her back at just the right angle to kiss her. His mouth descended swiftly. Reflexively Poppy arched and twisted away from him, nearly causing an awkward collision of their heads.

The evasion seemed to have stunned Harry. Sparks of wrath kindled in his eyes, as if she had been vastly unfair.

"A diamond necklace for one kiss. Is that such a bad bargain?"

"I've never denied you your marital rights," she said. "If you wish, I'll go to that bed willingly and do whatever you want, this very moment. But not because you gave me a necklace, as if it were part of some transaction."

Far from being appeased, Harry regarded her with gathering outrage. "The thought of you laid out like a martyr on the sacrificial altar is not what I had in mind."

"Why isn't it enough that I'm willing to submit to you?" Poppy asked, her own temper flaring. "Why must I be *eager* to lie with you, when you're not the husband I wanted?"

The very second the words left her lips, Poppy regretted them. But it was too late. Harry's eyes turned to ice. His lips parted, and she braced herself, knowing he was about to say something decimating.

Instead, he turned and walked from the room.

SUBMIT.

The word hovered, wasplike, in Harry's mind. Stinging repeatedly.

Submit to him . . . as if he were some loathsome toad, when some of the most beautiful women in London had begged for his attentions. Sensuous, accomplished women with clever mouths and hands, willing to satisfy his most exotic desires . . . in fact, he could have one of them tonight.

When his temper had eased enough that he could function normally, Harry went back into Poppy's bedroom and informed her that it was time to go down to supper. She sent him a wary glance, seeming to want to say something, but she had the sense to keep her mouth shut.

"You're not the husband I wanted."

And he never would be. No amount of scheming or manipulation could change it.

But Harry would continue to play out his hand. Poppy was legally his, and God knew he had money on his side. Time would have to take care of the rest.

The formal dinner was a great success. Every time Harry glanced at the other end of the long table, he saw that Poppy was acquitting herself splendidly. She was relaxed and smiling, taking part in conversation, appearing to charm her companions. It was exactly as Harry had expected: the same qualities that were considered faults in an unmarried girl were admired in a married woman. Poppy's acute observations and her enjoyment of lively debate made her far more interesting than a demure society miss with a modest downcast gaze.

She was breathtaking in the violet gown, her slender neck encircled with diamonds, her hair rich with dark fire. Nature had blessed her with abundant beauty. But it was her smile that made her irresistible, a smile so sweet and brilliant that it warmed him from the inside out.

Harry wished she would smile at him like that. She had, in the beginning. There had to be something that would induce her to warm to him, to like him again. Everyone had a weakness.

In the meantime, Harry stole glances of her whenever he could, his lovely and distant wife . . . and he drank in the smiles she gave to other people.

THE NEXT MORNING HARRY AWOKE AT HIS USUAL HOUR. HE washed and dressed, sat at the breakfast table with a newspaper, and glanced at Poppy's door. There was no sign of her. He assumed she would sleep late, since they had retired long after midnight.

"Don't wake Mrs. Rutledge," he told the maid. "She needs to rest this morning."

"Yes, sir."

Harry ate his breakfast alone, trying to focus on the newspaper, but his gaze kept dragging to Poppy's closed door.

He had gotten used to seeing her every morning. He liked to start his day with her. But Harry was aware that he had been nothing less than boorish the previous night, giving her jewelry and demanding a demonstration of gratitude. He should have known better.

It was just that he wanted her so damned badly. And he had become accustomed to having his way, especially where women were concerned. He reflected that it probably wouldn't hurt him to learn to consider someone else's feelings.

Especially if that would hasten the process of getting what he wanted.

After receiving the morning managers' reports from Jake Valentine, Harry went with him to the basement of the hotel to assess the damage from some minor flooding due to faulty drainage. "We'll need an engineering assessment," Harry said, "And I want an inventory of the damaged storage items."

"Yes, sir," Valentine replied. "Unfortunately there were some rolled-up Turkish carpets in the flooded area, but I don't know if the staining—"

"Mr. Rutledge!" An agitated housemaid descended to the bottom of the stairs and rushed over to them. She could barely speak between labored breaths. "Mrs. Pennywhistle said . . . to come fetch you because . . . Mrs. Rutledge . . ."

Harry looked at the housemaid sharply. "What is it?"

"She's injured, sir . . . took a fall . . ."

Alarm shot through him. "Where is she?"

"Your apartments, sir."

"Send for a doctor," Harry told Valentine, and he ran for the stairs, taking them two and three at a time. By the time he reached his apartments, full-scale panic roared through him. He tried to push it back enough to think clearly. There was a congregation of maids around the door, and he shouldered his way through them into the main room. "Poppy?"

Mrs. Pennywhistle's voice echoed from the tiled bathing room. "We're in here, Mr. Rutledge."

Harry reached the bathing room in three strides, his stomach lurching in fear as he saw Poppy on the floor, reclining against the housekeeper's supportive arms. Toweling had been draped over her for modesty's sake, but her limbs were naked and vulnerable looking in contrast to the hard gray tiling.

Harry dropped to his haunches beside her. "What happened, Poppy?"

"I'm sorry." She looked pained and mortified and apologetic. "It was so silly. I stepped out of the bath and slipped on the tiles, and my leg went out from beneath me."

"Thank heavens one of the maids had come to clear the breakfast dishes," Mrs. Pennywhistle told him, "and she heard Mrs. Rutledge cry out."

"I'm all right," Poppy said. "I just twisted my ankle a bit." She gave the housekeeper a gently chiding glance. "I'm perfectly capable of getting up, but Mrs. Pennywhistle won't let me."

"I was afraid to move her," the housekeeper told Harry.

"You were right to keep her still," Harry replied, examining Poppy's leg. The ankle was discolored and already beginning to swell. Even the light brush of his fingers was enough to make her flinch and inhale quickly.

"I don't think I'll need a doctor," Poppy said. "If you could just wrap it with a light binding, and perhaps I could have some willow bark tea—"

"Oh, you're seeing a doctor," Harry said, suffused with grim concern. Glancing at Poppy's face, he saw the residue of tears, and he reached out to her with extreme gentleness, his fingers caressing the side of her face. Her skin was as smooth as fine-milled soap. There was a red mark in the center of her lower lip, where she must have bitten it.

Whatever she saw in his expression caused her eyes to widen and her cheeks to flush.

Mrs. Pennywhistle eased up from the floor. "Well," she said briskly, "Now that she's in your care, Mr. Rutledge, shall I fetch some bandages and salve? We may as well treat the ankle until the doctor arrives."

"Yes," Harry said curtly. "And send for another doctor—I want a second opinion."

"Yes, sir." The housekeeper fled.

"We haven't even gotten a first opinion yet," Poppy protested. "And you're making far too much of this. It's just a minor sprain, and . . . what are you doing?"

Harry had laid two fingers on the top of her foot, two inches below the ankle, feeling for her pulse. "Making certain your circulation hasn't been compromised."

Poppy rolled her eyes. "My goodness. All I need is to sit somewhere with my foot up."

"I'm going to carry you to bed," he said, sliding one arm behind her back, the other beneath her knees. "Can you put your arms around my neck?"

She blushed from head to toe, and complied with an inarticulate murmur. He lifted her in a slow, easy movement. Poppy fumbled a little as the toweling began to slip from her body, and she gasped in pain.

"Did I jostle your leg?" Harry asked in concern.

"No. I think . . ." She sounded sheepish. "I think I may have hurt my back a little as well."

Harry let out a few quiet curses that caused her brows to raise, and he carried her into the bedroom. "From now on," he told her sternly, "you're not to step out of the bathing tub unless there's someone to help you."

"I can't do that," she protested.

"Why not?"

"I don't need help with my bath every night. I'm not a child!"

"Believe me," Harry said, "I'm aware of that." He set her

down gently and arranged the covers over her. After easing the damp towel away from her, he adjusted her pillows. "Where are your nightgowns?"

"The bottom dresser drawer."

Harry went to the dresser, jerked the drawer open, and pulled out a white gown. Returning to the bed, he helped Poppy into the nightgown, his face tautening with concern as she winced with every movement. She needed something for the pain. She needed a doctor.

Why the hell was it so *quiet* in the apartment? He wanted people running, fetching things. He wanted action.

After tucking the covers around Poppy, he left the room in rapid strides.

Three maids were still in the hallway, talking amongst themselves. Harry scowled, and the maids blanched simultaneously.

"S-sir?" one of them asked nervously.

"Why are you all standing here?" he demanded. "And where is Mrs. Pennywhistle? I want one of you to find her immediately, and tell her to hurry! And I want the other two of you to start fetching things."

"What kind of things, sir?" one of them quavered.

"Things for Mrs. Rutledge. A hot water bottle. Ice. Laudanum. A pot of tea. A book. I don't give a damn, just start bringing things!"

The maids scampered away like terrified squirrels.

A half minute passed, and still no one appeared.

Where the devil was the doctor? Why was everyone so bloody *slow?*

He heard Poppy calling for him, and he turned on his heels and raced back into the apartments. He was at her bedside in an instant.

Poppy was huddled in a small, motionless heap.

"Harry," her voice came from beneath the bedclothes, "are you yelling at people?"

"No," he said instantly.

"Good. Because this is not a serious situation, and it certainly doesn't merit—"

"It's serious to me."

Poppy pushed the covers away from her strained face and looked at him as if he were someone she had met before but couldn't quite place. A faint smile touched her lips. Tentatively her hand crept to Harry's, her small fingers curving around his palm.

That simple clasp did something strange to Harry's heartbeat. His pulse drove in erratic surges, and his chest turned hot with some unknown emotion. He took her entire hand in his, their palms gently pressing. He wanted to hold her in his arms, not in passion, but to give comfort. Even though his embrace was the last thing she wanted.

"I'll be back in a moment," he said, striding from the room. He rushed to a sideboard in his private library, poured a small glass of French brandy, and brought it back to Poppy. "Try this."

"What is it?"

"Brandy."

She tried to sit up, wincing with every movement. "I don't think I'll like it."

"You don't have to like it. Just drink it." Harry tried to help her, feeling unaccountably awkward . . . he, who had always navigated his way around the female form with absolute confidence. Carefully he wedged another pillow behind her back.

She sipped the brandy and made a face. "*Ugh.*"

Had Harry not been so worried, he might have found some amusement in her reaction to the brandy, a heritage vintage that had been aged at least a hundred years. As she continued to sip the brandy, Harry pulled a chair beside the bed.

By the time Poppy had finished the brandy, some of the fine-grooved tension had gone from her face. "That actually helped a bit," she said. "My ankle still hurts, but I don't think I care as much."

Harry took the glass from her and set it aside. "That's good," he said gently. "Would you mind if I left you again momentarily?"

"No, you're only going to yell at the staff again, and they're already doing their best. Stay with me." She reached for his hand.

That mystifying feeling again . . . the sense of puzzle pieces fitting together. Such an innocent connection, one hand in another, and yet it was enormously satisfying.

"Harry?" The soft way she said his name caused the hair to rise pleasurably on his arms and the back of his neck.

"Yes, love?" he asked hoarsely.

"Would you . . . would you mind rubbing my back?"

Harry fought to conceal his reaction. "Of course," he said, striving to keep his tone casual. "Can you turn to your side?" Reaching for her lower back, he found the little reefs of muscle on either side of her spine. Poppy pushed the pillows aside and lay flat on her stomach. He worked up to her upper shoulders, finding the knotted muscles.

A soft groan escaped her, and Harry paused.

"Yes, there," she said, and the full-throated pleasure in her voice went straight to Harry's groin. He continued to knead her back, his fingers coaxing and sure. Poppy sighed deeply. "I'm keeping you from your work."

"I have nothing planned."

"You always have at least ten things planned."

"Nothing's more important than you."

"You almost sound sincere."

"I am sincere. Why wouldn't I be?"

"Because your work is more important to you than anything, even people."

Annoyed, Harry held his tongue and continued to massage her.

"I'm sorry," Poppy said after a minute. "I didn't mean that. I don't know why I said it."

The words were an instant balm to Harry's anger. "You're hurting. And you're tipsy. It's all right."

Mrs. Pennywhistle's voice came from the threshold. "Here we are. Hopefully this will suffice until the doctor arrives." She brought a tray laden with supplies, including rolled linen bandages, a pot of salve, and two or three large green leaves.

"What are these for?" Harry asked, picking up one of the leaves. He gave the housekeeper a questioning glance. "Cabbage?"

"It's a very effective remedy," the housekeeper explained. "It reduces swelling and makes bruises disappear. Only make certain to break the spine of the leaf and crush it a bit, then wrap it around the ankle before you tie the bandage."

"I don't want to smell like cabbage," Poppy protested.

Harry gave her a severe glance. "I don't give a damn what it smells like, if it will make you better."

"That's because you're not the one who has to wear a vegetable leaf on your leg!"

But he had his way, of course, and Poppy reluctantly endured the poultice.

"There," Harry said, tying off a neat bandage around it. He drew the hem of Poppy's nightgown back over her knee. "Mrs. Pennywhistle, if you wouldn't mind—"

"Yes, I'll see if the doctor's arrived," the housekeeper said. "And I'll have a brief talk with the housemaids. For some reason they're piling the strangest assortment of objects near the doorway . . ."

The doctor had indeed arrived. Stoic soul that he was, he ignored Harry's muttered comment that he hoped the doctor didn't *always* take so long when there was a medical emergency, or half his patients would probably expire before he ever crossed the threshold.

After examining Poppy's ankle, the doctor diagnosed a light sprain, and he prescribed cold compresses for the swelling. He left a bottle of tonic for the pain, a pot of liniment for the pulled muscle in her shoulder, and advised that above all Mrs. Rutledge must rest.

Were it not for her discomfort, Poppy would have actually enjoyed the rest of the day. Apparently Harry had decided that she should be waited on hand and foot. Chef Broussard sent up a tray of pastry, fresh fruit, and creamed eggs. Mrs. Pennywhistle brought a selection of cushions to make her more comfortable. Harry had dispatched a footman to the bookshop, and the servant had returned with an armload of new publications.

Soon thereafter, a maid brought Poppy a tray of neat boxes tied with ribbons. Opening them, Poppy discovered that one was filled with toffee, another with boiled sweets, and another with Turkish delight. Best of all, one box was filled with a new confection called "eating-chocolates" that had been all the rage at the London Exhibition.

"Where did these come from?" Poppy asked Harry when he returned to her room after a brief visit to the front offices.

"From the sweet shop."

"No, *these*." Poppy showed him the eating-chocolates. "No one can obtain them. The makers, Fellows and Son, have closed their shop while they move to a new location. The ladies at the philanthropic luncheon were talking about it."

"I sent Valentine to the Fellows residence to ask them to make a special batch for you." Harry smiled as he saw the paper twists scattered across the counterpane. "I see you've sampled them."

"Have one," Poppy said generously.

Harry shook his head. "I don't like sweets." But he bent down obligingly as she gestured for him to come closer. She reached out to him, her fingers catching the knot of his necktie.

Harry's smile faded as Poppy exerted gentle tension, drawing him down. He was suspended over her, an impending weight of muscle and masculine drive. As her sugared breath blew against his lips, she sensed the deep tremor within him. And she was aware of a new equilibrium between them, a balance of will and curiosity. Harry held still, letting her do as she wished.

She tugged him closer until her mouth brushed his. The contact was brief but vital, striking a glow of heat.

Poppy released him carefully, and Harry drew back.

"You won't kiss me for diamonds," he said, his voice slightly raspy, "but you will for chocolates?"

Poppy nodded.

As Harry turned his face away, she saw his cheek tauten with a smile. "I'll put in a daily order, then."

Chapter Seventeen

Accustomed as Harry was to arranging everyone's schedule, he seemed to take it for granted that Poppy would allow him to do the same for her. When she told him that she preferred to make her own decisions about planning her days, Harry had countered that if she insisted on socializing with the hotel employees, he would find better uses for her time.

"I like to spend time with them," Poppy protested. "I can't treat everyone who lives and works here as nothing more than cogs in a machine."

"The hotel has been run this way for years," Harry said. "It's not going to change. As I've told you before, you'll create a management problem. From now on, no more visiting the kitchens. No more chats with the master gardener while he prunes the roses. No cups of tea with the housekeeper."

Poppy frowned. "Does it ever occur to you that your employees are people with thoughts and feelings? Have you thought to ask Mrs. Pennywhistle if her hand injury has healed?"

Harry frowned. "Hand injury?"

"Yes, she accidentally closed her fingers in the door. And when was the last time Mr. Valentine went on holiday?"

Harry's expression went blank.

"Three years," Poppy said. "Even the housemaids go on holiday to see their families, or go to the country. But Mr. Valentine is so devoted to his job that he forgoes all his personal time. And you've probably never offered a word of praise or thanks for it."

"I pay him a salary," Harry said indignantly. "Why the devil are you so interested in the personal lives of the hotel staff?"

"Because I can't live with people and see them day to day and not care about them."

"Then you can bloody well start with me!"

"You want me to care about you?" Her incredulous tone seemed to exasperate him.

"I want you to behave like a wife."

"Then stop trying to control me as you do everyone else. You've allowed me no choice in anything—not even the choice of whether or not to marry you in the first place!"

"And there's the heart of the matter," Harry said. "You'll never stop trying to punish me for taking you away from Michael Bayning. Has it occurred to you that it wasn't nearly as great a loss to him as it was to you?"

Poppy's eyes narrowed suspiciously. "What do you mean?"

"He's found consolation from any number of women since the wedding."

"I don't believe you," Poppy said, turning ashen. It wasn't possible. She couldn't conceive of Michael—*her* Michael—behaving in such a way.

"It's all over London," Harry said ruthlessly. "He drinks, gambles, and squanders money. And the devil knows how many bawdy-house diseases he's caught by now. It might console you that the viscount is probably regretting his decision to forbid the match between you and his son. At this rate, Bayning won't live long enough to inherit the title."

"You're lying."

"Ask your brother. You should thank me. Because as much as you despise me, I'm a better bargain than Michael Bayning."

"I should *thank* you?" Poppy asked thickly. "After what you've done to Michael?" A dazed smile crossed her lips, and she shook her head. She put her hands to her temples, as if to stave off an encroaching headache. "I need to see him. I must speak to him—" She broke off as he seized her arms in a harsh grip that was just short of painful.

"Try," Harry said softly, "and you'll both regret it."

Shoving his hands away, Poppy stared at his hard features and thought, *This is the man I'm married to.*

UNABLE TO ENDURE ONE MORE MINUTE OF PROXIMITY TO HIS wife, Harry left for the fencing club. He was going find someone, anyone, who wanted to practice, and he was going to fight until his muscles were sore and his frustration was spent. He was sick with need, half mad with it. But he didn't want Poppy to accept him out of duty. He wanted her willing. He wanted her warm and welcoming, the way she would have been with Michael Bayning. Harry would be damned if he'd take anything less.

There had never been a woman he'd wanted and hadn't gotten, until now. Why did his skills fail him when it came to seducing his own wife? It was becoming clear that as his craving for Poppy increased, his ability to charm her was decreasing at a proportionate rate.

The one brief kiss she'd given him had been more pleasurable than entire nights Harry had spent with other women. He could try to ease his needs with someone else, but that wouldn't begin to satisfy him. He wanted something that only Poppy seemed able to provide.

Harry spent two hours at the club, dueling at lightning speed, until the fencing master had flatly refused to allow anymore. "That's enough, Rutledge."

"I'm not finished," Harry said, tearing off his mask, his chest heaving with the force of his breaths.

"I say you are." Approaching him, the fencing master said quietly, "You're relying on brute force instead of using your head. Fencing requires precision and control, and this evening you're lacking both."

Offended, Harry schooled his features and said calmly, "Give me another chance. I'll prove you wrong."

The fencing master shook his head. "Go home, friend. Rest. You look tired."

The hour was late by the time Harry returned to the hotel. Still clad in fencing whites, he went into the hotel through the back entrance. Before he could ascend the stairs to his apartments, he was met by Jake Valentine.

"Good evening, Mr. Rutledge. How was your fencing?"

"Not worth discussing," Harry said shortly. His eyes narrowed as he saw the tension in his assistant's manner. "Is there anything the matter, Valentine?"

"A maintenance issue, I'm afraid."

"What is it?"

"The carpenter was repairing a section of flooring that happens to be located directly above Mrs. Rutledge's room. You see, the last guest who stayed there complained of a creaking board, and so I—"

"Is my wife all right?" Harry interrupted.

"Oh, *yes,* sir. Beg pardon, I didn't mean to worry you. Mrs. Rutledge is quite well. But unfortunately the carpenter struck a nail into a plumbing pipe, and there was a signifi-cant leak in the ceiling of Mrs. Rutledge's room. We had to take out a section of the ceiling to reach the pipe and stop the flooding. The bed and carpet are ruined, I'm afraid. And the room is uninhabitable at present."

"Bloody hell," Harry muttered, running a hand through his sweat-dampened hair. "How long until the repairs are done?"

"We estimate two to three days. The noise will undoubtedly be a problem for some of the guests."

"Apologize on behalf of the hotel and cut their room rates."

"Yes, sir."

With annoyance, Harry realized that Poppy would have to stay in his bedroom. Which meant that he would have to find another place to sleep. "I'll stay in a guest suite for the time being," he said. "Which ones are empty?"

Valentine's face was expressionless. "I'm afraid we're at full occupancy tonight, sir."

"There isn't one room available? In this *entire* hotel?"

"No, sir."

Harry scowled. "Set up a spare bed in my apartments, then."

Now the valet looked apologetic. "I've already thought of that, sir. But we have no spare beds. Three have been requested and set up in guest suites, and the other two were loaned to Brown's Hotel earlier in the week."

"Why did we do that?" Harry demanded incredulously.

"You told me that if Mr. Brown ever asked a favor, I should oblige him."

"I do too many damned favors for people!" Harry snapped.

"Yes, sir."

Rapidly Harry considered his alternatives . . . he could check into another hotel, he could prevail on a friend to allow him to stay overnight . . . but as he glanced at Valentine's implacable face, he knew how that would appear. And he'd go hang before he gave anyone reason to speculate he wasn't sleeping with his own wife. With a mumbled curse, he brushed by the valet and headed up the private staircase, his overworked leg muscles aching in vicious protest.

The apartment was ominously silent. Was Poppy asleep? No . . . a lamp had been lit in his room. His heart began to thud heavily as he followed the soft spill of light through the hallway. Reaching the doorway of his room, he looked inside.

Poppy was in his bed, an open book in her lap.

Harry filled his gaze with her, taking in the demure white nightgown, the frills of lace on her sleeves, the rope of shiny braided hair trailing over one shoulder. Her cheeks were stained with a high flush. She looked soft and sweet and clean, her knees drawn up beneath the covers.

Violent desire surged through him. Harry was afraid to move, afraid he might actually leap on her with no thought given to her virginal sensibilities. Appalled by the extent of his own need, Harry fought to restrain it. He tore his gaze away and stared hard at the floor, willing himself back into control.

"My bedroom was damaged." he heard Poppy say awkwardly. "The ceiling—"

"I heard." His voice was low and rough.

"I'm so sorry to inconvenience you—"

"It's not your fault." Harry brought himself to look at her again. A mistake. She was so pretty, so vulnerable, her slender throat rippling with a visible swallow. He wanted to ravish her. His body felt thick and hot with arousal, a merciless pulse pounding all through him.

Harry shook his head. "The hotel is fully occupied," he said gruffly.

She looked down at the book in her lap, remaining silent.

Harry saw how tightly Poppy was gripping the book, the tips of her fingers white. She wouldn't look at him.

She did not want him.

Why that mattered, he had no bloody idea.

But it did.

Bloody hell.

Somehow, with all his force of will, Harry mustered a cool tone. "I'll find somewhere else to sleep."

Leaving the bedroom, he went to the bathing room, to wash and douse himself with cold water. Repeatedly.

"WELL?" CHEF BROUSSARD ASKED AS JAKE VALENTINE entered the kitchen the next morning.

Mrs. Pennywhistle and Chef Rupert, who were standing by the long table, looked at him expectantly.

"I told you it was a bad idea," Jake said, glaring at the three of them. Sitting on a tall stool, he grabbed a warm croissant from a platter of pastries, and shoved half of it into his mouth.

"It didn't work?" the housekeeper asked gingerly.

Jake shook his head, swallowing the croissant and gesturing for a cup of tea. Mrs. Pennywhistle poured a cup, dropped in a lump of sugar, and gave it to him.

"From what I could tell," Jake growled, "Rutledge spent the night on the settee. I've never seen him in such a foul mood. He nearly took my head off when I brought him the managers' reports."

"Oh, dear," Mrs. Pennywhistle murmured.

Broussard shook his head in disbelief. "What is the matter with you British?"

"He's not British, he was born in America," Jake snapped.

"Oh, yes," Broussard said, recalling the indelicate fact. "Americans and romance. It's like watching a bird try to fly with one wing."

"What will we do now?" Chef Rupert asked in concern.

"*Nothing*," Jake said. "Not only has our meddling *not*

helped, it's made the situation worse. They're hardly speaking to each other."

POPPY WENT THROUGH THE DAY IN A STATE OF GLOOM, unable to stop worrying about Michael, knowing there was nothing she could do for him. Although his unhappiness was not her fault—and given the same choices, she wouldn't change anything she'd done—Poppy felt responsible all the same, as if by marrying Harry, she had assumed a portion of his guilt.

Except that Harry was incapable of feeling guilty about anything.

Poppy thought it would make things far less complicated if she could simply bring herself to hate Harry. But in spite of his innumerable flaws, something about him touched her, even now. His determined solitude . . . his refusal to make emotional connections to the people around him, or even to think of the hotel as his home . . . these things were alien to Poppy.

How in heaven's name, when all she had ever wanted was someone to share affection and intimacy with, had she ended up with a man who was capable of neither? All Harry wanted was the use of her body, and the illusion of a marriage.

Well, she had much more to give than that. And he would have to take all of her or nothing.

In the evening, Harry came to the apartments to have dinner with Poppy. He informed her that, after the meal was concluded, he was going to meet with visitors in their apartment library room.

"A meeting with whom?" Poppy asked.

"Someone from the War Office. Sir Gerald Hubert."

"May I ask what it's about?"

"I'd rather you didn't."

Staring into his inscrutable features, Poppy felt a chill of unease. "Am I to play hostess?" she asked.

"That won't be necessary."

The evening was cold and wet, rain striking in heavy sheets against the roof and windows, and washing the filth from the streets in muddy streams. The stilted dinner concluded, and a pair of maids cleared away the dishes and brought tea.

Stirring a spoonful of sugar into the dark liquid, Poppy stared at Harry thoughtfully. "What rank is Sir Gerald?"

"Assistant adjutant general."

"What is he in charge of?"

"Financial administration, personnel management, provost services. He's pushing for reforms to increase the army's strength. Badly needed reforms, in light of the tensions between the Russians and the Turks."

"If a war starts, will Britain be drawn into it?"

"Almost certainly. But it's possible that diplomacy will resolve the issue before it comes to war."

"Possible but not likely?"

Harry smiled cynically. "War is always more profitable than diplomacy."

Poppy sipped her tea. "My brother-in-law Cam told me that you improved the design of the standard army rifle. And now the War Office is indebted to you."

Harry shook his head to indicate that it had been nothing. "I scratched out a few ideas when the subject came up at a supper party."

"Obviously the ideas turned out to be very effective," Poppy said. "As most of your ideas are."

Harry turned a glass of port idly in his hands. His gaze lifted to hers. "Are you trying to ask something, Poppy?"

"I don't know. Yes. It seems likely that Sir Gerald will want to discuss weaponry with you, won't he?"

"Undoubtedly. He is bringing Mr. Edward Kinloch, who owns an arms manufactory." Seeing her expression, Harry gave her a quizzical glance. "You don't approve?"

"I think a brain as clever as yours should be put to better use than coming up with more efficient ways to kill people."

Before Harry could reply, there came a knock at the door, and the visitors were announced.

Harry stood and helped Poppy rise from her chair, and she went with him to welcome his guests.

Sir Gerald was a large and stocky man, his florid face supported by a scaffolding of thick white whiskers. He wore a silver gray military coat trimmed with regimental buttons. The scent of tobacco smoke and heavy cologne wafted from him with each movement.

"An honor, Mrs. Rutledge," he said with a bow. "I see the reports of your beauty are not at all exaggerated."

Poppy forced a smile. "Thank you, Sir Gerald."

Harry, standing beside her, introduced the other man. "Mr. Edward Kinloch."

Kinloch bowed impatiently. Clearly, meeting Harry Rutledge's wife was an unwelcome distraction. He wanted to get about the business at hand. Everything about him, the narrow, dark suit of clothes, the ungenerous tightness of his smile, the guarded eyes, even the flat hair subjugated by a gleaming layer of pomade, spoke of rigid containment. "Madam."

"Welcome, gentlemen," Poppy murmured. "I will leave you to your discussion. May I send for refreshments?"

"Why, thank you—" Sir Gerald began, but Kinloch interrupted.

"That is very gracious of you, Mrs. Rutledge, but it won't be necessary."

Sir Gerald's jowls drooped in disappointment.

"Very well," Poppy said pleasantly. "I will take my leave. I bid you good evening."

Harry showed the visitors to his library, while Poppy stared after them. She didn't like her husband's visitors, and she especially didn't like the subject they intended to discuss. Most of all, she loathed the idea of her husband's diabolical cleverness being applied to improve the art of war.

Retreating to Harry's bedroom, Poppy tried to read, but her mind kept returning to the conversation that was taking place in the library. Finally, she gave up the attempt and set the book aside.

She argued silently with herself. Eavesdropping was wrong. But really, in the spectrum of sin, how bad was it? What if one eavesdropped for a good reason? What if there was a beneficial result of the eavesdropping, such as preventing another person from making a mistake? Furthermore, wasn't it her duty as Harry's wife to be his helpmate whenever possible?

Yes, he might need her advice. And certainly the best way to be helpful was to find out what he was discussing with his guests.

Poppy tiptoed across the apartment to the library door, which had been left slightly ajar. Keeping herself tucked out of sight, she listened.

". . . you can feel the recoil power in the kick of the gun against your shoulder," Harry was saying in a matter-of-fact tone. "There might be a way to turn that to practical effect, using the recoil to draw in another bullet. Or better yet, I could devise a metallic casing that contains powder, bullet, and primer all in one. The recoil force would automatically eject the casing and draw in another, so the weapon could fire repeatedly. And it would have far more power and precision than any firearm yet developed."

His statements were met with silence. Poppy guessed that Kinloch and Sir Gerald, like herself, were struggling to take in what Harry had just described.

"My God," Kinloch finally said, sounding breathless. "That is so far beyond anything we . . . that is *leaps* ahead of what I'm currently manufacturing . . ."

"Can it be done?" Sir Gerald asked tersely. "Because if so, it would give us an advantage over every army in the world."

"Until they copy it," Harry said dryly.

"However," Sir Gerald continued, "in the time it would take them to reproduce our technology, we will have expanded the Empire . . . consolidated it so firmly . . . that our supremacy would be unchallenged."

"It wouldn't go unchallenged for long. As Benjamin Franklin once said, empire is like a great cake—most easily diminished around the edges."

"What do Americans know about empire building?" Sir Gerald asked with a scornful snort.

"I should remind you," Harry murmured, "that I'm American by birth."

Another silence.

"With whom do your loyalties lie?" Sir Gerald asked.

"With no country in particular," Harry replied. "Does that pose a problem?"

"Not if you'll give us the rights to the weapon design. And license it exclusively to Kinloch."

"Rutledge," came Kinloch's hard, eager voice, "how long would it take for you to develop these ideas and create a prototype?"

"I have no idea." Harry sounded amused by the other men's fervor. "When I have spare time, I'll work on it. But I can't promise you—"

"Spare time?" Now Kinloch was indignant. "A fortune

rests on this, not to mention the future of the Empire. By God, if I had your abilities, I wouldn't rest until I had brought this idea to fruition!"

Poppy felt ill as she heard the naked greed in his voice. Kinloch wanted profits. Sir Gerald wanted power.

And if Harry obliged them . . .

She couldn't bear to listen any longer. As the men continued to talk, she slipped away silently.

Chapter Eighteen

After bidding farewell to Sir Gerald and Edward Kinloch, Harry turned and set his back against the inside door of his apartments. The prospect of designing the new gun and integrated bullet casings would ordinarily have been an interesting challenge.

At present, however, it was nothing but an annoying distraction. There was only one problem he was interested in solving, and it had nothing to do with mechanical wizardry.

Rubbing the back of his neck, Harry went to his bedroom in search of a nightshirt. Although he usually slept naked, it would hardly be comfortable to do so on the settee. The prospect of spending another night there caused him to question his own sanity. He was faced with the choice of sleeping in a comfortable bed with his enticing wife, or alone on a narrow piece of furniture . . . and he was going to opt for the latter?

His wife regarded him from the bed, her gaze accusatory. "I can't believe you're even considering it," she said without preamble.

It took his distracted brain a moment to comprehend that she was not referring to their sleeping arrangements, but the meeting he'd just concluded. Had he not been so weary, Harry might have thought to advise his wife that now was not the night to pick an argument.

"How much did you hear?" he asked calmly, turning to rummage in one of the dresser drawers.

"Enough to understand that you may design a new kind of weapon for them. And if so, you would be responsible for so much carnage and suffering—"

"No, I wouldn't." Harry tugged off his necktie and coat, tossing them to the floor instead of laying them neatly on a chair. "The soldiers carrying the guns would be responsible for it. And the politicians and military men who sent them out there."

"Don't be disingenuous, Harry. If you didn't invent the weapons, no one would have them in the first place."

Giving up the search for the nightshirt, Harry untied his shoes and cast them on the heap of his discarded clothing. "Do you think people will ever stop developing new ways to kill each other? If I don't do this, someone else will."

"Then let someone else. Don't let it be your legacy."

Their gazes met, clashing. *For God's sake,* he wanted to beg her, *don't push me tonight.* The effort to carry on a coherent conversation was draining away what little self-restraint he had left.

"You know that I'm right," Poppy persisted, flinging back the covers and hopping out of bed to confront him. "You know how I feel about guns. Doesn't that matter to you at all?"

Harry could see the outline of her body in the thin white nightgown. He could even see the tips of her breasts, rosy and firm in the chill of the room. Right and wrong . . . no, he didn't give a damn about useless moralizing. But if it would soften her toward him, if it would cause her to yield even a little of herself, he would tell Sir Gerald and the entire British government to go swive themselves. And somewhere in the depths of his soul, a fracture began as he experienced something entirely new . . . the desire to please another person.

Yielding to the feeling before he even knew what it was, he opened his mouth to tell Poppy that she could have her way. He would send word to the War Office tomorrow that the deal was off.

Before he could get out a word, however, Poppy said quietly. "If you keep your promise to Sir Gerald, I'm going to leave you."

Harry wasn't aware of reaching out for her, only that she was in his grip, and that she was gasping. "That's not a choice for you," he managed to say.

"You can't make me stay if I don't want to," she said. "And I won't compromise on this, Harry. You will do as I ask, or I will leave."

All hell broke loose inside him. Leave him, would she?

Not in this life, or the next.

She thought him a monster . . . well, he would prove her right. He would be everything she thought him and worse. He jerked her against him, hot blood teeming in his groin as he felt the cambric slide over her firm, smooth body. Grasping her braid in his hand, he pulled the ribbon loose. His mouth went to the curve of her neck and shoulder, and the scents of soap and perfume and female skin inundated his senses.

"Before I make a decision," he said in a guttural tone, "I think I'll have a sample of what I might be forgoing."

Her hands came up to his shoulders as if to push him away.

But she wasn't struggling. She was holding onto him.

Harry had never been so aroused, desperate beyond pride. He held her, absorbing the feel of her with his whole body. Her hair was loose, fiery silk sliding over his arms.

He took handfuls of it, lifted the soft locks to his face. She smelled like roses, the intoxicating residue of perfumed soap or bath oil. He hunted for more of the scent, drawing it in with deep breaths.

Tugging the front of her nightgown open, Harry sent tiny cloth-covered buttons pattering to the carpet. Poppy quivered but offered no resistance as he tugged the garment to her waist, letting the sleeves trap her arms. His hand went to one of her breasts, their shapes lush and beautiful in the muted light. He touched her with the backs of his fingers, drifting down until one of the pink buds was caught lightly between his knuckles. He pulled, just a little. At the feel of the gentle tug, Poppy gasped and bit her lip.

Guiding Poppy backward, Harry stopped when her hips bumped against the edge of the mattress. "Lie down," he said, his voice rougher than he had intended. He helped her to lie back, supporting her with his arms, easing her to the bed. Bending over her flushed body, he savored all that rose-scented skin, wooing her with kisses . . . slow traveling kisses, wet and artful and fiendishly patient kisses. He licked his way to the tip of one breast and captured the taut point, flicking with his tongue. Poppy moaned, her body drawing into a helpless arch as he suckled her for long minutes.

Easing the muslin gown away from her, Harry dropped it to the floor. He stared at her with equal parts hunger and reverence. She was unspeakably beautiful, reclining in sweet abandon before him.

Harry tore off the rest of his clothing and lowered himself over her. "Touch me," he was mortified to hear himself rasp . . . something he had never asked of anyone before. "Please."

Slowly her arms lifted, one hand sliding around his neck. Her fingers laced through the shorter locks that curled slightly against his nape. The tentative caress drew a groan of pleasure from him. He lay beside her, easing a hand between her thighs.

Accustomed as he was to fine, intricate things, to delicate mechanisms, Harry was sensitive to every subtle response of her body. He discovered where and how she most liked to be stroked, what aroused her. What made her wet. Following the moisture, he slipped a finger inside, and she accepted it easily. When he tried to add another, however, she flinched and instinctively reached down to push his hand away. Withdrawing, he caressed her with a gentle palm, coaxing her to relax.

Pressing her back on the bed, Harry loomed over her. He heard her breathing quicken as he settled between her thighs. But he didn't try to enter her, only let her feel the pressure of him, the length fitting against the soft feminine rise. He knew how to tease, how to make her want him. He moved in the gentlest intimation of a thrust, sliding along dampness and sweetly vulnerable flesh, and then he rotated his hips slowly, every movement a syllable that added to a greater meaning.

Her lashes half lowered, and there was a faint, intent pull between her fine brows . . . she wanted what he was giving her, she wanted the tension and torment and relief. Desire had brought a mist of perspiration over her skin, until the scent of roses deepened and acquired a hint of musk, so wildly arousing and heady that he could have let himself go right then. But he rolled to his side, away from the enticing cradle of her hips.

He slid his hand over her mound and slipped his fingers inside her again, his touch coaxing and careful. This time her body relaxed and welcomed him. Kissing her throat, he caught the vibration of every moan against his lips. A faint, rhythmic clenching began around his knuckles as he thrust his fingers in her gently. Every time she took them to the hilt, he let the heel of his hand brush her intimately. She panted and began to lift upward repeatedly.

"Yes," Harry whispered, letting his hot breath fill the shell of her ear. "Yes. When I'm inside you, this is how you move. Show me what you want, and I'll give it to you, as much as you need, as long as you want . . ."

She clamped on his fingers, tightening, convulsing, coming in erotic shivers. He teased out every last luscious ripple, relishing her climax, lost in the feel of her.

Levering his body over hers, he pushed her thighs wide and lowered himself between them. Before her sated flesh had begun to close, he centered himself where she was wet and ready for him. He stopped thinking altogether. He pushed into the resisting ring, finding it even more difficult than he'd expected despite the abundant moisture.

Poppy whimpered in pained surprise, her body stiffening.

"Hold onto me," Harry said hoarsely. She obeyed, her arms coming around his neck. He reached down and pulled her hips upward, trying to make it easier for her as he pressed deeper, harder, her flesh unbelievably tight and hot and sweet, and he gave her more, unable to help himself, until he was fully buried in the soft heat of her.

"Oh, God," he whispered, shaking with the effort to hold still, to let her adjust around him.

Every nerve clamored for movement, for the sliding, teasing friction that would bring him release. He nudged gently. But Poppy grimaced, her legs straining on either side of his. He waited longer, caressing her with his hands.

"Don't stop," she choked. "It's all right."

But it wasn't. He pushed again, and a pained sound escaped her. Again, and she braced and clenched her teeth. Every time he moved, it caused her agony.

Resisting her tight grip on his neck, Harry drew back far enough to look at her face. Poppy was white with distress, her lips bloodless. Holy hell, was it this painful for all virgins?

"I'll wait," he said raggedly. "It will be easier in a moment."

She nodded, her mouth stiff, her eyes tightly shut.

And they both held still and fast, while he tried to soothe her. But nothing changed. Despite Poppy's compliance, this was sheer misery for her.

Harry buried his face in her hair and cursed. And he withdrew, despite the vicious protest of his loins, when every impulse screamed for him to hammer into her.

She couldn't stifle a gasp of relief as the painful intrusion was removed. Hearing the sound, Harry nearly exploded with frustration.

He heard her murmur his name, her voice questioning.

Ignoring her, Harry left the bed and staggered toward the bathing room. He braced his hands on the tiled wall and closed his eyes, struggling for self-control. After a few minutes, he drew water and washed himself. He found smears of blood . . . Poppy's blood. That was only to be expected. But the sight of it made him want to howl.

Because the last thing he wanted on earth was to cause his wife even a moment's pain. He would die before hurting her, no matter what the consequences to himself.

Dear God, what had happened to him? He had never wanted to feel this way about anyone, never even imagined it possible.

He had to make it stop.

SORE AND BEWILDERED, POPPY LAY ON HER SIDE AND listened to the sounds of Harry washing. It burned where he had taken her. The residue of blood was sticky between her thighs. She wanted to leave the bed and wash as well, but the thought of performing such an intimate task in front of Harry . . . no, she wasn't ready for that yet. And she was unsure, because even in her innocence, she knew that he had not finished making love to her.

But why?

Had there been something she should have done? Had she made some kind of mistake? Perhaps she should have been more stoic. She had tried her best, but it had hurt dreadfully, even though Harry had been gentle. Surely he knew that it was painful for a virgin the first time. Why, then, had he seemed angry with her?

Feeling inadequate and defensive, Poppy crept from the bed and found her nightgown. She put it on and hastily retreated beneath the covers as Harry came back into the room. Without a word, he picked up his discarded clothes and began to dress.

"You're going out?" she heard herself ask.

Harry didn't look at her. "Yes."

"Stay with me," she blurted out.

Harry shook his head. "I can't. We'll talk later. But right now I—" He broke off as if words failed him.

Poppy curled on her side, gripping the edges of the bed-clothes. Something was terribly wrong—she couldn't fathom what it was, and she was too afraid to ask.

Pulling on his coat, Harry started for the doorway.

"Where are you going?" Poppy asked unsteadily.

He sounded distant. "I don't know."

"When will you—"

"I don't know that, either."

She waited until he had left before she let a few tears slip out, and she blotted them with the sheet. Was Harry going to another woman?

Miserably, she reflected that her sister Win's advice about marital relations had been insufficient. There should have been a bit less about roses and moonlight and a bit more prac-tical information.

She wanted to see her sisters, especially Amelia. She wanted her family, who would pet and praise and make much of her, and offer the reassurance she badly needed. It was more than a little disheartening to have failed at marriage after a mere three weeks.

Most of all, she needed advice about husbands.

Yes, it was time to retreat and consider what to do. She would go to Hampshire.

A hot bath soothed her smarting flesh and eased the strained muscles on the insides of her thighs. After drying and powdering herself, she dressed in a wine-colored traveling gown. She packed a few belongings in a small valise, including undergarments and stockings, a silver-backed brush, a novel, and an automaton that Harry had made—a little woodpecker on a tree trunk—which she usually kept on her dressing table. However, she left the diamond necklace that Harry had given her, setting the velvet-lined case in a drawer.

When she was ready to depart, she rang the bellpull and sent a maid to fetch Jake Valentine.

The tall, brown-eyed young man appeared in an instant, making no effort to mask his concern. His gaze skimmed quickly over her traveling clothes. "May I be of service, Mrs. Rutledge?"

"Mr. Valentine, has my husband left the hotel?"

He nodded, a frown puckering his forehead.

"Did he tell you when he would return?"

"No, ma'am."

Poppy wondered if she could trust him. His loyalty to Harry was well-known. However, she had no choice but to ask for his help. "I must ask a favor of you, Mr. Valentine. However, I fear it may put you in a difficult position."

His brown eyes warmed with rueful amusement. "Mrs. Rutledge, I'm nearly always in a difficult position. Please don't hesitate to ask me for anything."

She squared her shoulders. "I need a carriage. I'm going to visit my brother at his terrace in Mayfair."

The smile vanished from his eyes. He glanced at the valise by her feet. "I see."

"I am very sorry to ask you to ignore your obligations to my husband but . . . I would prefer you didn't let him know where I've gone until morning. I will be perfectly safe in my brother's company. He is going to convey me to my family in Hampshire."

"I understand. Of course I will help you." Valentine paused, appearing to choose his words carefully. "I hope you will be returning soon."

"So do I."

"Mrs. Rutledge . . ." he started, and cleared his throat uncomfortably. "I shouldn't overstep my bounds. But I feel it necessary to say—" He hesitated.

"Go on," Poppy said gently.

"I've worked for Mr. Rutledge for more than five years. I daresay I know him as well as anyone. He's a complicated man . . . too smart for his own good, and he doesn't have much in the way of scruples, and he wants everyone around him to live by his terms. But he has changed many lives for the better. Including mine. I believe there's good in him, if one looks deep enough."

"I think so, too," Poppy said. "But that's not enough to found a marriage on."

"You mean something to him," Valentine insisted. "He's formed an attachment to you, and I've never seen that before. Which is why I don't think anyone in the world can manage him except for you."

"Even if that's true," Poppy managed to say, "I don't know if I *want* to manage him."

"Ma'am," Valentine said feelingly, "*someone* has to."

Amusement broke through Poppy's distress, and she

ducked her head to hide a smile. "I'll consider it," she said. "But at the moment I need some time away. What do they call it in the rope ring?"

"A breather," he said, bending to pick up her valise.

"Yes, a breather. Will you help me, Mr. Valentine?"

"Of course." Valentine bid her to wait but a few minutes, and went to summon the carriage. Comprehending the need for discretion, he had the vehicle brought to the back of the hotel, where Poppy could depart unobserved.

She felt a pang of regret, leaving the Rutledge and its employees. In no time at all it had become home . . . but things could not stay the way they were. Something would have to yield. And that something—or someone, rather—was Harry Rutledge.

Valentine returned to escort her to the back entrance. Opening an umbrella to shelter her from the rain, Valentine guided her outside to the waiting vehicle.

Poppy climbed onto the block step that had been placed beside the carriage, and turned to face the valet. With the added height of the step, they stood nearly eye to eye. Raindrops glittered in the light from the hotel as they fell in jewel-like strands from the points of the umbrella.

"Mr. Valentine . . ."

"Yes, ma'am?"

"You do think he'll follow me, don't you?"

"Only to the ends of the earth," he said gravely.

That drew a smile from her, and she turned to climb into the carriage.

Chapter Nineteen

It had taken Mrs. Meredith Clifton three months of dedicated pursuit before she had finally seduced Leo, Lord Ramsay. Or more accurately, was about to seduce him. As the young and nubile wife of a distinguished British naval officer, she was frequently left to her own devices while her husband was off at sea. Meredith had bedded every man in London worth bedding—excluding the handful of tiresomely faithful married ones, of course—but then she had heard about Ramsay, a man reputedly as sexually audacious as herself.

Leo was a man of tantalizing contradictions. He was a handsome man, dark haired and blue eyed, with a clean and wholesome appeal . . . and yet he was rumored to be capable of shocking debauchery. He was cruel but gentle, callous but perceptive, selfish but charming. And from what she had heard, he was a vastly accomplished lover.

Now, in Leo's bedroom, Meredith stood quietly while he undressed her. He took his time about unfastening the row of buttons at her back. Sidling back, she let the backs of her fingers brush his trousers. The feel of him caused her to purr.

She heard Leo laugh, and he pushed her exploring hand away. "Patience, Meredith."

"You can't know how much I've anticipated this night."

"That's a shame. I'm terrible in bed." Gently he spread her dress open.

She shivered as she felt the exploratory stroke of his fingertips on her upper back. "You're teasing, my lord."

"You'll find out soon, won't you?" He brushed aside the wisps of hair at her nape and kissed her there, letting his tongue brush her skin.

That light, erotic touch caused Meredith to gasp. "Are you ever serious about anything?" she managed to ask.

"No. I've found that life is far kinder to shallow people." Turning her, Leo drew her up against his tall, well-muscled frame.

And in one long, slow blaze of a kiss, Meredith realized that she had finally met a predator more seductive, less inhibited, than anyone she had ever met. His sensual power was no less potent for being completely devoid of emotion or tenderness. This was pure, unashamed physicality.

Consumed in the kiss, Meredith gave an agitated little cry when he stopped.

"The door," Leo said.

Another tentative knock.

"Ignore it," Meredith said, trying to slide her arms around his lean waist.

"I can't. My servants won't let me ignore them. Believe me, I've tried." Releasing her, Leo went to the door, opened it a crack, and said curtly, "There had better be a fire or a felony in progress, or I swear you'll be sacked."

Another murmur from the servant, and Leo's tone changed, the arrogant drawl vanishing. "Good God. Tell her I'll be down at once. Get her some tea or something." Raking his hand through the short dark brown layers of his hair, he went to a wardrobe and began to hunt through a row of jackets. "I'm afraid you'll have to ring for a maid to help you dress, Meredith. I'm sorry. When you're ready, my servants will make certain you're escorted out to your carriage at the back."

Her mouth fell open. "What? *Why*?"

"My sister has arrived unexpectedly." Pausing in his search, Leo threw an apologetic glance over his shoulder. "Another time, perhaps?"

"Most certainly not," Meredith said indignantly. "*Now*."

"Impossible." He pulled out a coat and shrugged into it. "My sister needs me."

"*I* need you! Tell her to return tomorrow. And if you don't send her away, you'll never have another chance with me."

Leo smiled. "My loss, I'm sure."

His indifference aroused Meredith even further. "Oh Ramsay, *please*," she said heatedly. "It's ungentlemanly to leave a lady wanting!"

"It's more than ungentlemanly, darling. It's a crime." Leo's face softened as he approached her. Taking her hand, he lifted it to kiss the backs of her fingers one by one. His eyes glinted with rueful amusement. "This is certainly not what I had planned for this evening. My apologies. Let's try again someday. Because, Meredith . . . I'm actually *not* terrible in bed." He kissed her lightly, and smiled with such skillfully manufactured warmth that she almost believed it was real.

POPPY WAITED IN THE SMALL FRONT PARLOR OF THE TERRACE. At the sight of her brother's tall form entering the room, she stood and flew to him. "Leo!"

He gathered her close. After a brief, hard hug, he held her at arms' length. His gaze swept over her. "You've left Rutledge?"

"Yes."

"You lasted a week longer than I expected," he said, not unkindly. "What's happened?"

"Well, to start with—" Poppy tried to sound pragmatic even though her eyes watered. "I'm not a virgin anymore."

Leo gave her a mock-shamed glance. "Neither am I," he confessed.

A reluctant giggle escaped her.

Leo rummaged in his coat for a handkerchief, without success. "Don't cry, darling. I have no handkerchief, and in any case, virginity is nearly impossible to find once you've lost it."

"That's not why I'm weepy," she said, blotting her wet cheek on his shoulder. "Leo . . . I'm in a muddle. I need to think about some things. Will you take me to Hampshire?"

"I've been waiting for you to ask."

"I'm afraid we'll have to depart immediately. Because if we wait too long, Harry may prevent us from going at all."

"Sweetheart, the devil himself couldn't stop me from taking you home. That being said . . . yes, we'll go right away. I prefer to avoid confrontation whenever possible. And I doubt Rutledge will take it well when he discovers you've left him."

"No," she said emphatically. "He'll take it quite badly. But I'm not leaving him because I want to end my marriage. I'm leaving him because I want to save it."

Leo shook his head, smiling. "There's Hathaway logic for you. What worries me is that I almost understand."

"You see—"

"No, you can explain once we're on our way. For the moment, wait here. I'll send for the driver and tell the servants to ready the carriage."

"I'm sorry to cause trouble—"

"Oh, they're used to it. I'm the master of hasty departures."

There must have been some truth to Leo's claim, because a trunk was packed and the carriage was readied with astonishing speed. Poppy waited by the parlor fire until Leo came to the doorway. "We'll be off now," he said. "Come."

He took her to his carriage, a comfortable and well-sprung vehicle with deep-upholstered seats. After arranging some cushions in the corner, Poppy settled back in preparation for a long journey. It would take the full night to reach Hampshire, and although the macadamized roadways were in decent repair, there were many rough stretches.

"I'm sorry to have come to you at such a late hour," she told her brother. "No doubt you would be sleeping soundly right now had I not arrived."

That produced a swift grin. "I'm not sure about that," Leo said. "But no matter—it's time to go to Hampshire. I want to see Win and that merciless brute she married, and I need to check on the estate and tenants."

Poppy smiled slightly, knowing how fond Leo was of the so-called "merciless brute." Merripen had earned Leo's everlasting gratitude for rebuilding and managing the estate. They communicated frequently by letter, maintained two or three running arguments at any given time, and thoroughly enjoyed baiting each other.

Reaching to the dark brown shade that covered the window nearest her, Poppy lifted it to glance at the broken buildings, brick facings plastered with bills, and battered shop fronts, all of them bathed in the twilight gloom of street lamps. London at night was unsavory, unsafe, uncontrolled. Harry was out there somewhere. She had no doubt he could take care of himself, but the thought of what he might be doing—or whom he might be doing it with—filled her with melancholy. She sighed heavily.

"I loathe London in the summer," Leo said. "The Thames is working up to an unholy stench this year." He paused, his gaze resting on her. "I suppose that look on your face isn't caused by worry over public sanitation. Tell me what you're thinking, sis."

"Harry left the hotel tonight after—" Poppy broke off,

unable to find a word to describe just what it was they had done. "I don't know how long he'll stay out, but at best, we're only about ten or twelve hours ahead of him. Of course, he may decide not to follow me, which would be rather anticlimactic but also a relief. Still—"

"He'll follow," Leo said flatly. "But you won't have to see him if you don't wish it."

Poppy shook her head morosely. "I've never had such mixed-up feelings about anyone. I don't understand him. Tonight in bed, he—"

"Wait," Leo said. "Some things are better discussed between sisters. I'm sure this is one of them. We'll reach Ramsay House by morning, and you can ask Amelia anything you like."

"I don't think she would know anything about this."

"Why not? She's a married woman."

"Yes, but it's . . . well . . . a masculine problem."

Leo blanched. "I wouldn't know anything about that, either. I don't have masculine problems. In fact, I don't even like saying the phrase 'masculine problems.'"

"Oh." Crestfallen, Poppy pulled a lap blanket over herself.

"Damn it. What exactly are we calling a 'masculine problem'? Did he have trouble running the flag up? Or did it fall to half-staff?"

"Do we have to speak about this metaphorically, or—"

"Yes," Leo said firmly.

"All right. He . . ." Poppy frowned in concentration as she searched for the right words, ". . . left me while the flag was still flying."

"Was he drunk?"

"No."

"Did you do or say something to make him leave?"

"Just the opposite. I asked him to stay, and he wouldn't."

Shaking his head, Leo rummaged in a side compartment

beside his seat and swore. "Where the blazes is my liquor? I told the servants to stock the carriage with drink for the journey. I'm going to fire the bloody lot of them."

"There's water, isn't there?"

"Water is for washing, not drinking." He muttered something about an evil conspiracy to keep him sober, and sighed. "One can only guess as to Rutledge's motivations. It's not easy for a man to stop in the middle of lovemaking. It puts us in a devil of a temper." Folding his arms across his chest, he watched her speculatively. "I propose the radical notion of actually asking Rutledge why he left you tonight, and discussing it like two rational beings. But before your husband reaches Hampshire, you'd better decide on something, and that's whether you're going to forgive him for what he did to you and Bayning."

She blinked in surprise. "Do you think I should?"

"The devil knows I wouldn't want to, were I in your place." He paused. "On the other hand, I've been forgiven for many things I should never have been forgiven for. The point is, if you can't forgive him, there's no use in trying to talk about anything else."

"I don't think Harry cares about being forgiven," Poppy said glumly.

"Of course he does. Men love to be forgiven. It makes us feel better about our inability to learn from our mistakes."

"I don't know if I'm ready," Poppy protested. "Why must I do it so soon? There's no time limit for forgiveness, is there?"

"Sometimes there is."

"Oh, Leo . . ." She felt crushed under a weight of uncertainty and hurt and yearning.

"Try to sleep," her brother murmured. "We'll have two hours, more or less, before it's time to change horses."

"I can't sleep for worrying," Poppy said, although a yawn had already overtaken her.

"There's no point in worrying. You already know what you want to do—you just aren't ready to admit it yet."

Poppy settled deeper into the corner, closing her eyes. "You know a lot about women, don't you, Leo?"

There was a smile in his voice. "I should hope so, with four sisters." And he watched over her while she slept.

After returning to the hotel drunk as a boiled owl, Harry staggered to his apartments. He had gone to a tavern, flamboyantly decorated with mirrors, tiled walls, and expensive prostitutes. It had taken approximately three hours to drink himself into a suitable state of numbness that he could go back home. Despite the artful advances of more than a few lightskirts, Harry took no notice of any of them.

He wanted his wife.

And he knew that Poppy would never soften toward him unless he began with a sincere apology for taking her away from Michael Bayning. The problem was, he couldn't. Because he wasn't at all sorry about what he'd done, he was only sorry that she was unhappy about it. He would never regret having done what was necessary to marry her, because she was what he had wanted most in his life.

Poppy was every fine, good, unselfish impulse that he would never have. She was every caring thought, loving gesture, happy moment, that he would never know. She was every minute of peaceful sleep that would forever elude him. According to the law of universal balance, Poppy had been put into the world to compensate for Harry and his wickedness. Which was probably why, as the opposite of two magnetic forces, Harry was so damnably drawn to her.

Therefore, the apology was not going to be sincere. But it would be made. And then he would ask to begin again with her.

Lowering himself to the narrow settee, which he loathed

with a passion, Harry fell into a drunken stupor that almost passed for sleep.

The morning light, weak though it was, entered his brain like a stiletto. Groaning, Harry cracked his eyes open and took inventory of his abused body. He was dry mouthed, exhausted, and aching, and if there had ever been a time in his life he had needed a shower bath more, he couldn't remember it. He slitted a glance at the closed door of his bedroom, where Poppy still slept.

Remembering her gasp of pain the previous night, when he had thrust into her, Harry felt a cold, sick heaviness in the pit of his stomach. She would be sore this morning. She might need something.

She probably hated him.

Swamped with dread, Harry lurched upward from the settee and went to the bedroom. He opened the door and let his eyes adjust to the semidarkness.

The bed was empty.

Harry stood there blinking while apprehension swept over him. He heard himself whisper her name.

In seconds he had reached the bellpull, but there was no need to call for anyone. As if by magic, Valentine was at the apartment door, his brown eyes alert in his lean face.

"Valentine," Harry began hoarsely, "where is—"

"Mrs. Rutledge is with Lord Ramsay. I believe they are traveling to Hampshire as we speak."

Harry grew very, very calm, as he always did when a situation was dire. "When did she leave?"

"Last night, while you were out."

Resisting the urge to kill his valet where he stood, Harry asked softly, "And you didn't tell me?"

"No, sir. She asked me not to." Valentine paused, looking momentarily bemused, as if he, too, couldn't believe that

Harry hadn't already killed him. "I have a carriage and team ready, if you intend to—"

"Yes, I intend to." Harry's tone was as crisp as the strike of a chisel through granite. "Pack my clothes. I'm leaving within the half hour."

Rage hovered nearby, so powerful that Harry could scarcely own it as his. But he shoved the feeling aside. Giving in to it would accomplish nothing. The undertaking for now was to wash and shave, change his clothes, and deal with the situation.

Any hint of concern or contrition burned to ashes. Any hope of being gentlemanly had gone. He would keep Poppy no matter how he had to do it. He would lay out the law, and when he was through, she would never dare leave him again.

POPPY AWAKENED FROM A JOLTING SLEEP AND SAT UP, RUB-bing her eyes. Leo was dozing in the seat opposite hers, his broad shoulders hunched and one arm curled behind his head as he leaned against a paneled wall.

Nudging aside the little curtain over one of the windows, Poppy saw her beloved Hampshire . . . sun crossed, green, peaceful. She had been in London too long—she had forgotten how beautiful the world could be. The carriage passed flushes of poppies and oxeye daisies and vibrant stands of lavender. The landscape was rich with wet meadows and chalk streams. Brilliant blue kingfishers and swifts darted through the sky, while green woodpeckers rattled the trees.

"Almost there," she whispered.

Leo awakened, yawning and stretching. His eyes narrowed in a protesting squint as he lifted a cloth panel for a glimpse of the passing countryside.

"Isn't it wonderful?" Poppy asked, smiling. "Have you ever seen such views?"

Her brother dropped the panel. "Sheep. Grass. Thrilling."

Before long the carriage reached the Ramsay lands and passed the gatekeeper's house, which had been constructed of blue gray brick and cream stone. Owing to recent and extensive renovations, the landscape and manor were new looking, although the house had retained its haphazard charm. The estate was not a large one, certainly nothing compared to the massive neighboring estate owned by Lord Westcliff. But it was a jewel, the land fertile and varied, with fields irrigated by channels that had been dug from a nearby stream to the upper fields.

Before Leo had inherited the title, the estate had fallen into decay and disrepair, abandoned by many of the tenants. Now, however, it had been turned into a thriving and progressive enterprise, mostly due to the efforts of Kev Merripen. And Leo, though he was almost embarrassed to admit it, had come to care about the estate and was doing his best to acquire the vast amounts of knowledge necessary to make it run efficiently.

Ramsay House was a cheerful combination of architectural styles. Originally an Elizabethan manor house, it had been altered as successive generations had grafted on additions and wings. The result was an asymmetrical building with bristling chimney stacks, rows of leaded-glass windows, and a gray slate roof with hips and bays. Inside, there were interesting niches and nooks, odd-shaped rooms, hidden doors and staircases, all adding to an eccentric charm that perfectly suited the Hathaway family.

Roses in bloom hugged the exterior of the house. Behind the manor, white-graveled walking paths led to gardens and fruit orchards. Stables and a livestock yard were set to one side of the manor, while at a farther distance there was a timber yard in full production.

The carriage stopped on the front drive before a set of timbered doors with glass insets. By the time the footmen had gone to alert the household of their arrival and Leo had assisted Poppy from the vehicle, Win had come running from the house. She flung herself at Leo. He grinned and caught her easily, swinging her around.

"Dear Poppy," Win exclaimed. "I missed you dreadfully!"

"What about me?" Leo asked, still holding her. "Haven't you missed me?"

"Perhaps a little," Win said with a grin, and kissed his cheek. She went to Poppy and embraced her. "How long will you stay?"

"I'm not sure," Poppy said.

"Where is everyone?" Leo asked.

Win kept her slender arm around Poppy's back as she turned to reply. "Cam is visiting Lord Westcliff at Stony Cross Park, Amelia is inside with the baby, Beatrix is roaming the woods, and Merripen is with some of the tenants, lecturing them on new techniques of hoeing."

The word caught Leo's attention. "I know all about that. If you don't want to go to a brothel, there are certain districts of London—"

"*Hoeing,* Leo," Win said. "Breaking ground with farm implements."

"Oh. Well, I know nothing about that."

"You'll find out a great deal about it once Merripen learns you're here." Win tried to look severe, although her eyes were twinkling. "I do hope you'll behave, Leo."

"Of course I will. We're in the country. There's nothing else to do." Heaving a sigh, Leo shoved his hands in his pockets and observed their picturesque surroundings as if he'd just been assigned a cell at Newgate. Then, with perfectly calibrated offhandedness he asked, "Where's Marks? You didn't mention her."

"She is well, but . . ." Win paused, obviously searching for words. "She had a small mishap today, and she's rather upset. Of course, any woman would be, considering the nature of the problem. Therefore, Leo, I insist that you *not* tease her. And if you do, Merripen has already said that he will give you such a drubbing—"

"Oh, please. As if I'd care enough to notice some problem of Marks's." He paused. "What is it?"

Win frowned. "I wouldn't tell you, except that the problem is obvious and you'll notice immediately. You see, Miss Marks dyes her hair, which I never knew before, but apparently—"

"Dyes her hair?" Poppy repeated in surprise. "But why? She's not old."

"I have no idea. She won't explain why. But there are some unfortunate women who start to gray in their twenties, and perhaps she's one of them."

"Poor thing," Poppy said. "It must embarrass her. She's certainly taken great pains to keep it secret."

"Yes, poor thing," Leo said, sounding not at all sympathetic. In fact, his eyes fairly danced with glee. "Tell us what happened, Win."

"We think the London apothecary who mixed her usual solution must have gotten the proportions wrong. Because when she applied the dye this morning, the result was . . . well, distressing."

"Did it fall out?" Leo asked. "Is she bald?"

"No, not at all. It's just that her hair is . . . green."

To look at Leo's face, one would think it was Christmas morning. "What shade of green?"

"Leo, *hush*," Win said urgently. "You are not to torment

her. It's been a very trying experience. We mixed a peroxide paste to take the green out, and I don't know if it worked or not. Amelia was helping her to wash it a little while ago. And no matter what the result is, you are to say *nothing*."

"You're telling me that tonight, Marks will be sitting at the supper table with hair that matches the asparagus, and I'm not supposed to remark on it?" He snorted. "I'm not that strong."

"Please, Leo," Poppy murmured, touching his arm. "If it were one of your sisters, you wouldn't mock."

"Do you think that little shrew would have any mercy on me, were the situations reversed?" He rolled his eyes as he saw their expressions. "Very well, I'll try not to jeer. But I make no promises."

Leo sauntered toward the house in no apparent hurry. He didn't deceive either of his sisters.

"How long do you think it will take him to find her?" Poppy asked Win.

"Two, perhaps three minutes," Win replied, and they both sighed.

In precisely two minutes and forty-seven seconds, Leo had located his archenemy in the fruit orchard behind the house. Marks sat on a low stone wall, her narrow frame slightly hunched, her elbows close together. She had some kind of cloth wrapped around her head, a knotted turban that concealed her hair entirely.

Seeing the dispirited droop of her slender frame, anyone else might have been moved to pity. But Leo had no compunction about taking a few jabs at Catherine Marks. From the beginning of their acquaintance, she had never missed an opportunity to nag, insult, or deflate him. On the few occasions he had said something charming or nice—purely as an experiment, of course—she willfully misinterpreted him.

Leo had never understood why they had started off on

such bad footing, or why she was so determined to hate him. And even more perplexing, why it mattered. Prickly, narrow-minded, sharp-tongued, secretive woman, with her stern mouth and haughty little nose . . . she *deserved* green hair, and she deserved to be mocked for it.

The time for revenge was at hand.

As Leo approached nonchalantly, Marks lifted her head, the sunlight flashing on the lenses of her spectacles. "Oh," she said sourly. "You're back."

She said it as if she had just discovered a vermin infestation.

"Hello, Marks," Leo said cheerfully. "Hmmm. You look different. What can it be?"

She glowered at him.

"Is it some new fashion, that wrapping on your head?" he asked with polite interest.

Marks maintained a stony silence.

The moment was delicious. He knew, and she knew that he knew, and mortified color was creeping over her face.

"I brought Poppy with me from London," Leo volunteered.

Her eyes turned alert behind the spectacles. "Did Mr. Rutledge come, too?"

"No. Although I imagine he's not far behind us."

The companion stood from the stone wall and brushed at her skirts. "I must see Poppy—"

"There'll be time for that." Leo moved to block her way. "But before we return to the house, I think you and I should reacquaint ourselves. How are things with you, Marks? Anything interesting happen lately?"

"You're no better than a ten-year-old," she said vehemently. "All ready to sneer at someone else's misfortune. You immature, mean-spirited—"

"I'm sure it's not that bad," Leo said kindly. "Let me have a look, and I'll tell you if—"

"Stay away from me!" she snapped, and tried to dart around him.

Leo blocked her easily, a muffled laugh escaping him as she tried to shove him. "Are you trying to push me out of the way? You don't have the strength of a butterfly. Here—your headgear is askew—let me help you with it—"

"Don't touch me!"

They struggled, one of them playful, the other frantic and flailing.

"One glance," Leo begged, a laugh ending in a grunt as she twisted and jabbed a sharp elbow against his midriff. He snatched at the kerchief, managing to loosen it. "Please. It's all I want from life, to see you with"—another swipe, and he snagged the edge of the cloth—"your hair all—"

But Leo broke off as the kerchief pulled free, and the hair that spilled out was not any conceivable shade of green. It was blond . . . pale amber and champagne and honey . . . and there was so much of it, cascading in shimmering waves to the middle of her back.

Leo went still, holding her in place as his astonished gaze raked over her. They both gulped for breath, worked up and winded like racehorses. Marks couldn't have looked more appalled if he had just stripped her naked. And the truth was, Leo couldn't have been any more confounded—or aroused—if he were actually viewing her naked. Though he certainly would have been willing to try it.

Such a commotion had risen in him, Leo hardly knew how to react. Just hair, just locks of hair . . . but it was like setting a previously undistinguished painting in the perfect frame, revealing its beauty in full luminous detail. Catherine Marks in the sunlight was a mythical creature, a nymph, with delicate features and opalescent eyes.

The most confounding realization was that it wasn't really hair color that had concealed all this from him . . . he had never noticed how stunning she was because she had deliberately kept him from seeing it.

"Why," Leo asked, his voice husky, "would you conceal something so beautiful?" Staring at her, nearly devouring her, he asked more softly still, "What are you hiding from?"

Her lips trembled, and she gave a brief shake of her head, as if to answer would prove fatal to them both. And, wrenching free of him, she picked up her skirts and ran headlong to the house.

Chapter Twenty

A melia," Poppy said as she lay her head on her sister's shoulder, "you've done me a terrible disservice, making marriage look so easy."

Amelia laughed softly, hugging her. "Oh, dear. If I've given that impression, I do apologize. It's not. Especially when both individuals are strong willed."

"The ladies' periodicals advise to let one's husband have his way most of the time."

"Oh, lies, lies. Only let your husband *think* he's having his way. That's the secret to a happy marriage."

They both snickered, and Poppy sat up.

Having put Rye down for his morning nap, Amelia had gone with Poppy to the family parlor, where they sat together on the settee. Although Win had been invited to join them, she had tactfully declined, sensitive to the fact that Amelia had a more maternal relationship with Poppy than she did.

During the two years that Win had spent away at a health clinic in France, recovering from the damages of scarlet fever, Poppy had grown even closer to their oldest sister. When Poppy wished to divulge her most private thoughts and problems, Amelia was the one she always felt most comfortable with.

A tea tray had been brought in, and there was a plate of treacle tarts made according to their mother's old recipe, strips of buttery shortbread topped with lemon syrup and sweet crumbs.

"You must be exhausted," Amelia remarked, putting a gentle hand to Poppy's cheek. "I think you need a nap more than little Rye."

Poppy shook her head. "Later. I must try to settle some things first, because I think Harry may arrive by nightfall. Of course, he may not, but—"

"He will," came a voice from the doorway, and Poppy looked up to behold her former companion. "Miss Marks," she exclaimed, jumping to her feet.

A brilliant smile broke out on Miss Marks's face, and she came to Poppy swiftly, catching her in a warm embrace. Poppy could tell that she had been outside. Instead of her usual pristine soap-and-starch smell, she carried the scents of earth and flowers and summer heat. "Nothing's the same without you here," Miss Marks said. "It's so much quieter."

Poppy laughed.

Drawing back, Miss Marks added hastily, "I didn't mean to imply—"

"Yes, I know." Still smiling, Poppy viewed her quizzically. "How pretty you look. Your hair . . ." Instead of being scraped back and tightly pinned, the thick, fine locks flowed around her back and shoulders. And the nondescript shade of brown had been lightened to brilliant pale gold. "Is that your natural color?"

A blush swept over Miss Marks's face. "I'm going to darken it again as soon as possible."

"Must you?" Poppy asked, perplexed. "It's so lovely this way."

Amelia spoke from the settee. "I wouldn't advise applying any chemicals for a while, Catherine. Your hair may be too fragile."

"You may be right," Miss Marks said with a frown, self-consciously reaching up to finger the light, glinting strands.

Poppy looked askance at them both, having never heard Amelia call the companion by her first name before.

"May I sit with you both?" Miss Marks asked Poppy gently. "I want very much to hear what has transpired since the wedding. And—" There was a quick, oddly nervous pause. "I have some things to tell you that I believe are relevant to your situation."

"Please do," Poppy said. Throwing a quick glance at Amelia, she saw that her older sister was already aware of what Miss Marks intended to tell her.

They sat together, the sisters on the settee and Catherine Marks on a nearby chair.

A long, supple shape streaked through the doorway and paused. It was Dodger, who caught sight of Poppy, did a few hops of joy, and raced to her.

"Dodger," Poppy exclaimed, almost happy to see the ferret. He loped to her, regarded her with bright eyes and chirped happily as she petted him. After a moment, he left her lap and stole toward Miss Marks.

The companion glanced at him sternly. "Don't come near me, you loathsome weasel."

Undeterred, he stopped by her feet and executed a slow roll, showing her his belly. It was a source of amusement to the Hathaways that Dodger adored Miss Marks, no matter that she despised him. "Go away," she told him, but the lovestruck ferret continued his efforts to entice her.

Sighing, she reached down and removed one of her shoes, a sturdy black leather affair that laced up to the ankle. "It's the only way to keep him quiet," she said dourly.

Immediately, the ferret's chatter ceased, and he buried his head inside the shoe.

Suppressing a grin, Amelia turned her attention to Poppy. "Did you have a row with Harry?" she asked gently.

"Not really. Well, it began as one, but—" Poppy felt a wash of heat over her face. "Ever since the wedding we've done nothing more than circle around each other. And then last evening it seemed that we would finally—" The words seemed to bottle up in her throat, and she had to force them out in a jumble. "I'm so afraid it will always be this way, this push and pull . . . I think he cares for me, but he doesn't want me to care for him. It's as if he both wants and fears affection. And that leaves me in an impossible position." She let out a shaky, mirthless laugh and looked at her sister with a helpless grimace, as if to ask *What can be done with such a man?*

Instead of replying, Amelia turned her gaze to Miss Marks.

The companion appeared vulnerable, uneasy, turmoil churning beneath the veneer of composure. "Poppy. I may be able to shed some light on the situation. On what makes Harry so unreachable."

Startled by the familiar way she had referred to Harry, Poppy stared at her without blinking. "You have some knowledge of my husband, Miss Marks?"

"Please call me Catherine. I would like very much for you to consider me as a friend." The fair-haired woman drew in a tense breath. "I was acquainted with him in the past."

"What?" Poppy asked faintly.

"I should have told you before. I'm sorry. It's not something I can speak of easily."

Poppy was silent with amazement. It wasn't often that someone she had known for a long time was suddenly revealed in a new and surprising way. A connection between Miss Marks and Harry? That was profoundly unnerving, especially since both of them had kept it secret. She suffered a chill of confusion as an awful thought occurred to her. "Oh, God. Were you and Harry—"

"*No*. Nothing like that. But it's a complicated story, and I'm not certain how to . . . well, let me start by telling you what I know about Harry."

Poppy responded with a dazed nod.

"Harry's father, Arthur Rutledge, was an exceptionally ambitious man," Catherine said. "He built a hotel in Buffalo, New York, around the time they had started to expand the port and the harbor. And he made a moderate success of it, although he was by all accounts a poor manager—proud and obstinate and domineering. Arthur didn't marry until he was in his forties. He chose a local beauty, Nicolette, known for her high spirits and charm. She was less than half his age, and they had little in common. I don't know if Nicolette married him solely for his money, or if there was affection between them at the beginning. Unfortunately, Harry was born a bit too early on in the marriage—there was a great deal of speculation as to whether or not Arthur was the father. I think the rumors helped to bring about an estrangement. Whatever the cause, the marriage turned bitter. After Harry's birth, Nicolette was indiscreet in her affairs, until finally she ran away to England with one of her lovers. Harry was four years old at the time."

Her expression turned pensive. She was so deep in thought, in fact, that she didn't appear to notice that the ferret had crawled into her lap. "Harry's parents had taken little enough notice of him before. After Nicolette left, however, he was utterly neglected. Worse than neglected—he was deliberately isolated. Arthur put him in a kind of invisible prison. The hotel staff was instructed to have as little to do with the boy as possible. He was often locked alone in his room. Even when he took his meals in the kitchen, the employees were afraid to talk to him, for fear of reprisal. Arthur had made certain that Harry was given food, clothing, and education. No one could say Harry was being maltreated, you see, because he wasn't beaten or starved. But there are ways to break someone's spirit other than physical punishment."

"But why?" Poppy asked with difficulty, trying to absorb the idea of it, a child being brought up in such a cruel manner. "Was the father so vindictive that he could blame a child for his mother's actions?"

"Harry was a reminder of past humiliation and disappointment. And in all likelihood, Harry isn't even Arthur's son."

"That's no excuse," Poppy burst out. "I wish . . . oh, someone should have helped him."

"Many of the hotel staff felt terrible guilt over what was being done to Harry. The housekeeper, in particular. At one point she noticed that she hadn't seen the child in two days, and she went looking for him. He had been locked in his room with no food . . . Arthur had been so busy, he had forgotten to let him out. And Harry was only five."

"No one had heard him crying? Hadn't he made any noise?" Poppy asked unsteadily.

Catherine looked down at the ferret, stroking him compulsively. "The cardinal rule of the hotel was never to bother the guests. It had been drilled into him since birth. So he waited quietly, hoping someone would remember him, and come for him."

"Oh, no," Poppy whispered.

"The housekeeper was so horrified," Catherine continued, "that she managed to find out where Nicolette had gone, and she wrote letters describing the situation in the hopes that they might send for him. Anything, even living with a mother like Nicolette, would be better than the terrible isolation that was imposed on Harry."

"But Nicolette never sent for him?"

"Not until much later, when it was too late for Harry. Too late for everyone, as it turned out. Nicolette took ill with a wasting disease. It was a long, slow decline, but when the end approached, it progressed quickly. She wanted to see what had become of her son before she died, and so she wrote asking him to come. He left for London on the next available ship. He was an adult by then, twenty years of age or so. I don't know what his motives for seeing his mother were. No doubt he had many questions. I suspect there was always an uncertainty in his mind, as to whether she had left because of him." She paused, momentarily preoccupied with her own thoughts. "Most often, children blame themselves for how they are treated."

"But it wasn't his fault," Poppy exclaimed, her heart wrenched with compassion. "He was only a little boy. No child deserves to be abandoned."

"I doubt anyone has ever said as much to Harry," Catherine said. "He won't discuss it."

"What did his mother say when he found her?"

Catherine looked away for a moment, seeming unable to speak. She stared at the curled-up ferret in her lap, stroking his sleek fur. Eventually she managed to reply in a strained voice, her gaze still averted. "She died the day before he reached London." Her fingers twined into a tight basket. "Forever eluding him. I suppose to Harry, any hope of finding answers, any hope of affection, died along with her."

The three women were silent.

Poppy was overwhelmed.

What would it do to a child, to be raised in such a barren and loveless environment? It must have seemed as if the world itself had betrayed him. What a cruel burden to carry.

I will never love you, she had told him on their wedding day. And his reply . . .

I've never wanted to be loved. And God knows no one's done it yet.

Poppy closed her eyes sickly. This was not a problem to be solved in a conversation, or in a day, or even a year. This was a wound to the soul.

"I wanted to tell you before," she heard Catherine say. "But I was afraid it might have inclined you more strongly in Harry's favor. You've always been so easily moved to compassion. And the truth is, Harry won't ever want your sympathy, and probably not your love. I don't think it likely that he can become the kind of husband you deserve. But I'm not entirely sure. I've never been sure about anything regarding Harry."

"Miss Marks—" Poppy began, and checked herself. "Catherine. How is it that you know all this about him?"

A curious series of expressions crossed Catherine's face . . . anxiety, sorrow, pleading. She began to tremble visibly, until the ferret in her lap awoke and hiccupped.

As the silence drew out, Poppy threw a questioning glance at Amelia, who gave her a subtle nod as if to say, *Be patient.*

Catherine removed her spectacles and polished the perspiration-misted edges of the lenses. Her entire face had gone damp with nervousness, the fine skin gleaming with the luster of a pearl. "A few years after Nicolette came to England with her paramour," she said, "she had another child. A daughter."

Poppy was left to make the connection on her own. She found herself pressing her knuckles gently against her mouth. "You?" she eventually managed to get out.

Catherine lifted her face, the spectacles still in her hand. A poetic, fine-boned face, but there was something direct and decisive in the lovely symmetry of her features. Yes, there was something of Harry in that face. And a quality in her reserve that spoke of deep-trammeled emotions.

"Why have you never mentioned it?" Poppy asked, bewildered. "Why hasn't my husband? Why is your existence a secret?"

"It's for my protection. I took a new name. No one can ever know why."

There was much more Poppy wanted to ask, but it seemed Catherine Marks had reached the limits of her tolerance. Murmuring another apology beneath her breath, and another, she stood and set the sleepy ferret onto the rug. Snatching up her discarded shoe, she left the room. Dodger shook himself awake and followed her instantly.

Left alone with her sister, Poppy contemplated the little pile of tarts on the nearby table. A long silence passed.

"Tea?" she heard Amelia ask.

Poppy responded with a distracted nod.

After the tea was poured, they both reached for tarts, using their fingers to cradle the heavy strips of pastry, biting carefully. Tart lemon, sugar syrup, the pie crust velvety and crumbly. It was one of the tastes of their childhood. Poppy washed it down with a sip of hot milky tea.

"Things that remind me of our parents," Poppy said absently, "and that lovely cottage in Primrose Place . . . they always make me feel better. Like eating these tarts. And flower-print curtains. And reading Aesop's fables."

"The smell of Apothecary's Roses," Amelia reminisced. "Watching the rain fall from the thatched eaves. And remember when Leo put glow-worms in jars, and we tried to use them as candlelight for supper?"

Poppy smiled. "I remember never being able to find the cake pan, because Beatrix was forever making it into a bed for her pets."

Amelia gave an unladylike snort of laughter. "What about the time one of the chickens was so frightened by the neighbor's dog, it lost all its feathers? And Bea asked Mother to knit a little jumper for it."

Poppy spluttered in her tea. "I was mortified. Everyone in the village came to see our bald chicken strutting about in a jumper."

"As far as I know," Amelia said with a grin, "Leo's never eaten poultry since. He says he can't have something for dinner if there's a chance it once wore clothes."

Poppy sighed. "I never realized how wonderful our childhood was. I wanted us to be ordinary, so people wouldn't refer to us as 'those peculiar Hathaways.'" She licked a tacky spot of syrup from a fingertip, and glanced ruefully at Amelia. "We're never going to be ordinary, are we?"

"No, dear. Although, I must confess, I've never fully understood your desire for an ordinary life. To me, the word implies dullness."

"To me, it means safety. Knowing what to expect. There have been so many terrible surprises for us, Amelia . . . Mother and Father dying, and the scarlet fever, and the house burning . . ."

"And you believe you would have been safe with Mr. Bayning?" Amelia asked gently.

"I thought so." Poppy shook her head in bemusement. "I was so certain that I would be content with him. But in retrospect, I can't help thinking . . . Michael didn't fight for me, did he? Harry said something to him on the morning of our wedding, right in front of me . . . 'She was yours, if you'd wanted her, but I wanted her more.' And even though I hated what Harry had done . . . part of me liked it that Harry didn't think of me as being beneath him."

Drawing her feet up onto the settee, Amelia regarded her with fond concern. "I suppose you know already that the family can't let you go back with Harry until we're satisfied that he'll be kind to you."

"But he has been," Poppy said. And she told Amelia about the day when she had sprained her ankle, and Harry had taken care of her. "He was thoughtful and gentle and . . . well, loving. And if that was a glimpse of who Harry really is, I . . ." She stopped and traced the edge of her teacup, staring intently into the empty bowl of it. "Leo said something to me on the way here, that I had to decide whether or not to forgive Harry for the way our marriage started. I think I must, Amelia. For my own sake as well as Harry's."

"To err is human," Amelia said, "to forgive, absolutely galling. But yes, I think it's a good idea."

"The problem is, *that* Harry—the one who took care of me that day—doesn't surface nearly often enough. He keeps himself ridiculously busy, and he meddles with everyone and everything in that blasted hotel to avoid having to think about anything personal. If I could get him away from the Rutledge, to some quiet, peaceful place, and just . . ."

"Keep him in bed for a week?" Amelia suggested, her eyes twinkling.

Glancing at her sister in surprise, Poppy flushed and tried to stifle a laugh.

"It might do wonders for your marriage," Amelia continued. "It's lovely to talk to your husband after you've been to bed together. They just lie there feeling grateful and say yes to everything."

"I wonder if I could convince Harry to stay here with me for a few days," Poppy mused. "Is the gamekeeper's cottage in the woods still empty?"

"Yes, but the caretaker's house is much nicer, and at a more convenient distance from the house."

"I wish . . ." Poppy hesitated. "But it would be impossible. Harry would never agree to stay away from the hotel so long."

"Make it a condition of your returning to London with him," Amelia suggested. "Seduce him. For heaven's sake, Poppy, it's not that difficult."

"I don't know anything about it," Poppy protested.

"Yes, you do. Seduction is merely encouraging a man to do something he already wants to do."

Poppy gave her a bemused glance. "I don't understand why you're giving me this advice now, when you were so against the marriage in the first place."

"Well, now that you're married, there's not much anyone can do except try to make the best of it." A thoughtful pause. "Sometimes when you're making the best of a situation, it turns out far better than you could have hoped for."

"Only you," Poppy said, "could make seducing a man sound like the most pragmatic option."

Amelia grinned and reached for another tart. "What I mean to suggest is, why don't you try making a headlong dash at him? Try to make a real go of it. Show him what kind of marriage you want."

"Charge at him," Poppy murmured, "like a rabbit at a cat."

Amelia gave her a perplexed glance. "Hmmm?"

Poppy smiled. "Something Beatrix advised me to do early on. Perhaps she's wiser than the rest of us."

"I wouldn't doubt it." Lifting her free hand, Amelia pushed aside the edge of a white lace curtain, sunlight falling over her shining sable hair, gilding her fine features. A laugh escaped her. "I see her now, coming back from her ramble in the wood. She'll be thrilled to discover that you and Leo are here. And it appears she's carrying something in her apron. Lord, it could be anything. Lovely, wild girl . . . Catherine has done wonders with her, but you know she'll never be more than half tame."

Amelia said this without worry or censure, merely accepting Beatrix for what she was, trusting that fate would be kind. Undoubtedly that was Cam's influence. He'd always had the good sense to give the Hathaways as much freedom as possible, making room for their eccentricities where someone else might have crushed them. The Ramsay estate was their safe harbor, their haven, where the rest of the world dared not intrude.

And Harry would be there soon.

Chapter Twenty-one

Harry's journey to Hampshire had been long, dull, and uncomfortable, with no companionship except his own smoldering thoughts. He had tried to rest, but as a man who found sleep difficult in even the best of circumstances, trying to doze in a jolting carriage in the daytime was impossible. He had occupied himself with making up extravagant threats to bully his wife into obedience. Then he had fantasized about what he would do to Poppy in her chastised state, until those thoughts had made him aroused and aggravated.

Damn her, he would not be *left*.

Harry had never been given to introspection, finding the territory of his own heart too treacherous and tricky to examine. But it was impossible to forget the earlier time in his life, when every bit of softness and pleasure and hope had disappeared, and he'd had to fend for himself. Survival had meant never allowing himself to need another person again.

Harry tried to divert his thoughts by staring at the passing scenery, the summer sky still light as the hour approached nine. Of all the places in England he had visited, he had not yet gone to Hampshire. They were traveling south of the Downs, toward the thick wood and fertile grasslands near the New Forest and Southampton. The prosperous market town of Stony Cross was located in one of the most picturesque regions of England. But the town and its environs possessed something more than mere scenic appeal—a mystical quality, something difficult to put his finger on. It seemed they were traveling to a place out of time, the ancient woods harboring creatures that could only exist in myth. As evening deepened, mist collected in the valley and crept across the roads in an otherworldly haze.

The carriage turned onto the private road of the Ramsay estate, past two sets of open gates and a caretaker's house made of blue gray stone. The main house was a composite of architectural styles that shouldn't have looked right together but somehow did.

Poppy was there. The knowledge spurred him, made him desperate to reach her. It was more than desperation. Losing Poppy was the one thing he couldn't recover from, and knowing that made him feel fearful and furious and caged. The feelings catalyzed into one impetus: He would not be kept apart from her.

With all the patience of a baited badger, Harry strode to the front door, not waiting for a footman. He shoved his way into the entrance hall, two stories high with immaculate cream paneling and a curving stone staircase at the back.

Cam Rohan was there to greet him, casually dressed in a collarless shirt, trousers, and an open leather jerkin. "Rutledge," he said pleasantly. "We were just finishing supper. Will you have some?"

Harry gave an impatient shake of his head. "How is Poppy?"

"Come, let's have some wine, and we'll discuss a few things—"

"Is she having supper as well?"

"No."

"I want to see her. Now."

Cam's pleasant expression didn't change. "I'm afraid you'll have to wait."

"Let me rephrase—I'm *going* to see her and make sure she's all right, if I have to turn this place into matchsticks."

Cam received this imperturbably, his shoulders hitching in a shrug. "Outside, then."

This ready acceptance of a brawl both surprised and gratified Harry.

Some part of his mind recognized that he wasn't quite himself, that the precise workings of his mind were off-kilter, his self-control dismantled. His usual cool logic had deserted him. All he knew was that he was worried about Poppy, and if he had to fight to be able to see her, so be it. He would fight until he bloody well dropped.

He followed Cam through the entrance, down a side hallway, and out to a small open conservatory and garden where a pair of torches burned.

"I'll say this for you," the Rom remarked conversationally, "it's in your favor that your first question was not 'Where is Poppy?' but *'How* is Poppy?'"

"Devil take you and your opinions," Harry growled, stripping off his coat and tossing it aside.

Cam turned to face him, the torchlight gleaming in his eyes and over the black layers of his hair. "She's part of my tribe," he said, beginning to circle him. "You'll go back without her, unless you can find a way to make her want you."

"I can't bloody well do that without talking to her!"

Harry threw the first punch, and Cam dodged easily. Adjusting, calculating, Harry retreated as Cam threw a right. A pivot, and then Harry connected with a left cross. Cam had reacted a fraction too late, deflecting some of the blow's force, but not all.

A quiet curse, a rueful grin, and Cam renewed his guard. "Hard and fast," he said approvingly. "Where did you learn to fight?"

"New York."

Cam lunged forward and flipped him to the ground. "West London," he returned.

Tucking into a roll, Harry gained his footing instantly. As he came up, he used his elbow in a backward jab into Cam's midriff.

Cam grunted. Grabbing Harry's arm, he hooked a foot around his ankle and took him down again. They rolled once, twice, until Harry sprang away and retreated a few steps.

Breathing hard, he watched as Cam leapt to his feet.

"You could have put a forearm to my throat," Cam pointed out, shaking a swath of hair from his forehead.

"I didn't want to crush your windpipe," Harry said acidly, "before I made you tell me where my wife is."

Cam grinned. Before he could reply, however, there was a commotion as all the Hathaways poured from the conservatory. Leo, Amelia, Win, Beatrix, Merripen, and Catherine Marks. Everyone except Poppy, Harry noted bleakly. Where the hell was she?

"Is this the after-dinner entertainment?" Leo asked sardonically, emerging from the group. "Someone might have asked me—I would have preferred cards."

"You're next, Ramsay," Harry said with a scowl. "After I finish with Rohan, I'm going to flatten you for taking my wife away from London."

"No," Merripen said with deadly calm, stepping forward, "I'm next. And I'm going to flatten *you* for taking advantage of my kinswoman."

Leo glanced from Merripen's grim face to Harry's, and rolled his eyes. "Forget it, then," he said, going back into the conservatory. "After Merripen's done, there won't be anything left of him." Pausing beside his sisters, he spoke quietly to Win out of the side of his mouth. "You'd better do something."

"Why?"

"Because Cam only wants to knock a bit of sense into him. But Merripen actually intends to kill him, which I don't think Poppy would appreciate."

"Why don't *you* do something to stop him, Leo?" Amelia suggested acidly.

"Because I'm a peer. We aristocrats always try to get someone else to do something before we have to do it ourselves." He gave her a superior look. "It's called *noblesse oblige*."

Miss Marks's brows lowered. "That's not the definition of *noblesse oblige*."

"It's my definition," Leo said, seeming to enjoy her annoyance.

"Kev," Win said calmly, stepping forward, "I would like to talk to you about something."

Merripen, attentive as always to his wife, gave her a frowning glance. "Now?"

"Yes, now."

"Can't it wait?"

"No," Win said equably. At his continued hesitation, she said, "I'm expecting."

Merripen blinked. "Expecting what?"

"A baby."

They all watched as Merripen's face turned ashen. "But

how . . . ,"? he asked dazedly, nearly staggering as he headed to Win.

"*How*?" Leo repeated. "Merripen, don't you remember that special talk we had before your wedding night?" He grinned as Merripen gave him a warning glance. Bending to Win's ear, Leo murmured, "Well done. But what are you going to tell him when he discovers it was only a ploy?"

"It's not a ploy," Win said cheerfully.

Leo's smile vanished, and he clapped a hand to his forehead. "Christ," he muttered. "Where's my brandy?" And he disappeared into the house.

"I'm sure he meant to say 'congratulations,' " Beatrix remarked brightly, following the group as they all went inside.

Cam and Harry were left alone.

"I should probably explain," Cam said to Harry, looking somewhat apologetic. "Win used to be an invalid, and although she's recovered, Merripen is still afraid that childbirth may be difficult for her." He paused. "We all are," he admitted. "But Win is determined to have children—and God help anyone who tries to say no to a Hathaway."

Harry shook his head in bemusement. "Your family—"

"I know," Cam said. "You'll get used to us eventually." A pause, and then he asked in a matter-of-fact tone, "Do you want to take up the fight again, or shall we dispense with the rest of it and go have a brandy with Ramsay?"

One thing was clear to Harry: His in-laws were not normal people.

ONE OF THE LOVELIEST ASPECTS OF HAMPSHIRE SUMMERS was that even when the days were sun drenched and warm, most evenings were cool enough for a fire. Alone in the caretaker's house, Poppy snuggled by the small, crackling hearth and read a book by lamplight. She read the same page repeatedly, unable to concentrate as she waited for Harry. She had seen his carriage pass the cottage on the way to Ramsay House, and she knew it was only a matter of time before they sent him to her. "You won't see him," Cam had told her, "until I've decided that his temper has cooled sufficiently."

"He would never hurt me, Cam."

"All the same, little sister, I intend to have a few words with him."

She wore a dressing gown borrowed from Win, a ruffled pale pink garment with a white lace inset at the top. The bodice was very low, exposing her cleavage, and since Win was more slender, the garment was a bit too snug, nearly causing her breasts to spill over the lace. Knowing that Harry liked her hair down, she had brushed it and left it loose, a feathery, fiery curtain.

There was a sound from outside, a hard strike against the door. Poppy looked up sharply, her heartbeat quickening, her stomach turning over in a lazy somersault. She set the book aside and went to the door, turning the key in the lock, pulling at the knob.

She found herself standing face-to-face with her husband, who was one step below the stoop.

This was a new version of Harry, exhausted and rumpled and brutish, a day beyond a shave. Somehow the masculine dishevelment suited him, giving his handsomeness a raw, unvarnished appeal. He looked as if he were contemplating at least a dozen ways to punish her for having escaped him. His gaze raised gooseflesh all over her.

With a deep, arid breath, she stood back to let Harry in. Carefully, she closed the door.

The silence was pressing, the air charged with emotions she couldn't even name. A pulse drummed in the backs of her knees, the insides of her elbows, and the pit of her belly as Harry's gaze raked over her. As Poppy stared at him, she felt a wave of tenderness. He looked so hard faced and alone. So in need of comfort.

Before she gave herself a chance to reconsider, she went forward in two strides, removing all distance between them. Taking his stiff jaw in her hands, she stood on her toes and brought herself against him, and silenced him with her mouth.

She felt the shock of that tender contact jolt all through Harry. His breath slammed in his throat, and he seized her upper arms, pushing her back just far enough to stare at her incredulously. She felt how strong he was, able to break her in two if he chose. He was motionless, riveted by whatever he saw in her expression.

Eager and intent, Poppy strained upward to put her mouth to his again. He allowed it for just a moment, then pushed her back. A swallow rippled visibly down his throat. If the first kiss had startled him into silence, the second had utterly disarmed him.

"Poppy," he said hoarsely, "I didn't want to hurt you. I tried to be gentle."

Poppy laid her hand softly along his cheek. "Is that why you think I left, Harry?"

He seemed stunned by the caress. His lips parted in a wordless question, his features stamped with exquisite frustration. She saw the moment when he stopped trying to make sense of anything.

Bending over her with a groan, he kissed her.

The shared heat of their mouths, the sinuous brush of tongue against tongue, filled her with pleasure. She answered him ardently, withholding nothing, letting him search and stroke inside her as he wished. His arms went around her, one hand clasping beneath her bottom to pull her closer.

Caught up on her toes, Poppy felt her body list forward,

chests, stomachs, hips pressing together. He was aggressively aroused, his flesh jutting boldly against her, every hint of friction wringing out deep and resonant delight.

His lips dragged along the side of her throat, and he bent her backward until her breasts strained the front of the dressing gown. He nuzzled into the valley of compressed flesh, stroking between her breasts with his tongue. His hot breath mingled in the white lace, his mouth dampening her skin. Roughly he sought the tip of her breast, but it was tucked too tightly beneath the soft pink fabric. She arched desperately, wanting his mouth there, everywhere, wanting everything.

She tried to say something, perhaps suggest they go to the bedroom, but it came out as a moan. Her knees were close to buckling. Harry tugged at the front of the bodice, discovering the row of concealed hook-and-eye closures. He opened the bodice with stunning swiftness and stripped the dressing gown away, leaving her naked.

Reaching for her, he turned her away from him and pushed the gleaming fall of her hair aside. His mouth descended to the nape of her neck, kissing, almost biting, his tongue playing, while his hands slid over her smooth front. He cupped a breast, gently pinching the hardening peak while his other hand slid between her thighs.

Poppy jumped a little, gasping in anticipation as he parted her. Instinctively she tried to widen her stance for him, offering herself, and his approving purr vibrated against her neck. He held her in a deep fondling embrace, feeling her, filling her with his fingers until she arched back against him, her bare bottom cradling the shape of his erection. He coaxed sensation from her, pleasuring her vulnerable flesh.

"Harry," she panted, "I'm going to f-fall—"

They sank to the carpeted floor in a sort of slow, grappling collapse, with Harry still behind her. He muttered against her back, imprinting words of need and praise against her skin. The texture of his mouth, wet velvet surrounded by the bristle of his jaw, caused her to shiver in pleasure. He kissed his way along the curve of her spine, following it to the small of her back.

Poppy turned around to reach for the placket of his shirt. Her fingers were unusually clumsy as she undid the four buttons. Harry held still, his chest rising and falling rapidly as he watched her with volatile green eyes. He stripped off his open waistcoat, pulled his leather braces to the sides, and tugged the shirt over his head. His chest was magnificent, broad reaches of curved muscle and tough-knit hardness covered by a light fleece of hair. She stroked him with a trembling hand and reached down to his trousers, trying to find the concealed placket at the front.

"Let me," Harry said brusquely.

"I will," she insisted, determined to learn this bit of wifely knowledge. She felt his stomach against her knuckles, hard as a board. Finding the elusive button, she worked on it with both hands while Harry forced himself to wait. They both jumped as her delving fingers inadvertently brushed against his erection.

He made a choked sound, something between a groan and a laugh. "Poppy." He was breathless. "Damn it, *please* let me do it."

"It wouldn't be so difficult—" she protested, finally managing to free the button, "—if your trousers weren't so tight."

"They're not usually."

Comprehending what he meant, she paused and met his gaze, and a shy, rueful grin curved her mouth. He took her head in his hands, staring at her with a longing that raised the hairs on the back of her neck.

"Poppy," he said raggedly, "I thought about you every minute of that twelve-hour carriage drive. About how to make you come back with me. I'll do anything. I'll buy you half of bloody London, if that will suffice."

"I don't want half of London," she said faintly. Her fingers tightened on the waist of his trousers. This was Harry as she had never seen him before, all defenses down, speaking to her with raw honesty.

"I know I should apologize for coming between you and Bayning."

"Yes, you should," she said.

"I can't. I'll never be sorry about it. Because if I hadn't done it, you'd be his now. And he only wanted you if it was easy for him. But I want you any way I can get you. Not because you're beautiful or clever or kind or adorable, although the devil knows you're all those things. I want you because there's no one else like you, and I don't ever want to start a day without seeing you."

As Poppy opened her mouth to reply, he smoothed his thumb across her lower lip, coaxing her to wait until he had finished. "Do you know what a balance wheel is?"

She shook her head slightly.

"There's one in every clock or watch. It rotates back and forth without stopping. It's what makes the ticking sound . . . what makes the hands move forward to mark the minutes. Without it, the watch wouldn't work. You're my balance wheel, Poppy." He paused, his fingers compulsively following the fine curve of her jaw up to the lobe of her ear. "I spent today trying to think of what I could apologize for and maybe sound at least half sincere. And I finally came up with something."

"What is it?" she whispered.

"I'm sorry I'm not the husband you wanted." His voice turned gravelly. "But I swear on my life, if you'll tell me what you need, I'll listen. I'll do anything you ask. Just don't leave me again."

Poppy stared at him in wonder. Perhaps most women wouldn't find this talk of watch mechanisms to be terribly romantic, but she did. She understood what Harry was trying to say, perhaps even more than he himself did.

"Harry," she said softly, daring to reach out and caress his jaw, "what am I to do with you?"

"Anything," he said with a heartfelt vehemence that almost made her laugh. Leaning forward, Harry pressed his face into the silky mass of her hair.

She continued to work on his trousers, popping the last two buttons from their holes. Her fingers trembled as she gripped him tentatively. He let out a growl of pleasure, his arms sliding around her back. Unsure of how to touch him, she clasped him, squeezed gently, drew her fingertips up the hot length. She was fascinated by him, the silk and hardness and contained force of him, the way his entire body shivered as she stroked him.

His mouth sought hers in a full-open kiss, obliterating all thought. He rose above her, powerful and predatory, famished for the pleasures that were still so new to her. As he lowered her to the carpet, she realized that he was going to take her, now, here, instead of seeking the more civilized comforts of the bedroom. But he hardly seemed aware of where they were, his eyes focused only on her, his color high, his lungs pumping like hearth bellows.

Murmuring his name, she lifted her arms to him. He struggled out of the rest of his clothes and bent to feast on her breasts . . . hot, wet mouth . . . restless tongue. She kept trying to pull him farther over her, seeking the weight of his body, needing to be anchored. She groped for the hard, aching length of him, and urged him against her.

"No," he said thickly. "Wait . . . I have to make sure you're ready."

But she was determined, her grip insistent, and somewhere amid his groans and pants, a husky laugh emerged. He mounted her, adjusted her hips, and paused as he struggled for a measure of self-restraint.

Poppy wriggled helplessly as she felt the gradual pressure of his entry . . . torturously slow . . . maddening, heavy, sweet.

"Does it hurt?" Harry panted, hanging over her, bracing his weight on his arms to keep from crushing her. "Shall I stop?"

The concern on his face was her undoing, filling her with warmth. Her arms slid around his neck, and she pressed kisses on his cheek, neck, ear, everywhere she could reach. Her body held him tightly down below. "I want more of you, Harry," she whispered. "All of you."

He groaned her name and surged into her, alert to every subtle response . . . lingering when it pleased her, pressing deeper when she lifted, every slow plunge tamping more sensation inside her. She let her hands glide over his sleek, flexing back, the burning silk of his skin, loving the feel of him.

Following the long lines of muscle, she went lower until her palms smoothed circles over the tight curves of his backside. His response was electric, his thrusts turning more forceful, a quiet grunt escaping his throat. He liked that, she thought with a smile, or would have smiled if her mouth hadn't been so thoroughly occupied with his. She wanted to discover more about him, all the ways to please him, but the accumulating pleasure reached a tipping point and began to spill powerfully, inundating her, drowning all thought.

Her body clenched him in strong spasms, extorting release, pulling it from him. He let out a harsh cry and sank into her with a last thrust, shuddering violently. It was indescribably satisfying to feel him climax inside her, his body powerful and yet vulnerable in that ultimate moment. And better still to have him lower into her arms, his head dropping on her soft shoulder. Here was the closeness she had always craved.

She cradled his head, his hair a silky tickle against her inner wrist, his breath flowing over her in hot rushes. His unshaven bristle was scratchy against the tender skin of her breast, but she wouldn't have moved him for all the world.

Their breathing slowed, and Harry's weight became crushingly heavy. Poppy realized he was falling asleep. She pushed at him. "Harry."

He lurched upward, blinking, his gaze disoriented.

"Come to bed," Poppy murmured, rising. "The bedroom is just over there." She murmured a few encouragements, urging him to follow. "Did you bring a traveling bag?" she asked. "Or a gentleman's case?"

Harry glanced at her as if she'd spoken in a foreign language. "Case?"

"Yes, with your clothes, toiletries, that sort of . . ." Perceiving how utterly exhausted he was, she smiled and shook her head. "Never mind. We'll sort it out in the morning." She towed him to the bedroom. "Come . . . we'll sleep . . . we'll talk later. A few more steps . . ."

The wooden bed was utilitarian, but easily large enough for two, and it was made up with quilts and fresh white linens. Harry went to it without hesitation, climbing beneath the covers—collapsing, really—and he fell asleep with startling immediacy.

Poppy paused to look down at the large, unshaven man

in her bed. Even in his unkempt state, his dark-angel handsomeness was breathtaking. His lids trembled infinitesimally as he succumbed to encroaching dreams. Complex, remarkable, driven man. Not incapable of love . . . not at all. He merely needed to be shown how.

And just as she had a few days earlier, Poppy thought, *This is the man I'm married to.*

Except that now, she felt a stirring of gladness.

Chapter Twenty-two

Harry had never known such sleep, so deep and restorative that it seemed he had never experienced real sleep before, only an imitation. He felt drugged when he awoke, drunk on sleep, steeped in it.

Squinting his eyes open, he discovered that it was morning, the curtained windows limned with sunlight. He felt no overwhelming need to leap out of bed as he usually did. Rolling to his side, he stretched lazily. His hand encountered empty space.

Had Poppy shared the bed with him? A frown gathered on his forehead. Had he slept all night with someone for the first time and missed it? Turning to his stomach, he levered himself to the other side of the bed, hunting for her scent. Yes . . . there was a flowery hint of her on the pillow, and the sheets carried a whiff of her skin, a lavender-tinged sweetness that aroused him with every breath.

He wanted to hold Poppy, to reassure himself that the previous night hadn't been a dream.

In fact, it had been so preposterously good that he felt a twinge of worry. *Had* it been a dream? Frowning, he sat up and scrubbed his fingers through his hair.

"Poppy," he said, not really calling out for her, just saying her name aloud. Quiet as the sound was, she appeared in the doorway as if she'd been waiting for him.

"Good morning." She was already dressed for the day in a simple blue gown, her hair in a loose braid tied with a white ribbon. How apt it was that she'd been named for the showiest of wildflowers, rich and vivid, a gleaming finish to the bloom. Her blue eyes surveyed him with such attentive warmth that he felt a catch in his chest, a dart of pleasure-pain.

"The shadows are gone," Poppy said softly. Seeing that he didn't follow, she added, "Beneath your eyes."

Self-consciously, Harry looked away and rubbed the back of his neck. "What time is it?" he asked gruffly.

Poppy went to a chair, where his clothes had been set in a folded pile, and rummaged for his pocket watch. Flipping open the gold case, she went to the windows and parted the curtains. Vigorous sunlight pushed into the room. "Half past eleven," she said, closing the watch with a decisive snap.

Harry stared at her blankly. Holy hell. Half the day was over. "I've never slept so late in my life."

His disgruntled surprise seemed to amuse Poppy. "No stack of managers' reports. No one rapping at the door. No questions or emergencies. Your hotel is a demanding mistress, Harry. But today, you belong to me."

Harry absorbed that, a tug of inner resistance quickly vanishing into the pull of his enormous attraction to her.

"Will you dispute it?" she asked, looking vastly pleased with herself. "That you're mine today?"

Harry found himself smiling back at her, unable to help himself. "Yours to command," he said. His smile turned rueful as he became uncomfortably aware of his unwashed state, his unshaven face. "Is there a bathing room?"

"Yes, through that door. The house is plumbed. There's

cold water pumped directly from a well to the bathtub, and I have cans of hot water ready on the cookstove." She tucked the watch back into his waistcoat. Straightening, she glanced over his naked torso with covert interest. "They sent your things from the main house this morning, along with some breakfast. Are you hungry?"

Harry had never been so ravenous. But he wanted to wash and shave, and put on fresh clothes. He felt out of his element, needing to recapture a measure of his usual equanimity. "I'll wash first."

"Very well." She turned to go to the kitchen.

"Poppy—" He waited until she glanced back at him. "Last night . . ." he forced himself to ask, ". . . after what we . . . was it all right?"

Comprehending his concern, Poppy's expression cleared. "Not all right." She paused only a second before adding, "It was wonderful." And she smiled at him.

HARRY ENTERED THE COTTAGE KITCHEN AREA, WHICH WAS essentially a portion of the main room, with a small cast-iron cookstove, a cupboard, a hearth, and a pine table that served both as workstation and dining surface. Poppy had set out a feast of hot tea, boiled eggs, Oxford sausages, and massive pasties—thick flaky crusts wrapped around fillings.

"These are a Stony Cross specialty," Poppy said, gesturing to a plate bearing two hefty baked loaves. "One side is filled with meat and sage, and the other side is filled with fruit. It's an entire meal. You start with the savory end, and . . ." Her voice faded as she glanced up at Harry, who was clean and dressed and freshly shaven.

He looked the same as always, and yet intrinsically different. His eyes were clear and unshadowed, the green irises brighter than hawthorn leaves. Every hint of tension had vanished from his face. It seemed as if he had been replaced by a Harry from a much earlier time in his life, before he'd mastered the art of hiding every thought and emotion. He was so devastating that Poppy felt hot flutters of attraction in her stomach, and her knees lost all their starch.

Harry glanced down at the oversized pastry with a crooked grin. "Which end do I start with?"

"I have no idea," she replied. "The only way to find out is to take a bite."

His hands went to her waist, and he turned her gently to face him. "I think I'll start with you."

As his mouth lowered to hers, she yielded easily, her lips parting. He drew in the taste of her, delighting in her response. The casual kiss deepened, altered into something patient and deeply hungering . . . heat opening into more heat, a kiss with the layered merosity of exotic flowers. Eventually Harry lifted his mouth, his hands coming to her face as if he were cupping water to drink. He had a unique way of touching, she thought dazedly, his fingers gentle and artful, sensitive to nuance.

"Your lips are swollen," he whispered, the tip of his thumb brushing the corner of her mouth.

Poppy pressed her cheek against one of his palms. "We've had many kisses to make up for."

"More than kisses," he said, and the look in those vivid eyes brought a heartbeat into her throat. "As a matter of fact—"

"Eat, or you'll starve," she said, trying to push him into a chair. He was so much larger, so solid, that the idea of compelling him to do anything was laughable. But he yielded to the urging of her hands, and sat, and began to peel an egg.

AFTER HARRY HAD CONSUMED AN ENTIRE PASTIE, TWO EGGS, an orange, and a mug of tea, they went for a walk. At Poppy's urging, he left off his coat and waistcoat. He even left the top buttons of his shirt undone and rolled up his sleeves.

Charmed by Poppy's eagerness, he took her hand and let her tug him outside.

They went across a field to a nearby wood, where a broad, leaf-carpeted path cut through the forest. The massive yews and furrowed oaks tangled their boughs in a dense roof, but the depth of shade was pierced by blades of sunlight. It was a place of abundant life, plants growing on plants. Pale green lichen frosted the oak branches, while tresses of woodbine dangled to the ground.

After Harry's ears had adjusted to the absence of city clamor, he became aware of new sounds . . . a rippling chorus of birdcalls, leaf rustlings, the burble of a nearby brook, and a rasp like a nail being drawn along the teeth of a comb.

"Cicadas," Poppy said. "This is the only place you'll see them in England. They're usually found only in the tropics. Only a male cicada makes that noise—it's said to be a mating song."

"How do you know he's not commenting on the weather?"

Sending him a provocative sideways glance, Poppy murmured, "Well, mating is rather a male preoccupation, isn't it?"

Harry smiled. "If there's a more interesting subject," he said, "I have yet to discover it."

The air was sweet, spiced heavily with woodbine and sun-heated leaves and flowers he didn't recognize. As they went deeper into the wood, it seemed they had left the world far behind them.

"I talked with Catherine," Poppy said.

Harry glanced at her alertly.

"She told me why you came to England," Poppy continued. "And she told me that she's your half sister."

Harry focused on the path before them. "Does the rest of the family know?"

"Only Amelia and Cam and I."

"I'm surprised," he admitted. "I would have thought she'd prefer death over telling anyone."

"She impressed upon us the need for secrecy, but she wouldn't explain why."

"And you want me to?"

"I was hoping you might," she said. "You know I would never say or do anything to harm her."

Harry was quiet, turning over thoughts in his mind, reluctant to refuse Poppy anything. And yet he had made a promise to Catherine. "They're not my secrets to reveal, love. May I talk to Cat first, and tell her what I'd like to explain to you?"

Her hand tightened on his. "Yes, of course." A quizzical smile curved her lips. "Cat? That's what you call her?"

"Sometimes."

"Do you . . . is there fondness between you?"

The hesitant question provoked a laugh as dry as the rustle of corn husks. "I don't know, actually. Neither of us is exactly comfortable with affection."

"She's a bit more comfortable with it than you, I think."

Glancing at her warily, Harry saw that there was no censure on her face. "I'm trying to improve," he said. "It's one of the things Cam and I discussed last evening—he said it's characteristic of Hathaway women, this need for demonstrations of affection."

Amused and fascinated, Poppy made a face. "What else did he say?"

Harry's mood altered with quicksilver speed. He threw her a dazzling grin. "He compared it to working with Arabian horses . . . they're responsive, quick, but they need their freedom. You never master an Arabian . . . you become its companion." He paused. "At least, I think that's what he said. I was half dead from exhaustion, and we were drinking brandy."

"That sounds like Cam." Poppy raised her gaze heavenward. "And after dispensing this advice, he sent you to me, the horse."

Harry stopped and pulled her against him, nudging her braid aside to kiss her neck. "Yes," he whispered. "And what a nice ride it was."

She flushed and squirmed with a protesting laugh, but he persisted in kissing her, working his way up to her mouth. His lips were warm, beguiling, determined. But as soon as he gained access to her mouth, he gentled, his mouth soft against hers. He liked to tease, to seduce. Warmth swept through her, arousal flowing through her veins, prickling sweetly in hidden places.

"I love kissing you," he murmured. "It was the worst punishment you could have devised, not letting me do this."

"It wasn't a punishment," Poppy protested. "It's just that a kiss means something special to me. And after what you'd done, I was afraid to be close to you."

All hint of amusement left Harry's expression. He smoothed her hair and drew the backs of his fingers softly along the side of her face. "I won't betray you again. I know you have no reason to trust me, but in time I hope—"

"I do trust you," she said earnestly. "I'm not afraid now."

Harry was baffled by her words, and even more by the intensity of his response to them. An unfamiliar feeling welled up in him, a deep, overwhelming ardor. His voice sounded a bit strange to his own ears as he asked, "How can you trust me when you have no way of knowing if I'm worthy of it?"

The corners of her lips tilted upward. "That's what trust is, isn't it?"

Harry couldn't help kissing her again, adoration and arousal pumping through him. He could barely feel the shape of her body through her skirts, and his hands shook with the urge to pull up the bunches of fabric, remove every obstruction between them. A quick glance along both directions of the path revealed that they were alone and unobserved. It would be so easy to lay her into the soft carpet of leaves and moss, push up her dress, and take her right there in the forest. He pulled her to the side of the path, his fingers clenching in a swath of her skirts.

But he forced himself to stop, breathing hard with the effort to check his desire. He had to be careful with Poppy, considerate of her. She deserved better than to have her husband throwing himself on her in the woods.

"Harry?" she murmured in confusion as he turned her to face away from him.

He held her from behind, his arms crossed around her front. "Say something to distract me," he said, only half joking. He took a deep breath. "I'm a hairsbreadth away from ravishing you right here."

Poppy was silent for a moment. Either she was struck mute with horror, or she was considering the possibility. Evidently it was the latter, because she asked, "It can be done outside?"

Despite his fierce arousal, Harry couldn't help smiling against her neck. "Love, there's hardly any place it can't be done. Against trees or walls, in chairs or bathtubs, on staircases or tables . . . balconies, carriages—" He let out a quiet groan. "Damn it, I've got to stop this, or I won't be able to walk back."

"None of those ways sound very comfortable," Poppy said.

"You'd like chairs. Chairs I can vouch for."

A chuckle rippled through her, causing her back to press against his chest.

They both waited until Harry had calmed himself sufficiently to let go of her. "Well," he said, "this has been a delightful walk. Why don't we go back, and—"

"But we're not even halfway done yet," she protested.

Harry glanced from her expectant face to the long path that extended before them, and he sighed. They linked hands and resumed traversing the ground woven with sun and shadows.

After a minute, Poppy asked, "Do you and Catherine visit each other, or correspond?"

"Hardly ever. We don't get on well."

"Why not?"

It wasn't a subject that Harry liked to think about, much less discuss. And this business of having to talk freely with someone, withholding nothing . . . it was like being perpetually naked, except that Harry would have preferred being literally naked in lieu of revealing his private thoughts and feelings. However, if that was the price of having Poppy, he'd bloody well pay it.

"At the time I first met Cat," he said, "she was in a difficult situation. I did as much as possible to help her, but I wasn't kind about it. I've never had much kindness to spare. I could have been better to her. I could have—" He gave an impatient shake of his head. "What's done is done. I did make certain that she would be financially independent for the rest of her life. She doesn't have to work, you know."

"Then why did she apply for a position with the Hathaways? I can't imagine why she would have wanted to subject herself to the hopeless task of making ladies of Beatrix and me."

"I imagine she wanted to be with a family. To know what it was like. And to keep from being lonely or bored." He stopped and gave her a questioning glance. "Why do you say it was a hopeless task? You're very much a lady."

"Three failed London seasons," she pointed out.

Harry made a scoffing sound. "That had nothing to do with being ladylike."

"Then why?"

"The biggest obstacle was your intelligence. You don't bother to hide it. One of the things Cat never taught you was how to flatter a man's vanity—because she doesn't have any damned idea of how to do it. And none of those idiots could tolerate the idea of having a wife who was smarter than himself. Second, you're beautiful, which meant they would always have to worry about you being the target of other men's attentions. On top of that, your family is . . . your family. Basically you were too much to manage, and they all knew they were better off finding dull, docile girls to marry. All except Bayning, who was so taken with you that the attraction eclipsed any other considerations. God knows I can't hold that against him."

Poppy gave him a wry glance. "If I'm so forbiddingly intelligent and beautiful, then why did *you* want to marry me?"

"I'm not intimidated by your brains, your family, or your beauty. And most men are too afraid of me to look twice at my wife."

"Do you have many enemies?" she asked quietly.

"Yes, thank God. They're not nearly as inconvenient as friends."

Although Harry was perfectly serious, Poppy seemed to find that highly amusing. After her laughter slowed, she stopped and turned to face him with her arms folded. "You need me, Harry."

He stopped before her, his head inclined over hers. "I've become aware of that."

The sounds of stonechats perched overhead filled the pause, their chirps sounding like pebbles being struck together.

"I've something to ask you," Poppy said.

Harry waited patiently, his gaze resting on her face.

"May we stay in Hampshire for a few days?"

His eyes turned wary. "For what purpose?"

She smiled slightly. "It's called a holiday. Haven't you ever gone on holiday before?"

Harry shook his head. "I'm not sure what I would do."

"You read, walk, ride, spend a morning fishing or shooting, perhaps go calling on the neighbors . . . tour the local ruins, visit the shops in town . . ." Poppy paused as she saw the lack of enthusiasm on his face. ". . . Make love to your wife?"

"Done," he said promptly.

"May we stay a fortnight?"

"Ten days."

"Eleven?" she asked hopefully.

Harry sighed. Eleven days away from the Rutledge. In close company with his in-laws. He was tempted to argue, but he wasn't fool enough to risk the ground he'd gained with Poppy. He'd come here with the expectation of a royal battle to get her back to London. But if Poppy would take him willingly into her bed, and then accompany him back with no fuss, it was worth a concession on his part.

Still . . . eleven days . . .

"Why not?" he muttered. "I'll probably go mad after three days."

"That's all right," Poppy said cheerfully. "No one around here would notice."

To Mr. Jacob Valentine
The Rutledge Hotel
Embankment and Strand
London

Valentine,

I hope this letter finds you well. I am writing to apprise you that Mrs. Rutledge and I have decided to remain in Hampshire until month's end.

In my absence, carry on as usual.

Yours truly,
J.H. Rutledge

Jake looked up from the letter with jaw-slackening disbelief. *Carry on as usual?*

Nothing was usual about this.

"Well, what does it say?" Mrs. Pennywhistle prompted, while nearly everyone in the front office strained to hear.

"They're not coming back until month's end," Jake said, dazed.

A strange, lopsided smile touched the housekeeper's lips. "Bless my soul. She's done it."

"Done what?"

Before she could reply, the elderly concierge sidled up to them and asked in a discreet tone, "Mrs. Pennywhistle, I couldn't help but overhear your conversation . . . am I to understand that Mr. Rutledge is taking a *holiday*?"

"No, Mr. Lufton," she said with an irrepressible grin. "He's taking a honeymoon."

Chapter Twenty-three

In the following days, Harry learned a great deal about his wife and her family. The Hathaways were an extraordinary group of individuals, lively and quick-witted, with an instant collective willingness to try any ideas that came to them. They teased and laughed and squabbled and debated, but there was an innate kindness in the way they treated each other.

There was something almost magical about Ramsay House. It was a comfortable, well-run home, filled with sturdy furniture and thick carpets, and piles of books everywhere . . . but that didn't account for the extra something. One felt it immediately after crossing the front threshold, something as intangible but life-giving as sunlight. A something that had always escaped Harry.

Gradually he came to realize that it was love.

THE SECOND DAY AFTER HARRY'S ARRIVAL IN HAMPSHIRE, Leo toured him around the estate. They rode to visit some of the tenant farms, and Leo stopped to talk to various tenants and laborers. He exchanged informed comments with them about the weather, the soil, and the harvest, displaying a depth of knowledge that Harry would not have expected.

In London, Leo played the part of disaffected rake to perfection. In the country, however, the mask of indifference dropped. It was clear that he cared about the families who lived and worked on the Ramsay estate, and he intended to make a success of it. He had designed a clever system of irrigation that brought water along stone channels they had dug from the nearby river, relieving many of the tenants of the chore of hauling water. And he was doing his utmost to bring modern methods to local farming, including convincing his tenants to plant a new variety of hybrid wheat developed in Brighton that produced higher yields and stronger straw.

"They're slow to accept change in these parts," Leo told Harry ruefully. "Many of them still insist on using the sickle and scythe instead of the threshing machine." He grinned. "I've told them the nineteenth century is going to be over before they ever decide to take part in it."

It occurred to Harry that the Hathaways were making a solid success of the estate not in spite of their lack of aristocratic heritage, but *because* of it. No traditions or habits had been passed on to them. There had been no one to protest "but this is how we've always done it." As a result, they approached estate management as both a business and a scientific undertaking, because they knew no other way to proceed.

Leo showed Harry the estate timber yard, where the backbreaking work of cutting, hauling, and adsizing logs was all done by hand. Massive logs were carried on shoulders or with lug hooks, creating countless opportunities for injury.

After supper that evening, Harry sketched some plans for moving timber with a system of rollers, run planks, and dollies. The system could be constructed at a relatively low expense, and it would allow for faster production and greater safety for the estate laborers. Merripen and Leo were both immediately receptive to the idea.

"It was very kind of you to draw up those schemes," Poppy told Harry later, when they had gone to the caretaker's house for the night. "Merripen was very appreciative."

Harry shrugged casually, unfastening the back of her gown and helping to draw her arms from the sleeves. "I merely pointed out a few obvious improvements they could make."

"Things that are obvious to you," she said, "aren't necessarily obvious to the rest of us. It was very clever of you, Harry." Stepping out of the gown, Poppy turned to face him with a satisfied smile. "I'm very glad my family is getting the chance to know you. They're beginning to like you. You're being very charming, and not at all condescending, and you don't make a fuss about things like finding a hedgehog in your chair."

"I'm not fool enough to compete with Medusa for chair space," he said, and she laughed. "I like your family," he said, unhooking the front of her corset, gradually freeing her from the web of cloth and stays. "Seeing you with them helps me to understand you better."

The corset made a soft *thwack* as he tossed it to the floor. Poppy stood before him in her chemise and drawers, flushing as he studied her intently.

An uncertain smile crossed her face. "What do you understand about me?"

Harry hooked a gentle finger beneath the strap of her chemise, easing it downward. "That it's your nature to form close attachments to the people around you." He moved his palm over the curve of her bared shoulder in a circling caress. "That you are sensitive, and devoted to those you love, and most of all . . . that you need to feel safe." He eased the other strap of her chemise down, and felt the shivers that chased through her body. He drew her against him, his arms closing around her, and she molded to him with a sigh.

After a while, he murmured softly into the pale, fragrant

curve of her neck. "I'm going to make love to you all night, Poppy. And the first time, you're going to feel very safe. But the second time, I'm going to be a little bit wicked . . . and you'll like that even more. And the third time . . ." He paused with a smile as he heard her breath catch. "The third time, I'm going to do things that will mortify you when you remember them tomorrow." He kissed her gently. "And you'll love that most of all."

POPPY COULDN'T QUITE FATHOM HARRY'S MOOD, DEVILISH yet tender as he finished undressing her. He laid her back on the mattress with her legs dangling, and stood between them as he leisurely removed his shirt. As his gaze traveled over her, she blushed and tried to cover herself with her arms.

Flashing a grin, Harry bent over her, pulling her hands away. "Love, if you only knew what pleasure it gives me to look at you . . ." He kissed her lips, teasing them open, his tongue slipping inside the warm interior of her mouth. The hair on his chest brushed over the tips of her breasts, a sweet and ceaseless stimulation that drew a moan from low in her throat.

His lips wandered along the arch of her throat to her breasts. Capturing a nipple, he stroked with his tongue, making it taut and stingingly sensitive. At the same time, his hand went to her other breast, his thumb circling and prodding the peak.

She strained upward, her body trembling and flushed. His hands drifted over her in light paths, across her stomach, lower, down to the place where a sweet erotic ache had centered. Finding the humid, delicately layered flesh, he teased her with his thumbs, opened her, making her ready for him.

Her knees drew up, and she reached for him with an incoherent sound, trying to draw him over her. Instead, he sank to his knees and gripped her hips, and she felt his mouth on her.

She quivered beneath the gentle articulation of his tongue, every intricate movement provoking, tormenting, until her eyes fluttered closed and she began to breathe in wrenching sighs. His tongue entered her and lingered for an excruciating moment. "Please," she whispered. "Please, Harry."

She felt him stand, heard the rustle of trousers and linens being dropped. There was hot, gentle pressure at the entrance of her body, and she made a shuddering sound of relief. He pushed inside as deeply as she could accept him, a deliciously substantial invasion. She was stretched, utterly filled, and she worked her hips against him, trying to take even more. A slow rhythm began, his body pressing hers at just the right angle, driving the pitch of feeling higher with each luscious ingress.

Her eyes flew open as the accumulated sensation rolled up to her, relentless in its strength and velocity, and she saw his sweat-misted face above hers. He was watching her, savoring her pleasure, bending to take her helpless cries into his mouth.

When the last spasms had faded, and she was as limp as a discarded stocking, Poppy found herself cradled in Harry's arms. They reclined together on the bed, her soft limbs tangled with his harder, longer ones.

She stirred in drowsy surprise as she felt that he was still aroused. He kissed her and sat up, his hand playing in the loose fire of her hair.

Gently he guided her head to his lap. "Make it wet," he whispered. Her mouth closed carefully over the pulsing head, slid as far down as she could, and lifted. Intrigued, she nuzzled the silken hardness, her tongue flicking out like a cat's.

Harry turned her so that she was positioned facedown on the mattress. Hoisting her hips upward, he covered her from behind, his fingers sliding between her thighs. She felt a leap of excitement, her body responding instantly to his touch.

"Now," he whispered into her hot ear, "I'm going to be wicked. And you'll let me do anything, won't you?"

"Yes, yes, yes . . ."

Harry held her with firm pressure, cupping her as he pulled her against his solid weight. She felt him move her in an insinuating rocking motion, with his aroused flesh poised at the wet cove of her body. He entered her, but just barely, and each time she rocked backward, he let her have a little more. Murmuring his name, she pushed back more strongly, trying to impale herself fully. But he only laughed softly and kept her where he wanted her, maintaining the voluptuous, metrical pitch.

He was utterly in control, appropriating her flesh with dizzying skill, letting her writhe and gasp for long minutes. Dragging the length of her hair to one side, he kissed the back of her neck, his mouth strong and gnawing. Everything he did drove her pleasure higher, and he knew it, gloried in it. Poppy felt the oncoming rush of fulfillment, her senses preparing for the hot tumble of release, and only then did he take her fully, driving hard and deep into her center.

Harry held her until she stopped trembling, her body limp with satisfaction. And then he pressed her to her back and whispered one word into her ear.

"Again."

It was a long and searing night, filled with unthinkable intimacy. After the third time, they snuggled in the darkness with Poppy's head on Harry's shoulder. It was lovely to lie with someone this way, talking about anything and everything, their bodies relaxed in the aftermath of passion.

"You fascinate me in every way," Harry whispered, his

hand playing gently in her hair. "There are mysteries in your soul that will take a lifetime to uncover . . . and I want to know every one of them."

No one had ever called her mysterious before. While Poppy didn't think of herself that way, she rather liked it. "I'm not all *that* mysterious, am I?"

"Of course you are." Smiling, he lifted her hand and pressed a kiss into the tender cup of her palm. "You're a woman."

Poppy went for a walk with Beatrix the next afternoon, while the rest of the family dispersed on various errands: Win and Amelia went to visit an ailing friend in the village, Leo and Merripen met with a prospective new tenant, and Cam had gone to a horse auction in Southampton.

Harry sat at a desk in the library with a detailed report from Jake Valentine. Relishing the peace and quiet—rare in the Hathaway household—he began to read. However, the sound of a floorboard creaking snagged his attention, and he looked toward the threshold.

Catherine Marks was standing there, book in hand, her cheeks pink. "Forgive me," she said. "I didn't mean to disturb you. I meant to return a book, but—"

"Come in," Harry said at once, rising from his chair. "You're not interrupting anything."

"I'll just be a moment." She hurried to a bookshelf, replaced the volume, and paused to glance at him. Light from the window gleamed on her spectacles, obscuring her eyes.

"Stay in here if you like," Harry said, feeling unaccountably awkward.

"No, thank you. It's a lovely day, and I thought I might walk through the gardens, or—" She stopped and shrugged uncomfortably.

God, how ill at ease they were with each other. Harry contemplated her for a moment, wondering what was troubling her. He had never known what to do with her, this unwanted half sister, what place in his life he could find for her. He had never wanted to care for Catherine, and yet she had always tugged at him, worried him, perplexed him.

"May I walk with you?" he asked huskily.

She blinked in surprise. Her answer was long in coming. "If you wish."

He went out with her to a small hedged garden, with heavy drifts of white and yellow daffodils all around. Squinting against the abundant sunshine, they walked along a graveled path.

Catherine gave him an unfathomable glance, her eyes like opals in the daylight. "I don't know you at all, Harry."

"You probably know me as well as anyone," Harry said. "Except for Poppy, of course."

"No, I don't," she said earnestly. "The way you've been this week . . . I would never have expected it of you. This affection you seem to have developed for Poppy—I find it quite astonishing."

"It's not an act," he said.

"I know. I can see that you're sincere. It's just that before the wedding, you said it didn't matter if Poppy's heart belonged to Mr. Bayning, as long as—"

"As long as I had the rest of her," Harry said, smiling in self-contempt. "I was an arrogant swine. I'm sorry, Cat." He paused. "I understand now why you feel so protective of Poppy and Beatrix. Of all of them. They're the closest thing to a family you've ever known."

"Or you."

An uncomfortable silence passed before Harry brought himself to admit, "Or I."

They stopped at a bench set alongside the path, and Catherine seated herself. "Will you?" she asked, gesturing to the space beside her.

He obliged, lowering to the bench and leaning forward with his elbows braced on his knees.

They were quiet but oddly companionable, both of them wishing for some kind of affinity, not knowing quite how to achieve it.

Harry decided to start with honesty. Taking a deep breath, he said gruffly, "I've never been kind to you, Cat. Especially when you needed it most."

"I would dispute that," she said, surprising him. "You rescued me from a very unpleasant situation, and you've given me the means to live handsomely without having to find employment. And you never demanded anything in return."

"I owed that much to you." He stared at her, taking in the rich golden glitter of her hair, the small oval of her face, the porcelain fineness of her skin. A frown pulled at his brow. Averting his gaze, he reached up to rub the back of his neck. "You look too damned much like our mother."

"I'm sorry," Catherine whispered.

"No, don't be sorry. You're beautiful, just as she was. More so. But sometimes it's difficult to see the resemblance, and not remember . . ." He let out a taut sigh. "When I found out about you, I resented you for having had so many more years with her than I'd had. It was only later that I realized I was the fortunate one."

A bitter smile touched her lips. "I don't think either of us could be accused of having had an excess of good fortune, Harry."

He responded with a humorless chuckle.

They continued to sit side by side, still and silent, close but not touching. The two of them had been raised not knowing how to give or receive love. The world had taught them lessons that would have to be unlearned. But sometimes life was unexpectedly generous, Harry mused. Poppy was proof of that.

"The Hathaways were a stroke of luck for me," Catherine

said, as if she had read his thoughts. She removed her spectacles and cleaned them with the edge of her sleeve. "Being with them these past three years . . . it's given me hope. It has been a time of healing."

"I'm glad of it," Harry said gently. "You deserve that, and more." He paused, searching for words. "Cat, I have something to ask you . . ."

"Yes?"

"Poppy wants to know more about my past. What may I tell her, if anything, about the part when I found you?"

Catherine replaced her spectacles and stared into a nearby blaze of daffodils. "Tell her everything," she said eventually. "She can be trusted with my secrets. And yours."

Harry nodded, silently amazed by a statement he once could never have imagined her making. "There's one more thing I want to ask of you. A favor. I understand the reasons we can't acknowledge each other in public. But in private, from now on, I hope you'll do me the honor of . . . well, letting me act as your brother."

She glanced at him with wide eyes, seeming too stunned to reply.

"We won't have to tell the rest of the family until you're ready," Harry said. "But I would rather not hide our relationship when we're in private. You're my only family."

Catherine reached beneath her spectacles to wipe at an escaping tear.

A feeling of compassion and tenderness came over Harry, something he had never felt for her before. Reaching out, he drew her close and kissed her forehead gently. "Let me be your big brother," he whispered.

SHE WATCHED IN WONDER AS HE WENT BACK TO THE HOUSE.

For a few minutes afterward Catherine sat alone on the bench, listening to the drone of a bee, the high, sweet chirps of common swifts, and the softer, more melodious twitters of skylarks. She wondered at the change that had come over Harry. She was half afraid he was playing some kind of game with her, with all of them, except . . . it had to be real. The emotion on his face, the sincerity in his eyes, all of it was undeniable. But how could someone's character alter so greatly?

Perhaps, she mused, it wasn't so much that Harry was being altered as he was being revealed . . . layer by layer, the defenses coming off. Perhaps Harry was becoming—or would become in time—the man he had always been meant to be. Because he had finally found someone who mattered.

Chapter Twenty-four

The mail coach had arrived at Stony Cross, and a footman was dispatched to fetch a stack of letters and parcels addressed to Ramsay House. The footman brought the deliveries to the back of the house, where Win and Poppy lounged on furniture that had been brought out to the brick-paved terrace. The largest parcel was addressed to Harry.

"More reports from Mr. Valentine?" Poppy asked, sipping sweet red wine as she curled next to Win on a chaise.

"It would appear so," Harry said with a self-mocking grin. "It appears the hotel is managing brilliantly in my absence. Perhaps I should have taken a holiday sooner."

Merripen went to Win and slipped his fingers beneath her chin. "How are you feeling?" he asked softly.

She smiled up at him. "Splendid."

He bent to kiss the top of Win's blond head, and sat in a nearby chair. One could see that he was trying to be at ease with the idea of his wife carrying a child, but his concern for her practically radiated from every pore.

Harry took the other chair and opened his parcel. After reading the first few lines of the top page, he made a sound of discomfort and winced visibly. "Good God."

"What is it?" Poppy asked.

"One of our regular guests—Lord Pencarrow—injured himself late last evening."

"Oh, dear." Poppy's brow furrowed. "And he's such a nice old gentleman. What happened? Did he take a fall?"

"Not exactly. He slid down the banister of the grand staircase, from the mezzanine level to the ground floor." Harry paused uncomfortably. "He made it all the way to the end of the balustrade—where he crashed into the pineapple ornament on top of the newel post."

"Why would a man in his eighties do such a thing?" Poppy asked in bewilderment.

Harry sent her a sardonic smile. "I imagine he was in his cups."

Merripen was cringing. "One can only be glad his child-siring years are behind him."

Harry paused to read a few more lines. "Apparently a doctor was summoned, and in his opinion the damage is not permanent."

"Is there any other news?" Win asked hopefully. "Something a bit more cheerful?"

Obligingly Harry continued to read, this time out loud. "I'm sorry to report another unfortunate incident that occurred Friday evening at eleven o'clock, involving—" He broke off, his gaze skimming swiftly down the page.

Before Harry managed to school his expression into impassiveness, Poppy saw that something was very wrong. He shook his head, not quite meeting her gaze. "It's nothing of interest."

"May I see?" Poppy asked gently, reaching for the page.

His fingers tightened on it. "It's not important."

"Let me," she insisted, tugging at the sheet of paper.

Win and Merripen were both quiet, exchanging a glance. Settling back on the chaise, Poppy glanced over the letter.

". . . involving Mr. Michael Bayning," she read aloud, "who appeared in the lobby without notice or warning, thoroughly inebriated and in a hostile temperament. He demanded to see you, Mr. Rutledge, and refused to accept that you were not in the hotel. To our alarm, he brandished a—" She stopped and took an extra breath. "A revolver, and made threats against you. We tried to bring him to the front office to calm him in private. A scuffle ensued, and regrettably Mr. Bayning was able to fire a shot before I was able to disarm him. Thankfully no one was injured, although there were many anxious queries from hotel patrons afterward, and the office ceiling must be repaired. Mr. Lufton took a bad fright from the incident and experienced pains in his chest, but the doctor prescribed a day of bed rest and said he should be right as rain tomorrow. As for Mr. Bayning, he was returned home safely, and I took the initiative to reassure his father that no charges would be pressed, as the viscount seemed quite concerned about the possibility of scandal . . ."

Poppy fell silent, feeling ill, shivering even though the sun was warm.

"Michael," she whispered.

Harry glanced sharply at her.

The carefree young man she had known would never have resorted to such sordid, irresponsible melodrama. Part of her ached for him, and part of her was appalled, and part was simply furious. Coming to her home—for that was how she thought of the hotel—making a scene, and worst of all, endangering people. He might have seriously injured someone, perhaps even killed someone. Dear God, there were children in the hotel—hadn't Michael spared a thought for their safety? And he had frightened poor Mr. Lufton into apoplexy.

Poppy's throat went tight, anger and misery stinging like pepper. She wished she could go to Michael right then and shout at him. And she wanted to shout at Harry as well, because no one could deny that the incident was a consequence of his perfidy.

Occupied with her roiling thoughts, she wasn't aware of how much time had passed before Harry broke the silence.

He spoke in the way she most hated: the amused, silky, callous tone of a man who didn't give a damn about anything.

"He ought to be more clever in his murder attempt. Done properly, he could make a wealthy widow of you, and then you'd both have your happy ending."

HARRY KNEW INSTANTLY THAT HE SHOULDN'T HAVE SAID it—the comment was the kind of cold-blooded sarcasm he had always resorted to when he felt the need to defend himself. He regretted it even before he saw Merripen out of the periphery of his vision. The Rom was giving him a warning shake of his head and drawing a finger across his throat.

Poppy was red faced, her brows drawn in a scowl. "What a dreadful thing to say!"

Harry cleared his throat. "I'm sorry," he said brusquely. "I was joking. It was in poor—" He ducked as something came flying at him. "What the devil—"

She had thrown something at him, a cushion.

"I don't want to be a widow, I don't want Michael Bayning, and I don't want you to joke about such things, you tactless *clodpole*!"

As all three of them stared at her openmouthed, Poppy leapt up and stalked away, her hands drawn into fists.

Bewildered by the immediate force of her fury—it was like being stung by a butterfly—Harry stared after her dumbly. After a moment, he asked the first coherent thought that came to him. "Did she just say she doesn't want Bayning?"

"Yes," Win said, a smile hovering on her lips. "That's what she said. Go after her, Harry."

Every cell in Harry's body longed to comply. Except that

he had the feeling of standing on the edge of a cliff, with one ill-chosen word likely to send him over. He gave Poppy's sister a desperate glance. "What should I say?"

"Be honest with her about your feelings," Win suggested.

A frown settled on Harry's face as he considered that. "What's my second option?"

"I'll handle this," Merripen told Win before she could reply. Standing, he slung a great arm across Harry's shoulders and walked him to the side of the terrace. Poppy's furious form could be seen in the distance. She was walking down the drive to the caretaker's house, her skirts and shoes kicking up tiny dust storms.

Merripen spoke in a low, not unsympathetic tone, as if compelled to guide a hapless fellow male away from danger. "Take my advice, *gadjo* . . . never argue with a woman when she's in this state. Tell her you were wrong and you're sorry as hell. And promise never to do it again."

"I'm still not exactly certain what I did," Harry said.

"That doesn't matter. Apologize anyway." Merripen paused and added in whisper, "And whenever your wife is angry . . . for God's sake, don't try logic."

"I heard that," Win said from the chaise.

HARRY CAUGHT UP WITH POPPY BY THE TIME SHE WAS halfway to the caretaker's house. She didn't glance at him, only glared ahead with her jaw set.

"You think I drove him to it," Harry said quietly, keeping pace with her. "You think I ruined his life as well as yours."

That fueled Poppy's outrage until she wasn't certain whether she might cry or slap him. Blast him, he was going to drive her mad.

She had been in love with a prince, and she had ended up in the arms of a villain, and it would be so much easier if she could continue to view everything in those simplistic terms. Except that her prince was not nearly as perfect as he had seemed . . . and her villain was a caring, passionate man.

It was finally becoming clear to her that love wasn't about finding someone perfect to marry. Love was about seeing through to the truth of a person, and accepting all their shades of light and dark. Love was an ability. And Harry had it in abundance, even if he wasn't ready to come to terms with it yet.

"Don't presume to tell me what I think," she said. "You're wrong on both counts. Michael is responsible for his own behavior, which in this case was—" she paused to deliver a vicious kick to a stray pebble, "—revoltingly self-indulgent. Immature. I'm sorely disappointed in him."

"I can't blame him," Harry said. "I would have done far worse, were I in his position."

"Of that I have no doubt," Poppy said acidly.

He scowled but remained silent.

Approaching another pebble, Poppy kicked it with a vicious swipe of her foot. "I hate it when you say cynical things," she burst out. "That stupid remark about making me a wealthy widow—"

"I shouldn't have," Harry said quickly. "That was unfair, and wrong. I should have considered that you were distressed because you still care for him, and—"

Poppy stopped dead in her tracks, staring at him with scornful astonishment. "*Oh*! How a man whom everyone considers so intelligent can be such an *imbecile*—" Shaking her head, she continued to storm along the drive.

Bewildered, Harry followed at her heels.

"Does it not occur to you," her words came winging over her shoulder like angry bats, "that I might not like the idea of someone making threats against your life? That I might be just the *least* little bit bothered by someone coming to our home waving a gun about with the intention of shooting you?"

It took Harry a long time to answer. In fact, they had nearly reached the house by the time he replied, his voice thick and odd. "You're concerned for my safety? For . . . me?"

"Someone has to be," she muttered, stomping to the front door. "I'm sure I don't know why it's me."

Poppy reached for the handle, but Harry stunned her by flinging it open, whisking her inside, and slamming it shut. Before she could even draw breath, he had pushed her back up against the door, a bit rough in his eagerness.

She had never seen him look quite this way, incredulous, anxious, yearning.

His body crowded hers, his breath falling in swift strikes against her cheek. She saw a visible pulse in the strong plane of his throat. "Poppy . . . are you . . ." He was forced to pause, as if he were fumbling to speak in a foreign language.

Which he was, in a way.

Poppy knew what Harry wanted to ask, and yet she didn't want him to. He was forcing the issue—it was too soon—she wanted to beg him to be patient, for both their sakes.

He managed to get the words out. "Are you starting to care for me, Poppy?"

"No," she said firmly, but that didn't seem to put him off at all.

Harry leaned his face against hers, his lips parting against her cheek in a nuzzling half kiss. "Not even a little?" he whispered.

"Not the slightest bit."

He pressed the side of his cheek to hers, his lips playing with the wisps of hair at her ear. "Why won't you say it?"

He was so large and warm, and everything in her wanted to surrender to him. A fine trembling started inside her, radiating outward from her bones to her skin. "Because if I did, you wouldn't be able to run from me fast enough."

"I would never run from you."

"Yes, you would. You'd turn distant and push me away, because you're not nearly ready to take such a risk yet."

Harry pressed the front of his body all along hers, his forearms braced on either side of her head. "Say it," he urged, tender and predatory. "I want to hear what it sounds like."

Poppy had never thought it was possible to be amused and aroused at the same time. "No, you don't." Slowly, her arms went around his lean waist.

If only Harry knew the extent of what she felt for him. The very second she judged that he was ready, the moment she was certain it wouldn't cause their marriage to lose ground, she would tell him how dearly she loved him. She could hardly wait.

"I'll make you say it," Harry said, his sensuous mouth covering hers, his hands going to the fastenings of her bodice.

Poppy couldn't control a shiver of anticipation. No, he wouldn't . . . but for the next few hours, she would certainly enjoy letting him try.

Chapter Twenty-five

To the Hathaways' general surprise, Leo elected to return to London the same day as the Rutledges. His original intention had been to stay in Hampshire the remainder of the summer, but he had decided instead to take on a small commission to design a conservatory addition to a Mayfair mansion. Poppy wondered privately if his change of plan had anything to do with Miss Marks. She suspected they had quarreled, because it seemed they were going to great extremes to avoid each other now. Even more than usual.

"You can't go," Merripen had said in outrage when Leo told him he was heading back to London. "We're preparing to sow the turnip crop. There is much to be decided, including the composition of the manure, and how best to approach the harrowing and plowing, and—"

"Merripen," Leo had interrupted sarcastically, "I know you consider my help to be invaluable in these matters, but I believe that somehow you'll all manage to drill turnip seed competently without my involvement. As for the manure composition, I can't help you there. I have a very democratic view of excrement—it's all shit to me."

Merripen had responded with a volley of Romany that

no one except Cam could understand. And Cam refused to translate a word of it, claiming there were no English equivalents and that was a good thing.

After making his farewells, Leo left for London in his carriage. Harry and Poppy were slower to depart, having a last cup of tea, a last lingering glimpse of the green summer-dressed estate.

"I'm almost surprised you're letting me take her," Harry said to Cam after handing his wife into the carriage.

"Oh, we voted this morning, and it was a unanimous decision," his brother-in-law replied in a matter-of-fact tone.

"You voted on my marriage?"

"Yes, we decided you fit in with the family quite well."

"Oh, God," Harry said, just as Cam closed the carriage door.

AFTER A PLEASANT AND UNEVENTFUL JOURNEY, THE RUT-ledges arrived in London. To discerning outsiders, particularly the hotel employees, it was clear that Poppy and Harry had acquired the mysterious and intangible bond of two people who had made a promise to each other. They were a couple.

Although Poppy was happy to return to the Rutledge, she had a few private concerns about how her relationship with Harry would proceed—if perhaps he might slip back into his former habits. To her reassurance, Harry had firmly set a new course, and he seemed to have no intention of deviating from it.

The differences in him were observed with gratified wonder by the hotel staff the first full day of his return. Poppy had brought back gifts, including jars of honey for the managers and everyone in the front office, a length of bobbin lace for Mrs. Pennywhistle, cured Hampshire hams and sides of smoked bacon for Chef Broussard and Chef Rupert and the kitchen staff, and for Jake Valentine, a sheep hide that had been tanned and polished with smooth stones until the material had been worked into butter-soft glove leather.

After delivering the presents, Poppy sat in the kitchen and chattered animatedly about her visit to Hampshire. ". . . and we found a dozen truffles," she told Chef Broussard, "each one nearly as large as my fist. All at the roots of a beech tree, and barely a half inch beneath the soil. And guess how we discovered them? My sister's pet ferret! He ran over to them and started nibbling."

Broussard sighed dreamily. "When I was a boy, I lived in Périgord for a time. The truffles there would make one weep. So delicious and dear, they were usually only eaten by nobles and their kept women." He looked at Poppy expectantly. "How did you prepare them?"

"We chopped some leeks and sautéed them in butter and cream, and—" She paused as she noticed the staff in a sudden flurry of activity, scrubbing, chopping, stirring. Glancing over her shoulder, she saw that Harry had entered the kitchen.

"Sir," Mrs. Pennywhistle said, while she and Jake stood to face him.

Harry motioned for them to stay seated. "Good morning," he said with a slight smile. "Forgive me for interrupting." He came to stand beside Poppy, who was perched on a stool. "Mrs. Rutledge," he murmured, "I wonder if I might steal you away for just a few minutes? There's a . . ." His voice faded as he stared into his wife's face. She had looked up at him with a flirting little grin that had apparently disrupted his train of thought.

And who could blame him? Jake Valentine thought, both amused and similarly mesmerized. Although Poppy Rutledge had always been a beautiful woman, there was an extra glow about her now, a new brilliance in her blue eyes.

"The carriage maker," Harry said, recollecting himself. "They've just delivered your carriage. I hoped you might come look at it, and make certain everything is to your satisfaction."

"Yes, I'd love to." Poppy took another bite of her brioche, a warm puff of glazed bread touched with butter and jam. She held the last bit up to Harry's lips. "Help me finish?"

They all watched in astonishment as Harry took the tidbit obligingly into his mouth. And, holding her wrist in his hand, he nipped at her fingertip to remove a little spot of jam. "Delicious," he said, helping her from the stool. He glanced at the three of them. "I'll return her shortly. And Valentine . . ."

"Yes, sir?"

"It's come to my attention that you haven't gone on holiday in far too long. I want you to arrange something for yourself immediately."

"I wouldn't know what to do on holiday," Jake protested, and Harry smiled.

"That, Valentine, is why you need one."

After Harry had escorted his wife from the kitchen, Jake looked at the others with a dumbfounded expression. "He's an entirely different man," he said dazedly.

Mrs. Pennywhistle smiled. "No, he'll always be Harry Rutledge. It's just that now . . . he's Harry Rutledge with a heart."

As the hotel was a virtual clearinghouse of gossip, Poppy was privy to scandals and private disclosures concerning people from every part of London. To her dismay, there were persistent rumors about the continuing decline of Michael Bayning . . . his frequent public drunkenness, gambling, brawling, and all manner of behavior unbecoming to a man of his position. Some of the rumors were linked to

Poppy, of course, and her precipitate wedding to Harry. It saddened Poppy profoundly to hear what a mess Michael was making of his life, and she wished there were something she could do about it.

"It's the one subject I can't discuss with Harry," she told Leo, visiting his terrace one afternoon. "It puts him in a dreadful temper—he gets very quiet and stern faced, and last night we actually quarreled about it."

Taking a cup of tea from her, Leo arched a sardonic brow at the information. "Sis, as much as I would prefer to take your side in all things . . . why should you *want* to discuss Michael Bayning with your husband? And what the devil is there to argue about? That chapter in your life is closed. Were I married—and thank God I never will be—I wouldn't welcome the subject of Bayning with any more enthusiasm than Harry apparently does."

Poppy frowned into her own cup of tea, slowly stirring a sugar lump into the steaming amber liquid. She waited until it had thoroughly dissolved before replying. "I'm afraid Harry took exception to a request I made. I said I wanted to visit Michael, and that perhaps I might be able to talk some sense into him." As she saw Leo's expression, she added defensively, "Only for a few minutes! A *supervised* visit. I even told Harry he was welcome to accompany me. But he forbade me in a very overbearing manner, without even letting me explain why I—"

"He should have put you over his knee," Leo informed her. As her mouth fell open, he set his tea down, made her do the same, and took both her hands in his. His expression was a comical mixture of reproof and sympathy. "Darling Poppy, you have a kind heart. And I've no doubt that for you, visiting Bayning is a mission of mercy comparable to Beatrix rescuing a rabbit from a snare. But this is where it becomes clear that you are still woefully ignorant of men. Since it falls to me to explain to you . . . we're not nearly as civilized as you seem to think. In fact, we were much happier in the days when we could simply chase off a rival at spearpoint. Therefore, asking Harry to allow you—by all accounts, the only person on earth he actually gives a damn about—to visit Bayning and soothe his wounded feelings . . ." Leo shook his head.

"But Leo," Poppy protested, "you remember the days when you were doing the same things that Michael is doing. I would have thought you'd have sympathy for him."

Letting go of her hands, Leo smiled, but it didn't reach his eyes. "The circumstances were a bit different. I had to watch a girl I loved die in my arms. And yes, afterward I behaved very badly. Even worse than Bayning. But a man on that path can't be rescued, sweetheart. He has to follow it off a cliff. Perhaps Bayning will survive the fall, perhaps not. In either case . . . no, I have no sympathy for him."

Poppy picked up her tea and took a hot, bracing swallow. Presented with Leo's viewpoint, she felt uncertain and even a bit sheepish. "I'll let the matter drop, then," she said. "I may have been wrong to ask it of Harry. Perhaps I should apologize to him."

"Now that," Leo said softly, "is one of the things I've always adored about you, sis. The willingness to reconsider, and even change your mind."

After her visit to her brother had concluded, Poppy went to the jeweler's shop on Bond Street. She retrieved a gift that she'd had made for Harry, and returned to the hotel.

Thankfully, she and Harry had planned to have supper sent up to their apartment that night. It would allow her the time and privacy she needed to discuss their argument of the previous evening. And she would apologize. In her desire to help Michael Bayning, she hadn't stopped to consider Harry's feelings, and she wanted very much to atone.

The situation reminded her of something her mother had often said about marriage: "Never remember his mistakes, but always remember your own."

After taking a perfumed bath, Poppy donned a light blue dressing gown and brushed out her hair, leaving it loose in the way he liked.

Harry entered the apartment as the clock struck seven. He looked more like the Harry she remembered from the beginning of their marriage, his face grim and tired, his gaze wintry.

"Hello," she murmured, going to kiss him. Harry held still, not rebuffing her, but he was hardly warm or encouraging. "I'll send for dinner," she said. "And then we can—"

"None for me, thank you. I'm not hungry."

Taken aback by his flat tone, Poppy regarded him with concern. "Did something happen today? You look all in."

Harry shrugged out of his coat and laid it on a chair. "I've just returned from a meeting at the War Office, where I told Sir Gerald and Mr. Kinloch that I've decided not to work on the new gun design. They receive my decision as nothing short of treason. Kinloch even threatened to lock me in a room somewhere until I'd come up with a set of drawings."

"I'm sorry." Poppy grimaced in sympathy. "That must have been dreadful. Are you . . . are you disappointed that you won't be doing the work for them?"

Harry shook his head. "As I told them, there are better things I could do for my fellow countrymen. Working on agricultural technology, for one thing. Putting food in a man's belly is a vast improvement over inventing a more efficient way to put a bullet in him."

Poppy smiled. "That was well done of you, Harry."

But he didn't return the smile, only leveled a cool, speculative stare at her. His head tilted a bit. "Where were you today?"

Poppy's pleasure dissolved as she understood.

He was suspicious of her.

He thought she had gone to visit Michael.

The injustice of that, and the hurt of being mistrusted, caused her face to stiffen. She answered in a brittle voice. "I went out for an errand or two."

"What kind of errand?"

"I'd rather not say."

Harry's face was hard and implacable. "I'm afraid I'm not giving you a choice. You will tell me where you went and whom you saw."

Reddening in outrage, Poppy whirled away from him and clenched her fists. "I don't have to account for every minute of my day, not even to you."

"Today you do." His eyes narrowed. "Tell me, Poppy."

She laughed incredulously. "So you can verify my statements, and decide whether I'm lying to you?"

His silence was answer enough.

Hurt and furious, Poppy went to her reticule, which had been set on a small table, and rummaged in it. "I went to visit Leo," she snapped without looking at him. "He'll vouch for me, and so will the driver. And afterward I went to Bond Street to pick up something I had bought for you. I had wanted to wait for an appropriate moment to give it to you, but apparently that's not possible now."

Extracting an object encased in a small velvet pouch, she resisted the temptation to throw it at him. "Here's your proof," she muttered, pushing it into his hands. "I knew you would never get one of these on your own."

Harry opened the pouch slowly, and let the object slide into his hand.

It was a pocket watch with a solid gold casing, exquisitely simple except for the engraved initials *JHR* on the lid.

There was a perplexing lack of reaction from Harry. His

dark head was bent so that Poppy couldn't even see his face. His fingers closed around the watch, and he let out a long, deep breath.

Wondering if she had done the wrong thing, Poppy turned blindly to the bellpull. "I hope you like it," she said evenly. "I'll ring for dinner now. I'm hungry, even if you're—"

All at once Harry seized her from behind, wrapping his arms around her, one hand still gripped around the watch. His entire body was trembling, powerful muscles threatening to crush her. His voice was low and remorseful.

"I'm sorry."

Poppy relaxed against him as he continued to hold her. She closed her eyes.

"Damn it," he said into the loose sheaf of her hair, "I'm so sorry. It's just that the thought of you having any feelings for Bayning . . . it . . . doesn't bring out the best in me."

"There's an understatement," Poppy said darkly. But she turned in his arms and pressed against him, her hand sliding up to the back of his head.

"It tortures me," he admitted gruffly. "I don't want you to care for any man but me. Even if I don't deserve it."

Poppy's hurt faded as she reflected that the experience of being loved was still very new to Harry. The problem wasn't a lack of trust in her, it was a result of his own self-doubt. Harry would probably always be possessive where she was concerned.

"Jealous," she accused softly, pulling his head down to her shoulder.

"Yes."

"Well, there's no need for it. The only feelings I have for Michael Bayning are pity and kindness." She brushed her lips against his ear. "Did you see the engraving on the watch? No? . . . It's inside the lid. Look."

But Harry didn't move, didn't do anything except hold her

as if she were a lifeline. She suspected he was too overcome to do anything at the moment. "It's a quote by Erasmus," she said helpfully. "My father's favorite monk, after Roger Bacon. The watch is inscribed, 'It is the chiefest point of happiness that a man is willing to be what he is.'" At Harry's continued silence, she couldn't help throwing more words into the void. "I want you to be happy, you exasperating man. I want you to understand that I love you for exactly what you are."

Harry's breathing turned hard and rough. He held her in a grip that would have taken a hundred men to break. "I love you, Poppy," he said raggedly. "I love you so much that it's absolute hell."

She tried to suppress a smile. "Why is it hell?" she asked sympathetically, stroking his nape.

"Because I have so much to lose now. But I'm going to love you anyway, because there doesn't seem to be any way to stop doing it." He kissed her forehead, eyelids, cheeks. "I have so much love for you, I could fill rooms with it. Buildings. You're surrounded by it wherever you go, you walk through it, breathe it . . . it's in your lungs, and under your tongue, and between your fingers and toes . . ." His mouth moved passionately over hers, urging her lips apart.

It was a kiss to level mountains and shake stars from the sky. It was a kiss to make angels faint and demons weep . . . a passionate, demanding, soul-searing kiss that nearly knocked the earth off its axis.

Or at least that was how Poppy felt about it.

Harry swept her up in his arms and carried her to the bed. He lowered over her and smoothed the rich tumble of her hair. "I never want to be apart from you," he said. "I'm going to buy an island and take you there. A ship will come once a month with supplies. The rest of the time it will be just the two of us, wearing leaves and eating exotic fruit and making love on the beach . . ."

"You'd start a produce export business and organize a local economy within a month," she said flatly.

Harry groaned as he recognized the truth of it. "God. Why do you tolerate me?"

Poppy grinned and slid her arms around his neck. "I like the side benefits," she told him. "And really, it's only fair since you tolerate *me*."

"You're perfect," Harry said with heated earnestness. "Everything about you, everything you do or say. And even if you have a little flaw here or there . . ."

"Flaws?" she asked in mock indignation.

". . . I love those best of all."

Harry undressed her, his efforts hindered by the fact that Poppy was trying to undress him at the same time. They rolled and struggled with their clothing, and despite the intensity of their mutual need, a few gasps of laughter escaped as they found themselves in a hopeless tangle of fabric and limbs. Finally, they both emerged naked and panting.

Harry hooked a hand beneath her knee, widening the spread of her thighs, and he took possession of her in a forceful plunge. Poppy cried out, quivering in surprise at the power of his rhythm. His body was elegant and strong, claiming her in demanding thrusts. Her breasts were cupped in his hands, his mouth covering a taut peak, and he suckled her in time to the lunges of his hips.

A deep flush came over her, the hard slide of his flesh in hers offering exquisite relief and erotic torment. She moaned and struggled to match his rhythm as ripples of pleasure went through her, stronger and stronger until she couldn't move at all. And he drank in her sobs with his mouth, making love to her until she eventually quieted, her body replete with sensation.

Harry stared down at her intently, his face gleaming with perspiration, eyes tiger bright. Poppy wrapped her arms and legs around him, trying to absorb him, wanting him as close as physically possible. "I love you, Harry," she said. The words made him catch his breath, shudders resounding through his body. "I love you," she repeated, and he surged inside her, hard and deep, and found his release. She curled up against him afterward, while his hand played gently in her hair. They slept together, dreamed together, all barriers finally gone.

And the next day, Harry disappeared.

Chapter Twenty-six

For a man who revered schedules as much as Harry, being late was not only unusual, it was akin to atrocity. Therefore, when he didn't return to the hotel from an afternoon visit to his fencing club, Poppy was more than a little concerned. When three hours had passed and her husband still wasn't back, she rang for Jake Valentine.

The assistant came at once, his expression perturbed, his brown hair in disarray as if he'd been tugging on it distractedly.

"Mr. Valentine," Poppy said with a frown, "do you know anything about Mr. Rutledge's whereabouts at present?"

"No, ma'am. The driver just returned without him."

"What?" she asked, bewildered.

"The driver waited at the usual time and place, and when Mr. Rutledge didn't appear after an hour, he went inside the club to make inquiries. A search was done. Apparently Mr. Rutledge was nowhere to be found on the premises. The master of the fencing club asked various members if they had seen Mr. Rutledge go off with someone, perhaps enter a carriage, or even mention his plans, but no one had seen or heard anything after Mr. Rutledge finished his practice." Valentine paused and drew the side of his fist over his mouth, a nervous gesture Poppy had never seen him make before. "He seems to have vanished."

"Has this ever happened before?" she asked.

Valentine shook his head.

They stared at each other in the mutual recognition that something was very wrong.

"I'll go back to the club and search again," Valentine said. "Someone had to have seen something."

Poppy steeled herself to wait. Perhaps it was nothing, she told herself. Perhaps Harry had gone somewhere with an acquaintance, and he would return any moment. But she knew instinctively that something had happened to him. It seemed her blood had turned to ice water . . . she was shaky, numb, terrified. She paced around the apartments, and then she went downstairs to the front office, where the receptionist and concierge were similarly distracted.

Evening had settled deeply over London by the time Valentine finally returned. "Not a trace of him anywhere," he said.

Poppy felt a chill of fear. "We must notify the police."

He nodded. "I already have. I once received instructions from Mr. Rutledge in case something like this ever occurred. I've notified a Special Constable who works from the Bow Street office, and also a South London cracksman named William Edgar."

"Cracksman? What is that?"

"Thief. And from time to time he does a bit of smuggling. Mr. Edgar is familiar with every street and rookery in London."

"My husband instructed you to contact a constable and a criminal?"

Valentine looked a bit sheepish. "Yes, ma'am."

Poppy put her fingertips to her temples, trying to calm her

racing thoughts. A painful sob rose in her throat before she could swallow it back down. She dragged a sleeve across her wet eyes. "If he's not found by morning," she said, taking the handkerchief he handed to her, "I want to post a reward for any information that leads to his safe return." She blew her nose indelicately. "Five thousand—no, ten thousand pounds."

"Yes, ma'am."

"And we should give a list to the police."

Valentine looked at her blankly. "A list of what?"

"Of all the people who might wish to do him harm."

"That won't be easy," Valentine muttered. "Most of the time I can't tell the difference between his friends and his enemies. Some of his friends would love to kill him, and one or two of his enemies have actually named their children after him."

"I think Mr. Bayning should be considered a suspect," Poppy said.

"I had thought of that," Valentine admitted. "In light of the recent threats he's made."

"And the meeting at the War Office yesterday—Harry said they were displeased with him, and he—" Her breath stopped. "He said something about Mr. Kinloch, that he wanted to lock Harry away somewhere."

"I'll go tell the Special Constable immediately," Valentine said. Seeing the way Poppy's eyes flooded and her mouth contorted, he added hastily, "We'll find him. I promise. And remember that whatever Mr. Rutledge is dealing with, he knows how to take care of himself."

Unable to reply, Poppy nodded and pressed the wadded-up handkerchief to her nose.

As soon as Valentine had departed, she spoke to the concierge in a tear-clotted voice. "Mr. Lufton, may I write a note at your desk?"

"Oh, certainly, ma'am!" He arranged paper, ink, and a pen with a steel nib on the desk, and stood back respectfully as she began to write.

"Mr. Lufton, I want this taken to my brother, Lord Ramsay, immediately. He is going to help me search for Mr. Rutledge."

"Yes, ma'am, but . . . do you think that wise at this hour? I'm sure Mr. Rutledge would not want you to compromise your safety by going out at night."

"I'm sure he wouldn't, Mr. Lufton. But I can't wait here without doing something. I'll go mad."

To Poppy's vast relief, Leo came at once, his cravat askew and his waistcoat unbuttoned, as if he'd dressed hastily. "What's going on?" he asked shortly. "And what did you mean, 'Harry's gone missing?' "

Poppy described the situation as quickly as possible, and curled her fingers into his sleeve. "Leo, I need you to take me somewhere."

She saw from her brother's face that he understood immediately. "Yes, I know." He let out a taut sigh. "I had better start praying that Harry won't be found for a good long while. Because when he learns that I took you to see Michael Bayning, my life won't be worth a tin of oysters."

After questioning Michael's manservant as to his whereabouts, Leo and Poppy went to Marlow's, a club so exclusive that one could only belong if his grandfather and father had been counted among its former members. The ennobled crowd at Marlow's looked down on the rest of the populace—including less-privileged bluebloods—with undiluted disdain. Having always been curious to see the inside of the place, Leo was more than pleased to go there in search of Michael Bayning.

"You won't be allowed past the door," Poppy said. "You're precisely the kind of person they want to keep out."

"I'll merely tell them Bayning is a suspect in a kidnapping plot, and if they don't let me look for him, I'll see that they're charged as accessories."

Poppy watched through the carriage window as Leo went up to the Marlow's classical white stone and stucco façade. After a minute or two of conversation with the doorman, Leo went into the club.

Folding her arms tightly, Poppy tried to warm herself. She felt cold from the inside out, ill with panic. Harry was somewhere in London, perhaps injured, and she couldn't reach him. She couldn't do anything for him. Remembering what Catherine had told her about Harry's childhood, that he had been locked in a room for two days with no one giving a thought to him, she nearly burst into tears.

"I'll find you," she whispered, rocking a little in her seat. "I'll be there soon. Just a little longer, Harry."

The carriage door was wrenched open with startling suddenness.

Leo stood there with Michael Bayning, who was shockingly ravaged by his recent habits of excess. His fine clothes and meticulously tied cravat only served to accentuate the bloat of his jaw and the ruddy web of broken capillaries on his cheeks.

Poppy stared at him blankly. "Michael?"

"He's halfway pickled," Leo told her, "but coherent."

"Mrs. Rutledge," Michael said, his lip curling in a sneer. As he spoke, the scent of strong spirits wafted into the carriage. "Your husband's gone missing, has he? It seems I'm supposed to spout some kind of information about it. Problem is . . ." He averted his face and suppressed a quiet belch. "I haven't any."

Poppy's eyes narrowed. "I don't believe you. I think you had something to do with his disappearance."

He gave her a distorted smile. "I've been here for the past

four hours, and before that I was at my home. I'm sorry to say I haven't arranged any underhanded plot to harm him."

"You've made no secret of your animosity," Leo pointed out. "You've made threats against him. You even came to the hotel with a revolver. You're the most likely person to have been involved in his disappearance."

"Much as I'd like to claim responsibility," Michael said, "I can't. The satisfaction of killing him isn't worth being hanged for it." His bloodshot eyes focused on Poppy. "How do you know he hasn't decided to spend the evening with some lightskirt? He's probably tired of you now. Go home, Mrs. Rutledge, and pray that he doesn't come back. You're better off without the bastard."

Poppy blinked as if she'd been slapped.

Leo interceded coolly. "You'll be answering scores of questions about Harry Rutledge in the next day or two, Bayning. Everyone, including your friends, will be pointing fingers in your direction. By tomorrow morning, half of London will be looking for him. You could spare yourself a great deal of trouble by helping us resolve the matter now."

"I've told you, I had nothing to do with it," Michael snapped. "But I hope to hell that he's found soon—facedown in the Thames."

"*Enough*," Poppy cried in outrage. Both men glanced at her in surprise. "That is beneath you, Michael! Harry wronged both of us, it's true, but he apologized and tried to make reparations."

"Not to me, by God!"

Poppy gave him an incredulous glance. "You want an apology from him?"

"No." He glared at her, and then a hoarse note of pleading entered his voice. "I want you."

She flushed with fury. "That will never be possible. And

it never was. Your father wouldn't have consented to have me as his daughter-in-law, because he considered me beneath him. And the truth is that you did, too, or you would have managed everything far differently than you did."

"I'm not a snob, Poppy. I'm conventional. There's a difference."

She shook her head impatiently—it was an argument she didn't want to waste precious time on. "It doesn't matter. I've come to love my husband. I will never leave him. So for your sake as well as mine, stop making a spectacle and a nuisance of yourself, and go on with your life. You were meant for better things than this."

"Well said," Leo muttered, climbing into the carriage. "Let's go, Poppy. We'll get nothing else out of him."

Michael grabbed the edge of the door before Leo could close it. "Wait," he said to Poppy. "If it turns out that something has happened to your husband . . . will you come to me?"

She looked into his pleading face and shook her head, unable to believe he would ask such a thing. "No, Michael," she said quietly. "I'm afraid you're too conventional to suit me."

And Leo closed the door in Michael Bayning's astonished face.

Poppy stared at her brother desperately. "Do you think Michael had anything to do with Harry's disappearance?"

"No." Leo reached up to signal the driver. "He's not in a condition to plot anything other than where he's going to find his next drink. I think he's essentially a decent lad, drowning in self-pity." Seeing her distraught expression, he took her hand and squeezed it comfortingly. "Let's go back to the hotel. Perhaps there'll be some word about Harry."

She was silent and bleak, her thoughts taking the shape of nightmares.

As the carriage jounced along the street, Leo sought for

a remark to distract her. "The interior of Marlow's wasn't nearly as pleasant as I'd expected. Oh, there was quite bit of mahogany paneling and nice carpeting, but the air was difficult to breathe."

"Why?" Poppy asked glumly. "Was it filled with cigar smoke?"

"No," he said. "Smugness."

BY MORNING, HALF OF LONDON WAS INDEED LOOKING FOR Harry. Poppy had spent a sleepless night waiting for news of her husband, while Leo and Jake Valentine had been out searching gentlemen's clubs, taverns, and gaming halls. Although Poppy was frustrated by her own enforced inactivity, she knew that everything possible was being done. The cracksman, Mr. Edgar, had promised to use his network of thieves to find any possible scrap of information about Harry's disappearance.

Special Constable Hembrey, for his part, had been exceedingly busy. Sir Gerald at the War Office had confirmed that Edward Kinloch had threatened Harry during their meeting. Subsequently, Hembrey had procured a search warrant from one of the Bow Street magistrates, and had questioned Kinloch early in the morning. However, a thorough search of Kinloch's residence had revealed no trace of Harry.

The Home Secretary, who was the acting head of the Metropolitan Police Force, had directed his Criminal Investigation Unit—comprised of two inspectors and four sergeants—to apply their skills to the case. They were all engaged in questioning various individuals, including employees at the fencing club and some of Edward Kinloch's servants.

"It's as if he's disappeared into thin air," Jake Valentine said wearily, lowering himself into a chair in the Rutledge apartment, taking a cup of tea from Poppy. He gave her a haggard glance. "Are there any problems with the hotel? I haven't seen the managers' reports—"

"I went over them this morning," Poppy said scratchily, understanding that Harry would want his business to continue as usual. "It gave me something to do. There are no problems with the hotel." She rubbed her face with both hands. "No problems," she repeated bleakly, "except that Harry is missing."

"He'll be found," Valentine said. "Soon. There's no way he can *not* be found."

Their conversation was interrupted as Leo entered the apartment. "Come with me, Valentine," he said. "Bow Street has just sent word they have at least three men claiming to be Harry Rutledge, along with their 'rescuers.' It's assumed they're all impostors, but I thought we'd go have a look at them in any case."

"I'm going, too," Poppy said.

Leo gave her a dark look. "You wouldn't ask to go if you knew what kind of riffraff parades through that office every day."

"I'm not asking," Poppy said. "I'm telling you that you're not going without me."

Leo contemplated her for a moment, and sighed. "Fetch your cloak."

The Bow Street court was universally regarded as the foremost London magistrates' court, where the most publicized criminal cases were investigated and prosecuted. The Metropolitan Police Act had been passed more than twenty years earlier, resulting in the formation of what was still called the "New Police."

However, there still remained a few law enforcement establishments outside the Home Secretary's direct control, and Bow Street was one of them. Its mounted patrol and half-dozen Runners were answerable only to the Bow Street magistrates. Oddly, the Bow Street enforcement office had never been given a statutory basis for its authority. But that didn't seem to matter to anyone. When results were needed, one went to Bow Street.

The two buildings that comprised the court and office, nos. 3 and 4, were plain and unassuming, giving little hint as to the power that was wielded inside.

Poppy approached Bow Street with Leo and Valentine, her eyes widening as she saw throngs of people milling around the building and along the street. "Don't speak to anyone," Leo told her, "don't stand close to anyone, and if you hear, smell, or see something offensive, don't say you weren't warned."

As they entered no. 3, they were surrounded by the mingled smells of bodies, sweat, brass polish, and plaster. A narrow hallway led to various holding rooms, charge rooms, and offices. Every inch of the hallway was occupied with jostling bodies, the air thick with exclamations and complaints.

"Hembrey," Jake Valentine called out, and a lean man with close-cropped gray hair turned toward him. The man possessed a long, narrow face and intelligent dark eyes. "He's the Special Constable," Valentine told Poppy as the man made his way toward them.

"Mr. Valentine," Hembrey said, "I've just arrived to discover this lunatic gathering."

"What's happening?" Leo asked.

Hembrey's attention switched to him. "My lord, Mr. Rutledge's disappearance was reported in the *Times* this morning, along with the promise of reward money. And his physical description was given. With the result that every tall, dark-haired swindler in London will appear at Bow Street today. The same thing is occurring at Scotland Yard."

Poppy's jaw dropped as she glanced at the gathering in the hallway and realized that at least half of them were men who vaguely resembled her husband. "They're . . . they're all claiming to be Harry?" she asked dazedly.

"It would seem so," Leo said. "Accompanied by their heroic rescuers, who have their hands out for the reward money."

"Come to my office," Special Constable Hembrey urged, leading them along the hallway. "We'll have more privacy there, and I'll apprise you of my latest information. Leads have been pouring in . . . people claiming to have seen Rutledge drugged and put aboard a ship to China, or robbed at some brothel, things of that nature . . ."

Poppy and Valentine followed Leo and Hembrey. "This is abominable," she told Valentine in a low tone, glancing at the line of imposters. "All of them posturing and lying, hoping to profit from someone else's misfortune."

They were forced to pause as Hembrey tried to clear a path to the doorway of his office.

One of the black-haired men nearest Poppy bowed theatrically. "Harry Rutledge, at your service. And who might you be, my fair creature?"

Poppy glared at him. "Mrs. Rutledge," she said curtly.

Immediately another man exclaimed, "Darling!" He held his arms out to Poppy, who shrank away and gave him an appalled glance.

"Idiots," Hembrey muttered, and raised his voice. "Clerk! Find some place to put all these damned Rutledges so they don't crowd the hallway."

"Yes, sir!"

They entered the office, and Hembrey closed the door firmly. "A pleasure to make your acquaintance, Mrs. Rutledge. I assure you, we're doing everything possible to locate your husband."

"My brother, Lord Ramsay," she said, and Hembrey bowed respectfully.

"What is the latest information?" Leo asked.

Hembrey went to pull out a chair for Poppy, speaking all the while. "A stable boy in the mews behind the fencing club said that around the time of Mr. Rutledge's disappearance, he saw two men carrying a body through the alley out to a waiting carriage."

Poppy sat hard in the chair. "A body?" she whispered, cold sweat breaking out on her face, nausea rising.

"I'm sure he was only unconscious," Valentine told her hastily.

"The stableboy had a glimpse of the carriage," Hembrey continued, returning to his side of the desk. "He described it to us as black lacquer with a small pattern of rosemaled scrollwork across the boot. The description matches a brougham in the mews of Mr. Kinloch's Mayfair residence."

"What next?" Leo asked, his blue eyes hard.

"I intend to bring him here for questioning. And we'll proceed by taking inventory of Mr. Kinloch's other properties—his arms manufactory, realty he may own in town—and obtain warrants to search them methodically."

"How do you know for certain that Rutledge isn't being held in the Mayfair house?" Leo asked.

"I went over every inch of it personally. I can assure you that he is not there."

"Is the warrant still valid?" Leo persisted.

"Yes, my lord."

"Then you can return to Kinloch's house for another search? Right now?"

The Special Constable looked perplexed. "Yes, but why?"

"I'd like to have a go at it, if I may."

A flicker of annoyance appeared in Hembrey's dark eyes. Clearly he regarded Leo's request as nothing more than a bit of self-important showmanship. "My lord, our previous search of the house and grounds was comprehensive."

"I have no doubt of that," Leo replied. "But I trained as

an architect several years ago, and I'll be able to look at the place from a draftsman's perspective."

Jake Valentine spoke then. "You think there's a hidden room, my lord?"

"If there is," Leo said steadily, "I'll find it. And if not, at least we'll annoy the devil out of Kinloch, which should have some entertainment value."

Poppy held her breath as they waited for the Special Constable's reply.

"Very well," Hembrey finally said. "I can send you in with a constable while I bring Mr. Kinloch in for questioning. However, I will insist that you abide by our codes of practice during the execution of the search—and the constable will make certain you are aware of those rules."

"Oh, have no fear," Leo replied gravely. "I always follow the rules."

The Special Constable seemed rather unconvinced by the claim. "If you'll wait but a moment," he said, "I will confer with one of the magistrates, and he will assign the constable to escort you."

As soon as he left the office, Poppy leapt up from her chair. "Leo," she said, "I'm—"

"Yes, I know. You're going, too."

THE KINLOCH HOME WAS LARGE AND FASHIONABLY GLOOMY, the interiors done in dark crimson and green, the walls oak paneled. The cavernous entrance hall was paved with uncovered stone slabs that caused their footsteps to echo repeatedly.

What Poppy found most distinctive and unnerving about Edward Kinloch's house, however, was that instead of adorning the rooms and hallways with traditional artwork, he had filled the place with an astonishingly vast array of game trophies. They were everywhere, dozens of pairs of glass eyes staring down at Poppy, Leo, Jake Valentine, and the constable assigned to accompany them. In the entrance hall alone there were heads from a ram, a rhino, two lions, a tiger, as well as a stag, elk, caribou, leopard, and zebra, and other species that were entirely unfamiliar to her.

Poppy hugged her arms around her middle as she turned a slow circle. "I'm glad Beatrix can't see this."

She felt Leo's hand settle comfortingly on her back.

"Apparently Mr. Kinloch enjoys sport hunting," Valentine commented, gazing at the ghastly assortment.

"Large game hunting isn't a sport," Leo said. "It's only a sport when both sides are equally armed."

Poppy felt cold prickles of unease as she stared at the tiger's frozen snarl. "Harry is here," she said.

Leo glanced at her. "Why are you so certain?"

"Mr. Kinloch likes to display his power. To dominate. And this house is where he brings all his trophies." She shot her brother a glance of barely suppressed panic. Her voice was very quiet. "Find him, Leo."

He gave her a short nod. "I'm going to walk around the outside perimeter of the house."

Jake Valentine touched Poppy's elbow and said, "We'll go through the rooms on this floor and inspect the molding and paneling to see if there are discrepancies that would indicate a concealed door. And we'll also look behind the larger pieces of furniture, such as bookcases or wardrobes."

"And fireplaces," Poppy said, remembering the one at the hotel.

Valentine smiled briefly. "Yes." After conferring with the constable, he accompanied Poppy to the parlor.

They spent a half hour investigating every minute crack, edge, and surface elevation, running their hands over the walls, getting on their hands and knees, lifting edges of carpet.

"May I ask," came Valentine's muffled voice as he looked behind a settee, "did Lord Ramsay really study architecture, or was he more of a . . ."

"Dilettante?" Poppy supplied, moving every object on the fireplace mantel. "No, he's quite accomplished, actually. He attended the Académie des Beaux-Arts in Paris for two years, and worked as a draftsman for Rowland Temple. My brother loves to play the part of featherbed aristocrat, but he's far more clever than he lets on."

Eventually Leo came back inside. He went from room to room, pacing the distance from one wall to another, pausing to make notes. Poppy and Valentine continued to search diligently, progressing from the parlor to the entrance hall stairwell. With every minute that passed, Poppy's anxiety sharpened. From time to time a housemaid or footman passed, glancing at them curiously but remaining silent.

Surely one of them had to know something, Poppy thought in frustration. Why weren't they helping to find Harry? Did their misplaced loyalty to their master preclude any sense of human decency?

As a young housemaid wandered by with an armload of folded linens, Poppy lost her patience. "Where is it?" she exploded, glaring at the girl.

The maid dropped the linens in surprise. Her eyes went as round as saucers. "Wh-where is what, ma'am?" she asked in a squeaky voice.

"A hidden door. A secret room. There is a man being kept against his will somewhere in this house, *and I want to know where he is!*"

"I don't know noffing, ma'am," the housemaid quavered, and burst into tears. Scooping up the fallen linens, she fled up the stairs.

Valentine spoke quietly, his brown eyes filled with understanding. "The servants have already been questioned," he said. "Either they don't know, or they don't dare betray their employer."

"Why would they keep their silence about something like this?"

"There's little hope for a servant who is dismissed without references to find a job nowadays. It could mean devastation. Starvation."

"I'm sorry," Poppy said, gritting her teeth. "But at the moment I don't care about anyone or anything save my husband's welfare. And I know he's here somewhere, and I'm not leaving until he's found! I'll tear the house apart if I must—"

"That won't be necessary," came Leo's voice as he strode into the entrance hall. He jerked his head purposefully in the direction of a hallway that branched off the main entrance. "Come to the library. Both of you."

Galvanized, they hurried after him, while the constable followed as well.

The library was a rectangular room filled with heavy mahogany furniture. Three of the walls were fitted with shelved alcoves and bookcases, all topped by a cornice that was continuous with the wall joinery. The area of oak flooring uncovered by carpet was scarred and mellow with age.

"This house," Leo said, going straight to the draped windows, "is a classical Georgian, which means that every design feature in this half of the house is a perfect reflection of the other half. Any deviation is felt as a deep flaw. And according to the form of strict symmetrical arrangement, this room should have three windows on that wall, to match the corresponding room on the other side of the house. But obviously there are only two in here." Deftly he tied back the drapes to admit as much daylight as possible.

Waving impatiently at a cloud of dust motes in the air, Leo went to the second window, fastening those drapes as well.

"So I went outside and noticed that the brickwork is different on the section of the wall where a third window should be. And if you pace out this room and the one beside it—and compare the measurements with the exterior dimensions of the house—it appears there's an eight- to ten-foot space between these rooms with no apparent access."

Poppy flew to the wall of bookcases, examining them desperately. "Is there a door here? How do we find it?"

Leo joined her, lowering to his haunches and staring at the floor. "Look for fresh scuff marks. The floorboards are never level in these older houses. Or look for fibers caught in the seams between the cases. Or—"

"Harry!" Poppy shouted, using her fist to bang on a bookcase frame. *"Harry!"*

They were all still, listening intently for a response.

Nothing.

"Here," the constable said, pointing to a small white crescent scuff on the floor. "This is a new mark. And if the bookcase swung out, it would correspond."

All four of them gathered around the bookcase. Leo pried, pushed, and pounded on the edge of the frame, but the unit remained firmly in place. He scowled. "I know how to find the room, but I'll be damned if I know how to break inside."

Jake Valentine began to pull books from the shelves and toss them heedlessly to the floor. "The concealed doors we have at the hotel," he said, "are locked according to a pulley-and-dowel mechanism, with a wire running to a nearby object. When you tilt the object, the wire lifts the dowel and frees a doorstop wedge, and the door opens."

Poppy grabbed books and tossed them aside as well. One of the volumes she found was stuck in place. "This one," she said breathlessly.

Valentine slid his hand over the top of the book, found the wire, and pulled gently.

The entire bookcase swung open with stunning ease, revealing a locked door.

Leo pounded on the door with a heavy thump of his fist. *"Rutledge?"*

They were all electrified by a distant, nearly inaudible reply, and the quiet vibration of the door being pounded from the other side.

A few openmouthed servants gathered at the library doorway, watching the proceedings.

"He's in there," Poppy said, her heart thundering. "Can you open the door, Leo?"

"Not without a bloody key."

"Excuse me," Valentine said, shouldering his way to the door and pulling a small rolled cloth from his coat pocket. He extracted two thin metal implements, knelt beside the door, and set to work on the lock. Within thirty seconds, they heard a distinct *clack* as the tumblers shifted.

The door opened.

Poppy sobbed in relief as Harry emerged, dressed in fencing whites that were gray with dust. Her husband was pale and dirt smudged, but remarkably composed considering the circumstances. Poppy launched herself at him, and he caught her and said her name hoarsely.

Squinting in the brightness of the room, Harry kept Poppy against him as he reached out to shake the other men's hands in turn. "Thank you. I didn't think you'd be able to find me." His voice was ragged and rough, as if he'd been shouting for some time. "The room is insulated with slag wool to muffle sound. Where's Kinloch?"

The constable replied. "He's at the Bow Street Office, sir, being questioned. What do you say to accompanying us there and making a report, so we can detain him indefinitely?"

"It would be my pleasure," Harry said feelingly.

Ducking behind him, Leo ventured into the dark room.

"Quite professional," the constable told Valentine, as he re-placed the lock picks in his pocket. "I don't know whether to commend you or arrest you. Where did you learn to do that?"

Valentine sent a grin in Harry's direction. "My employer."

Leo emerged from the concealed room. "Little more than a desk, a chair, and a blanket," he said grimly. "Commissioned you to do a bit of mechanical engineering, did he?"

Harry nodded ruefully, reaching up to touch a tender spot on his skull. "The last thing I was aware of was something crashing down on my skull at the fencing club. I awoke here with Kinloch standing over me, ranting. I gathered the plan was to keep me locked away until I had developed a set of drawings that would result in a workable gun prototype."

"And after that," Valentine said darkly, "when you were no longer useful . . . what did he intend to do with you then?"

Harry smoothed his hand over Poppy's back as he felt her tremble. "We didn't discuss that part."

"Have you any idea whom his accomplices were?" the constable asked.

Harry shook his head. "I didn't see anyone else."

"I promise you, sir," the constable vowed, "we'll have Kinloch in the Bow Street strong room within the hour, and we'll obtain the names of everyone involved in this wretched business."

"Thank you."

"Are you hurt?" Poppy asked anxiously, lifting her head from Harry's chest. "Are you well enough to go to Bow Street? Because if not—"

"I'm fine, love," he murmured, smoothing a stray wisp of hair back from her face. "Just thirsty . . . and I wouldn't mind having some dinner when we return to the hotel."

"I was afraid for you," Poppy said, and her voice broke.

Harry pulled her close with a comforting murmur, tucking her body into his, clasping her head against his shoulder.

In tacit agreement, the other men drew away to allow them a moment of privacy.

There was much to be said between them—too much—so Harry simply held her against him. There would be time later to disclose what was in their hearts.

A lifetime, if he had his way.

Harry lowered his mouth to Poppy's flushed ear. "The princess rescues the villain," he whispered. "It's a nice variation on the story."

AFTER WHAT SEEMED AN INTERMINABLE TIME AT BOW Street, Harry was finally allowed to return to the Rutledge. As he and Poppy left the police office, they were told that Edward Kinloch and two of his servants were already being held in the strong room, with Runners in pursuit of another, yet unnamed suspect. And every last one of the charlatans trying to claim Harry's identity had been banished from the building.

"If there's one thing that today has made clear," Special Constable Hembrey quipped, "it's that the world needs only one Harry Rutledge."

The hotel employees were overjoyed at Harry's return, crowding around him before he could go upstairs to his apartments. They displayed a level of affectionate familiarity that they once wouldn't have dared, shaking Harry's hand, patting his back and shoulders, exclaiming their relief over his safe return.

Harry seemed a bit bemused by the demonstrations, but he tolerated it all quite willingly. It was Poppy who finally put a stop to the happy uproar, saying firmly, "Mr. Rutledge needs food and rest."

"I'll have a tray sent up at once," Mrs. Pennywhistle declared, dispersing the employees efficiently.

The Rutledges went to their private apartments, where Harry took a shower bath, shaved, and donned a dressing robe. He wolfed down a meal without even seeming to taste it, drained a glass of wine, and sat back in his chair looking exhausted but content.

"Bloody hell," he said, "I love being home."

Poppy went to sit on his lap, curling her arms around his neck. "Is that how you think of the hotel now?"

"Not the hotel. Just wherever you are." He kissed her, his lips gentle at first, but heat rose swiftly between them. He became more demanding, almost savaging her mouth, and she responded with an ardent sweetness that set fire to his blood. His head lifted, his breathing uncontrolled, and his arms cradled her tightly against him. Beneath her hips, she felt the insistent pressure of his arousal.

"Harry," she said breathlessly, "you need sleep far more than this."

"I never need sleep more than this." He kissed her head, nuzzling into the glowing locks of her hair. His voice softened, deepened. "I thought I'd go mad if I had to spend another minute in that blasted room. I was worried about you. I sat there thinking that all I want in life is to spend as much time with you as possible. And then it occurred to me that you had visited this hotel for three seasons in a row—*three*—and I'd never met you. All that time I wasted, when we could have been together."

"But Harry . . . even if we had met and married three years ago, you'd still say it wasn't enough time."

"You're right. I can't think of a single day of my life that wouldn't have been improved with you in it."

"Darling," she whispered, her fingertips coming up to stroke his jaw, "that's lovely. Even more romantic than comparing me to watch parts."

Harry nipped at her finger. "Are you mocking me?"

"Not at all," Poppy said, smiling. "I know how you feel about gears and mechanisms."

Lifting her easily, Harry brought her into the bedroom. "And you know what I like to do with them," he said softly. "Take them apart . . . and put them back together again. Shall I show you, love?"

"Yes . . . yes . . ."

And they put off sleep just a little longer.

Because people in love know that time should never be wasted.

Epilogue

I'm late," Poppy said thoughtfully, tying the sash of her white dressing gown as she approached the breakfast table.

Harry stood and held a chair for her, stealing a kiss when she was seated. "I wasn't aware you had an appointment this morning. There's nothing on the schedule."

"No, not that kind of late. The other kind of late." Seeing his incomprehension, Poppy smiled. "I'm referring to a certain monthly occurrence . . ."

"Oh." Harry stared at her fixedly, his expression unfathomable.

Poppy poured her tea and dropped a lump of sugar in it. "It's only two or three days past the usual time," she said, her voice deliberately casual, "but I've never been late before." She lightened her tea with milk and sipped it cautiously. Glancing at her husband over the rim of the china cup, she tried to gauge his reaction to the information.

Harry swallowed and blinked, and stared at her. His color had heightened, making his eyes look unusually green. "Poppy . . ." He was forced to stop by the necessity of taking an extra breath. "Do you think you could be expecting?"

She smiled, her excitement tempered with a flutter of nervousness. "Yes, I think it's possible. We won't know for certain until a bit more time has passed." Her smile turned uncertain as Harry remained silent. Perhaps it was too soon . . . perhaps he wasn't entirely receptive to the idea. "Of course," she said, trying to sound prosaic, "it may take some time for you to become accustomed to the idea, and that's only natural—"

"I don't need time."

"You don't?" Poppy gasped as she was snatched off the chair and hauled into his lap. His arms went fast around her. "You want a baby, then?" she asked. "You wouldn't mind?"

"*Mind?*" Harry pressed his face against her chest, feverishly kissing her exposed skin, her shoulder, her throat. "Poppy, there are no words to describe how much I want it." His head lifted, the depth of emotion in his eyes making her breath catch. "For most of my life, I thought I'd always be alone. And now to have you . . . and a baby . . ."

"It's not entirely certain yet," Poppy said, smiling as he scattered kisses over her face.

"I'll make certain, then." Still holding her, Harry stood from the chair and began to carry her back into the bedroom.

"What about the morning schedule?" she protested.

And Harry Rutledge uttered three words he had never said in his life. "Damn the schedule."

At that moment the door reverberated with a brisk knock. "Mr. Rutledge?" came Jake Valentine's voice. "I have the managers' reports—"

"Later, Valentine," Harry replied, not pausing as he took Poppy to the bedroom. "I'm occupied."

The assistant's voice was muffled by the door. "Yes, sir."

Crimson from head to toe, Poppy said, "Harry, *really!* Do you know what he must be thinking at this moment?"

Lowering her to the bed, he tugged her dressing robe open. "No, tell me."

Poppy squirmed in protest, a helpless giggle escaping her as he began to kiss his way down her body. "You are the most *wicked* man . . ."

"Yes," Harry murmured in satisfaction.

They both knew she wouldn't have him any other way.

LATER THAT DAY . . .

Leo's unexpected return to Hampshire had set Ramsay House into happy turmoil, maids hurrying to ready his usual room, a footman setting another place at the table. The family welcomed him warmly. Merripen poured glasses of excellent wine as they gathered in the parlor for a few minutes of conversation before dinner was served.

"What about the commission for the conservatory?" Amelia asked. "Did you change your mind?"

Leo shook his head. "The project is so small, I sketched something on the spot. They seemed pleased with it. I'll work out the details here, and send the final plans back to London. But never mind that. I have some news I think you'll find of interest . . ." He proceeded to regale the family with the story of Harry's abduction and rescue, and Edward Kinloch's subsequent arrest. They reacted with expressions of amazement and concern, and praised Leo for his part in the affair.

"How is Poppy?" Amelia asked. "So far this has certainly not been the calm, serene life she was hoping for."

"Happier than I've ever seen her," Leo replied. "I think Poppy has reconciled herself to the idea that one can't avoid the storms and calamities of life, but one can at least find the right partner to face them with."

Cam smiled at that, holding his dark-haired son against his chest. "Well said, *phral*."

Leo stood and set aside his wineglass. "I'll go wash before the meal is served." Glancing around the room, he affected an expression of mild surprise. "I don't see Marks. I hope she'll come down to supper—I have need of a good argument."

"The last time I saw her," Beatrix replied, "she was looking all around the house for her garters. Dodger stole every last one of them out of her dresser."

"Bea," Win murmured, "it's better not to mention the word 'garters' in mixed company."

"All right. But I don't understand why. Everyone knows we wear them—why do we have to pretend it's a secret?"

As Win tried to explain tactfully, Leo grinned and went upstairs. Instead of heading to his own room, however, he went to the end of the hallway, turned to the right, and tapped on the door. Without waiting for an answer, he pushed his way in.

Catherine Marks whirled to face him, gasping. "How dare you come into my room without . . ." Her voice faded as Leo closed the door and approached her. Dampening her lips with the tip of her tongue, she backed away until she had come up against the edge of a small dressing table. Her hair fell in pale silk streamers over her shoulders, her eyes darkening to the blue gray of a turbulent ocean. As she stared at him, a flush rose in her cheeks.

"Why did you come back?" she asked weakly.

"You know why." Slowly Leo braced his hands on the table, on either side of her. She shrank backward until no further movement was possible. The scent of her skin, mingled with bath soap and fresh garden blossoms, rose to his nostrils. The memory of sensation hovered around them, between them. As Leo saw the shiver that went through her, he felt a rush of unwanted heat, his blood turning to liquid fire.

Struggling for self-discipline, Leo took a deep, steadying breath.

"Cat . . . we have to talk about what happened."